# Short Stories from the Irish Renaissance

# Short Stories from the Irish Renaissance

## An Anthology

edited by
Alexander G. Gonzalez

The Whitston Publishing Company
Troy, New York
1993

PR
8876
.S56
1993

Copyright 1993
Alexander G. Gonzalez

Library of Congress Catalog Card Number 91-75023

ISBN 0-87875-421-0 (Cloth)
ISBN 0-87875-442-3 (Paper)

Printed in the United States of America

"Spring Sowing" and "The Tramp" from *Spring Sowing* by Liam O'Flaherty, reprinted by permission of Harcourt Brace Jovanovich, Inc.

"Her Table Spread" from *The Collected Stories of Elizabeth Bowen* by Elizabeth Bowen. Copyright © 1981 by Curtis Brown Ltd., Literary Executors of the Estate of Elizabeth Bowen. Reprinted by permission of Alfred A. Knopf, Inc.

"The Fall of Joseph Timmins" by Liam O'Flaherty reprinted by permission of Peters, Fraser, and Dunlop.

CANISIUS COLLEGE LIBRARY
BUFFALO, N.Y.

For Cristina, Kevin, Brian, and Jack

# Acknowledgements

I would like to thank a number of persons involved, knowingly or unknowingly, in the development of this project. Robert Rhodes read the introduction and offered his usual useful commentary. Barton R. Friedman recommended that I read Stephens's stories and broaden my scope in studying the Irish short story. Richard Finneran encouraged me to continue working on O'Kelly when I was at a rather unsure stage. Morris Beja has long supported my work on Joyce's contemporaries. And Edmund Epstein and Joseph Hynes were the ones who first nurtured my interest in this field.

I would also like to thank the office staff at the SUNY College at Cortland: Susan Stout and Marilyn Bradley for typing assistance and general spiritual uplifting; and Cynthia Pilok for huge amounts of xeroxing of texts.

Further, I feel that thanks—in addition to formal acknowledgement elsewhere in this book—is due to Maire Colum O'Sullivan, Christopher Plant, Oliver Weldon, and Jed Clauss for their kindness and encouragement while granting permission to use copyrighted material. For helping me track down copyright holders I must thank Sanford Sternlicht, Francis Doherty, Robert Spoo, Frances Hickson, and Lauren Stiles.

I am also grateful to Eberhard Alsen for his professional courtesy, without which this project might never have come to fruition.

The help and interest of all is greatly appreciated.

# Contents

Acknowledgements ..................................................................... vi

Introduction ................................................................................. 1

**George Moore**
    Dublin ..................................................................................... 10
    An Eviction ............................................................................ 21
    "Emma Bovary" ..................................................................... 29
    Some Parishioners ................................................................ 37
    The Exile ............................................................................... 90
    Home Sickness .................................................................... 110
    The Wild Goose ................................................................. 122
    Father Moling and the Immaculate Conception ............. 179

**W. B. Yeats**
    The Heart of the Spring .................................................... 201
    Red Hanrahan ..................................................................... 206

**James Joyce**
    An Encounter ...................................................................... 215
    Araby .................................................................................... 223
    Eveline ................................................................................. 229
    A Little Cloud ..................................................................... 234
    Clay ...................................................................................... 247
    The Dead ............................................................................. 253

**James Stephens**
    The Triangle ........................................................................ 293
    The Blind Man .................................................................... 300
    Desire ................................................................................... 306
    Hunger ................................................................................. 314

**Padraic Colum**
  Eilis: A Woman's Story ........................................................ 328
  The Death of the Rich Man ................................................. 334
  The Slopes of Tara ............................................................. 339
  Three Men ......................................................................... 345

**Seumas O'Kelly**
  The Building ...................................................................... 364
  The Haven .......................................................................... 379
  The Derelict ....................................................................... 387
  Both Sides of the Pond ...................................................... 400
  The Weaver's Grave .......................................................... 409

**Daniel Corkery**
  Vanity ................................................................................. 455
  The Cobbler's Den ............................................................. 461
  Carrig-an-Afrinn ................................................................ 490
  A Looter of the Hills ......................................................... 507
  The Priest ........................................................................... 516

**Liam O'Flaherty**
  Spring Sowing ................................................................... 526
  The Tramp .......................................................................... 532
  The Outcast ........................................................................ 543
  The Fall of Joseph Timmins .............................................. 548

**Brinsley MacNamara**
  The Smiling Faces .............................................................. 558
  The Sisters .......................................................................... 566
  In the Window ................................................................... 574

**Elizabeth Bowen**
  Her Table Spread ............................................................... 584

# Introduction

The Irish Renaissance is a rich literary period. Extending approximately 1890-1930, it is an era well known for its innovations in poetry, in drama, and, if James Joyce is considered, in fiction. However, such qualification of the last genre is too often typically assumed, and there is sometimes a tendency to forget that it was during these years that the Irish short story was born—long before Joyce's *Dubliners* was finally published in 1914. Joyce both grew out of and contributed significantly to a remarkable tradition of short-story writing. Besides gathering together most of the period's finest stories, many of which are out of print, this anthology's purpose is to create a context for Joyce's work—to show clearly that he was not an isolated genius in the realm of the Irish short story—so that any study of the Irish short story's origins will be facilitated. The number of quality Irish stories out of print is staggering.

Joyce long resented George Moore, the author almost universally acknowledged as the originator of the short story in Ireland. Modelled on Turgenev's *Sportsman's Sketches* (1852), Moore's *The Untilled Field* (Gaelic 1902, English 1903) is considered the first modern collection of Irish short stories ever published, and this is certainly true if we think in terms of collections of discrete stories that make some attempt at thematic unity. Moore's first efforts in establishing the genre came in *Parnell and His Island* (1887), a vicious and immature series of sketches that pillories both urban and rural Ireland. Taking the nineteenth-century naturalist writer's approach, Moore mercilessly limned the worst and most degrading scenes he could, which gained him lasting enmity among his countrymen—of both the upper and lower classes. "Dublin" and "An Eviction," each taken from this collection, are adequate examples included in this anthology first so that anyone studying Moore's artistic development will have a complete sampling of his range as short-story writer and secondly so that we can see the beginnings of a dominating cultural symbol: the image of physical paralysis or sluggishness as a representation of spiritual inertia. This theme became a virtually lifelong preoccupation with Moore, who also became the first writer to link paralysis with exile: those who could escape the disease before becoming trapped by their own weakness and lack of resolve did so. Until relatively recently, Joyce received all the credit for originating and developing this thematic dialectic, but nowadays Moore is generally acknowledged as the first to base a literary work upon it, both in novel form—*A Drama in Muslin* (1886) and *The Lake* (1905)—and in the genre of the short story with *Celibates* (1895) and *The Untilled Field*. Because of the latter collection's importance in terms of quality and literary-historical value, four of its stories are represented here, with the exile theme figuring most strongly. "The Wild Goose" is included, despite some sentimental excesses, because it shows Moore working in the genre of the long short-story or novella. Two other stories complete the George Moore section: "'Emma Bovary'" was first published in *Lippincott's Magazine* in 1902 and is included because of its sheer literary excellence. "Father Moling and the Immaculate Conception" is a title I have created for an excerpt from *A Storyteller's Holiday* (1918), a long collection of stories in two volumes that are woven together as told by an old Irish storyteller to his engrossed upper-class listener. Emulating the form of the oral tradition, Moore created the collection as one long, continuous piece of work so that excerpting one story is an unavoidably disruptive and arbitrary process. Nevertheless, it is necessary to do so if we are to obtain a full sampling of Moore's tremendous range as story teller, for in *A Storyteller's Holiday* we find evidence of Moore's humor—lacking in virtually all of Moore's previously written stories—of his frequent tendency to delve into the past for creative materials, and of his continued, indeed lifelong, anticlerical posture. Some readers will perhaps be surprised at Moore's versatility in short-story writing, exceeding that of even Joyce; generally Joyce may give us higher quality, but Moore attempts more forms—usually succeeding in those attempts—and employs a far broader scope of subject matter, including both urban and rural perspectives on his themes.

Both of the Yeats stories included were published in different collections in 1897. With their occult focus, they are, of course, radically different types of stories from those composed by Moore and Joyce. "The Heart of the Spring" (from *The Secret Rose*) may involve the Sidhe and a wizard, but it also clearly takes a sarcastic poke at the inadequacy of Catholicism as an all-explaining religion. It is the kind of story Moore is likely to have been fond of. The other story, "Red Hanrahan" (from *The Stories of Red Hanrahan*), is set in "modern" times and, indeed, much of the story is told surrealistically with several portions reading much like Flann O'Brien's *The Third Policeman* (1967). These stories are engaging in themselves, but they also suggest Yeats had a greater influence on—or maintained less of a distance from—the fiction writers of his time than has heretofore been assumed.

The reader of this anthology would be well served to be familiar with all the stories in Joyce's landmark collection, *Dubliners*. The six selected here are intended to be as representative as possible of the entire book, but they cannot substitute for a full awareness of Joyce's short-story masterpiece collection. "An Encounter" and "Araby" are two of the trilogy of stories on childhood epiphanies. The former is also a story that, in miniature, broaches the central themes of paralysis and exile, while the latter demonstrates one of the most memorable moments of sudden illumination in the entire collection. "Eveline," a tale about young adulthood, is the story that perhaps most obviously establishes that thematic dialectic at the heart of *Dubliners*: the title character is a young woman whose paralysis prevents her spiritually liberating exile from occurring, even though all she must do is step aboard the ship that will bring that liberation about. "A Little Cloud," whose focus—in keeping with the book's progression in terms of the ages of the protagonists—is a relatively newlywed adult whose epiphany involves an awareness of his own paralysis. "Clay" is a moving story about a spinster entering the living death of her middle age. And, finally, the crowning story in *Dubliners* is "The Dead," a story involving what is perhaps the most intimate epiphany in all of Irish literature. Whether Gabriel Conroy can, as a result of his epiphany, rouse himself from his somnambulistic existence is frequently a subject for lengthy debate with no hope of resolution—unless an agreement to disagree is struck or the debaters conclude that the story equally invites both interpretations.

James Stephens, a good friend of Joyce's, also wrote strikingly original short stories, and of the four presented here none is more bizarre than "Desire," taken from Stephens's 1928 collection, *Etched in Moonlight*. It is perhaps the only story in this anthology that stands in complete isolation from the traditions established in the Irish short-story genre prior to 1930. The originality of "Hunger," a story from the same collection, may seem less by comparison, but it too has a unique way of portraying the naturalistic decline of an entire family in one of Ireland's turn-of-the-century urban ghettoes. Highly effective use of animal imagery is only a contributing factor in a story that virtually defines the meaning of extreme hunger. "The Triangle" and "The Blind Man" are both from Stephens's 1913 collection, *Here Are Ladies*; each is a well structured story, but the latter is perhaps the more interesting for its darkly comic outlook on a man naturalistically dragged down by women into a state of drunkenness and general catatonia. As is common in Stephens's fiction, the tale is hardly at all visual, tending instead to the aphoristic.

The first of four stories by Padraic Colum, "Eilis: A Woman's Story," was originally published in *Studies* in 1907. Parts of the story's concerns remarkably suggest Seumas O'Kelly's novella, "The Weaver's Grave," especially the weaver's death and the fact that Eilis herself is said to be "too young to be a widow"—and she is also, like O'Kelly's widow, one who follows duty over other considerations. Surprisingly, the story also suggests James Joyce in two significant ways: first, the man Eilis marries is named Michael Conroy, prefiguring Joyce's Gabriel Conroy and Michael Furey from "The Dead"; secondly, when Eilis is unable to run off with Shaun Gorman, she sounds much like Eveline: "My knees failed, and I couldn't pass." Nets similar to Eveline's prevent her departure: parental expectations and religion keep her safely planted in "the sweet County of Fermanagh." Five years later Colum published "The Death of the Rich Man," a naturalistic tale that is thoroughly original in calling attention to greedy peasant materialism, a theme later developed in far more detail in the fiction of O'Kelly and Daniel Corkery. "The Slopes of Tara," published in *The Road Round Ireland* (1926), is strongly reminiscent of Yeats's "Red Hanrahan" in its surrealistically occult ending and its own apparent digression that focuses upon a seemingly meaningless card game. Finally, "Three Men" (1930) is an urban story with a familiar atmosphere of paralysis and general naturalistic seediness that reminds us of *Dubliners*, as do the characters, who are bursting with the self-importance born of shallowness and insecurity.

Seumas O'Kelly is probably the most significant writer of rural Irish fiction to emerge from the Renaissance years. His output of quality stories is remarkable, especially given his untimely death near the age of forty. 1912 saw the publication of three important stories. "The Derelict" constitutes one of the strongest indictments of peasant miserliness and acquisitiveness ever to come out of the new Ireland, which now allowed peasants to earn and save more money than before and to own more property; the story becomes utterly grotesque as we see a disturbed father literally valuing his moldy old roll of banknotes over the life of his own daughter. "The Haven" is a plotless tale surprisingly suggestive of T. S. Eliot's *The Waste Land* (1921), particularly with its atmosphere of paralysis and its setting—a pub where the customers are reluctant to leave despite frequent admonitions to do so. In "The Building" we see the often devastating effects of exile on those left behind, a theme reminiscent of Moore's story, "The Exile." The story is also impressive for its early use of epiphany when the time comes for Martin Cosgrave to realize his own excesses. Despite his realization, Martin does remain in Ireland, as does old Pat Phelan in Moore's story, but in "Both Sides of the Pond" (from *Waysiders*, 1917) we find that the steadily depopulated countryside provides a self-propagating impetus for others to go into exile rather than remain in a land becoming barren of people as well as of gainful employment. O'Kelly's anti-exile posture remains intact, however, as his exiled protagonist is ultimately unhappy and jaded in his Bowery environment—having lost his peasant dignity, which had seemed previously to be innate. Indeed, the story's repulsive second part, contrasting strongly with the beautiful, simple scenes set earlier in the first part, seems to have been intended to provide Irish readers with an epiphany—a sudden realization that emigrating Irishmen might be giving up far more than they could possibly gain abroad. This intention surely must have seemed highly idealistic to peasants struggling unsuccessfully to keep themselves fed, but O'Kelly wanted at least to make an attempt to counteract the highly romantic and widely held view that once outside Ireland financial success and spiritual rejuvenation necessarily followed. The final story included in this anthology, "The Weaver's Grave" (1919), is long and complex enough to be considered actually a novella, and indeed has been compared by critics to Joseph Conrad's *Heart of Darkness* (1902) in terms only of its sheer quality, for despite its very serious dimensions it is foremost a comic story whose characters are warmly remembered by most readers. It is a story admired greatly by Joyce, perhaps in part because of the utter brilliance of the widow's epiphany and the unobtrusive way in which it sadly chronicles the passing of rural Irish occupations and traditions, for the title's grave is not only that of one weaver, but of all weavers, now that automation has come to the linen industry.

It is not clear whether or not Daniel Corkery was aware of O'Kelly's early stories when he published *A Munster Twilight* in 1916, but many of the stories in this collection echo the themes and techniques earlier developed by O'Kelly. The link between poverty and paralysis is effectively explored in "Vanity," a tale that is also a subtle psychological inquiry into the peasant mentality in a new Ireland. "The Cobbler's Den" is a series of very short tales that with some success captures the spirit of the oral tradition, as Moore had tried to do in his far longer *A Storyteller's Holiday*. But Corkery's most engaging stories are those found in his 1929 collection, *The Stormy Hills*. Generally regarded as the strongest of these is "The Priest," a story that poignantly and succinctly renders rural Ireland's depopulation, paralysis, and acquisitiveness—and in the process offers us a brilliant epiphany brought about by a priest's voyage to and realization of his own heart of darkness. The process, symbolically reinforced by the landscape through which he travels, strips the comfortable old cleric of his habitual complacency and forces him to confront his own paralysis as well as the horrifying poverty of the long-neglected outer reaches of his parish. Another excellent story is "Carrig-an-Afrinn," which translates into English as "Rock of the Mass," an obvious reference to Ireland's old penal laws that once forbade the celebration of Mass in Ireland; the title's "rock" is the place where Mass was then secretly and defiantly held until the laws eventually changed. To the head of the story's household, this rock has become deeply symbolic as we watch his family in the process of dissolution over several generations. The pathetic final blow will be the dynamiting of the rock in order to allow for the highway to be widened: thus do old, venerated traditions become extinct before the spectre of "progress" in the new Ireland. The improved standard of living necessarily signals the loss of a noble culture and way of life. The final story taken from this collection is "A Looter of the

Hills," considered by some to be a relatively minor story but included nonetheless for its forceful descriptions of urban life in Cork's tenements: the opening descriptions, which border on the claustrophobic, suggest a paralysis as devastating as anything out of Joyce's Dublin.

Liam O'Flaherty, writing toward the end of the Renaissance period, is not surprisingly the author who, despite his own originality, was most clearly influenced by a number of his predecessors. The title story from *Spring Sowing* (1924) is beautifully written and is as much a paean to the robust spirit of rural Irishmen as is the first half of O'Kelly's "Both Sides of the Pond." "The Tramp," also taken from the same collection, gives an idea of O'Flaherty's versatility, for this story about urban life seems almost as if plucked right out of the pages of *Dubliners*: it exposes the protagonist's spiritual paralysis and then, as in Joyce's "Eveline," reveals the symbolic corresponding physical paralysis as Duignan cannot make his legs move to follow his potential savior out of degradation and into a spiritually hardy way of life. It is probably the single Renaissance story most like one of Joyce's. In "The Outcast," taken from *The Tent* (1926), we see an extension of the anticlerical tradition among writers of Irish fiction; this story, more savage and less balanced than anything out of Moore, is not at all subtle in its rendering of an unmarried pregnant girl's trials after she has been denounced from the altar by her parish priest—trials that can lead only to her suicide. And finally, "The Fall of Joseph Timmins," from *The Mountain Tavern* (1929), humorously shows the hypocrisy that dwells in the hearts of society's most "upright" citizens and creates the most odiously excessive religious atmosphere of any Irish story I can recall. Once again we have a paralytic sufferer—victim of his own repulsive piety—coming to an awareness of his spiritually diseased condition but unable to extricate himself from the nets that hold him firmly in place.

The three Brinsley MacNamara stories are taken from *The Smiling Faces* and are thematically linked: they all deal with the spiritual suffering of the unmarried, a minor theme in *Dubliners* that is vigorously pursued by MacNamara quite successfully. For all the spinsters or unmarried men we find in *Dubliners*, MacNamara gives us even more, not only in this 1929 collection but throughout much of his entire canon. One of his stories, "The Sisters," obviously even echoes the title of the opening story in Joyce's collection, though the spinsters in MacNamara's tale are younger. "In the Window" details the paralysis of a spinster who—ironically—is employed in making wedding gowns; her suffering and bitterness are poignantly rendered. The collection's title story tells the tale of a pathetic creature whose paralysis stems from an unrequited love for a beautiful young barmaid with whom he has absolutely nothing in common. Clearly MacNamara is a writer as vitally concerned with the spiritual condition of the Irish people as Moore and Joyce. In fact, MacNamara emerges as an author continuing to explore in meaningful new ways the interrelated themes of paralysis and celibacy—extending the tradition established by his better-known predecessors. Perhaps the most significant difference between MacNamara's approach and theirs is that non-marriage is the dominant theme, while the resulting paralysis is treated as a subordinate component of the unmarried state; in the work of Moore and Joyce, Ireland's paralysis is each author's primary concern, with spinsterhood merely being one frequent attendant condition among many.

The lone story by Elizabeth Bowen, "Her Table Spread" (1930), was one of the very few Irish stories published by her during this period. Not only is it an engrossing and rewarding work of literary art in its own right, but it also reveals yet one more Irish contemporary of Joyce's who was clearly influenced by him. Upon a first glance, the story would appear to have nothing Joycean about it, since it involves Ireland's Protestant upper class during the twenties; Dublin's slums and middle-class neighborhoods are nowhere in sight. However, many solid connections eventually become evident, especially when we consider Bowen's use of paralysis as theme and symbol—Mr. Alban is in many ways a counterpart to Gabriel Conroy from "The Dead"—and her nearly perfect orchestration of a deeply significant and, for the protagonist, perhaps life-changing epiphany.

This is quite an array of authors, all of whom have also written impressively in a variety of other literary forms ineligible for inclusion here. What this anthology is in part intended to confirm is that the Renaissance period was indeed wonderfully rich in terms of literary masterpieces, but that the fiction, especially the short stories, needs no apology prefatory to its inclusion in the Renaissance canon. The Irish short-story tradition has continued to flourish with such writers as Sean O'Faolain, Frank O'Connor, Mary Lavin, Michael McLaverty, and Wiliam Trevor. Many of these writers openly acknowledge their debt to their Irish predecessors. With this anthology's appearance, the clear lines of influence will be more easily traced between the Renaissance and the present, since no anthology has previously appeared that concentrates in any depth upon the work of the originators of the Irish short-story tradition. The reading is intellectually stimulating, the discovery of literary connections exciting, and the stories frequently very moving. Work of such calibre deserves to be in print and available for study.

# George Moore

## *Dublin*

This is Dalkey, a suburb of Dublin. From where I stand I look down upon the sea as on a cup of blue water; it lies two hundred feet below me like a great smooth mirror; it lies beneath the blue sky as calm, as mysteriously still, as an enchanted glass in which we may read the secrets of the future. How perfectly cuplike is the bay! Blue mountains, blue embaying mountains, rise on every side, and amorously the sea rises up to the lip of the land. These mountains of the north, these Turner-like mountains, with their innumerable aspects, hazy perspectives lost in delicate grey, large and trenchant masses standing out brutally in the strength of the sun, are as the mailed arms of a knight leaning to a floating siren whose flight he would detain and of whom he asks still an hour of love. I hear the liquid murmur of the sea; it sings to the shore as softly as a turtle-dove to its mate. I see white sails scattered over the grey backgrounds of the sky, and through the dissolving horizon other sails appear and disappear, lighter than the large wings of the sea-gull that floats and plunges, sometimes within a few feet of the cliff's edge, a moment after there are a hundred feet between it and the sea. My thoughts turn involuntarily to the Bay of Naples, which I have never seen, but perfect though it be—Nature's fullest delight above which no desire may soar—it cannot be more beautiful than the scene which now lies blue and translucid before me.

I am two hundred feet above a sea striped with purple and violet; and above my head the rocks rise precipitously. From every side the mountains press with voluptuous arms the voluptuous sea: above my head the villas are perched like birds amid the rocks. There I see a bouquet of trees, here I see a green sward where the white dresses of the young girls playing tennis float this way and that. From villa to villa a white road winds, like a thread leading through the secrets of a labyrinth; sometimes it is lost in a rocky entanglement, sometimes it vanishes in the dark and long shadows of a pine wood; sometimes it is suspended, it is impossible to say how, out of the mountain-side, and higher still spread out on the clear sky, and crowning the mountain-brow is the imperial heather.

In the exquisite clarity of the day every detail is visible; and as my glance passes from the highest heights down to the depths of the shore I see women in long bathing-dresses crawling up the strand far away: they appear like flies: the naked flesh of some boys bathing shines in the sun ray, they are climbing up the black sides of a boat,—that one on the prow joins his hands above his head and disappears in the purple of the waves. On the terrace by me stands a fat man, the type of commercial prosperity (he is a distiller); his family is about him, enjoying the delicate listlessness of this summer afternoon. Now I hear the rushing rumble of a train, the strident whistle tears the air and is repeated high and far through the sonorous distances of this strange mountain. The eye follows the white steam across the bridge; then the train is lost in a tunnel; now it re-appears and turning and twisting it scuttles away like a rabbit through the rocks.

No town in the world has more beautiful surroundings than Dublin. Seeing Dalkey one dreams of Monte Carlo, or better still of the hanging gardens of Babylon, of marble balustrades, of white fountains, of innumerable yachts, of courts of love, and of sumptuous pleasure places; but alas, all that meets the eye are some broken-down villas! The white walls shine in the sun and deceive you, but if you approach you will find a front-door where the paint is peeling, and a ruined garden.

And in such ruin life languishes here! The inhabitants of the villas are, for the most part, landlords whom circumstances have forced to shut up their houses and to come here to economise; or, they may belong to the second class of landlords: widows living on jointures paid by the eldest sons, or mortgagees upon money placed by them or by their ancestors upon the land. For in Ireland there is nothing but the land; with the exception of a few distillers and brewers in Dublin, who live upon the drunkenness of the people, there is no way in Ireland of getting money except through the peasant.

The socialistic axiom that capital is only a surplus-value coming from unpaid labour, either in the past or in the present, is in other countries mitigated and lost sight of in the multiplicity of ways through which money passes before falling into the pockets of the rich; but in Ireland the passage direct and brutal of money from the horny hands of the peasant to the delicate hands of the proprietor is terribly suggestive of serfdom. In England the landlord lays out the farm and builds the farm-buildings. In Ireland he does absolutely nothing. He gives the bare land to the peasant, and sends his agent to collect the half-yearly rent; in a word he allows the peasant to keep him in ease and luxury. "I am an Irish landlord, I have done this, I do this, and I shall continue to do this, for it is as impossible for me as for the rest of my class to do otherwise; but that doesn't prevent me from recognising the fact that it is a worn-out system, no longer possible in the nineteenth century, and one whose end is nigh." In Ireland every chicken eaten, every glass of champagne drunk, every silk dress trailed in the street, every rose worn at a ball, comes straight out of the peasant's cabin. A few years ago this tribute (for in Ireland rent is a tribute and nothing else) was accepted without astonishment, without an after-thought, absolutely—as in other ages the world accepted slavery and feudalism.

But one day, suddenly, without warning, the scales fell from the eyes of the people, and the people resolved to rid themselves of this plague. Visible hitherto only to a small number, and they denied its existence save in the poorest districts, this plague-spot is apparent today to every eye; it is visible everywhere, even in the heart of the slums as in the most elegant suburb; it was as if a veil had been drawn revealing the boils with which the flesh of Ireland is covered.

You see that coarse, common man dressed in a greasy, worn-out tweed jacket, smoking a black pipe at the end of the weed-grown terrace of the dilapidated villa which he has hired for the season? He is speaking to his daughter, a sad-looking girl dressed in a long red cashmere buttoned down the back; she tells him that she wants a new dress to go to a tennis party in the neighborhood. He grumbles, he thinks she had better not accept any more tennis parties this year. Does he want her to remain an old maid? Nothing is done for her that she may get a husband; no parties are given for her, never is there a young man invited to the house. Finally he draws from his pocket a roll of bank-notes black and greasy, notes with worn-out edges, notes cut in two and stuck together, notes which smell of the smoke of the cabin, notes that are rancid of the sweat of the fields, notes which have been spat upon at fairs for good luck, notes which are an epitome of the sufferings of the peasant of the west of Ireland.

The young girl runs away skipping with three or four of these notes to buy a dress, to dream of the husband which she will never get; the man sinks into gloom, dreaming of the Land League and of the possibility of getting out of the tenants in the autumn what they refused to pay in the spring; and I dreaming of the bank-notes, of the husband-hunting girl, of the ruined proprietor, of the villa in ruins. I read in all this, as in an epitaph upon a tomb, the history of a vanished civilisation. Then as my thoughts return to the beautiful landscape—with its broken rocks full of lights and shades, its bits of white road and the strange railway suspended as if by magic above the blue bay, and the violet mountains standing out against the silver clouds, I dream of Paris and of what Paris would be if within a few miles of so beautiful a panorama. Paris would sing in this bay; Paris would dance on these terraces; columns and palaces, balustrades, arches and cupolas would extend from height to height the enchantment of their architecture. The calm and sombre waters of the bay, illuminated by gondolas coming and gondolas going—white beneath the moon, yellow and gold beneath the lamps—would be a floating dream; fireworks darting from the abrupt hollows of the dark hill-side, would jewel the forehead of the night, detonations of champagne, cries of the dancers, blaring of the *cors de chasse* and the sonorous mountain echoing with the various sounds of festival.

And still dreaming of my Irish France I listened to the monotonous cry of a broken barrel-organ, and, looking at the poor devil of an Italian, I know well that nobody here, except perhaps the distiller, is rich enough to throw him a penny.

Far away those are the Wicklow mountains. Bound about Dublin like a blue scarf, they are as bright notes of joy in the pale monotony of the pale dim streets.

The character of Dublin is the absence of any characteristic touch. Dublin is neither ugly, nor pretty, nor modern, nor ancient, but all these qualifications might be applied to it as to an "old-clo' shop." Yes, Dublin reminds me of an old-clothes shop where ball-dresses, dress coats, morning trowsers, riding habits, wellington boots, lace shawls are to be let or sold. Nothing seems really to belong to anyone. Everybody might have owned everything—language, dress, and manners—at one time or another. The streets are built of pale brown bricks, a pale poor brown—poor but honest. Nor are they built at hazard, improvised like London streets, but set out artificially in squares and monotonous lines, like a town that a tired child might have improvised out of a box of bricks. Here you find no architectural surprises, like in other towns; no alleys or curious courts filled with life—strange, picturesque, and enigmatic; none of those singular byways with reft of sky in the brick entanglement, sometimes bulging out into courts; where shops of fried fish, coal shops, shops of old iron and old paper, lean one against the other in giddy confusion; sometimes slipping into passages narrow and twisted, where bands of little children dance joyously to the sound of a friendly organ.

"We are the poor but honest," the houses cry aloud, and in their faded elegance they bend and bow like ladies who have seen better times. Others who would give themselves fashionable airs trail their finery like a middle-aged coquette in a provincial town. The flower-boxes rot in the windows, the rose-coloured window-blinds are torn, the railings rot with rust, the areas exhale the fœtid odours of unemptied dust-bins; add to this the noise of a hundred pianos; imagine a society of ill-bred young girls, making love to a few briefless barristers, their clerks, the employés in the breweries; beat this all up to waltz music from four-o'clock in the afternoon till four in the morning, with an interval of three hours or so for dinner, and you will have realised the exterior aspect of Dublin society.

The following conversation which I overheard in "the best society," will give an idea of the general culture and the normal *esprit* of Dublin girls.

Scene, a ball-room. Dramatis personæ, two officers and a charming girl. First officer: "By Jove, what a pretty girl you have been dancing with! She is really a Juno, she is superb. You must introduce me to her."

Second officer: "She is not ugly, but I don't think you would care about her, she's rather common."

"Common with that face, impossible!"

The two men approach the beauty. He who thinks her common leaves her with him who considers her divine. I listen to see how this acquaintance, so happily begun, will end. Overcome with emotion the lover seeks for words; should he begin by speaking of the weather, or of the excellence of the floor? Important question! At last the young girl breaks silence, and whilst her admirer is still seeking for a transitional phrase to lead up to more important matter, she says, after having examined him from head to foot: "Ah Captain, what a little foot you've got!"

In the sombre and sad streets of Dublin there are two open spaces—Stephen's Green and Merrion Square. The first—which has lately been reclaimed from its Indian-jungle-like state and decorated with mounds and bridges and ponds, and presented to the city by a rich nobleman—resembles in its present state a school-treat for charity children; the other still flourishes in all its ancient dilapidation; rusty iron railings, decrepit trees, and a few lamentable tennis players; in the deep ruts of the roads two or three outside cars lie hidden—that singular vehicle which defies description, two wheels with seats suspended on either side and from which you will certainly be thrown if you don't hold on with all your might.

On every door in Merrion Square there is a brass plate. For there are more doctors and lawyers in Dublin than any other city in the world. Dublin is a town of officials. Every man wears the red ribbon of the castle in his button-hole; and more than one woman wears it instead of a garter.

Nobody reads, nobody thinks. To be considered a man of the world, it is only necessary to have seen one or two plays in London before they are six months old, and to curse the Land League. In the "best society" I have met with young men who have never read "Vanity Fair" and young women who have never heard of Leonardo da Vinci. Once I was dining with a Mr. Ryan; on the club table there were two photographs, one was of Richard Wagner and the other was of Beethoven.

Mr. Ryan: "Who is that?"

I: "That is Wagner."

Mr. Ryan: "Who is Wagner?"

I (recovering myself with an effort): "Don't you know? Richard Wagner, the great breeder of shorthorns!"

Mr. Ryan: "Begorra 'tis strange I niver came across him in Ballinasloe; and who is the other?"

I: "That is Beethoven."

Mr. Ryan: "Who is Beethoven?"

I: "Don't you know? He is the great breeder of cobs."

Mr. Ryan: "And I niver met him at the Dublin horse show; does he niver go there? Tell me—are you listening to me?—what sort of stock does he go in for?"

Dublin is in a barbarous state, and, what is worse, in a retrograde state.

    \*  \*  \*  \*  \*

Dublin is divided into four parts: The Castle, the Shelbourne Hotel, the Kildare Street Club, and Mrs. Rusville the fashionable dressmaker.

### *The Castle*

To describe the Castle it is only necessary to compare it to an immense police barrack. It is devoid of all architecture, and the brick walls are as bare and as bald as an official document; everything, even to the red coats of the sentinels, reminds you of the red tape with which these documents are tied. The Castle rises like a upas tree amid ruins and death; the filth of the surrounding streets is extreme. The Castle dominates the Liffey—a horrible canal or river flowing between two stone embankments. Curious and characteristic details: between the bridges great sea-gulls fly back and forwards with a mechanical regularity, diving from time to time after the rubbish which the current bears away to the sea.

On either side there are sombre and sinister streets, aged and decrepit buildings filled with old books rotting in dark and fœtid confusion; dark holes where, in Rembrandt *chiaroscuro*, you see the form of a hag groping amidst heaps of something—something that may be clothes; shops where suspicious-looking women pretend to sell cheap cigars; others where placards announce the excellence of obscene goods manufactured on the premises; then the perspective floats in a slight curve, and is lost in the smoke of breweries and distilleries, an appropriate horizon for this town of miserable vice and hideous decrepitude.

From the Castle the law in Ireland is administered, and it is there that the Viceroy holds his mock Court; every sort of religious ceremony may be turned into ridicule, but it is certain, when a man not a king is forced to mimic royalty as far as possible, that everything that is grotesque in the original becomes in the imitation a caricature. The Viceroy is not an actor who consents to play a part, nor a Messiah audacious enough to declare himself God, but something indefinable between the two that says: "Of course you know that I am not a king, but I hope you will consider me one, and you will address me as such." Such an anomaly necessitates a multitude of situations which are very suggestive of a Palais Royal farce. Although the Viceroy plays the part of a king, his wife is not authorised to play that of a queen.

How, therefore, is a drawing-room to be held? It is clear that the ladies who are presented cannot kiss the hand of the Viceroy as they kiss the hand of the Queen in Buckingham Palace. A difficult situation of which this is the solution: the Viceroy must kiss the ladies. It is impossible to imagine anything more absurd than this Viceroy, an English nobleman, chosen for the post by the Government actually in power, standing upon a daïs surrounded by red guardsmen, all the ladies of the household behind him upon an estrade, kissing an interminable procession of women, young and old, fat and thin, as they are announced by the Chamberlain who reads out their names like a Doge's secretary in an opera bouffe.

And then how are all the innumerable sinecures of the Castle disposed of? Underlings, hirelings, of all sorts, swarm about this mock Court like flies about a putrefying carcass. A sight indeed it is to see them marching in procession through the drawing-rooms after the presentations. The A. D. C.'s, the Medical Department, the Private Secretary, the Military Private Secretary, the Assistant Under-Secretary, the Gentleman-in-Waiting, the Master of the Horse, the Dean of the Chapel Royal, the Chamberlain, the Gentlemen Ushers, the Controller, the State Steward walking with a wand, etc . . . It is easy, therefore, to understand the hatred of the people for the corruptions and injustices of the Castle.

The Castle is for the National party—to employ a comparison whose success is unquestionable—what a red flag is for a bull. This mock Court is considered as an absurdity by all classes of society except fashionable women to whom the fêtes of the Castle are of all importance. There are no mothers in Ireland as there are in France; it is not in the circle of their friends that they search for possible husbands for their daughters. As soon as a young girl has left school she is taken to Dublin, kissed by the Lord-Lieutenant, and let loose of the ball-rooms of the Castle to flirt as extravagantly or as discreetly as she thinks proper. In France the chaperon has a meaning; in England and Ireland she is a nonentity: from the moment a chaperon enters the ballroom till the time she leaves it she sees nothing of her charges. Still, nevertheless, the young girl passes four or five hours dancing; or, when an occasion presents itself, searches for a favourite corner hidden at the end of a dark corridor. The young girls without any great moral conscience make their way at the Castle, and those who are well introduced may amuse themselves, but for the majority it is a place of torture and despair. The girls outnumber the men in a proportion of three to one, the competition is consequently severe; and it is pitiable to see these poor muslin martyrs standing at the door, their eyes liquid with invitation, striving to inveigle, to stay the steps of the men as they pass by. But although these balls are little else for the young girls than a series of heart-breaks, nevertheless the most abject basenesses are committed to secure an invitation.

### *The Shelbourne Hotel*

The Shelbourne is a large and commodious hotel. On entering, a winter garden on the first floor strikes a pleasant note of green, and a little fountain murmurs pleasantly amid grey stone frogs. The pen of Balzac would be necessary to describe the Shelbourne Hotel; it is the *pension* of Madame Vanquier placed in aristocratic circles. For three pounds a week you can live there; and this liberality on the part of the proprietor is singularly appreciated by widows and old maids of all sorts. The ladies' drawing-room is on the right, and Flaubert's celebrated phrase may be applied to it, "It was the moral centre of the house." The walls are decorated with Swiss landscapes—mountains, chamois, cascades, and lakes. About the chimney-piece there are a great number of low chairs, chairs for invalid ladies, chairs made for novel reading and for wool-work. Nothing is spoken of but men and marriages; it is here that all the scandals of Dublin are laid and are hatched.

At this moment the drawing-room wears its most habitual air. Two old ladies are seated on the sofa knitting. Two old maids who come up every year husband-hunting, are sitting artlessly advancing their little slippered feet, between them is the chaperon who has brought them to Dublin for the Castle season.

"Oh, so you have all come up to the Castle, and are going to be presented! Well, you'll find the rooms very grand and the suppers very good, and if you know a lot of people, particularly the officers quartered here, you will find the Castle balls very amusing. The best way to do it is to come to town a month before the drawing-room and give a ball; and in that way you get to know all the men. If you haven't done that I'm afraid you won't get many partners. Even if you do get introduced they will only ask you to dance, and you will never see them again. Dublin is like a race-course, men come and speak to you and pass on. It is pleasant enough if you know people, but as for marriages there are none, I assure you. I know lots of girls, and very nice girls too, who have been going up for six or seven years, and have not been able to pull it off."

"And ay," said a girl speaking with a terrible brogue, "the worst of it is that the stock is for iver increasing; ivery year we are growing more and more numerous, and the men seem to be getting fewer. Nowadays a man won't look at you unless you have at least two thousand a year."

At the Shelbourne the fashionable world stays during the Castle season. The hotel is then as full of girls as a beehive of bees; their clear voices are heard in the corridors, and the staircase is gay with passing and rustling silk; and then, too, is made manifest the morality which is so characteristic of all English-speaking countries where young girls have acquired the same liberty as men. Complete freedom of speech is granted them. In Dublin a virgin is scarcely a favourable specimen of virginity: scandals, divorce cases, and invitations to the Castle are the sole themes of her conversation.

*The Kildare Street Club*

The Kildare Street Club is one of the most important institutions in Dublin. It represents in the most complete acceptation of the word the rent party in Ireland; better still, it represents all that is respectable, that is to say, those who are gifted with an oyster-like capacity for understanding this one thing; that they should continue to get fat in the bed in which they were born. This club is a sort of oyster-bed into which all the eldest sons of the landed gentry fall as a matter of course. There they remain spending their days, drinking sherry and cursing Gladstone in a sort of dialect, a dead language which the larva-like stupidity of the club has preserved. The green banners of the League are passing, the cries of a new Ireland awaken the dormant air, the oysters rush to their window—they stand there open-mouthed, real pantomime oysters, and from the corner of Frederick Street a group of young girls watch them in silent admiration.

### Mrs. Rusville

To this sympathetic dressmaker all fashionable figures are confided, and all highbred griefs and scandals.

When the giggling countess leaves, the sighing marchioness is received with genial sympathy.

"My dear Helen, I can bear up no longer; my husband is a brute! It is only here I find any comfort; you only are kind." Overcome with emotion the women fall into each other's arms and they kiss fervently. Finally, they retire to Mrs. Rusville's boudoir, a delicious little retreat hung with Japanese draperies. Reclining gracefully, sometimes hand in hand laid gently, they drink their afternoon stimulants. In delicately cut glasses gin loses much of its vulgarity, but when sportswomen are announced, brandy and sodas are ordered, and telling of adventures and disappointments they watch with dreamy eyes great crabs crawling through the long sea-weeds, and a flight of wild geese that hide with their wings the silver disc of the moon.

As may be supposed, the business could not but suffer by these long hours passed in drunkenness and scandalmongery, but Mrs. Rusville had three daughters to bring out, and she hoped—when she had disposed of her shop, and her feet were set on the redoubtable staircase of Cork Hill—that her aristocratic friend would extend to her a cordial helping hand. Mrs. Rusville is one of the myriad little schemes with which Dublin is honeycombed.

The Castle is the head, the Shelbourne Hotel the body, the Kildare Street Club and Mrs. Rusville's Shop the members of the miserable creature covered with bleeding sores that is called Dublin Society. To-day it trembles with sullen fear, and listens to savage howling of the pack in kennels set in a circle about the Castle, the Hotel, the Club, and the Shop; and as Gladstone advances, the barking springs to meet him; the fierce teeth are heard upon the wood-work. Will he lift the latch and let the hounds rush in on the obscene animal?

# George Moore

## *An Eviction*

A strange woman lives in the west of Ireland; a sort of she-Nero besotted with drink and maddened with lust of cruelty. She is a woman with pale blue eyes, so pale that they look like porcelain; she is middle-aged, she is fat, she is dressed in man's clothes. Iron-grey hair grows thinly over large scabs of dirt, the red flesh of the cheeks is loose and hanging, and something shapeless moves beneath the long, filthy jacket which falls like a petticoat and is bound about her with a leathern strap; her legs are covered in a pair of corduroy trousers, patched and greased and stained with abominable stains; and the thick, coarse hand, which looks as if it were all thumbs, twitches at the hem of the discoloured jacket.

The judge (to the solicitor): "You might grant the tenant time if he promises to pay."

Miss Barrett (in a bellowing, half-drunken tone): "Certainly not. A decree of ejectment is granted."

And the pale blue eyes catch expression horribly indicative of cruelty and rapacity, but only to fade a moment after into the usual helpless semi-idiotic stare. Other cases have to be heard, and Miss Barrett consults with her companion, Miss McCoy, a tall, raw-boned Scotchwoman, so tightly buttoned up in a brown, mud-smeared ulster, that it is difficult to say if her undergarment is a petticoat or a pair of trousers.

The night is falling, and the people are coming out of the court-house. The sullen faces of the peasants are hardly visible in the gloom, but their exclamations of hatred are very audible: "You dirty old petticoated brandy vessels; oh, the filthy animals!"

But paying no attention to these jeers, the two women pass with their guard of police and their bailiffs to the nearest public-house; and from public-house to public-house they go, drinking and cursing with ever-increasing ardour until at last the glass slips from their hands and the oath dies on their lips, and they fall helpless on the ground. Then they are piled up and tied on a car by the police and driven home to sleep off the effects of their drunken bout.

Many are the legends concerning Miss Barrett. It is said that she was once—a quarter of a century ago—a pretty and graceful Irish girl, whose blue eyes and merry voice were the delight of her friends, and particularly of a young English painter with whom she was passionately in love. It is suggested that he painted her as Ophelia and that the picture still exists in London; but her father, so report goes, would not hear of the marriage and sent his daughter abroad in the charge of a companion. A few weeks after he died, and Miss Barrett came travelling back, as fast as express trains could bring her, to bury her father and marry her painter. But the painter had already married another, and Miss Barrett returned to her Western home and spoke of founding a convent. That there is some truth in these stories is probable enough, for it is certain that Miss Barrett was not only born, but once lived, as a lady, but the cause of her decline into the sewer of debauchery is not known, and it is impossible to trace the steps by which she descended into these lowest and most horrible depths. Golden fortune has however always attended her; relative after relative died, leaving her their properties, which they could not will away from her, and she is now possessed of vast wealth, which she has no power or way of spending except in an occasional drinking-bout with her bailiffs and caretakers in a county town.

Her house and grounds once differed nowise from those of the surrounding gentry; but the same changes have taken place in them as in herself. How dissolute, how degraded! All the trees have been cut down, and the hewn stumps show naked out of the great green field. In large scabs the cement is falling from the wall; the windows are broken and are barricaded on the inside with rough boards. The hall-door is nailed up, and there are great beams of wood and stones lying about; clearly the only entrance used is the back one. Inside there is but filth and barrenness. You can tell which was the drawing-room by the broken piano, by the gilt cornices that strew the floor. A patch of carpet remains, a deal table stands in the middle of the room. Apparently washing was once done here, for a wash-tub stands on a fragile Chippendale chair that somehow escaped destruction before the room was abandoned. In the bedrooms only the huge four-posters remain; foul earthy odours assail your nostrils; damp, decay, and dust meet you alternately and in combination. Bottles and broken glasses grow more frequent as you descend to the kitchen—now the principal apartment of Miss Barrett and her sister-in arms, Miss McCoy; and there their herdsmen and bailiffs come of an evening and are made riotous with whisky,—and the lampless Irish night grows shrill with shriekings, and the echoes of orgie follow the traveller across the desolate bogs.

The house is surrounded by immense pasture-lands—thousands of acres, from which the tenants have been driven at different times. These are stocked with herds of sheep and cattle. Dressed as a man, in her dreadful corduroy trousers and felt hat, Miss Barrett attends the fairs, and counselled by her herdsmen she buys and sells, spitting and swearing and drinking out of a flask, while she drives the bargain. The sexual economy of animals has no secrets for her; she goes down before the rams are turned into the fold, and it is she who often passes the usual coat of red paint over the animals' bellies. Miss Barrett is delighted as little as she is disgusted by the procreation of beasts; she merely declines to acknowledge the mystery with which we occidentals have surrounded such things, and having chosen to become a herdsman she accepts the duties in all their completeness. Against her virtue not a word has ever been said; she is execrated in the county in which she lives, but it is for drunkenness and cruelty that she is so violently and vehemently abused. To evict her tenants is her one desire, to harass them with summonses for trespass is her sole amusement. She watches them collectively and individually, and when an unfortunate one is a few months in arrear he is at once served with a writ, law costs are run up, every effort is made to render it impossible for him to save himself from ejectment. If by any chance the money should be scraped together and the tenant saved Miss Barrett is wofully disappointed, for she looks forward to an eviction as men did to cock-fights in the old days...

\* \* \* \* \*

# An Eviction

The streets of a county town are swarming with police, they are driving in on cars from all sides—great, big, brawny fellows clad in black cloth and armed with rifles and sword-bayonets. They come thronging in from all parts of the country: sergeant and constables from Ballina, Ballinrobe, Ballindine, Clarenorris, Kelimach, Louisburg, Newport—in fact from every station in Mayo, for it is not known if the peasantry will resist eviction. Three car-loads of police are now crossing the railway bridge. The station is deserted, the platform is empty, a single grey line stretches to and is lost in the interminable bog. Nearer the town there are a few green fields belonging to a landlord who keeps a dairy farm. Then come some filthy cottages where roofs are falling and pigs run grunting from the horses' hoofs. The road is flowing with mud. Suddenly a pavement and stone houses appear, then the market-place and the court-house, and then the spire of the church; and grey houses follow as untidily as dirty shirts and towels hung out on a line in a back yard. Dark and dingy goods, thick boots and shoes, coarse clothes, etc., are piled up in the shop windows, but nowhere is seen a flower-vase, a balcony, a fantastic gable.

At the cross roads of Logafoil, about a mile distant on the other side of the town, we perceive long lines of policemen, about a hundred in all. They are drawn up in lines, headed by their different officers and commanded by Major Murphy. Surrounded by a special guard the gaunt hungry Scotchwoman, Miss McCoy, gives her arm to Miss Barrett—that strange creature in corduroy trousers strapped round her with a belt; fat and bloated she is with drink, and her blue eyes stare with the vagueness of coming idiocy. But she wakes up a little when the order to march is given, and as she whispers to her friend an expression of atrocious cruelty steals over the faces of the women. On the other side there is her bailiff—a man named Pratt, whom the peasants assail, as we march, with the bitterest reproaches concerning his birth and the applications he had made for the post of hangman.

"At all events I have gentleman's blood in my veins, even if it did not come to me through the marriage ring, and that is more than any of you can say."

"The devil a drop, the Colonel disowned you, your _____ of a mother was caught by a policeman one night in a ditch: that's more like it."

And with such lively passages of wit, varied with sarcastic

allusions of a like delicate nature, the tedium of our walk is enlivened. Hundreds of people have assembled, there is some blowing of horns on the hill-side and at first we think the police will have to charge the people. But having been fired upon lately they are frightened, and allow themselves to be driven back with the butt-ends of the rifles, and the little army is posted about the wretched hut from which a human family is to be driven. So horrible is the place that it seems a mockery, a piece of ferocious cynicism to suggest that the possession of it is about to be contested, and that to restore it to its rightful owner an army has to be gathered together. It lies under the potato-field, and the space between bank and wall is a stream of mud and excrement. The incessant rain has rotted the straw of the roof, and at one end it droops ready to slip down at every moment. The weak walls lean this way and that, and their foundations are clearly sinking away into the wet bog. Hard by the dung-heap, in front of the door, where the pig strives to find a place dry enough to lie in, the mud and filth have lapsed into green liquid where some ducks are paddling; under the thatch there is mould and damp, about the door and window-holes blackness and ooze, mud permeates and soaks through every crevice; the place seems like a rat's nest built on the edge of a cesspool. Not a tree is to be seen, not even a bush. There is the brown bog far away, and the flashes of water where lapwings are flying; there are the tumble-down little walls which separate the fields that the peasants scratch rather than till; there is the desolate lake where waves are breaking and rushes are blown in the wild wind. And this chilling landscape is bound with the usual sash of blue mountains.

Only the voice of a child crying is heard. Pratt and a one-armed man, upon whom the peasants continued to shower the strangest abuse, approach and ask for admittance.

"I'll not open it. 'Tis not like the last day, when you boasted you caught the buck in the house."

"Now, Thomas," says Pratt, "the easy way is the best. If you don't open I'll have to force the door."

"You hang-in-bone dog! You may thank the law, or you wouldn't come this way to my door; I would scatter your brains on the street, you dirty bloodhound and nameless bastard! My father and grandfather were reared here, and you want to put me out of it—a fellow who couldn't tell who was *his* grandfather. When your old mother called you after Colonel Pratt, to try and knock money out of him, he always denied that you had a drop of his blood in you, and you have not, *Billeen Sollagh*." This speech is received with roars of laughter, and Pratt puts his shoulder to the door, but it does not give way and paying no heed to the sarcastic suggestion that he might fetch a long ladder and get down the chimney, he seeks about for a stone. Selecting the largest he can find he launches it against the door. There is a cry from the children within, but the door has not given way. The missile is hurled again and again, and when he starts a plank he levels his next throw at the same place; a piece of wood snaps off short; he is invited to put his hand inside, but he wisely refrains. And all the while the children are crying, and the mother utters unceasingly that long wail traditional with the Gaelic people and always used by them in times of mourning; and on the dung-heap and on the road there is jeering; and wild curses are showered on the extraordinary creature—the lumpy, wornout debauchee, who stands staring vaguely, her bloated face now and then lighting up in an expression of cruelty, her trembling hand twitching nervously at the hem of her abominable dress. At last the door gives way, and Pratt, the one-handed assistant, and a couple of police, force their way into the black den. There is the father, the wife and her six half-naked children. The father, covered only with a pair of trousers, his hairy shoulders showing through the ragged shirt, rushes out like a wild beast to strangle Pratt, but he is seized by the policemen; and the clearing of the house of furniture is commenced—an iron pot, a few plates, three logs of wood that are used as seats, a chair, a cradle, and some straw and rags on which the whole family slept; Miss Barrett looks on with manifest satisfaction. Here are a few remarks snatched as it were out of the crowd: "McCoy, have you anything in that flask? You ought to give a drop to your neighbours. Barrett, you buy this old cradle, it was a very lucky one! Who knows what might turn up for you yet, in the shape of some old devil of a husband as ugly as yourself but not so great a drunkard?"

Then the family has to follow the furniture. The father struggles, held fast by two policemen, the children are soon shoved out of the door, but the woman offers a stubborn resistance. She is a strong, stout, shapeless creature. A red petticoat falls to her knees, a shawl is wrapped round her shoulders, and she carries a baby in her arms.

"Ah, you dirty illegitimate beast, I dare you to lay a hand

on me; I am an honest woman and not a dirty slut like your mother... Don't touch me! Will you? you are breaking my back... You are killing the innocent child. Leave go of me! Is there no one here to save me?"

"Now you had better go for the asking; we don't want to hurt you, but out you must go."

"You don't want to hurt me? I tell ye you are breaking my back. The death of the child be on your head; he isn't a dirty bastard like you. Will you leave me go?"

Pratt pushes her from behind, the one-armed man pulls her in front, but she always manages to evade the door-way. It is a marvel how she jerks up the child when it seems on the point of slipping from her. The woman writhes to and fro; she shrieks and shrieks again, the red petticoat is twisted round her waist, and she appears, as she struggles across the doorway in strong and savage nakedness.

But her strength is beginning to fail her, and at last, uttering a wild cry, she slips on the ground, screaming that Pratt has kicked her in the stomach, that she is dying. Leaving his shirt in the hands of the police the husband slips out of their grasp and he would have probably done for Pratt had he not been again seized.

Howls and execrations! Pratt swears he never touched her; the husband swears he saw him; the one-armed man calls God to witness to a number of things; and Major Murphy orders his men to disperse the crowd. Then many things happen: Miss Barrett loses her brandy-flask, a neighbour brings a saucepan of milk, and the wounded woman is consoled and questioned.

"And where did he kick you, awornine?"

"I'm loth to tell you with all the people about."

It is infinitely pitiful and infinitely grotesque. The woman, no doubt, hit herself in her conflict with the bailiff, but she is evidently pretending to worse injuries than she received. For her wailing is more horrible than natural; and the suffering of the little children crying on the dung-heap is more heart-rending. An hour and a half passes. At last she allows herself to be helped out of the house, and she is laid down on some straw under a wall. It seems as if it never could end. The husband goes from group to group collecting evidence against Pratt; the wife shrieks she is bleeding to death—"that she can feel it running down her inside"—and the little boys mock at Miss Barrett's breeches, taunt her with her drunkenness, and Pratt with his bastardy.  At last the doctor arrives.  But how is he to examine her?  Those who after so much trouble have possessed themselves of her house refuse to readmit her even for a few minutes on any pretext whatever.  The woman writhes on the straw, her red petticoat twisted about her naked red legs; and Pratt, still swearing that he never laid a hand or a foot on her, suggests that the Major should clear away the crowd so that the doctor might examine her at once.

"The woman is not a sheep or a cow and cannot be examined in the open air. . ."

"He is thinking of his old mother, your honour; many a time she was examined in the open air; and more is the pity the wall did not tumble upon her and the Colonel, and we wouldn't have him here—Billy, the bad begot!"

Meanwhile a large hole is being made in the roof, the rafters are being torn up, and the woman in breeches and pot-hat, who it is said was once in love with a painter and sat for a picture of Ophelia, puts a padlock on the door.

# George Moore

## *"Emma Bovary"*

The Misses O'Hara arrived at Aix-les-Bains by the afternoon express from Mâcon. The month was September, the air was moveless and warm, and Ismena hoped that Letitia would be benefited by the change. Letitia had never been abroad before. Ismena had been to Paris in early youth to study art, and the drawings she had done in Julien's were tied up in a portfolio, and it lay in a cupboard in their house in Dublin. But this was more than twenty years ago, and Ismena had discovered in the course of the journey to Aix that she had forgotten a good deal of her French. As they drove to the *pension* Letitia said she was glad they were going to stay where English was spoken; she had been a little bored by her sister's attempt to speak French, and when the fly stopped and the proprietress came forward she asked her in triumphant English if they could have a double-bedded room.

"I am very sorry, Mesdames, but we have not a room with two beds in it vacant, but we can give you two small rooms on the same floor."

The sisters stood looking at each other. They had been accustomed for many years to retire at the same hour, and Ismena wondered what it would be like to awaken in the middle of the night and to feel herself alone; and Letitia thought it would be very strange to undress by herself, and to go to sleep without saying good-night to her sister.

"Your rooms will be in the same corridor," the proprietress said.

And Ismena, thinking that she read in Letitia's eyes acquiescence in this arrangement, said—

"If you don't mind, Letitia."

Ismena was tall and straight, and she was better looking than her sister. Her nose was slender and the nostrils were shapely, her eyes were clear and intelligent, her teeth were in good order, and she would not have looked her age had her hair not turned white. Letitia was stouter than her sister, her complexion was muddier, she was less distinguished looking, and her features corresponded to her character—neither was clear-cut. Her hair was an iron grey and her teeth were not so well preserved as Ismena's; the front tooth looked as if it would not last much longer, there was an ominous black speck in it.

In early youth they had lived in the west, and their habit had been to come up to Dublin in the spring and to stop for a month at a hotel. They said they came to Dublin to buy dresses, but their friends said that they came up to Dublin to look for husbands. Whatever their intentions in coming to Dublin may have been, it is certain that they received no proposals of marriage in the drawing-room of their hotel. Neither received a proposal until Ismena went to study art in Julien's and Letitia was left alone in their lodge in the west. In this interval both were on the point of being married, but, unfortunately, Ismena thought it necessary to rush back to Ireland to see her sister and to bring her suitor with her; Letitia brought her suitor from the country; and when the young men saw the sisters together neither loved his betrothed as much as he had done before. There was no wish to change over, together neither sister seemed to please, and the young men broke off their engagements.

After this miserable adventure their visits to Dublin became more private, they stayed only a few days in town, returning to the country as soon as their clothes came home from the dressmaker's. Many years passed, and when they were middle-aged they had inherited a house in Stanhope Terrace, and they came to live in Dublin for good. They often said they would go abroad, but they had never dared to go until Letitia had been ordered abroad by the doctor. But now that they had got as far as Aix, there was no saying they might not go on to Rome when the season at Aix was over and if Letitia's health had been benefited by the waters. They especially looked forward to going to Geneva, and regretted Mont Blanc could not be seen from Aix. Ismena consoled Letitia. She must put Mont Blanc out of her head. She must think of nothing but her health. They went to the baths every morning after mass, and after a short walk they returned to the *pension* for lunch; in the afternoon they went for drives around the green lake and admired the mountains; in the evening there was always some music in the drawing-room, and though Letitia and Ismena neither played nor sang, they were fond of music.

True that they missed their reading a little, but about a week after their arrival they discovered there was an English library in the town.

They had begun reading Mrs Henry Wood before they left Dublin; Letitia was in the middle of the twelfth and Ismena was finishing the thirteenth volume. The librarian said he could supply them with all her works, and both women had begun to think that their journey south was a complete success. Nothing happened to mar their happiness except that they were forced to sleep in different rooms, and now the little blot on it was about to be wiped away, the people who occupied the double-bedded room were going, and the question arose if they should leave their single rooms.

Ismena, though not impatient to share her nights with her sister, was surprised to hear Letitia say it would be hardly worth while changing, now that they were returning home so soon, and she questioned her sister sharply in the baths that morning, but without obtaining any other answer from her.

Letitia had found a book in her room, and a book that had interested her more than any book she had ever read. She had had occasion to move the chest of drawers, and the book dropped down. It was a French novel of many hundred pages and very closely written, but Letitia's attention had been caught at once. She had opened the book at a page where the French was easy, and she had read of a farmer's beautiful daughter who was going to marry a country doctor. The writer mentioned that when Emma put up her silk parasol the last drops splashed on the distended silk. Letitia had never read anything like this in Sir Walter Scott or in Mrs Henry Wood. The rain-drops splashing upon the distended silk parasol excited her wonderment, the sensation was so near that she could feel and hear the cold rain on the silk, and that afternoon her sister noticed that she was a little distracted as they drove about the sailless green lake. Ismena admired the vines and thought it exciting to be in the south at the time of the vintage, but Letitia was thinking of the pages she had read before coming out to drive with her sister. They described the farmer's daughter after her marriage. One day Emma was walking in some meadows wondering if her life would always be the same, and her thoughts ran round and round in circles, like the little Italian greyhound in front of her. Letitia had been impressed by the passage, and she felt that she must read this book, not once, but many times. But they were returning to Dublin in a few days, and she could not read the book in that time, nor yet in twenty days. She felt she must read the passage about the greyhound again. The book had probably been forgotten by some former occupant of the room. She did not like to take what did not belong to her, and she could not leave it behind, for then the people in the hotel would think that she had bought the book, that it was hers, and the last three days were spent in thinking of what she should do with it. She could not put it into that trunk; Ismena would be sure to find it, and she did not want Ismena to know that she had read it; she did not want Ismena to read this book; she did not want to discuss this book with Ismena. One can discuss Scott or Dickens or Thackeray, but one cannot discuss emotions that one ought never to have felt with one's sister. Eventually she put the book into the pocket that she wore under her skirt, and it seriously inconvenienced her during the journey. It was difficult for her to get her purse when Ismena asked her for it at the ticket-offices, and the book thumped her legs when she walked, but she did not mind the inconvenience; she was troubled by the thought that she had stolen the book, but her anxiety to know what became of Emma was intense. She thought of the pleasure it would be to read this book in the garden, and almost the first thing she did was to hide her book in the tool-house. It was only in the garden she could read it; in the drawing-room she read Scott with Ismena. There was a rosewood table in the middle of the worn carpet, and the wall-paper was stained and dusty and covered with bad engravings of sentimental pictures, and there were some coloured lithographs of Pyrenean peasants and forgotten prima-donnas. It was in this drawing-room, sitting on the little green sofa or on the old armchairs, sheltered from the flare of the fire by tapestry screens, that Ismena and Letitia read the books that came every week from the circulating library. They always read the same authors, for if they read different authors they would have nothing to talk about, and they enjoyed discussing the heroes and the heroines in the evening before they took their candle and went to their bedroom. It was Ismena who decided which author they should read; her mind was more methodical than Letitia's, and she believed that to derive any considerable benefit from an author he should be read from the earliest to the latest works. Her preference for authors of historical tendencies enabled her to overrule Letitia's taste for modern sentimentalities, and she was now forcing a thorough reading of the Waverley novels upon her sister. Most of their reading was done in the afternoons and evenings. The sisters took the housekeeping and the gardening in turns. At half-past ten every morning they separated for a while. One took up the key-basket, the other looked to see if it were raining; if it were not, she put on her gardening gloves.

"You don't seem to care for *Old Mortality*?"

"I admire it, but I don't care to read it. How many more novels are there, Ismena, in this edition?"

"Thirteen or fourteen, I think, dear; we ought to get through them all before February."

In those fourteen novels Letitia saw nothing but breast-plates and ramparts, and she made up her mind to skip a number of pages when Ismena went to the kitchen.

"Before we went to Aix we began Mrs Henry Wood. You insisted on reading her and you did not finish her works."

"I read eighteen, and then I began to get confused about the characters and to muddle up the stories. I have read now a dozen volumes of Scott, and I don't seem to have learned anything."

"What do you mean, Letitia?"

"Well, one learns nothing of life."

There seemed to be some truth in Letitia's remark, and Ismena thought before she answered—

"You did not like *Felix Holt*, you never finished it, and you said that a novel was intended to amuse rather than to instruct."

"*Felix Holt*, if I remember right, is about democracy, socialism, and Methodism. I should like to read about life, about what people really feel. I cannot express myself any better, Ismena. Don't you understand that one would like to read about one's own life or about something that might have been one's life?"

"But no one could write a novel about our lives; nothing very much seems to have happened in them."

Letitia heard her go downstairs to the kitchen, and she put the marker twenty and odd pages farther than she had read. She turned on the sofa and looked out of the window. There were clouds, but it was still fine, and Letitia decided that this was the moment to go into the garden.

Their garden was a small square facing the street in which they lived. It looked as if it should be the common property of those living in the street, but the landlord had found that if he allowed all the tenants to walk in the garden no one walked in it at all. For it to be enjoyed by someone it had to become the exclusive property of one house, and it had been given to the Misses O'Hara to keep in order. They had a pretty taste in gardening, and they kept it in beautiful order.

Along the street there were hawthorn-trees and along one wall many lilac-bushes and some apple-trees, and the lilacs grew in such abundance that their branches joined overhead, making a shady little avenue. The tool-house was at the end of this avenue, and Letitia could read there in safety; her sister could not come upon her unawares; the moment the garden gate opened Letitia could hide her novel behind the loose planks.

She could generally get about one hour a day by herself in the garden, and she read about Emma's love of Rudolph, and the scene where she sees him for the last time in the garden impressed her very much, and while talking to her sister of things that did not interest her she remembered how the ripe peach had broken from its stalk and had fallen with a thud in the quiet midnight. She had read of the passionate yearning of this wife of the country doctor, the wife always looking to something beyond her life and the husband quite contented in his life. The sensation that the book exhaled of Emma's empty days was extraordinarily intense. There was a description of how Emma looked out of the window in the morning, how she watched her husband ride away to visit his patients. Later, a clerk came to fill her empty days with desire again, and Letitia was extraordinarily impressed by a passage describing how the husband, lying by his wife's side, thinks of the child in the cradle, what she will be like when she grows up, etc., while Emma dreams of a romantic elopement in a coach drawn through mountain passes by four horses. Letitia read that Emma hardly heard her husband's breathing, so intently did she listen to the tinkling of the postilion bells and the sound of distant water-falls.

Rudolph was a neighbour, and Emma had been able to see Rudolph in her own house or in his, but she had to go to Rouen to see the clerk, and to go to Rouen she required money, and

Letitia read how Emma used to borrow from a usurer. When the usurer gave her the money all she saw in it, all it represented to her, was a number of visits to Rouen. Emma used to meet her lover in a hotel. The descriptions of their meetings frightened Letitia, and she sometimes thought she was not justified in reading any more, but her scruple died from her in an extraordinary sense of bewilderment and curiosity.

The garden gate closed with a snap, and she slipped the book behind the loose woodwork of the shed and, catching up a rake, went to meet her sister.

Ismena had come to ask her sister if she had seen the French dictionary. She had been writing to some of her friends in Aix and wanted to know how to spell a word. Letitia told her sister that she thought she would find the dictionary in the study, and she resolved to put it there when they went in to lunch.

They walked across the sward to the bare borders. The sunflowers had died and the dahlias had been put away for the winter, but the chrysanthemums were still flowering.

After lunch Ismena brought her sister out with her to pay some visits, and next day it rained. It rained all the week, and they read the Waverley novels under the great Victorian chandelier. Letitia often thought of putting on her water-proof and running down to the tool-house to fetch her book. The Waverley novels were books, and Mrs Henry Wood's novels were books, but this book was life or very nearly. Letitia knew she never would get nearer life than this book, and she waited impatiently for another dry day. Whenever there was a dry hour Ismena was with her, and it looked as if the Waverley novels would be finished before she got into the garden again. She was now trying to read *The Talisman*, but she seemed to make no progress, and she had to move her marker on several pages in order to deceive Ismena. While skipping the last half of this book she had to deceive Ismena further. She held the book as if she were reading it, and fixed her thoughts on Emma and the usurer. There could be but one end—the convent, or her husband might die and she might marry the clerk. But then she would not be punished for her sins! Then Rudolph was her first love, and to marry him not only the husband but the clerk would have to die. But these endings were the endings that Scott or Mrs Henry Wood would have chosen, and Letitia wondered.

At last a fine day came, but that morning Letitia awoke with a bad throat, and her throat grew worse all day. Next day she could hardly speak, and Ismena had to send for their doctor; but he assured her there was no cause for alarm, that her sister was not suffering from diphtheria. An hour later the parlour maid said to a visitor—

"Miss O'Hara is ill, she is in bed, but Miss Ismena would like to see you."

Ismena explained that, although her sister could not speak, there was no cause for alarm; the doctor said so. The visitor thought she would send in a specialist, but Ismena never permitted any interference, and two days after Letitia was dead. She died the evening of the following day. About four o'clock she made signs that she wanted to write, and Ismena handed her a sheet of note-paper and a pencil, and she wrote, "*There is a brown-paper parcel in the summer-house.*" She thought that if she got better, she could read the book in bed; if she got worse, she would ask the nurse to burn it.

But it took Ismena a very long time to find the book, so securely had it been hidden, and during that time Letitia's throat had inflamed still further, and when Ismena returned Letitia was dead.

Had it not been for the garden Ismena would not have lived; it was the garden that helped her to forget her grief. She digged in the garden all the spring, and in June Ismena's flower-beds were the admiration of the neighbourhood. But one day as she crossed the sward going to the tool-house she remembered that she had gone there to fetch a brown-paper parcel for her sister. She had taken a long time to find it, and when she brought it to her sister, her sister was dead. She left the garden and searched for it; she remembered that it looked like a book. At last she found it, and it was a book. She had read it in France long ago; she remembered who had given her the book, and wondering what had become of him she stood for a long time watching the trees waving in the garden.

"But how did Letitia come upon this book? Who could have given it to her? Now I know why she sat in the garden so often. Now I know what became of the French dictionary. Oh," she said, "who ever would have thought this of Letitia!"

# George Moore

*Some Parishioners*

I

The way before Father Maguire was plain enough, yet his uncle's apathy and constitutional infirmity of purpose seemed at times to thwart him. Some two or three days ago, he had come running down from Kilmore with the news that a baby had been born out of wedlock, and Father Stafford had shown no desire that his curate should denounce the girl from the altar.

"The greatest saints," he said, "have been kind, and have found excuses for the sins of others."

And a few days later, when he told his uncle that the Salvationists had come to Kilmore, and that he had walked up the village street and slit their drum with a carving knife, his uncle had not approved of his conduct, and what had especially annoyed Father Tom was that his uncle seemed to deplore the slitting of the drum in the same way as he deplored that the Kavanaghs had a barrel of porter in every Saturday, as one of those regrettable excesses to which human nature is liable. On being pressed he had agreed with his nephew that dancing and drinking were no preparation for the Sabbath, but he would not agree that evil could be suppressed by force. He had even hinted that too strict a rule brought about a revolt against the rule, and when Father Tom had expressed his disbelief at any revolt against the authority of the priest, Father Stafford said:—

"They may just leave you, they may just go to America."

"Then you think that it is our condemnation of sin that is driving the people to America."

"My dear Tom, you told me the other day that you met a

lad and a lass walking along the roadside, and that you drove them home. You told me you were sure they were talking about things they should not talk about; you have no right to assume these things. You're asking of the people an abstinence you don't practise yourself. Sometimes your friends are women."

"Yes. But—"

Father Tom's anger prevented him from finding an adequate argument. Father Stafford pushed the tobacco bowl towards his nephew.

"You're not smoking, Tom."

"Your point is that a certain amount of vice is inherent in human nature, and that if we raise the standard of virtuous living our people will escape from us to New York or London."

"The sexes mix freely everywhere in Western Europe; only in Ireland and Turkey is there any attempt made to separate them."

Later in the evening Father Tom insisted that the measure of responsibility was always the same.

"I should be sorry," said his uncle, "to say that those who inherit drunkenness bear the same burden of responsibility as those who come of parents who are quite sane—"

"You cannot deny, uncle John, that free will and predestination—"

"My dear Tom, I really must go to bed. It is after midnight."

As he walked home, Father Maquire thought of the great change he perceived in his uncle. Father Stafford liked to go to bed at eleven; the very name of St. Thomas seemed to bore him; fifteen years ago he would sit up till morning. Father Maguire remembered the theological debates, sometimes prolonged till after three o'clock, and the passionate scholiast of Maynooth seemed to him unrecognisable in the esurient Vicar-General, only occasionally interested in theology, at certain hours and when he felt particularly well. He could not reconcile the two ages, his mind not being sufficiently acute to see that after all no one can discuss theology for more than five and twenty years without wearying of the subject.

The moon was shining among the hills and the mystery of the landscape seemed to aggravate his sensibility, and he asked himself if the guardians of the people should not fling themselves into the forefront of the battle. Men came to preach heresy in his parish—was he not justified in slitting their drum?

He had recourse to prayer, and he prayed for strength and for guidance. He had accepted the Church, and in the Church he saw only apathy, neglect, and bad administration on the part of his superiors . . . He had read that great virtues are, like large sums of money, deposited in the bank, whereas humility is like the pence, always at hand, always current. Obedience to our superiors is the sure path. He could not persuade himself that it was right for him to allow the Kavanaghs to continue a dissolute life of drinking and dancing. They were the talk of the parish; and he would have spoken against them from the altar, but his uncle had advised him not to do so. Perhaps his uncle was right; he might be right regarding the Kavanaghs. In the main he disagreed with his uncle, but in this particular instance it might be well to wait and pray that matters might improve.

Father Tom believed Ned Kavanagh to be a good boy. Ned was going to marry Mary Byrne, and Father Tom had made up this marriage. The Byrnes did not care for the marriage—they were prejudiced against Ned on account of his family. But he was not going to allow them to break off the marriage. He was sure of Ned, but in order to make quite sure he would get him to take the pledge. Next morning when the priest had done his breakfast, the servant opened the door, and told him that Ned Kavanagh was outside, and wanted to see him.

It was a pleasure to look at this nice, clean boy, with his winning smile, and the priest thought that Mary could not wish for a better husband. The priest had done his breakfast, and was about to open his newspaper, but he wanted to see Ned Kavanagh, and he told his servant to let him in. Ned's smile seemed a little fainter than usual, and his face was paler; the priest wondered, and presently Ned told the priest that he had come to confession, and, going down on his knees, he told the priest that he had been drunk last Saturday night, and that he had come to take the pledge. He would never do any good while he was at home, and one of the reasons he gave for wishing to marry Mary Byrne was his desire to leave home. The priest asked him if matters were mending, and if his sister showed any signs of wishing to be married.

"Sorra sign," said Ned.

"That's bad news you're bringing me," said the priest, and he walked up and down the room, and they talked over Kate's wilful character.

"From the beginning she did not like living at home," said the priest.

"I don't care about living at home," said Ned.

"But for a different reason," said the priest. "You want to leave home to get married, and have a wife and children, if God is pleased to give you children."

Kate had been in numerous services, and the priest sat thinking of the stories he had heard. He had heard that Kate had come back from her last situation in a cab, wrapped up in blankets, saying she was ill. On inquiry it was found that she had only been three or four days in her situation; three weeks had to be accounted for. He had questioned her himself regarding this interval, but had not been able to get any clear and definite answer from her.

"She and mother never stop quarrelling about Pat Connex."

"It appears," said the priest, "that your mother went out with a jug of porter under her apron, and offered a sup of it to Pat Connex, who was talking with Peter M'Shane, and now he is up at your cabin every Saturday."

"That's it," said Ned.

"Mrs. Connex was here the other day, and I can tell you that if Pat marries your sister he will find himself cut off with a shilling."

"She's been agin us all the while," said Ned. "Her money has made her proud, but I don't blame her. If I had the fine house she has, maybe I would be as proud as she."

"Maybe you would," said the priest. "But what I am thinking of is your sister Kate. She will never get Pat Connex. Pat will never go against his mother."

"Well, you see he comes up and plays the melodion on Saturday night," said Ned, "and she can't stop him from doing that."

"Then you think," said the priest, "that Pat will marry your sister?"

"I don't think she wants to marry him."

"If she doesn't want to marry him, what's all this talk about?"

"She likes to meet Pat in the evenings and go for a walk with him, and she likes him to put his arm round her waist and kiss her, saving your reverence's presence."

"It is strange that you should be so unlike. You come here

and ask me to speak to Mary Byrne's parents for you, and that I'll do, Ned, and it will be all right. You will make a good husband, and though you were drunk last night, you have taken the pledge to-day, and I will make a good marriage for Kate, too, if she'll listen to me."

"And who may your reverence be thinking of?"

"I'm thinking of Peter M'Shane. He gets as much as six shillings a week and his keep on Murphy's farm, and his mother has got a bit of money, and they have a nice, clean cabin. Now listen to me. There is a poultry lecture at the school house to-night. Do you think you could bring your sister with you?"

"We used to keep a great many hens at home, and Kate had the feeding of them, and now she's turned agin them, and she wants to live in town, and she even tells Pat Connex she would not marry a farmer, however much he was worth."

"But if you tell her that Pat Connex will be at the lecture, will she come?"

"Yes, your reverence, if she believes me."

"Then do as I bid you," said the priest; "you can tell her that Pat Connex will be there."

II

After leaving the priest Ned crossed over the road to avoid the publichouse. He went for a walk on the hills, and it was about five when he turned towards the village. On his way there he met his father, and Ned told him that he had been to see the priest, and that he was going to take Mary to the lecture.

Michael Kavanagh wished his son God-speed. He was very tired; and he thought it was pretty hard to come home after a long day's work to find his wife and daughter quarrelling.

"I am sorry your dinner is not ready, father, but it won't be long now. I'll cut the bacon."

"I met Ned on the road," said her father. "He has gone to fetch Mary. He is going to take her to the lecture on poultry-keeping at the schoolhouse."

"Ah, he has been to the priest, has he?" said Kate, and her mother asked her why she said that, and the wrangle began again.

Ned was the peacemaker; there was generally quiet in the

cabin when he was there. He came in with Mary, a small, fair girl, and a good girl, who would keep his cabin tidy. His mother and sisters were broad-shouldered women with blue-black hair and red cheeks, and it was said that he had said he would like to bring a little fair hair into the family.

"We've just come in for a minute," said Mary, "Ned said that perhaps you'd be coming with us."

"All the boys in the village will be there to-night," said Ned. "You had better come with us." And pretending he wanted to get a coal of fire to light his pipe, Ned whispered to Kate as he passed her, "Pat Connex will be there."

She looked at the striped sunshade she had brought back from the dressmaker's—she had once been apprenticed to a dressmaker—but Ned said that a storm was blowing and she had better leave the sunshade behind.

The rain beat in their faces and the wind came sweeping down the mountain and made them stagger. Sometimes the road went straight on, sometimes it turned suddenly and went up-hill. After walking for a mile they came to the schoolhouse. A number of men were waiting outside, and one of the boys told them that the priest had said they were to keep a look out for the lecturer, and Ned said that he had better stay with them, that his lantern would be useful to show her the way. They went into a long, smoky room. The women had collected into one corner, and the priest was walking up and down, his hands thrust into the pockets of his overcoat. Now he stopped in his walk to scold two children who were trying to light a peat fire in a tumbled-down grate.

"Don't be tired, go on blowing," he said. "You are the laziest child I have seen this long while."

Ned came in and blew out his lantern, but the lady he had mistaken for the lecturer was a lady who had come to live in the neighbourhood lately, and the priest said:—

"You must be very much interested in poultry, ma'am, to come out on such a night as this."

The lady stood shaking her waterproof.

"Now, then, Lizzie, run to your mother and get the lady a chair."

And when the child came back with the chair, and the lady was seated by the fire, he said:—

"I'm thinking there will be no lecturer here to-night, and that it would be kind of you if you were to give the lecture yourself. You have read some books about poultry, I am sure?"

"Well, a little—but—"

"Oh, that doesn't matter," said the priest. "I'm sure the book you have read is full of instruction."

He walked up to the room towards a group of men and told them they must cease talking, and coming back to the young woman he said:—

"We shall be much obliged if you will say a few words about poultry. Just say what you have in your mind about the different breeds."

The young woman again protested, but the priest said:—

"You will do it very nicely." And he spoke like one who is not accustomed to being disobeyed. "We will give the lecturer five minutes more."

"Is there no farmer's wife who could speak," the young lady said in a fluttering voice. "She would know much more than I. I see Biddy M'Hale there. She has done very well with her poultry."

"I daresay she has," said the priest, "but the people would pay no attention to her. She is one of themselves. It would be no amusement to them to hear her."

The young lady asked if she might have five minutes to scribble a few notes. The priest said he would wait a few minutes, but it did not matter much what she said.

"But couldn't some one dance or sing," said the young lady.

"Dancing and singing!" said the priest. "No!"

And the young lady hurriedly scribbled a few notes about fowls for laying, fowls for fattening, regular feeding, warm houses, and something about a percentage of mineral matter. She had not half finished when the priest said:—

"Now will you stand over there near the harmonium. Whom shall I announce?"

The young woman told him her name, and he led her to the harmonium and left her talking, addressing most of her instruction to Biddy M'Hale, a long, thin, pale-faced woman, with wistful eyes.

"This won't do," said the priest, interrupting the lecturer, —"I'm not speaking to you, miss, but to my people. I don't see one of you taking notes, not even you, Biddy M'Hale, though you have made a fortune out of your hins. Didn't I tell you from the pulpit that you were to bring pencil and paper and write down all you heard. If you had known years ago all this young lady is going to tell you you would be rolling in your carriages to-day."

Then the priest asked the lecturer to go on, and the lady explained that to get hens to lay about Christmas time, when eggs fetched the best price, you must bring on your pullets early.

"You must," she said, "set your eggs in January."

"You hear that," said the priest. "Is there anyone who has got anything to say about that? Why is it that you don't set your eggs in January?"

No one answered, and the lecturer went on to tell of the advantages that would come to the poultry keeper whose eggs were hatched in December.

As she said this, the priest's eyes fell upon Biddy M'Hale, and, seeing that she was smiling, he asked her if there was any reason why eggs could not be hatched in the beginning of January.

"No, Biddy, you must know all about this, and I insist on your telling us. We are here to learn."

Biddy did not answer.

"Then what were you smiling at?"

"I wasn't smiling, your reverence."

"Yes; I saw you smiling. Is it because you think there isn't a brooding hin in January?"

It had not occurred to the lecturer that hens might not be brooding so early in the year, and she waited anxiously. At last Biddy said:—

"Well, your reverence, it isn't because there are no hins brooding. You'll get brooding hins at every time in the year; but, you see, you can't rear chickens earlier than March. The end of February is the earliest I have ever seen. But, of course, if you could rear them in January, all that the young lady said would be quite right. I have nothing to say agin it. I have no fault to find with anything she says, your reverence."

"Only that it can't be done," said the priest. "Well, you ought to know, Biddy."

The villagers were laughing.

"That will do," said the priest. "I don't mind your having a bit of amusement, but you're here to learn."

And as he looked round the room, quieting the villagers into silence, his eyes fell on Kate. "That's all right," he thought, and he looked for the others, and spied Pat Connex and Peter

M'Shane near the door. "They're here, too," he thought. "When the lecture is over I will see them and bring them all together. Kate Kavanagh won't go home until she promises to marry Peter. I have had enough of her goings on in my parish."

But Kate had caught sight of Peter. She would get no walk home with Pat that night, and she suspected her brother of having done this for a purpose. She got up to go.

"I don't want anyone to leave this room," said the priest. "Kate Kavanagh, why are you going? Sit down till the lecture is over."

And as Kate had not strength to defy the priest she sat down, and the lecturer continued for a little while longer. The priest could see that the lecturer had said nearly all she had to say, and he had begun to wonder how the evening's amusement was to be prolonged. It would not do to let the people go home until Michael Dunne had closed his public-house, and the priest looked round the audience thinking which one he might call upon to say a few words on the subject of poultry-keeping.

From one of the back rows a voice was heard:—

"What about the pump, your reverence?"

"Well, indeed, you may ask," said the priest.

And immediately he began to speak of the wrong they had suffered by not having a pump in the village. The fact that Almighty God had endowed Kilmore with a hundred mountain streams did not release the authorities from the obligation of supplying the village with a pump. Had not the authorities put up one in the neighbouring village?

"You should come out," he said, "and fight for your rights. You should take off your coats like men, and if you do I'll see that you get your rights," and he looked round for someone to speak.

There was a landlord among the audience, and as he was a Catholic the priest called upon him to speak. He said that he agreed with the priest in the main. They should have their pump, if they wanted a pump; if they didn't, he would suggest that they asked for something else. Farmer Byrne said he did not want a pump, and then everyone spoke his mind, and things got mixed. The Catholic landlord regretted that Father Maguire was against allowing a poultry-yard to the patients in the lunatic asylum. If, instead of supplying a pump, the Government would sell them eggs for hatching at a low price, something might be gained. If the Government would not do this, the Government might be induced to supply books on poultry free of charge. It took the Catholic landlord half an hour to express his ideas regarding the asylum, the pump, and the duties of the Government, and in this way the priest succeeded in delaying the departure of the audience till after closing time. "However fast they walk," he said to himself, "they won't get to Michael Dunne's public-house in ten minutes, and he will be shut by then." It devolved upon him to bring the evening's amusement to a close with a few remarks, and he said:

"Now, the last words I have to say to you I'll address to the women. Now listen to me. If you pay more attention to your poultry you'll never be short of half a sovereign to lend your husbands, your sons, or your brothers."

These last words produced an approving shuffling of feet in one corner of the room, and seeing that nothing more was going to happen the villagers got up and they went out very slowly, the women curtseying and the men lifting their caps to the priest as they passed him.

He had signed to Ned and Mary that he wished to speak to them, and after he had spoken to Ned he called Kate and reminded her that he had not seen her at confession lately.

"Pat Connex and Peter M'Shane, now don't you be going. I will have a word with you presently."

And while Kate tried to find an excuse to account for her absence from confession, the priest called to Ned and Mary, who were talking at a little distance. He told them he would be waiting for them in church tomorrow, and he said he had never made a marriage that gave him more pleasure. He alluded to the fact that they had come to him. He was responsible for this match, and he accepted the responsibility gladly. His uncle, the Vicar-General, had delegated all the work of the parish to him.

"Father Stafford," he said abruptly, "will be very glad to hear of your marriage, Kate Kavanagh."

"My marriage," said Kate.... "I don't think I shall ever be married."

"Now, why do you say that?" said the priest.

Kate did not know why she had said that she would never be married. However, she had to give some reason, and she said:

"I don't think, your reverence, anyone would have me."

"You are not speaking your mind," said the priest, a little

sternly. "It is said that you don't want to be married, that you like courting better."

"I'd like to be married well enough," said Kate.

"Those who wish to make safe, reliable marriages consult their parents and they consult the priest. I have made your brother's marriage for him. Why don't you come to me and ask me to make up a marriage for you?"

"I think a girl should make her own marriage, your reverence."

"And what way do you go about making up a marriage? Walking about the roads in the evening, and going into public-houses, and leaving your situations. It seems to me, Kate Kavanagh, you have been a long time making up this marriage."

"Now, Pat Connex, I've got a word with you. You're a good boy, and I know you don't mean any harm by it; but I have been hearing tales about you. You've been up to Dublin with Kate Kavanagh. Your mother came up to speak to me about this matter yesterday, and she said: 'Not a penny of my money will he ever get if he marries her,' meaning the girl before you. Your mother said: 'I've got nothing to say against her, but I've got a right to choose my own daughter-in-law.' These are your mother's very words, Pat, so you had better listen to reason. Do you hear me, Kate?"

"I hear your reverence."

"And if you hear me, what have you got to say to that?"

"He's free to go after the girl he chooses, your reverence," said Kate.

"There's been courting enough," the priest said. "If you aren't going to be married you must give up keeping company. I see Paddy Boyle outside the door. Go home with him. Do you hear what I'm saying, Pat? Go straight home, and no stopping about the roads. Just do as I bid you; go straight home to your mother."

Pat did not move at the bidding of the priest. He stood watching Kate as if he were waiting for a sign from her, but Kate did not look at him.

"Do you hear what I'm saying to you?" said the priest.

"Yes, I hear," said Pat.

"And aren't you going?" said the priest.

Everyone was afraid Pat would raise his hand against the priest, and they looked such strong men, both of them, that everyone wondered which would get the better of the other.

"You won't go home when I tell you to do so. We will see if I can't put you out of the door then."

"If you weren't a priest," said Pat, "the devil a bit of you would put me out of the door."

"If I weren't a priest I would break every bone in your body for talking to me like that. Now out you go," he said, taking him by the collar, and he put him out.

"And now, Kate Kavanagh," said the priest, coming back from the door, "you said you didn't marry because no man would have you. Peter has been waiting for you ever since you were a girl of sixteen years old, and I may say it for him, since he doesn't say much himself, that you have nearly broken his heart."

"I'm sure I never meant it. I like Peter."

"You acted out of recklessness without knowing what you were doing."

A continual smile floated round Peter's moustache, and he looked like a man to whom rebuffs made no difference. His eyes were patient and docile; and whether it was the presence of this great and true love by her side, or whether it was the presence of the priest, Kate did not know, but a great change came over her, and she said:

"I know that Peter has been very good, that he has cared for me this long while. . . . If he wishes to make me his wife—"

When Kate gave him her hand there was a mist in his eyes, and he stood trembling before her.

III

Next morning, as Father Maguire was leaving the house, his servant handed him a letter. It was from an architect who had been down to examine the walls of the church. The envelope that Father Maguire was tearing open contained his report, and Father Maguire read that it would require £200 to make the walls secure. Father Maguire was going round to the church to marry Mary Byrne and Ned Kavanagh, and he continued to read the report until he arrived at the church. The wedding party was waiting, but the architect's report was much more important than a wedding, and he wandered round the old walls examining the cracks as he went. He could see they were crumbling, and he believed the architect was right, and that it would be better to build a new church. But to build a new church three or four thousand pounds would be required, and the architect might as well suggest that he should collect three or four millions.

And Ned and Mary noticed the dark look between the priest's eyes as he came out of the sacristy, and Ned regretted that his reverence should be out of his humour that morning, for he had spent three out of the five pounds he had saved to pay the priest for marrying him. He had cherished hopes that the priest would understand that he had had to buy some new clothes, but the priest looked so cross that it was with difficulty that he summoned courage to tell him that he had only two pounds left.

"I want two hundred pounds to make the walls of the church safe. Where is the money to come from? All the money in Kilmore goes into drink, and," he added bitterly, "into blue trousers. No, I won't marry you for two pounds. I won't marry you for less than five. I will marry you for nothing or I will marry you for five pounds," he added, and Ned looked round the wedding guests; he knew that none had five shillings in his pocket, and he did not dare to take the priest at his word and let him marry him for nothing.

Father Maguire felt that his temper had got the better of him, but it was too late to go back on what he said. Marry them for two pounds with the architect's letter in the pocket of his cassock! And if he were to accept two pounds, who would pay five to be married? If he did not stand out for his dues the marriage fee would be reduced from five pounds to one pound. . . . And if he accepted Ned's two pounds his authority would be weakened; he would not be able to get them to subscribe to have the church made safe. On the whole he thought he had done right, and his servant was of the same opinion.

"They'd have the cassock off your back, your reverence, if they could get it."

"And the architect writing to me that the walls can't be made safe under £200, and the whole lot of them earning not less than thirty shillings a week, and they can't pay the priest five pounds for marrying them."

In the course of the day he went to Dublin to see the architect; and next morning it occurred to him that he might have to go to America to get the money to build a new church, and as he sat thinking the door was opened and the servant said that Biddy M'Hale wanted to see his reverence.

She came in curtseying, and before saying a word she took ten sovereigns out of her pocket and put them upon the table. The priest thought she had heard of the architect's report, and he said—

"Now, Biddy, I am glad to see you. I suppose you have brought me this for my church. You have heard of the money it will cost to make the walls safe."

"No, your reverence, I did not hear any more than that there were cracks in the walls."

"But you have brought me this money to have the cracks mended?"

"Well, no your reverence. I have been thinking a long time of doing something for the church, and I thought I would like to have a window put up in the church with coloured glass in it."

Father Maguire was touched by Biddy's desire to do something for the church, and he thought he would have no difficulty in persuading her. He could get this money for the repairs, and he told her that her name would be put on top of the subscription list.

"A subscription from Miss M'Hale—£10. A subscription from Miss M'Hale."

Biddy did not answer, and the priest could see that it would give her no pleasure whatever to subscribe to mending the walls of his church, and it annoyed him to see her sitting in his own chair stretching out her hands to take the money back. He could see that her wish to benefit the church was merely a pretext for the glorification of herself, and the priest began to argue with the old woman. But he might have spared himself the trouble of explaining that it was necessary to have a new church before you could have a window. She understood well enough it was useless to put a window up in a church that was going to fall down. But her idea still was St. Joseph in a red cloak and the Virgin in blue with a crown of gold on her head, and forgetful of everything else, she asked him whether her window in the new church should be put over the high altar, or if it should be a window lighting a side altar.

"But, my good woman, £10 will not pay for a window. You couldn't get anything to speak of in the way of a window for less than fifty pounds."

He had expected to astonish Biddy, but she did not seem astonished. She said that although fifty pounds was a great deal of money she would not mind spending all that money if she were to have her window all to herself. She had thought at first of only putting in part of the window, a round piece at the top of the window, and she had thought that that could be bought for ten pounds. The priest could see that she had been thinking a good deal of this window, and she seemed to know more about it than he expected. "It is extraordinary," he said to himself, "how a desire of immortality persecutes these second-class souls. A desire of temporal immortality," he said, fearing he had been guilty of a heresy.

"If I could have the whole window to myself, I would give you fifty pounds, your reverence."

The priest had no idea she had saved as much money as that.

"The hins have been very good to me, your reverence, and I would like to put up the window in the new church better than in the old church."

"But I've got no money, my good woman, to build the church."

"Ah, won't your reverence go to America and get the money. Aren't our own kith and kin over there, and aren't they always willing to give us money for our churches."

The priest spoke to her about statues, and suggested that perhaps a statue would be a more permanent gift, but the old woman knew that stained glass was more permanent, and that it could be secured from breakage by means of wire netting.

"Do you know, Biddy, it will require three or four thousand pounds to build a new church. If I go to America and do my best to get the money, how much will you help me with?"

"Does your reverence mean for the window?"

"No, Biddy, I was thinking of the church itself."

And Biddy said that she would give him five pounds to help to build the church and fifty pounds for her window, and, she added, "if the best gilding and paint costs a little more I would be sorry to see the church short."

"Well, you say, Biddy, you will give five pounds towards the church. Now, let us think how much money I could get in this parish."

He had a taste for gossip, and he liked to hear everyone's domestic details. She began by telling him she had met Kate

Kavanagh on the road, and Kate had told her that there had been great dancing last night.

"But there was no wedding," said the priest.

"I only know, your reverence, what Kate Kavanagh told me. There had been great dancing last night. The supper was ordered at Michael Dunne's, and the cars were ordered, and they went to Enniskerry and back."

"But Michael Dunne would not dare to serve supper to people who were not married," said the priest.

"The supper had been ordered, and they would have to pay for it whether they ate it or not. There was a pig's head, and the cake cost eighteen shillings, and it was iced."

"Never mind the food," said the priest, "tell me what happened."

"Kate said that after coming back from Enniskerry, Michael Dunne said, 'Is this the wedding party?' and that Ned jumped off the car, and said: 'To be sure. Amn't I the wedded man.' And they had half a barrel of porter."

"Never mind the drink," said the priest, "what then?"

"There was dancing first and fighting after. Pat Connex and Peter M'Shane were both there. You know Pat plays the melodion, and he asked Peter to sing, and Peter can't sing a bit, and he was laughed at. So he grabbed a bit of stick and hit Pat on the head, and hit him badly, too. I hear the doctor had to be sent for."

"That is always the end of their dancing and drinking," said the priest. "And what happened then, what happened? After that they went home?"

"Yes, your reverence, they went home."

"Mary Byrne went home with her own people, I suppose, and Ned went back to his home."

"I don't know, your reverence, what they did."

"Well, what else did Kate Kavanagh tell you?"

"She had just left her brother and Mary, and they were going towards the Peak. That is what Kate told me when I met her on the road."

"Mary Byrne would not go to live with a man to whom she was not married. But you told me that Kate said she had just left Mary Byrne and her brother."

"Yes, they were just coming out of the cabin," said Biddy. "She passed them on the road."

"Out of whose cabin?" said the priest.

"Out of Ned's cabin. I know it must have been out of Ned's cabin, because she said she met them at the cross roads."

He questioned the old woman, but she grew less and less explicit.

"I don't like to think this of Mary Byrne, but after so much dancing and drinking, it is impossible to say what might not have happened."

"I suppose they forgot your reverence didn't marry them."

"Forgot!" said the priest. "A sin has been committed, and through my fault."

"They will come to your reverence to-morrow when they are feeling a little better."

The priest did not answer, and Biddy said:—

"Am I to take away my money, or will your reverence keep it for the stained glass window."

"The church is tumbling down, and before it is built up you want me to put up statues."

"I'd like a window as well or better."

"I've got other things to think of now."

"Your reverence is very busy. If I had known it I would not have come disturbing you. But I'll take my money with me."

"Yes, take your money," he said. "Go home quietly, and say nothing about what you have told me. I must think over what is best to be done."

Biddy hurried away gathering her shawl about her, and this great strong man who had taken Pat Connex by the collar and could have thrown him out of the schoolroom, fell on his knees and prayed that God might forgive him the avarice and anger that had caused him to refuse to marry Ned Kavanagh and Mary Byrne.

"Oh! my God, oh! my God," he said, "Thou knowest that it was not for myself that I wanted the money, it was to build up Thine Own House."

He remembered that his uncle had warned him again and again against the sin of anger. He had thought lightly of his uncle's counsels, and he had not practised the virtue of humility, which, as St. Teresa said, was the surest virtue to seek in this treacherous world.

"Oh, my God, give me strength to conquer anger."

The servant opened the door, but seeing the priest upon his knees, she closed it quietly, and the priest prayed that if sin had been committed he might bear the punishment.

And on rising from his knees he felt that his duty was to seek out the sinful couple. But how to speak to them of their sin? The sin was not theirs. He was the original wrong-doer. If Ned Kavanagh and Mary Byrne were to die and lose their immortal souls, how could the man who had been the cause of the loss of two immortal souls save his own, and the consequences of his refusal to marry Ned Kavanagh and Mary Byrne seemed to reach to the very ends of Eternity.

He walked to his uncle's with great swift steps, hardly seeing his parishioners as he passed them on the road.

"Is Father Stafford in?"

"Yes, your reverence."

"Uncle John, I have come to consult you."

The priest sat huddled in his arm chair over the fire, and Father Maguire noticed that his cassock was covered with snuff, and he noticed the fringe of reddish hair about the great bald head, and he noticed the fat inert hands. And he noticed these things more explicitly than he had ever noticed them before, and he wondered why he noticed them so explicitly, for his mind was intent on a matter of great spiritual importance.

"I have come to ask you," Father Tom said, "regarding the blame attaching to a priest who refuses to marry a young man and a young woman, there being no impediment of consanguinity or other."

"But have you refused to marry anyone because they couldn't pay your dues?"

"Listen, the church is falling."

"My dear Tom, you should not have refused to marry them," he said, as soon as his soul-stricken curate had laid the matter before him.

"Nothing can justify my action in refusing to marry them," said Father Tom, "nothing. Uncle John, I know that you can extenuate, that you are kind, but I do not see it is possible to look at it from any other side."

"My dear Tom, you are not sure they remained together; the only knowledge you have of the circumstances you obtained from that old woman, Biddy M'Hale, who cannot tell a story properly. An old gossip, who manufactures stories out of the slightest materials . . . but who sells excellent eggs; her eggs are always fresh. I had two this morning."

"Uncle John, I did not come here to be laughed at."

"I am not laughing at you, my dear Tom; but really you know very little about this matter."

"I know well enough that they remained together last night. I examined the old woman carefully, and she had just met Kate Kavanagh on the road. There can be no doubt about it," he said.

"But," said Father John, "they intended to be married; the intention was there."

"Yes, but the intention is no use. We are not living in a country where the edicts of the Council of Trent have not been promulgated."

"That's true," said Father John. "But how can I help you? What am I to do?"

"Are you feeling well enough for a walk this morning? Could you come up to Kilmore?"

"But it is two miles—I really—"

"The walk will do you good. If you do this for me, Uncle John—"

"My dear Tom, I am, as you say, not feeling very well this morning, but—"

He looked at his nephew, and seeing that he was suffering, he said—

"I know what these scruples of conscience are; they are worse than physical suffering."

But before he decided to go with his nephew to seek the sinners out, he could not help reading him a little lecture.

"I don't feel as sure as you do that a sin has been committed, but admitting that a sin has been committed, I think you ought to admit that you set your face against the pleasure of these poor people too resolutely."

"Pleasure," said Father Tom. "Drinking and dancing, hugging and kissing each other about the lanes."

"You said dancing—now, I can see no harm in it."

"There is no harm in dancing, but it leads to harm. If they only went back with their parents after the dance, but they linger in the lanes."

"It was raining the other night, and I felt sorry, and I said, 'Well, the boys and girls will have to stop at home to-night, there will be no courting to-night.' If you do not let them walk about the lanes and make their own marriages, they marry for money. These walks at eventide represent all the aspiration that may come into their lives. After they get married, the work of the world grinds all the poetry out of them."

"Walking under the moon," said Father Tom, "with their arms round each other's waists, sitting for hours saying stupid things to each other—that isn't my idea of poetry. The Irish find poetry in other things than sex."

"Mankind," said Father John, "is the same all the world over. The Irish are not different from other races; do not think it. Woman represents all the poetry that the ordinary man is capable of appreciating.

"And what about ourselves?"

"We are different. We have put this interest aside. I have never regretted it, and you have not regretted it either."

"Celibacy has never been a trouble to me."

"But Tom, your own temperament should not prevent you from sympathy with others. You are not the whole of human nature; you should try to get a little outside yourself."

"Can one ever do this?" said Father Tom.

"Well, you see what a difficulty your narrow mindedness has brought you into."

"I know all that," said Father Tom. "It is no use insisting upon it. Now will you come with me? They must be married this morning. Will you come with me? I want you to talk to them. You are kinder than I am. You sympathise with them more than I do, and it wasn't you who refused to marry them."

Father John got out of his arm chair and staggered about the room on his short fat legs, trying to find his hat. Father Tom said—

"Here it is. You don't want your umbrella. There's no sign of rain."

"No," said his uncle, "but it will be very hot presently. My dear Tom, I can't walk fast."

"I am sorry, I didn't know I was walking fast."

"You are walking at the rate of four miles an hour at the least."

"I am sorry, I will walk slower."

At the cross roads inquiry was made, and the priests were told that the cabin Ned Kavanagh had taken was the last one.

"That's just another half mile," said Father John.

"If we don't hasten we shall be late."

"We might rest here," said Father John, "for a moment," and he leaned against a gate. "My dear Tom, it seems to me you're agitating yourself a little unnecessarily about Ned

Kavanagh and his wife—I mean the girl he is going to marry.

"I am quite sure. Ned Kavanagh brought Mary back to his cabin. There can be no doubt."

"Even so," said Father John. "He may have thought he was married."

"How could he have thought he was married unless he was drunk, and that cannot be put forward as an excuse. No, my dear uncle, you are inclined for subtleties this morning."

"He may have thought he was married. Moreover, he intended to be married, and if through forgetfulness—"

"Forgetfulness!" cried Father Maguire. "A pretty large measure of forgetfulness!"

"I shouldn't say that a mortal sin has been committed; a venial one. . . . If he intended to be married—"

"Oh, my dear uncle, we shall be late, we shall be late!"

Father Stafford repressed the smile that gathered in the corner of his lips, and he remembered how Father Tom had kept him out of bed till two o'clock in the morning, talking to him about St. Thomas Aquinas.

"If they're to be married to-day we must be getting on." And Father Maguire's stride grew more impatient. "I'll walk on in front."

At last he spied a woman in a field, and she told him that the married couple had gone towards the Peak. Most of them had gone for a walk, but Pat Connex was in bed, and the doctor had to be sent for.

"I've heard," said Father Tom, "of last night's drunkenness. Half a barrel of porter; there's what remains," he said, pointing to some stains on the roadway. "They were too drunk to turn off the tap."

"I heard your reverence wouldn't marry them," the woman said.

"I am going to bring them down to the church at once."

"Well if you do," said the woman, "you won't be a penny the poorer; you will have your money at the end of the week. And how do you do, your reverence." The woman dropped a curtsey to Father Stafford. "It's seldom we see you up here."

"They have gone towards the Peak," said Father Tom, for he saw his uncle would take advantage of the occasion to gossip. "We shall catch them up there."

"I am afraid I am not equal to it, Tom. I'd like to do this

for you, but I am afraid I am not equal to another half mile uphill."

Father Maguire strove to hypnotize his parish priest.

"Uncle John, you are called upon to make this effort. I cannot speak to these people as I should like to."

"If you spoke to them as you would like to, you would only make matters worse," said Father John.

"Very likely, I'm not in a humour to contest these things with you. But I beseech you to come with me. Come," he said, "take my arm."

They went a few hundred yards up the road, then there was another stoppage, and Father Maguire had again to exercise his power of will, and he was so successful that the last half mile of the road was accomplished almost without a stop.

At Michael Dunne's, the priests learned that the wedding party had been there, and Father Stafford called for a lemonade.

"Don't fail me now, Uncle John. They are within a few hundred yards of us. I couldn't meet them without you. Think of it. If they were to tell me that I had refused to marry them for two pounds, my authority would be gone for ever. I should have to leave the parish."

"My dear Tom, I would do it if I could, but I am completely exhausted."

At that moment sounds of voices were heard.

"Listen to them, Uncle John." And the curate took the glass from Father John. "They are not as far as I thought, they are sitting under these trees. Come," he said.

And they walked some twenty yards, till they came to a spot where the light came pouring through the young leaves, and all the brown leaves of last year were spotted with light. There were light shadows amid the rocks and pleasant mosses, and the sounds of leaves and water, and from the top of a rock Kate listened while Peter told her they would rebuild his house.

"The priests are after us," she said.

And she gave a low whistle, and the men and boys looked round, and seeing the priests coming, they dispersed, taking several paths, and none but Ned and Mary were left behind. Ned was dozing, Mary was sitting beside him fanning herself with her hat; they had not heard Kate's whistle, and they did not see the priests until they were by them.

"Now, Tom, don't lose your head, be quiet with them."

"Will you speak to them, or shall I?" said Father Tom.

In the excitement of the moment he forgot his own imperfections and desired to admonish them.

"I think you had better let me speak to them," said Father John. "You are Ned Kavanagh," he said, "and you are Mary Byrne, I believe. Now, I don't know you all, for I am getting an old man, and I don't often come up this way. But notwithstanding my age, and the heat of the day, I have come up, for I have heard that you have not acted as good Catholics should. I don't doubt for a moment that you intended to get married, but you have, I fear, been guilty of a great sin, and you've set a bad example."

"We were on our way to your reverence now," said Mary. "I mean to his reverence."

"Well," said Father Tom, "you are taking your time over it, lying here half asleep under the trees."

"We hadn't the money," said Mary, "it wasn't our fault."

"Didn't I say I'd marry you for nothing."

"But sure, your reverence, that's only a way of speaking."

"There's no use lingering here," said Father Tom. "Ned, you took the pledge the day before yesterday, and yesterday you were tipsy."

"I may have had a drop of drink in me, your reverence. Pat Connex passed me the mug of porter and I forgot myself."

"And once," said the priest, "you tasted the porter you thought you could go on taking it."

Ned did not answer, and the priests whispered together.

"We are half way now," said Father Tom, "we can get there before twelve o'clock."

"I don't think I'm equal to it," said Father John. "I really don't think—"

The sounds of wheels were heard, and a peasant driving a donkey cart came up the road.

"You see it is all up-hill," said Father John. "See how the road ascends. I never could manage it."

"The road is pretty flat at the top of the hill once you get to the top of the hill, and the cart will take you to the top."

It seemed undignified to get into the donkey cart, but his nephew's conscience was at stake, and the Vicar-General got in, and Father Tom said to the unmarried couple—

"Now walk on in front of us, and step out as quickly as you can."

And on the way to the church Father Tom remembered

that he had caught sight of Kate standing at the top of the rock talking to Peter M'Shane. In a few days they would come to him to be married, and he hoped that Peter and Kate's marriage would make amends for this miserable patchwork, for Ned Kavanagh and Mary Byrne's marriage was no better than patchwork.

## IV

Mrs. Connex promised the priest to keep Pat at home out of Kate's way, and the neighbours knew it was the priest's wish that they should do all they could to help him to bring about this marriage, and everywhere Kate went she heard nothing talked of but her marriage.

The dress that Kate was to be married in was a nice grey silk. It had been bought at a rummage sale, and she was told that it suited her. But Kate had begun to feel that she was being driven into a trap. In the week before her marriage she tried to escape. She went to Dublin to look for a situation; but she did not find one. She had not seen Pat since the poultry lecture, and his neglect angered her. She did not care what became of her.

On the morning of her wedding she turned round and asked her sister if she thought she ought to marry Peter, and Julia said it would be a pity if she didn't. Six cars had been engaged, and, feeling she was done for, she went to the church, hoping it would fall down on her. Well, the priest had his way, and Kate felt she hated him and Mrs. M'Shane, who stood on the edge of the road. The fat were distributed alongside of the lean, and the bridal party drove away, and there was a great waving of hands and Mrs. M'Shane waited until the last car was out of sight.

Her husband had been dead many years, and she lived with her son in a two-roomed cabin. She was one of those simple, kindly natures that everyone likes and that everyone despises, and she returned home like a lonely goose, waddling slowly, a little overcome by the thought of the happiness that awaited her son. There would be no more lonely evenings in the cabin; Kate would be with him now, and later on there would be some children, and she waddled home thinking of the cradle and the joy it would be to her to take her grandchildren upon her knee. When she returned to the cottage she sat down, so that she might dream over her happiness a little longer. But she had not been sitting long when she remembered there was a great deal of work to be done. The cabin would have to be cleaned from end to end, there was the supper to be cooked, and she did not pause in her work until everything was ready. At five the pig's head was on the table, and the sheep's tongues; the bread was baked; the barrel of porter had come, and she was expecting the piper every minute. As she stood with her arms akimbo looking at the table, thinking of the great evening it would be, she thought how her old friend, Annie Connex, had refused to come to Peter's wedding. Wasn't all the village saying that Kate would not have married Peter if she had not been driven to it by the priest and by her mother.

"Poor boy," she thought "his heart is so set upon her that he has no ears for any word against her."

She could not understand why people should talk ill of a girl on her wedding day. "Why shouldn't a girl be given a chance," she asked herself. "Why should Annie Connex prevent her son from coming to the dance." If she were to go to her now and ask her if she would come? and if she would not come herself, if she would let Pat come round for an hour? If Annie would do this all the gossips would have their tongues tied. Anyhow she could try to persuade her. And she locked her door and walked up the road and knocked at Mrs. Connex's.

Prosperity in the shapes of pig styes and stables had collected round Annie's door, and Mrs. M'Shane was proud to be a visitor in such a house.

"I came round, Annie, to tell you they're married."

"Well, come in, Mary," she said, "if you have the time."

The first part of the sentence was prompted by the news that Kate was safely married and out of Pat's way; and the second half of the sentence, "if you have the time," was prompted by a wish that Mary should see that she need not come again for some time at least.

To Annie Connex the Kavanagh family was abomination. The father got 18s. a week for doing a bit of gardening. Ned had been a quarry man now he was out of work and did odd jobs. The Kavanaghs took in a baby and they got 5s. or 6s. a week for that. Mrs. Kavanagh sold geraniums at more than their value, and she got more than the market value for her chickens—she sold them to charitable folk who were anxious to encourage poultry farming; and now Julia, the second daughter, had gone in for lace making, and she made a lace that looked as if it were cut out of paper, and sold it for three times its market value.

And to sell above market value was abominable to Annie Connex. Her idea of life was order and administration, and the village she lived in was thriftless and idle. The Kavanaghs received out-door relief; they got 2s. a week off the rates, though every Saturday evening they bought a quarter barrel of porter, and Annie Connex could not believe in the future of a country that would tolerate such a thing. If her son had married a Kavanagh her life would have come to an end, and the twenty years she had worked for him would have been wasted years. Thank God Kate was out of her son's way, and on seeing Mary she resolved that Pat should never cross the M'Shane's threshold.

Mrs. M'Shane looked round the comfortable kitchen, with sides of bacon and home-cured hams hanging from the rafters. She had not got on in life as well as Mrs. Connex, and she knew she would never have a beautiful closed range, but an open hearth, till the end of her days. She could never have a nice dresser with a pretty carved top. The dresser in her kitchen was deal, and had no nice shining brass knobs on it. She would never have a parlour, and this parlour had in it a mahogany table and a grandfather's clock that would show you the moon on it just the same as it was in the sky, and there was a glass over the fire place. This was Annie Connex's own parlour. The parlour on the other side of the house was even better furnished, for in the summer months Mrs. Connex bedded and boarded her lodgers for one pound or one pound five shillings a week.

"So she was married to-day, and Father Maguire married her after all. I never thought he would have brought her to it. Well, I'm glad she's married." It rose to Mary's lips to say, "you are glad she didn't marry your son," but she put back the words. "It comes upon me as a bit of surprise, for sure and all I could never see her settling down in the parish."

"Them that are the wildest before marriage are often the best after, and I think it will be like that with Kate."

"I hope so," said Annie. "And there is reason why it should be like that. She must have liked Peter better than we thought; you will never get me to believe that it was the priest's will or anybody's will that brought Kate to do what she did."

"I hope she'll make my boy a good wife."

"I hope so, too," said Annie, and the women sat over the fire thinking it out.

Annie Connex wore an apron, and a black straw hat; and her eyes were young, and kind, and laughing, but Mrs. M'Shane, who had known her for twenty years, often wondered what Annie would have been like if she had not got a kind husband, and if good luck had not attended her all through life.

"We never had anyone like her before in the parish. I hear she turned round to her sister Julia, who was dressing her, and said, 'Now am I to marry him, or shall I go to America?' And she was putting on her grey dress at the time."

"She looked well in that grey dress; there was lace on the front of it, and everyone said that a handsomer girl hasn't been married in the parish for years. There isn't a man in the parish that would not be in Peter's place to-day if he only dared."

"I don't catch your meaning, Mary."

"Well, perhaps I oughtn't to have said it now that she's my own daughter, but I think many would have been a bit afraid of her after what she said to the priest three days ago."

"She did have her tongue on him. People are telling all ends of stories."

"'Tis said that Father Maguire was up at the Kavanagh's three days ago, and I heard that she hunted him. She called him a policeman, and a tax collector, and a landlord, and if she said this she said more to a priest than anyone ever said before. 'There are plenty of people in the parish,' she said, 'who believe he could turn them into rabbits if he liked.' As for the rabbits she isn't far from the truth, though I don't take it on myself to say if it be a truth or a lie. But I know for a fact that Patsy Rogan was going to vote for the Unionist to please his landlord, but the priest had been to see his wife, who was going to be confined, and didn't he tell her that if Patsy voted for the wrong man there would be horns on the new baby, and Mrs. Rogan was so frightened that she wouldn't let her husband go when he came in that night till he had promised to vote as the priest wished."

"Patsy Rogan is an ignorant man," said Annie, "there are many like him even here."

"Ah, sure there will be always some like him. Don't we like to believe the priest can do all things."

"But Kate doesn't believe the priest can do these things. Anyhow she's married, and there will be an end to all the work that has been going on."

"That's true for you, Annie, and that's just what I came to talk to you about. I think now she's married we ought to give her a chance. Every girl ought to get her chance, and the way to put an end to all this talk about her will be for you to come round to the dance to-night."

"I don't know that I can do that. I am not friends with the Kavanaghs, though I always bid them the time of day when I meet them on the road."

"If you come in for a few minutes, or if Pat were to come in for a few minutes. If Peter and Pat aren't friends they'll be enemies."

"Maybe they'd be worse enemies if I don't keep Pat out of Kate's way. She's married Peter; but her mind is not settled yet."

"Yes, Annie, I've thought of all that; but they'll be meeting on the road, and, if they aren't friends, there will be quarrelling, and some bad deed may be done."

Annie did not answer, and, thinking to convince her, Mary said:

"You wouldn't like to see a corpse right over your window."

"It ill becomes you, Mary, to speak of corpses after the blow that Peter gave Pat with his stick at Ned Kavanagh's wedding. No; I must stand by my son, and I must keep him out of the low Irish, and he won't be safe until I get him a good wife."

"The low Irish! indeed, Annie, it ill becomes you to talk in that way of your neighbours. Is it because none of us have brass knockers on our doors? I have seen this pride growing up in you, Annie Connex, this long while. There isn't one in the village now that you've any respect for except the grocer, that black Protestant, who sits behind his counter and makes money, and knows no enjoyment in life at all."

"That's your way of looking at it; but it isn't mine. I set my face against my son marrying Kate Kavanagh, and you should have done the same."

"Something will happen to you for the cruel words you have spoken to me this day."

"Mary, you came to ask me to your son's wedding, and I had to tell you—"

"Yes, and you've told me that you won't come and that you hate the Kavanaghs, and you've said all you could against them. I should not have listened to all you said; if I did, it is because we have known each other these twenty years. Don't I remember well the rags you had on your back when you came to this village. It ill becomes—"

Mrs. M'Shane got up and went out and Annie followed her to the gate.

The sounds of wheels and hoofs were heard, and the wedding party passed by, and on the first car whom should they see but Kate sitting between Pat and Peter.

"Good-bye, Annie. I see that Pat's coming to our dance after all. I must hurry down the road to open the door to him."

And she laughed as she waddled down the road, and she could not speak for want of breath when she got to the door. They were all there, Pat and the piper and Kate and Peter and all their friends; and she could not speak, and hadn't the strength to find the key. She could only think of the black look that had come over Annie's face when she saw Pat sitting by Kate on the car. She had told Annie that she would be punished, and Mrs. M'Shane laughed as she searched for the key, thinking how quickly her punishment had come.

She searched for the key, and all the while they were telling her how they had met Pat at Michael Dunne's.

"When he saw us he tried to sneak into the yard; but I went after him. And don't you think I did right?" Kate said, as they went into the house. And when they were all inside, she said: "Now I'll get the biggest jug of porter, and one shall drink one half and the other the other."

Peter was fond of jugs, and had large and small; some were white and brown, and some were gilt, with pink flowers. At last she chose the great brown one.

"Now, Peter, you'll say something nice."

"I'll say, then," said Peter, "this is the happiest day of my life, as it should be, indeed; for haven't I got the girl that I wanted, and hasn't Pat forgiven me for the blow I struck him? For he knows well I wouldn't hurt a hair of his head. Weren't we boys together? But I had a cross drop in me at the time, and that was how it was."

Catching sight of Kate's black hair and rosy cheeks, which were all the world to him, he stopped speaking and stood looking at her, unheedful of everything; and he looked so good and foolish at that time that more than one woman thought it would be a weary thing to live with him.

"Now, Pat, you must make a speech, too," said Kate.

"I haven't any speech in me," he said. "I'm glad enough

to be here; but I'm sore afraid my mother saw me sitting on the car, and I think I had better be going home and letting you finish this marriage."

"What's that you're saying," said Kate. "You won't go out of this house till you've danced a reel with me, and now sit down at the table next to me; and, Peter, you sit on the other side of him, so that he won't run away to his mother."

Her eyes were as bright as coals of fire, and she called to her father, who was at the end of the table, to have another slice of pig's head, and to the piper, who was having his supper in the window, to have a bit more; and then she turned to Pat, who said never a word, and laughed at him for having nothing to say.

It seemed to them as if there was no one in the room but Kate; and afterwards they remembered things. Ned remembered that Kate had seemed to put Pat out of her mind. She had stood talking to her husband, and she had said that he must dance with her, though it was no amusement to a girl to dance opposite Peter. And Mary, Ned's wife, remembered how Kate, though she had danced with Peter in the first reel, had not been able to keep her eyes from the corner where Pat sat sulking, and that, sudden-like, she had grown weary of Peter. Mary remembered she had seen a wild look pass in Kate's eyes, and that she had gone over to Pat and pulled him out.

It was a pleasure for a girl to dance opposite to Pat, so cleverly did his feet move to the tune. And everyone was admiring them when Pat cried out:

"I'm going home. I bid you all good-night; here, finish this wedding as you like."

And before anyone could stop him he had run out of the house.

"Peter, go after him," Kate said; "bring him back. It would be ill luck on our wedding night for anyone to leave us like that."

Peter went out of the door, and was away some time; but he came back without Pat.

"The night is that dark, I lost him," he said.

Then Kate did not seem to care what she said. Her black hair fell down, and she told Peter he was a fool, and that he should have run faster. Her mother said it was the porter that had been too much for her; but she said it was the priest's blessing, and this frightened everyone. But, after saying all this, she went to her husband, saying that he was very good to her, and she had no fault to find with him. But no sooner were the words out of her mouth than her mind seemed to wander, and everyone had expected her to run out of the house. But she went into the other room instead, and shut the door behind her. Everyone knew then there would be no more dancing that night; and the piper packed up his pipes. And Peter sat by the fire, and he seemed to be crying. They were all sorry to leave him like this; and, so that he might not remember what had happened, Ned drew a big jug of porter, and put it by him.

He drank a sup out of it, but seemed to forget everything, and the jug fell out of his hand.

"Never mind the pieces, Peter," his mother said. "You can't put them together; and it would be better for you not to drink any more porter. Go to bed. There's been too much drinking this night."

"Mother, I want to know why she said I didn't run fast enough after Pat. And didn't she know that if I hit Pat so hard it was because there were knobs on his stick; and didn't I pick up his stick by mistake of my own."

"Sure, Peter, it wasn't your fault; we all know that, and Kate knows it too. Now let there be no more talking or drinking. No, Peter, you've had enough porter for to-night."

He looked round the kitchen, and seeing that Kate was not there, he said:—

"She's in the other room, I think; mother, you'll be wantin' to go to bed."

And Peter got on his feet and stumbled against the wall, and his mother had to help him towards the door.

"Is it drunk I am, mother? Will you open the door for me?"

But Mrs. M'Shane could not open the door, and she said:—

"I think she's put a bit of stick in it."

"A bit of stick in the door? And didn't she say that she didn't want to marry me? Didn't she say something about the priest's blessing?"

And then Peter was sore afraid that he would not get sight of his wife that night, and he said:—

"Won't she acquie-esh-sh?"

And Kate said:—

"No, I won't."

And then he said:—

"We were married in church—to-day, you acquieshed."

And she said:—

"I'll not open the door to you. You're drunk, Peter, and not fit to enter a decent woman's room."

"It isn't because I've a drop too much in me that you should have fastened the door on me; it is because you're thinking of the blow I've gave Pat. But Kate, it was because I loved you so much that I struck him. Now will you open—the door?"

"No, I'll not open the door to-night," she said. "I'm tired and want to go to sleep."

And when he said he would break open the door, she said:—

"You're too drunk, Peter, and sorra bit of good it will do you. I'll be no wife to you to-night, and that's as true as God's in heaven."

"Peter," said his mother, "don't trouble her to-night. There has been too much dancing and drinking."

"It's a hard thing . . . shut out of his wife's room."

"Peter, don't vex her to-night. Don't hammer her door any more."

"Didn't she acquie-esh? Mother, you have always been agin me. Didn't she acquie-esh?"

"Oh, Peter, why do you say I'm agin you?"

"Did you hear her say that I was drunk. If you tell me I'm drunk I'll say no more. I'll acquie-esh."

"Peter, you must go to sleep."

"Yes, go to sleep. . . . I want to go to sleep, but she won't open the door."

"Peter, never mind her."

"It isn't that I mind; I'm getting sleepy, but what I want to know, mother, before I go to bed, is if I'm drunk. Tell me I'm not drunk on my wedding night, and, though Kate—and I'll acquie-esh in all that may be put upon me."

He covered his face with his hands and his mother begged him not to cry. He became helpless, she put a blanket under his head and covered him with another blanket, and went up the ladder and lay down in the hay. She asked herself what had she done to deserve this trouble? and she cried a great deal; and the poor, hapless old woman was asleep in the morning when Peter stumbled to his feet. And, after dipping his head in a pail of water, he remembered that the horses were waiting for him in the farm. He walked off to his work, staggering a little, and as soon as he was gone Kate drew back the bolt of the door and came into the kitchen.

"I'm going, mother," she called up to the loft.

"Wait a minute, Kate," said Mrs. M'Shane, and she was half way down the ladder when Kate said:—

"I can't wait, I'm going."

She walked up the road to her mother's, and she hardly saw the fields or the mountains, though she knew she would never look upon them again. And her mother was sweeping out the house. She had the chairs out in the pathway. She had heard that the rector was coming down that afternoon, and she wanted to show him how beautifully clean she kept the cabin.

"I've come, mother, to give you this," and she took the wedding ring off her finger and threw it on the ground. "I don't want it; I shut the door on him last night, and I'm going to America to-day. You see how well the marriage that you and the priest made up together has turned out."

"Going to America," said Mrs. Kavanagh, and it suddenly occurred to her that Kate might be going to America with Pat Connex, but she did not dare to say it.

Kate stood looking at the bushes that grew between their cottage and the next one, and she remembered how she and her brother used to cut the branches of the alder to make pop guns, for the alder branches are full of sap, and when the sap is expelled there is a hole smooth as the barrel of a gun.

"I'm going," she said suddenly, "there's nothing more to say. Good-bye."

She walked away quickly, and her mother said "she's going with Pat Connex." But Kate had no thought of going to America with him. It was not until she met him a little further on, at the cross roads, that the thought occurred to her that he might like to go to America with her. She called him, and he came to her, and he looked a nice boy, but she thought he was better in Ireland. And the country seemed far away, though she was still in it, and the people too, though she was still among them.

"I'm going to America, Pat."

"You were married yesterday."

"Yes, that was the priest's doing and mother's, and I thought they knew best. But I'm thinking one must go one's own way, and there's no judging for one's self here. That's why I'm going. You'll find some other girl, Pat."

"There's not another girl like you in the village. We're a dead and alive lot. You stood up to the priest."

"I didn't stand up to him enough. You're waiting for someone. Who are you waiting for?"

"I don't like to tell you, Kate."

She pressed him to answer her, and he told her he was waiting for the priest. His mother had said he must marry, and the priest was coming to make up a marriage for him.

"Everthing's mother's."

"That's true, Pat, and you'll give a message for me. Tell my mother-in-law that I've gone."

"She'll be asking me questions and I'll be sore set for an answer."

She looked at him steadily, but she left him without speaking, and he stood thinking.

He had had good times with her, and all such times were ended for him for ever. He was going to be married and he did not know to whom. Suddenly he remembered he had a message to deliver, and he went down to the M'Shanes' cabin.

"Ah, Mrs. M'Shane," he said, "it was a bad day for me when she married Peter. But this is a worse one, for we've both lost her."

"My poor boy will feel it sorely."

And when Peter came in for dinner his mother said:—

"Peter, she's gone, she's gone to America, and you're well rid of her."

"Don't say that, mother, I am not well rid of her, for there's no other woman in the world for me except her that's gone. Has she gone with Pat Connex?"

"No, he said nothing about that, and it was he who brought the message."

"I've no one, mother, to blame but myself. I was drunk last night, and how could she let a drunken fellow like me into her room."

He went out to the back yard, and his mother heard him crying till it was time for him to go back to work.

## V

As he got up to go to his work he caught sight of Biddy M'Hale coming up the road; he rushed past her lest she should ask him what he was crying about, and she stood looking after him for a moment, and went into the cabin to inquire what had happened.

"Sure she wouldn't let her husband sleep with her last night," said Mrs. M'Shane, "and you'll be telling the priest that. It will be well if he should know it at once."

Biddy would have liked to have heard how the wedding party had met Pat Connex on the road, and what had happened after, but the priest was expecting her, and she did not dare to keep him waiting much longer. But she was not sorry she had been delayed, for the priest only wanted to get her money to mend the walls of the old church, and she thought that her best plan would be to keep him talking about Kate and Peter. He was going to America to-morrow or the day after, and if she could keep her money till then it would be safe.

His front door was open, he was leaning over the green paling that divided his strip of garden from the road, and he looked very cross indeed.

She began at once:

"Sure, your reverence, there's terrible work going on in the village, and I had to stop to listen to Mrs. M'Shane. Kate Kavanagh, that was, has gone to America, and she shut her door on him last night, saying he was drunk."

"What's this you're telling me?"

"If your reverence will listen to me—"

"I'm always listening to you, Biddy M'Hale. Go on with your story."

It was a long time before he fully understood what had happened, but at last all the facts seemed clear, and he said:—

"I'm expecting Pat Connex."

Then his thoughts turned to the poor husband weeping in the backyard, and he said:—

"I made up this marriage so that she might not go away with Pat Connex."

"Well, we've been saved that," said Biddy.

"Ned Kavanagh's marriage was bad enough, but this is worse. It is no marriage at all."

"Ah, your reverence, you musn't be taking it to heart. If

the marriage did not turn out right it was the drink."

"Ah, the drink—the drink," said the priest, and he declared that the brewer and the distiller were the ruin of Ireland.

"That's true for you; at the same time we musnt forget that they have put up many a fine church."

"It would be impossible, I suppose, to prohibit the brewing of ale and the distillation of spirit." The priest's brother was a publican and had promised a large subscription. "And now, Biddy, what are you going to give me to make the walls secure. I don't want you all to be killed while I am away."

"There's no fear of that, your reverence; a church never fell down on anyone."

"Even so, if it falls down when nobody's in it where are the people to hear the Mass?"

"Ay, won't they be going down to hear Mass at Father Stafford's?"

"If you don't wish to give anything say so."

"Your reverence, amn't I—?"

"We don't want to hear about that window."

Biddy began to fear she would have to give him a few pounds to quiet him. But, fortunately, Pat Connex came up the road, and she thought she might escape after all.

"I hear, Pat Connex, you were dancing with Kate Kavanagh, I should say Kate M'Shane, and she went away to America this morning. Have you heard this?"

"I have, your reverence. She passed me on the road this morning."

"And you weren't thinking you might stop her?"

"Stop her," said Pat. "Who could stop Kate from doing anything she wanted to do?"

"And now your mother writes to me, Pat Connex, to ask if I will get Lennon's daughter for you."

"I see your reverence has private business with Pat Connex. I'll be going," said Biddy, and she was many yards down the road before he could say a word.

"Now, Biddy M'Hale, don't you be going." But Biddy pretended not to hear him.

"Will I be running after her," said Pat, "and bringing her back."

"No, let her go. If she doesn't want to help to make the walls safe I'm not going to go on my knees to her. . . . You'll all have to walk to Father Stafford's to hear Mass. Have you heard your mother say what she's going to give towards the new church, Pat Connex?"

"I think she said, your reverence, she was going to send you ten pounds."

"That's very good of her," and this proof that a public and religious spirit was not yet dead in his parish softened the priest's temper, and, thinking to please him and perhaps escape a scolding, Pat began to calculate how much Biddy had saved.

"She must be worth, I'm thinking, close on one hundred pounds to-day." As the priest did not answer, he said, "I wouldn't be surprised if she was worth another fifty."

"Hardly as much as that," said the priest.

"Hadn't her aunt the house we're living in before mother came to Kilmore, and they used to have the house full of lodgers all the summer. It's true that her aunt didn't pay her any wages, but when she died she left her a hundred pounds, and she has been making money ever since."

This allusion to Biddy's poultry reminded the priest that he had once asked Biddy what had put the idea of a poultry farm into her head, and she had told him that when she was taking up the lodgers' meals at her aunt's she used to have to stop and lean against the banisters, so heavy were the trays.

"One day I slipped and hurt myself, and I was lying on my back for more than two years, and all the time I could see the fowls pecking in the yard, for my bed was by the window. I thought I would like to keep fowls when I was older."

The priest remembered the old woman standing before him telling him of her accident, and while listening he had watched her, undecided whether she could be called a hunchback. Her shoulders were higher than shoulders usually are, she was jerked forward from the waist, and she had the long, thin arms, and the long, thin face, and the pathetic eyes of the hunchback. Perhaps she guessed his thoughts. She said:—

"In those days we used to go blackberrying with the boys. We used to run all over the hills."

He did not think she had said anything else, but she had said the words in such a way that they suggested a great deal— they suggested that she had once been very happy, and that she had suffered very soon the loss of all her woman's hopes. A few weeks, a few months, between her convalescence and her disappointment had been all her woman's life. The thought that life is but a little thing passed across the priest's mind, and then he looked at Pat Connex and wondered what was to be done with him. His conduct at the wedding would have to be inquired into and the marriage that was being arranged would have to be broken off if Kate's flight could be attributed to him.

"Now, Pat Connex, we will go to Mrs. M'Shane. I shall want to hear her story."

"Sure what story can she tell of me? Didn't I run out of the house away from Kate when I saw what she was thinking of? What more could I do?"

"If Mrs. M'Shane tells the same story as you do we'll go to your mother's, and afterwards I'll go to see Lennon about his daughter."

Pat's dancing with Kate and Kate's flight to America had reached Lennon's ears, and it did not seem at all likely that he would consent to give his daughter to Pat Connex, unless, indeed, Pat Connex agreed to take a much smaller dowry than his mother had asked for.

These new negotiations, his packing, a letter to the Bishop, and the payment of bills, fully occupied the last two days, and the priest did not see Biddy again till he was on his way to the station. She was walking up and down her poultry-yard, telling her beads, followed by her poultry; and it was with difficulty that he resisted the impulse to ask her for a subscription, but the driver said if they stopped they would miss the train.

"Very well," said the priest, and he drove past her cabin without speaking to her.

In the bar-rooms of New York, while trying to induce a recalcitrant loafer to part with a dollar, he remembered that he had not met anyone so stubborn as Biddy. She had given very little, and yet she seemed to be curiously mixed up with the building of the church. She was the last person he saw on his way out, and, a few months later, he was struck by the fact that she was the first parishioner he saw on his return. As he was driving home from the station in the early morning whom should he see but Biddy, telling her beads, followed by her poultry. The scene was the same except that morning was substituted for evening. This was the first impression. On looking closer he noticed that she was not followed by as many Plymouth Rocks as on the last occasion. "She seems to be going in for Buff Orpingtons," he said to himself.

"It's a fine thing to see you again, and your reverence is looking well. I hope you've been lucky in America?"

"I have brought home some money anyhow, and the church will be built, and you will tell your beads under your window one of these days."

"Your reverence is very good to me, and God is very good."

And she stood looking after him, thinking how she had brought him round to her way of thinking. She had always known that the Americans would pay for the building, but no one else but herself would be thinking of putting up a beautiful window that would do honour to God and Kilmore. And it wasn't her fault if she didn't know a good window from a bad one, as well as the best of them. And it wasn't she who was going to hand over her money to the priest or his architect to put up what window they liked. She had been inside every church within twenty miles of Kilmore, and would see that she got full value for her money.

At the end of the week she called at the priest's house to tell him the pictures she would like to see in the window, and the colours. But the priest's servant was not certain whether Biddy could see his reverence.

"He has a gentleman with him."

"Isn't it the architect he has with him? Don't you know it is I who am putting up the window?"

"To be sure," said the priest; "show her in." And he drew forward a chair for Miss M'Hale, and introduced her to the architect. The little man laid his pencil aside, and this encouraged Biddy, and she began to tell him of the kind of window she had been thinking of. But she had not told him half the things she wished to have put into the window when he interrupted her, and said there would be plenty of time to consider what kind of window should be put in when the walls were finished and the roof was upon them.

"Perhaps it is a little premature to discuss the window, but you shall choose the subjects you would like to see represented in the window, and as for the colours, the architect and designer will advise you. But I am sorry to say, Biddy, that this gentleman says that the four thousand pounds the Americans were good enough to give me will not do much more than build the walls."

"They're waiting for me to offer them my money, but I won't say a word," Biddy said to herself; and she sat fidgetting with her shawl, coughing from time to time, until the priest lost his patience.

"Well, Biddy, we're very busy here, and I'm sure you want to get back to your fowls. When the church is finished we'll see if we want your window."

The priest had hoped to frighten her, but she was not the least frightened. Her faith in her money was abundant; she knew that as long as she had her money the priest would come to her for it on one pretext or another, sooner or later. And she was as well pleased that nothing should be settled at present, for she was not quite decided whether she would like to see Christ sitting in judgment, or Christ crowning His Virgin Mother; and during the next six months she pondered on the pictures and the colours, and gradually the design grew clearer.

And every morning, as soon as she had fed her chickens, she went up to Kilmore to watch the workmen. She was there when the first spadeful of earth was thrown up, and as soon as the walls showed above the ground she began to ask the workmen how long it would take them to reach the windows, and if a workman put down his trowel and wandered from his work she would tell him it was God he was cheating; and later on, when the priest's money began to come to an end and he could not pay the workmen full wages, she told them they were working for God's Own House, and that He would reward them in the next world.

"Hold your tongue," said a mason. "If you want the church built why don't you give the priest the money you're saving, and let him pay us?"

"Keep a civil tongue in your head, Pat Murphy. It isn't for myself I am keeping it back. Isn't it all going to be spent?"

The walls were now built, and amid the clatter of the slaters' hammers Biddy began to tell the plasterers of the beautiful pictures that would be seen in her window; and she gabbled on, mixing up her memories of the different windows she had seen, until at last her chatter grew wearisome, and they threw bits of mortar, laughing at her for a crazy old woman, or the priest would suddenly come upon them, and they would scatter in all directions, leaving him with Biddy.

"What were they saying to you, Biddy?"

"They were saying, your reverence, that America is a great place."

"You spend a great deal of your time here, Biddy, and I suppose you are beginning to see that it takes a long time to build a church. Now you are not listening to what I am saying.

You are thinking about your window; but you must have a house before you can have a window."

"I know that very well, your reverence; but, you see, God has given us the house."

"God's House consists of little more than walls and a roof."

"Indeed it does, your reverence; and amn't I saving up all my money for the window."

"But, my good Biddy, there is hardly any plastering done yet. The laths have come in, and there isn't sufficient to fill that end of the church, and I have no more money."

"Won't your reverence be getting the rest of the money in America? And I am thinking a bazaar would be a good thing. Wouldn't we all be making scapulars, and your reverence might get medals that the Pope had blessed."

Eventually he drove her out of the church with his umbrella. But as his anger cooled he began to think that perhaps Biddy was right—a bazaar might be a good thing, and a distribution of medals and scapulars might induce his workmen to do some overtime. He went to Dublin to talk over this matter with some pious Catholics, and an old lady wrote a cheque for fifty pounds, two or three others subscribed smaller sums, and the plasterers were busy all next week. But these subscriptions did not go nearly as far towards completing the work as he had expected. The architect had led him astray, and he looked round the vast barn that he had built and despaired. It seemed to him it would never be finished in his lifetime. A few weeks after he was again running short of money, and he was speaking to his workmen one Saturday afternoon, telling them how they could obtain a plenary indulgence by subscribing so much towards the building of the church, and by going to Confession and Communion on the first Sunday of the month, and if they could not afford the money they could give their work. He was telling them how much could be done if every workman were to do each day an hour of overtime, when Biddy suddenly appeared, and, standing in front of the men, she raised up her hands and said that they should not pass her until they had pledged themselves to come to work on Monday.

"But haven't we got our wives and little ones, and haven't we to think of them?" said a workman.

"Ah, one can live on very little when one is doing the work of God," said Biddy.

The man called her a vain old woman, who was starving herself so that she might put up a window, and they pushed her aside and went away, saying they had to think of their wives and children.

The priest turned upon her angrily and asked her what she meant by interfering between him and his workmen.

"Now don't be angry with me, your reverence. I will say a prayer, and you will say a word or two in your sermon tomorrow."

And he spoke in his sermon of the disgrace it would be to Kilmore if the church remained unfinished. The news would go over to America, and what priest would be ever able to get money there again to build a church?

"Do you think a priest likes to go about the barrooms asking for dollars and half-dollars? Would you make his task more unpleasant? If I have to go to America again, what answer shall I make if they say to me:—'Well, didn't your workmen leave you at Kilmore? They don't want churches at Kilmore. Why should we give you money for a church?'"

There was a great deal of talking that night in Michael Dunne's, and they were all of one mind, that it would be a disgrace to Kilmore if the church were not finished; but no one could see that he could work for less wages than he was in the habit of getting. As the evening wore on the question of indulgences was raised, and Ned Kavanagh said:—

"The devil a bit of use going against the priest, and the indulgences will do us no harm."

"The devil a bit, but maybe a great deal of good," said Peter M'Shane, and an hour later they were staggering down the road swearing they would stand by the priest till the death.

But on Monday morning nearly all were in their beds; only half a dozen came to the work, and the priest sent them away, except one plasterer. There was one plasterer who, he thought, could stand on the scaffold.

"If I were to fall I'd go straight to Heaven," the plasterer said, and he stood so near the edge, and his knees seemed so weak under him, that Biddy thought he was going to fall.

"It would be better for you to finish what you are doing; the Holy Virgin will be more thankful to you."

"Aye, maybe she would," he said, and he continued his work mechanically.

He was working at the clustered columns about the window Biddy had chosen for her stained glass and she did not take her eyes off him. The priest returned a little before twelve o'clock, as the plasterer was going to his dinner, and he asked him if he were feeling better.

"I'm all right, your reverence, and it won't occur again."

"I hope he won't go down to Michael Dunne's during his dinner hour," he said to Biddy. "If you see any further signs of drink upon him when he comes back you must tell me."

"He is safe enough, your reverence. Wasn't he telling me while your reverence was having your breakfast that if he fell down he would go straight to Heaven, and he opened his shirt and showed me he was wearing the scapular of the Holy Virgin."

And Biddy began to advocate a sale of scapulars.

"A sale of scapulars will not finish my church. You're all a miserly lot here, you want everything done for you."

"Weren't you telling me, your reverence, that a pious lady in Dublin—"

"The work is at a stand-still. If I were to go to America tomorrow it would be no use unless I could tell them it was progressing."

"Sure they don't ask any questions in America, they just give their money."

"If they do, that's more than you're doing at home. I want to know, Biddy, what you are going to do for this church. You're always talking about it; you're always here and you have given less than any one else."

"Didn't I offer your reverence a sovereign once since I gave you the five pounds."

"You don't seem to understand, Biddy, that you can't put up your window until the plastering is finished."

"I think I understand that well enough, but the church will be finished."

"How will it be finished? When will it be finished?"

She did not answer, and nothing was heard in the still church but her irritating little cough.

"You're very obstinate. Well, tell me where you would like to have your window."

"It is there I shall be kneeling, and if you will let me put my window there I shall see it when I look up from my beads. I should like to see the Virgin and I should like to see St. John with her. And don't you think, your reverence, we might have

St. Joseph as well. Our Lord would have to be in the Virgin's arms, and I think, your reverence, I would like Our Lord coming down to judge us, and I should like to have Him on His throne on the day of Judgment up at the top of the window."

"I can see you've been thinking a good deal about this window," the priest said.

She began again, and the priest heard the names of the different saints she would like to see in stained glass, and he let her prattle on. But his temper boiled up suddenly, and he said:—

"You'd go on like this till midnight if I let you. Now, Biddy M'Hale, you've been here all the morning delaying my workman. Go home to your fowls."

And she ran away shrinking like a dog, and the priest walked up and down the unfinished church. "She tries my temper more than anyone I ever met," he said to himself. At that moment he heard some loose boards clanking, and, thinking it was the old woman coming back, he looked round, his eyes flaming. But the intruder was a short and square-set man, of the type that one sees in Germany, and he introduced himself as an agent of a firm of stained glass manufacturers. He told Father Maguire they had heard in Germany of the beautiful church he was building. "I met an old woman on the road, and she told me that I would find you in the church considering the best place for the window she was going to put up. She looks very poor."

"She's not as poor as she looks; she's been saving money all her life for this window. Her window is her one idea, and, like people of one idea, she's apt to become a little tiresome."

"I don't quite understand."

He began telling the story, and seeing that the German was interested in the old woman he began to acquire an interest in her himself, an unpremeditated interest; he had not suspected that Biddy was so interesting. The German said she reminded him of the quaint sculpture of Nuremburg, and her character reminded him of one of the German saints, and talking of Biddy and mediævalism and Gothic art and stained glass the priest and the agent for the manufacture of stained glass in Munich walked up and down the unfinished church until the return of the plasterer reminded the priest of his embarrassments, and he took the German into his confidence.

"These embarrassments always occur," said the agent, "but there is no such thing as an unfinished church in Ireland; if you were to let her put up the window subscriptions would pour in."

"How is that?"

"A paragraph in the newspaper describing the window, the gift of a local saint. I think you told me her name was M'Hale, and that she lives in the village."

"Yes, you pass her house on the way to the station."

The German took his leave abruptly, and when he was half-way down the hill he asked some children to direct him.

"Is it Biddy M'Hale, that has all the hins, and is going to put up a window in the church, that you're wanting?"

The German said that that was the woman he wanted, and the eldest child said:—

"You will see her feeding her chickens, and you must call to her over the hedge."

And he did as he was bidden.

"Madam . . . the priest has sent me to show you some designs for a stained glass window."

No one had ever addressed Biddy as madam before. She hastened to let him into the house, and wiped the table clean so that he could spread the designs upon it. The first designs he showed her were the four Evangelists, but he would like a woman's present to her church to be in a somewhat lighter style, and he showed her a picture of St. Cecilia that fascinated her for a time; and then he suggested that a group of figures would look handsomer than a single figure. But she could not put aside the idea of the window that had grown up in her mind, and after some attempts to persuade her to accept a design they had in stock he had to give way and listen.

At the top of the picture, where the window narrowed to a point, Our Lord sat dressed in white on a throne, placing a golden crown on the head of the Virgin kneeling before him. About him were the women who had loved him, and the old woman said she was sorry she was not a nun, and hoped that Christ would not think less of her. As far as mortal sin was concerned she could say she had never committed one. At the bottom of the window there were suffering souls. The cauldrons that Biddy wished to see them in, the agent said, would be difficult to introduce—the suffering of the souls could be artistically indicated by flames.

"I shall have great joy," she said, "seeing the blessed women standing about Our Divine Lord, singing hymns in his praise, and the sight of sinners broiling will make me be sorrowful."

She insisted on telling the German of the different churches she had visited, and the windows she had seen, and she did not notice that he was turning over his designs and referring to his note book while she was talking. Suddenly he said:—

"Excuse me, but I think we have got the greater part of the window you wish for in stock, and the rest can be easily made up. Now the only question that remains is the question of the colours you care about."

"I've always thought there's no colour like blue. I'd like the Virgin to wear a blue cloak."

She did not know why she had chosen that colour, but the agent told her that she was quite right; blue signified chastity; and when the German had gone she sat thinking of the Virgin and her cloak. The Minorcas, and Buff Orpingtons, and Plymouth Rocks came through the door cackling, and while feeding them she sat, her eyes fixed on the beautiful evening sky, wondering if the blue in the picture would be as pale, or if it would be a deeper blue.

She remembered suddenly that she used to wear a blue ribbon when she went black-berrying among the hills; she found it in an old box and tied it round her neck. The moment she put it on her memory was as if lighted up with memories of the saints and the miracles they had performed, and she went to Father Maguire to tell him of the miracle. That the agent should have in stock the very window she had imagined seemed a miracle, and she was encouraged to think some miraculous thing had happened when the priest asked her to tell him exactly what her window was like. She had often told him before but he had never listened to her. But now he recognised her window as an adaptation of Fra Angelico's picture, and he told her how the saint had wandered from monastery to monastery painting pictures on the walls. More he could not tell her, but he promised to procure a small biography of the saint. She received the book a few days after, and as she turned over the leaves she heard the children coming home from school, and she took the book out to them, for her sight was failing, and they read bits of it aloud, and she frightened them by dropping on her knees and crying out that God had been very good to her.

She wandered over the country visiting churches, returning to Kilmore suddenly. She was seen as usual at sunrise and at sunset feeding her poultry, and then she went away again, and the next time she was heard of was in a church near Dublin celebrated for its stained glass. A few days after Ned Kavanagh met her hurrying up the road from the station, and she told him she had just received a letter from the Munich agent saying he had forwarded her window. It was to arrive to-morrow.

It was expected some time about mid-day, but Biddy's patience was exhausted long before, and she walked a great part of the way to Dublin to meet the dray. She returned with it, walking with the dray men, but within three miles of Kilmore she was so tired that they had to put her on the top of the boxes, and a cheer went up from the villagers when she was lifted down. She called to the workmen to be careful in unpacking the glass; and when they were putting it up she went down on her knees and prayed that no accident might happen.

At sunset the church had to be closed, and it was with difficulty she was persuaded to leave it. Next morning at sunrise she was knocking at the door of the woman who was charged with the cleaning of the church, asking for the key.

And from that day she was hardly ever out of the church; the charwoman began to complain that she could not get on with her work, and she was telling the priest that Biddy was always at her elbow, asking her to come to her window, saying she would show her things she had not seen before, when their conversation was interrupted by Biddy. She seemed a little astray, a little exalted, and Father Maguire watched her as she knelt with up-lifted face, telling her beads. He noticed that her fingers very soon ceased to move; and that she held the same bead a long time between her fingers. Minutes passed, but her lips did not move; her eyes were fixed on the panes and her look was so enraptured that he began to wonder if Paradise were being revealed to her.

And while the priest wondered, Biddy listened to music inconceivably tender. She had been awakened from her prayers by the sound of a harp string touched very gently; and the note had floated down like a flower, and all the vibrations were not dead when the same note floated down the aisles once more. Biddy listened, anxious to hear it a third time. Once more she heard it, and the third time she saw the saint's fingers moving over the strings; and she played a little tune of six notes. And it was at the end of the second playing of the tune that the priest touched Biddy on the shoulder. She looked up and it was a long while before she saw him, and she was greatly grieved that she had been awakened from her dream. She said it was a dream, because her happiness had been so great; and she stood looking at the priest, fain, but unable, to tell how she had been borne beyond her usual life, that her whole being had answered to the music the saint played, and looking at him, she wondered what would have happened if he had not awakened her.

Next day was Sunday, and she was in the church at sunrise listening for the music. But she heard and saw nothing until the priest had reached the middle of the Mass. The acolyte had rung the bell to prepare the people for the Elevation, and it was then that she heard a faint low sound that the light wire emitted when the saint touched her harp, and she noticed that it was the same saint that had played yesterday, the tall saint with the long fair hair who stood apart from the others, looking more intently at Our Blessed Lord than the others. She touched her harp again and the note vibrated for a long while, and when the last vibrations died she touched the string again. The note was sweet and languid and intense, and it pierced to the very core of Biddy. The saint's hand passed over the strings, producing faint exquisite sounds, so faint that Biddy felt no surprise they were not heard by anyone else; it was only by listening intently that she could hear them. Yesterday's little tune appeared again a little tune of six notes, and it seemed to Biddy even more exquisite than it had seemed when she first heard it. The only difference between today and yesterday was, that to-day all the saints struck their harps, and after playing for some time the music grew white like snow and remote as star-fire, and yet Biddy heard it more clearly than she had heard anything before, and she saw Our Lord more clearly than she had ever seen anybody else. She saw Him look up when He had placed the crown on His Mother's head; she heard Him sing a few notes, and then the saints began to sing. The window filled up with song and colour, and all along the window there was a continual transmutation of colour and song. The figures grew taller, and they breathed extraordinary life. It sang like a song within them, and it flowed about them and out of them in a sort of pearl-coloured mist. The vision clove the church along and across, and through it she could see the priest saying his Mass, and when he raised the Host above his head, Biddy saw Our Lord look at her, and His eyes brightened as if with love of her. He seemed to have forgotten the saints that sang His praises so beautifully, and when he bent towards her and she felt His presence about her, she cried out.

"He is coming to take me in His arms!"

And it was then that Biddy fell out of her place and lay at length on the floor of the church, pale as a dead woman. The clerk went to her, but he could not carry her out; she lay rigid as one who had been dead a long while, and she muttered "He is coming to put the gold crown on my head." The clerk moved away, and she swooned again.

Her return to her ordinary perceptions was slow and painful. The people had left long ago, and she tottered out of the empty church and followed the road to her cabin without seeing it or the people whom she met on the road. At last a woman took her by the arm and led her into her cabin, and spoke to her. She could not answer at first, but she awoke gradually, and she began to remember that she had heard music in the window and that Our Lord had sung to her. The neighbour left her babbling. She began to feed her chickens, and was glad when she had fed them. She wanted to think of the great and wonderful sights she had seen. She could not particularize, preferring to remember her vision as a whole, unwilling to separate the music from the colour, or the colour and the music from the adoration of the saints.

As the days went by her life seemed to pass more and more out of the life of the ordinary day. She seemed to live, as it were, on the last verge of human life; the mortal and the immortal mingled; she felt she had been always conscious of the immortal, and that nothing had happened except the withdrawing of a veil. The memory of her vision was still intense in her, but she wished to renew it; and waited next Sunday breathless with anticipation. The vision began at the same moment, the signal was the same as before; the note from the harp string floated down the aisles and when it had been repeated three times the saintly figures moved over the strings, and she heard the beautiful little tune.

Every eye was upon her, and forgetful of the fact that the priest was celebrating Mass, they said "Look, she hears the saints singing about her. She sees Christ coming." The priest heard Biddy cry out "Christ is coming," and she fell prone and none dared to raise her up, and she lay there till the Mass was finished. When the priest left the altar she was still lying at length, and the people were about her; and knowing how much she would feel the slightest reproof, he did not say a word that would throw doubt on her statement. He did not like to impugn a popular belief, but he felt himself obliged to exercise clerical control.

"Now Biddy, I know you are a very pious woman, but I cannot allow you to interrupt the Mass."

"If the Lord comes to me am I not to receive Him, your reverence?"

"In the first place I object to your dress; you are not properly dressed."

She wore a bright blue cloak, she seemed to wear hardly anything else, and tresses of dirty hair hung over her shoulders.

"The Lord has not said anything to me about my dress, your reverence, and He put His gold crown on my head to-day."

"Biddy, is all this true?"

"As true as you're standing there."

"I am not asking you if your visions are true. I have my opinion about that. I am asking if they are true to you."

"True to me, your reverence?" I don't rightly understand."

"I want to know if you think Our Lord put a gold crown on your head to-day."

"To be sure He did, your reverence."

"If He did, where is it?"

"Where is it, your reverence? It is with Him, to be sure. He wouldn't be leaving it on my head and me walking about the parish—that would not be reasonable at all, I am thinking. He doesn't want me to be robbed."

"There is no one in the parish who would rob you."

"Maybe some one would come out of another parish, if I was walking about with a gold crown on my head. And such a crown as He put upon it!—I am sorry you did not see it, but your reverence was saying the holy Mass at the time."

And she fell on her knees and clung to his cassock.

"And you saw the crown, Biddy?"

"I had it on my head, your reverence."

"And you heard the saints singing."

"Yes, and I will tell you what they were singing," and she began crooning. "Something like that your reverence. You don't believe me, but we have only our ears and our eyes to guide us."

"I don't say I don't believe you, Biddy, but you may be deceived."

"Sorra deceiving, your reverence, or I've been deceived all my life. And now, your reverence, if you have no more business with me I will go, for they are waiting in the chapel yard to hear me tell them about the crown that was put upon my head."

"Well, Biddy, I want you to understand that I cannot have you interrupting the Mass. I cannot permit it. The visions may be true, or not true, but you must not interrupt the Mass. Do you hear me?"

The acolyte had opened the door of the sacristy, she slipped through it, and the priest took off his cassock. As he did so, he noticed that the acolytes were anxious to get out; they were at the window watching, and when the priest looked out of the window he saw the people gathered about Biddy and could see she had obtained an extraordinary hold on the popular imagination; no one noticed him when he came out of the sacristy; they were listening to Biddy, and he stood unnoticed amid the crowd for a few minutes.

"She's out of her mind," he said. "She's as good as mad. What did she tell me—that Our Lord put a crown on her head."

It was difficult to know what to do. News of her piety had reached Dublin. People had been down to Kilmore to see her and had given subscriptions, and he understood that Biddy had enabled him to furnish his church with varnished pews and holy pictures. A pious Catholic lady had sent him two fine statues of Our Lady and St. Joseph. St. Joseph was in a purple cloak and Our Lady wore a blue cloak, and there were gold stars upon it. He had placed these two statues on the two side altars. But there were many things he wanted for his church, and he could only get them through Biddy. It was, therefore, his interest to let her remain in Kilmore, only she could not be allowed to interrupt the Mass, and he felt that he must be allowed to pass in and out of his church without having to put up with extravagant salutations.

He was going home to his breakfast, and a young man extremely interested in ecclesiastical art was coming to breakfast with him. The young man had a great deal to say about Walter Pater and Chartres Cathedral, and Father Maguire feared he was cutting but a very poor figure in the eyes of this young man, for he could not keep his thoughts on what the young man was saying, he was thinking of Biddy; he hardly thought of anything else now; she was absorbing the mind of his entire parish, she interrupted the Mass, he could not go into his church without being accosted by this absurd old woman, and this young man, a highly cultivated young man, who had just come from Italy and who took the highest interest in architecture would not be able to see his church in peace. As soon as they entered it they would be accosted by this old woman; she would follow them about asking them to look at her window, telling them her visions, which might or might not be true. She had a knack of hiding herself—he often came upon her suddenly behind the pillars, and sometimes he found her in the confessional. As soon as he crossed the threshold he began to look for her, and not finding her in any likely place, his fears subsided, and he called the young man's attention to the altar that had been specially designed for his church. And the young man had begun to tell the priest of the altars he had seen that spring in Italy, when suddenly he uttered a cry; he suddenly felt a hand upon his shoulder.

"Your honour will be well rewarded if you will come to my window. Now why should I tell you a lie, your reverence?"

She threw herself at the priest's feet and besought him to believe that the saints had been with her, and that every word she was speaking was the truth.

"Biddy, if you don't go away at once I will not allow you inside the church to-morrow."

The young man looked at the priest, surprised at his sternness, and the priest said:—

"She has become a great trial to us at Kilmore. Come aside and I will tell you about her."

And when the priest had told the young man about the window the young man asked if Biddy would have to be sent away.

"I hope not, for if she were separated from her window she would certainly die. It came out of her savings, out of the money she made out of chickens."

"And what has become of the chickens?"

"She has forgotten all about them; they wandered away or died. She has been evicted, and she lives now in an out-house. She lives on the bits of bread and the potatoes the neighbours give her. The things of this world are no longer realities to her. Her realities are what she sees and hears in that window. She told me last night the saints were singing about her. I don't like to encourage her to talk, but if you would like to hear her—Biddy, come here!"

The old woman came back as a dog comes to its master, joyful, and with brightening eyes.

"Tell us what you saw last night."

"Well, your reverence, I was asleep, and there suddenly came a knocking at the door, and I got up, and then I heard a voice say, 'open the door.' There was a beautiful young man outside, his hair was yellow and curly, and he was dressed in white. He came into the room first, and he was followed by other saints, and they had harps in their hands, and they sang for a long while; they sang beautiful music. Come to the window and you will hear it for yourselves. Someone is always singing it in the window, not always as clearly as they did last night."

"We'll go to see your window presently."

The old woman crept back to her place and the priest and the young man began to talk about the possibilities of miracles in modern times, and they talked on until the sudden sight of Biddy gave them pause.

"Look at her," said the young man, "can you doubt that she sees Heaven quite plainly, and that the saints visited her just as she told us."

"No doubt, no doubt. But she's a great trial to us at Mass. . . . The Mass must not be interrupted."

"I suppose even miracles are inconvenient at times, Father Maguire. Be patient with her, let her enjoy her happiness."

And the two men stood looking at her, trying vainly to imagine what her happiness might be.

# George Moore

## *The Exile*

### I

Pat Phelan's bullocks were ready for the fair, and so were his pigs; but the two fairs happened to come on the same day, and it was the pigs he would prefer to sell himself. His eldest son, James, was staying at home to help Catherine Ford with her churning; Peter, his second son, was not much of a hand at a bargain; it was Pat and James who managed the farm, and when Peter had gone to bed they began to wonder if Peter would be able to sell the bullocks. Pat said Peter had been told what was the lowest price he could take, James said there was a good demand for cattle, and at last they decided that Peter could not fail to sell the beasts.

Pat was to meet Peter at the cross-roads about twelve o'clock in the day. But he had sold his pigs early, and was half an hour in front of him, and sitting on the stile waiting for his son, he thought if Peter got thirteen pounds apiece for the bullocks he would say he had done very well. A good jobber, he thought, would be able to get ten shillings apiece more for them; and he went on thinking of what price Peter would get, until, suddenly looking up the road, whom should he see but Peter coming down the road with the bullocks in front of him. He could hardly believe his eyes, and it was a long story that Peter told him about two men who wanted to buy the bullocks early in the morning. They had offered him eleven pounds ten, and when he would not sell them at that price they had stood laughing at the bullocks and doing all they could to keep off other buyers. Peter was quite certain it was not his fault, and he began to argue. But Pat Phelan was too disappointed to argue with him, and he let him go on talking. At last Peter ceased talking, and this seemed to Pat Phelan a good thing.

The bullocks trotted in front of them. They were seven miles from home, and fifteen miles are hard on fat animals, and he could truly say he was at a loss of three pounds that day if he took into account the animals' keep.

Father and son walked on, and not a word passed between them till they came to Michael Quinn's public-house. "Did you get three pounds apiece for the pigs, father?"

"I did, and three pounds five."

"We might have a drink out of that."

It seemed to Peter that the men inside were laughing at him or at the lemonade he was drinking, and, seeing among them one who had been interfering with him all day, he told him he would put him out of the house, and he would have done it if Mrs. Quinn had not told him that no one put a man out of her house without her leave.

"Do you hear that, Peter Phelan?"

"If you can't best them at the fair," said his father, "it will be little good for you to put them out of the public-house afterwards."

And on that Peter swore he would never go to a fair again, and they walked on until they came to the priest's house.

"It was bad for me when I listened to you and James. If I hadn't I might have been in Maynooth now."

"Now, didn't you come home talking of the polis?"

"Wasn't that after?"

They could not agree as to when his idea of life had changed from the priesthood to the police, nor when it had changed back from the police to the priesthood, and Peter talked on, telling of the authors he had read with Father Tom—Caesar, Virgil, even Quintillian. The priest had said that Quintillian was too difficult for him, and Pat Phelan was in doubt whether the difficulty of Quintillian was a sufficient reason for preferring the police to the priesthood.

"Any way it isn't a girl that's troubling him," he said to himself, and he looked at Peter, and wondered how it was that Peter did not want to be married. Peter was a great big fellow, over six feet high, that many a girl would take a fancy to, and Pat Phelan had long had his eye on a girl who would marry him. And his failure to sell the bullocks brought all the advantages of this marriage to Pat Phelan's mind, and he began to talk to his son. Peter listened, and seemed to take an interest in all that was said, expressing now and then a doubt if the girl would marry him; the possibility that she might seemed to turn his thoughts again towards the priesthood.

The bullocks had stopped to graze, and Peter's indecisions threw Pat Phelan fairly out of his humour.

"Well, Peter, I am tired listening to you. If it's a priest you want to be, go in there, and Father Tom will tell you what you must do, and I'll drive the bullocks home myself."

And on that Pat laid his hand on the priest's green gate, and Peter walked through.

II

There were trees about the priest's house, and there were two rooms on the right and left of the front door. The parlour was on the left, and when Peter came in the priest was sitting reading in his mahogany armchair. Peter wondered if it were this very mahogany chair that had put the idea of being a priest into his head. Just now, while walking with his father, he had been thinking that they had not even a wooden armchair in their house, though it was the best house in the village—only some stools and some plain wooden chairs.

The priest could see that Peter had come to him for a purpose. But Peter did not speak; he sat raising his pale, perplexed eyes, looking at the priest from time to time, thinking that if he told Father Tom of his failure at the fair, Father Tom might think he only wished to become a priest because he had no taste for farming.

"You said, Father Tom, if I worked hard I should be able to read Quintillian in six months."

The priest's face always lighted up at the name of a classical author, and Peter said he was sorry he had been taken away from his studies. But he had been thinking the matter over, and his mind was quite made up, and he was sure he would sooner be a priest than anything else.

"My boy, I knew you would never put on the policeman's belt. The bishop will hold an examination for the places that are vacant in Maynooth." Peter promised to work hard, and he already saw himself sitting in an armchair, in a mahogany armchair, reading classics, and winning admiration for his learning.

He walked home, thinking that everything was at last decided, when suddenly, without warning, when he was thinking of something else, his heart misgave him. It was as if he heard a voice saying: "My boy, I don't think you will ever put on the cassock. You will never walk with the biretta on your head." The priest had said that he did not believe he would ever buckle on the policeman's belt. He was surprised to hear the priest say this, though he had often heard himself thinking the same thing. What surprised and frightened him now was that he heard himself saying he would never put on the cassock and the biretta. It is frightening to hear yourself saying you are not going to do the thing you have just made up your mind you will do.

He had often thought he would like to put the money he would get out of the farm into a shop, but when it came to the point of deciding he had not been able to make up his mind. He had always had a great difficulty in knowing what was the right thing to do. His uncle William had never thought of anything but the priesthood. James never thought of anything but the farm. A certain friend of his had never thought of anything but going to America. Suddenly he heard some one call him.

It was Catherine, and Peter wondered if she were thinking to tell him she was going to marry James.

For she always knew what she wanted. Many said that James was not the one she wanted, but Peter did not believe that, and he looked at Catherine and admired her face, and thought what a credit she would be to the family. No one wore such beautifully knitted stockings as Catherine, and no one's boots were so prettily laced.

But not knowing exactly what to say, he asked her if she had come from their house, and he went on talking, telling her that she would find nobody in the parish like James. James was the best farmer in the parish, none such a judge of cattle; and he said all this and a great deal more, until he saw that Catherine did not care to talk about James at all.

"I daresay all you say is right, Peter; but you see he's your brother."

And then, fearing she had said something hurtful, she

told him that she liked James as much as a girl could like a man who was not going to be her husband.

"And are you sure, Catherine, that James is not going to be your husband?"

"Yes," she said, "quite sure."

Their talk had taken them as far as Catherine's door, and Peter went away wondering why he had not told her he was going to Maynooth; for no one would have been able to advise him as well as Catherine, she had such good sense.

III

There was a quarter of a mile between the two houses, and while Peter was talking to Catherine, Pat Phelan was listening to his son James, who was telling his father that Catherine had said she would not marry him.

Pat was over sixty, but he did not give one the impression of an old man. The hair was not grey, there was still a little red in the whiskers. James, who sat opposite to him holding his hands to the blaze, was not as good-looking a man as his father, the nose was not as fine, nor were the eyes as keen. There was more of the father in Peter than in James.

When Peter opened the half-door, awaking the dozen hens that roosted on the beam, he glanced from one to the other, for he suspected that his father was telling James how he had failed to sell the bullocks. But the tone of his father's voice when he asked him what had detained him on the road told him he was mistaken; and then he remembered that Catherine had said she would not marry James, and he began to pity his brother.

"I met Catherine on the road, and I could do no less than walk as far as her door with her."

"You could do no less than that, Peter," said James.

"And what do you mean by that, James?"

"Only this, that it is always the crooked way, Peter; for if it had been you that had asked her she would have had you and jumping."

"She would have had me!"

"And now don't you think you had better run after her, Peter, and ask her if she'll have you?"

"I'll never do that; and it is hurtful, James, that you should think such a thing of me, that I would go behind your back and try to get a girl from you."

"I did not mean that, Peter; but if she won't have me, you had better try if you can get her."

And suddenly Peter felt a resolve come into his heart, and his manner grew exultant.

"I've seen Father Tom, and he said I can pass the examination. I'm going to be a priest."

And when they were lying down side by side Peter said, "James, it will be all right." Knowing there was a great heart-sickness on his brother, he put out his hand. "As sure as I lie here she will be lying next you before this day twelvemonths. Yes, James, in this very bed, lying here where I am lying now."

"I don't believe it, Peter."

Peter loved his brother, and to bring the marriage about he took some money from his father and went to live at Father Tom's, and he worked so hard during the next two months that he passed the bishop's examination. And it was late one night when he went to bid them good-bye at home.

"What makes you so late, Peter?"

"Well, James, I didn't want to meet Catherine on the road."

"You are a good boy, Peter," said the father, "and God will reward you for the love you bear your brother. I don't think there are two better men in the world. God has been good to me to give me two such sons."

And then the three sat round the fire, and Pat Phelan began to talk family history.

"Well, Peter, you see, there has always been a priest in the family, and it would be a pity if there's not one in this generation. In '48 your grand-uncles joined the rebels, and they had to leave the country. You have an uncle a priest, and you are just like your uncle William."

And then James talked, but he did not seem to know very well what he was saying, and his father told him to stop—that Peter was going where God had called him.

"And you will tell her," Peter said, getting up, "that I have gone."

"I haven't the heart for telling her such a thing. She will be finding it out soon enough."

Outside the house—for he was sleeping at Father Tom's

that night—Peter thought there was little luck in James's eyes; inside the house Pat Phelan and James thought that Peter was settled for life.

"He will be a fine man standing on an altar," James said, "and perhaps he will be a bishop some day."

"And you'll see her when you're done reaping, and you won't forget what Peter told you," said Pat Phelan.

And, after reaping, James put on his coat and walked up the hillside, where he thought he would find Catherine.

"I heard Peter has left you," she said, as he opened the gate to let the cows through.

"He came last night to bid us good-bye."

And they followed the cows under the tall hedges.

"I shall be reaping to-morrow," he said. "I will see you at the same time."

And henceforth he was always at hand to help her to drive her cows home; and every night, as he sat with his father by the fire, Pat Phelan expected James to tell him about Catherine. One evening he came back overcome, looking so wretched that his father could see that Catherine had told him she would not marry him.

"She won't have me," he said.

"A man can always get a girl if he tries long enough," his father said, hoping to encourage him.

"That would be true enough for another. Catherine knows she will never get Peter. Another man might get her, but I'm always reminding her of Peter.

She told him the truth one day, that if she did not marry Peter she would marry no one, and James felt like dying. He grew pale and could not speak.

At last he said, "How is that?"

"I don't know. I don't know, James. But you mustn't talk to me about marriage again."

And he had to promise her not to speak of marriage again, and he kept his word. At the end of the year she asked him if he had any news of Peter.

"The last news we had of him was about a month ago, and he said he hoped to be admitted into the minor orders."

And a few days afterwards he heard that Catherine had decided to go into a convent.

"So this is the way it has ended," he thought. And he seemed no longer fit for work on the farm. He was seen about the road smoking, and sometimes he went down to the ball-alley, and sat watching the games in the evening. It was thought that he would take to drink, but he took to fishing instead, and was out all day in his little boat on the lake, however hard the wind might blow. The fisherman said he had seen him in the part of the lake where the wind blew the hardest, and that he could hardly pull against the waves.

"His mind is away. I don't think he'll do any good in this country," his father said.

And the old man was very sad, for when James was gone he would have no one, and he did not feel he would be able to work the farm for many years longer. He and James used to sit smoking on either side of the fireplace, and Pat Phelan knew that James was thinking of America all the while. One evening, as they were sitting like this, the door was opened suddenly.

"Peter!" said James. And he jumped up from the fire to welcome his brother.

"It is good for sore eyes to see the sight of you again," said Pat Phelan. "Well, tell us the news. If we had known you were coming we would have sent the cart to meet you."

As Peter did not answer, they began to think that something must have happened. Perhaps Peter was not going to become a priest after all, and would stay at home with his father to learn to work on the farm.

"You see, I did not know myself until yesterday. It was only yesterday that—"

"So you are not going to be a priest? We are glad to hear that, Peter."

"How is that?"

He had thought over what he should say, and without waiting to hear why they were glad, he told them the professor, who overlooked his essays, had refused to recognise their merits—he had condemned the best things in them; and Peter said it was extraordinary that such a man should be appointed to such a place. Then he told them that the Church afforded little chances for the talents of young men unless they had a great deal of influence.

And they sat listening to him, hearing how the college might be reformed. He had a gentle, winning way of talking, and his father and brother forgot their own misfortunes thinking how they might help him.

"Well, Peter, you have come back none too soon."

"And how is that? What have you been doing since I went away? You all wanted to hear about Maynooth."

"Of course we did, my boy. Tell him, James."

"Oh! it is nothing particular," said James. "It is only this, Peter—I am going to America."

"And who will work the farm?"

"Well, Peter, we were thinking that you might work it yourself."

"I work the farm! Going to America, James! But what about Catherine?"

"That's what I'm coming to, Peter. She has gone into a convent. And that's what's happened since you went away. I can't stop here, Peter—I will never do a hand's turn in Ireland—and father is getting too old to go to the fairs. That's what we were thinking when you came in."

There was a faint tremble in his voice, and Peter saw how heartsick his brother was.

"I will do my best, James."

"I knew you would."

"Yes, I will," said Peter; and he sat down by the fire. And his father said:—

"You are not smoking, Peter."

"No," he said; "I've given up smoking."

"Will you drink something?" said James. "We have got a drain of whiskey in the house."

"No, I have had to give up spirits. It doesn't agree with me. And I don't take tea in the morning. Have you got any cocoa in the house?"

It was not the kind of cocoa he liked, but he said he would be able to manage.

## IV

And when the old man came through the doorway in the morning buttoning his braces, he saw Peter stirring his cocoa. There was something absurd as well as something attractive in Peter, and his father had to laugh when he said he couldn't eat American bacon.

"My stomach wouldn't retain it. I require very little, but that little must be the best."

And when James took him into the farmyard, he noticed that Peter crossed the yard like one who had never been in a farmyard before; he looked less like a farmer than ever, and when he looked at the cows, James wondered if he could be taught to see the difference between an Alderney and a Durham.

"There's Kate," he said; "she's a good cow; as good a cow as we have, and we can't get any price for her because of that hump on her back."

They went to the styes; there were three pigs there and a great sow with twelve little bonhams, and the little ones were white with silky hair, and Peter asked how old they were, and when they would be fit for killing. And James told Peter there were seven acres in the Big field.

"Last year we had oats in the Holly field; next year you'll sow potatoes there." And he explained the rotation of crops. "And, now," he said, "we will go down to Crow's Oak. You have never done any ploughing, Peter; I will show you."

It was extraordinary how little Peter knew. He could not put the harness on the horse, and he reminded James that he had gone into the post office when he left school. James gave in to him that the old red horse was hard to drive, but James could drive him better than Peter could lead him; and Peter marvelled at the skill with which James raised his hand from the shaft of the plough and struck the horse with the rein whilst he kept the plough steady with the other hand.

"Now, Peter, you must try again."

At the end of the headland where the plough turned, Peter always wanted to stop and talk about something; but James said they would have to get on with the work, and Peter walked after the plough, straining after it for three hours, and then he said: "James, let me drive the horse. I can do no more."

"You won't feel it so much when you are accustomed to it," said James.

Anything seemed to him better than a day's ploughing: even getting up at three in the morning to go to a fair.

He went to bed early, as he used to, and they talked of him over the fire, as they used to. But however much they talked, they never seemed to find what they were seeking—his vocation—until one evening an idea suddenly rose out of their talk.

"A good wife is the only thing for Peter," said Pat. And they went on thinking.

"A husband would be better for her," said Pat Phelan, "than a convent."

"I cannot say I agree with you there. Think of all the good them nuns are doing."

"She isn't a nun yet," said Pat Phelan.

And the men smoked on a while, and they ruminated as they smoked.

"It would be better, James, that Peter got her than that she would stay in a convent."

"I wouldn't say that," said James.

"You see," said his father, "she did not go into the convent because she had a calling, but because she was crossed in love."

And after another long while James said, "It is a bitter dose, I am thinking, father, but you must go and tell her that Peter has left Maynooth."

"And what would the Reverend Mother be saying to me if I went to her with such a story as that? Isn't your heart broken enough already, James, without wanting me to be breaking it still more? Sure, James, you could never see her married to Peter?"

"If she were to marry Peter I should be able to go to America, and that is the only thing for me."

"That would be poor consolation for you, James."

"Well, it is the best I shall get, to see Peter settled, and to know that there will be some one to look after you, father."

"You are a good son, James."

They talked on, and as they talked it became clearer to them that some one must go to-morrow to the convent and tell Catherine that Peter had left Maynooth.

"But wouldn't it be a pity," said Pat Phelan, "to tell her this if Peter is not going to marry her in the end?"

"I will have him out of his bed," said James, "and he'll tell us before this fire if he will or won't."

"It's a serious thing you are doing, James, to get a girl out of a convent, I am thinking."

"It will be on my advice that you will be doing this, father; and now I'll go and get Peter out of his bed."

And Peter was brought in, asking what they wanted of him at this hour of the night; and when they told him what they had been talking about and the plans they had been making, he said he would be catching his death of cold, and they threw some sods of turf on the fire.

"It is against myself that I am asking a girl to leave the convent, even for you, Peter," said James. "But we can think of nothing else."

"Peter will be able to tell us if it is a sin that we'd be do

"It is only right that Catherine should know the truth before she made her vows," Peter said. "But this is very unexpected, father. I really—"

"Peter, I'd take it as a great kindness. I shall never do a hand's work in this country. I want to get to America. It will be the saving of me."

"And now, Peter," said his father, "tell us for sure if you will have the girl?"

"Faith I will, though I never thought of marriage, if it be to please James." Seeing how heart sick his brother was, he said, "I can't say I like her as you like her; but if she likes me I will promise to do right by her. James, you're going away; we may never see you again. It is all very sad. And now you'll let me go back to bed."

"Peter, I knew you would not say no to me; I can't bear this any longer."

"And now," said Peter, "let me go back to bed. I am catching my death."

And he ran back to his room, and left his brother and father talking by the fire.

### V

Pat thought the grey mare would take him in faster than the old red horse; and the old man sat, his legs swinging over the shaft, wondering what he should say to the Reverend Mother, and how she would listen to his story; and when he came to the priest's house a great wish came upon him to ask the priest's advice. The priest was walking up his little lawn reading his breviary, and a great fear came on Pat Phelan, and he thought he must ask the priest what he should do.

The priest heard the story over the little wall, and he was sorry for the old man.

It took him a long time to tell the story, and when he was finished the priest said:—

"But where are you going, Pat?"

"That's what I stopped to tell you, your reverence. I was thinking I might be going to the convent to tell Catherine that Peter has come back."

"Well it wasn't yourself that thought of doing such a thing as that, Pat Phelan."

But at every word the priest said Pat Phelan's face grew more stubborn, and at last he said:—

"Well, your reverence, that isn't the advice I expected from you," and he struck the mare with the ends of the reins and let her trot up the hill. Nor did the mare stop trotting till she had reached the top of the hill, and Pat Phelan had never known her to do such a thing before. From the top of the hill there was a view of the bog, and Pat thought of the many fine loads of turf he had had out of that bog, and the many young fellows he had seen there cutting turf. "But every one is leaving the country," the old man said to himself, and his chin dropped into his shirt-collar, and he held the reins loosely, letting the mare trot or walk as she liked. And he let many pass him without bidding them the hour of the day, for he was too much overcome by his own grief to notice any one.

The mare trotted gleefully; soft clouds curled over the low horizon far away, and the sky was blue overhead; and the poor country was very beautiful in the still autumn weather, only it was empty. He passed two or three fine houses that the gentry had left to caretakers long ago. The fences were gone, cattle strayed through the woods, the drains were choked with weeds, the stagnant water was spreading out into the fields, and Pat Phelan noticed these things, for he remembered what this country was forty years ago. The devil a bit of lonesomeness there was in it then.

He asked a girl if they would be thatching the house that autumn; but she answered that the thatch would last out the old people, and she was going to join her sister in America.

"She's right—they're all there now. Why should anyone stop here?" the old man said.

The mare tripped, and he took this to be a sign that he should turn back. But he did not go back. Very soon the town began, in broken pavements and dirty cottages; going up the hill there were some slated roofs, but there was no building of any importance except the church.

At the end of the main street, where the trees began again,

the convent stood in the middle of a large garden, and Pat Phelan remembered he had heard that the nuns were doing well with their dairy and their laundry.

He knocked, and a lay-sister peeped through the grating, and then she opened the door a little way, and at first he thought he would have to go back without seeing either Catherine or the Reverend Mother. For he had got no further than "Sister Catherine," when the lay-sister cut him short with the news that Sister Catherine was in retreat, and could see no one. The Reverend Mother was busy.

"But," said Pat, "you're not going to let Catherine take vows without hearing me."

"If it is about Sister Catherine's vows—."

"Yes, it is about them I've come, and I must see the Reverend Mother."

The lay-sister said Sister Catherine was going to be clothed at the end of the week.

"Well, that is just the reason I've come here."

On that the lay-sister led him into the parlour, and went in search of the Reverend Mother.

The floor was so thickly bees-waxed that the rug slipped under his feet, and, afraid lest he might fall down, he stood quite still, impressed by the pious pictures on the walls, and by the large books upon the table, and by the poor-box, and by the pious inscriptions. He began to think how much easier was this pious life than the life of the world—the rearing of children, the failure of crops, and the loneliness. Here life slips away without one perceiving it, and it seemed a pity to bring her back to trouble. He stood holding his hat in his old hands, and the time seemed very long. At last the door opened, and a tall woman with sharp, inquisitive eyes came in.

"You have come to speak to me about Sister Catherine?"

"Yes, my lady."

"And what have you got to tell me about her?"

"Well, my son thought and I thought last night—we were all thinking we had better tell you—last night was the night that my son came back."

At the word Maynooth a change of expression came into her face, but when he told that Peter no longer wished to be a priest her manner began to grow hostile again, and she got up from her chair and said:

"But really, Mr. Phelan, I have got a great deal of business to attend to."

"But, my lady, you see that Catherine wanted to marry my son Peter, and it is because he went to Maynooth that she came here. I don't think she'd want to be a nun if she knew that he didn't want to be a priest."

"I cannot agree with you, Mr. Phelan, in that. I have seen a great deal of Sister Catherine—she has been with us now for nearly a year—and if she ever entertained the wishes you speak of, I feel sure she has forgotten them. Her mind is now set on higher things."

"Of course you may be right, my lady; very likely. It isn't for me to argue with you about such things; but you see I have come a long way, and if I could see Catherine herself—"

"That is impossible. Catherine is in retreat."

"So the lay-sister told me; but I thought—"

"Sister Catherine is going to be clothed next Saturday, and I can assure you, Mr. Phelan, that the wishes you tell me of are forgotten. I know her very well. I can answer for Sister Catherine."

The rug slipped under the peasant's feet and his eyes wandered round the room; and the Reverend Mother told him how busy she was, she really could not talk to him any more that day.

"You see, it all rests with Sister Catherine herself."

"That's just it," said the old man; "that's just it, my lady. My son Peter, who has come from Maynooth, told us last night that Catherine should know everything that has happened, so that she may not be sorry afterwards, otherwise I wouldn't have come here, my lady. I wouldn't have come to trouble you."

"I am sorry, Mr. Phelan, that your son Peter has left Maynooth. It is sad indeed when one finds that one has not a vocation. But that happens sometimes. I don't think it will be Catherine's case. And now, Mr. Phelan, I must ask you to excuse me," and the Reverend Mother persuaded the unwilling peasant into the passage, and he followed the lay-sister down the passage to the gate and got into his cart again.

"No wonder," he thought, "they don't want to let Catherine out, now that they have got that great farm, and not one among them, I'll be bound, who can manage it except Catherine."

At the very same moment the same thoughts passed through the Reverend Mother's mind. She had not left the parlour yet, and stood thinking how she should manage if Catherine were to leave them. "Why," she asked, "should he choose to leave Maynooth at such a time? It is indeed unfortunate. There is nothing," she reflected, "that gives a woman so much strength as to receive the veil. She always feels stronger after her clothing. She feels that the world is behind her."

The Reverend Mother reflected that perhaps it would be better for Catherine's sake and for Peter's sake—indeed, for everyone's sake—if she were not to tell Catherine of Pat Phelan's visit until after the clothing. She might tell Catherine three months hence. The disadvantage of this would be that Catherine might hear that Peter had left Maynooth. In a country place news of this kind cannot be kept out of a convent. And if Catherine were going to leave, it were better that she should leave them now than leave them six months hence, after her clothing.

"There are many ways of looking at it," the Reverend Mother reflected. "If I don't tell her, she may never hear it. I might tell her later, when she has taught one of the nuns how to manage the farm." She took two steps towards the door and stopped to think again, and she was thinking when a knock came to the door. She answered mechanically, "Come in," and Catherine wondered at the Reverend Mother's astonishment.

"I wish to speak to you, dear Mother," she said timidly. But seeing the Reverend Mother's face change expression, she said, "Perhaps another time will suit you better."

The Reverend Mother stood looking at her, irresolute; and Catherine, who had never seen the Reverend Mother irresolute before, wondered what was passing in her mind.

"I know you are busy, dear mother, but what I have come to tell you won't take very long."

"Well, then, tell it to me, my child."

"It is only this, Reverend Mother. I had better tell you now, for you are expecting the bishop, and my clothing is fixed for the end of the week, and—"

"And," said the Reverend Mother, "you feel that you are not certain of your vocation."

"That is it, dear mother. I thought I had better tell you." Reading disappointment in the nun's face, Catherine said, "I hesitated to tell you before. I had hoped that the feeling would pass away; but, dear mother, it isn't my fault; everyone has not a vocation."

Then Catherine noticed a softening in the Reverend

Mother's face, and she asked Catherine to sit down by her; and Catherine told her she had come to the convent because she was crossed in love, and not as the others came, because they wished to give up their wills to God.

"Our will is the most precious thing in us, and that is why the best thing we can do is to give it up to you, for in giving it up to you, dear mother, we are giving it up to God. I know all these things, but—"

"You should have told me of this when you came here, Catherine, and then I would not have advised you to come to live with us."

"Mother, you must forgive me. My heart was broken, and I could not do otherwise. And you have said yourself that I made the dairy a success."

"If you had stayed with us, Catherine, you would have made the dairy a success; but we have got no one to take your place. However, since it is the will of God, I suppose we must try to get on as well as we can without you. And now tell me, Catherine, when it was that you changed your mind. It was only the other day you told me you wished to become a nun. You said you were most anxious for your clothing. How is it that you have changed your mind?"

Catherine's eyes brightened, and speaking like one illuminated by some inward light, she said:

"It was the second day of my retreat, mother. I was walking in the garden where the great cross stands amid the rocks. Sister Angela and Sister Mary were with me, and I was listening to what they were saying, when suddenly my thoughts were taken away and I remembered those at home. I remembered Mr. Phelan, and James, who wanted to marry me, but whom I would not marry; and it seemed to me that I saw him leaving his father—it seemed to me that I saw him going away to America. I don't know how it was—you will not believe me, dear mother—but I saw the ship lying in the harbour, that is to take him away. And then I thought of the old man sitting at home with no one to look after him, and it was not a seeming, but a certainty mother. It came over me suddenly that my duty was not here, but there. Of course you can't agree with me, but I cannot resist it, it was a call."

"But the Evil One, my dear child, calls us too; we must be careful not to mistake the devil's call for God's call."

"Mother, I daresay." Tears came to Catherine's eyes, she

began to weep. "I can't argue with you, mother, I only know—" She could not speak for sobbing, and between her sobs she said, "I only know that I must go home."

She recovered herself very soon, and the Reverend Mother took her hand and said:

"Well, my dear child, I shall not stand in your way."

Even the Reverend Mother could not help thinking that the man who got her would get a charming wife. Her face was rather long and white, and she had long female eyes with dark lashes, and her eyes were full of tenderness. She had spoken out of so deep a conviction that the Reverend Mother had begun to believe that her mission was perhaps to look after this hapless young man; and when she told the Reverend Mother that yesterday she had felt a conviction that Peter was not going to be a priest, the Reverend Mother felt that she must tell her of Pat Phelan's visit.

"I did not tell you at once, my dear child, because I wished to know from yourself how you felt about this matter," the nun said; and she told Catherine that she was quite right, that Peter had left Maynooth. "He hopes to marry you, Catherine."

A quiet glow came into the postulant's eyes, and she seemed engulfed in some deep joy.

"How did he know that I cared for him?" the girl said, half to herself, half to the nun.

"I suppose his father or his brother must have told him," the nun answered.

And then Catherine, fearing to show too much interest in things that the nun deemed frivolous, said, "I am sorry to leave before my work is done here. But, mother, so it has all come true; it was extraordinary what I felt that morning in the garden," she said, returning to her joy. "Mother, do you believe in visions?"

"The saints, of course, have had visions. We believe in the visions of the saints."

"But after all, mother, there are many duties besides religious duties."

I suppose, Catherine, you feel it to be your duty to look after this young man?"

"Yes, I think that is it. I must go now, mother, and see Sister Angela, and write out for her all I know about the farm, and what she is to do, for if one is not very careful with a farm one loses a great deal of money. There is no such thing as making two ends meet. One either makes money or loses money."

And then Catherine again seemed to be engulfed in some deep joy, out of which she roused herself with difficulty.

## VI

When her postulant left the room, the Reverend Mother wrote to Pat Phelan, asking him to come next morning with his cart to fetch Catherine. And next morning, when the lay sister told Catherine that he was waiting for her, the Reverend Mother said:

"We shall be able to manage, Catherine. You have told Sister Angela everything, and you will not forget to come to see us, I hope."

"Mr. Phelan," said the lay sister, "told me to tell you that one of his sons is going to America to-day. Sister Catherine will have to go at once if she wishes to see him."

"I must see James. I must see him before he leaves for America. "Oh," she said, turning to the Reverend Mother, "do you remember that I told you I had seen the ship? Everything has come true. You can't believe any longer that it is not a call."

Her box was in the cart, and as Pat turned the mare round he said: "I hope we won't miss James at the station. That's the reason I came for you so early. I thought you would like to see him."

"Why did you not come earlier?" she cried. "All my happiness will be spoilt if I don't see James."

The convent was already behind her, and her thoughts were now upon poor James, whose heart she had broken. She knew that Peter would never love her as well as James, but this could not be helped. Her vision in the garden consoled her, for she could no longer doubt that she was doing right in going to Peter, that her destiny was with him.

She knew the road well, she knew all the fields, every house and every gap in the walls. Sign after sign went by; at last they were within sight of the station. The signal was still up, and the train had not gone yet; at the end of the platform she saw James and Peter. She let Pat Phelan drive the cart round; she could get to them quicker by running down the steps and crossing the line. The signal went down.

"Peter," she said, "we shall have time to talk presently. I want to speak to James now."

And they walked up to the platform, leaving Peter to talk to his father.

"Paddy Maguire is outside," Pat said; "I asked him to stand at the mare's head."

"James," said Catherine, "it is very sad you are going away. We may never see you again, and there is no time to talk, and I've much to say to you."

"I am going away, Catherine, but maybe I will be coming back some day. I was going to say maybe you would be coming over after me; but the land is good land, and you'll be able to make a living out of it."

And then they spoke of Peter. James said he was too great a scholar for a farmer, and it was a pity he could not find out what he was fit for—for surely he was fit for something great after all.

And Catherine said:

"I shall be able to make something out of Peter."

His emotion almost overcame him and Catherine looked aside so that she should not see his tears.

"This is no time for talking of Peter," she said. "You are going away, James, but you will come back. You will find another woman better than I am in America, James. I don't know what to say to you. The train will be here in a minute. I am distracted. But one day you will be coming back, and we shall be very proud of you when you come back. I shall rebuild the house, and we shall be all happy then. Oh! here's the train. Good-bye; you have been very good to me. Oh, James! shall I ever see you again?"

Then the crowd swept them along, and James had to take his father's hand and his brother's hand. There were a great many people in the station—hundreds were going away in the same ship that James was going in. The train was followed by wailing relatives. They ran alongside of the train, waving their hands until they could no longer keep up with the train. James waved a red handkerchief until the train was out of sight. It disappeared in a cutting, and a moment after Catherine and Peter remembered they were standing side by side. They were going to be married in a few days! They started a little, hearing a step beside them. It was old Phelan.

"I think," he said, "it is time to be getting home."

# George Moore

## *Home Sickness*

### I

He told the doctor he was due in the bar-room at eight-o'clock in the morning; the bar-room was in a slum in the Bowery; and he had only been able to keep himself in health by getting up at five o'clock and going for long walks in the Central Park.

"A sea voyage is what you want," said the doctor. "Why not go to Ireland for two or three months?"

"I'd like to see Ireland again."

And he began to wonder how the people at home were getting on. The doctor was right. He thanked him, and three weeks afterwards he landed in Cork.

As he sat in the railway carriage he recalled his native village—he could see it and its lake, and then the fields one by one, and the roads. He could see a large piece of rocky land—some three or four hundred acres of headland stretching out into the winding lake. Upon this headland the peasantry had been given permission to build their cabins by former owners of the Georgian house standing on the pleasant green hill. The present owners considered the village a disgrace; but the villagers paid high rents for their plots of ground, and all the manual labour that the Big House required came from the village: the gardeners, the stable helpers, the house and the kitchen maids.

Bryden had been thirteen years in America, and when the train stopped at his station, he looked round to see if there were any changes in it. It was just the same blue limestone station-house as it was thirteen years ago. The platform and the sheds were the same, and there were five miles of road from the station to Duncannon. The sea voyage had done him good, but five miles were too far for him to-day; the last time he had walked the road, he had walked it in an hour and a half, carrying a heavy bundle on a stick.

He was sorry he did not feel strong enough for the walk; the evening was fine, and he would meet many people coming home from the fair, some of whom he had known in his youth, and they would tell him where he could get a clean lodging. But the carman would be able to tell him that; he called the car that was waiting at the station, and soon he was answering questions about America. But he wanted to hear of those who were still living in the old country, and after hearing the stories of many people he had forgotten, he heard that Mike Scully, who had been away in a situation for many years as a coachman in the King's county, had come back and built a fine house with a concrete floor. Now there was a good loft in Mike Scully's house, and Mike would be pleased to take in a lodger.

Bryden remembered that Mike had been in a situation at the Big House; he had intended to be a jockey, but had suddenly shot up into a fine tall man, and had had to become a coachman instead. Bryden tried to recall the face, but he could only remember a straight nose, and a somewhat dusky complexion. Mike was one of the heroes of his childhood, and now his youth floated before him, and he caught glimpses of himself, something that was more than a phantom and less than a reality. Suddenly his reverie was broken: the carman pointed with his whip, and Bryden saw a tall, finely-built, middle-aged man coming through the gates, and the driver said:

"There's Mike Scully."

Mike had forgotten Bryden even more completely than Bryden had forgotten him, and many aunts and uncles were mentioned before he began to understand.

"You've grown into a fine man, James," he said, looking at Bryden's great width of chest. "But you are thin in the cheeks, and you're very sallow in the cheeks too."

"I haven't been very well lately—that is one of the reasons I have come back; but I want to see you all again."

Bryden paid the carman, wished him "God-speed," and he and Mike divided the luggage between them, Mike carrying the bag and Bryden the bundle, and they walked round the lake, for the townland was at the back of the demesne; and while they walked, James proposed to pay Mike ten shillings a week for his board and lodging.

He remembered the woods thick and well-forested; now they were windworn, the drains were choked, and the bridge leading across the lake inlet was falling away. Their way led between long fields where herds of cattle were grazing; the road was broken—Bryden wondered how the villagers drove their carts over it, and Mike told him that the landlord could not keep it in repair, and he would not allow it to be kept in repair out of the rates, for then it would be a public road, and he did not think there should be a public road through his property.

At the end of many fields they came to the village, and it looked a desolate place, even on this fine evening, and Bryden remarked that the county did not seem to be as much lived in as it used to be. It was at once strange and familiar to see the chickens in the kitchen; and, wishing to re-knit himself to the old habits, he begged of Mrs. Scully not to drive them out, saying he did not mind them. Mike told his wife that Bryden was born in Duncannon, and when she heard Bryden's name she gave him her hand, after wiping it in her apron, saying he was heartily welcome, only she was afraid he would not care to sleep in a loft.

"Why wouldn't I sleep in a loft, a dry loft! You're thinking a good deal of America over here," said he, "but I reckon it isn't all you think it. Here you work when you like and you sit down when you like; but when you have had a touch of blood-poisoning as I had, and when you have seen young people walking with a stick, you think that there is something to be said for old Ireland."

"Now won't you be taking a sup of milk? You'll be wanting a drink after travelling," said Mrs. Scully.

And when he had drunk the milk Mike asked him if he would like to go inside or if he would like to go for a walk.

"Maybe it is sitting down you would like to be."

And they went into the cabin, and started to talk about the wages a man could get in America, and the long hours of work.

And after Bryden had told Mike everything about America that he thought of interest, he asked Mike about Ireland. But Mike did not seem to be able to tell him much that was of interest. They were all very poor—poorer, perhaps, than when he left them.

"I don't think anyone except myself has a five pound note to his name."

Bryden hoped he felt sufficiently sorry for Mike. But after all Mike's life and prospects mattered little to him. He had come back in search of health; and he felt better already; the milk had done him good, and the bacon and cabbage in the pot sent forth a savoury odour. The Scullys were very kind, they pressed him to make a good meal; a few weeks of country air and food, they said, would give him back the health he had lost in the Bowery; and when Bryden said he was longing for a smoke, Mike said there was no better sign than that. During his long illness he had never wanted to smoke, and he was a confirmed smoker.

It was comfortable to sit by the mild peat fire watching the smoke of their pipes drifting up the chimney, and all Bryden wanted was to be let alone; he did not want to hear of anyone's misfortunes, but about nine o'clock a number of villagers came in, and their appearance was depressing. Bryden remembered one or two of them—he used to know them very well when he was a boy; their talk was as depressing as their appearance, and he could feel no interest whatever in them. He was not moved when he heard that Higgins the stone mason was dead; he was not affected when he heard that Mary Kelly, who used to go to do the laundry at the Big House, had married; he was only interested when he heard she had gone to America. No, he had not met her there; America is a big place. Then one of the peasants asked him if he remembered Patsy Carabine, who used to do the gardening at the Big House. Yes, he remembered Patsy well. Patsy was in the poor-house. He had not been able to do any work on account of his arm; his house had fallen in; he had given up his holding and gone into the poor-house. All this was very sad, and to avoid hearing any further unpleasantness, Bryden began to tell them about America. And they sat round listening to him; but all the talking was on his side; he wearied of it; and looking round the group he recognised a ragged hunchback with grey hair; twenty years ago he was a young hunchback, and, turning to him, Bryden asked him if he were doing well with his five acres.

"Ah, not much. This has been a bad season. The potatoes failed; they were watery—there is no diet in them."

These peasants were all agreed that they could make nothing out of their farms. Their regret was that they had not gone to America when they were young; and after striving to take an interest in the fact that O'Connor had lost a mare and foal worth forty pounds Bryden began to wish himself back in the slum.

When they left the house he wondered if every evening would be like the present one. Mike piled fresh sods on the fire, and he hoped it would show enough light in the loft for Bryden to undress himself by.

The cackling of some geese in the road kept him awake, and the loneliness of the country seemed to penetrate to his bones, and to freeze the marrow in them. There was a bat in the loft—a dog howled in the distance—and then he drew the clothes over his head. Never had he been so unhappy, and the sound of Mike breathing by his wife's side in the kitchen added to his nervous terror. Then he dozed a little; and lying on his back he dreamed he was awake, and the men he had seen sitting round the fireside that evening seemed to him like spectres come out of some unknown region of morass and reedy tarn. He stretched out his hands for his clothes, determined to fly from this house, but remembering the lonely road that led to the station he fell back on his pillow. The geese still cackled, but he was too tired to be kept awake any longer. He seemed to have been asleep only a few minutes when he heard Mike calling him. Mike had come half way up the ladder and was telling him that breakfast was ready. "What kind of breakfast will he give me?" Bryden asked himself as he pulled on his clothes. There were tea and hot griddle cakes for breakfast, and there were fresh eggs; there was sunlight in the kitchen, and he liked to hear Mike tell of the work he was going to do in the fields. Mike rented a farm of about fifteen acres, at least ten of it was grass; he grew an acre of potatoes and some corn, and some turnips for his sheep. He had a nice bit of meadow, and he took down his scythe, and as he put the whetstone in his belt Bryden noticed a second scythe, and he asked Mike if he should go down with him and help him to finish the field.

"You haven't done any mowing this many a year; I don't think you'd be of much help. You'd better go for a walk by the lake, but you may come in the afternoon if you like and help to turn the grass over."

Bryden was afraid he would find the lake shore very lonely, but the magic of returning health is sufficient distraction for the convalescent, and the morning passed agreeably. The weather was still and sunny. He could hear the ducks in the reeds. The days dreamed themselves away, and it became his habit to go to the lake every morning. One morning he met the landlord, and they walked together, talking of the country, of what it had been, and the ruin it was slipping into. James Bryden told him that ill health had brought him back to Ireland; and the landlord lent him his boat, and Bryden rowed about the islands, and resting upon his oars he looked at the old castles, and remembered the pre-historic raiders that the landlord had told him about. He came across the stones to which the lake dwellers had tied their boats, and these signs of ancient Ireland were pleasing to Bryden in his present mood.

As well as the great lake there was a smaller lake in the bog where the villagers cut their turf. This lake was famous for its pike, and the landlord allowed Bryden to fish there, and one evening when he was looking for a frog with which to bait his line he met Margaret Dirken driving home the cows for the milking. Margaret was the herdsman's daughter, and she lived in a cottage near the Big House; but she came up to the village whenever there was a dance, and Bryden had found himself opposite to her in the reels. But until this evening he had had little opportunity of speaking to her, and he was glad to speak to someone, for the evening was lonely, and they stood talking together.

"You're getting your health again," she said. "You'll soon be leaving us."

"I'm in no hurry."

"You're grand people over there. I hear a man is paid four dollars a day for his work."

"And how much," said James, has he to pay for his food and for his clothes?"

Her cheeks were bright and her teeth small, white and beautifully even; and a woman's soul looked at Bryden out of her soft Irish eyes. He was troubled and turned aside, and catching sight of a frog looking at him out of a tuft of grass he said:

"I have been looking for a frog to put upon my pike line."

The frog jumped right and left, and nearly escaped in some bushes, but he caught it and returned with it in his hand.

"It is just the kind of frog a pike will like," he said. "Look at its great white belly and its bright yellow back."

And without more ado he pushed the wire to which the hook was fastened through the frog's fresh body, and dragging it through the mouth he passed the hooks through the hind legs and tied the line to the end of the wire.

"I think," said Margaret, "I must be looking after my cows; it's time I got them home."

"Won't you come down to the lake while I set my line?"
She thought for a moment and said:—
"No, I'll see you from here."

He went down to the reedy tarn, and at his approach several snipe got up, and they flew above his head uttering sharp cries. His fishing-rod was a long hazel stick, and he threw the frog as far as he could into the lake. In doing this he roused some wild ducks; a mallard and two ducks got up, and they flew toward the larger lake. Margaret watched them; they flew in a line with an old castle; and they had not disappeared from view when Bryden came toward her, and he and she drove the cows home together that evening.

They had not met very often when she said, "James, you had better not come here so often calling to me."

"Don't you wish me to come?"

"Yes, I wish you to come well enough, but keeping company is not the custom of the country, and I don't want to be talked about."

"Are you afraid the priest would speak against us from the altar?"

"He has spoken against keeping company, but it is not so much what the priest says, for there is no harm in talking."

"But if you are going to be married there is no harm in walking out together."

"Well, not so much, but marriages are made differently in these parts; there is not much courting here."

And next day it was known in the village that James was going to marry Margaret Dirken.

His desire to excel the boys in dancing had caused a stir of gaiety in the parish, and for some time past there had been dancing in every house where there was a floor fit to dance upon; and if the cottager had no money to pay for a barrel of beer, James Bryden, who had money, sent him a barrel, so that Margaret might get her dance. She told him that they sometimes crossed over into another parish where the priest was not so averse to dancing, and James wondered. And next morning at Mass he wondered at their simple fervour. Some of them held their hands above their head as they prayed, and all this was very new and very old to James Bryden. But the obedience of these people to their priest surprised him. When he was a lad they had not been so obedient, or he had forgotten their obedience; and he listened in mixed anger and wonderment to the priest, who was scolding his parishioners, speaking to them by name, saying that he had heard there was dancing going on in their homes. Worse than that, he said he had seen boys and girls loitering about the roads, and the talk that went on was of one kind—love. He said that newspapers containing love stories were finding their way into the people's houses, stories about love, in which there was nothing elevating or ennobling. The people listened, accepting the priest's opinion without question. And their submission was pathetic. It was the submission of a primitive people clinging to religious authority, and Bryden contrasted the weakness and incompetence of the people about him with the modern restlessness and cold energy of the people he had left behind him.

One evening, as they were dancing, a knock came to the door, and the piper stopped playing, and the dancers whispered:—

"Some one has told on us; it is the priest."

And the awe-stricken villagers crowded round the cottage fire, afraid to open the door. But the priest said that if they did not open the door he would put his shoulder to it and force it open. Bryden went towards the door, saying he would allow no one to threaten him, priest or no priest, but Margaret caught his arm and told him that if he said anything to the priest, the priest would speak against them from the altar, and they would be shunned by the neighbours. It was Mike Scully who went to the door and let the priest in, and he came in saying they were dancing their souls into hell.

"I've heard of your goings on," he said—" of your beer-drinking and dancing. I will not have it in my parish. If you want that sort of thing you had better go to America."

"If that is intended for me, sir, I will go back to-morrow. Margaret can follow."

"It isn't the dancing, it's the drinking I'm opposed to," said the priest, turning to Bryden.

"Well, no one has drunk too much, sir," said Bryden.

"But you'll sit here drinking all night," and the priest's eyes went toward the corner where the women had gathered, and Bryden felt that the priest looked on the women as more dangerous than the porter. "It's after midnight," he said, taking out his watch.

By Bryden's watch it was only half-past eleven, and while they were arguing about the time Mrs. Scully offered Bryden's umbrella to the priest, for in his hurry to stop the dancing the priest had gone out without his; and, as if to show Bryden that he bore him no ill-will, the priest accepted the loan of the umbrella, for he was thinking of the big marriage fee that Bryden would pay him.

"I shall be badly off for the umbrella to-morrow," Bryden said, as soon as the priest was out of the house. He was going with his father-in-law to a fair. His father-in-law was learning him how to buy and sell cattle. And his father-in-law was saying that the country was mending, and that a man might become rich in Ireland if he only had a little capital. Bryden had the capital, and Margaret had an uncle on the other side of the lake who would leave her all he had, that would be fifty pounds, and never in the village of Duncannon had a young couple begun life with so much prospect of success as would James Bryden and Margaret Dirken.

Some time after Christmas was spoken of as the best time for the marriage; James Bryden said that he would not be able to get his money out of America before the spring. The delay seemed to vex him, and he seemed anxious to be married, until one day he received a letter from America, from a man who had served in the bar with him. This friend wrote to ask Bryden if he were coming back. The letter was no more than a passing wish to see Bryden again. Yet Bryden stood looking at it, and everyone wondered what could be in the letter. It seemed momentous, and they hardly believed him when he said it was from a friend who wanted to know if his health were better. He tried to forget the letter, and he looked at the worn fields, divided by walls of loose stones, and a great longing came upon him.

The smell of the Bowery slum had come across the Atlantic, and had found him out in this western headland; and one night he awoke from a dream in which he was hurling some drunken customer through the open doors into the darkness. He had seen his friend in his white duck jacket throwing drink from glass into glass amid the din of voices and strange accents; he had heard the clang of money as it was swept into the till, and his sense sickened for the bar-room. But how should he tell Margaret Dirken that he could not marry her? She had built her life upon this marriage. He could not tell her that he would not marry her . . . yet he must go. He felt as if he were being hunted; the thought that he must tell Margaret that he could not marry her hunted him day after day as a weasel hunts a rabbit. Again and again he went to meet her with the intention of telling her that he did not love her, that their lives were not for one another, that it had all been a mistake, and that happily he had found out it was a mistake soon enough. But Margaret, as if she guessed what he was about to speak of, threw her arms about him and begged him to say he loved her, and that they would be married at once. He agreed that he loved her, and that they would be married at once. But he had not left her many minutes before the feeling came upon him that he could not marry her—that he must go away. The smell of the bar-room hunted him down. Was it for the sake of the money that he might make there that he wished to go back? No, it was not the money. What then? His eyes fell on the bleak country, on the little fields divided by bleak walls; he remembered the pathetic ignorance of the people, and it was these things that he could not endure. It was the priest who came to forbid the dancing. Yes, it was the priest. As he stood looking at the line of the hills the bar-room seemed by him. He heard the politicians, and the excitement of politics was in his blood again. He must go away from this place—he must get back to the bar-room. Looking up, he saw the scanty orchard, and he hated the spare road that led to the village, and he hated the little hill at the top of which the village began, and he hated more than all other places the house where he was to live with Margaret Dirken—if he married her. He could see it from where he stood—by the edge of the lake, with twenty acres of pasture land about it, for the landlord had given up part of his demesne land to them.

He caught sight of Margaret, and he called her to come through the stile.

"I have just had a letter from America."

"About the money?" she said.

"Yes, about the money. But I shall have to go over there."

He stood looking at her, seeking for words; and she guessed from his embarrassment that he would say to her that he must go to America before they were married.

"Do you mean, James, you will have to go at once?"

"Yes," he said, "at once. But I shall come back in time to be married in August. It will only mean delaying our marriage a month."

They walked on a little way talking, and every step he took James felt he was a step nearer the Bowery slum. And when they came to the gate Bryden said:—

"I must hasten or I shall miss the train."

"But," she said, "you are not going now—you are not going to-day?"

"Yes, this morning. It is seven miles. I shall have to hurry not to miss the train."

And then she asked him if he would ever come back.

"Yes," he said, "I am coming back."

"If you are coming back, James, why not let me go with you?"

"You could not walk fast enough. We should miss the train."

"One moment, James. Don't make me suffer; tell me the truth. You are not coming back. Your clothes—where shall I send them?"

He hurried away, hoping he would come back. He tried to think that he liked the country he was leaving, that it would be better to have a farmhouse and live there with Margaret Dirken than to serve drinks behind a counter in the Bowery. He did not think he was telling her a lie when he said he was coming back. Her offer to forward his clothes touched his heart, and at the end of the road he stood and asked himself if he should go back to her. He would miss the train if he waited another minute, and he ran on. And he would have missed the train if he had not met a car. Once he was on the car he felt himself safe—the country was already behind him. The train and the boat to Cork were mere formulæ; he was already in America.

The moment he landed he felt the thrill of home that he had not found in his native village, and he wondered how it was that the smell of the bar seemed more natural than the smell of fields, and the roar of crowds were more welcome than the silence of the lake's edge. He offered up a thanksgiving for his escape, and entered into negotiations for the purchase of the bar-room.

\* \* \* \* \*

He took a wife, she bore him sons and daughters, the bar-room prospered, property came and went; he grew old, his wife died, he retired from business, and reached the age when a man begins to feel there are not many years in front of him, and that all he has had to do in life has been done. His children married, lonesomeness began to creep about him in the evening and when he looked into the fire-light, a vague, tender reverie floated up, and Margaret's soft eyes and name vivified the dusk. His wife and children passed out of mind, and it seemed to him that a memory was the only real thing he possessed, and the desire to see Margaret again grew intense. But she was an old woman, she had married, maybe she was dead. Well, he would like to be buried in the village where he was born.

There is an unchanging, silent life within every man that none knows but himself, and his unchanging, silent life was his memory of Margaret Dirken. The bar-room was forgotten and all that concerned it and the things he saw most clearly were the green hillside, and the bog lake and the rushes about it, and the greater lake in the distance, and behind it the blue line of wandering hills.

# George Moore

## *The Wild Goose*

He remembered a green undulating country out of which the trees seemed to emerge like vapours, and a line of pearl-coloured mountains showing above the horizon on fine days. And this was all. But this slight colour memory had followed him through all his wanderings. His parents had emigrated to Manchester when he was nine, and when he was sixteen he felt that he must escape from Manchester, from the overwhelming dreariness of the brick chimneys and their smoke cloud. He had joined a travelling circus on its way to the Continent and he crossed with it from New Haven to Dieppe in charge of the lions. The circus crossed in a great storm; Ned was not able to get about, the tossing of the vessel closed the ventilating slides, and when they arrived at Dieppe the finest lion was dead.

"Well, there are other things to do in life besides feeding lions," he said, and taking up his fiddle he became interested in it. He played it all the way across the Atlantic, and everyone said there was no reason why he should not play in the opera house. But an interview with the music conductor dispelled illusions. Ned learnt from him that improvisations were not admissible in an opera house; and when the conductor told him what would be required of him he began to lose interest in his musical career. As he stood jingling his pence on the steps of the Opera House a man went by who had crossed with Ned, and the two getting into conversation, Ned was asked if he could draw a map according to scale. It would profit him nothing to say no; he remembered he had drawn maps in the school in Manchester. A bargain was struck! He was to get ten pounds for his map! He ordered a table; he pinned out the paper, and the map was finished in a fortnight. It was of a mining district, and having nothing to do when he finished he thought he would like to see the mine; the owners encouraged him to go there, and he did some mining in the morning—in the evenings he played his fiddle. Eventually he became a journalist.

He wandered and wrote, and wandered again, until one day, finding himself in New York, he signed an agreement and edited a newspaper. But he soon wearied of expressing the same opinions, and as the newspaper could not change its opinions Ned volunteered to go to Cuba and write about the insurgents. And he wrote articles that inflamed the Americans against the Spaniards, and went over to the American lines to fight when the Americans declared war against Spain, and fought so well that he might have become a general if the war had lasted. But it was over, and, overpowered by an extraordinary dislike to New York, he felt he must travel. He wanted to see Europe again, and remembering the green plain of Meath, he said:—"I'll go to Ireland."

His father and mother were dead, and without a thought of his relations, he read the legends of Meath on his way out; he often sat considering his adventures: the circus, the mining camp, his sympathy with the Cubans in their revolt against Spain, convinced him of his Gaelic inheritance and that something might be done with Ireland. England's power was great, but Spain's power had been great too, and when Spain thought herself most powerful the worm had begun. Everything has its day, and as England decayed, Ireland would revive. A good time might be on its way to Ireland; if so he would like to be there or thereabouts; for he always liked to be in the van of a good time.

He went straight to Tara, his mind bending rather to pagan than to Christian Ireland. Traces of Cormac's banqueting hall were pointed out to him, and he imagined what this great hall, built entirely of wood and hung about with skins, must have been. He was shown the Rath of Kings and the Rath of Grania. Her name brought to his mind her flight with Diarmuid and how when they had had to cross a stream and her legs were wetted, she had said to Diarmuid, who would not break his oath to Finn, "Diarmuid, you are a great warrior, but this water is braver than you!" "Perhaps this very stream!" he said, looking towards a stream that flowed from the well of Neamhtach or Pearly. But he was told it was this stream that had turned the first water mill in Ireland, and that Cormac had put up the mill to save a beautiful bond-maid from toiling at the quern.

The morning was spent in seeking the old sites, and in the afternoon he went to the inn and found a good number of villagers in the tap-room. He learned from them that there were cromlechs and Druid altars within walking distance of Tara, and decided on a walking tour. He wandered through the beautiful country, interested in Ireland's slattern life, touched by the kindness and simplicity of the people. "Poor people," he thought, "how touching it is to find them learning their own language," and he began to think out a series of articles about Ireland.

"They talk of Cuchulain," he said, "but they prefer an Archbishop, and at every turn in their lives they are paying the priest. The title of my book shall be 'A Western Thibet,' an excellent title for my book!" and leaning on a gate, and looking across a hay-field he saw the ends of chapters.

Now that he had a book to write, his return to America was postponed; a postponement was to Ned an indefinite period, and he was glad he was not returning to America till the spring, for he had found pleasant rooms in a farm-house. He would make them his head-quarters; for it was only by living in a farmhouse he could learn the life of the people and its real mind. And he would have written his book just as he had planned it if he had not met Ellen Cronin.

She was the only daughter of a rich farmer in the neighbourhood. He had heard so much about her learning and her pretty face that he was disposed to dispute her good looks; but in spite of his landlady's praise he had liked her pretty oval face. "Her face is pretty when you look at it," he said to his landlady. But this admission did not satisfy her "Well, enthusiasm is pleasant," he thought, and he listened to her rambling talk.

"She used to like to come to tea here, and after her tea she and my son James, who was the same age, used to make paper boats under the alder trees."

And the picture of Ellen making boats under alder trees pleased Ned's fancy, and he encouraged the landlady to tell him more about her. She told him that Ellen had not taken to study till she was twelve, and that it was the priest who had set her reading books and had taught her Latin.

Ned lay back in his chair smiling, listening to the landlady telling him about Ellen. She had chosen her own school. She had inquired into the matter, and had taken her father into her confidence one day by telling him of the advantages of this school. But this part of the story did not please Ned, and he said he did not like her a bit better for having chosen her own school. Nor did he like her better because her mistress had written to her father to say she had learned all that she could learn in Ireland. He liked her for her love of Ireland and her opposition to her father's ideas. Old Cronin thought Ireland a miserable country and England the finest in the world, whereas Ellen thought only of Irish things, and she had preferred the Dublin University to Oxford or Cambridge. He was told that her university career had been no less brilliant than her school career, and he raised his eyebrows when the landlady said that Miss Ellen used to have her professors staying at Mount Laurel, and that they used to talk Latin in the garden.

But she was long ago done with the professors, and Ned asked the landlady to tell him what change had come over the mind of this somewhat pedantic young woman. And he was told that Ellen had abandoned her studies and professors for politics and politicians, and that these were a great trial to her father, into whose house no Nationalist member of Parliament had ever put his foot before. "Now the very men that Mr. Cronin used to speak of as men who were throwing stones at the police three years ago are dining with him to-day," and worse than her political opinions, according to Mr. Cronin, was her resolution to speak the language of her own country. "When he had heard her talking it to a boy she had up from the country to teach her, Mr. Cronin stuck both his hands into his stubbly hair and rushed out the house like a wild man."

It was pleasant to listen to the landlady's babble about the Cronins, for he was going to spend the evening with them; he had been introduced to her father, a tall, thin, taciturn man, who had somewhat gruffly, but not unkindly, asked him to come to spend the evening with them, saying that some friends were coming in, and there would be some music.

Ned's life had been lived in newspaper offices, in theatres, circuses and camps. He knew very little of society—nothing at all of European society—and was curious to see what an Irish country house was like. The Cronins lived in a dim, red brick, eighteenth-century house. It stood in the middle of a large park, and the park was surrounded by old grey walls and Ned liked to lean on these walls, for in places they had crumbled, and admire the bracken in the hollows and the wind-blown hawthorn trees growing on the other side of the long winding drive. He had long wished to walk in the park and now he was there. The hawthorns were in bloom and the cuckoo was calling. The sky was dark overhead, but there was light above the trees, and long herds of cattle wandered and life seemed to Ned extraordinarily lovely and desirable at that moment. "I wonder what she is like, living in this beautiful place, walking among these mysterious hollows and these abundant hawthorn groves?"

The young lady had been pointed out to him as she went by, and he was impatient to be introduced to Ellen, but she was talking to some friends near the window, and she did not see him. He liked her white dress, there were pearls round her neck, and her red hair was pinned up with a tortoiseshell comb. She and her friends were looking over a photograph album, and Ned was left with Mr. Cronin to talk to him as best he could; for it was difficult to talk to this hard, grizzled man, knowing nothing about the war in Cuba nor evincing any interest in America. When Ned asked him about Ireland he answered in short sentences, which brought the conversation to abrupt closes. America and Ireland having failed to draw him out, Ned began to talk of his landlady. But it was not until he related the conversation he had had with her that evening about Miss Cronin that the old farmer began to talk a little. Ned could see he was proud of his daughter; he regretted that she had not gone to Oxford, and said she would have carried all before her if she had gone there. Ned could see that what his landlady had told him was true—that old Cronin thought very little of Ireland. He hoped to get three minutes' conversation, at least, out of Girton, but the old farmer seemed to have said everything he had to say on the subject. The conversation failed again, and Ned was forced to speak to him of the interest that Miss Cronin took in the Irish language and her desire to speak it. At the mention of the Irish language, the old man grew gruffer, and remembering that the landlady had said that Miss Cronin was very religious, Ned spoke of the priests—there were two in the room—and he asked Mr. Cronin which of them had encouraged Miss Cronin to learn Irish. He had never heard the language spoken, and would like to hear it.

"I believe Mr. Cronin, it was Father Egan who taught your daughter Latin?"

"It was so," said Mr. Cronin; "but he might have left the Irish alone, and politics, too. We keep them as fat as little bonhams, and they ought to be satisfied with that."

Ned did not know what were little bonhams, and pretended a great interest when he was told that bonham was the Irish for sucking pig, and glancing at the priests he noticed they were fat indeed, and he said, "There is nothing like faith for fattening. It is better than any oil cake."

Mr. Cronin gave a grunt and Ned thought he was going to laugh at this sally, but he suddenly moved away and Ned wondered what had happened. It was Ellen who had crossed the room to speak to her father, and Ned could see that she had heard his remark, and he could see that the remark had angered her, that she thought it in bad taste. He prepared quickly a winning speech which would turn the edge of her indignation, but before he had time to speak the expression of her face changed and a look of pleasure passed into it; he could see that the girl liked him, and he hastened to tell her that his landlady had told him about the paper boats and the alder trees. And Ellen began to speak about the landlady, saying she was a very good kind woman, and she wanted to know if Ned were comfortable at the farm house. But she seemed to have some difficulty in speaking, and then, as if moved by some outside influence, they walked across the room towards the window and sat under the shadow of the red damask curtain. A gentle breeze was blowing and the curtains filled with it and sank back with a mysterious rustle. And beyond them the garden lay dark and huddled in the shadows of great trees. He heard her say she was sorry that James, the landlady's son, had gone to America, and then they spoke of the forty thousand that were leaving Ireland every year. It was Ned who continued the conversation, but he could see that what he said hardly entered her ear at all. Yet she heard his voice in her heart, and he, too, heard her voice in his heart, and several times she felt she could not go on talking and once she nearly lost consciousness and must have swayed a little, for he put out his hand to save her.

They went into the garden and walked in the dusk. He told her about the war in Cuba and about the impulse which had brought him back to Ireland, and his tale seemed to her the most momentous thing she had ever heard. She listened to his first impressions about Tara, and every moment it seemed to her that she was about to hear a great secret, a secret that had been troubling her a long while; every moment she expected to hear him speak it, and she almost cried when her father came to ask Ned if he would play for them.

Ellen was not a musician, and another woman would

have to accompany him. How tall and thin he was and what manly hands! She could hardly look at his hands without shuddering, so beautiful were they when they played the violin; and that night music said something more to her than it had ever said before. She heard again the sounds of birds and insects, and she saw again the gloom of the trees, and she felt again and more intensely the overpowering ecstasy, and she yielded herself utterly and without knowing why. When he finished playing he came to her and sat by her, and everything she said fell from her lips involuntarily. She seemed to have lost herself utterly, she seemed to have become fluid, she yielded herself like a fluid; it was like dying: for she seemed to pass out of herself to become absorbed in the night. How the time passed she knew not, and when her guests came to bid her good-bye she hardly saw them, and listened to their leave-taking with a little odd smile on her lips, and when everyone was gone she bade her father goodnight absent-mindedly, fearing, however, that he would speak to her about Ned. But he only said good-night, and she went up the wide staircase conscious that the summer night was within the house and without it; that it lay upon the world, a burden sweet and still, like happiness upon the heart.

She opened her window, and sat there hoping that something would come out of the night and whisper in her ear the secret that tormented her. The stars knew! If she could only read them! She felt she was feeling a little more than she was capable of understanding. The ecstasy grew deeper, and she waited for the revelation. But none came, and feeling a little ashamed she got up to close the window and it was then that the revelation broke upon her. She had met the man who was to lead the Irish people! They wanted a new leader, a leader with a new idea; the new leader must come from the outside, and he had come to them from America, and her emotion was so great that she would have liked to have awakened her father. She would have liked to have gone into the country waking the people up in the cottages, telling them that the leader had come. She stood entranced, remembering all he had said to her. He had told her he had been moved to return to Ireland after the war in Cuba, and she had not understood. The word married passed through her mind before she could stay it. But she was necessary to this man, of this she was sure; the Voice had told her. She was feeling more than she could understand, and she lay down in her bed certain that she had accomplished the first stage of her journey.

Just then Ned was leaning on the garden gate. The summer night was sweet and still, and he wanted to think of this girl who had come so suddenly into his life. The idea of marriage flitted across his mind as it had flitted across hers, and he tried to remember the exact moment in Cuba when the wish to see Ireland had come into his mind. To believe in fate and predestination is an easy way out of life's labyrinth, and if one does not believe in something of the kind the figures will not come right. How did he know that he had not met this girl for some unknown purpose. He could see a great white star through a vista in the trees, and he said: "I believe that that star knows. Why will it not tell me?"

And then he walked into the woods, and out under the moon, between the little grey fields. Some sheep had come out on the road and were lying upon it. "I suppose it's all very natural," he said; "the circus aspiring to the academy and the academy spying the circus. Now, what am I going to do tomorrow? I suppose I must go to see her."

He had visited all the ruins and pondered by all the cromlechs, and was a little weary of historic remains; the girl was too much in his mind to permit of his doing much writing. He might go to Dublin, where he had business, and in the morning he looked out the trains, but none seemed to suit his convenience, and at five o'clock he was at Laurel Hill listening to Ellen. She was anxious to talk to him about the political opportunity he could seize if he were so minded.

"Men have always believed in fate," Ned said, and, interrupting him suddenly, she asked him if he would come to see a pretty house in the neighbourhood—a house that would suit him perfectly, for he must have a house if he intended to go in for politics.

They came back in the dusk, talking of painting and papering and the laying out of the garden. Ellen was anxious that the garden should be nice, and he had been much interested in the old family furniture at Laurel Hill, not in the spindle-legged Sheraton sideboard, but in the big Victorian furniture which the Cronins thought ugly. He liked especially the black mahogany sideboards in the diningroom, and he was enthusiastic about the four-post bed that Mr. Cronin had slept in for thirty years without ever thinking it was a beautiful thing. This massive furniture represented a life that Ned perceived for the first time, a sedate monotonous life; and he could see these people accomplishing the same tasks from daylight to dark; he admired the well-defined circle of their interests and the calm security with which they spoke of the same things every evening, deepening the tradition of their country and their own characters; and he conceived a sudden passion for tradition, and felt he would like to settle down in these grass lands in an eighteenth-century house, living always amid heavy mahogany furniture, sleeping every night in a mahogany four-post bed; and he could not help thinking that if he did not get the mahogany four-post bed with the carved top perhaps he would not care to marry Ellen at all.

The next time he saw her their talk turned upon the house she had found for him, and she said if he did not take it he would certainly go back to America in the spring. She forgot herself a little; her father had to check her, and Ned returned home sure in his mind that she would marry him—if he asked her. And the next day he chose a pair of trousers that he thought becoming—they were cut wide in the leg and narrow over the instep. He looked out for a cravat that she had not seen him wear, and he chose the largest, and he put on his braided coat. He could see that his moustache was not in keeping with his clothes; he had often intended to shave it, but to-day was not the day for shaving. She had liked his moustache, and he thought it would be a pity she should not enjoy it, however reprehensible her taste for it might be. And he pondered his side whiskers, remembering they were in keeping with his costume (larger whiskers would be still more in keeping), and amused by his own fantastic notions, he thought he was beginning to look like the gentleman of seventy or eighty years ago that he had seen in varnished maplewood frames in the drawing-room at the Cronins'. His trousers were of a later period, but they were, nevertheless, contemporaneous with the period of the mahogany sideboard, and that was what he liked best.

Suddenly he stopped, remembering that he had never wished to be married, because he never thought that he could love the same woman always, and now he asked himself if Ellen were an exception, and if he had been led back to Ireland to marry her. He had grown tired of women before, but it seemed to him that he never could grow tired of her. That remained to be seen, the one certain thing was that he was going to propose to her.

He was told she was in the garden, and he was glad to dispense with the servant's assistance; he would find his way there himself, and, after some searching, he found the wicket. When he had a garden he would have a wicket. He had already begun to associate Ellen with her garden. She was never so much herself as when attending her flowers, and to please her he had affected an interest in them, but when he had said that the flowers were beautiful his eyes went to the garden walls and Ellen had seen that they interested him more than the flowers. He had said that the buttresses were of no use; they had been built because in those days people took a pleasure in making life seem permanent. The buttresses had enabled him to admire the roses planted between them, and he had grown enthusiastic; but she had laughed at his enthusiasm, seeing quite clearly that he admired the flowers because they enhanced the beauty of the walls.

At the end of the garden there was a view of the Dublin mountains, and the long walk that divided the garden had been designed in order to draw attention to them. The contrast between the wild mountain and the homely primness of the garden appealed to his sense of the picturesque; and even now though the fate of his life was to be decided in a few minutes he could not but stay to admire the mysterious crests and hollows. In this faint day the mountains seemed more like living things, more mysterious and moving, than he had ever seen them before, and he would have stood looking at them for a long while if he had not had to find Ellen. She was at the furthest end of the garden, where he had never been, beyond the rosery, beyond the grass plot, and she was walking up and down. She seemed to have a fishing net in her hand. But how could she be fishing in her garden? Ned did not know that there was a stream at the end of it; for the place had once belonged to monks, and they knew how to look after their bodily welfare and had turned the place into a trout preserve. But when Mr. Cronin had bought the property the garden was waste and the stream overgrown with willow weed and meadow-sweet and every kind of brier. And it was Ellen who had discovered that the bottom of the stream was flagged and she had five feet of mud taken out of it, and now the stream was as bright and clear as in the time of the monks, and as full of trout. She had just caught two which lay on the grass panting, their speckled bellies heaving painfully.

"There is a great big trout here," Ellen said, "he must be a pound weight, and we tried to catch him all last season but he is very cunning, he dives and gets under the net."

"I think we shall be able to catch him," said Ned, "if he is in the stream and if I could get another net."

"The gardener will give you one."

And presently Ned came back with a net, and they beat up the stream from different ends, Ellen taking the side next the wall. There was a path there nearly free from briers, and she held her light summer dress round her tightly. Ned thought he had never seen anyone so prettily dressed. She wore a striped muslin variegated with pink flowers; there were black bows in her hat and black ribbon was run round the bottom of her dress; she looked very pretty against the old wall touched here and there with ivy. And the grace of her movement enchanted Ned when she leaned forward and prevented the trout from escaping up the stream. But Ned's side of the stream was overgrown with briers and he could not make his way through them. Once he very nearly slipped into the stream, and only saved himself by catching some prickly biers and Ellen had to come over to take the thorns out of his hand. Then they resumed their fishing, hunting the trout up and down the stream but the trout had been hunted so often that he knew how to escape the nets, and dived at the right moment. At last wearied out he let Ned drive him against the bank. Ellen feared he would jump out of the net at the last moment, but he was tired and they landed him safely.

And proud of having caught him they sat down beside him on the grass and Ellen said that the gardener and the gardener's boy had tried to catch him many times; that whenever they had company to dinner her father said it was a pity they had not the big trout on the table.

The fishing had been great fun, principally on account of Ellen's figure, which Ned admired greatly, and now he admired her profile—its gravity appealed to him—and her attitude full of meditation. He watched her touching the gasping trout with the point of her parasol. She had drawn one leg under her. Her eyes were small and grey and gem-like, and there was a sweet look of interrogation in them now and then.

"I like it, this lustreless day," said Ned, "and those swallows pursuing their food up and down the boding sky. It all seems like a fairy tale, this catching of the fish, you and I. The day so dim," he said, "so quiet and low, and the garden hushed. These things would be nothing to me were it not for you," and he put his hand upon her knee.

She withdrew her knee quickly and a moment after got

up, and Ned got up and followed her across the grass plot and through the rosery; not a word was said, and she began to wonder he did not plead to be forgiven. She felt she should send him away, but she could not find words to tell him to go. His conduct was so unprecedented; no one had ever taken such a liberty before. It was shameful that she was not more angry, for she knew she was only trying to feel angry.

"But," he said, suddenly, as if he divined her thoughts, "we've forgotten the fish; won't you come back and help me to carry them. I cannot carry three trout by myself."

She was about to answer severely but as she stood looking at him her thoughts yielded before an extraordinary feeling of delight; she tried in vain to collect her scattered mind—she wished to reproach him.

"Are you going to answer me, Ellen," and he took her hand.

"Ned, are you a Catholic?" she said, turning suddenly.

"I was born one, but I have thought little about religion. I have had other things to think about. What does it matter? Religion doesn't help us to love one another."

"I should like you better if you were a good Catholic."

"I wonder how that is?" he said, and he admired the round hand and its pretty articulations, and she closed her hand on his with a delicious movement.

"I could like you better, Ned, if you were a Catholic. . . . I think I could."

"What has my being a good Catholic got to do with your love of me?"

And he watched the small and somewhat severe profile looking across the old grey wall into the flat grey sky.

"I did not say I loved you," she said, almost angrily; "but, if I did love you," she said, looking at him tenderly, "and you were religious, I should be loving something eternal. You don't understand what I mean? What I am saying to you must seem like nonsense."

"No, it doesn't, Ellen, only I am content with the reality. I can love you without wings."

He watched for the look of annoyance in her face that he knew his words would provoke, but her face was turned away.

"I like you, but I am afraid of you. It is a very strange feeling. You ran away with a circus and you let the lion die and you went to fight in Cuba. You have loved other women, and I have never loved anyone. I never cared for a man until I saw you, until I looked up from the album."

"I understand very well, Ellen; I knew something was going to happen to me in Ireland."

She turned; he was glad to see her full face again. Her eyes were fixed upon him, but she saw through him, and jealous of her thought he drew her towards him.

"Let us go into the arbour," he said. "I have never been into the arbour of clipped limes with you."

"Why do you want to go into the arbour?"

"I want to kiss you. . . . The gardener can see us now; a moment ago he was behind the Jerusalem artichokes."

"I hadn't noticed the gardener; I hadn't thought about him."

She had persuaded herself before she went into the arbour, and coming out of the arbour she said:—

"I don't think father will raise any objection."

"But you will speak to him. Hello! we're forgetting the fish, and it was the fish that brought all this about. Was it to bring this about that they lived or to be eaten to-night at dinner?"

"Ned, you take a strange pleasure in making life seem wicked."

"I'm sorry I've been so unsuccessful, but will you ask your father to invite me, Ellen? and I'll try and make life seem nice—and the trout will try, too."

Ellen did not know whether she liked or disliked Ned's levity, but when she looked at him an overpowering emotion clouded her comprehension and she walked in silence, thinking of when he would kiss her again. At the end of the walk she stopped to bind up a carnation that had fallen from its stake.

"Father will be wondering what has become of us."

"I think," said Ned, and his own cowardice amused him, "I think you had better tell your father yourself. You will tell him much better than I."

"And what will you do?" she said, turning suddenly and looking at him with fervid eyes. "Will you wait here for me?"

"No, I will go home, and do you come and fetch me—and don't forget to tell him I caught the trout and have earned an invitation to dinner."

His irresponsibility enchanted her in spite of herself—Ned had judged the situation rightly when he said: "It is the circus aspiring to the academy and the academy spying the circus." His epigram occurred to him as he walked home and it amused him, and he thought of how unexpected their lives would be, and he hummed beautiful music as he went along the roads, Schumann's *Lotus Flower* and *The Moonlight*. Then he recalled the beautiful duet, Siegmund's and Sieglinde's *May Time*, and turning from sublimity suddenly into triviality he chanted the somewhat common but expressive duet in Mireille, and the superficiality of its emotion pleased him at the moment and he hummed it until he arrived at the farm house.

Mrs. Grattan could tell his coming from afar, for no one in the country whistled so beautifully as Mr. Carmady, she said, "every note is clear and distinct; and it does not matter how many there are in the tune he will not let one escape him and there is always a pleasant look in his face when you open the door to him;" and she ran to the door.

"Mrs. Grattan, won't you get me a cup of tea?" And then he felt he must talk to some one. "You needn't bring it upstairs, I will take it in the kitchen if you'll let me."

Mrs. Grattan had a beautiful kitchen. It had an old dresser with a carved top and a grandfather's clock, and Ned liked to sit on the table and watch the stove. She poured him out a cup of tea and he drank it, swinging his legs all the time.

"Well, Mrs. Grattan, I'll tell you some news—I think I am going to marry Miss Cronin."

"Well," said she, "it doesn't astonish me," but she nearly let the teapot drop. "From the first day you came here I always thought something was going to happen to you."

He had no sooner told her the news than he began to regret he had told her, and he said that Miss Cronin had gone to her father to ask his consent. Of course, if he did not give it, there would be no marriage.

"But he will give it. Miss Ellen does exactly as she likes with him, and it's a fine fortune you will be having with her."

"It isn't of that I am thinking," said Ned, "but of her red hair."

"And you wouldn't believe me when I said that she was the prettiest girl in the country. Now you will see for yourself."

Ned hadn't finished his when there was a knock at the door.

"And how do you do, Miss Ellen?" said Mrs. Grattan, and Ellen guessed from her manner that Ned had told her.

"Well, Mrs. Grattan, I am glad that you are the first person to bear the news to. I have just asked my father's consent and he has given it. I am going to marry Mr. Carmady."

Mrs. Grattan was sorry there was no cake on the table, but there was some buttered toast in the oven; and Ellen reminded her of the paper boats and the alder trees, and they spoke for a long time about her son James and about people that Ned knew nothing of, until Ned began to feel bored and went to the window. Every now and again he heard a word referring to their marriage, and when the women had done their talk, Ellen said:—

"Father says you are to come back to dinner."

"Mrs. Grattan," said Ned, "we caught three trout this afternoon," and Ellen wondered why Ned should linger to explain how they had caught the big trout.

As they walked down the road Ellen said: "As our love began in a love of Ireland, we might go for a tour round Ireland and see the places that Ireland loves best."

She was eager for a change of scene, and as soon as the wedding was over they began their wanderings. The first place they visited was Tara, and, standing on the Mound of the Hostages, Ellen pointed out the Rath of Grania. All over Ireland there are cromlechs, and the people point to those as the places where the lovers had rested in their flight. Grania became one of Ned's heroines, and he spoke so much of her that Ellen grew a little jealous. They talked of her under the ruins of Dun Angus and under the arches of Cormac's Chapel, the last and most beautiful piece of Irish architecture.

"We were getting on very well," Ned said, "until the English came. This was the last thing we did and after this no more."

On another occasion he ascribed the failure of the Irish in art and literature to the fact that they had always loved the next world, and that the beautiful world under their feet had been neglected or given over to priests. "I hope, Ned," said she, "that you will soon be at the head of affairs."

He took her hand and they wandered on amid the ruins, saying that as soon as their honeymoon was over they would be furnishing a pretty house at the foot of the Dublin mountains.

Her father had offered to make her an allowance, but she preferred a lump sum, and this lump sum of many thousands of pounds had been invested in foreign securities, for Ellen wished that Ned should be free to advocate whatever policy he judged best for Ireland.

"My dear, shall we buy this table?"

And while the price and the marquetry were discussed she remembered suddenly that a most experienced electioneering agent was coming to dinner.

"I wish you hadn't asked him," said Ned; "I looked forward to spending the evening with you," and he watched happiness flash into her eyes.

"There are plenty of evenings before us, and I hope you won't be tired of spending them with me." He said he never wished for better company, and they strolled on through the show rooms.

Turning from some tapestried curtains, he told her he was weary of the life of the camp. One night in Cuba they had crossed a mountain by a bridle path. At the top of the mountain they had come to a ledge of rock three feet high and had to leap their horses one by one up this ledge, and the enemy might have attacked them at any moment. And this incident was typical of what his life had been for the last few years. It had been a skein of adventure, and now his wife was his adventure. Flowers stood in pretty vases on his table in the summer time and around the room were his books, and on the table his pens and paper. The dining room was always a little surprise, so profusely was the table covered with silver. There were beautiful dinner and dessert services to look at; the servants were well trained, they moved about the table quickly—in a word his home was full of grace and beauty. Lately he had been a great deal from home and had come to look on Ellen as a delicious recompense for the fatigue of a week's electioneering in the West. The little train journey from Dublin was an extraordinary excitement, the passing of the stations one by one, the discovery of his wife on the platform, and walking home through the bright evening, telling how his speech had been received.

Ellen always took Ned round the garden before they went into dinner, and after dinner he went to the piano; he loved his music as she loved her garden. She would listen to him for a while, pleased to find that she liked music. But she would steal away to her garden in a little while and he would go on playing for a long while before he would notice her absence; then he would follow her.

"There were no late frosts this year and I have never seen

so many caterpillars!" she said one evening when he joined her; "See they have eaten this flower nearly all away."

"How bright the moon is, we can find them by the light of the moon."

Ellen passed behind the hollyhocks and threw the snails to Ned, not liking to tread upon them herself; she was intent on freeing her flowers from gnawing insects and Ned tried to feel interested, but he liked the moonlight on the hills far better than the flowers. He could not remember which was Honesty and which was Rockit, though the difference had been pointed out to him many times. He liked Larkspur and Canterbury bells, may be it was their names that he liked, for he sometimes mistook one for the other just as Ellen mistook one sonata for another, yet she always liked the same sonatas.

"In another month the poppies will be over everything," she said, "and my pansies are beautiful—see these beautiful yellow pansies! But you're not looking at my garden."

They went towards their apple tree, and Ellen said it was the largest she had ever seen; its boughs were thickest over the seat, and shot straight out, making as it were a little roof. The moon was brilliant among the boughs that night, and they left their seat and passed out of the garden by the wicket, moved by a desire to see the long fields with the woods sloping down to the shore.

And they stood on the hill-side, thinking that they had never seen the sea so beautiful before. On the other side was the dim hill, and the moon led them up the hill-side, up the little path by a ruined church and over a stream that was difficult to cross, for the stepping-stones were placed crookedly. Ellen took Ned's hand and a little further on there were ash trees and not a wind in the boughs.

"How grey the moonlight is on the mountain," Ned said. They went through the furze where the cattle were lying, and the breath of the cattle was odorous in the night like the breath of the earth itself, and Ned said that the cattle were part of the earth. They sat on a druid stone and wondered at the chance that brought them together, and wondered how they could have lived if chance had not brought them together.

Now, the stone they were sitting upon was a druid stone, and it was from Ellen's lips that Ned heard how Brian had conquered the Danes, and how a century later a traitor had brought the English over; and she told the story of Ireland's betrayal with such fervour that Ned felt she was the support his character required, the support he had been looking for all his life; her self-restraint and her gravity were the supports his character required, and these being thrown into the scale life stood at equipoise. The women who had preceded Ellen were strange, fantastic women, counterparts of himself, but he had always aspired to a grave and well-mannered woman who was never ridiculous.

She protested, saying that she wished Ned to express his own ideas. He pleaded that he was learning Ireland from her lips and that his own ideas about Ireland were superficial and false. Every day he was catching up new ideas and every day he was shedding them. He must wait until he had re-knit himself firmly to the tradition, and in talking to her he felt that she was the tradition and was sure that he could do no better than accept her promptings, at least for the present.

"We shall always think the same. Do you not feel that?" and when they returned to the house he fetched a piece of paper and pencil and begged of her to dictate, and then begged of her to write what she would like him to say. He said that the sight of her handwriting helped him, and he thought his life would crumble to pieces if she were taken from him.

He told her that she had said he would be a success. He was a success! Success had begun to revolve about him, and he had begun to feel that he was the centre of things: Everyone listened when he spoke; his opinion was sought out, and he could see the people looking towards him for guidance. It pleased Ellen that he should confide in her and his confidence seemed complete. We do not tell all because we do not know all and Ned was only half aware of the little dissatisfaction dormant in his heart. He knew that he had given himself as hostage—half of himself was in his wife's keeping—and he sometimes wondered if he would break out of her custody in spite of his vows.

He had told her that though he was no friend of the church, he was not its active enemy, and he believed he was speaking the truth. The fight for free will would have to be fought in Ireland some day, and this fight was the most vital; but he agreed with her that other fights would have to be fought and won before the great fight could be arranged for. The order of the present day was for lesser battles, and he promised again and again he would not raise the religious question, and every time he promised his wife his life seemed to vanish. The lesser battles were necessary, but it was the fight for free will that interested him. A politician is the man who does the day's work; he must not forget that; and he was a politician. So he agreed to go to America to speechify and to get money for the lesser battles. He was the man who could get the money—what better man could they send than an Irish-American? An American soldier and a journalist! These were the words that were on everyone's lips, but after speaking them everyone paused, for, notwithstanding Ellen's care, Ned was suspected; the priests had begun to suspect him, but there were no grounds for opposing him.

He was despondent, but Ellen was enthusiastic. Her knowledge of Irish politics enabled her to see that his chance had come.

"If you succeed in America, you'll come back the first man in Ireland."

"Even so," said Ned, "it would be more natural for you to be sorry that I am going."

"I cannot be sorry and glad at the same time."

"You will be lonely."

"Very likely; but, Ned, I shall not be looking very well for the next two months."

"You mean on account of the baby. The next few months will be a trying time for you and I should be with you."

They continued to walk round and round their apple tree and Ellen did not answer for a long while.

"I want you to go to America, I don't care that you should see me losing my figure."

"We have spent many pleasant hours under this apple tree."

"Yes, it has been a dear tree," she said.

"And in about six years there will be one who will appreciate this tree as we have never appreciated it. I can see the little chap running after the apples."

"But, Ned, it may be a girl."

"Then it will be like you, dear."

She said she would send a telegram and Ned shook the boughs, and their apple-gathering seemed portentous. The sound of apples falling in the dusk garden, and a new life coming into the world!

"Men have gathered apples and led their fruitful wives towards the house since the beginning of time." He said these words as he looked over the waste of water seeing Ireland melting away.

A new life was about to begin and he was glad of that. "For the next three months I shall be carried along on the tide of human affairs. In a week I shall be dining in a restaurant." He turned and entered into conversation with some people who interested him, and the day passed in conversation. "It is a curious change," he said, three weeks later, as he walked home from a restaurant; and he enjoyed the change so much that he wondered if his love for his wife would be the same when he returned. "Yes, that will be another change." He was carried like a piece of wreckage from hotel to hotel. "How different this life is from the life in Ireland," he said one night as he dressed to go to a meeting, and he began to wonder. And he had not been thinking five minutes when a knock came to the door, and he was handed a telegram containing two words: "A boy." He had always felt it was going to be a boy. "Though it does cost a shilling a word they might have let me know how she is," he thought. He lay back in his chair thinking of his wife—indulging in sensations of her beauty, seeing her gem-like eyes, her pretty oval face, and her red hair scattered about the pillow. At first he was not certain whether the baby was lying by the side of the mother, but now he saw it, and he thrilled with a sense of wonder. The commonest of all occurrences never ceases to be the most wonderful, and there lay his wife and child in the room he knew so well—the curtains with a fruit pattern upon them, the pale wallpaper with roses climbing up a trellis, and pretty blue ribbons intervening between each line of roses. The room was painted white, and he knew the odour of the room well, and the sensation of the carpet. He could see the twilight, and the bulky nurse passing to and fro; and his thoughts went back to his child, and he began to wonder if it were like him or like its mother. It was probably like both. His eyes went to the clock, and he thought of the meeting he was going to. The notes of his speech were upon the table, but he found great difficulty in rousing himself out of his chair; it was so pleasant to lie there, thinking of his wife, of his home, and of his child. But into this vague wandering sensation of happy and beautiful things there came a sudden vision and a thought. He saw his wife take the baby and put it to her breast and he could not bear to think that that beautiful breast, so dear to him, should suffer harm. He had often thought of Ellen as a beautiful marble—she was as full of exquisite lines as any marble—and only very rarely had he thought of her as a mother; the thought had never been entertained long, for it was never wholly sympathetic.

Now his thoughts quickened, and it seemed urgent that he must communicate at once with his wife. She must not suckle the baby! Only by telegram could he reach her soon enough, but it was not possible to telegraph such a thing. He must write, but the letter would take six days to reach her, and he stood thinking. The post was going out: if he wrote at once she would get his letter in a week. He was due at the meeting in about twenty minutes; the notes of his speech lay on the table, and he gathered them up and put them in his pocket, and drawing a sheet of paper towards him, he began a hurried letter. But as soon as he dipped his pen in the ink, he experienced great difficulty in expressing his feelings; they were intense enough, but they were vague, and he must find reasons. He must tell her that he loved her beauty, and that it must suffer no disfigurement from a baby's lips. No sooner did he put his feelings into words than they shocked him, and he knew how much more they would shock Ellen, and he wondered how he could think such things about his own child. The truth was, there was little time for thinking, and he had to tell Ellen what she must do. It so happened that he had heard only the other day that goat's milk was the exact equivalent to human, but it was often difficult to procure. "You will find no difficulty," he said, "at the foot of the Dublin mountains in procuring goat's milk." His thoughts rushed on, and he remembered the peasant women. One could easily be found who would put her baby on goat's milk and come and nurse his child for a few shillings—ten or fifteen shillings a week; Ellen's beauty was worth a great deal more. The hands of the clock went on, he had to close his letter and post it; and no sooner was it posted than he was beset by qualms of conscience. During the meeting he wondered what Ellen would think of his letter, and he feared it would shock her and trouble her; for, while considering the rights of the child, she would remember his admiration of her.

He passed the following days uneasily, and when the seventh day came he had no difficulty in imagining Ellen reading his letter, and the scene he imagined was very like what really happened. His letter troubled Ellen greatly. She had been thinking only of her baby, she had been suckling it for several days, and it had given her pleasure to suckle it. She had not thought of herself at all, and Ned's order that she should pass her child on to another, and consider her personal charm for him, troubled her even to tears; and when she told the nurse her husband's wishes the nurse was sorry that Mrs. Carmady had been troubled, for she was still very weak. Now the child was crying; Ellen put it to her little cup-like breast, which was, nevertheless, full of milk, and it was for the nurse to tell her that a foster-mother could easily be found in the village, but this did not console her and she cried very bitterly. The doctor called. He did not think there was anything strange in Ned's letter. He approved of it! He said that Ellen was delicate and had nursed her baby long enough, and it appeared that he had been thinking of recommending a nurse to her, and he spoke of a peasant woman he had just seen. He spoke with so much assurance that Ellen was soothed, but he had not left her very long before she felt that medical opinion would not satisfy her, that she must have theological opinion as well, and she wrote a letter to Father Brennan asking him to come down to see her, mentioning that she had had a baby and could not go to see him. It would be a great relief to her to see him for a few minutes, and if he would come at once she would consider it a great favour. If it were possible for him to come down that very afternoon she would be deeply grateful. She wished to consult him, and on a matter on which she felt very deeply, and nothing, she said, but a priest's advice could allay her scruples.

The nurse gave her a sheet of paper and a pencil, and she scribbled a letter as best she could in her bed, and lay back fatigued. The nurse said she must not fret, that Father Brennan would be sure to come to her at once if he were at home, and Ellen knew that that was so; she felt that she was peevish, but she felt that Ned ought not to have written her that letter.

The hours that afternoon were very long and she restless and weary of them, and she asked the nurse many times to go to the window to see if Father Brennan were coming. At last he came, and she told him of the letter she had received, not wishing to show him the letter, for it was somewhat extravagant, and she did not like a priest to read Ned's praise of her body. She was anxious, however, to give him a true account of the letter, and would have talked a long while if the priest had not stopped her, saying the matter was one for the doctor to decide. The church had never expressed any views on the subject; whether a mother was justified in nursing her child or in passing it over to a foster-mother. It was entirely a question for the doctor, and if the doctor advised such a course she would be wrong not to follow it. Ellen felt that she had been misunderstood, and she tried to tell the priest that Ned's letter had been inspired by his admiration of her, and that this seemed to her selfish. She wondered how a father could consider his wife before the child, but when she said this she did not feel she was speaking quite sincerely, and this troubled her; she was on the verge of tears, and the nurse came in and said she had spoken enough that afternoon, and the priest bade her good-bye. The doctor came in soon after; there was some whispering, and Ellen knew that the woman he had brought with him was the foster-mother, and the baby was taken from her, and she saw it fix its gluttonous little lips on the foster-mother's breast.

Now that the priest had ordered her conscience, she got well rapidly, and it was a pleasure to her to prepare herself for her husband's admiration. The nurse thought he would perceive no difference in her, but when they put on her stays it was quite clear that she had grown stouter, and she cried out, "I'm quite a little mother!" But the nurse said her figure would come back all right. Ned's return had been delayed, and this she regarded as fortunate, for there was no doubt that in a month she would be able to meet him, slight and graceful as she had ever been.

As soon as she was able she went for long walks on the hills and every day she improved in health and in figure; and when she read Ned's letter saying he would be in Cork in a few days she felt certain he would see no change in her. She opened her dress and could discern no difference; perhaps a slight wave in the breast's line; she was not quite sure and she hoped Ned would not notice it. And she chose a white dress. Ned liked her in white, and she tied it with a blue sash; she put on a white hat trimmed with china roses, and the last look convinced her that she had never looked prettier.

"I never wore so becoming a hat," she said. She walked slowly so as not to be out of breath, and, swinging her white parasol over the tops of her tan boots, she stood at the end of the platform waiting for the train to come up.

"I had expected to see you pale," he said, "and perhaps a little stouter, but you are the same, the very same." And saying that he would be able to talk to her better if he were free from his bag, he gave it to a boy to carry. And they strolled down the warm dusty road.

They lived about a mile and a half from the station, and there were great trees and old crumbling walls, and, beyond the walls, water meadows, and it was pleasant to look over the walls and watch the cattle grazing peacefully. And to-day the fields were so pleasant that Ned and Ellen could hardly speak from the pleasure of looking at them.

"You've seen nothing more beautiful in America, have you, Ned?"

There was so much to say it was difficult to know where to begin, and it was delicious to be stopped by the scent of the honeysuckle. Ned gathered some blossoms to put into his wife's dress, but while admiring her dress and her hat and her pretty red hair he remembered the letter he had written to her in answer to her telegram.

"I've had many qualms about the letter I wrote you in answer to your telegram. After all a child's right upon the mother is the first right of all. I wrote the letter in a hurry, and hardly knew what I was saying."

"We got an excellent nurse, Ned, and the boy is doing very well."

"So you said in your letters. But after posting my letter I said to myself: if it causes me trouble, how much more will it cause her?"

"Your letter did trouble me, Ned. I was feeling very weak that morning and the baby was crying for me, for I had been nursing him for a week. I did not know what to do. I was torn both ways, so I sent up a note to Father Brennan asking him to come to see me, and he came down and told me that I was quite free to give my baby to a foster mother."

"But what does Father Brennan know about it more than anyone of us?"

"The sanction of the Church, Ned—"

"The sanction of the Church! What childish nonsense is this?" he said. "The authority of a priest. So it was not for me, but because a priest—"

"But, Ned, there must be a code of morality, and these men devote their lives to thinking out one for us."

He could see that she was looking more charming than she had ever looked before, but her beauty could not crush the anger out of him; and she never seemed further from him not even when the Atlantic divided them.

"Those men devote their lives to thinking out a code of morality for us! You submit your soul to their keeping. And what remains of you when you have given over your soul?"

"But, Ned, why this outbreak? You knew I was a Catholic when you married me."

"Yes, . . . of course, and I'm sorry, Ellen, for losing my temper. But it is only in Ireland that women submit themselves body and soul. It is extraordinary; it is beyond human reason."

They walked on in silence, and Ned tried to forget that his wife was a Catholic. Her religion did not prevent her from wearing a white dress and a hat with roses in it.

"Shall I go up-stairs to see the baby, or will you bring him down?"

"I'll bring him down."

And it was a great lump of white flesh with blue eyes and a little red down on its head that she carried in her arms.

"And now, Ned, forget the priest and admire your boy."

"He seems a beautiful boy, so healthy and sleepy."

"I took him out of his bed but he never cries. Nurse said she never heard of a baby that did not cry. Do you know I'm sometimes tempted to pinch him to see if he can cry."

She sat absorbed looking at the baby; and she was so beautiful and so intensely real at that moment that Ned began to forget that she had given the child out to nurse because the priest had told her that she might do so without sin.

"I called him after you, Ned. It was Father Stafford who baptised him."

"So he has been baptised!"

"He was not three days old when he was baptised."

"Of course. He could not have gone to heaven if he had not been baptised."

"Ned, I don't think it kind of you to say these things to me. You never used to say them."

"I am sorry Ellen; I'll say no more, and I'm glad it was Father Stafford who baptised him. He is the most sensible priest we have. If all the clergy were like him I should find it easier to believe."

"But religion has nothing to do with the clergy. It is quite possible to think the clergy foolish and yet to believe that the religion is the true one."

"I like the clergy far better than their religion, and believe them to be worthy of a better one. I like Father Stafford, and you like having a priest to dinner. Let us ask him."

"I'm afraid, Ned, that Father Stafford is getting old. He rarely leaves the house now, and Father Maguire does all the work of the parish."

She liked clerical gossip, and she told him that the church was finished, and how Biddy heard the saints singing in the window made a fine tale.

"So now we have a local saint."

"Yes, and miracles!"

"But do you believe in miracles?"

"I don't know. I shouldn't like to say. One is not obliged to believe in them."

"I'm sure you would enjoy believing in Biddy."

"Oh, Ned, how aggressive you are, and the very day you come back."

But why hadn't she asked him about America and about his speeches? He had looked forward to telling her about them. She seemed to care nothing about them; even when she spoke about them after dinner, he could see that she was not as much interested in politics as she used to be. However, she wore a white dress and black stockings; her red hair was charmingly pinned up with a tortoiseshell comb, and taking her upon his knee he thought it would be well to please himself with her as she was and forget what she was not.

Next morning when he picked up the newspaper and the daily instalment of a cardinal's tour through Ireland caught his eye, he remembered that Ellen had sent for a theologian. . . . His eyes went down the columns of the newspaper and he said, "All the old flummery. Ireland's fidelity to her religion, etc., her devotion to Rome, etc.,—to everything," he said, "except herself. Propagations of the faith, exhortations to do as our ancestors had done, to do everything except make life joyous and triumphant." Looking across the page his eye was caught by the headline, "Profession of Irish Nuns in France." Further on in large letters, "Killmessan Cathedral: Bazaar." And these items of news were followed by a letter from a Bishop. "What a lot of Bishops!" he said. He read of "worthy" parish priests, and a little further on of "brilliant" young clergymen, and at every meeting the chair was taken by the "worthy" or by the "good" parish priest.

"Well," he said, "if the newspaper reflects the mind of the people there is no hope."

And he heard daily of new churches and new convents and the acquisition of property by the clergy. He heard tales of esuriency and avarice, and the persecution of the dancing girl and the piper.

"The clergy," he said, "are swallowing up the country," and he looked for some means whereby he might save the Gael.

About this time an out-cry was made against the ugliness of modern ecclesiastical architecture, and a number of enthusiasts were writing to the newspapers proposing a revival of Irish romanesque; they instanced Cormac's Chapel as the model that should be followed. Ned joined in the outcry that no more stained glass should be imported from Birmingham, and wrote to the newspapers many times that good sculpture and good painting and good glass were more likely to produce a religious fervour than bad. His purpose was to point a finger of scorn at the churches, and he hoped to plead a little later that there were too many churches, and that no more should be built until the population had begun to increase again. He looked forward to the time when he would be able to say right out that the Gael had spent enough of money on his soul, and should spend what remained to him on his body. He looked forward to the time when he should tell the Gael that his soul was his greatest expense, but the time was far off when he could speak plainly.

The clergy were prepared to admit that German glass was not necessary for their successful mediation, but they were stubborn when Ned asked them to agree that no more churches were necessary. They were not moved by the argument that the population was declining and would not admit that there were too many churches or even that there were churches enough. The ecclesiastical mind is a subtle one and it knows that when men cease to build churches they cease to be religious. The instinct of the clergy was against Ned, but they had to make concessions, for the country was awakening to its danger, and Ned began to think that all its remaining energies were being concentrated in an effort of escape.

Long years ago in America he had watched a small snake trying to swallow a frog. The snake sucked down the frog, and the frog seemed to acquiesce until the half of his body was down the snake's gullet, and the frog bestirred himself and succeeded in escaping. The snake rested awhile and the next day he renewed his attack. At last the day came when the weary frog delayed too long and Ned watched him disappear down the snake's gullet.

A good deal of Ireland was down the clerical throat and all would go down if Ireland did not bestir herself. Ireland was weakening daily, and every part of her that disappeared made it more difficult for her to extricate herself. Ned remembered that life and death, sickness and health, success and failure are merely questions of balance. A nation is successful when its forces are at balance, and nations rise and fall because the centre of gravity shifts. A single Spaniard is as good as a single German, but the centre of gravity is in Spain no longer.

Ned did not look upon religion as an evil; he knew religion to be necessary; but it seemed to him that the balance had been tilted in Ireland.

He threw himself more and more into the education of the people, and politics became his chief interest. At last he had begun to live for his idea, and long absence from home and long drives on outside cars and evenings spent in inn parlours were accepted without murmuring; these discomforts were no longer perceived, whereas when he and Ellen used to sit over the fire composing speeches together, the thought of them filled him with despair. He used to complain that Ellen was always sending him away from home and to hard mutton shops and dirty bed rooms. He reminded her no more of these discomforts. He came back and spent a day or two with her, and went away again. She had begun to notice that he did not seem sorry to leave, but she did not reproach him, because he said he was working for Ireland. He tried to think the explanation a sufficient one. Did he not love his home? His home was a delightful relaxation. The moment he crossed the threshold his ideas went behind him and in the hour before dinner he played with his child and talked to Ellen about the house and the garden and the things he thought she was most interested in. After dinner she read or sewed and he spent an hour at the piano, and then he took her on his knees.

And sometimes in the morning as he walked, with Ellen at his side to catch the train, he wondered at his good fortune—the road was so pleasant, so wide and smooth and shaded, in fact just as he imagined the road should be, and Ellen was the very pleasantest companion a man could wish for. He looked on her, on his child and his house at the foot of the Dublin mountains, as a little work of art which he had planned out and the perfection of which entitled him to some credit. He compared himself to one who visits a larder, who has a little snack of something and then puts down the cover, saying, "Now that's all right, that's safe for another week."

Nevertheless he could see a little shadow gathering. His speeches were growing more explicit, and sooner or later his wife would begin to notice that he was attacking the clergy. Had she no suspicion? She was by nature so self-restrained that it was impossible to tell. He knew she read his speeches, and if she read them she must have noticed their anti-clerical tone. Last Saturday he had spoken to her about politics, but she had allowed the conversation to drop, and that had puzzled him. He was not well reported. The most important parts of his speech were omitted and for these omissions he looked upon the reporters and the editors as his best friends. He had managed to steer his way very adroitly up to the present, but the day of reckoning could not much longer be postponed, and one day coming home from a great meeting he remembered that he had said more than he intended to say, though he had intended to say a good deal. This time the reporter could not save him, and when his wife would read the newspaper to-morrow an explanation could hardly be avoided.

He had thrown a book on the seat opposite, and he put it into his bag. Its Nihilism had frightened him at first but he had returned to the book again and again and every time the attraction had become stronger. The train passed the signal box, and Ned was thinking of the aphorisms—the new Gospel was written in aphorisms varying from three to twenty lines in length—and he thought of these as meat lozenges each containing enough nutriment to make a gallon of weak soup suitable for invalids, and of himself as a sort of illicit dispensary.

Ellen was not on the platform; something had delayed her, and he could see the road winding under trees, and presently he saw her white summer dress and her parasol aslant. There was no prettier, no more agreeable woman than Ellen in Ireland, and he thought it a great pity to have to worry her and himself with explanations about politics and about religion. To know how to sacrifice the moment is wisdom, and it would be better to sacrifice their walk than that she should read unprepared what he had said. But the evening would be lost! It would be lost in any case, for his thoughts would be running all the while on the morning paper.

And they walked on together, he a little more silent than usual, for he was thinking how he could introduce the subject on which he had decided to speak to her, and Ellen more talkative, for she was telling how the child had delayed her, and it was not until they reached the prettiest part of the road that she notice that Ned was answering perfunctorily.

"What is the matter, dear? I hope you are not disappointed with the meeting?"

"No, the meeting was well enough. There were a great number of people present and my speech was well received."

"I am glad of that," she said, "but what is the matter, Ned?"

"Nothing. I was thinking about my speech. I hope it will not be misunderstood. People are so stupid, and some will understand it as an attack on the clergy, whereas it is nothing of the kind."

"Well," she said, "if it isn't it will be different from your other speeches."

"How is that?"

"All your speeches lately have been an attack upon the clergy direct or indirect. I daresay many did not understand them but anyone who knows your opinions can read between the lines."

"If you had read between the lines, Ellen, you would have seen that I have been trying to save the clergy from themselves. They are so convinced of their own importance that they forget that after all there must be a laity."

Ellen answered very quietly, and there was a sadness in her gravity which Ned had some difficulty in appreciating. He went on talking, telling her that some prelate had pointed out lately, and with approbation, that although the population had declined the clergy had been increasing steadily year after year.

"I am really," he said, "trying to save them from themselves. I am only pleading for the harmless and the necessary laity."

Ellen did not answer him for a long while.

"You see, Ned, I am hardly more to you now than any other woman. You come here occasionally to spend a day or two with me. Our married life has dwindled down to that. You play with the baby and you play with the piano, and you write your letters. I don't know what you are writing in them. You never speak to me of your ideas now. I know nothing of your politics."

"I haven't spoken about politics much lately, Ellen, because I thought you had lost interest in them."

"I have lost interest in nothing that concerns you. I have not spoken to you about politics because I know quite well that my ideas don't interest you any longer. You're absorbed in your own ideas, and we're divided. You sleep now in the spare room, so that you may have time to prepare your speeches."

"But I sometimes come to see you in your room, Ellen."

"Sometimes," she said, sadly, "but that is not my idea of marriage, nor is it the custom of the country, nor is it what the Church wishes."

"I think Ellen you are very unreasonable, and you are generally so reasonable."

"Well, don't let us argue any more," she said. "We shall never agree, I'm afraid."

Ned remembered that he once used to say to her, "Ellen, we are agreed in everything."

"If I had only known that it was going to turn out so disagreeable as this," Ned said to himself, "I should have held my tongue," and he was sorry for having displeased Ellen, so pretty did she look in her white dress and her hat trimmed with china roses; and though he did not care much for flowers he liked to see Ellen among her flowers; he liked to sit with her under the shady apple tree, and the hollyhocks were making a fine show up in the air.

"I think I like hollyhocks better than any flowers, and the sunflowers are coming out," he said.

He hesitated whether he should speak about the swallows, Ellen did not care for birds. The swallows rushed around the garden in groups of six and seven filling the air with piercing shrieks. He had never seen them so restless. He and Ellen walked across the sward to their seat and then Ellen asked him if he would like to see the child.

"I've kept him out of bed and thought you might like to see him."

"Yes," he said, "go fetch the baby and I will shake the boughs, and it will amuse him to run after the apples."

"Differences of opinion arise," he said to himself, "for the mind changes and desire wanes, but the heart is always the same, and what an extraordinary bond the child is," he said, seeing Ellen leading the child across the sward. He forgot Ireland, forgot priests and forgot politics, forgot everything. He lifted his little son in his arms and shook the boughs and saw the child run after the falling apples, stumbling and falling but never hurting himself.

The quarrels of the day died down; the evening grew more beautiful under the boughs, and this intimate life round their apple tree was strangely intense, and it grew more and more intense as the light died. Every now and then the child came to show them an apple he had picked up, and Ned said: "He thinks he has found the largest apples that have ever been seen." The secret of their lives seemed to approach and at every moment they expected to hear it. The tired child came to his mother and asked to be taken on her lap. An apple fell with a thud, the stars came out, and Ned carried his son, now half asleep, into the house, and they undressed him together, having forgotten, seemingly, their differences of opinion.

But after dinner when they were alone in the drawing room their relations grew strained again. Ned wanted to explain to Ellen that his movement was not anticlerical, but he could see she did not wish to hear. He watched her take up her work and wondered what he could say to persuade her, and after a little while he began to think of certain pieces of music. But to go to the piano would be like a hostile act. The truth was that he had looked forward to the evening he was going to spend with her, he had imagined an ideal evening with her and could not reconcile himself to the loss. "The hour we passed in the garden was extraordinarily intense," he said to himself, and he regretted ever having talked to her about anything except simple things. "It is unwise of a man to make a comrade of his wife.... Now I wonder if she would be angry with me if I went to the piano—if I were to play something very gently? Perhaps a book would seem less aggressive." He went into his study and fetched his book, and very soon forgot Ellen. But she had not forgotten him, and she raised her eyes to look at him from time to time, knowing quite well that he was reading the book out of which he drew the greater part of his doctrine that he had alluded to on his way home, and that he had called the Gospel of Life.

He turned the pages, and seeing that his love of her had been absorbed by the book, she stuck her needle in her work, folded it up, and put it into the work basket.

"I am going to bed, Ned." He looked up, and she saw he had returned from a world that was unknown to her, a world in which she had no part, and did not want to have a part, knowing it to be wicked. "You have been reading all the evening. You prefer your book to me. Good-night."

She had never spoken to him so rudely before. He wondered awhile and went to the piano. She had gone out of the room very rudely. Now he was free to do what he liked, and what he liked most was to play Bach. The sound of the piano would reach her bedroom! Well, if it did—he had not played Bach for four weeks and he wanted to play Bach. Yes, he was playing Bach to please himself. He knew the piano would annoy her. And he was right.

She had just lighted the candles on her dressing table, and she paused and listened. It annoyed her that he should go to the piano the moment she left him, and that he should play dry intellectual Bach, for he knew that Bach did not interest her. She was tempted to ring for her maid, and would have sent down word to Ned that she would be obliged if he would stop playing, had it not seemed undignified to do so.

As she undressed she lost control over herself, and lying in bed it seemed to her that Ned had hidden himself in a veil of kindness and good humour, and that the man she had married was a man without moral qualities, a man who would leave her without resentment, without disgust, who would say good-bye to her as to some brief habit. She could hear Bach's interminable twiddles, and this exasperated her nerves and she wept through many preludes and fugues. Later on she must have heard the fugues in a dream, for the door opened; it passed over the carpet softly; and she heard Ned saying that he hoped the piano had not kept her awake. She heard him lay the candle on the table and come over to her bedside, and, leaning over her, he begged of her to turn round and speak to him.

"My poor little woman, I hope I have not been cross with you this evening."

She turned away petulantly, but he took her hand and held it and whispered to her, and gradually tempted her out of her anger, and taking some of her red hair from the pillow he kissed it. She still kept her head turned from him but she could not keep back her happiness; it followed her like fire, enfolding her, and at last, raising herself up in the bed, she said:—

"Oh, Ned, do you still love me?"

When he came into the bed she slipped down so that she could lie upon his breast, and they fell asleep thinking of the early train he would have to catch in the morning.

He was going to Dublin, and the servant knocked at the door at seven o'clock; Ellen roused a little asking if he must go to Dublin. She would like him to stay with her. But he could not stay, and she felt she must give him his breakfast. While tying her petticoats she went to the door of Ned's dressing-room asking him questions, for she liked to talk to him while he was shaving. After breakfast they walked to the station together, and she stood on the platform smiling and waving farewells.

She turned home, her thoughts chattering like the sunshine among the trees; she leaned over the low, crumbling walls and looked across the water meadows. Two women were spending the morning under the trees; they were sewing. A man lying at length talking to them. This group was part of external nature. The bewitching sunlight found a way into her heart, and it seemed to her that she would never be happy again.

Ned had told her that he was not going to say anything about the priests at this meeting. Ah, if she were only sure he would not attack religion she would not mind him criticising the priests. They were not above criticism; they courted criticism, approving of a certain amount of lay criticism. But it was not the priests that Ned hated, it was religion; and his hatred of religion had increased since he began to read those books—she had seen him put one into his bag, and the rest of the set were in his study. When she got home she paused a moment, and, without knowing exactly why, she turned aside and did not go into his study.

But next day the clock in the drawingroom stopped and, wanting to know the time, she went into the study and looked at the clock, trying to keep her eyes from the book case. But in spite of herself she looked. The books were there: they had been thrust so far back that she could not read the name of the writer. Well, it did not matter, she did not care to know the name of the writer—Ned's room interested her more than the books. There was his table covered with his papers; and the thought passed through her mind that he might be writing the book he had promised her not to write. What he was writing was certainly for the printer—he was writing only on one side of the paper—and one of these days what he was writing would be printed.

The study was on the ground floor, its windows overlooking the garden, and she glanced to see if the gardener were by, but her wish to avoid observation reminded her that she was doing a dishonourable action, and, standing with the papers in her hand, she hoped she would go out of the study without reading them. She began to read.

The papers in her hand were his notes for the book he was writing, and the title caught her eye, "A Western Thibet." "So he is writing the book he promised me not to write," she said. But she could feel no anger, so conscious was she of her own shame. And she did not forget her shame until she remembered that it was her money that was supporting the agitation. He had been spending a great deal of money lately—they were rich now; her father had died soon after their marriage and all his money had come to her, and Ned was spending it on an anti-religious agitation. She had let Ned do what he liked; she had not cared what happened so long as she kept his love, and her moral responsibility became clearer and clearer. She must tell Ned that she could give him no more money unless he promised he would not say anything against the priests. He would make no such promise, and to speak about her money would exhibit her in a mean light, and she would lose all her influence. Now that they were reconciled she might win him back to religion; she had been thinking of this all yesterday. How could she tell him that she would take all her money away from him? Ned was the last person in the world who would be influenced by a threat.

And looking round the room she asked herself why she had ever come into it to commit a dishonourable act! and much trouble had come upon her. But two thousand a year of her money was being spent in robbing the people of Ireland of their religion! Maybe thousands of souls would be lost—and through her fault.

Ellen feared money as much as her father had loved it.

"Good Heavens," she murmured to herself, "what am I to do?" Confession . . . Father Brennan. She must consult him. The temptation to confide her secret became more decisive. Confession! She could ask the priest what she liked in confession, and without betraying Ned. And it was not ten o'clock yet. She would be in time for eleven o'clock Mass, Father Brennan would be hearing confessions after Mass, and she could get to Dublin on her bicycle in an hour. In three quarters of an hour she was at the presbytery, and before the attendant could answer she caught sight of Father Brennan running down-stairs.

"I only want to speak to you for a few minutes."

"I am just going into church."

"Can't I say a word to you before you go in?"

And seeing how greatly agitated she was, he took her into the parlour, and she told him that though she trusted him implicitly she could not consult him on this particular question except in the confessional.

"I shall be hearing confessions after Mass."

If the priest told her she must withdraw her money from Ned, her marriage was a broken one. It was she who had brought Ned into politics; she had often spoken of her money in order to induce him to go into politics, and now it was her money that was forcing her to betray him. She had not thought of confession in her present difficulty as a betrayal, but it was one, and a needless one; Father Brennan could only tell her to withdraw her money; yet she must consult the priest—nothing else would satisfy her. She lacked courage: his advice would give her courage. But when she had told Ned that she could give him no more money, she would have to tell him she was acting on the priest's advice, for she could not go on living with him and not tell him everything. A secret would poison her life, and she had no difficulty in imagining how she would remember it; she could see it stopping her suddenly as she crossed the room when she was thinking of something quite different. The hardest confession of all would be to tell Ned that she had consulted the priest, and she did not think he would ever love her again. But what matter, so long as she was not weak and contemptible in the eyes of God. That is what she had to think of. The love of one's husband is of this world and temporary, but the love of God is for all eternity. All things are in the will of God. It was God that had sent her into Ned's room. She had been compelled, and now she was compelled again. It was God that had sent her to the priest; she was a mere puppet in the hands of God, and she prayed that she might be reconciled to His will, only daring to implore His mercy with one "Our Father" and one "Hail Mary." Further imploration would be out of place, she must not insist too much. God was all wisdom, and would know if the love of her husband might be spared to her, and she hoped she would be reconciled to His will even if her child should be taken from her.

There were two penitents before her. One a woman, faded by time and deformed by work. From the black dress, come down to her through a succession of owners and now as nondescript as herself, Ellen guessed the woman to be one of the humblest class of servants, one of those who get their living by going out to work by the day. She leaned over the bench, and Ellen could see she was praying all the while, and Ellen wondered how Ned could expect this poor woman, earning a humble wage in humble service, to cultivate what he called "the virtue of pride." Was it not absurd to expect this poor woman to go through life trying to make life "exuberant and triumphant?" And Ellen wished she could show Ned this poor woman waiting to go into the confessional. In the confessional she would find a refined and learned man to listen to her, and he would have patience with her. Where else would she find a patient listener? Where else would she find consolation? "The Gospel of Life," indeed! How many may listen to the gospel of life, and for how long may anyone listen? Sooner or later we are that poor woman waiting to go into the confessional; she is the common humanity.

The other penitent was a girl about sixteen. Her hair was not yet pinned up, and her dress was girlish even for her age, and Ellen judged her to be one of the many girls who come up to Dublin from the suburbs to an employment in a shop or in a lawyer's office, and who spend a few pence in the middle of the day in tea rooms. The girl looked round the church so frequently that Ellen could not think of her as a willing penitent, but as one who had been sent to confession by her father and mother. At her age sensuality is omnipresent, and Ellen thought of the check confession is at such an age. If that girl overstepped the line she would have to confess everything, or face the frightful danger of a bad confession, and that is a danger that few Catholic girls are prepared to face.

The charwoman spent a long time in the confessional, and Ellen did not begrudge her the time she spent, for she came out like one greatly soothed, and Ellen remembered that Ned had once described the soothed look which she noticed on the poor woman's face as "a look of foolish ecstasy, wholly divorced from the intelligence." But what intellectual ecstasy did he expect from this poor woman drifting towards her natural harbour—the poor house?

It was extraordinary that a man so human as Ned was in many ways should become so inhuman the moment religion was mentioned, and she wondered if the sight of that poor woman leaving the confessional would allay his hatred of the sacrament. At that moment the young girl came out. She hurried away, and Ellen went into the confessional to betray her husband.

She was going to betray Ned, but she was going to betray him under the seal of confession, and entertained no thought that the priest would avail himself of any technicality in her confession to betray her. She was, nevertheless, determined that her confession should be technically perfect. She went into the confessional to confess her sins, and one of the sins she was going to confess was her culpable negligence regarding the application of her money. There were other sins. She had examined her conscience, and had discovered many small ones. She had lost her temper last night, and her temper had prevented her from saying her prayers, her temper and her love of Ned; for it were certainly a sin to desire anything so fervidly that one cannot give to God the love, the prayers, that belong to Him.

During Mass the life of her soul had seemed to her strange and complex, and she thought that her confession would be a long one; but on her knees before the priest her soul seemed to vanish, and all her interesting scruples and phases of thought dwindled to almost nothing—she could not put her soul into words. The priest waited, but the matter on which she had come to consult him had put everything else out of her head.

"I am not certain that what I am going to tell you is a sin, but I consider it as part of my confession," and she told him how she had given Ned her money and allowed him to apply it without inquiring into the application. "Since my child was born I have not taken the interest I used to take in politics. I don't think my husband is any longer interested in my ideas, and now he has told me that some kind of religious reformation is necessary in Ireland."

"When did he tell you that?"

"Yesterday—the day before. I went to the station to meet him and he told me as we walked home. For a long time I believed him: I don't mean that he told me falsehoods; he may have deceived himself. Anyhow he used to tell me that though his agitation might be described as anti-clerical no one could call it anti-religious. But this morning something led me into his room and I looked through his papers. I daresay I had no right to do so but I did."

"And you discovered from his papers that his agitation was directed against religion?"

Ellen nodded.

"I cannot think of anything more unfortunate," said the priest.

Father Brennan was a little fat man with small eyes and a punctilious deferential manner, and his voice was slightly falsetto.

"I cannot understand how your husband can be so unwise. I know very little of him, but I did not think he was capable of making so grave a mistake. The country is striving to unite itself, and we have been uniting, and now that we have a united Ireland, or very nearly, it appears that Mr. Carmady has come from America to divide us again. What can he gain by these tactics? If he tells the clergy that the moment Home Rule is granted an anti-religious party will rise up and drive them out of the country, he will set them against Home Rule, and if the clergy are not in favour of Home Rule who, I would ask Mr. Carmady, who will be in favour of it? And I will ask you, my dear child, to ask him—I suggest that you should ask him to what quarter he looks for support?"

"Ned and I never talk politics; we used to, but that is a long time ago."

"He will only ruin himself. But I think you said you came to consult me about something?"

"Yes. You see a very large part of my money is spent in politics and I am not certain that I should not withdraw my money. It is for that I have come to consult you."

Ellen had been addressing the little outline of the priest's profile, but when he heard the subject on which she had come to consult him he turned and she saw his large face, round and mottled. A little light gathered in his wise and kindly eyes, and Ellen guessed that he had begun to see his way out of the difficulty, and she was glad of it, for she reckoned her responsibility at a number of souls. The priest spoke very kindly, he seemed to understand how difficult it would be for her to tell her husband that she could not give him any more money unless he promised not to attack the clergy or religion, but she must do so. He pointed out that to attack one was to attack the other, for the greater mass of mankind understands religion only through the clergy.

"You must not only withdraw your money," he said, "but you must use your influence to dissuade him."

"I am afraid," said Ellen, "that when I tell him that I must withdraw my money, and that you have told me to do so—"

"You need not say that I told you to do so."

"I cannot keep anything back from my husband. I must

tell him the truth," she said. "And when I tell him everything, I shall not only lose any influence that may remain, but I doubt very much if my husband will continue to live with me."

"But your marriage was a love marriage?"

"Yes, but that is a long time ago. It is four years ago."

"I don't think your husband will separate himself from you, but even so I think—"

"You will give me absolution?"

She said this a little defiantly, and the priest wondered, and she left the confessional perplexed and a little ashamed and very much terrified.

There was nothing for her to do in Dublin, she must go home and wait for her husband. He was not coming home until evening, and she rode home wondering how the day would pass, thinking the best time to tell him would be after dinner when he left the piano. If he were very angry with her she would go to her room. He would not go on living with her, she was sure of that, and her heart seemed to stand still when she entered the house and saw the study door open and Ned looking through the papers.

"I have come back to look for some papers," he said. "It is very annoying. I have lost half the day," and he went on looking among his papers and she could see that he suspected nothing. "Do you know when is the next train?"

She looked out the trains for him, and she could see that he suspected nothing, and after he had found the papers he wanted they went into the garden.

She talked of her flowers with the same interest as she had done many times before, and when he asked her to go for a walk with him on the hill she consented, although it was almost unbearable to walk with him for the last time through the places where they had walked so often, thinking that their lives would move on to the end unchanged; and they walked about the hill talking of Irish history, their eyes often resting on the slender outlines of Howth, until it was time for Ned to go to the station.

"I shall be back in time for dinner. You will wait dinner a little for me, I may have to come back by a later train."

And they walked down the hill together, Ned bidding her good-bye at the garden gate, saying she had walked enough that day, and she feeling the moment was at hand.

"But, Ned, why are you going to Dublin? You are only

going to see people who are anti-Catholic, who hate our religion, who are prejudiced against it."

"But," he said, "why do you talk of these things. We have got on very much better since we have ceased to discuss politics together. We are agreed in everything else."

She did not answer for a long while and then she said:—

"But I don't see how we are to avoid discussing them, for it is my money that supports the agitation."

"I never thought of that. So it is. Do you wish to withdraw it?"

"You are not angry with me, Ned? You won't think it mean of me to withdraw my money? How are you are going to go on without my money? You see I am wrecking your political career."

"Oh," he said. "I shall be able to get on without it. Now, goodbye."

"May I go to the station with you?"

"If you like, only let us talk of something else. Everyone's conscience is his own law and you must act accordingly."

She trotted by his side, and she begged of him not to laugh at her when he said that to be truly logical she would have to turn him out of the house, or at least to charge him for his board and lodging.

The intonation of his voice laid her heart waste; she felt she was done for, and she walked home repeating the words, "I am done for."

As she passed through her garden she saw that her flowers were dying for want of water, and she gave them a few cans of water; but she could not do much work, and though the cans were heavy, they were not as heavy as her heart. She sat down under the apple tree and remembered her life. Her best days were her school days. Then life was beginning. Now it seemed to her nearly over, and she only five-and-twenty. She never could take the same interest in politics as she had once taken, nor in books. She felt that her intelligence had declined. She was cleverer as a girl than she was as a woman.

Ned was coming home for dinner, and some time that evening she would have to tell him that she had read his manuscript. She would have liked to meet him at the station, but thought it would be better not to go. The day wore away. Ned was in his best humour, and when she told him why she did not go to the station to meet him, he said it was foolish of her not to have come, for there was nothing he liked better than to stroll home with her in the evening, the road was so pleasant, etc.

She could see that he had not noticed her dress or what he was eating, and it was irritating to see him sitting there with his spoon full of soup telling her how the Irish people would have to reduce their expenditure and think a little less of priests—for a while, at least—unless they were minded to pass away, to become absorbed in America.

"I like Brennan," he said, throwing himself back in his chair. "He is a clever man. Brennan knows as well as I do there's too much money spent upon religion in Ireland. But, tell me, did he tell you explicitly that you should give me no more money?"

"Yes. But, Ned—"

"No, no, I am not in the least angry," he said, "I shall always get money to carry on politics. But what a game it is! And I suppose, Ellen, you consult him on every detail of your life?"

Her admission that Father Brennan had taken down books and put on his spectacles delighted him.

"Taking down tomes!" he said. "Splendid! Some of these gentlemen would discuss theology with God. I can see Father Brennan getting up: 'Sire, my reason for entering the said sin as a venial sin, etc.'"

Very often during the evening the sewing dropped from her hands, and she sat thinking. Sooner or later she would have to tell Ned she had read his manuscript. He would not mind her reading his manuscript, and though he hated the idea that anyone should turn to a priest and ask him for his interpretation regarding right and wrong, he had not, on the whole, been as angry as she had expected.

At last she got up. "I am going to bed, Ned."

"Isn't it very early?"

"There is no use my stopping here. You don't want to talk to me; you'll go on playing till midnight."

"Now, why this petulancy, Ellen? I think it shows a good deal of forgiveness for me to kiss you after the way you behaved."

She held a long string of grease in her fingers, and was melting it and when she could no longer hold it in her fingers, she threw the end into the flame.

"I've forgiven you, Ellen. . . . You never tell me anything

of your ideas now; we never talk to each other, and if this last relation is broken there will be nothing . . . will there?"

"I sought Father Brennan's advice under the seal of confession, that was all. You don't think that—"

"There are plenty of indirect ways in which he will be able to make use of the information he has got from you."

"You have not yet heard how it happened, and perhaps when you do you will think worse of me. I went into your room to see what books you were reading. There was no harm in looking at a book; but you had put the books so far into the bookcase that I could not see the name of the author. I took up the manuscript from the table and glanced through it. I suppose I ought not to have done that: a manuscript is not the same as a book. And now good-night."

He imagined her going slowly up the stairs and knew she would not expect him. Well, the sensual coil was broken, and if he did not not follow her now she would understand that it was broken. He had wanted freedom this long while. They had come to the end of the second period, and there are three—a year of mystery and passion, and then some years of passion without mystery. The third period is one of resignation. The lives of the parents pass into the children, and the mated journey on, carrying their packs. Seldom, indeed, the man and the woman weary of the life of passion at the same time and turn instinctively into the way of resignation like animals. Sometimes it is the man who turns first, sometimes it is the woman. In this case it was the man. He had his work to do, and Ellen had her child to think of, and each must think of his and her task from henceforth. Their tasks were not the same. Each had a different task; she had thrown, or tried to throw, his pack from his shoulders. She had thwarted him, or tried to thwart him. He grew angry as he thought of what she had done. She had gone into his study and read his papers, and she had then betrayed him to a priest. He lay awake thinking how he had been deceived by Ellen; thinking that he had been mistaken; that her character was not the noble character he had imagined. But at the bottom of his heart he was true to the noble soul that religion could not extinguish nor even his neglect.

She said one day: "Is it because I read your manuscript and told the priest, that you would not come to my room, or is it because you are tired of me?"

"I cannot tell you; and, really, this conversation is very

painful. I am engaged upon my work, and I have no thoughts for anything but it."

Another time when he came from the piano and sat opposite to her she raised her eyes from her sewing and sat looking at him, and then getting up suddenly she put her hands to her forehead and said to herself: "I will conquer this," and she went out of the room.

And from that day she did not trouble him with love. She obtained control over herself, and he remembered a mistress who had ceased to love him, and he had persecuted her for a long while with supplication. "She is at one with herself always," he said, and he tried to understand her. "She is one of those whose course through life is straight, and not zig-zag, as mine is." He liked to see her turn and look at the baby, and he said, "That love is the permanent and original element of things, it is the universal substance;" and he could trace Ellen's love of her child in her love of him; these loves were not two loves, but one love. And when walking one evening through the shadows, as they spoke about the destiny we can trace in our lives, about life and its loneliness, the conversation verged on the personal, and she said, with a little accent of regret, but not reproachfully:

"But, Ned, you could not live with anyone, at least not always. I think you would sooner not live with anyone."

He did not dare to contradict her; he knew that she had spoken the truth; and Ned was sorry he was giving pain to Ellen, for there was no one he would have liked to please better. He regretted that he was what he was, that his course was zig-zag. For a moment he regretted that such a fate should have befallen Ellen. "I am not the husband that would have suited her," he said. . . . And then, after a moment's reflection, "I was her instinct; constancy is not everything. It's a pity I cannot love her always, for none is more worthy of being loved."

They became friends; he knew there was no danger of her betraying him again. Her responsibility ended with her money, and he told her how the agitation was progressing.

"Oh, Ned, if I were only sure that your agitation was not directed against religion I would follow you. But you will never believe in me."

"Yes, I believe in you. Come to Dublin with me; come to the meeting. I'd like you to hear my speech."

"I would like to hear you speak, Ned; but I don't think I can go to the meeting."

They were on their way to the station, and they walked some time without speaking. Then, speaking suddenly and gravely as if prompted by some deep instinct, Ellen said:—

"But if you fail, Ned, you will be an outcast in Ireland, and if that happens you will go away, and I shall never see you again."

He turned and stood looking at her. That he should fail and become an outcast were not at all unlikely. Her words seemed to him like a divination! But it is the unexpected that happens, she said to herself, and the train came up to the station, and he bade her good-bye, and settled himself down in a seat to consider his speech for the last time.

"I shall say everything I dare, the moment is ripe: and the threat to hold out is, that Ireland is becoming a Protestant country. And the argument to use is that the Catholics are leaving because there is no joy in Ireland.

He went through the different sections of his speech introducing the word joy: Is Ireland going to become joyous? She has dreamed long enough among dead bones and ancient formulae. The little stations went by and the train rolled into Harcourt Street. He called a car. He was speaking at the Rotunda.

He was speaking on the depopulation question, and he said that his question came before every other question. Ireland was now confronted with the possibility that in five-and-twenty years the last of Ireland would have disappeared in America. There were some who attributed the Irish emigration to economic causes: that was a simple and obvious explanation, one that could be understood by everybody; but these simple and obvious explanations are not often, if they are ever, the true ones. The first part of Ned's speech was taken up with the examination of the economic causes, and proving that these were not the origin of the evil. The country was joyless; man's life is joyless in Ireland. In every other country there were merry-makings. "You have only to go into the National Gallery" he said, "to see how much time the Dutch spent in merry-makings." All their pictures with the exception of Rembrandt's treated of joyful subjects, of peasants dancing under trees, peasants drinking and singing songs in taverns, and caressing servant girls. Some of their merry-makings were not of a very refined character, but the ordinary man is not refined and in the most refined men there is often admiration and desire for common pleasure. In the country districts Irish life is one of stagnant melancholy, the only aspiration that comes into their lives is a religious one. "Of course it will be said that the Irish are too poor to pay for pleasure, but they are not too poor to spend fifteen millions a year upon religion." He was the last man in the world who would say that religion was not necessary, but if he were right in saying that numbers were leaving Ireland because Ireland was joyless he was right in saying that it was the duty of every Irishman to spend his money in making Ireland a joyful country. He was speaking now in the interests of religion. A country is antecedent to religion. To have religion you must first have a country, and if Ireland was not made joyful Ireland would become a Protestant country in about twenty-five years. In support of this contention he produced figures showing the rate at which the Catholics were emigrating. But not only were the Catholics emigrating—those who remained were becoming nuns and priests. As the lay population declined the clerics became more numerous. "Now," he said, "there must be a laity. It is a very commonplace thing to say, but this very commonplace truth is forgotten or ignored, and I come here to plead to-day for the harmless and the necessary laity." He knew that these words would get a laugh, and that the laugh would get him at least two or three minutes grace, and these two or three minutes could not be better employed than with statistics, and he produced some astonishing figures. These figures were compiled, he said, by a prelate bearing an Irish name, but whose object in Ireland was to induce Irish men and Irish women to leave Ireland. This would not be denied, though the pretext on which he wished Irish men and women to leave Ireland would be pleaded as justification. "But of this I shall speak," Ned said, "presently. I want you first to give your attention to the figures which this prelate produced, and with approbation. According to him there were ten convents and one hundred nuns in the beginning of the century, now there were twelve hundred convents and twenty thousand nuns. The prelate thinks that this is a matter for us to congratulate ourselves on. In view of our declining population I cannot agree, and I regret that prelates should make such thoughtless observations. Again I have to remind you of a fact that cannot be denied, but which is ignored, and it is that celibate clergy cannot continue the population, and that if the population be not continued the tail of the race will disappear in

America in about twenty-five years. . . . Not only does this prelate think that we should congratulate ourselves on the fact that while the lay population is decreasing the clerical population is increasing, but he thinks that Ireland should still furnish foreign missions. He came to Ireland to get recruits, to beseech Irishmen and Irishwomen to continue their noble work of the conversion of the world. No doubt the conversion of the world is a noble work. My point now is that Ireland has done her share in this noble work, and that Ireland can no longer spare one single lay Irishman or cleric or any Irishwoman. If the foreign mission is to be recruited it must be recruited at the expense of some other country."

Ned suggested Belgium as the best recruiting ground. But it was the prelate's own business to find recruits, it was only Ned's business to say that Ireland had done enough for the conversion of the world. And this prelate with the Irish name and cosmopolitan heart, who thought it an admirable thing that the clerical population should increase, while the lay population declined; who thought that with the declining population Ireland should still send out priests and nuns to convert the world—was no true Irishman. He cared not a jot what became of his country, so long as Ireland continued to furnish him with priests and nuns for the foreign mission. This prelate was willing to bleed Ireland to death to make a Roman holiday. Ireland did not matter to him, Ireland was a speck—Ned would like to have said, a chicken that the prelate would drop into the caldron which he was boiling for the cosmopolitan restaurant; but this would be an attack upon religion, it would be too direct to be easily understood by the audience, and as the words came to his lips he changed the phrase and said, "a pinch of snuff in the Roman snuff box." After this, Ned passed on to perhaps the most important part of his speech—to the acquisition of wealth by the clergy. He said that if the lay population had declined, and if the clerical population had increased, there was one thing that had increased with the clergy and that was the wealth of the clergy. "I wish the cosmopolitan prelate had spoken upon this subject. I wonder if he inquired how much land has passed into the hands of the clergy in the last twenty years, and how many mortgages the religious hold upon the land. I wonder if he inquired how many poultry farms the nuns and the friars are adding to their convents and their monasteries; and now they are starting new manufactories for weaving—the weaving industry is falling into their hands. And there are no lay teachers in Ireland, now all the teaching is done by clerics. The Church is very rich in Ireland. If Ireland is the poorest country in the world, the Irish Church is richer than any other. All the money in Ireland goes into religion. There is only one other trade that can compete with it. Heaven may be for the laity, but this world is certainly for the clergy."

More money was spent upon religion in Ireland than in any other country. Too much money was spent for the moment in building churches, and the great sums of money that were being spent on religion were not fairly divided. And passing rapidly on Ned very adroitly touched upon the relative positions of the bishops and the priests and the curates. He told harrowing stories of the destitution of the curates, and he managed so well that his audience had not time to stop him. Everything he thought that they could not agree with he sandwiched between things that he knew they would agree with.

Father Murphy stood a little distance on his right, a thick-set man, and as the sentences fell from Ned's lips he could see that Father Murphy was preparing his answer, and he guessed what Father Murphy's answer would be like. He knew Father Murphy to be an adroit speaker, and the priest began in a low key as Ned had expected him to do. He began by deploring the evils of emigration, and Mr. Carmady deserved their best thanks for attracting popular attention to this evil. They were indebted to him for having done this. Others had denounced the evil, but Mr. Carmady's eloquence had enabled him to do so as well, perhaps even better than it had been done before. He complimented Mr. Carmady on the picturesque manner in which he described the emptying of the country, but he could not agree with Mr. Carmady regarding the causes that had brought about this lamentable desire to leave the fatherland. Mr. Carmady's theory was that the emptying of Ireland was due to the fact that the Irish priests had succeeded in inducing men to refrain from the commission of sin. Mr. Carmady did not reproach the priests with having failed; he reproached them with having succeeded. A strange complaint. The cause of the emigration, which we all agreed in deploring, was, according to Mr. Carmady, the desire of a sinless people for sin. A strange accusation. The people, according to Mr. Carmady, were leaving Ireland because they wished to indulge in indecent living. Mr. Carmady did not use these words; the words he used were "The joy of life," but the meaning of the words was well known.

"No race," he said, "had perhaps ever been libelled as the Irish race had been, but of all the libels that had ever been levelled against it, no libel had ever equalled the libel which he had heard uttered to-day, that the Irish wasere leaving Ireland in search of sin.

"They had heard a great deal about the dancing girl, and according to Mr. Carmady it would seem that a nation could save itself by jigging."

"He is speaking very well, from his point of view," said Ned to himself.

Father Murphy was a stout, bald-headed man with small pig-like eyes, and a piece seemed to have been taken from the top of his bony forehead. He was elegantly dressed in broad cloth and he wore a gold chain and he dangled his chain from time to time. He was clearly the well-fed, well-housed cleric who was making, in this world, an excellent living of his advocacy for the next, and Ned wondered how it was that the people did not perceive a discrepancy between Father Murphy's appearance and the theories he propounded. "The idealism of the Irish people," said the priest, "was inveterate," and he settled himself on his short legs and began his peroration.

Ned had begun to feel that he had failed, he began to think of his passage back to America. Father Murphy was followed by a young curate, and the curate began by saying that Mr. Carmady would be able to defend his theories, and that he had no concern with Mr. Carmady's theories, though, indeed, he did not hear Mr. Carmady say anything which was contrary to the doctrine of our "holy religion." Father Murphy had understood Mr. Carmady's speech in quite a different light, and it seemed to the curate that he, Father Murphy, had put a wrong interpretation upon it; at all events he had put one which the curate could not share. Mr. Carmady had ventured, and, he thought, very properly, to call attention to the number of churches that were being built and the number of people who were daily entering the orders. He did not wish to criticise men and women who gave up their lives to God, but Mr. Carmady was quite right when he said that without a laity there could be no country. In Ireland the clergy were apt to forget this simple fact that celibates do not continue the race. Mr. Carmady had quoted from a book written by a priest in which the distinguished author had said he looked forward to the day when Ireland would be one vast monastery, and the curate agreed with Mr. Carmady that no more foolish wish had ever found its way into a book. He agreed with Mr. Carmady that a real vocation is a rare thing. No country had produced many painters or many sculptors or many poets, and a true religious vocation was equally rare. Mr. Carmady had pointed out that although the population had diminished the nuns and priests had increased, and Father Murphy must hold that Ireland must become one vast monastery, and the laity ought to become extinct, or he must agree with Mr. Carmady that there was a point when a too numerous clergy would over-balance the laity.

Altogether an unexpected and plucky little speech, and long before it closed Ned saw that Father Murphy's triumph was not complete. Father Murphy's face told the same tale.

The curate's argument was taken up by other curates, and Ned began to see he had the youth of the country on his side.

He was speaking at the end of the week at another great meeting, and received even better support at this meeting than he had done at the first, and he returned home wondering what his wife was thinking of his success. But what matter? Ireland was waking from her sleep. . . . The agitation was running from parish to parish, it seemed as if the impossible were going to happen, and that the Gael was going to be free.

The curates had grievances, and he applied himself to setting the inferior clergy against their superiors, and as the agitation developed he told the curates that they were no better than ecclesiastical serfs, that although the parish priests dozed in comfortable arm chairs and drank champagne, the curates lived by the wayside and ate and drank very little and did all the work.

One day at Maynooth it was decided that curates had legitimate grievances, and that the people had grievances that were likewise legitimate. And at this great council it was decided that the heavy marriage fees and the baptismal fees demanded by the priests should be reduced. Concessions were accompanied by threats. Even so it required all the power of the Church to put down the agitation. Everyone stood agape, saying the bishops must win in the end. An indiscretion on Ned's part gave them the victory. In a moment of excitement he was unwise enough to quote John Mitchel's words "that the Irish would be free long ago only for their damned souls." A priest wrote to the newspapers pointing out that after these words there could be no further doubt that it was the doctrine of the French Revolution that Mr.

Carmady was trying to force upon a Christian people. A bishop wrote saying that the words quoted were fit words for Anti-Christ. After that it was difficult for a priest to appear on the same platform and the curates whose grievances had been redressed deserted, and the fight became an impossible one.

Very soon, Ned's meetings were interrupted, disagreeable scenes began to happen, and his letters were not admitted to the newspapers. A great solitude formed about him.

"Well," he said one morning, "I suppose you have read the account in the paper of my ignominious escape. That is what they called it."

"The wheel," Ellen said, "is always going round. You may be at the bottom now, but the wheel is going round, only there is no use opposing the people in their traditions, in their instinct. ... And whether the race is destined to disappear or to continue it's certain that the last Gael will die a Catholic."

"And the Red Indian will die with the scalp at his girdle."

"We won't talk about religion, we'll talk about things we are agreed upon. I have heard you say yourself that you would not go back to America again, that you never enjoyed life until you came here."

"That was because I met you, Ellen."

"I have heard you praise Ireland as being the most beautiful and sympathetic country in the world."

"It is true that I love these people, and I wish I could become one of them."

"You would become one of them and yet you would tear them to pieces because they are not what you want them to be."

Sometimes he thought he would like to write "A Western Thibet," but he was more a man of action than of letters. His writings had been so long confined to newspaper articles that he could not see his way from chapter to chapter. He might have overcome the difficulty, but doubt began to poison his mind. "Every race," he said, "has its own special genius. The Germans have or have had music. The French and Italians have or have had painting and sculpture. The English have or have had poetry. The Irish had, and alas! they still have their special genius, religious vocation."

He used to go for long walks on the hills, and one day, lying in the furze amid the rough grass, his eyes following the course of the ships in the bay, he said: "Was it accident or my own fantastic temperament that brought me back from Cuba?"

It seemed as if a net had been thrown over him and he had been drawn along like a fish in a net. "For some purpose," he said, "But for what purpose? I can perceive none, and yet I cannot believe that an accident brought me to Ireland and involved me in the destiny of Ireland for no purpose."

And he did not need to take the book from his pocket, he knew the passage well, and he repeated it word for word while he watched the ships in the bay.

> We were friends and we have become strangers one to the other. Ah, yes; but it is so, and we do not wish to hide our strangerhood, or to dissemble as if we were ashamed of it. We are two ships each with a goal and a way; and our ways may draw together again and we may make holiday as before. And how peacefully the good ships used to lie in the same harbour, under the same sun; it seemed as if they had reached their goal, and it seemed as if there was a goal. But soon the mighty sway of our tasks laid on us as from of old sundered and drove us into different seas and different zones; and it may be that we shall never meet again and it may be that we shall meet and not know each other, so deeply have the different seas and suns changed us. The law that is over us decreed that we must become strangers one to the other; and for this we must reverence each other the more, and for this the memory of our past friendship become more sacred. Perhaps there is a vast invisible curve and orbit and our different goals and ways are parcel of it, infinitesimal segments. Let us uplift ourselves to this thought! But our life is too short and our sight too feeble for us to be friends except in the sense of this sublime possibility. So, let us believe in our stellar friendship though we must be enemies on earth.

"A deep and mysterious truth," he said, "I must go, I must go," he said to himself. "My Irish life is ended. There is a starry orbit and Ireland and I are parts of it, 'and we must believe in our stellar friendship though we are enemies upon earth.'"

He wandered about admiring the large windless evening and the bright bay. Great men had risen up in Ireland and had failed before him, and it were easy to account for their failure by saying they were not close enough to the tradition of their race, that they had just missed it, but some of the fault must be the fault of Ireland. . . . The anecdote varies, but substantially it is always the same story: The interests of Ireland sacrificed to the interests of Rome.

There came a whirring sound, and high overhead he saw three great birds flying through the still air, and he knew them to be wild geese flying south. . . .

War had broken out in South America, Irishmen were going out to fight once again; they were going to fight the stranger abroad when they could fight him at home no longer. The birds died down on the horizon, and there was the sea before him, bright and beautiful, with ships passing into the glimmering dusk, and among the hills a little mist was gathering. He remembered the great pagans who had wandered over these hills before scapulars and rosaries were invented. His thoughts came in flashes, and his happiness grew intense. He had wanted to go and the birds had shown him where he might go. His instinct was to go, he was stifling in Ireland. He might never find the country he desired, but he must get out of Ireland, "a mean ineffectual atmosphere," he said, "of nuns and rosaries."

A mist was rising, and the lovely outlines of Howth reminded him of pagan Ireland; "they're like music," he said, and he thought of Usheen and his harp. "Will Usheen ever come again?" he said. "Better to die than to live here." The mist thickened—he could see Howth no longer. "The land is dolorous," he said, and as if in answer to his words the most dolorous melody he had ever heard came out of the mist. "The wailing of an abandoned race," he said. "This is the soul-sickness from which we are fleeing." And he wandered about calling to the shepherd, and the shepherd answered, but the mist was so thick in the hollows that neither could find the other. After a little while the shepherd began to play his flute again; and Ned listened to it, singing it after him, and he walked home quickly, and the moment he entered the drawingroom he said to Ellen, "Don't speak to me; I am going to write something down," and this is what he wrote:—

## THE WILD GOOSE.

"A mist came on suddenly, and I heard a shepherd playing this folk tune. Listen to it. Isn't it like the people? Isn't it like Ireland? Isn't it like everything that has happened? It is melancholy enough in this room, but no words can describe its melancholy on a flute played by a shepherd in the mist. It is the song of the exile; it is the cry of one driven out in the night—into a night of wind and rain. It is night, and the exile on the edge of the waste. It is like the wind sighing over bog water. It is a prophetic echo and final despair of a people who knew they were done for from the beginning. A mere folk tune, mere nature, raw and unintellectual; and these raw folk tunes are all that we shall have done: and by these, and these alone, shall we be remembered."

"Ned," she said at last, "I think you had better go away. I can see you're wearing out your heart here."

"Why do you think I should go? What put that idea into your head?"

"I can see you are not happy."

"But you said that the wheel would turn, and that what was lowest would come to the top."

"Yes, Ned, but sometimes the wheel is a long time in turning, and maybe it would be better for you to go away for a while."

He told her that he had seen wild geese on the hill.

"And it was from you I heard about the wild geese. You told me the history of Ireland, sitting on a druid stone?"

"You want to go, Ned? And the desire to go is as strong in you as in the wild geese."

"Maybe; but I shall come back, Ellen."

"Do you think you will, Ned? How can you if you go to fight for the Boers?"

"There's nothing for me to do here. I want new life. It was you who said that I should go."

"For five years you have been devoted to Ireland, and now you and Ireland are separated like two ships."

"Yes, like two ships. Ireland is still going Rome-ward, and Rome is not my way."

"You are the ship, Ned, and you came to harbour in Ireland. But you and I are like two ships that have lain side by side in the harbour, and now—"

"And now what, Ellen? Go on!"

"It seemed to me that we were like two ships."

"That is the very thing I was thinking on the hills. The comparison of two ships rose up in my mind on the hill, and then I remembered a passage." And when he had repeated it she said—

"So there is no hope for us on earth. We are but segments of a starry curve, and must be content with our stellar friendship. But, Ned, we shall never be enemies on earth. I am not your enemy, and never shall be. So we have nothing to think of now but our past friendship. The memory of our past—is all that remains? And it was for that you left America after the Cuban war? There is our child. You love the little boy, don't you, Ned?"

"Yes," he said, "I love the little boy. . . . But you'll bring him up a Catholic. You'll bring him up to love the things that I hate."

"Let there be no bitterness between us to-night, Ned dear. Let there be only love. If not love, affection at least. This is our last night."

"How is that?"

"Because, Ned, when one is so bent upon going as you are it is better he should go at once. I give you your freedom. You can go in the morning or when you please. But remember, Ned, that you can come back when you please, that I shall be always glad to see you."

They went upstairs and looked for some time on the child, who was sleeping. Ellen took him out of his bed, and she looked very pretty, Ned thought, holding the half-awakened child, and she kept the little quilt about him so that he might not catch cold.

He put his hands into his eyes and looked at his father, and then hid his face in his mother's neck, for the light blinded him and he wished to go to sleep.

"Let me put him back in his bed," Ned said, and he took his son and put him back, and he kissed him. As he did so he wondered how it was that he could feel so much affection for his son and at the same time desire to leave his home.

"Now, Ned, you must kiss me, and do not think I am angry with you for going. I know you are dull here, that you have got nothing further to do in Ireland, but it will be different when you come back."

"And is it possible that you aren't angry with me, Ellen, for going?"

"I am sorry you are going, Ned—in a way, but I should be more sorry to see you stay here and learn to hate me."

"You are very wise, Ellen. But why did you read that manuscript?"

"I suppose because God wished me to."

One thing Ireland had done for him, and for that he would be always grateful to Ireland—Ireland had revealed a noble woman to him; and distance would bring a closer and more intimate appreciation of her.

He left early next morning before she was awake in order to save her the pain of farewells, and all that day in Dublin he walked about, possessed by the great joyful yearning of the wild goose when it rises one bright morning from the warm marshes, scenting the harsh north through leagues of air, and goes away on steady wing-beats. But he did not feel he was a free soul until the outlines of Howth began to melt into the grey drift of evening. There was a little mist on the water, and he stood watching the waves tossing in the mist thinking that it were well that he had left home—if he had stayed he would have come to accept all the base moral coinage in circulation; and he stood watching the green waves tossing in the mist, at one moment ashamed of what he had done, at the next overjoyed that he had done it.

# George Moore

## *Father Moling and the Immaculate Conception*

The story Alec was cherishing of the saint who came out of the wilderness in search of temptations, like Scothine, but who, unlike Scothine, failed to conquer them, diverted my attention from the trees to Alec's anxious face, and putting together all my knowledge of Alec, gathered, it is true, in a week's intimacy, and adding to it my instinctive comprehension of what is lowly and remote, I concluded, rightly or wrongly, I know not which, but I concluded that outside of his gift of story-telling he differed little if at all from the first peasant that might catch my eye in Westport on market day; and that if I considered him closely I should discover that very little of his gift of story-telling is personal to him—to himself. But can anyone say: This much belongs to me and to no one else? Is not all reflection and derivation? My refusal, however, was firm not to be led into this blind alley, and fixing my thoughts firmly on Alec, striving to see him steadily and to see him whole, as a good mid-Victorian should, I said: His gift of story-telling amuses me because it is new to me, but it is as old as the hills themselves, flowing down the generations since yonder hills were piled up. Sheep paths worn among the hills. His grandfather or granduncle, whichever the Dublin scholar was, trimmed these paths a little. Sheep paths, nothing else. Alec is a creature of circumstance, and like myself can be accounted for. He tells stories against the priests and nuns of the twelfth century, for these are not far removed, in his knowledge and imagination, from druids and druidesses. It was only a few centuries before the twelfth that the druids began to discard the oak leaves for the biretta; but in the thirteenth and fourteenth centuries they were full-bellied roman priests; by that time the word had become flesh; it is just touch and go if he tells me the story he is brooding over or refrains from telling it. I can do nothing.

On this thought I raised my eyes for another look at him, and as I did so Alec said: Mind he must have been one of the greatest saints that ever fell out in Ireland, for it was the great deed he did, saving a soul from the devil himself. I told your honour, as I should have done, that it was at the end of his life; he came out of the wilderness, where he had been along with the hermits since he was a bit of a gossoon living on cress and gulls' eggs. It was after twenty years of the tough eating that he came to rest his bones in the convent that you saw this day. A man between fifty and sixty, yet the diet did not seem to have taken a feather out of him, for his hair was as black as you like, and it hung down on his shoulders in fine curls, and the pair of eyes in his head were as shiny as a young cat's. A spare, wiry little man that no one would believe to be so old. But it was just as I'm telling you. He came out of the wilderness between fifty-five and sixty to hear the confessions of nuns by the lake beyond; he came down from the crags above Old Head. You know Old Head, your honour. Mr. Tuttledge goes there every summer with the children to swim. It was there Moling had been living many a year the way I told you. A queer place it is too, and he thought that his rest was well-earned anyhow. But there was no rest for him in this world, poor man, from the day he waved his hat at the crags above Old Head, and came down at the trot to Loch Conn to confess the nuns of Cuthmore. And then didn't the bad luck start up in the most unlikely place, in the mind of Sister Ligach, as pious a one as ever wore out a pair of knees on the top of this earth. I've come, Father, she said, dropping down on the same bones, I've come with a great sin stuck in my conscience; but I've faith in the sacrament to relieve me. Well you might, said Moling, for you are the one got well instructed. On these words, he settled his stole and cocked his ear, and wasn't it a relief to him to learn that the only thing that was wrong with her was this, that she wasn't able to pray to the saints to put in a word for herself and the sisters in the convent. A light sin, surely, but being a priest he had to blame her, and tell her she'd be better off remembering the saints that stand by us when the word of death is in our throats, singing and praying round the throne of God to spare them that do be passing away from the world, or if that cannot be owing to mortal sin, getting their share of purgatory a bit easy.

After saying all this he thought he had done with her and that she would get up from her knees, but there wasn't a move out of her. My child, said he, what are you waiting for? Well, Father, said herself, what good would it be for me to be leaving you and I not making a clean breast of it? I confessed that I can't pray to the saints any longer, but I've worse than that in my head. Well the priest puckered up his lips and a thoughtful look came into his eyes. No more than to the saints am I able to pray to the holy virgin to succour us. Are you telling me that you can't pray to the holy virgin, the mother of the blessed God! said the priest, and he in fright. Not to herself who bore the son of God in her womb? It is like that, Father, indeed. The priest next to jumped out of his skin at that, and the chair he'd been sitting on fell behind him. Pick up your chair, Father, and hear me out, said Ligach, or you'll be sorry afterwards. I can pray to no one but to Jesus himself, said she. To no better could you nor anyone else be praying, said the priest; but don't forget that there is no one could put in a word better or quicker for you and for us all than his own mother. Tell me, my child, who would he be likely to be listening to more than to his own mother? To which Ligach replied: The truth indeed, Father, but I've no thought for anybody but himself, and there's no use giving a prayer when your thoughts aren't in it. I wouldn't say so far as that, said the priest, for by saying the prayers themselves the sinner brings himself under the rule of the Church, and the frozen waters of his heart will loosen and burst. It is as you say, Father, but you haven't heard all yet. I can't say a prayer at Mass; my thoughts aren't on the Mass that you're saying, but out in the garden.

At the words "out in the garden" Moling's brow blackened, and maybe it was the quiet drawl of the girl got him on the raw as much as anything else. Is it that your thoughts are out gallivanting in the garden when I'm calling down God into the bread and wine? But, Father, isn't it much of a much? Isn't it the same thing? Jesus gave us the sacrament, and if I'm thinking of him I'm thinking of what is going on at the altar too. It is of the upper chamber in which he ordered the sacrament, cried the priest, that you should be thinking; and it would be better still if your thoughts were on the miracle and me at it. My child, I'm afraid I don't understand you. I haven't got the rights of it yet. Well, it's like this, Father; all the time you're saying your Mass I'm thinking of Jesus on the cross, and he suffering great torments for me. A very good thought that is, Moling answered; a holy thought indeed; but you ought to be thinking too that it was himself ordered the apostles to celebrate Mass when he was gone. I believe all that, said Ligach, but it's the way that his suffering on the cross puts every other thing out of my head, for am I not his bride whom he will take in his arms? That's true for you, said the priest, but you mustn't be thinking too much of your meeting with him in heaven. It is well enough for you, Father, to say that, but 'tis of our meeting in heaven I'm thinking all the time, and there's nothing will ever get that thought out of my mind.

All the same I won't be refusing you absolution, said he. But, Father, will you be hearing me out first, for I've not told you the lot of it yet? A great part of my prayers to Jesus is that he will be giving me a sign, a nod of the head or the like. Faith, said the priest, I do not come to this place to listen to nonsense and rameis. Say your prayers and obey the rule, and let me be hearing the rest of the parish. How many more are there waiting to come in to me? Three of us, Father. And now, Ligach, if you want my absolution, bend your head; for you see, your honour, Moling was a hot-tempered man, and Ligach one of those that would work up a passion in the greatest saint in heaven. All the same, said she, I'd be glad of a sign. But what would the like of you be wanting a sign for? Haven't you heard that humility is the top of the virtues? Be off with you. But Ligach wasn't to be outdone. I'm afraid, Father, without a sign— Without a sign of what? snapped out Moling. The day may come, Ligach continued, when I shall not feel as sure as I do now that he suffered all those torments for me. I want to believe always and to be sure of it, never thinking of anything but my belief in the son of God our redeemer. You're wanting a lot and plenty, said the priest— to live on earth as we shall live hereafter in heaven. But it's not a bit too much, surely, when we remember the death he died, which I can never let out of my thoughts. You're a good little nun, said the priest; I used to be like that myself in the years back. You'll give me absolution, Father? Faith, I will, said the priest, startled, for he'd been away.

Other penitents were waiting; he shrove them all without giving much of his mind to their sins, for he was thinking of Ligach all the time, and on leaving the chapel who did he meet but Ligach and the Mother Abbess coming in from the garden, Ligach dripping like a spaniel that had been in the river. Father, cried Mother Abbess, I'll ask you to refuse her absolution if she doesn't give in and be biddable. Look at the way she is in, and you wouldn't guess where I found her in three guesses—in front of the cross kneeling down in a pool of water. See the way she's in—out there in the teeming rain, catching her death of cold. Go and change your clothes at once, my child, and remember that the first duty of a nun is to give in to her superiors. To back up the Mother Abbess, Moling said he never remembered so severe a winter, and when Ligach came to confess to him he wasn't a bit surprised to hear a bad cough. The cough was followed up by another, and before she could confess one of her sins, she was taken with such a fit of coughing and sneezing that Moling said: My child, that's the bad cold you've got, and a cough on the top of it. Yes, I suppose I got it in the garden, for it's been wet enough there lately. But didn't I hear the Mother Abbess tell you that you weren't to go there? You did, Father. But it was for a sign I was praying, and if I do not get one I may fall into a worse sin than that of disobedience. Now what sign are you wanting? asked Moling. A sign that he is waiting for me in heaven. You've got a bad cold, a very bad one, the priest repeated. Faith, I have, but a cold is a small matter compared to what he suffered on the cross. 'Tis true for you, said Moling, but a cold may put an end to you just as well as a thrust of a spear. You wouldn't be comparing myself to himself, would you? said the nun. Of course not, the priest snapped out, and began to speak hard and stiff about her folly in wanting God to grant her special favours. You're sinning in the sight of God, said he, by endangering your life in the way you're doing. Be off with you now; and Ligach just bowed her head, and her cough was so bad as she left the chapel that the priest would have taken his words back if he could, and not being able to do that, he rang the parlour bell as soon as he had had dinner and asked for herself.

Now, said he to herself, Ligach has as bad a cough as I've ever heard in my born days, and the Mother Abbess answered: True for you, Father; it keeps us all awake at night. We can hear her all over the convent barking, and now there are three other sisters and the lot almost as bad as Ligach, and there will be more laid up, for be it wet or cold, they're all kneeling round the cross catching their full of cramps. Well, I was like that myself once; and Moling began to tell of the years he spent among the gulls on the crags above Old Head, and the twenty-three years in the woods living on water-grass. For thirty years I didn't sleep under a roof, but as the years go by we begin to weary of the things that we hung on to in our youth. But our lives are in God's hand; we belong to God, who has given life into our keeping, and expects us to look after it. I'm altogether of the same idea as yourself, the Mother Abbess replied, but it will be no change while that same cross is left in the garden. A better place for it, said the priest, would be in the chapel. Now you've said it, Father, and as soon as we can get a little help we will have the cross—Put up in one of the side chapels, the priest interjected. I'll show you the place.

And it was a fortnight after the shifting of the cross that Sister Ligach crawled out of her cell more dead than alive; the others were well before her. And what did she do? Out with her into the garden to kneel down in front of the cross that had nearly cost her her life, and finding it gone out of the garden, she cried: How are we to keep our thoughts from wandering from him who died for our sins and waits for us in heaven? Do we know that he got the best of health always when he lived on this earth? Not a word in the scripture; not a word. And such was her canter till Mother Abbess had to say: Now, Ligach, obedience is the first rule in a convent. But, Mother, think what he suffered for me and I not allowed into the garden for his sake. Well, that is my rule, said herself, but to make matters lighter for Ligach, she gave the young nun permission to rise out of her bed at eleven o'clock and go into the chapel and do an hour's devotion before the nuns rose out of the beds for matins. At which indulgence the tears came into Ligach's eyes, and she said: May the Lord have mercy upon you for that. It is all I can give you, the Abbess answered; make the best of it, Ligach. Faith and troth I will, and you won't be left out of the prayers, Mother Abbess. And every night Ligach was on her knees before the cross praying for a sign. But not the sign of a sign nor the ghost of a sign came near her, and when she next went to confession, she said: No sign has come to me, Father, and the temptation is always pushing me from behind. What temptation is that one, my child? the priest asked. The devil himself and not one of his bailiffs either, telling me always that if I can't get a sign from Jesus, I must be getting one from himself, which would do me as well. My child, my child, do you know what you're saying? I do indeed, she answered, and I cannot help myself much longer. Every time the thought comes into my head I shake it and say: Hail Mary, but it doesn't help me at all. If I were you I'd give myself a pinch in some soft spot, said the priest, or a pin I'd stick into me when the temptation came around; here's one for Satan, you will be saying, as the pin goes into your thigh or your bosom; and if you aren't hurt enough push the pin into the sorest place you can find, under one of your nails, and if that doesn't stop the black fellow I'll have to put on my considering cap and think it out, but do what I tell you first.

It must be the devil, he said, as he walked home thinking what he could do to save her soul; and if, said he, his thoughts taking a sudden turn, I were a bit of a carpenter I might make something with a pulley that would let the head nod at her when she's on her knees asking for a sign; a nod of the head is all that's wanted to save her soul. Bad luck to it, for I am an unhandy man, said the saint—for he was a saint, or a sort of a saint, your honour, though a sinner into the bargain. I'm no good at carpentering; there isn't one in the town of Westport that could learn me in a year what the little boy playing among the shavings knows already. So I needn't be getting a pain in my head thinking about pulleys and the like. I'll get another thought soon, and a better one. Nor was he long waiting for a second thought; in five minutes, neither more nor less, he had it, and it frightening the life out of him—the queerest thought that ever came into a man's head, one that left him without a prayer to throw at the devil. Let me at all events be pulling myself into a shape of prayer, he said, and if the thought isn't driven off while I'm down on the knees, I'll know for certain it was sent to me by the Lord Jesus—for what he was thinking was that he had just the figure for the deed. It is as like as not, he thought, his hair was as black as mine, he being from the country of the Jews, but they always paint him with fair hair. But maybe she'll be too deep in her prayers to take much notice of the colour of my hair, if any colour be showing. As soon as she lifts her eyes to me I'll give a nod of the head to her from above and she'll get enough faith out of that nod to last her till she's called up before the throne of God. But if she comes kissing my feet and begging me to come down to her it will be the great temptation I shall be overcoming, getting thereby a higher place in paradise than them gone before me; and for a chance like this one it was well worth my while to have come out of the wilderness.

The priest's thoughts broke off suddenly, and after one or two more turns up and down his garden he went back to the house with the fear on him that Jesus might not be wishing his cross interfered with. How do I know that it isn't Satan is tempting me? he asked, and going to the holy-water stoop he splashed nearly all the water in it about him. But aren't I the fool? said he; for why should the devil be prompting me to save a soul and he wanting as many as he can get hold of? It is God himself is putting this thought into my head, relying on me to outdo the devil, who has a mighty big wish on him at present to get Sister Ligach's soul, one of the beautifullest that ever looked out of a human face. A great prize she'd be to him, surely. The face of a saint if there be one walking about on two legs in holy Ireland. But if I lose my soul in the saving of hers! cried Moling. But it is the old boy himself that is putting that fear into my head, for who ever lost his soul while at the work of robbing the devil of a soul he set his heart on? I'll lead her out of the chapel quietly, and bid her tell no one. Risks there are, he said a few minutes after, in every hour of life, but a holier one than mine, which is to rob the devil, I don't know of. Nor can anybody tell me it won't be Jesus himself that will be thanking me for the robbing on the day of judgment.... But I'm bet after all—how will I fix myself up on the cross? The image is nailed there—nails in the hands and the feet, but my feet aren't made of wood, and must have a support; and for my hands I must have two rings of rope, and Moling, not being much of a handy man, as I've said, spent many hours more than another would have done making them rings.

At last they were twisted and hidden away in the chapel, where he was himself at half-past ten, removing our Lord from his cross and fixing himself up in his place, which he had just time to do before Ligach came in to her devotions; and he might have dropped down from the cross so great was his fear that she might see the loincloth was missing from his body, for he'd forgotten it in his hurry, and, says he to himself, if Ligach wasn't innocent of the difference in the make of a man and a woman, I'd be fairly caught. But he was safe enough, Ligach having no thought but for him that is in heaven. Christ with me, Christ before me, Christ behind me, Christ in me, Christ beneath me, Christ above me, Christ on my right, Christ on my left, Christ when I lie down, Christ when I sit down, Christ when I arise. Thou'lt not deny me a sign, said she, lifting her eyes to the cross; it will increase my faith in thee till thou shalt be in him that sees me, in him that I see, in him that speaks to me, in him that I am speaking to, in him that I hear and in him that hears me. And seeing and hearing naught but thee, so would I live and die aloof from all else, from the world. Dear God, I would be unto thee on earth as I shall be in heaven. A sign, a sign of thy love of me. A sign that will save me from the temptation of thinking that the devil would answer me if I were to pray to him.

On hearing them terrible words the priest took such a fright that he slipped his hands out of the ropes and came down to her, sure and certain that he'd be able to quiet her. But while he was telling her of the great meeting it would be for them both up in heaven, she kept saying: Am not I up in heaven now? the sparks flying out of her eyes all the time as you might see them in Jimmy Kilcoin's forge when he pulls at the bellows. Am not I Christ's bride? she kept calling to the poor man, trying his best to get to the holy water; and if he'd got there 'tis a different story I'd be telling, but the senses failed on him, and he no more than a yard off the stoop, and when they came back the nun was beside him in a faint so deadly that he mistook it for her death. It's a poor thing to be tempted like this, surely, says he; but no more than a venial sin can it be, for 'tis the intention that counts. But I must be attending to her, and it took a lot of sprinkling and calling into her ears that she must obey him before her lips opened and she muttered: Thy will be done, Lord. Open your eyes, Ligach, said he; and she opened them, but only to see what she was minded to see, and, led to the door of the chapel, she heard him say: What has fallen out this night must be kept to yourself. One word of it to anybody and the sign that you got tonight will lose its power, and the blessing will be changed into a curse altogether. Return to your cell, Ligach, and close the door behind you.

And no sooner was she out of the chapel than the priest put the image back and made off with himself in the great fright of his life, as well it might be, for by dint of what had passed he didn't seem to know himself rightly at all; his thoughts were all astray, and he couldn't get them together in his poor head. At one moment he was thinking that he had planned the lot from the beginning, and the next that if he hadn't got down off the cross and made her his bride she would have come to her right reason and found out what a trick he was working on her. Her faith would have gone for good and all, he cried out, and instead of saving a soul I'd have well damned one for ever. As soon as she came to kiss my feet, I was bound to come down. But the rest? All right from her side, but maybe my soul is lost. But it is the intention that counts; and all night he was asking Jesus if a sin committed with a good intention could be a sin. The sins of the flesh, he began again, are small ones compared with the sins of the spirit; her sin was of the spirit, mine was of the flesh. The flesh has redeemed the spirit, a thing which doesn't often happen, for it is usually the spirit that redeems the flesh. But in this world things often fall out contrary-like. She won't tell anybody, not even myself, he murmured; she will keep her sin dark; but there was no sin on her side, only on mine, and on mine but a venial sin, if my intention was to save a soul, which it was, and a man should be judged by his intentions, so it is said.

Before long it seemed to the nuns that Moling hurried them up in their confessions; they missed the bits of kindly reproof, and left him wondering, saying: His mind is off; our sins don't seem to matter to him. It's your turn now, Ligach; and seeing a light on her face that made them think of the sun shining on the sea, they said: What's wrong with Ligach this time? Father, she said, dropping on her knees, a sign has been given to me, and a greater one than I hoped for, and, the nun went on: He came down from his cross and took me in his arms. But no sooner were the words across her lips than a great fear and a great fright came over her. Oh, but I've been told not to speak of all this; he put a bond on me, and I've broken the bond. It would have been broken, the priest answered, if you'd spoken to anybody but myself. Every secret is safe with me. Don't you know the seal of the confession has never yet been broken and never will be? But, Father, a bond was put upon me never to reveal what passed between us by himself at the door of the chapel. Am I not the representative of Christ on earth? Moling asked, and when you tell me what happened between you, you're telling it to himself. Haven't I the power to bid him come down from heaven into the bread and wine? Must he not obey? I know that, said Ligach, I know it well. And don't I absolve sins that are committed? 'Tis true for you, said the nun. But it is hard to tell. He came down from his cross, and he took me in his arms, and made me his bride in life as he will afterwards in heaven. 'Tis a great honour he did to you, surely. It is that, she replied, and one that I wouldn't have dared to think of if it hadn't happened to me, but it is just as I told it to your

Reverence, just as I told it, and no way else. But not a word out of you about this, cried the priest. I won't say a word, Father, Ligach replied, for I was told not to. And now, said Moling, I'll be giving you absolution. But would you be giving me absolution for being visited by himself? I forgot that, said the priest, but mind what I'm telling you: Let not a word out of your mouth to anyone of this, or he'll never visit you again. Visit me again? said Ligach; what would he come to me again for? though indeed I'd be glad if he did. The priest did not answer, and she repeated: For what, I'm asking you, Father, would he visit me again? And the priest still not saying a word she kept on at him. For what, I'm asking you? for why should he be treating me different from Mary, who was visited only once so far as the scriptures goes. True, true, said Moling, he will never come to you again. But something will come to me, for it wasn't for nothing he came down from his cross. Time will prove me right. I was forgetting, said the priest. A strange thing to be forgetting, a thing that doesn't happen once in every thousand years, she replied.

What did she say, Moling asked himself, when Ligach rose up from her knees and left the chapel; what did she say about expecting? Will there be a child? he asked. And on his way home he asked himself if he came down from the cross because he was afraid that if Ligach did not get the sign she had been praying for so long her belief might fade. Did she not tell him that the temptation was pressing her from behind that if she addressed herself to the devil she'd get an answer? O Lord, have mercy upon me, he muttered, and he knew that all the colour was out of his face, and that his hand was trembling. I'm bet and bothered with it all, said he. If I've sinned, forgive me, Lord. But who is to tell me if I be in mortal sin or venial sin? Not a bishop in Ireland could tell me that, nor the Pope of Rome himself, for what happened last night never happened to anybody in this world before. He walked on a bit and then stopped again. I'm the most miserable man in all the world, and will not be able to pull through this business. He went on walking ahead, mile after mile, without a prayer in his heart and his thoughts tormenting him, buzzing in his poor mind like flies, stinging him, stopping him in his walk, making him drop his knife and fork out of his hand when he was at his dinner, leaving him staring across the room, thinking of the good days he spent with the hermits living on water-grass, and the better ones when he was on his own picking seagulls' eggs from out of the rocks. Them were fine days, he said, and I had the good health then, but it is all going now, though I'll not be what you would call an old, ancient man for a good while yet. It is the fear that I am in mortal sin is destroying me and wasting my bones. And then he would stop to ask himself what she meant when she said that something would happen to her. Was it a child? Of course it was that same, and he hadn't much longer to wait for the news from herself in the convent. Father, I think I'm with child. Women that live in chastity are often troubled with fancies, and to speak of such a thing and it not the truth might— How could it be else, said Ligach, he after coming down from his cross to me? All the same keep it to yourself till the child leaps in your womb, if 'tis there he is, he said to her, and to himself: The news will soon be out; the nuns will soon know all about it. Highly favoured, they will say, is our convent. And, Ligach, now will you be telling the others that I can hear no more confessions to-day. Oh, my Lord Jesus Christ, cried Moling, as soon as the nun closed the door behind her, the torture is in the waiting! And from that day out he'd be saying: Another day has gone by and I'm one day nearer to the day when the Mother Abbess will come with her nuns, Ligach in the middle of them, to tell me about the great miracle: Ligach in the family way though she has never known a man.

The weeks went by and he counting them till the week came when he said to himself: She must be seven months gone, yet the nuns haven't come to me, though her appearance is great. As these very words were passing through his mind the parlour door opened and in came the Mother Abbess, surrounded by her nuns, with Ligach in the middle of them. Father, said the Mother Abbess, we have come to tell you something you will find it hard to believe, yet it is true. It's a miracle, surely, said Moling, after he had heard the Mother Abbess, and at these words the nuns were so overjoyed that they linked their hands and danced round Ligach for all the world like a lot of children. It is not for me, said Moling, as soon as a little quiet had been gotten, to discourage your faith in the miracles that God grants to us sometimes so that we should not altogether forget him, but I call upon you to be mindful that you all keep this a secret among yourselves, for if the miracle you speak of should not prove to be as great a miracle as you think it is, we shall be—But, Father, they began, it is either a great miracle or it's no miracle at all, and you're the last man that should say a word against Ligach. I am indeed, said Moling, the very last in the world; her sweet face tells that she knew no kind of man any more than the virgin herself did till the birth of our Lord. But in this world it's not so easy to find believers; there are always gabby tongues, and this neighbourhood is not freer from them than another. But who, Mother Abbess asked the priest, would say a word against our little Ligach, whose conception is as miraculous as Mary's? and the priest, without a word in his chops, stood looking at the nun. Her conception is certainly a great mystery, he said at last, and until we learn more about it my advice to you all is to keep this secret from everybody. But, said the Mother Abbess, what do you mean, Father Moling, when you say till we know more about it? Well, this is what I mean, said he, that the boy himself will be proof enough of his miraculous birth when he grows up. Let us hope so. But we don't know, said Mother Abbess, whether it will be a girl or a boy. A boy, a boy, cried the nuns, clapping their hands, and they began to argue that it could not be else than a boy, for that no woman had ever borne a girl miraculously. Oh, said the priest, I'm afraid we're travelling on a road that will carry us into a fine heresy; but after thinking a while he saw he was mistaken, for St. Anne herself wasn't conceived miraculously, only without sin. There will be a child for sure, but, as I've told you already, until we learn more about it, I'd be advising you to speak to none about the miracle that God has been pleased to work for us. The Mother Abbess was of the priest's way of thinking, and having gotten a promise from them all in the name of Jesus, Mary and Joseph, the priest said to himself: Well, God knows how all this will turn out, and we must leave it to him.

At times he was tempted to hope that she might die, for only her death and the death of his child could stop the scandal; but he was a saint as well as a sinner, and every time the thought came he shook his head, for he knew it was the devil that sent it, and he kept the holy water going about him all the time. His real torment was that, thinking over the reason for his sin, he didn't know if he was guilty of a mortal sin or venial sin, or of no sin at all. Be this as it may, he often said: I'm doing a good share of my purgatory on the earth, and these were the words he was speaking to himself the day the Mother Abbess came into him with the joyful tidings that Ligach had been delivered of a fine boy, and with no more than two hours' trouble before he came: no more than a little uneasiness. Didn't we tell you, cried the nuns, that Ligach would bear a boy and not a girl? and the priest, not knowing what to say to all this, asked if the child was a weakling; and, a bit surprised that he should ask that, the Mother Abbess answered: There's nothing weak about him barring that he has a strong weakness for the breast, even if it was a virgin bore him into the world. Is a virgin's child different? he asked, not knowing very much what he was saying, and the two of them fell to talking of the christening, which was to be at the end of the week, the priest thinking his mind would be easier when it was over. But from this hour out he never got an easy minute, and he put in a week before the christening thinking of his sermon, which would all be about miracles and mysteries. Said he: I mustn't say a word against one or t'other, for the sisters are right in this, that to say her case was not miraculous is much the same as taking away her character and she a nun enclosed in the Convent of Cuthmore. And he began to think of the men they'd suspect if the miracle were denied, but he could think only of the gardener and the gardener's boy. No one, he muttered, would believe that Ligach—the Nuns won't be cheated out of their miracle, and the best I can do is to persuade them to let the child be put out to nurse. We can say it was found by the convent door; left there by someone that didn't want it. A moment after, he remembered a woman down the road who had lost her child: She would be glad to rear it for us, if Ligach—But will she consent to be separated from her child? And the nuns give in to part with it? Not a chance of it, poor childless women, and they are looking forward to this child, and not one of them but is already a mother in her heart; the most I'll be able to do will be to get them to promise to keep the secret of Ligach's miraculous conception to themselves till the boy begins to show what sort of a man he'll be stretching into; and mind you, he kept on telling them, for though the way she got him is a miracle we don't know for sure and certain who he was got by. But, Father, would you have us think that Satan had a finger in it? cried Mother Abbess, and the nuns dropped their hands and eyes. I'm the last man in the world who'd be putting a sore thought into your minds, said Moling. I'm all for taking things easy, saying nothing about the miracle and letting him grow up naturally without any cramming up of Latin and Greek. But, Father, he must get the education.

The priest heaved a big sigh, for he knew well there was to be no rest for him on this earth, and hardly was the boy four years of age before he could read his native Irish tongue, and when he was seven or eight he could con the Latin and Greek; and between ten and eleven he was running down to his father's house taking out the books into the garden, reading and learning and refusing to be a shepherd or a carpenter or a blacksmith. Not one of the decent trades that Moling offered him could he be got to take up. It was only books that he had a thought for, and it was great delight to the nuns when he began to read the scriptures to them, and he only fourteen years of age. After this proof of his learning there was no holding the good sisters, and nothing the priest could say could stop their blabbing tongues. One and all of them went about telling how the boy had given out the scriptures to them in the Greek and the Latin, asking if that wasn't sign enough that a great prophet he would be in time to come: One who would hunt the heretics out of Ireland? Prophet! said the priest, who was now at his wit's end to quiet them. And what would there be wonderful in that? said the Mother Abbess. Only this, said the priest, if Ligach conceived miraculously it would not be a prophet that she'd bring into the world but a Messiah; and no sooner were the words out of him than he saw he had made a mistake, for, as the Mother Abbess put it to him and to the nuns, by means of the Holy Ghost God begot a son that was neither greater nor lesser than himself, and full equal to the Ghost. But we're not asked, said she, to give in that the Son, with or without the help of the Ghost, can beget himself a son? Sure, being God, the priest answered, he could do anything. That is so, said the nun, but this is the vexation: have we got to believe that our little Martin is God's grandson? If we believe him to be a grandson aren't we upsetting the Trinity, a thing that no person here would have hand or part in? Bothered and badgered we are, thinking out the same question, and I'd like to know if the doctrine, as I'm giving it to you, will hold good at the Court of Rome.

Well, now, said the priest, I'll think that over, for it's a tough point indeed, and one that won't be untied in a month of days, with the parishioners dropping in, to say nothing of yourselves banging away at my door on one business or another. A knotty point which a man must give the whole of his head to.

And where, would you tell me, can a man give his mind to a deep matter like the Trinity, unless it's in the wilderness that I came out of years ago, and where I am going back to think the whole thing out? If I make any head on it I'll come back with the news. But the nuns were very fond of Father Moling, and at that they started in to weep and wail and cry aloud, a fair keening it was; all ochon ceo go deo, and woeful is the day, very distressful to the priest, who, to quiet them, reminded them of the forty days Jesus spent in the desert. We'll pray that God will not keep you waiting, cried the nuns. And I'll make a prayer too, he said, that will be the dead image of the one you're making, and now my blessing be upon you all, and on our little Martin, whom I give into your charge, and if you don't see my face again—We will, we will, they all cried, for be the word, and the Mother Abbess took a grip and a swing out of his cassock, but he hauled it off her with a rip in it maybe, and their eyes rested on him for the last time as he stood for a moment at the edge of the wood with his bundle on his shoulder, and he waving a farewell sign to them.

May God speed him, cried the Mother Abbess, on his way, and help him to untie the knot, for it's a knot of the knots, and I'm dead sure that he is too old to stand the hardships of the wilderness, with them joints and them bones. May God send him back safe to us, said another nun. I'm thinking now, said the Mother Abbess—And the nuns cried out to know what she was thinking. What will we be doing ourselves without a priest and he gone? Without confessions, without Mass we will be lost entirely. True for you, said a nun, and the others added: We never thought of that Mother. We'll have to write to the Bishop, and tell him of the loss of our pastor, who has gone into the wilderness to think out a hard bit of doctrine, one so knotty, said the Mother abbess in her letter, that he may be away for long enough. Se we should be glad of a temporary priest if it would be convenient to your lordship to send us one.


The man that goes into the wilderness in his youth returns to it in his old age, and I doubt if they'll ever see him again the Bishop remarked, as he passed the letter on to his clerk. A man of seventy-five hasn't got it in him to spend his nights on the hill-side in draughty huts. But no more than that did he think about it, except, of course, to send them a priest, and when the priest came, Manchin was his name, the first talk was about the disappearance of Moling into the wilderness, and the great and holy man that he was. The last words his lordship spake to me, said he to the nuns, were: The wilderness is no place for a man of his age, and all the nuns cried out that they thought the same. But there was no holding Moling with them for the knot he had to untie—What knot? said Manchin. And bit by bit the story came out, the priest's face getting more and more troubled and queer-looking, till at last the Mother Abbess cried out; I can see by your Reverence's eye that you'll have none of the miracle, and that you think our little Martin is somebody's leavings. I wouldn't be saying that, said the priest, and he had a long talk with Ligach, who gave him the story as well as she could for the water in her eyes, and she guessing that the priest didn't swallow much of her story; and afterwards he wrote to the Bishop saying that a great heresy might arise out of this story that was going the round, and a great many souls be lost in it. The Bishop was fairly put out by the news, and wrote to his brother bishops, and seven or eight of them came, and they went at it.

The news had travelled far and wide; pilgrims were coming all the time, the whole country was talking of the miracle, and nothing else. As the bishops didn't want to disappoint the people there is no knowing what mightn't have happened if, just as the bishops were leaving, their mitres on their heads and their crosiers in their hands, three long-bearded old men hadn't come down out of the wilderness and begun talking. The story they had come to tell was that Father Moling was doing penance for the great sin he had fallen into in the years back with a nun of the name of Ligach, whom he had deceived and had a child by. Enough, enough, cried the bishops; it was God sent you, lest a great heresy should eat the Church the way a wolf eats a lamb. And the nuns and the bishops and all the country went after the Archbishop into the church, which was fuller that day than it ever was before or since.

Well this is the way it was: the Archbishop began to tell them out of the pulpit that it must have been God sent the three hermits with the news of Moling's sin, and that they didn't come a bit too soon either, for they, the bishops, were about to give it up as a bad job without coming to any judgment, none of them liking to say a word for or a thing against the story of such an out-of-the-way miracle as a miraculous conception, though there wasn't a man jack of them but agreed that such a thing was less likely than one of the little miracles the Church is always willing to accept, such as the curing of palsy with a touch, the giving back of sight and hearing with a spit, the setting of one that has not been able to go about without crutches for years on his feet again; for not like any of these little miracles are the greater miracles, such as the lifting of a dead man alive out of his tomb, or a woman that has never known a man bearing a child; these great miracles were done once in the Eastern world for the saving of the world. So it isn't likely that God would let his greater miracles happen again: for if a woman bore a child all by herself, or if a corpse lifted himself out of the tomb alive, the great truth of the Church would not be the plain pikestaff that it is to everyone that cares to open one of his two eyes. You may be sure and certain, my brethren, you may give in to it once for all, that no woman will get a child that way again, and whosoever says she has done it is just trying to disturb people in their faith. It is with sorrow that I give it out, but Father Moling was guilty of the crime; but let it be remembered always that he was punished for his sin year in year out, day after day, minute by minute, expecting all the time, and sure and certain of it, that something would happen to drag the secret out of him, till at last he could bear the torment no longer, and took himself off to the wilderness to pray for forgiveness.

The people were reminded by the Bishop that God had forgiven Moling, and that they were bound to believe this, for Moling had confessed his sin and sent three holy men with tidings of his confession to them, the only thing he could do to make up for his sin. The three holy men will tell you of Moling's repentance as they heard it from the lips of Father Moling himself. They will stand up. Up the hermits, said he, but not a hermit of the hermits moved, and as nobody stirred the people began looking here and there for the men, but they were not in the chapel, and so the Bishop sent out to see if they were in the yard. But they were not in the yard either, and all the news that they could get about them was from a shepherd who had seen them sloping away with themselves into the wood; thinking, the Bishop said, their mission was finished. Which it was indeed. All that was wanted, he went on, was proof that no miraculous conception had fallen out in this parish, and they had that. I would have liked you all to hear the story again from their lips, but it isn't the will of God that you should; for these holy men have gone back to the wilderness they came out of.

The Bishop was a great hand at a sermon, and he said much more than I'm telling your honour, and would have said more than he did if a commotion had not begun in the chapel, Ligach suddenly falling faint or dead, it wasn't certain at first; so white and still was she, that many began saying that the news that her son was a by-blow had finished her. Water was sprinkled on to her face, and she was well rubbed; they got a drop of whisky between her teeth, and as soon as she opened her eyes the Bishop began to take pity on her, and he told the people that she wasn't a bit to blame nor a scrap in the wrong. She had been, he said, a victim, and next door to a martyr, but a victim she was, one of Satan's many victims, for the devil never flinched from doing a big wrong if he could only get his own way, which, in this case, was the soul of a man who, until he gave in to temptation, had been a good man and a very good man; one who had left the wilderness because the health failed on him, who had sinned, but we must not judge a man by a single case, but by his whole life; Moling had sinned, not a doubt of that, but he had gone back to the wilderness to repent, he had not hummed nor hawed about it, old man though he was, and the Bishop churned on till Ligach had another faint.

This time her son carried her to the door of the church, putting back all the people who would help him, saying to them: Let none lay a finger on my mother, I am here to care for her and to stick by her. At the chapel door he kissed her and at that she opened her eyes, and they put words in his mouth, and leading her back till they were on the threshold, he stood up to the Bishop in the pulpit, asking his lordship was a story told by three hermits to be believed rather than the story that the nuns of Cuthmore had known to be true for the last fourteen years. If the hermits had the rights of it why have they disappeared like evil spirits? he asked, and the people thought well of that, and the priests were frightened. Let the Bishop call the hermits back. At that the Bishop interrupted Martin, and said that he didn't know a thing about these hermits. Then why, asked Martin, do you believe them before the words of every sister in this convent? Women my mother lived with from her young youth, always known to them to be as pious as any nun of the nuns, often going stricter than the rule of the convent in her wish to please God, putting her life in the danger too. My mother's life is well known, so it is, and you said yourself, my lord, that a man's life ought not to be judged by a single deed. Why then should the whole of my mother's life be struck out as nothing? No one accused your mother of sin: we hold her to be blameless, cried the Bishop from the pulpit. And by that you hold her to be a silly woman who believed a living man got up on the cross and let on to be God himself. My mother has never been known as an omadhaun, and if it was true would not the hermits have stood their ground here and had it out with me? If they went off with themselves it is because they were afraid of my questions! Let them be called back here if they are hermits itself, coming here and dropping their bad egg and skedaddling off with themselves. All the people gave in to the rights of that, saying: True for you, my boy, more power to the gossoon, and who hid the hermits?

The mistake Martin made was speaking of the hermits as if maybe they weren't hermits at all; for that gave the bishops the handle they wanted and they called on the people not to hear another word from the man who accused the clergy of calling the devil to give a hand, which was the way the clergy got the people over to their side, and seeing that he and his mother hadn't a defender in the world, Martin said: I'll go on the track of the hermits and I'll bring Father Moling back with me too, and he'll tell you that the three hermits told a lie. So off he went with himself into the wilderness, and if I were to begin to tell your honour of the adventures he met and the queer things that happened to him we'd be here until the day after to-morrow morning; for Ireland was a wild place in the days gone by, and it was through the wildest parts he had to be trotting his boots in search of the hermits and Moling, looking for them in the forests and glens, along the naked seashores and from lake island to lake island, but sorra sight or light he could get of one of them, for Ireland is too big a place for one man to go visiting the whole of it; and it was with a belly full of disappointment and a grown man that he came again to Loch Conn, the only place in the wide world he had a memory of. His heart was sick and sore, I'm telling you, as he stood in the place you stood in to-day, your honour, and he looking on a few ruined walls. Is it, says he to the goatherd that was passing by at the time, is it that these walls are all that are left of the Convent of Cuthmore? There was a convent here one time, I've heard tell of it, the goatherd answered; but the nuns left it years ago because a nun of them thought she had been put in the straw by the lord himself, but it turned out to be by a robber that came through the chapel while she was praying before the cross. The woman that is buried here was my mother, said Martin to the goatherd, and I have gone Ireland up and down and back and forth for the last seven years of my life, through forests and mountains, trying to come up with the hermits that brought the news that killed her. Bad and real bad the same news must have been, said the goatherd; what kind of news was it at all, and it that deadly? It was the news that Moling, who was the priest in the convent while my mother was carrying, went to the hermits in the wilderness to repent his sin, and confessed to them that he was my father, and they came along afterwards and told the bishops. It's not likely at all, said the goatherd, for who ever heard in the world of a confession being told; if Moling had told that to the hermits they couldn't have told it to the bishops, and you can take it from me that if the nun buried under this stone was your mother indeed, then your father was a robber that done a climb in through a window on a dark night and played his trick! Not a bit of it, said Martin, and a great argument and a great row began between the pair of them, and how it would have turned out I don't know, only that the goatherd had to make off after his goats.

As soon as he got the one hobbled that was setting the others astray, he came back to ask Martin who the this and the that was his father, if it was neither the priest nor the robber, and they must have talked a bit before they separated: but the man my grandfather had the story from, and who got it from his father before him, told my grandfather that Martin believed his soul had come down from a star and went into Ligach's body while she was at her prayers—it's the queer thoughts do be in the heads of them heretics. Heretics, Alec? Heretic he was, sir, surely, though I wouldn't be saying anything about the soul coming down from a star, for can't the power of the devil work up above as well as down below? But he told the goatherd that his mother's name was under his own special care, and that everybody would believe in her virginity, for it was part of the new religion he was going to set up, with himself at the head of it. And the new religion? I asked. It is said that Martin went off to Germany, Alec answered, and that he got married to an escaped nun, for you couldn't set up a new religion or do any of them tricks in Ireland. Are you telling me, Alec, that he married Catherine Bora? That might be her name indeed, for the religion itself was no better than a whore. You don't mean that Ligach's son was Martin Luther? Faith, I wouldn't be saying anything or too much, and we standing at the edge of her grave, still and all the German Martin might easy have been one of the sons of our Martin, but here's the grave beside us, and you have the story as well as I can give it to you.

# W. B. Yeats

## The Heart of the Spring

A very old man, whose face was almost as fleshless as the foot of a bird, sat meditating upon the rocky shore of the flat and hazel-covered isle which fills the widest part of Lough Gill. A russet-faced boy of seventeen years sat by his side, watching the swallows dipping for flies in the still water. The old man was dressed in threadbare blue velvet and the boy wore a frieze coat and had a rosary about his neck. Behind the two, and half hidden by trees, was a little monastery. It had been burned down a long while before by sacrilegious men of the Queen's party, but had been roofed anew with rushes by the boy, that the old man might find shelter in his last days. He had not set his spade, however, into the garden about it, and the lilies and the roses of the monks had spread out until their confused luxuriance met and mingled with the narrowing circle of the fern. Beyond the lilies and the roses the ferns were so deep that a child walking among them would be hidden from sight, even though he stood upon his toes; and beyond the fern rose many hazels and small oak-trees.

"Master," said the boy, "this long fasting, and the labour of beckoning after nightfall to the beings who dwell in the waters and among the hazels and oak-trees, is too much for your strength. Rest from all this labour for a little, for your hand this day seemed more heavy upon my shoulder and your feet less steady than I have known them. Men say that you are older than the eagles, and yet you will not seek the rest that belongs to age." He spoke eagerly, as though his heart were in the words; and the old man answered slowly and deliberately, as though his heart were in distant days and events.

"I will tell you why I have not been able to rest," he said. "It is right that you should know, for you have served me faithfully these five years, and even with affection, taking away thereby a little of the doom of loneliness which always falls upon the wise. Now, too, that the end of the labour and the triumph of my hopes is at hand, it is more needful for you to have this knowledge."

"Master, do not think that I would question you. It is my life to keep the fire alight, and the thatch close that the rain may not come in, and strong, that the wind may not blow it among the trees; and to take down the heavy books from the shelves, and to possess an incurious and reverent heart. God has made out of His abundance a separate wisdom for everything which lives, and to do these things is my wisdom."

"You are afraid," said the old man, and his eyes shone with a momentary anger.

"Sometimes at night," said the boy, "when you are reading, with a stick of mountain ash in your hand, I look out of the door and see, now a great grey man driving swine among the hazels, and now many little people in red caps who come out of the lake driving little white cows before them. I do not fear these little people so much as the grey man; for, when they come near the house, they milk the cows, and they drink the frothing milk, and begin to dance; and I know there is good in the heart that loves dancing; but I fear them for all that. And I fear the tall white-armed ladies who come out of the air, and move slowly hither and thither, crowning themselves with the roses or with the lilies, and shaking about them their living hair, which moves, for so I have heard them tell the little people, with the motion of their thoughts, now spreading out and now gathering close to their heads. They have mild, beautiful faces, but I am afraid of the Sidhe, and afraid of the art which draws them about us."

"Why," said the old man, "do you fear the ancient gods who made the spears of your father's fathers to be stout in battle, and the little people who came at night from the depth of the lakes and sang among the crickets upon their hearths? And in our evil day they still watch over the loveliness of the earth. But I must tell you why I have fasted and laboured when others would sink into the sleep of age, for without your help once more I shall have fasted and laboured to no good end. When you have done for me this last thing, you may go and build your cottage and till your fields, and take some girl to wife, and forget the ancient gods, for I shall leave behind me in this little house money to make strong the roof-tree of your cottage and to keep cellar and larder full. I have sought through all my life to find the secret of life. I was not happy in my youth, for I knew that it would pass; and I was not happy in my manhood, for I knew that age was coming; and so I gave myself, in youth and manhood and age, to the search for the Great Secret. I longed for a life whose abundance would fill centuries, I scorned the life of fourscore winters. I would be—no, I *will* be!—like the ancient gods of the land. I read in my youth, in a Hebrew manuscript I found in a Spanish monastery, that there is a moment after the Sun has entered the Ram and before he has passed the Lion, which trembles with the Song of the Immortal Powers, and that whosoever finds this moment and listens to the Song shall become like the Immortal Powers themselves; I came back to Ireland and asked the faery men, and the cow-doctors, if they knew when this moment was; but though all had heard of it, there was none could find the moment upon the hour-glass. So I gave myself to magic, and spent my life in fasting and in labour that I might bring the gods and the Men of Faery to my side; and now at last one of the Men of Faery has told me that the moment is at hand. One, who wore a red cap and whose lips were white with the froth of the new milk, whispered it into my ear. To-morrow, a little before the close of the first hour after dawn, I shall find the moment, and then I will go away to a southern land and build myself a palace of white marble amid orange-trees, and gather the brave and the beautiful about me, and enter into the eternal kingdom of my youth. But, that I may hear the whole Song, I was told by the little fellow with the froth of the new milk on his lips that you must bring great masses of green boughs and pile them about the door and the window of my room; and you must put fresh green rushes upon the floor, and cover the table and the rushes with the roses and the lilies of the monks. You must do this to-night, and in the morning at the end of the first hour after dawn, you must come and find me."

"Will you be quite young then? said the boy.

"I will be as young then as you are, but now I am still old and tired, and you must help me to my chair and to my books."

When the boy had left the wizard in his room, and had lighted the lamp which, by some contrivance, gave forth a sweet odour as of strange flowers, he went into the wood and began cutting green boughs from the hazels, and great bundles of rushes from the western border of the isle, where the small rocks gave place to gently sloping sand and clay. It was nightfall before he had cut enough for his purpose, and wellnigh midnight before he had carried the last bundle to its place, and gone back for the roses and the lilies. It was one of those warm, beautiful nights when everything seems carved of precious stones. Sleuth Wood away to the south looked as though cut out of green beryl, and the waters that mirrored it shone like pale opal. The roses he was gathering were like glowing rubies, and the lilies had the dull lustre of pearl. Everything had taken upon itself the look of something imperishable, except a glow-worm, whose faint flame burnt on steadily among the shadows, moving slowly hither and thither, the only thing that seemed alive, the only thing that seemed perishable as mortal hope. The boy gathered a great armful of roses and lilies, and thrusting the glow-worm among their pearl and ruby, carried them into the room, where the old man sat in a half slumber. He laid armful after armful upon the floor and above the table, and then, gently closing the door, threw himself upon his bed of rushes, to dream of a peaceful manhood with a desirable wife and laughing children. At dawn he got up, and went down to the edge of the lake, taking the hour-glass with him. He put some bread and wine into the boat, that his master might not lack food at the outset of his journey, and then sat down to wait the close of the first hour after dawn. Gradually the birds began to sing, and when the last grains of sand were falling, everything suddenly seemed to overflow with their music. It was the most beautiful and living moment of the year; one could listen to the spring's heart beating in it. He got up and went to find his master. The green boughs filled the door, and he had to make a way through them. When he entered the room the sunlight was falling in flickering circles on floor and walls and table, and everything was full of soft green shadows. But the old man sat clasping a mass of roses and lilies in his arms, and with his head sunk upon his breast. On the table, at his left hand, was a leather wallet full of gold and silver pieces, as for a journey, and at his right hand was a long staff. The boy touched him and he did not move. He lifted the hands, but they were quite cold, and they fell heavily.

"It were better for him," said the lad, "to have said his prayers and kissed his beads!" He looked at the threadbare blue velvet, and he saw it was covered with the pollen of the flowers, and while he was looking at it a thrush, who had alighted among the boughs that were piled against the window, began to sing.

# W. B. Yeats

## *Red Hanrahan*

Hanrahan, the hedge schoolmaster, a tall, strong, red-haired young man, came into the barn where some of the men of the village were sitting on Samhain eve. It had been a dwelling-house, and when the man that owned it had built a better one, he had put the two rooms together, and kept it for a place to store one thing or another. There was a fire on the old hearth, and there were dip candles stuck in bottles, and there was a black quart bottle upon some boards that had been put across two barrels to make a table. Most of the men were sitting beside the fire, and one of them was singing a long wandering song, about a Munster man and a Connacht man that were quarrelling about their two provinces.

Hanrahan went to the man of the house and said, "I got your message"; but when he had said that, he stopped, for an old mountainy man that had a shirt and trousers of unbleached flannel, and that was sitting by himself near the door, was looking at him, and moving an old pack of cards about in his hands and muttering. "Don't mind him," said the man of the house; "he is only some stranger came in a while ago, and we bade him welcome, it being Samhain night, but I think he is not in his right wits. Listen to him now and you will hear what he is saying."

They listened then, and they could hear the old man muttering to himself as he turned the cards, "Spades and Diamonds, Courage and Power; Clubs and Hearts, Knowledge and Pleasure."

"That is the kind of talk he has been going on with for the last hour," said the man of the house, and Hanrahan turned his eyes from the old man as if he did not like to be looking at him.

"I got your message," Hanrahan said then. "'He is in the barn with his three first cousins from Kilchriest," the messenger said, "and there are some of the neighbours with them.'"

"It is my cousin over there is wanting to see you," said the man of the house, and he called over a young frieze-coated man, who was listening to the song, and said, "This is Red Hanrahan you have the message for."

"It is a kind message, indeed," said the young man, "for it comes from your sweetheart, Mary Lavelle."

"How would you get a message from her, and what do you know of her?"

"I don't know her, indeed, but I was in Loughrea yesterday, and a neighbour of hers that had some dealings with me was saying that she bade him send you word, if he met any one from this side in the market, that her mother has died from her, and if you have a mind yet to join with herself, she is willing to keep her word to you."

"I will go to her indeed," said Hanrahan.

"And she bade you make no delay, for if she has not a man in the house before the month is out, it is likely the little bit of land will be given to another."

When Hanrahan heard that, he rose up from the bench he had sat down on. "I will make no delay indeed," he said; "there is a full moon, and if I get as far as Kilchriest to-night, I will reach to her before the setting of the sun to-morrow."

When the others heard that, they began to laugh at him for being in such haste to go to his sweetheart, and one asked him if he would leave his school in the old lime-kiln, where he was giving the children such good learning. But he said the children would be glad enough in the morning to find the place empty, and no one to keep them at their task; and as for his school he could set it up again in any place, having as he had his little inkpot hanging from his neck by a chain, and his big Virgil and his primer in the skirt of his coat.

Some of them asked him to drink a glass before he went, and a young man caught hold of his coat, and said he must not leave them without singing the song he had made in praise of Venus and of Mary Lavelle. He drank a glass of whiskey, but he said he would not stop but would set out on his journey.

"There's time enough, Red Hanrahan," said the man of the house. "It will be time enough for you to give up sport when you are after your marriage, and it might be a long time before we will see you again."

"I will not stop," said Hanrahan; "my mind would be on the roads all the time, bringing me to the woman that sent for me, and she lonesome and watching till I come."

Some of the others came about him, pressing him that had been such a pleasant comrade, so full of songs and every kind of trick and fun, not to leave them till the night would be over, but he refused them all, and shook them off, and went to the door. But as he put his foot over the threshold, the strange old man stood up and put his hand that was thin and withered like a bird's claw on Hanrahan's hand, and said: "It is not Hanrahan, the learned man and the great songmaker, that should go out from a gathering like this, on a Samhain night. And stop here, now," he said, "and play a hand with me; and here is an old pack of cards has done its work many a night before this, and old as it is, there has been much of the riches of the world lost and won over it."

One of the young men said, "It isn't much of the riches of the world has stopped with yourself, old man," and he looked at the old man's bare feet, and they all laughed. But Hanrahan did not laugh, but he sat down very quietly, without a word. Then one of them said, "So you will stop with us after all, Hanrahan"; and the old man said, "He will stop indeed, did you not hear me asking him?"

They all looked at the old man then as if wondering where he came from. "It is far I am come," he said; "through France I have come, and through Spain, and by Lough Greine of the hidden mouth, and none has refused me anything." And then he was silent and nobody liked to question him, and they began to play. There were six men at the boards playing, and the others were looking on behind. They played two or three games for nothing, and then the old man took a fourpenny bit, worn very thin and smooth, out from his pocket, and he called to the rest to put something on the game. Then they all put down something on the boards, and little as it was it looked much, from the way it was shoved from one to another, first one man winning it and then his neighbour. And sometimes the luck would go against a man and he would have nothing left, and then one or another would lend him something, and he would pay it again out of his winnings, for neither good nor bad luck stopped long with any one.

And once Hanrahan said as a man would say in a dream,

"It is time for me to be going the road"; but just then a good card came to him, and he played it out, and all the money began to come to him. And once he thought of Mary Lavelle, and he sighed; and that time his luck went from him, and he forgot her again.

But at last the luck went to the old man and it stayed with him, and all they had flowed into him, and he began to laugh little laughs to himself, and to sing over and over to himself, "Spades and Diamonds, Courage and Power," and so on, as if it was a verse of a song.

And after a while any one looking at the men, and seeing the way their bodies were rocking to and fro, and the way they kept their eyes on the old man's hands, would think they had drink taken, or that the whole store they had in the world was put on the cards; but that was not so, for the quart bottle had not been disturbed since the game began, and was nearly full yet, and all that was on the game was a few sixpenny bits and shillings, and maybe a handful of coppers.

"You are good men to win and good men to lose," said the old man; "you have play in your hearts." He began then to shuffle the cards and to mix them, very quick and fast, till at last they could not see them to be cards at all, but you would think him to be making rings of fire in the air, as little lads would make them with whirling a lighted stick; and after that it seemed to them that all the room was dark, and they could see nothing but his hands and the cards.

And all in a minute a hare made a leap out from between his hands, and whether it was one of the cards that took that shape, or whether it was made out of nothing in the palms of his hands, nobody knew, but there it was running on the floor of the barn, as quick as any hare that ever lived.

Some looked at the hare, but more kept their eyes on the old man, and while they were looking at him a hound made a leap out between his hands, the same way as the hare did, and after that another hound and another, till there was a whole pack of them following the hare round and round the barn.

The players were all standing up now, with their backs to the boards, shrinking from the hounds, and nearly deafened with the noise of their yelping, but as quick as the hounds were they could not overtake the hare, but it went round, till at the last it seemed as if a blast of wind burst open the barn door, and the hare doubled and made a leap over the boards where the men had been playing, and went out of the door and away through the night, and the hounds over the boards and through the door after it.

Then the old man called out, "Follow the hounds, follow the hounds, and it is a great hunt you will see to-night," and he went out after them. But used as the men were to go hunting after hares, and ready as they were for any sport, they were in dread to go out into the night, and it was only Hanrahan that rose up and that said, "I will follow, I will follow on."

"You had best stop here, Hanrahan," the young man that was nearest him said, "for you might be going into some great danger." But Hanrahan said, "I will see fair play, I will see fair play," and he went stumbling out of the door like a man in a dream, and the door shut after him as he went.

He thought he saw the old man in front of him, but it was only his own shadow that the full moon cast on the road before him, but he could hear the hounds crying after the hare over the wide green fields of Granagh, and he followed them very fast, for there was nothing to stop him; and after a while he came to smaller fields that had little walls of loose stones around them, and he threw the stones down as he crossed them, and did not wait to put them up again; and he passed by the place where the river goes underground at Ballylee, and he could hear the hounds going before him up towards the head of the river. Soon he found it harder to run, for it was uphill he was going, and clouds came over the moon, and it was hard for him to see his way, and once he left the path to take a short-cut, but his foot slipped into a bog-hole and he had to come back to it. And how long he was going he did not know, or what way he went, but at last he was up on the bare mountain, with nothing but the rough heather about him, and he could neither hear the hounds nor any other thing. But their cry began to come to him again, at first far off and then very near, and when it came quite close to him, it went up all of a sudden into the air, and there was the sound of hunting over his head; then it went away northward till he could hear nothing at all. "That's not fair," he said, "that's not fair." And he could walk no longer, but sat down on the heather where he was, in the heart of Slieve Echtge, for all the strength had gone from him, with the dint of the long journey he had made.

And after a while he took notice that there was a door close to him, and a light coming from it, and he wondered that being so close to him he had not seen it before. And he rose up, and tired as he was he went in at the door, and although it was night-time outside, it was daylight he found within. And presently he met with an old man that had been gathering summer thyme and yellow flag-flowers, and it seemed as if all the sweet smells of the summer were with them. And the old man said, "It is a long time you have been coming to us, Hanrahan the learned man and the great songmaker."

And with that he brought him into a very big shining house, and every grand thing Hanrahan had ever heard of, and every colour he had ever seen, was in it. There was a high place at the end of the house, and on it there was sitting in a high chair a woman, the most beautiful the world ever saw, having a long pale face and flowers about it, but she had the tired look of one that had been long waiting. And there were sitting on the step below her chair four grey old women, and the one of them was holding a great cauldron in her lap; and another a great stone on her knees, and heavy as it was it seemed light to her; and another of them had a very long spear that was made of pointed wood; and the last of them had a sword that was without a scabbard.

Hanrahan stood looking at them for a long time, but none of them spoke any word to him or looked at him at all. And he had it in his mind to ask who that woman in the chair was, that was like a queen, and what she was waiting for; but ready as he was with his tongue and afraid of no person, he was in dread now to speak to so beautiful a woman, and in so grand a place. And then he thought to ask what were the four things the four grey old women were holding like great treasures, but he could not think of the right words to bring out.

Then the first old woman rose up, holding the cauldron between her two hands, and she said, "Pleasure," and Hanrahan said no word. Then the second old woman rose up with the stone in her hands, and she said, "Power"; and the third old woman rose up with a spear in her hand, and she said, "Courage"; and the last of the old women rose up having the sword in her hands, and she said, "Knowledge." And every one, after she had spoken, waited as if for Hanrahan to question her, but he said nothing at all. And then the four old women went out of the door, bringing their four treasures with them, and as they went out one of them said, "He has no wish for us"; and another said, "He is weak, he is weak"; and another said, "He is afraid"; and the last said, "His wits are gone from him." And then they all said, "Echtge, daughter of the Silver Hand, must stay in her sleep. It is a pity, it is a great pity."

And then the woman that was like a queen gave a very sad sigh, and it seemed to Hanrahan as if the sigh had the sound in it of hidden streams; and if the place he was in had been ten times grander and more shining than it was, he could not have hindered sleep from coming on him; and he staggered like a drunken man and lay down there and then.

When Hanrahan awoke, the sun was shining on his face, but there was white frost on the grass around him, and there was ice on the edge of the stream he was lying by, and that goes running on through Doire-caol and Drim-na-rod. He knew by the shape of the hills and by the shining of Lough Greine in the distance that he was upon one of the hills of Slieve Echtge, but he was not sure how he came there; for all that had happened in the barn had gone from him, and all of his journey but the soreness of his feet and the stiffness in his bones.

It was a year after that, there were men of the village of Cappaghtagle sitting by the fire in a house on the roadside, and Red Hanrahan that was now very thin and worn, and his hair very long and wild, came to the half-door and asked leave to come in and rest himself; and they bid him welcome because it was Samhain night. He sat down with them, and they gave him a glass of whiskey out of a quart bottle; and they saw the little inkpot hanging about his neck, and knew he was a scholar, and asked for stories about the Greeks.

He took the Virgil out of the big pocket of his coat, but the cover was very black and swollen with the wet, and the page when he opened it was very yellow, but that was no great matter, for he looked at it like a man that had never learned to read. Some young man that was there began to laugh at him then, and to ask why did he carry so heavy a book with him when he was not able to read it.

It vexed Hanrahan to hear that, and he put the Virgil back in his pocket and asked if they had a pack of cards among them, for cards were better than books. When they brought out the cards he took them and began to shuffle them, and while he was shuffling them something seemed to come into his mind, and he put his hand to his face like one that is trying to remember, and he said, "Was I ever here before, or where was I on a night like this?" and then of a sudden he stood up and let the cards fall to the floor, and he said, "Who was it brought me a message from Mary Lavelle?"

"We never saw you before now, and we never heard of Mary Lavelle," said the man of the house. "And who is she," he said, "and what is it you are talking about?"

"It was this night a year ago, I was in a barn, and there were men playing cards, and there was money on the table, they were pushing it from one to another here and there—and I got a message, and I was going out of the door to look for my sweetheart that wanted me, Mary Lavelle." And then Hanrahan called out very loud, "Where have I been since then? Where was I for the whole year?"

"It is hard to say where you might have been in that time," said the oldest of the men, "or what part of the world you may have travelled; and it is like enough you have the dust of many roads on your feet; for there are many go wandering and forgetting like that," he said, "when once they have been given the touch."

"That is true," said another of the men. "I knew a woman went wandering like that through the length of seven years; she came back after, and she told her friends she had often been glad enough to eat the food that was put in the pig's trough. And it is best for you to go to the priest now," he said, "and let him take off you whatever may have been put upon you."

"It is to my sweetheart I will go, to Mary Lavelle," said Hanrahan; "it is too long I have delayed, how do I know what might have happened her in the length of a year?"

He was going out of the door then, but they all told him it was best for him to stop the night, and to get strength for the journey; and indeed he wanted that, for he was very weak, and when they gave him food he ate it like a man that had never seen food before, and one of them said, "He is eating as if he had trodden on the hungry grass." It was in the white light of the morning he set out, and the time seemed long to him till he could get to Mary Lavelle's house. But when he came to it, he found the door broken, and the thatch dropping from the roof, and no living person to be seen. And when he asked the neighbours what had happened her, all they could say was that she had been put out of the house, and had married some labouring man, and they had gone looking for work to London or Liverpool or some big place. And whether she found a worse place or a better he never knew, but anyway he never met with her or with news of her again.

# James Joyce

## *An Encounter*

It was Joe Dillon who introduced the Wild West to us. He had a little library made up of old numbers of *The Union Jack, Pluck* and *The Halfpenny Marvel.* Every evening after school we met in his back garden and arranged Indian battles. He and his fat young brother Leo the idler held the loft of the stable while we tried to carry it by storm; or we fought a pitched battle on the grass. But, however well we fought, we never won siege or battle and all our bouts ended with Joe Dillon's war dance of victory. His parents went to eight-o'clock mass every morning in Gardiner Street and the peaceful odour of Mrs. Dillon was prevalent in the hall of the house. But he played too fiercely for us who were younger and more timid. He looked like some kind of an Indian when he capered round the garden, an old teacosy on his head, beating a tin with his fist and yelling:

"Ya! yaka, yaka, yaka!"

Everyone was incredulous when it was reported that he had a vocation for the priesthood. Nevertheless it was true.

A spirit of unruliness diffused itself among us and, under its influence, differences of culture and constitution were waived. We banded ourselves together, some boldly, some in jest and some almost in fear: and of the number of these latter, the reluctant Indians who were afraid to seem studious or lacking in robustness, I was one. The adventures related in the literature of the Wild West were remote from my nature but, at least, they opened doors of escape. I liked better some American detective stories which were traversed from time to time by unkempt fierce and beautiful girls. Though there was nothing wrong in these stories and though their intention was sometimes literary they were circulated secretly at school. One day when Father Butler was hearing the four pages of Roman History clumsy Leo Dillon was discovered with a copy of *The Halfpenny Marvel*.

"This page or this page? This page? Now, Dillon, up!" *Hardly had the day* . . . "Go on! What day?" *Hardly had the day dawned* . . . "Have you studied it? What have you there in your pocket?"

Everyone's heart palpitated as Leo Dillon handed up the paper and everyone assumed an innocent face. Father Butler turned over the pages, frowning.

"What is this rubbish?" he said. *The Apache Chief!* "Is this what you read instead of studying your Roman History? Let me not find any more of this wretched stuff in this college. The man who wrote it, I suppose, was some wretched scribbler that writes these things for a drink. I'm surprised at boys like you, educated, reading such stuff. I could understand it if you were . . . National School boys. Now, Dillon, I advise you strongly, get at your work or . . . "

This rebuke during the sober hours of school paled much of the glory of the Wild West for me and the confused puffy face of Leo Dillon awakened one of my consciences. But when the restraining influence of the school was at a distance I began to hunger again for wild sensations, for the escape which those chronicles of disorder alone seemed to offer me. The mimic warfare of the evening became at last as wearisome to me as the routine of school in the morning because I wanted real adventures to happen to myself. But real adventures, I reflected, do not happen to people who remain at home: they must be sought abroad.

The summer holidays were near at hand when I made up my mind to break out of the weariness of school-life for one day at least. With Leo Dillon and a boy named Mahony I planned a day's miching. Each of us saved up sixpence. We were to meet at ten in the morning on the Canal Bridge. Mahony's big sister was to write an excuse for him and Leo Dillon was to tell his brother to say he was sick. We arranged to go along the Wharf Road until we came to the ships, then to cross in the ferryboat and walk out to see the Pigeon House. Leo Dillon was afraid we might meet Father Butler or someone out of the college; but Mahony asked, very sensibly, what would Father Butler be doing out at the Pigeon House. We were reassured: and I brought the first stage of the plot to an end by collecting sixpence from the other two, at the same time showing them my own sixpence. When we were making the last arrangements on the eve we were all vaguely excited. We shook hands, laughing, and Mahony said:

"Till to-morrow, mates."

That night I slept badly. In the morning I was firstcomer to the bridge as I lived nearest. I hid my books in the long grass near the ashpit at the end of the garden where nobody ever came and hurried along the canal bank. It was a mild sunny morning in the first week of June. I sat up on the coping of the bridge admiring my frail canvas shoes which I had diligently pipeclayed overnight and watching the docile horses pulling a tramload of business people up the hill. All the branches of the tall trees which lined the mall were gay with little light green leaves and the sunlight slanted through them on to the water. The granite stone of the bridge was beginning to be warm and I began to pat it with my hands in time to an air in my head. I was very happy.

When I had been sitting there for five or ten minutes I saw Mahony's grey suit approaching. He came up the hill, smiling, and clambered up beside me on the bridge. While we were waiting he brought out the catapult which bulged from his inner pocket and explained some improvements which he had made in it. I asked him why he had brought it and he told me he had brought it to have some gas with the birds. Mahony used slang freely, and spoke of Father Butler as Bunsen Burner. We waited on for a quarter of an hour more but still there was no sign of Leo Dillon. Mahony, at last, jumped down and said:

"Come along. I knew Fatty'd funk it."

"And his sixpence . . . ?" I said.

"That's forfeit," said Mahony. "And so much the better for us—a bob and a tanner instead of a bob."

We walked along the North Strand Road till we came to the Vitriol Works and then turned to the right along the Wharf Road. Mahony began to play the Indian as soon as we were out of public sight. He chased a crowd of ragged girls, brandishing his unloaded catapult and, when two ragged boys began, out of chivalry, to fling stones at us, he proposed that we should charge them. I objected that the boys were too small, and so we walked on, the ragged troop screaming after us: *Swaddlers! Swaddlers!* thinking that we were Protestants because Mahony, who was dark-complexioned, wore the silver badge of a cricket club in his cap. When we came to the Smoothing Iron we arranged a siege; but it was a failure because you must have at least three. We revenged ourselves on Leo Dillon by saying what a funk he was and guessing how many he would get at three o'clock from Mr. Ryan.

We came then near the river. We spent a long time walking about the noisy streets flanked by high stone walls, watching the working of cranes and engines and often being shouted at for our immobility by the drivers of groaning carts. It was noon when we reached the quays and, as all the labourers seemed to be eating their lunches, we bought two big currant buns and sat down to eat them on some metal piping beside the river. We pleased ourselves with the spectacle of Dublin's commerce—the barges signalled from far away by their curls of woolly smoke, the brown fishing fleet beyond Ringsend, the big white sailing-vessel which was being discharged on the opposite quay. Mahony said it would be right skit to run away to sea on one of those big ships and even I, looking at the high masts, saw, or imagined, the geography which had been scantily dosed to me at school gradually taking substance under my eyes. School and home seemed to recede from us and their influences upon us seemed to wane.

We crossed the Liffey in the ferryboat, paying our toll to be transported in the company of two labourers and a little Jew with a bag. We were serious to the point of solemnity, but once during the short voyage our eyes met and we laughed. When we landed we watched the discharging of the graceful threemaster which we had observed from the other quay. Some bystander said that she was a Norwegian vessel. I went to the stern and I tried to decipher the legend upon it but, failing to do so, I came back and examined the foreign sailors to see had any of them green eyes for I had some confused notion.... The sailors' eyes were blue and grey and even black. The only sailor whose eyes could have been called green was a tall man who amused the crowd on the quay by calling out cheerfully every time the planks fell:

"All right! All right!"

When we were tired of this sight we wandered slowly into Ringsend. The day had grown sultry, and in the windows of the grocers' shops musty biscuits lay bleaching. We bought some biscuits and chocolate which we ate sedulously as we wandered through the squalid streets where the families of the fishermen live. We could find no dairy and so we went into a huckster's shop and bought a bottle of raspberry lemonade each. Refreshed by this, Mahony chased a cat down a lane, but the cat escaped into a wide field. We both felt rather tired and when we reached the field we made at once for a sloping bank over the ridge of which we could see the Dodder.

It was too late and we were too tired to carry out our project of visiting the Pigeon House. We had to be home before four o'clock lest our adventure should be discovered. Mahony looked regretfully at his catapult and I had to suggest going home by train before he regained any cheerfulness. The sun went in behind some clouds and left us to our jaded thoughts and the crumbs of our provisions.

There was nobody but ourselves in the field. When we had lain on the bank for some time without speaking I saw a man approaching from the far end of the field. I watched him lazily as I chewed one of those green stems on which girls tell fortunes. He came along the bank slowly. He walked with one hand upon his hip and in the other hand he held a stick with which he tapped the turf lightly. He was shabbily dressed in a suit of greenish-black and wore what we used to call a jerry hat with a high crown. He seemed to be fairly old for his moustache was ashen-grey. When he passed at our feet he glanced up at us quickly and then continued his way. We followed him with our eyes and saw that when he had gone on for perhaps fifty paces he turned about and began to retrace his steps. He walked towards us very slowly, always tapping the ground with his stick, so slowly that I thought he was looking for something in the grass.

He stopped when he came level with us and bade us goodday. We answered him and he sat down beside us on the slope slowly and with great care. He began to talk of the weather, saying that it would be a very hot summer and adding that the seasons had changed greatly since he was a boy—a long time ago. He said that the happiest time of one's life was undoubtedly one's schoolboy days and that he would give anything to be young again. While he expressed these sentiments which bored us a little we kept silent. Then he began to talk of school and of books. He asked us whether we had read the poetry of Thomas Moore or the works of Sir Walter Scott and Lord Lytton. I pretended that I had read every book he mentioned so that in the end he said:

"Ah, I can see you are a bookworm like myself." "Now,"

he added, pointing to Mahony who was regarding us with open eyes, "he is different; he goes in for games."

He said he had all Sir Walter Scott's works and all Lord Lytton's works at home and never tired of reading them. Of course, he said, there were some of Lord Lytton's works which boys couldn't read. Mahony asked why couldn't boys read them—a question which agitated and pained me because I was afraid the man would think I was as stupid as Mahony. The man, however, only smiled. I saw that he had great gaps in his mouth between his yellow teeth. Then he asked us which of us had the most sweethearts. Mahony mentioned lightly that he had three totties. The man asked me how many had I. I answered that I had none. He did not believe me and said he was sure I must have one. I was silent.

"Tell us," said Mahony pertly to the man, "how many have you yourself?"

The man smiled as before and said that when he was our age he had lots of sweethearts.

"Every boy," he said, "has a little sweetheart."

His attitude on this point struck me as strangely liberal in a man of his age. In my heart I thought that what he said about boys and sweethearts was reasonable. But I disliked the words in his mouth and I wondered why he shivered once or twice as if he feared something or felt a sudden chill. As he proceeded I noticed that his accent was good. He began to speak to us about girls, saying what nice soft hair they had and how soft their hands were and how all girls were not so good as they seemed to be if one only knew. There was nothing he liked, he said, so much as looking at a nice young girl, at her nice white hands and her beautiful soft hair. He gave me the impression that he was repeating something which he had learned by heart or that, magnetised by some words of his own speech, his mind was slowly circling round and round in the same orbit. At times he spoke as if he were simply alluding to some fact that everybody knew, and at times he lowered his voice and spoke mysteriously as if he were telling us something secret which he did not wish others to overhear. He repeated his phrases over and over again, varying them and surrounding them with his monotonous voice. I continued to gaze towards the foot of the slope, listening to him.

After a long while his monologue paused. He stood up slowly, saying that he had to leave us for a minute or so, a few minutes, and without changing the direction of my gaze, I saw him walking away from us towards the near end of the field. We remained silent when he had gone. After a silence of a few minutes I heard Mahony exclaim:

"I say! Look what he's doing!"

As I neither answered nor raised my eyes Mahony exclaimed again:

"I say . . . He's a queer old josser!"

"In case he asks us for our names," I said, "let you be Murphy and I'll be Smith."

We said nothing further to each other. I was still considering whether I would go away or not when the man came back and sat down beside us again. Hardly had he sat down when Mahony, catching sight of the cat which had escaped him, sprang up and pursued her across the field. The man and I watched the chase. The cat escaped once more and Mahony began to throw stones at the wall she had escaladed. Desisting from this, he began to wander about the far end of the field, aimlessly.

After an interval the man spoke to me. He said that my friend was a very rough boy and asked did he get whipped often at school. I was going to reply indignantly that we were not National School boys to be *whipped*, as he called it; but I remained silent. He began to speak on the subject of chastising boys. His mind, as if magnetised again by his speech, seemed to circle slowly round and round its new centre. He said that when boys were that kind they ought to be whipped and well whipped. When a boy was rough and unruly there was nothing would do him any good but a good sound whipping. A slap on the hand or a box on the ear was no good: what he wanted was to get a nice warm whipping. I was surprised at this sentiment and involuntarily glanced up at his face. As I did so I met the gaze of a pair of bottle-green eyes peering at me from under a twitching forehead. I turned my eyes away again.

The man continued his monologue. He seemed to have forgotten his recent liberalism. He said that if ever he found a boy talking to girls or having a girl for a sweetheart he would whip him and whip him; and that would teach him not to be talking to girls. And if a boy had a girl for a sweetheart and told lies about it then he would give him such a whipping as no boy ever got in this world. He said that there was nothing in this world he would like so well as that. He described to me how he would whip such a boy as if he were unfolding some elaborate mystery. He would love that, he said, better than anything in this world; and his voice, as he led me monotonously through the mystery, grew almost affectionate and seemed to plead with me that I should understand him.

I waited till his monologue paused again. Then I stood up abruptly. Lest I should betray my agitation I delayed a few moments pretending to fix my shoe properly and then, saying that I was obliged to go, I bade him good-day. I went up the slope calmly but my heart was beating quickly with fear that he would seize me by the ankles. When I reached the top of the slope I turned round and, without looking at him, called loudly across the field:

"Murphy!"

My voice had an accent of forced bravery in it and I was ashamed of my paltry stratagem. I had to call the name again before Mahony saw me and hallooed in answer. How my heart beat as he came running across the field to me! He ran as if to bring me aid. And I was penitent; for in my heart I had always despised him a little.

# James Joyce

## *Araby*

North Richmond Street, being blind, was a quiet street except at the hour when the Christian Brothers' School set the boys free. An uninhabited house of two storeys stood at the blind end, detached from its neighbours in a square ground. The other houses of the street, conscious of decent lives within them, gazed at one another with brown imperturbable faces.

The former tenant of our house, a priest, had died in the back drawing-room. Air, musty from having been long enclosed, hung in all the rooms, and the waste room behind the kitchen was littered with old useless papers. Among these I found a few paper-covered books, the pages of which were curled and damp: *The Abbot*, by Walter Scott, *The Devout Communicant* and *The Memoirs of Vidocq*. I liked the last best because its leaves were yellow. The wild garden behind the house contained a central apple-tree and a few straggling bushes under one of which I found the late tenant's rusty bicycle-pump. He had been a very charitable priest; in his will he had left all his money to institutions and the furniture of his house to his sister.

When the short days of winter came dusk fell before we had well eaten our dinners. When we met in the street the houses had grown sombre. The space of sky above us was the colour of ever-changing violet and towards it the lamps of the street lifted their feeble lanterns. The cold air stung us and we played till our bodies glowed. Our shouts echoed in the silent street. The career of our play brought us through the dark muddy lanes behind the houses where we ran the gantlet of the rough tribes from the cottages, to the back doors of the dark dripping gardens where odours arose from the ashpits, to the dark odorous stables where a coachman smoothed and combed the horse or shook music from the buckled harness. When we returned to the street, light from the kitchen windows had filled the areas. If my uncle was seen turning the corner we hid in the shadow until we had seen him safely housed. Or if Mangan's sister came out on the doorstep to call her brother in to his tea we watched her from our shadow peer up and down the street. We waited to see whether she would remain or go in and, if she remained, we left our shadow and walked up to Mangan's steps resignedly. She was waiting for us, her figure defined by the light from the half-opened door. Her brother always teased her before he obeyed and I stood by the railings looking at her. Her dress swung as she moved her body and the soft rope of her hair tossed from side to side.

Every morning I lay on the floor in the front parlour watching her door. The blind was pulled down to within an inch of the sash so that I could not be seen. When she came out on the doorstep my heart leaped. I ran to the hall, seized my books and followed her. I kept her brown figure always in my eye and, when we came near the point at which our ways diverged, I quickened my pace and passed her. This happened morning after morning. I had never spoken to her, except for a few casual words, and yet her name was like a summons to all my foolish blood.

Her image accompanied me even in places the most hostile to romance. On Saturday evenings when my aunt went marketing I had to go to carry some of the parcels. We walked through the flaring streets, jostled by drunken men and bargaining women, amid the curses of labourers, the shrill litanies of shop-boys who stood on guard by the barrels of pigs' cheeks, the nasal chanting of street-singers, who sang a *come-all-you* about O'Donovan Rossa, or a ballad about the troubles in our native land. These noises converged in a single sensation of life for me. I imagined that I bore my chalice safely through a throng of foes. Her name sprang to my lips at moments in strange prayers and praises which I myself did not understand. My eyes were often full of tears (I could not tell why) and at times a flood from my heart seemed to pour itself out into my bosom. I thought little of the future. I did not know whether I would ever speak to her or not or, if I spoke to her, how I could tell her of my confused adoration. But my body was like a harp and her words and gestures were like fingers running upon the wires.

One evening I went into the back drawing-room in which the priest had died. It was a dark rainy evening and there was no sound in the house. Through one of the broken panes I heard the rain impinge upon the earth, the fine incessant needles of water playing in the sodden beds. Some distant lamp or lighted window gleamed below me. I was thankful that I could see so little. All my senses seemed to desire to veil themselves and, feeling that I was about to slip from them, I pressed the palms of my hands together until they trembled, murmuring: *O love! O love!* many times.

At last she spoke to me. When she addressed the first words to me I was so confused that I did not know what to answer. She asked me was I going to *Araby*. I forget whether I answered yes or no. It would be a splendid bazaar, she said; she would love to go.

"And why can't you?" I asked.

While she spoke she turned a silver bracelet round and round her wrist. She could not go, she said, because there would be a retreat that week in her convent. Her brother and two other boys were fighting for their caps and I was alone at the railings. She held one of the spikes, bowing her head towards me. The light from the lamp opposite our door caught the white curve of her neck, lit up her hair that rested there and, falling, lit up the hand upon the railing. It fell over one side of her dress and caught the white border of a petticoat, just visible as she stood at ease.

"It's well for you," she said.

"If I go," I said, "I will bring you something."

What innumerable follies laid waste my waking and sleeping thoughts after that evening! I wished to annihilate the tedious intervening days. I chafed against the work of school. At night in my bedroom and by day in the classroom her image came between me and the page I strove to read. The syllables of the word *Araby* were called to me through the silence in which my soul luxuriated and cast an Eastern enchantment over me. I asked for leave to go to the bazaar Saturday night. My aunt was surprised and hoped it was not some Freemason affair. I answered few questions in class. I watched my master's face pass from amiability to sternness; he hoped I was not beginning to idle. I could not call my wandering thoughts together. I had hardly any patience with the serious work of life which, now that it stood between me and my desire, seemed to me child's play, ugly monotonous child's play.

On Saturday morning I reminded my uncle that I wished to go to the bazaar in the evening. He was fussing at the hallstand, looking for the hat-brush, and answered me curtly:

"Yes, boy, I know."

As he was in the hall I could not go into the front parlour and lie at the window. I left the house in bad humour and walked slowly towards the school. The air was pitilessly raw and already my heart misgave me.

When I came home to dinner my uncle had not yet been home. Still it was early. I sat staring at the clock for some time and, when its ticking began to irritate me, I left the room. I mounted the staircase and gained the upper part of the house. The high cold empty gloomy rooms liberated me and I went from room to room singing. From the front window I saw my companions playing below in the street. Their cries reached me weakened and indistinct and, leaning my forehead against the cool glass, I looked over at the dark house where she lived. I may have stood there for an hour, seeing nothing but the brown-clad figure cast by my imagination, touched discreetly by the lamplight at the curved neck, at the hand upon the railings, and at the border below the dress.

When I came downstairs again I found Mrs. Mercer sitting at the fire. She was an old garrulous woman, a pawnbroker's widow, who collected used stamps for some pious purpose. I had to endure the gossip of the tea-table. The meal was prolonged beyond an hour and still my uncle did not come. Mrs. Mercer stood up to go: she was sorry she couldn't wait any longer, but it was after eight o'clock and she did not like to be out late, as the night air was bad for her. When she had gone I began to walk up and down the room, clenching my fists. My aunt said:

"I'm afraid you may put off your bazaar for this night of Our Lord."

At nine o'clock I heard my uncle's latchkey in the halldoor. I heard him talking to himself and heard the hallstand rocking when it had received the weight of his overcoat. I could interpret these signs. When he was midway through his dinner I asked him to give me the money to go to the bazaar. He had forgotten.

"The people are in bed and after their first sleep now," he said.

I did not smile. My aunt said to him energetically:

"Can't you give him the money and let him go? You've kept him late enough as it is."

My uncle said he was very sorry he had forgotten. He said he believed in the old saying: *All work and no play makes Jack a dull boy*. He asked me where I was going and, when I had told him a second time, he asked me did I know *The Arab's Farewell to his Steed*. When I left the kitchen he was about to recite the opening lines of the piece to my aunt.

I held a florin tightly in my hand as I strode down Buckingham Street towards the station. The sight of the streets thronged with buyers and glaring with gas recalled to me the purpose of my journey. I took my seat in a third-class carriage of a deserted train. After an intolerable delay the train moved out of the station slowly. It crept onward among ruinous houses and over the twinkling river. At Westland Row Station a crowd of people pressed to the carriage doors; but the porters moved them back, saying that it was a special train for the bazaar. I remained alone in the bare carriage. In a few minutes the train drew up beside an improvised wooden platform. I passed out on to the road and saw by the lighted dial of a clock that it was ten minutes to ten. In front of me was a large building which displayed the magical name.

I could not find any sixpenny entrance and, fearing that the bazaar would be closed, I passed in quickly through a turnstile, handing a shilling to a weary-looking man. I found myself in a big hall girdled at half its height by a gallery. Nearly all the stalls were closed and the greater part of the hall was in darkness. I recognised a silence like that which pervades a church after a service. I walked into the centre of the bazaar timidly. A few people were gathered about the stalls which were still open. Before a curtain, over which the words *Café Chantant* were written in coloured lamps, two men were counting money on a salver. I listened to the fall of the coins.

Remembering with difficulty why I had come I went over to one of the stalls and examined porcelain vases and flowered tea-sets. At the door of the stall a young lady was talking and laughing with two young gentlemen. I remarked their English accents and listened vaguely to their conversation.

"O, I never said such a thing!"

"O, but you did!"

"O, but I didn't!"

"Didn't she say that?"
"Yes. I heard her."
"O, there's a . . . fib!"

Observing me the young lady came over and asked me did I wish to buy anything. The tone of her voice was not encouraging; she seemed to have spoken to me out of a sense of duty. I looked humbly at the great jars that stood like eastern guards at either side of of the dark entrance to the stall and murmured:

"No, thank you."

The young lady changed the position of one of the vases and went back to the two young men. They began to talk of the same subject. Once or twice the young lady glanced at me over her shoulder.

I lingered before her stall, though I knew my stay was useless, to make my interest in her wares seem the more real. Then I turned away slowly and walked down the middle of the bazaar. I allowed the two pennies to fall against the sixpence in my pocket. I heard a voice call from one end of the gallery that the light was out. The upper part of the hall was now completely dark.

Gazing up into the darkness I saw myself as a creature driven and derided by vanity; and my eyes burned with anguish and anger.

# James Joyce

## *Eveline*

She sat at the window watching the evening invade the avenue. Her head was leaned against the window curtains and in her nostrils was the odour of dusty cretonne. She was tired.

Few people passed. The man out of the last house passed on his way home; she heard his footsteps clacking along the concrete pavement and afterwards crunching on the cinder path before the new red houses. One time there used to be a field there in which they used to play every evening with other people's children. Then a man from Belfast bought the field and built houses in it—not like their little brown houses but bright brick houses with shining roofs. The children of the avenue used to play together in that field—the Devines, the Waters, the Dunns, little Keogh the cripple, she and her brothers and sisters. Ernest, however, never played: he was too grown up. Her father used often to hunt them in out of the field with his blackthorn stick; but usually little Keogh used to keep *nix* and call out when he saw her father coming. Still they seemed to have been rather happy then. Her father was not so bad then; and besides, her mother was alive. That was a long time ago; she and her brothers and sisters were all grown up; her mother was dead. Tizzie Dunn was dead, too, and the Waters had gone back to England. Everything changes. Now she was going to go away like the others, to leave her home.

Home! She looked round the room, reviewing all its familiar objects which she had dusted once a week for so many years, wondering where on earth all the dust came from. Perhaps she would never see again those familiar objects from which she had never dreamed of being divided. And yet during all those years she had never found out the name of the priest whose yellowing photograph hung on the wall above the broken harmonium beside the coloured print of the promises made to Blessed Margaret Mary Alacoque. He had been a school friend of her father. Whenever he showed the photograph to a visitor her father used to pass it with a casual word:

"He is in Melbourne now."

She had consented to go away, to leave her home. Was that wise? She tried to weigh each side of the question. In her home anyway she had shelter and food; she had those whom she had known all her life about her. Of course she had to work hard both in the house and at business. What would they say of her in the Stores when they found out that she had run away with a fellow? Say she was a fool, perhaps; and her place would be filled up by advertisement. Miss Gavan would be glad. She had always had an edge on her, especially whenever there were people listening.

"Miss Hill, don't you see these ladies are waiting?"

"Look lively, Miss Hill, please."

She would not cry many tears at leaving the Stores.

But in her new home, in a distant unknown country, it would not be like that. Then she would be married—she, Eveline. People would treat her with respect then. She would not be treated as her mother had been. Even now, though she was over nineteen, she sometimes felt herself in danger of her father's violence. She knew it was that that had given her the palpitations. When they were growing up he had never gone for her, like he used to go for Harry and Ernest, because she was a girl; but latterly he had begun to threaten her and say what he would to to her only for her dead mother's sake. And now she had nobody to protect her. Ernest was dead and Harry, who was in the church decorating business, was nearly always down somewhere in the country. Besides, the invariable squabble for money on Saturday nights had begun to weary her unspeakably. She always gave her entire wages—seven shillings—and Harry always sent up what he could but the trouble was to get any money from her father. He said she used to squander the money, that she had no head, that he wasn't going to give her his hard-earned money to throw about the streets and much more, for he was usually fairly bad of a Saturday night. In the end he would give her the money and ask her had she any intention of buying Sunday's dinner. Then she had to rush out as quickly as she could and do her marketing, holding her black leather purse tightly in her hand as she elbowed her way through the crowds and returning home late under her load of provisions. She had hard work to keep the house together and to see that the two young children who had been left to her charge went to school regularly and got their meals regularly. It was hard work—a hard life—but now that she was about to leave it she did not find it a wholly undesirable life.

She was about to explore another life with Frank. Frank was very kind, manly, open-hearted. She was to go away with him by the night-boat to be his wife and to live with him in Buenos Ayres where he had a home waiting for her. How well she remembered the first time she had seen him; he was lodging in a house on the main road where she used to visit. It seemed a few weeks ago. He was standing at the gate, his peaked cap pushed back on his head and his hair tumbled forward over a face of bronze. Then they had come to know each other. He used to meet her outside the Stores every evening and see her home. He took her to see *The Bohemian Girl* and she felt elated as she sat in an unaccustomed part of the theatre with him. He was awfully fond of music and sang a little. People knew that they were courting and, when he sang about the lass that loves a sailor, she always felt pleasantly confused. He used to call her Poppens out of fun. First of all it had been an excitement for her to have a fellow and then she had begun to like him. He had tales of distant countries. He had started as a deck boy at a pound a month on a ship of the Allan Line going out to Canada. He told her the names of the ships he had been on and the names of the different services. He had sailed through the Straits of Magellan and he told her stories of the terrible Patagonians. He had fallen on his feet in Buenos Ayres, he said, and had come over to the old country just for a holiday. Of course, her father had found out the affair and had forbidden her to have anything to say to him.

"I know these sailor chaps," he said.

One day he had quarrelled with Frank and after that she had to meet her lover secretly.

The evening deepened in the avenue. The white of two letters in her lap grew indistinct. One was to Harry; the other was to her father. Ernest had been her favourite but she liked Harry too. Her father was becoming old lately, she noticed; he would miss her. Sometimes he could be very nice. Not long before, when she had been laid up for a day, he had read her out a ghost story and made toast for her at the fire. Another day, when their mother was alive, they had all gone for a picnic to the Hill of Howth. She remembered her father putting on her mother's bonnet to make the children laugh.

Her time was running out but she continued to sit by the window, leaning her head against the window curtain, inhaling the odour of dusty cretonne. Down far in the avenue she could hear a street organ playing. She knew the air. Strange that it should come that very night to remind her of the promise to her mother, her promise to keep the home together as long as she could. She remembered the last night of her mother's illness; she was again in the close dark room at the other side of the hall and outside she heard a melancholy air of Italy. The organ-player had been ordered to go away and given sixpence. She remembered her father strutting back into the sickroom saying:

"Damned Italians! coming over here!"

As she mused, the pitiful vision of her mother's life laid its spell on the very quick of her being—that life of commonplace sacrifices closing in final craziness. She trembled as she heard again her mother's voice saying constantly with foolish insistence:

"Derevaun Seraun! Derevaun Seraun!"

She stood up in a sudden impulse of terror. Escape! She must escape! Frank would save her. He would give her life, perhaps love, too. But she wanted to live. Shy should she be unhappy? She had a right to happiness. Frank would take her in his arms, fold her in his arms. He would save her.

\* \* \* \* \*

She stood among the swaying crowd in the station at the North Wall. He held her hand and she knew that he was speaking to her, saying something about the passage over and over again. The station was full of soldiers with brown baggages. Through the wide doors of the sheds she caught a glimpse of the black mass of the boat, lying in beside the quay wall, with illumined portholes. She answered nothing. She felt her cheek pale and cold and, out of a maze of distress, she prayed to God to direct her, to show her what was her duty. The boat blew a long mournful whistle into the mist. If she went, to-morrow she would be on the sea with Frank, steaming toward Buenos Ayres.

Their passage had been booked. Could she still draw back after all he had done for her? Her distress awoke a nausea in her body and she kept moving her lips in silent fervent prayer.

A bell clanged upon her heart. She felt him seize her hand:

"Come!"

All the seas of the world tumbled about her heart. He was drawing her into them: he would drown her. She gripped with both hands at the iron railing.

"Come!"

No! No! No! It was impossible. Her hands clutched the iron in frenzy. Amid the seas she sent a cry of anguish!

"Eveline! Evvy!"

He rushed beyond the barrier and called to her to follow. He was shouted at to go on but he still called to her. She set her white face to him, passive like a helpless animal. Her eyes gave him no sign of love or farewell or recognition.

# James Joyce

## *A Little Cloud*

Eight years before he had seen his friend off at the North Wall and wished him godspeed. Gallaher had got on. You could tell that at once by his travelled air, his well-cut tweed suit and fearless accent. Few fellows had talents like his and fewer still could remain unspoiled by such success. Gallaher's heart was in the right place and he had deserved to win. It was something to have a friend like that.

Little Chandler's thoughts ever since lunch-time had been of his meeting with Gallaher, of Gallaher's invitation and of the great city London where Gallaher lived. He was called Little Chandler because, though he was but slightly under the average stature, he gave one the idea of being a little man. His hands were white and small, his frame was fragile, his voice was quiet and his manners were refined. He took the greatest care of his fair silken hair and moustache and used perfume discreetly on his handkerchief. The half-moons of his nails were perfect and when he smiled you caught a glimpse of a row of childish white teeth.

As he sat at his desk in the King's Inns he thought what changes those eight years had brought. The friend whom he had known under a shabby and necessitous guise had become a brilliant figure on the London Press. He turned often from his tiresome writing to gaze out of the office window. The glow of a late autumn sunset covered the grass plots and walks. It cast a shower of kindly golden dust on the untidy nurses and decrepit old men who drowsed on the benches; it flickered upon all the moving figures—on the children who ran screaming along the gravel paths and on everyone who passed through the gardens.

He watched the scene and thought of life; and (as always happened when he thought of life) he became sad. A gentle melancholy took possession of him. He felt how useless it was to struggle against fortune, this being the burden of wisdom which the ages had bequeathed to him.

He remembered the books of poetry upon his shelves at home. He had bought them in his bachelor days and many an evening, as he sat in the little room off the hall, he had been tempted to take one down from the bookshelf and read out something to his wife. But shyness had always held him back; and so the books had remained on their shelves. At times he repeated lines to himself and this consoled him.

When his hour had struck he stood up and took leave of his desk and of his fellow-clerks punctiliously. He emerged from under the feudal arch of the King's Inns, a neat modest figure, and walked swiftly down Henrietta Street. The golden sunset was waning and the air had grown sharp. A horde of grimy children populated the street. They stood or ran in the roadway or crawled up the steps before the gaping doors or squatted like mice upon the thresholds. Little Chandler gave them no thought. He picked his way deftly through all that minute vermin-like life and under the shadow of the gaunt spectral mansions in which the old nobility of Dublin had roistered. No memory of the past touched him, for his mind was full of a present joy.

He had never been in Corless's but he knew the value of the name. He knew that people went there after the theatre to eat oysters and drink liqueurs; and he had heard that the waiters there spoke French and German. Walking swiftly by at night he had seen cabs drawn up before the door and richly dressed ladies, escorted by cavaliers, alight and enter quickly. They wore noisy dresses and many wraps. Their faces were powdered and they caught up their dresses, when they touched earth, like alarmed Atalantas. He had always passed without turning his head to look. It was his habit to walk swiftly in the street even by day and whenever he found himself in the city late at night he hurried on his way apprehensively and excitedly. Sometimes, however, he courted the causes of his fear. He chose the darkest and narrowest streets and, as he walked boldly forward, the silence that was spread about his footsteps troubled him, the wandering silent figures troubled him; and at times a sound of low fugitive laughter made him tremble like a leaf.

He turned to the right towards Capel Street. Ignatius Gallaher on the London Press! Who would have thought it possible eight years before? Still, now that he reviewed the past, Little Chandler could remember many signs of future greatness in his friend. People used to say that Ignatius Gallaher was wild. Of course, he did mix with a rakish set of fellows at that time, drank freely and borrowed money on all sides. In the end he had got mixed up in some shady affair, some money transaction: at least, that was one version of his flight. But nobody denied him talent. There was always a certain . . . something in Ignatius Gallaher that impressed you in spite of yourself. Even when he was out at elbows and at his wits' end for money he kept up a bold face. Little Chandler remembered (and the remembrance brought a slight flush of pride to his cheek) one of Ignatius Gallaher's sayings when he was in a tight corner:

"Half time, now, boys," he used to say light-heartedly. "Where's my considering cap?"

That was Ignatius Gallaher all out; and, damn it, you couldn't but admire him for it.

Little Chandler quickened his pace. For the first time in his life he felt himself superior to the people he passed. For the first time his soul revolted against the dull inelegance of Capel Street. There was no doubt about it: if you wanted to succeed you had to go away. You could do nothing in Dublin. As he crossed Grattan Bridge he looked down the river towards the lower quays and pitied the poor stunted houses. They seemed to him a band of tramps, huddled together along the river-banks, their old coats covered with dust and soot, stupefied by the panorama of sunset and waiting for the first chill of night to bid them arise, shake themselves and begone. He wondered whether he could write a poem to express his idea. Perhaps Gallaher might be able to get it into some London paper for him. Could he write something original? He was not sure what idea he wished to express but the thought that a poetic moment had touched him took life within him like an infant hope. He stepped onward bravely.

Every step brought him nearer to London, farther from his own sober inartistic life. A light began to tremble on the horizon of his mind. He was not so old—thirty two. His temperament might be said to be just at the point of maturity. There were so many different moods and impressions that he wished to express in verse. He felt them within him. He tried to weigh his soul to see if it was a poet's soul. Melancholy was the dominant note of his temperament, he thought, but it was a melancholy tempered by recurrences of faith and resignation and simple joy. If he could give expression to it in a book of poems perhaps men would listen. He would never be popular: he saw that. He could not sway the crowd but he might appeal to a little circle of kindred minds. The English critics, perhaps, would recognise him as one of the Celtic school by reason of the melancholy tone of his poems; besides that, he would put in allusions. He began to invent sentences and phrases from the notices which his book would get. *Mr Chandler has the gift of easy and graceful verse. . . . A wistful sadness pervades these poems. . . . The Celtic note.* It was a pity his name was not more Irish-looking. Perhaps it would be better to insert his mother's name before the surname: Thomas Malone Chandler, or better still: T. Malone Chandler. He would speak to Gallaher about it.

He pursued his revery so ardently that he passed his street and had to turn back. As he came near Corless's his former agitation began to overmaster him and he halted before the door in indecision. Finally he opened the door and entered.

The light and noise of the bar held him at the doorway for a few moments. He looked about him, but his sight was confused by the shining of many red and green wineglasses. The bar seemed to him to be full of people and he felt that the people were observing him curiously. He glanced quickly to right and left (frowning slightly to make his errand appear serious), but when his sight cleared a little he saw that nobody had turned to look at him: and there, sure enough, was Ignatius Gallaher leaning with his back against the counter and his feet planted far apart.

"Hallo, Tommy, old hero, here you are! What is it to be? What will you have? I'm taking whisky: better stuff than we get across the water. Soda? Lithia? No mineral? I'm the same. Spoils the flavour. . . . Here, *garçon*, bring us two halves of malt whisky, like a good fellow. . . . Well, and how have you been pulling along since I saw you last? Dear God, how old we're getting! Do you see any signs of aging in me—eh, what? A little grey and thin on the top—what?"

Ignatius Gallaher took off his hat and displayed a large closely cropped head. His face was heavy, pale and cleanshaven. His eyes, which were of bluish slate-colour, relieved his unhealthy pallor and shone out plainly above the vivid orange tie he wore. Between these rival features the lips appeared very long and shapeless and colourless. He bent his head and felt with two sympathetic fingers the thin hair at the crown. Little Chandler shook his head as a denial. Ignatius Gallaher put on his hat again.

"It pulls you down," he said, "Press life. Always hurry and scurry, looking for copy and sometimes not finding it: and then, always to have something new in your stuff. Damn proofs and printers, I say, for a few days. I'm deuced glad, I can tell you, to get back to the old country. Does a fellow good, a bit of a holiday. I feel a ton better since I landed again in dear dirty Dublin.... Here you are, Tommy. Water? Say when."

Little Chandler allowed his whisky to be very much diluted.

"You don't know what's good for you, my boy," said Ignatius Gallaher. "I drink mine neat."

"I drink very little as a rule," said Little Chandler modestly. "An odd half-one or so when I meet any of the old crowd: that's all."

"Ah, well," said Ignatius Gallaher, cheerfully, "here's to us and to old times and old acquaintance."

They clinked glasses and drank the toast.

"I met some of the old gang to-day," said Ignatius Gallaher. "O'Hara seems to be in a bad way. What's he doing?"

"Nothing," said Little Chandler. "He's gone to the dogs."

"But Hogan has a good sit, hasn't he?"

"Yes; he's in the Land Commission."

"I met him one night in London and he seemed to be very flush.... Poor O'Hara! Boose, I suppose?"

"Others things, too," said Little Chandler shortly.

Ignatius Gallaher laughed.

"Tommy," he said, "I see you haven't changed an atom. You're the very same serious person that used to lecture me on Sunday mornings when I had a sore head and a fur on my tongue. You'd want to knock about a bit in the world. Have you never been anywhere, even for a trip?"

"I've been to the Isle of Man," said Little Chandler.

Ignatius Gallaher laughed.

"The Isle of Man!" he said. "Go to London or Paris: Paris, for choice. That'd do you good."

"Have you seen Paris?"

"I should think I have! I've knocked about there a little."

"And is it really so beautiful as they say?" asked Little Chandler.

He sipped a little of his drink while Ignatius Gallaher finished his boldly.

"Beautiful?" said Ignatius Gallaher, pausing on the word and on the flavour of his drink. "It's not so beautiful, you know. Of course, it is beautiful. . . . But it's the life of Paris; that's the thing. Ah, there's no city like Paris for gaiety, movement, excitement. . . ."

Little Chandler finished his whisky and, after some trouble, succeeded in catching the barman's eye. He ordered the same again.

"I've been to the Moulin Rouge," Ignatius Gallaher continued when the barman had removed their glasses, "and I've been to all the bohemian cafés. Hot stuff! Not for a pious chap like you, Tommy."

Little Chandler said nothing until the barman returned with the two glasses: then he touched his friend's glass lightly and reciprocated the former toast. He was beginning to feel somewhat disillusioned. Gallaher's accent and way of expressing himself did not please him. There was something vulgar in his friend which he had not observed before. But perhaps it was only the result of living in London amid the bustle and competition of the Press. The old personal charm was still there under this new gaudy manner. And, after all, Gallaher had lived, he had seen the world. Little Chandler looked at his friend enviously.

"Everything in Paris is gay," said Ignatius Gallaher. "They believe in enjoying life—and don't you think they're right? If you want to enjoy yourself properly you must go to Paris. And, mind you, they've a great feeling for the Irish there. When they heard I was from Ireland they were ready to eat me, man."

Little Chandler took four or five sips from his glass.

"Tell me," he said, "is it true that Paris is so . . . immoral as they say?"

Ignatius Gallaher made a catholic gesture with his right arm.

"Every place is immoral," he said. "Of course you do find spicy bits in Paris. Go to one of the students' balls, for instance. That's lively, if you like, when the *cocottes* begin to let themselves loose. You know what they are, I suppose?"

"I've heard of them," said Little Chandler.

Ignatius Gallaher drank off his whisky and shook his head.

"Ah," he said, "you may say what you like. There's no woman like the Parisienne—for style, for go."

"Then it is an immoral city," said Little Chandler, with timid insistence. "I mean, compared with London or Dublin?"

"London!" said Ignatius Gallaher. "It's six of one and half-a-dozen of the other. You ask Hogan, my boy. I showed him a bit about London when he was over there. He'd open your eye. . . . I say, Tommy, don't make punch of that whisky: liquor up."

"No, really. . . ."

"O, come on, another one won't do you any harm. What is it? The same again, I suppose?"

"Well . . . all right."

"*François*, the same again. . . . Will you smoke, Tommy?"

Ignatius Gallaher produced his cigar-case. The two friends lit their cigars and puffed at them in silence until their drinks were served.

"I'll tell you my opinion," said Ignatius Gallaher, emerging after some time from the clouds of smoke in which he had taken refuge, "it's a rum world. Talk of immorality! I've heard of cases—what am I saying?—I've known them: cases of . . . immorality. . . ."

Ignatius Gallaher puffed thoughtfully at his cigar and then, in a calm historian's tone, he proceeded to sketch for his friend some pictures of the corruption which was rife abroad. He summarised the vices of many capitals and seemed inclined to award the palm to Berlin. Some things he could not vouch for (his friends had told him), but of others he had had personal experience. He spared neither rank nor caste. He revealed many of the secrets of religious houses on the Continent and described some of the practices which were fashionable in high society and ended by telling, with details, a story about an English duchess— a story which he knew to be true. Little Chandler was astonished.

"Ah, well," said Ignatius Gallaher, "here we are in old jog-along Dublin where nothing is known of such things."

"How dull you must find it," said Little Chandler, "after all the other places you've seen!"

"Well," said Ignatius Gallaher, "it's a relaxation to come over here, you know. And, after all, it's the old country, as they say, isn't it? You can't help having a certain feeling for it. That's human nature. . . . But tell me something about yourself. Hogan told me you had . . . tasted the joys of connubial bliss. Two years ago, wasn't it?"

Little Chandler blushed and smiled.

"Yes," he said. "I was married last May twelve months."

"I hope it's not too late in the day to offer my best wishes," said Ignatius Gallaher. "I didn't know your address or I'd have done so at the time."

He extended his hand, which Little Chandler took.

"Well, Tommy," he said, "I wish you and yours every joy in life, old chap, and tons of money, and may you never die till I shoot you. And that's the wish of a sincere friend, an old friend. You know that?"

"I know that," said Little Chandler.

"Any youngsters?" said Ignatius Gallaher.

Little Chandler blushed again.

"We have one child," he said.

"Son or daughter?"

"A little boy."

Ignatius Gallaher slapped his friend sonorously on the back.

"Bravo," he said, "I wouldn't doubt you, Tommy."

Little Chandler smiled, looked confusedly at his glass and bit his lower lip with three childishly white front teeth.

"I hope you'll spend an evening with us," he said, "before you go back. My wife will be delighted to meet you. We can have a little music and—"

"Thanks awfully, old chap," said Ignatius Gallaher, "I'm sorry we didn't meet earlier. But I must leave to-morrow night."

"To-night, perhaps . . . ?"

"I'm awfully sorry, old man. You see I'm over here with another fellow, clever young chap he is too, and we arranged to go to a little card-party. Only for that . . . "

"O, in that case. . . ."

"But who knows?" said Ignatius Gallaher considerately. "Next year I may take a little skip over here now that I've broken the ice. It's only a pleasure deferred."

"Very well," said Little Chandler, "the next time you come we must have an evening together. That's agreed now, isn't it?"

"Yes, that's agreed," said Ignatius Gallaher. "Next year if I come, *parole d'honneur.*"

"And to clinch the bargain," said Little Chandler, "we'll just have one more now."

Ignatius Gallaher took out a large gold watch and looked at it.

"Is it to be the last?" he said. "Because you know, I have an a.p."

"O, yes, positively," said Little Chandler.

"Very well, then," said Ignatius Gallaher, "let us have another one as a *deoc an doruis*—that's good vernacular for a small whisky, I believe."

Little Chandler ordered the drinks. The blush which had risen to his face a few moments before was establishing itself. A trifle made him blush at any time; and now he felt warm and excited. Three small whiskies had gone to his head and Gallaher's strong cigar had confused his mind, for he was a delicate and abstinent person. The adventure of meeting Gallaher after eight years, of finding himself with Gallaher in Corless's surrounded by lights and noise, of listening to Gallaher's stories and of sharing for a brief space Gallaher's vagrant and triumphant life, upset the equipoise of his sensitive nature. He felt acutely the contrast between his own life and his friend's, and it seemed to him unjust. Gallaher was his inferior in birth and education. He was sure that he could do something better than his friend had ever done, or could ever do, something higher than mere tawdry journalism if he only got the chance. What was it that stood in his way? His unfortunate timidity! He wished to vindicate himself in some way, to assert his manhood. He saw behind Gallaher's refusal of his invitation. Gallaher was only patronising him by his friendliness just as he was patronising Ireland by his visit.

The barman brought their drinks. Little Chandler pushed one glass towards his friend and took up the other boldly.

"Who knows?" he said, as they lifted their glasses. "When you come next year I may have the pleasure of wishing long life and happiness to Mr and Mrs Ignatius Gallaher."

Ignatius Gallaher in the act of drinking closed one eye expressively over the rim of his glass. When he had drunk he smacked his lips decisively, set down his glass and said:

"No blooming fear of that, my boy. I'm going to have my fling first and see a bit of life and the world before I put my head in the sack—if I ever do."

"Some day you will," said Little Chandler calmly.

Ignatius Gallaher turned his orange tie and slate-blue eyes full upon his friend.

"You think so?" he said.

"You'll put your head in the sack," repeated Little Chandler stoutly, "like everyone else if you can find the girl."

He had slightly emphasised his tone and he was aware that he had betrayed himself; but, though the colour had heightened in his cheek, he did not flinch from his friend's gaze. Ignatius Gallaher watched him for a few moments and then said:

"If ever it occurs, you may bet your bottom dollar there'll be no mooning and spooning about it. I mean to marry money. She'll have a good fat account at the bank or she won't do for me."

Little Chandler shook his head.

"Why, man alive," said Ignatius Gallaher, vehemently, "do you know what it is? I've only to say the word and tomorrow I can have the woman and the cash. You don't believe it? Well, I know it. There are hundreds—what am I saying?—thousands of rich Germans and Jews, rotten with money, that'd only be too glad.... You wait a while, my boy. See if I don't play my cards properly. When I go about a thing I mean business, I tell you. You just wait."

He tossed his glass to his mouth, finished his drink and laughed loudly. Then he looked thoughtfully before him and said in a calmer tone:

"But I'm in no hurry. They can wait. I don't fancy tying myself up to one woman, you know."

He imitated with his mouth the act of tasting and made a wry face.

"Must get a bit stale, I should think," he said.

\* \* \* \* \*

Little Chandler sat in the room off the hall, holding a child in his arms. To save money they kept no servant but Annie's young sister Monica came for an hour or so in the morning and an hour or so in the evening to help. But Monica had gone home long ago. It was quarter to nine. Little Chandler had come home late for tea and, moreover, he had forgotten to bring Annie home the parcel of coffee from Bewley's. Of course she was in a bad humour and gave him short answers. She said she would do without any tea but when it came near the time at which the shop at the corner closed she decided to go out herself for a quarter of a pound of tea and two pounds of sugar. She put the sleeping child deftly in his arms and said:

"Here. Don't waken him."

A little lamp with a white china shade stood upon the table and its light fell over a photograph which was enclosed in a frame of crumpled horn. It was Annie's photograph. Little Chandler looked at it, pausing at the thin tight lips. She wore the pale blue summer blouse which he had brought her home as a present one Saturday. It had cost him ten and elevenpence; but what an agony of nervousness it had cost him! How he had suffered that day, waiting at the shop door until the shop was empty, standing at the counter and trying to appear at his ease while the girl piled ladies' blouses before him, paying at the desk and forgetting to take up the odd penny of his change, being called back by the cashier, and, finally, striving to hide his blushes as he left the shop by examining the parcel to see if it was securely tied. When he brought the blouse home Annie kissed him and said it was very pretty and stylish; but when she heard the price she threw the blouse on the table and said it was a regular swindle to charge ten and elevenpence for that. At first she wanted to take it back but when she tried it on she was delighted with it, especially with the make of the sleeves, and kissed him and said he was very good to think of her.

Hm! . . .

He looked coldly into the eyes of the photograph and they answered coldly. Certainly they were pretty and the face itself was pretty. But he found something mean in it. Why was it so unconscious and lady-like? The composure of the eyes irritated him. They repelled him and defied him: there was no passion in them, no rapture. He thought of what Gallaher had said about rich Jewesses. Those dark Oriental eyes, he thought, how full they are of passion, of voluptuous longing! . . . Why had he married the eyes in the photograph?

He caught himself up at the question and glanced nervously round the room. He found something mean in the pretty furniture which he had bought for his house on the hire system. Annie had chosen it herself and it reminded him of her. It too was prim and pretty. A dull resentment against his life awoke within him. Could he not escape from his little house? Was it too late for him to try to live bravely like Gallaher?

Could he go to London? There was the furniture still to be paid for. If he could only write a book and get it published, that might open the way for him.

A volume of Byron's poems lay before him on the table. He opened it cautiously with his left hand lest he should waken the child and began to read the first poem in the book:

> Hushed are the winds and still the evening gloom,
> Not e'en a Zephyr wanders through the grove,
> Whilst I return to view my Margaret's tomb
> And scatter flowers on the dust I love.

He paused. He felt the rhythm of the verse about him in the room. How melancholy it was! Could he, too, write like that, express the melancholy of his soul in verse? There were so many things he wanted to describe: his sensation of a few hours before on Grattan Bridge, for example. If he could get back again into that mood....

The child awoke and began to cry. He turned from the page and tried to hush it: but it would not be hushed. He began to rock it to and fro in his arms but its wailing cry grew keener. He rocked it faster while his eyes began to read the second stanza:

> Within this narrow cell reclines her clay
> That clay where once ...

It was useless. He couldn't read. He couldn't do anything. The wailing of the child pierced the drum of his ear. It was useless, useless! He was a prisoner for life. His arms trembled with anger and suddenly bending to the child's face he shouted:

"Stop!"

The child stopped for an instant, had a spasm of fright and began to scream. He jumped up from his chair and walked hastily up and down the room with the child in his arms. It began to sob piteously, losing its breath for four or five seconds, and then bursting out anew. The thin walls of the room echoed the sound. He tried to soothe it but it sobbed more convulsively. He looked at the contracted and quivering face of the child and began to be alarmed. He counted seven sobs without a break between them and caught the child to his breast in fright. If it died! ...

The door was burst open and a young woman ran in, panting.

"What is it? What is it?" she cried.

The child, hearing its mother's voice, broke out into a paroxysm of sobbing.

"It's nothing, Annie . . . it's nothing. . . . He began to cry . . ."

She flung her parcels on the floor and snatched the child from him.

"What have you done to him?" she cried, glaring into his face.

Little Chandler sustained for one moment the gaze of her eyes and his heart closed together as he met the hatred in them. He began to stammer:

"It's nothing. . . . He . . . he began to cry. . . . I couldn't . . . I didn't do anything. . . . What?"

Giving no heed to him she began to walk up and down the room, clasping the child tightly in her arms and murmuring:

"My little man! My little mannie! Was 'ou frightened, love? . . . There now, love! There now! . . . Lambabaun! Mamma's little lamb of the world! . . . There now!"

Little Chandler felt his cheeks suffused with shame and he stood back out of the lamplight. He listened while the paroxysm of the child's sobbing grew less and less; and tears of remorse started to his eyes.

# James Joyce

## *Clay*

The matron had given her leave to go out as soon as the women's tea was over and Maria looked forward to her evening out. The kitchen was spick and span: the cook said you could see yourself in the big copper boilers. The fire was nice and bright and on one of the side-tables were four very big barmbracks. These barmbracks seemed uncut; but if you went closer you would see that they had been cut into long thick even slices and were ready to be handed round at tea. Maria had cut them herself.

Maria was a very, very small person indeed but she had a very long nose and a very long chin. She talked a little through her nose, always soothingly: "Yes, my dear," and "No, my dear." She was always sent for when the women quarrelled over their tubs and always succeeded in making peace. One day the matron had said to her:

"Maria, you are a veritable peace-maker!"

And the sub-matron and two of the Board ladies had heard the compliment. And Ginger Mooney was always saying what she wouldn't do to the dummy who had charge of the irons if it wasn't for Maria. Everyone was so fond of Maria.

The women would have their tea at six o'clock and she would be able to get away before seven. From Ballsbridge to the Pillar, twenty minutes; from the Pillar to Drumcondra, twenty minutes; and twenty minutes to buy the things. She would be there before eight. She took out her purse with the silver clasps and read again the words *A Present from Belfast*. She was very fond of that purse because Joe had brought it to her five years before when he and Alphy had gone to Belfast on a Whit-Monday trip. In the purse were two half-crowns and some coppers. She would have five shillings clear after paying tram fare. What a nice evening they would have, all the children singing! Only she hoped that Joe wouldn't come in drunk. He was so different when he took any drink.

Often he had wanted her to go and live with them; but she would have felt herself in the way (though Joe's wife was ever so nice with her) and she had become accustomed to the life of the laundry. Joe was a good fellow. She had nursed him and Alphy too; and Joe used often say:

"Mamma is mamma but Maria is my proper mother."

After the break-up at home the boys had got her that position in the *Dublin by Lamplight* laundry, and she liked it. She used to have such a bad opinion of Protestants but now she thought they were very nice people, a little quiet and serious, but still very nice people to live with. Then she had her plants in the conservatory and she liked looking after them. She had lovely ferns and wax-plants and, whenever anyone came to visit her, she always gave the visitor one or two slips from her conservatory. There was one thing she didn't like and that was the tracts on the walls; but the matron was such a nice person to deal with, so genteel.

When the cook told her everything was ready she went into the women's room and began to pull the big bell. In a few minutes the women began to come in by twos and threes, wiping their steaming hands in their petticoats and pulling down the sleeves of their blouses over their red steaming arms. They settled down before their huge mugs which the cook and the dummy filled up with hot tea, already mixed with milk and sugar in huge tin cans. Maria superintended the distribution of the barmbrack and saw that every woman got her four slices. There was a great deal of laughing and joking during the meal. Lizzie Fleming said Maria was sure to get the ring and, though Fleming had said that for so many Hallow Eves, Maria had to laugh and say she didn't want any ring or man either; and when she laughed her grey-green eyes sparkled with disappointed shyness and the tip of her nose nearly met the tip of her chin. Then Ginger Mooney lifted up her mug of tea and proposed Maria's health while all the other women clattered with their mugs on the table, and said she was sorry she hadn't a sup of porter to drink it in. And Maria laughed again till the tip of her nose nearly met the tip of her chin and till her minute body nearly shook itself asunder because she knew that Mooney meant well though, of course, she had the notions of a common woman.

But wasn't Maria glad when the women had finished their tea and the cook and the dummy had begun to clear away the tea-things! She went into her little bedroom and, remembering that the next morning was a mass morning, changed the hand of the alarm from seven to six. Then she took off her working skirt and her house-boots and laid her best skirt out on the bed and her tiny dress-boots beside the foot of the bed. She changed her blouse too and, as she stood before the mirror, she thought of how she used to dress for mass on Sunday morning when she was a young girl; and she looked with quaint affection at the diminutive body which she had so often adorned. In spite of its years she found it a nice tidy little body.

When she got outside the streets were shining with rain and she was glad of her old brown raincloak. The tram was full and she had to sit on the little stool at the end of the car, facing all the people, with her toes barely touching the floor. She arranged in her mind all she was going to do and thought how much better it was to be independent and to have your own money in your pocket. She hoped they would have a nice evening. She was sure they would but she could not help thinking what a pity it was Alphy and Joe were not speaking. They were always falling out now but when they were boys together they used to be the best of friends; but such was life.

She got out of her tram at the Pillar and ferreted her way quickly among the crowds. She went into Downes's cakeshop but the shop was so full of people that it was a long time before she could get herself attended to. She bought a dozen of mixed penny cakes, and at last came out of the shop laden with a big bag. Then she thought what else would she buy: she wanted to buy something really nice. They would be sure to have plenty of apples and nuts. It was hard to know what to buy and all she could think of was cake. She decided to buy some plumcake but Downes's plumcake had not enough almond icing on top of it so she went over to a shop in Henry Street. Here she was a long time in suiting herself and the stylish young lady behind the counter, who was evidently a little annoyed by her, asked her was it wedding-cake she wanted to buy. That made Maria blush and smile at the young lady; but the young lady took it all very seriously and finally cut a thick slice of plumcake, parcelled it up and said:

"Two-and-four, please."

She thought she would have to stand in the Drumcondra tram because none of the young men seemed to notice her but an elderly gentleman made room for her. He was a stout gentleman and he wore a brown hard hat; he had a square red face and a greyish moustache. Maria thought he was a colonel-looking gentleman and she reflected how much more polite he was than the young men who simply stared straight before them. The gentleman began to chat with her about Hallow Eve and the rainy weather. He supposed the bag was full of good things for the little ones and said it was only right that the youngsters should enjoy themselves while they were young. Maria agreed with him and favoured him with demure nods and hems. He was very nice with her, and when she was getting out at the Canal Bridge she thanked him and bowed, and he bowed to her and raised his hat and smiled agreeably; and while she was going up along the terrace, bending her tiny head under the rain, she thought how easy it was to know a gentleman even when he has a drop taken.

Everybody said: "O, here's Maria!" when she came to Joe's house. Joe was there, having come home from business, and all the children had their Sunday dresses on. There were two big girls in from next door and games were going on. Maria gave the bag of cakes to the eldest boy, Alphy, to divide and Mrs. Donnelly said it was too good of her to bring such a big bag of cakes and made all the children say:

"Thanks, Maria."

But Maria said she had brought something special for papa and mamma, something they would be sure to like, and she began to look for her plumcake. She tried in Downes's bag and then in the pockets of her raincloak and then on the hall-stand but nowhere could she find it. Then she asked all the children had any of them eaten it—by mistake, of course—but the children all said no and looked as if they did not like to eat cakes if they were to be accused of stealing. Everybody had a solution for the mystery and Mrs. Donnelly said it was plain that Maria had left it behind her in the tram. Maria, remembering how confused the gentleman with the greyish moustache had made her, coloured with shame and vexation and disappointment. At the thought of the failure of her little surprise and of the two and fourpence she had thrown away for nothing she nearly cried outright.

But Joe said it didn't matter and made her sit down by the fire. He was very nice with her. He told her all that went on in his office, repeating for her a smart answer which he had made to the manager. Maria did not understand why Joe laughed so much over the answer he had made but she said the manager must have been a very overbearing person to deal with. Joe said he wasn't so bad when you knew how to take him, that he was a decent sort so long as you didn't rub him the wrong way. Mrs. Donnelly played the piano for the children and they danced and sang. Then the two next-door girls handed round the nuts. Nobody could find the nutcrackers and Joe was nearly getting cross over it and asked how did they expect Maria to crack nuts without a nutcracker. But Maria said she didn't like nuts and that they weren't to bother about her. Then Joe asked would she take a bottle of stout and Mrs. Donnelly said there was port wine too in the house if she would prefer that. Maria said she would rather they didn't ask her to take anything: but Joe insisted.

So Maria let him have his way and they sat by the fire talking over old times and Maria thought she would put in a good word for Alphy. But Joe cried that God might strike him stone dead if ever he spoke a word to his brother again and Maria said she was sorry she had mentioned the matter. Mrs. Donnelly told her husband it was a great shame for him to speak that way of his own flesh and blood but Joe said that Alphy was no brother of his and there was nearly being a row on the head of it. But Joe said he would not lose his temper on account of the night it was and asked his wife to open some more stout. The two next-door girls had arranged some Hallow Eve games and soon everything was merry again. Maria was delighted to see the children so merry and Joe and his wife in such good spirits. The next-door girls put some saucers on the table and then led the children up to the table, blindfold. One got the prayerbook and the other three got the water; and when one of the next-door girls got the ring Mrs. Donnelly shook her finger at the blushing girl as much as to say: "O, I know all about it!" They insisted then on blindfolding Maria and leading her up to the table to see what she would get; and, while they were putting on the bandage, Maria laughed and laughed again till the tip of her nose nearly met the tip of her chin.

They led her up to the table amid laughing and joking and she put her hand out in the air as she was told to do. She moved her hand about here and there in the air and descended on one of the saucers. She felt a soft wet substance with her fingers and was surprised that nobody spoke or took off her bandage. There was a pause for a few seconds; and then a great deal of scuffling and whispering. Somebody said something about the garden, and at last Mrs. Donnelly said something very cross to one of the next-door girls and told her to throw it out at once: that was no play. Maria understood that it was wrong that time and so she had to do it over again: and this time she got the prayer-book.

After that Mrs. Donnelly played Miss McCloud's Reel for the children and Joe made Maria take a glass of wine. Soon they were all quite merry again and Mrs. Donnelly said Maria would enter a convent before the year was out because she had got the prayer-book. Maria had never seen Joe so nice to her as he was that night, so full of pleasant talk and reminiscences. She said they were all very good to her.

At last the children grew tired and sleepy and Joe asked Maria would she not sing some little song before she went, one of the old songs. Mrs. Donnelly said "Do, please, Maria!" and so Maria had to get up and stand beside the piano. Mrs. Donnelly bade the children be quiet and listen to Maria's song. Then she played the prelude and said "Now, Maria!" and Maria, blushing very much, began to sing in a tiny quavering voice. She sang *I Dreamt that I Dwelt,* and when she came to the second verse she sang again:

> *I dreamt that I dwelt in marble halls*
> *With vassals and serfs at my side*
> *And of all who assembled within those walls*
> *That I was the hope and the pride.*
> *I had riches too great to count, could boast*
> *Of a high ancestral name,*
> *But I also dreamt, which pleased me most,*
> *That you loved me still the same.*

But no one tried to show her her mistake; and when she had ended her song Joe was very much moved. He said that there was no time like the long ago and no music for him like poor old Balfe, whatever other people might say; and his eyes filled up so much with tears that he could not find what he was looking for and in the end he had to ask his wife to tell him where the corkscrew was.

# James Joyce

## *The Dead*

Lily, the caretaker's daughter, was literally run off her feet. Hardly had she brought one gentleman into the little pantry behind the office on the ground floor and helped him off with his overcoat than the wheezy hall-door bell clanged again and she had to scamper along the bare hallway to let in another guest. It was well for her she had not to attend to the ladies also. But Miss Kate and Miss Julia had thought of that and had converted the bathroom upstairs into a ladies' dressing-room. Miss Kate and Miss Julia were there, gossiping and laughing and fussing, walking after each other to the head of the stairs, peering down over the banisters and calling down to Lily to ask her who had come.

It was always a great affair, the Misses Morkan's annual dance. Everybody who knew them came to it, members of the family, old friends of the family, the members of Julia's choir, any of Kate's pupils that were grown up enough and even some of Mary Jane's pupils too. Never once had it fallen flat. For years and years it had gone off in splendid style as long as anyone could remember; ever since Kate and Julia, after the death of their brother Pat, had left the house in Stoney Batter and taken Mary Jane, their only niece, to live with them in the dark gaunt house on Usher's Island, the upper part of which they had rented from Mr. Fulham, the cornfactor on the ground floor. That was a good thirty years ago if it was a day. Mary Jane, who was then a little girl in short clothes, was now the main prop of the household for she had the organ in Haddington Road. She had been through the Academy and gave a pupils' concert every year in the upper room of the Antient Concert Rooms. Many of her pupils belonged to better-class families on the Kingstown and Dalkey line. Old as they were, her aunts also did their share. Julia, though she was quite grey, was still the leading soprano in Adam and Eve's, and Kate, being too feeble to go about much, gave music lessons to beginners on the old square piano in the back room. Lily, the caretaker's daughter, did housemaid's work for them. Though their life was modest they believed in eating well; the best of everything: diamond-bone sirloins, three-shilling tea and the best bottled stout. But Lily seldom made a mistake in the orders so that she got on well with her three mistresses. They were fussy, that was all. But the only thing they would not stand was back answers.

Of course they had good reason to be fussy on such a night. And then it was long after ten o'clock and yet there was no sign of Gabriel and his wife. Besides they were dreadfully afraid that Freddy Malins might turn up screwed. They would not wish for worlds that any of Mary Jane's pupils should see him under the influence; and when he was like that it was sometimes very hard to manage him. Freddy Malins always came late but they wondered what could be keeping Gabriel: and that was what brought them every two minutes to the banisters to ask Lily had Gabriel or Freddy come.

"O, Mr. Conroy," said Lily to Gabriel when she opened the door for him, "Miss Kate and Miss Julia thought you were never coming. Good-night, Mrs. Conroy."

"I'll engage they did," said Gabriel, "but they forget that my wife here takes three mortal hours to dress herself."

He stood on the mat, scraping the snow from his goloshes, while Lily led his wife to the foot of the stairs and called out:

"Miss Kate, here's Mrs. Conroy."

Kate and Julia came toddling down the dark stairs at once. Both of them kissed Gabriel's wife, said she must be perished alive and asked was Gabriel with her.

"Here I am as right as the mail, Aunt Kate! Go on up. I'll follow," called out Gabriel from the dark.

He continued scraping his feet vigorously while the three women went upstairs, laughing, to the ladies' dressing-room. A light fringe of snow lay like a cape on the shoulders of his overcoat and like toecaps on the toes of his goloshes; and, as the buttons of his overcoat slipped with a squeaking noise through the snow-stiffened frieze, a cold fragrant air from out-of-doors escaped from crevices and folds.

"Is it snowing again, Mr. Conroy?" asked Lily.

She had preceded him into the pantry to help him off with his overcoat. Gabriel smiled at the three syllables she had given his surname and glanced at her. She was a slim, growing girl, pale in complexion and with hay-coloured hair. The gas in the pantry made her look still paler. Gabriel had known her when she was a child and used to sit on the lowest step nursing a rag doll.

"Yes, Lily," he answered, "and I think we're in for a night of it."

He looked up at the pantry ceiling, which was shaking with the stamping and shuffling of feet on the floor above, listened for a moment to the piano and then glanced at the girl, who was folding his overcoat carefully at the end of a shelf.

"Tell me, Lily," he said in a friendly tone, "do you still go to school?"

"O no, sir," she answered. "I'm done schooling this year and more."

"O, then," said Gabriel gaily, "I suppose we'll be going to your wedding one of these fine days with your young man, eh?"

The girl glanced back at him over her shoulder and said with great bitterness:

"The men that is now is only all palaver and what they can get out of you."

Gabriel coloured as if he felt he had made a mistake and, without looking at her, kicked off his goloshes and flicked actively with his muffler at his patent-leather shoes.

He was a stout tallish young man. The high colour of his cheeks pushed upwards even to his forehead where it scattered itself in a few formless patches of pale red; and on his hairless face there scintillated restlessly the polished lenses and the bright gilt rims of the glasses which screened his delicate and restless eyes. His glossy black hair was parted in the middle and brushed in a long curve behind his ears where it curled slightly beneath the groove left by his hat.

When he had flicked lustre into his shoes he stood up and pulled his waistcoat down more tightly on his plump body. Then he took a coin rapidly from his pocket.

"O Lily," he said, thrusting it into her hands, "it's Christmas-time, isn't it? Just . . . here's a little. . . ."

He walked rapidly towards the door.

"O no, sir!" cried the girl, following him. "Really, sir, I wouldn't take it."

"Christmas-time! Christmas-time!" said Gabriel, almost trotting to the stairs and waving his hand to her in deprecation.

The girl, seeing that he had gained the stairs, called out after him:

"Well, thank you, sir."

He waited outside the drawing-room door until the waltz should finish, listening to the skirts that swept against it and to the shuffling of feet. He was still discomposed by the girl's bitter and sudden retort. It had cast a gloom over him which he tried to dispel by arranging his cuffs and the bows of his tie. Then he took from his waistcoat pocket a little paper and glanced at the headings he had made for his speech. He was undecided about the lines from Robert Browning for he feared they would be above the heads of his hearers. Some quotation that they could recognise from Shakespeare or from the Melodies would be better. The indelicate clacking of the men's heels and the shuffling of their soles reminded him that their grade of culture differed from his. He would only make himself ridiculous by quoting poetry to them which they could not understand. They would think that he was airing his superior education. He would fail with them just as he had failed with the girl in the pantry. He had taken up a wrong tone. His whole speech was a mistake from first to last, an utter failure.

Just then his aunts and his wife came out of the ladies' dressing-room. His aunts were two small plainly dressed old women. Aunt Julia was an inch or so taller. Her hair, drawn low over the tops of her ears, was grey; and grey also, with darker shadows, was her large flaccid face. Though she was stout in build and stood erect her slow eyes and parted lips gave her the appearance of a woman who did not know where she was or where she was going. Aunt Kate was more vivacious. Her face, healthier than her sister's, was all puckers and creases, like a shrivelled red apple, and her hair, braided in the same old-fashioned way, had not lost its ripe nut colour.

They both kissed Gabriel frankly. He was their favourite nephew, the son of the dead elder sister, Ellen, who had married T. J. Conroy of the Port and Docks.

"Gretta tells me you're not going to take a cab back to Monkstown to-night, Gabriel," said Aunt Kate.

"No," said Gabriel, turning to his wife, "we had quite enough of that last year, hadn't we. Don't you remember, Aunt Kate, what a cold Gretta got out of it? Cab windows rattling all the way, and the east wind blowing in after we passed Merrion. Very jolly it was. Gretta caught a dreadful cold."

Aunt Kate frowned severely and nodded her head at every word.

"Quite right, Gabriel, quite right," she said. "You can't be too careful."

"But as for Gretta there," said Gabriel, "she'd walk home in the snow if she were let."

Mrs. Conroy laughed.

"Don't mind him, Aunt Kate," she said. "He's really an awful bother, what with green shades for Tom's eyes at night and making him do the dumb-bells, and forcing Eva to eat the stirabout. The poor child! And she simply hates the sight of it! ... O, but you'll never guess what he makes me wear now!"

She broke out into a peal of laughter and glanced at her husband, whose admiring and happy eyes had been wandering from her dress to her face and hair. The two aunts laughed heartily too, for Gabriel's solicitude was a standing joke with them.

"Goloshes!" said Mrs. Conroy. "That's the latest. Whenever it's wet underfoot I must put on my goloshes. To-night even he wanted me to put them on, but I wouldn't. The next thing he'll buy me will be a diving suit."

Gabriel laughed nervously and patted his tie reassuringly while Aunt Kate nearly doubled herself, so heartily did she enjoy the joke. The smile soon faded from Aunt Julia's face and her mirthless eyes were directed towards her nephew's face. After a pause she asked:

"And what are goloshes, Gabriel?"

"Goloshes, Julia!" exclaimed her sister. "Goodness me, don't you know what goloshes are? You wear them over your ... over your boots, Gretta, isn't it?"

"Yes," said Mrs. Conroy. "Guttapercha things. We both have a pair now. Gabriel says everyone wears them on the continent."

"O, on the continent," murmured Aunt Julia, nodding her head slowly.

Gabriel knitted his brows and said, as if he were slightly angered:

"It's nothing very wonderful but Gretta thinks it very funny because she says the word reminds her of Christy Minstrels."

"But tell me, Gabriel," said Aunt Kate, with brisk tact. "Of course, you've seen about the room. Gretta was saying . . ."

"O, the room is all right," replied Gabriel. "I've taken one in the Gresham."

"To be sure," said Aunt Kate, "by far the best thing to do. And the children, Gretta, you're not anxious about them?"

"O, for one night," said Mrs. Conroy. "Besides, Bessie will look after them."

"To be sure," said Aunt Kate again. "What a comfort it is to have a girl like that, one you can depend on! There's that Lily, I'm sure I don't know what has come over her lately. She's not the girl she was at all."

Gabriel was about to ask his aunt some questions on this point but she broke off suddenly to gaze after her sister who had wandered down the stairs and was craning her neck over the banisters.

"Now, I ask you," she said, almost testily, "where is Julia going? Julia! Julia! Where are you going?"

Julia, who had gone halfway down one flight, came back and announced blandly:

"Here's Freddy."

At the same moment a clapping of hands and a final flourish of the pianist told that the waltz had ended. The drawing-room door was opened from within and some couples came out. Aunt Kate drew Gabriel aside hurriedly and whispered into his ear:

"Slip down, Gabriel, like a good fellow and see if he's all right, and don't let him up if he's screwed. I'm sure he's screwed. I'm sure he is."

Gabriel went to the stairs and listened over the banisters. He could hear two persons talking in the pantry. Then he recognised Freddy Malins' laugh. He went down the stairs noisily.

"It's such a relief," said Aunt Kate to Mrs. Conroy, "that Gabriel is here. I always feel easier in my mind when he's here. . . . Julia, there's Miss Daly and Miss Power will take some refreshment. Thanks for your beautiful waltz, Miss Daly. It made lovely time."

A tall wizen-faced man, with a stiff grizzled moustache and swarthy skin, who was passing out with his partner said:

"And may we have some refreshment, too, Miss Morkan?"

"Julia," said Aunt Kate summarily, "and here's Mr. Browne and Miss Furlong. Take them in, Julia, with Miss Daly and Miss Power."

"I'm the man for the ladies," said Mr. Browne, pursing his lips until his moustache bristled and smiling in all his wrinkles. "You know, Miss Morkan, the reason they are so fond of me is—"

He did not finish his sentence, but, seeing that Aunt Kate was out of earshot, at once led the three young ladies into the back room. The middle of the room was occupied by two square tables placed end to end, and on these Aunt Julia and the caretaker were straightening and smoothing a large cloth. On the sideboard were arrayed dishes and plates, and glasses and bundles of knives and forks and spoons. The top of the closed square piano served also as a sideboard for viands and sweets. At a smaller sideboard in one corner two young men were standing, drinking hopbitters.

Mr. Browne led his charges thither and invited them all, in jest, to some ladies' punch, hot, strong and sweet. As they said they never took anything strong he opened three bottles of lemonade for them. Then he asked one of the young men to move aside, and, taking hold of the decanter, filled out for himself a goodly measure of whisky. The young men eyed him respectfully while he took a trial sip.

"God help me," he said, smiling, "it's the doctor's orders."

His wizened face broke into a broader smile, and the three young ladies laughed in musical echo to his pleasantry, swaying their bodies to and fro, with nervous jerks of their shoulders. The boldest said:

"O, now, Mr. Browne, I'm sure the doctor never ordered anything of the kind."

Mr. Browne took another sip of his whisky and said, with sidling mimicry:

"Well, you see, I'm like the famous Mrs. Cassidy, who is reported to have said: *Now, Mary Grimes, if I don't take it, make me take it, for I feel I want it.*"

His hot face had leaned forward a little too confidentially and he had assumed a very low Dublin accent so that the young ladies, with one instinct, received his speech in silence. Miss Furlong, who was one of Mary Jane's pupils, asked Miss Daly what was the name of the pretty waltz she had played; and Mr. Browne, seeing that he was ignored, turned promptly to the two young men who were more appreciative.

A red-faced young woman, dressed in pansy, came into the room, excitedly clapping her hands and crying:

"Quadrilles! Quadrilles!"

Close on her heels came Aunt Kate, crying:

"Two gentlemen and three ladies, Mary Jane!"

"O, here's Mr. Bergin and Mr. Kerrigan," said Mary Jane. "Mr. Kerrigan, will you take Miss Power? Miss Furlong, may I get you a partner, Mr. Bergin. O, that'll just do now."

"Three ladies, Mary Jane," said Aunt Kate.

The two young gentlemen asked the ladies if they might have the pleasure, and Mary Jane turned to Miss Daly.

"O, Miss Daly, you're really awfully good, after playing for the last two dances, but really we're so short of ladies to-night."

"I don't mind in the least, Miss Morkan."

"But I've a nice partner for you, Mr. Bartell D'Arcy, the tenor. I'll get him to sing later on. All Dublin is raving about him."

"Lovely voice, lovely voice!" said Aunt Kate.

As the piano had twice begun the prelude to the first figure Mary Jane led her recruits quickly from the room. They had hardly gone when Aunt Julia wandered slowly into the room, looking behind her at something.

"What is the matter, Julia?" asked Aunt Kate anxiously. "Who is it?"

Julia, who was carrying in a column of table-napkins, turned to her sister and said, simply, as if the question had surprised her:

"It's only Freddy, Kate, and Gabriel with him."

In fact right behind her Gabriel could be seen piloting Freddy Malins across the landing. The latter, a young man of about forty, was of Gabriel's size and build, with very round shoulders. His face was fleshy and pallid, touched with colour only at the thick hanging lobes of his ears and at the wide wings of his nose. He had coarse features, a blunt nose, a convex and receding brow, tumid and protruded lips. His heavy-lidded eyes and the disorder of his scanty hair made him look sleepy. He was laughing heartily in a high key at a story which he had been telling Gabriel on the stairs and at the same time rubbing the knuckles of his left fist backwards and forwards into his left eye.

"Good-evening, Freddy," said Aunt Julia.

Freddy Malins bade the Misses Morkan good-evening in

what seemed an offhand fashion by reasons of the habitual catch in his voice and then, seeing that Mr. Browne was grinning at him from the sideboard, crossed the room on rather shaky legs and began to repeat in an undertone the story he had just told to Gabriel.

"He's not so bad, is he?" said Aunt Kate to Gabriel.

Gabriel's brows were dark but he raised them quickly and answered:

"O no, hardly noticeable."

"Now, isn't he a terrible fellow!" she said. "And his poor mother made him take the pledge on New Year's Eve. But come on, Gabriel, into the drawing-room."

Before leaving the room with Gabriel she signalled to Mr. Browne by frowning and shaking her forefinger in warning to and fro. Mr. Browne nodded in answer and, when she had gone, said to Freddy Malins:

"Now, then, Teddy, I'm going to fill you out a good glass of lemonade just to buck you up."

Freddy Malins, who was nearing the climax of his story, waved the offer aside impatiently but Mr. Browne, having first called Freddy Malins' attention to a disarray in his dress, filled out and handed him a full glass of lemonade. Freddy Malins' left hand accepted the glass mechanically, his right hand being engaged in the mechanical readjustment of his dress. Mr. Browne, whose face was once more wrinkling with mirth, poured out for himself a glass of whisky while Freddy Malins exploded, before he had well reached the climax of his story, in a kink of high-pitched bronchitic laughter and, setting down his untasted and overflowing glass, began to rub the knuckles of his left fist backwards and forwards into his left eye, repeating words of his last phrase as well as his fit of laughter would allow him.

\* \* \* \* \*

Gabriel could not listen while Mary Jane was playing her Academy piece, full of runs and difficult passages, to the hushed drawing-room. He liked music but the piece she was playing had no melody for him and he doubted whether it had any melody for the other listeners, though they had begged Mary Jane to play something. Four young men, who had come from the refreshment-room to stand in the door-way at the sound of the piano, had gone away quietly in couples after a few minutes.

The only persons who seemed to follow the music were Mary Jane herself, her hands racing along the key-board or lifted from it at the pauses like those of a priestess in momentary imprecation, and Aunt Kate standing at her elbow to turn the page.

Gabriel's eyes, irritated by the floor, which glittered with beeswax under the heavy chandelier, wandered to the wall above the piano. A picture of the balcony scene in *Romeo and Juliet* hung there and beside it was a picture of the two murdered princes in the Tower which Aunt Julia had worked in red, blue and brown wools when she was a girl. Probably in the school they had gone to as girls that kind of work had been taught, for one year his mother had worked for him as a birthday present a waistcoat of purple tabinet, with little foxes' heads upon it, lined with brown satin and having round mulberry buttons. It was strange that his mother had had no musical talent though Aunt Kate used to call her the brains carrier of the Morkan family. Both she and Julia had always seemed a little proud of their serious and matronly sister. Her photograph stood before the pierglass. She held an open book on her knees and was pointing out something in it to Constantine who, dressed in a man-o'-war suit, lay at her feet. It was she who had chosen the names for her sons for she was very sensible of the dignity of family life. Thanks to her, Constantine was now senior curate in Balbriggan and, thanks to her, Gabriel himself had taken his degree in the Royal University. A shadow passed over his face as he remembered her sullen opposition to his marriage. Some slighting phrases she had used still rankled in his memory; she had once spoken of Gretta as being country cute and that was not true of Gretta at all. It was Gretta who had nursed her during all her last long illness in their house at Monkstown.

He knew that Mary Jane must be near the end of her piece for she was playing again the opening melody with runs of scales after every bar and while he waited for the end the resentment died down in his heart. The piece ended with a trill of octaves in the treble and a final deep octave in the bass. Great applause greeted Mary Jane as, blushing and rolling up her music nervously, she escaped from the room. The most vigorous clapping came from the four young men in the doorway who had gone away to the refreshment-room at the beginning of the piece but had come back when the piano had stopped.

Lancers were arranged. Gabriel found himself partnered with Miss Ivors. She was a frank-mannered talkative young lady, with a freckled face and prominent brown eyes. She did not wear a low-cut bodice and the large brooch which was fixed in the front of her collar bore on it an Irish device.

When they had taken their places she said abruptly:

"I have a crow to pluck with you."

"With me?" said Gabriel.

She nodded her head gravely.

"What is it?" asked Gabriel, smiling at her solemn manner.

"Who is G. C.?" answered Miss Ivors, turning her eyes upon him.

Gabriel coloured and was about to knit his brows, as if he did not understand, when she said bluntly:

"O, innocent Amy! I have found out that you write for *The Daily Express*. Now, aren't you ashamed of yourself?"

"Why should I be ashamed of myself?" asked Gabriel, blinking his eyes and trying to smile.

"Well, I'm ashamed of you," said Miss Ivors frankly. "To say you'd write for a rag like that. I didn't think you were a West Briton."

A look of perplexity appeared on Gabriel's face. It was true that he wrote a literary column every Wednesday in *The Daily Express*, for which he was paid fifteen shillings. But that did not make him a West Briton surely. The books he received for review were almost more welcome than the paltry cheque. He loved to feel the covers and turn over the pages of newly printed books. Nearly every day when his teaching in the college was ended he used to wander down the quays to the second-hand booksellers, to Hickey's on Bachelor's Walk, to Webb's or Massey's on Aston's Quay, or to O'Clohissey's in the by-street. He did not know how to meet her charge. He wanted to say that literature was above politics. But they were friends of many years' standing and their careers had been parallel, first at the University and then as teachers: he could not risk a grandiose phrase with her. He continued blinking his eyes and trying to smile and murmured lamely that he saw nothing political in writing reviews of books.

When their turn to cross had come he was still perplexed and inattentive. Miss Ivors promptly took his hand in a warm grasp and said in a soft friendly tone:

"Of course, I was only joking. Come, we cross now."

When they were together again she spoke of the University question and Gabriel felt more at ease. A friend of hers had shown her his review of Browning's poems. That was how she had found out the secret: but she liked the review immensely. Then she said suddenly:

"O, Mr. Conroy, will you come for an excursion to the Aran Isles this summer? We're going to stay there a whole month. It will be splendid out in the Atlantic. You ought to come. Mr. Clancy is coming, and Mr. Kilkelly and Kathleen Kearney. It would be splendid for Gretta too if she'd come. She's from Connacht, isn't she?"

"Her people are," said Gabriel shortly.

"But you will come, won't you?" said Miss Ivors, laying her warm hand eagerly on his arm.

"The fact is," said Gabriel, "I have already arranged to go—"

"Go where," asked Miss Ivors.

"Well, you know, every year I go for a cycling tour with some fellows and so—"

"But where?" asked Miss Ivors.

"Well, we usually go to France or Belgium or perhaps Germany," said Gabriel awkwardly.

"And why do you go to France and Belgium," said Miss Ivors, "instead of visiting your own land?"

"Well," said Gabriel, "it's partly to keep in touch with the languages and partly for a change."

"And haven't you your own language to keep in touch with—Irish?" asked Miss Ivors.

"Well," said Gabriel, "if it comes to that, you know, Irish is not my language."

Their neighbours had turned to listen to the cross-examination. Gabriel glanced right and left nervously and tried to keep his good humour under the ordeal which was making a blush invade his forehead.

"And haven't you your own land to visit," continued Miss Ivors, "that you know nothing of, your own people, and your own country?"

"O, to tell you the truth," retorted Gabriel suddenly, "I'm sick of my own country, sick of it!"

"Why?" asked Miss Ivors.

Gabriel did not answer for his retort had heated him.

"Why?" repeated Miss Ivors.

They had to go visiting together and, as he had not

answered her, Miss Ivors said warmly:

"Of course, you've no answer."

Gabriel tried to cover his agitation by taking part in the dance with great energy. He avoided her eyes for he had seen a sour expression on her face. But when they met in the long chain he was surprised to feel his hand firmly pressed. She looked at him from under her brows for a moment quizzically until he smiled. Then, just as the chain was about to start again, she stood on tiptoe and whispered into his ear:

"West Briton!"

When the lancers were over Gabriel went away to a remote corner of the room where Freddy Malins' mother was sitting. Her voice had a catch in it like her son's and she stuttered slightly. She had been told that Freddy had come and that he was nearly all right. Gabriel asked her whether she had had a good crossing. She lived with her married daughter in Glasgow and came to Dublin on a visit once a year. She answered placidly that she had had a beautiful crossing and that the captain had been most attentive to her. She spoke also of the beautiful house her daughter kept in Glasgow, and of all the nice friends they had there. While her tongue rambled on Gabriel tried to banish from his mind all memory of the unpleasant incident with Miss Ivors. Of course the girl or woman, or whatever she was, was an enthusiast but there was a time for all things. Perhaps he ought not to have answered her like that. But she had no right to call him a West Briton before people, even in joke. She had tried to make him ridiculous before people, heckling him and staring at him with her rabbit's eyes.

He saw his wife making her way towards him through the waltzing couples. When she reached him she said into his ear:

"Gabriel, Aunt Kate wants to know won't you carve the goose as usual. Miss Daly will carve the ham and I'll do the pudding."

"All right," said Gabriel.

"She's sending in the younger ones first as soon as this waltz is over so that we'll have the table to ourselves."

"Were you dancing?" asked Gabriel.

"Of course I was. Didn't you see me? What words had you with Molly Ivors?"

"No words. Why? Did she say so?"

"Something like that. I'm trying to get that Mr. D'Arcy to sing. He's full of conceit, I think."

"There were no words," said Gabriel moodily, "only she wanted me to go for a trip to the west of Ireland and I said I wouldn't."

His wife clasped her hands excitedly and gave a little jump.

"O, do go, Gabriel," she cried. "I'd love to see Galway again."

"You can go if you like," said Gabriel coldly.

She looked at him for a moment, then turned to Mrs. Malins and said:

"There's a nice husband for you, Mrs. Malins."

While she was threading her way back across the room Mrs. Malins, without adverting to the interruption, went on to tell Gabriel what beautiful places there were in Scotland and beautiful scenery. Her son-in-law brought them every year to the lakes and they used to go fishing. Her son-in-law was a splendid fisher. One day he caught a fish, a beautiful big big fish, and the man in the hotel boiled it for their dinner.

Gabriel hardly heard what she said. Now that supper was coming near he began to think again about his speech and about the quotation. When he saw Freddy Malins coming across the room to visit his mother Gabriel left the chair free for him and retired into the embrasure of the window. The room had already cleared and from the back room came the clatter of plates and knives. Those who still remained in the drawing-room seemed tired of dancing and were conversing quietly in little groups. Gabriel's warm trembling fingers tapped the cold pane of the window. How cool it must be outside! How pleasant it would be to walk out alone, first along by the river and then through the park! The snow would be lying on the branches of the trees and forming a bright cap on the top of the Wellington Monument. How much more pleasant it would be there than at the supper-table!

He ran over the headings of his speech: Irish hospitality, sad memories, the Three Graces, Paris, the quotation from Browning. He repeated to himself a phrase he had written in his review: *One feels that one is listening to a thought-tormented music.* Miss Ivors had praised the review. Was she sincere? Had she really any life of her own behind all her propagandism? There had never been any ill-feeling between them until that night. It unnerved him to think that she would be at the supper-table, looking up at him while he spoke with her critical quizzing eyes. Perhaps she would not be sorry to see him fail in his speech. An idea came into his mind and gave him courage. He would say, alluding to Aunt Kate and Aunt Julia: *Ladies and Gentlemen, the generation which is now on the wane among us may have had its faults but for my part I think it had certain qualities of hospitality, of humour, of humanity, which the new and very serious and hypereducated generation that is growing up around us seems to me to lack.* Very good: that was one for Miss Ivors. What did he care that his aunts were only two ignorant old women?

A murmur in the room attracted his attention. Mr. Browne was advancing from the door, gallantly escorting Aunt Julia, who leaned upon his arm, smiling and hanging her head. An irregular musketry of applause escorted her also as far as the piano and then, as Mary Jane seated herself on the stool, and Aunt Julia, no longer smiling, half turned so as to pitch her voice fairly into the room, gradually ceased. Gabriel recognised the prelude. It was that of an old song of Aunt Julia's—*Arrayed for the Bridal*. Her voice, strong and clear in tone, attacked with great spirit the runs which embellish the air and though she sang very rapidly she did not miss even the smallest of the grace notes. To follow the voice, without looking at the singer's face, was to feel and share the excitement of swift and secure flight. Gabriel applauded loudly with all the others at the close of the song and loud applause was borne in from the invisible suppertable. It sounded so genuine that a little colour struggled into Aunt Julia's face as she bent to replace in the music-stand the old leather-bound songbook that had her initials on the cover. Freddy Malins, who had listened with his head perched sideways to hear her better, was still applauding when everyone else had ceased and talking animatedly to his mother who nodded her head gravely and slowly in acquiescence. At last, when he could clap no more, he stood up suddenly and hurried across the room to Aunt Julia whose hand he seized and held in both his hands, shaking it when words failed him or the catch in his voice proved too much for him.

"I was just telling my mother," he said, "I never heard you sing so well, never. No, I never heard your voice so good as it is to-night. Now! Would you believe that now? That's the truth. Upon my word and honour that's the truth. I never heard your voice sound so fresh and so . . . so clear and fresh, never."

Aunt Julia smiled broadly and murmured something about compliments as she released her hand from his grasp. Mr. Browne extended his open hand towards her and said to those who were near him in the manner of a showman introducing a prodigy to an audience:

"Miss Julia Morkan, my latest discovery!"

He was laughing very heartily at this himself when Freddy Malins turned to him and said:

"Well, Browne, if you're serious you might make a worse discovery. All I can say is I never heard her sing half so well as long as I am coming here. And that's the honest truth."

"Neither did I," said Mr. Browne. "I think her voice has greatly improved."

Aunt Julia shrugged her shoulders and said with meek pride:

"Thirty years ago I hadn't a bad voice as voices go."

"I often told Julia," said Aunt Kate emphatically, "that she was simply thrown away in that choir. But she never would be said by me."

She turned as if to appeal to the good sense of the others against a refractory child while Aunt Julia gazed in front of her, a vague smile of reminiscence playing on her face.

"No," continued Aunt Kate, "she wouldn't be said or led by anyone, slaving there in that choir night and day, night and day. Six o'clock on Christmas morning! And all for what?"

"Well, isn't it for the honour of God, Aunt Kate?" asked Mary Jane, twisting round on the piano-stool and smiling.

Aunt Kate turned fiercely on her niece and said:

"I know all about the honour of God, Mary Jane, but I think it's not at all honourable for the pope to turn out the women out of the choirs that have slaved there all their lives and put little whipper-snappers of boys over their heads. I suppose it is for the good of the Church if the pope does it. But it's not just, Mary Jane, and it's not right."

She had worked herself into a passion and would have continued in defence of her sister for it was a sore subject with her but Mary Jane, seeing that all the dancers had come back, intervened pacifically:

"Now, Aunt Kate, you're giving scandal to Mr. Browne who is of the other persuasion."

Aunt Kate turned to Mr. Browne, who was grinning at this allusion to his religion, and said hastily:

"O, I don't question the pope's being right. I'm only a stupid old woman and I wouldn't presume to do such a thing. But there's such a thing as common everyday politeness and gratitude. And if I were in Julia's place I'd tell that Father Healy straight up to his face . . . "

"And besides, Aunt Kate," said Mary Jane, "we really are all hungry and when we are hungry we are all very quarrelsome."

"And when we are thirsty we are also quarrelsome," added Mr. Browne.

"So that we had better go to supper," said Mary Jane, "and finish the discussion afterwards."

On the landing outside the drawing-room Gabriel found his wife and Mary Jane trying to persuade Miss Ivors to stay for supper. But Miss Ivors, who had put on her hat and was buttoning her cloak, would not stay. She did not feel in the least hungry and she had already overstayed her time.

"But only for ten minutes, Molly," said Mrs. Conroy. "That won't delay you."

"To take a pick itself," said Mary Jane, "after all your dancing."

"I really couldn't," said Miss Ivors.

"I am afraid you didn't enjoy yourself at all," said Mary Jane hopelessly.

"Ever so much, I assure you," said Miss Ivors, "but you really must let me run off now."

"But how can you get home?" asked Mrs. Conroy.

"O, it's only two steps up the quay."

Gabriel hesitated a moment and said:

"If you will allow me, Miss Ivors, I'll see you home if you really are obliged to go."

But Miss Ivors broke away from them.

"I won't hear of it," she cried. "For goodness sake go in to your suppers and don't mind me. I'm quite well able to take care of myself."

"Well, you're the comical girl, Molly," said Mrs. Conroy frankly.

"*Beannacht libh*," cried Miss Ivors, with a laugh, as she ran down the staircase.

Mary Jane gazed after her, a moody puzzled expression on her face, while Mrs. Conroy leaned over the banisters to listen for the hall-door. Gabriel asked himself was he the cause of her abrupt departure. But she did not seem to be in ill humour; she had gone away laughing. He stared blankly down the staircase.

At that moment Aunt Kate came toddling out of the supper-room, almost wringing her hands in despair.

"Where is Gabriel?" she cried. "Where on earth is Gabriel? There's everyone waiting in there, stage to let, and nobody to carve the goose!"

"Here I am, Aunt Kate!" cried Gabriel, with sudden animation, ready to carve a flock of geese, if necessary.

A fat brown goose lay at one end of the table and at the other end, on a bed of creased paper strewn with sprigs of parsley, lay a great ham, stripped of its outer skin and peppered over with crust crumbs, a neat paper frill round its shin and beside this was a round of spiced beef. Between these rival ends ran parallel lines of side-dishes: two little minsters of jelly, red and yellow; a shallow dish full of blocks of blancmange and red jam, a large green leaf-shaped dish with a stalk-shaped handle, on which lay bunches of purple raisins and peeled almonds, a companion dish on which lay a solid rectangle of Smyrna figs, a dish of custard topped with grated nutmeg, a small bowl full of chocolates and sweets wrapped in gold and silver papers and a glass vase in which stood some tall celery stalks. In the centre of the table there stood, as sentries to a fruit-stand, which upheld a pyramid of oranges and American apples, two squat old-fashioned decanters of cut glass, one containing port and the other dark sherry. On the closed square piano a pudding in a huge yellow dish lay in waiting and behind it were three squads of bottles of stout and ale and minerals, drawn up according to the colours of their uniforms, the first two black, with brown and red labels, the third and smallest squad white, with transverse green sashes.

Gabriel took his seat boldly at the head of the table and, having looked to the edge of the carver, plunged his fork firmly into the goose. He felt quite at ease now for he was an expert carver and liked nothing better than to find himself at the head of a well-laden table.

"Miss Furlong, what shall I send you?" he asked. "A wing or a slice of the breast?"

"Just a small slice of the breast."

"Miss Higgins, what for you?"

"O, anything at all, Mr. Conroy."

While Gabriel and Miss Daly exchanged plates of goose and plates of ham and spiced beef Lily went from guest to guest with a dish of hot floury potatoes wrapped in a white napkin. This was Mary Jane's idea and she had also suggested apple sauce for the goose but Aunt Kate had said that plain roast goose without apple sauce had always been good enough for her and she hoped she might never eat worse. Mary Jane waited on her pupils and saw that they got the best slices and Aunt Kate and Aunt Julia opened and carried across from the piano bottles of stout and ale for the gentlemen and bottles of minerals for the ladies. There was a great deal of confusion and laughter and noise, the noise of orders and counter-orders, of knives and forks, of corks and glass-stoppers. Gabriel began to carve second helpings as soon as he had finished the first round without serving himself. Everyone protested loudly so that he compromised by taking a long draught of stout for he had found the carving hot work. Mary Jane settled down quietly to her supper but Aunt Kate and Aunt Julia were still toddling round the table, walking on each other's heels, getting in each other's way and giving each other unheeded orders. Mr. Browne begged of them to sit down and eat their suppers and so did Gabriel but they said there was time enough so that, at last, Freddy Malins stood up and, capturing Aunt Kate, plumped her down on her chair amid general laughter.

When everyone had been well served Gabriel said, smiling:

"Now, if anyone wants a little more of what vulgar people call stuffing let him or her speak."

A chorus of voices invited him to begin his own supper and Lily came forward with three potatoes which she had reserved for him.

"Very well," said Gabriel amiably, as he took another preparatory draught, "kindly forget my existence, ladies and gentlemen, for a few minutes."

He set to his supper and took no part in the conversation with which the table covered Lily's removal of the plates. The subject of talk was the opera company which was then at the Theatre Royal. Mr. Bartell D'Arcy, the tenor, a dark-complexioned young man with a smart moustache, praised very highly the leading contralto of the company but Miss Furlong thought she had a rather vulgar style of production. Freddy Malins said there was a negro chieftain singing in the second part of the

Gaiety pantomime who had one of the finest tenor voices he had ever heard.

"Have you heard him?" he asked Mr. Bartell D'Arcy across the table.

"No," answered Mr. Bartell D'Arcy carelessly.

"Because," Freddy Malins explained, "now I'd be curious to hear your opinion of him. I think he has a grand voice."

"It takes Teddy to find out the really good things," said Mr. Browne familiarly to the table.

"And why couldn't he have a voice too?" asked Freddy Malins sharply. "Is it because he's only a black?"

Nobody answered this question and Mary Jane led the table back to the legitimate opera. One of her pupils had given her a pass for *Mignon*. Of course it was very fine, she said, but it made her think of poor Georgina Burns. Mr. Browne could go back farther still, to the old Italian companies that used to come to Dublin—Tietjens, Ilma de Murzka, Campanini, the great Trebelli, Giuglini, Ravelli, Aramburo. Those were the days, he said, when there was something like singing to be heard in Dublin. He told too of how the top gallery of the old Royal used to be packed night after night, of how one night an Italian tenor had sung five encores to *Let Me Like a Soldier Fall*, introducing a high C every time, and of how the gallery boys would sometimes in their enthusiasm unyoke the horses from the carriage of some great *prima donna* and pull her themselves through the streets to her hotel. Why did they never play the grand old operas now, he asked, *Dinorah*, *Lucrezia Borgia*? Because they could not get the voices to sing them: that was why.

"O, well," said Mr. Bartell D'Arcy, "I presume there are as good singers to-day as there were then."

"Where are they?" asked Mr. Browne defiantly.

"In London, Paris, Milan," said Mr. Bartell D'Arcy warmly. "I suppose Caruso, for example, is quite as good, if not better than any of the men you have mentioned."

"Maybe so," said Mr. Browne. "But I may tell you I doubt it strongly."

"O, I'd give anything to hear Caruso sing," said Mary Jane.

"For me," said Aunt Kate, who had been picking a bone, "there was only one tenor. To please me, I mean. But I suppose none of you ever heard of him."

"Who was he, Miss Morkan?" asked Mr. Bartell D'Arcy politely.

"His name," said Aunt Kate, "was Parkinson. I heard him when he was in his prime and I think he had then the purest tenor voice that was ever put into a man's throat."

"Strange," said Mr. Bartell D'Arcy. "I never even heard of him."

"Yes, yes, Miss Morkan is right," said Mr. Browne. "I remember hearing of old Parkinson but he's too far back for me."

"A beautiful pure sweet mellow English tenor," said Aunt Kate with enthusiasm.

Gabriel having finished, the huge pudding was transferred to the table. The clatter of forks and spoons began again. Gabriel's wife served out spoonfuls of the pudding and passed the plates down the table. Midway down they were held up by Mary Jane, who replenished them with raspberry or orange jelly or with blancmange and jam. The pudding was of Aunt Julia's making and she received praises for it from all quarters. She herself said that it was not quite brown enough.

"Well, I hope, Miss Morkan," said Mr. Browne, "that I'm brown enough for you because, you know, I'm all brown."

All the gentlemen, except Gabriel, ate some of the pudding out of compliment to Aunt Julia. As Gabriel never ate sweets the celery had been left for him. Freddy Malins also took a stalk of celery and ate it with his pudding. He had been told that celery was a capital thing for the blood and he was just then under doctor's care. Mrs. Malins, who had been silent all through the supper, said that her son was going down to Mount Melleray in a week or so. The table then spoke of Mount Melleray, how bracing the air was down there, how hospitable the monks were and how they never asked for a penny-piece from their guests.

"And do you mean to say," asked Mr. Browne incredulously, "that a chap can go down there and put up there as if it were a hotel and live on the fat of the land and then come away without paying a farthing?"

"O, most people give some donation to the monastery when they leave," said Mary Jane.

"I wish we had an institution like that in our Church," said Mr. Browne candidly.

He was astonished to hear that the monks never spoke, got up at two in the morning and slept in their coffins. He asked what they did it for.

"That's the rule of the order," said Aunt Kate firmly.

"Yes, but why?" asked Mr. Browne.

Aunt Kate repeated that it was the rule, that was all. Mr. Browne still seemed not to understand. Freddy Malins explained to him, as best he could, that the monks were trying to make up for the sins committed by all the sinners in the outside world. The explanation was not very clear for Mr. Browne grinned and said:

"I like that idea very much but wouldn't a comfortable spring bed do them as well as a coffin?"

"The coffin," said Mary Jane, "is to remind them of their last end."

As the subject had grown lugubrious it was buried in a silence of the table during which Mrs. Malins could be heard saying to her neighbour in an indistinct undertone:

"They are very good men, the monks, very pious men."

The raisins and almonds and figs and apples and oranges and chocolates and sweets were now passed about the table and Aunt Julia invited all the guests to have either port or sherry. At first Mr. Bartell D'Arcy refused to take either but one of his neighbours nudged him and whispered something to him upon which he allowed his glass to be filled. Gradually as the last glasses were being filled the conversation ceased. A pause followed, broken only by the noise of the wine and by unsettlings of chairs. The Misses Morkan, all three, looked down at the tablecloth. Someone coughed once or twice and then a few gentlemen patted the table gently as a signal for silence. The silence came and Gabriel pushed back his chair and stood up.

The patting at once grew louder in encouragement and then ceased altogether. Gabriel leaned his ten trembling fingers on the tablecloth and smiled nervously at the company. Meeting a row of upturned faces he raised his eyes to the chandelier. The piano was playing a waltz tune and he could hear the skirts sweeping against the drawing-room door. People, perhaps, were standing in the snow on the quay outside, gazing up at the lighted windows and listening to the waltz music. The air was pure there. In the distance lay the park where the trees were weighted with snow. The Wellington Monument wore a gleaming cap of snow that flashed westward over the white field of Fifteen Acres.

He began:

"Ladies and Gentlemen.

"It has fallen to my lot this evening, as in years past, to

perform a very pleasing task but a task for which I am afraid my poor powers as a speaker are all too inadequate."

"No, no!" said Mr. Browne.

"But, however that may be, I can only ask you tonight to take the will for the deed and to lend me your attention for a few moments while I endeavour to express to you in words what my feelings are on this occasion.

"Ladies and Gentlemen. It is not the first time that we have gathered together under this hospitable roof, around this hospitable board. It is not the first time that we have been the recipients—or perhaps, I had better say, the victims—of the hospitality of certain good ladies."

He made a circle in the air with his arm and paused. Everyone laughed or smiled at Aunt Kate and Aunt Julia and Mary Jane who all turned crimson with pleasure. Gabriel went on more boldly:

"I feel more strongly with every recurring year that our country has no tradition which does it so much honour and which it should guard so jealously as that of its hospitality. It is a tradition that is unique as far as my experience goes (and I have visited not a few places abroad) among the modern nations. Some would say, perhaps, that with us it is rather a failing than anything to be boasted of. But granted even that, it is, to my mind, a princely failing, and one that I trust will long be cultivated among us. Of one thing, at least, I am sure. As long as this one roof shelters the good ladies aforesaid—and I wish from my heart it may do so for many and many a long year to come—the tradition of genuine warm-hearted courteous Irish hospitality, which our forefathers have handed down to us and which we in turn must hand down to our descendants, is still alive among us."

A hearty murmur of assent ran round the table. It shot through Gabriel's mind that Miss Ivors was not there and that she had gone away discourteously: and he said with confidence in himself:

"Ladies and Gentlemen.

"A new generation is growing up in our midst, a generation actuated by new ideas and new principles. It is serious and enthusiastic for these new ideas and its enthusiasm, even when it is misdirected, is, I believe, in the main sincere. But we are living in a sceptical and, if I may use the phrase, a thought-tormented age: and sometimes I fear that this new generation, educated or hypereducated as it is, will lack those qualities of humanity, of hospitality, of kindly humour which belonged to an older day. Listening to-night to the names of all those great singers of the past it seemed to me, I must confess, that we were living in a less spacious age. Those days might, without exaggeration, be called spacious days: and if they are gone beyond recall let us hope, at least, that in gatherings such as this we shall still speak of them with pride and affection, still cherish in our hearts the memory of those dead and gone great ones whose fame the world will not willingly let die."

"Hear, hear!" said Mr. Browne loudly.

"But, yet," continued Gabriel, his voice falling into a softer inflection, "there are always in gatherings such as this sadder thoughts that will recur to our minds: thoughts of the past, of youth, of changes, of absent faces that we miss here to-night. Our path through life is strewn with many such sad memories: and were we to brood upon them always we could not find the heart to go on bravely with our work among the living. We have all of us living duties and living affections which claim, and rightly claim, our strenuous endeavours.

"Therefore, I will not linger on the past. I will not let any gloomy moralising intrude upon us here to-night. Here we are gathered together for a brief moment from the bustle and rush of our everyday routine. We are met here as friends, in the spirit of good-fellowship, as colleagues, also to a certain extent, in the true spirit of *camaraderie,* and as the guests of—what shall I call them?—the Three Graces of the Dublin musical world."

The table burst into applause and laughter at this sally. Aunt Julia vainly asked each of her neighbours in turn to tell her what Gabriel had said.

"He says we are the Three Graces, Aunt Julia," said Mary Jane.

Aunt Julia did not understand but she looked up, smiling, at Gabriel, who continued in the same vein:

"Ladies and Gentlemen.

"I will not attempt to play to-night the part that Paris played on another occasion. I will not attempt to choose between them. The task would be an invidious one and one beyond my poor powers. For when I view them in turn, whether it be our chief hostess herself, whose good heart, whose too good heart, has become a byword with all who know her, or her sister, who seems to be gifted with perennial youth and whose singing must have been a surprise and a revelation to us all to-night, or, last but not least, when I consider our youngest hostess, talented, cheerful, hard-working and the best of nieces, I confess, Ladies and Gentlemen, that I do not know to which of them I should award the prize."

Gabriel glanced down at his aunts and, seeing the large smile on Aunt Julia's face and the tears which had risen to Aunt Kate's eyes, hastened to his close. He raised his glass of port gallantly, while every member of the company fingered a glass expectantly, and said loudly:

"Let us toast them all three together. Let us drink to their health, wealth, long life, happiness and prosperity and may they long continue to hold the proud and self-won position which they hold in their profession and the position of honour and affection which they hold in our hearts."

All the guests stood up, glass in hand, and, turning towards the three seated ladies, sang in unison, with Mr. Browne as leader:

> *For they are jolly gay fellows,*
> *For they are jolly gay fellows,*
> *For they are jolly gay fellows,*
> *Which nobody can deny.*

Aunt Kate was making frank use of her handkerchief and even Aunt Julia seemed moved. Freddy Malins beat time with his pudding-fork and the singers turned towards one another, as if in melodious conference, while they sang, with emphasis:

> *Unless he tells a lie,*
> *Unless he tells a lie.*

Then, turning once more towards their hostesses, they sang:

> *For they are jolly gay fellows,*
> *For they are jolly gay fellows,*
> *For they are jolly gay fellows,*
> *Which nobody can deny.*

The acclamation which followed was taken up beyond the door of the supper-room by many of the other guests and renewed time after time, Freddy Malins acting as officer with his fork on high.

\* \* \* \* \*

The piercing morning air came into the hall where they were standing so that Aunt Kate said:

"Close the door, somebody. Mrs. Malins will get her death of cold."

"Browne is out there, Aunt Kate," said Mary Jane.

"Browne is everywhere," said Aunt Kate, lowering her voice.

Mary Jane laughed at her tone.

"Really," she said archly, "he is very attentive."

"He has been laid on here like the gas," said Aunt Kate in the same tone, "all during the Christmas."

She laughed herself this time good-humouredly and then added quickly:

"But tell him to come in, Mary Jane, and close the door. I hope to goodness he didn't hear me."

At that moment the hall-door was opened and Mr. Browne came in from the doorstep, laughing as if his heart would break. He was dressed in a long green overcoat with mock astrakhan cuffs and collar and wore on his head an oval fur cap. He pointed down the snow-covered quay from where the sound of shrill prolonged whistling was borne in.

"Teddy will have all the cabs in Dublin out," he said.

Gabriel advanced from the little pantry behind the office, struggling into his overcoat and, looking round the hall, said:

"Gretta not down yet?"

"She's getting on her things, Gabriel," said Aunt Kate.

"Who's playing up there?" asked Gabriel.

"Nobody. They're all gone."

"O no, Aunt Kate," said Mary Jane. "Bartell D'Arcy and Miss O'Callaghan aren't gone yet."

"Someone is strumming at the piano, anyhow," said Gabriel.

Mary Jane glanced at Gabriel and Mr. Browne and said with a shiver:

"It makes me feel cold to look at you two gentlemen muffled up like that. I wouldn't like to face your journey home at this hour."

"I'd like nothing better this minute," said Mr. Browne stoutly, "than a rattling fine walk in the country or a fast drive with a good spanking goer between the shafts."

"We used to have a very good horse and trap at home," said Aunt Julia sadly.

"The never-to-be-forgotten Johnny," said Mary Jane, laughing.

Aunt Kate and Gabriel laughed too.

"Why, what was wonderful about Johnny?" asked Mr. Browne.

"The late lamented Patrick Morkan, our grandfather, that is," explained Gabriel, "commonly known in his later years as the old gentleman, was a glue-boiler."

"O, now, Gabriel," said Aunt Kate, laughing, "he had a starch mill."

"Well, glue or starch," said Gabriel, "the old gentleman had a horse by the name of Johnny. And Johnny used to work in the old gentleman's mill, walking round and round in order to drive the mill. That was all very well; but now comes the tragic part about Johnny. One fine day the old gentleman thought he'd like to drive out with the quality to a military review in the park."

"The Lord have mercy on his soul," said Aunt Kate compassionately.

"Amen," said Gabriel. "So the old gentleman, as I said, harnessed Johnny and put on his very best tall hat and his very best stock collar and drove out in grand style from his ancestral mansion somewhere near Back Lane, I think."

Everyone laughed, even Mrs. Malins, at Gabriel's manner and Aunt Kate said:

"O now, Gabriel, he didn't live in Back Lane, really. Only the mill was there."

"Out from the mansion of his forefathers," continued Gabriel, "he drove with Johnny. And everything went on beautifully until Johnny came in sight of King Billy's statue: and whether he fell in love with the horse King Billy sits on or whether he thought he was back again in the mill, anyhow he began to walk round the statue."

Gabriel paced in a circle round the hall in his goloshes amid the laughter of the others.

"Round and round he went," said Gabriel, "and the old gentleman, who was a very pompous old gentleman, was highly indignant. *Go on, sir! What do you mean, sir? Johnny! Johnny! Most extraordinary conduct! Can't understand the horse!*"

The peals of laughter which followed Gabriel's imitation of the incident were interrupted by a resounding knock at the hall-door. Mary Jane ran to open it and let in Freddy Malins. Freddy Malins, with his hat well back on his head and his shoulders humped with cold, was puffing and steaming after his exertions.

"I could only get one cab," he said.

"O, we'll find another along the quay," said Gabriel.

"Yes," said Aunt Kate. "Better not keep Mrs. Malins standing in the draught."

Mrs. Malins was helped down the front steps by her son and Mr. Browne and, after many manœuvres, hoisted into the cab. Freddy Malins clambered in after her and spent a long time settling her on the seat, Mr. Browne helping him with advice. At last she was settled comfortably and Freddy Malins invited Mr. Browne into the cab. There was a good deal of confused talk, and then Mr. Browne got into the cab. The cabman settled his rug over his knees, and bent down for the address. The confusion grew greater and the cabman was directed differently by Freddy Malins and Mr. Browne, each of whom had his head out through a window of the cab. The difficulty was to know where to drop Mr. Browne along the route and Aunt Kate, Aunt Julia and Mary Jane helped the discussion from the door-step with cross-directions and contradictions and abundance of laughter. As for Freddy Malins he was speechless with laughter. He popped his head in and out of the window every moment, to the great danger of his hat, and told his mother how the discussion was progressing till at last Mr. Browne shouted to the bewildered cabman above the din of everybody's laughter:

"Do you know Trinity College?"

"Yes, sir," said the cabman.

"Well, drive bang up against Trinity College gates," said Mr. Browne, "and then we'll tell you where to go. You understand now?"

"Yes, sir," said the cabman.

"Make like a bird for Trinity College."

"Right, sir," cried the cabman.

The horse was whipped up and the cab rattled off along the quay amid a chorus of laughter and adieus.

Gabriel had not gone to the door with the others. He was in a dark part of the hall gazing up the staircase. A woman was standing near the top of the first flight, in the shadow also. He could not see her face but he could see the terracotta and salmonpink panels of her skirt which the shadow made appear black and white. It was his wife. She was leaning on the banisters, listening to something. Gabriel was surprised at her stillness and strained his ear to listen also. But he could hear little save the noise of laughter and dispute on the front steps, a few chords struck on the piano and a few notes of a man's voice singing.

He stood still in the gloom of the hall, trying to catch the air that the voice was singing and gazing up at his wife. There was grace and mystery in her attitude as if she were a symbol of something. He asked himself what is a woman standing on the stairs in the shadow, listening to distant music, a symbol of. If he were a painter he would paint her in that attitude. Her blue felt hat would show off the bronze of her hair against the darkness and the dark panels of her skirt would show off the light ones. *Distant Music* he would call the picture if he were a painter.

The hall-door was closed; and Aunt Kate, Aunt Julia and Mary Jane came down the hall, still laughing.

"Well, isn't Freddy terrible?" said Mary Jane. "He's really terrible."

Gabriel said nothing but pointed up the stairs towards where his wife was standing. Now that the hall-door was closed the voice and the piano could be heard more clearly. Gabriel held up his hand for them to be silent. The song seemed to be in the old Irish tonality and the singer seemed uncertain both of his words and of his voice. The voice, made plaintive by distance and by the singer's hoarseness, faintly illuminated the cadence of the air with words expressing grief:

> *O, the rain falls on my heavy locks*
> *And the dew wets my skin,*
> *My babe lies cold . . .*

"O," exclaimed Mary Jane. "It's Bartell D'Arcy singing and he wouldn't sing all the night. O, I'll get him to sing a song before he goes."

"O do, Mary Jane," said Aunt Kate.

Mary Jane brushed past the others and ran to the staircase but before she reached it the singing stopped and the piano was closed abruptly.

"O, what a pity!" she cried. "Is he coming down, Gretta?"

Gabriel heard his wife answer yes and saw her come down towards them. A few steps behind her were Mr. Bartell D'Arcy and Miss O'Callaghan.

"O, Mr. D'Arcy," cried Mary Jane, "it's downright mean of you to break off like that when we were all in raptures listening to you."

"I have been at him all the evening," said Miss O'Callaghan, "and Mrs. Conroy too and he told us he had a dreadful cold and couldn't sing."

"O, Mr. D'Arcy," said Aunt Kate, "now that was a great fib to tell."

"Can't you see that I'm as hoarse as a crow?" said Mr. D'Arcy roughly.

He went into the pantry hastily and put on his overcoat. The others, taken aback by his rude speech, could find nothing to say. Aunt Kate wrinkled her brows and made signs to the others to drop the subject. Mr. D'Arcy stood swathing his neck carefully and frowning.

"It's the weather," said Aunt Julia, after a pause.

"Yes, everybody has colds," said Aunt Kate readily, "everybody."

"They say," said Mary Jane, "we haven't had snow like it for thirty years; and I read this morning in the newspapers that the snow is general all over Ireland."

"I love the look of snow," said Aunt Julia sadly.

"So do I," said Miss O'Callaghan. "I think Christmas is never really Christmas unless we have the snow on the ground."

"But poor Mr. D'Arcy doesn't like the snow," said Aunt Kate, smiling.

Mr. D'Arcy came from the pantry, full swathed and buttoned, and in a repentant tone told them the history of his cold. Everyone gave him advice and said it was a great pity and urged him to be very careful of his throat in the night air. Gabriel watched his wife who did not join in the conversation. She was standing right under the dusty fanlight and the flame of the gas lit up the rich bronze of her hair which he had seen her drying at the fire a few days before. She was in the same attitude and seemed unaware of the talk about her. At last she turned towards them and Gabriel saw that there was colour on her cheeks and that her eyes were shining. A sudden tide of joy went leaping out of his heart.

"Mr. D'Arcy," she said, "what is the name of that song you were singing?"

"It's called *The Lass of Aughrim*," said Mr. D'Arcy, "but I couldn't remember it properly. Why? Do you know it?"

"*The Lass of Aughrim*," she repeated. "I couldn't think of the name."

"It's a very nice air," said Mary Jane. "I'm sorry you were not in voice to-night."

"Now, Mary Jane," said Aunt Kate, "don't annoy Mr. D'Arcy. I won't have him annoyed."

Seeing that all were ready to start she shepherded them to the door where good-night was said:

"Well, good-night, Aunt Kate, and thanks for the pleasant evening."

"Good-night, Gabriel. Good-night, Gretta!"

"Good-night, Aunt Kate, and thanks ever so much. Good-night, Aunt Julia."

"O, good-night, Gretta, I didn't see you."

"Good-night, Mr. D'Arcy. Good-night, Miss O'Callaghan."

"Good-night, Miss Morkan."

"Good-night, again."

"Good-night, all. Safe home."

"Good-night. Good-night."

The morning was still dark. A dull yellow light brooded over the houses and the river; and the sky seemed to be descending. It was slushy underfoot; and only streaks and patches of snow lay on the roofs, on the parapets of the quay and on the area railings. The lamps were still burning redly in the murky air and, across the river, the palace of the Four Courts stood out menacingly against the heavy sky.

She was walking on before him with Mr. Bartell D'Arcy, her shoes in a brown parcel tucked under one arm and her hands holding her skirt up from the slush. She had no longer any grace of attitude but Gabriel's eyes were still bright with happiness. The blood went bounding along his veins; and the thoughts went rioting through his brain, proud, joyful, tender, valorous.

She was walking on before him so lightly and so erect that he longed to run after her noiselessly, catch her by the shoulders and say something foolish and affectionate into her ear. She seemed to him so frail that he longed to defend her against something and then to be alone with her. Moments of their secret life together burst like stars upon his memory. A heliotrope envelope was lying beside his breakfast-cup and he was caressing it with his hand. Birds were twittering in the ivy and the sunny web of the curtain was shimmering along the floor: he could not eat for happiness. They were standing on the crowded platform and he was placing a ticket inside the warm palm of her glove. He was standing with her in the cold, looking in through a grated window at a man making bottles in a roaring furnace. It was very cold. Her face, fragrant in the cold air, was quite close to his; and suddenly she called out to the man at the furnace:

"Is the fire hot, sir?"

But the man could not hear her with the noise of the furnace. It was just as well. He might have answered rudely.

A wave of yet more tender joy escaped from his heart and went coursing in warm flood along his arteries. Like the tender fires of stars moments of their life together, that no one knew of or would ever know of, broke upon and illumined his memory. He longed to recall to her those moments, to make her forget the years of their dull existence together and remember only their moments of ecstasy. For the years, he felt, had not quenched his soul or hers. Their children, his writing, her household cares had not quenched all their souls' tender fire. In one letter that he had written to her then he had said: *Why is it that words like these seem to me so dull and cold? Is it because there is no word tender enough to be your name?*

Like distant music these words that he had written years before were borne towards him from the past. He longed to be alone with her. When the others had gone away, when he and she were in their room in the hotel, then they would be alone together. He would call her softly:

"Gretta!"

Perhaps she would not hear at once: she would be undressing. Then something in his voice would strike her. She would turn and look at him. . . .

At the corner of Winetavern Street they met a cab. He was glad of its rattling noise as it saved him from conversation. She was looking out of the window and seemed tired. The others spoke only a few words, pointing out some building or street. The horse galloped along wearily under the murky morning sky, dragging his old rattling box after his heels, and Gabriel was again in a cab with her, galloping to catch the boat, galloping to their honeymoon.

As the cab drove across O'Connell Bridge Miss O'Callaghan said:

"They say you never cross O'Connell Bridge without seeing a white horse."

"I see a white man this time," said Gabriel.

"Where?" asked Mr. Bartell D'Arcy.

Gabriel pointed to the statue, on which lay patches of snow. Then he nodded familiarly to it and waved his hand.

"Good-night, Dan," he said gaily.

When the cab drew up before the hotel Gabriel jumped out and, in spite of Mr. Bartell D'Arcy's protest, paid the driver. He gave the man a shilling over his fare. The man saluted and said:

"A prosperous New Year to you, sir."

"The same to you," said Gabriel cordially.

She leaned for a moment on his arm in getting out of the cab and while standing at the curbstone, bidding the others goodnight. She leaned lightly on his arm, as lightly as when she had danced with him a few hours before. He had felt proud and happy then, happy that she was his, proud of her grace and wifely carriage. But now, after the kindling again of so many memories, the first touch of her body, musical and strange and perfumed, sent through him a keen pang of lust. Under cover of her silence he pressed her arm closely to his side; and, as they stood at the hotel door, he felt that they had escaped from their lives and duties, escaped from home and friends and run away together with wild and radiant hearts to a new adventure.

An old man was dozing in a great hooded chair in the hall. He lit a candle in the office and went before them to the stairs. They followed him in silence, their feet falling in soft thuds on the thickly carpeted stairs. She mounted the stairs behind the porter, her head bowed in the ascent, her frail shoulders curved as with a burden, her skirt girt tightly about her. He could have flung his arms about her hips and held her still for his arms were trembling with desire to seize her and only the stress of his nails against the palms of his hands held the wild impulse of his body in check. The porter halted on the stairs to settle his guttering candle. They halted too on the steps below him. In the silence Gabriel could hear the falling of the molten wax into the tray and the thumping of his own heart against his ribs.

The porter led them along a corridor and opened a door.

Then he set his unstable candle down on a toilet-table and asked at what hour they were to be called in the morning.

"Eight," said Gabriel.

The porter pointed to the tap of the electric-light and began a muttered apology but Gabriel cut him short.

"We don't want any light. We have light enough from the street. And I say," he added, pointing to the candle, "you might remove that handsome article, like a good man."

The porter took up his candle again, but slowly for he was surprised by such a novel idea. Then he mumbled good-night and went out. Gabriel shot the lock to.

A ghostly light from the street lamp lay in a long shaft from one window to the door. Gabriel threw his overcoat and hat on a couch and crossed the room towards the window. He looked down into the street in order that his emotion might calm a little. Then he turned and leaned against a chest of drawers with his back to the light. She had taken off her hat and cloak and was standing before a large swinging mirror, unhooking her waist. Gabriel paused for a few moments, watching her, and then said:

"Gretta!"

She turned away from the mirror slowly and walked along the shaft of light towards him. Her face looked so serious and weary that the words would not pass Gabriel's lips. No, it was not the moment yet.

"You looked tired," he said.

"I am a little," she answered.

"You don't feel ill or weak?"

"No, tired: that's all."

She went on to the window and stood there, looking out. Gabriel waited again and then, fearing that diffidence was about to conquer him, he said abruptly:

"By the way, Gretta!"

"What is it?"

"You know that poor fellow Malins?" he said quickly.

"Yes. What about him?"

"Well, poor fellow, he's a decent sort of chap after all," continued Gabriel in a false voice. "He gave me back that sovereign I lent him and I didn't expect it really. It's a pity he wouldn't keep away from that Browne, because he's not a bad fellow at heart."

He was trembling now with annoyance. Why did she

seem so abstracted? He did not know how he could begin. Was she annoyed, too, about something? If she would only turn to him or come to him of her own accord! To take her as she was would be brutal. No, he must see some ardour in her eyes first. He longed to be master of her strange mood.

"When did you lend him the pound?" she asked, after a pause.

Gabriel strove to restrain himself from breaking out into brutal language about the sottish Malins and his pound. He longed to cry to her from his soul, to crush her body against his, to overmaster her. But he said:

"O, at Christmas, when he opened that little Christmas-card shop in Henry Street."

He was in such a fever of rage and desire that he did not hear her come from the window. She stood before him for an instant, looking at him strangely. Then, suddenly raising herself on tiptoe and resting her hands lightly on his shoulders, she kissed him.

"You are a very generous person, Gabriel," she said.

Gabriel, trembling with delight at her sudden kiss and at the quaintness of her phrase, put his hands on her hair and began smoothing it back, scarcely touching it with his fingers. The washing had made it fine and brilliant. His heart was brimming over with happiness. Just when he was wishing for it she had come to him of her own accord. Perhaps her thoughts had been running with his. Perhaps she had felt the impetuous desire that was in him and then the yielding mood had come upon her. Now that she had fallen to him so easily he wondered why he had been so diffident.

He stood, holding her head between his hands. Then, slipping one arm swiftly about her body and drawing her towards him, he said softly:

"Gretta dear, what are you thinking about?"

She did not answer nor yield wholly to his arm. He said again, softly:

"Tell me what it is, Gretta. I think I know what is the matter. Do I know?"

She did not answer at once. Then she said in an outburst of tears:

"O, I am thinking about that song, *The Lass of Aughrim*."

She broke loose from him and ran to the bed and, throwing her arms cross the bed-rail, hid her face. Gabriel stood stock-still for a moment in astonishment and then followed her. As he passed in the way of the cheval-glass he caught sight of himself in full length, his broad, well-filled, shirt-front, the face whose expression always puzzled him when he saw it in a mirror and his glimmering gilt-rimmed eyeglasses. He halted a few paces from her and said:

"What about the song? Why does that make you cry?"

She raised her head from her arms and dried her eyes with the back of her hand like a child. A kinder note than he had intended went into his voice.

"Why, Gretta?" he asked.

"I am thinking about a person long ago who used to sing that song."

"And who was the person long ago?" asked Gabriel, smiling.

"It was a person I used to know in Galway when I was living with my grandmother," she said.

The smile passed away from Gabriel's face. A dull anger began to gather again at the back of his mind and the dull fires of his lust began to glow angrily in his veins.

"Someone you were in love with?" he asked ironically.

"It was a young boy I used to know," she answered, "named Michael Furey. He used to sing that song, *The Lass of Aughrim*. He was very delicate."

Gabriel was silent. He did not wish her to think that he was interested in this delicate boy.

"I can see him so plainly," she said after a moment. "Such eyes as he had: big dark eyes! And such an expression in them— an expression!"

"O then, you were in love with him?" said Gabriel.

"I used to go out walking with him," she said, "when I was in Galway."

A thought flew across Gabriel's mind.

"Perhaps that was why you wanted to go to Galway with that Ivors girl?" he said coldly.

She looked at him and asked in surprise:

"What for?"

Her eyes made Gabriel feel awkward. He shrugged his shoulders and said:

"How do I know? To see him perhaps."

She looked away from him along the shaft of light towards the window in silence.

"He is dead," she said at length. "He died when he was only seventeen. Isn't it a terrible thing to die so young as that?"

"What was he?" asked Gabriel, still ironically.

"He was in the gasworks," she said.

Gabriel felt humiliated by the failure of his irony and by the evocation of this figure from the dead, a boy in the gasworks. While he had been full of memories of their secret life together, full of tenderness and joy and desire, she had been comparing him in her mind with another. A shameful consciousness of his own person assailed him. He saw himself as a ludicrous figure, acting as a pennyboy for his aunts, a nervous well-meaning sentimentalist, orating to vulgarians and idealising his own clownish lusts, the pitiable fatuous fellow he had caught a glimpse of in the mirror. Instinctively he turned his back more to the light lest she might see the shame that burned upon his forehead.

He tried to keep up his tone of cold interrogation but his voice when he spoke was humble and indifferent.

"I suppose you were in love with this Michael Furey, Gretta," he said.

"I was great with him at that time," she said.

Her voice was veiled and sad. Gabriel, feeling now how vain it would be to try to lead her whither he had purposed, caressed one of her hands and said, also sadly:

"And what did he die of so young, Gretta? Consumption, was it?"

"I think he died for me," she answered.

A vague terror seized Gabriel at this answer as if, at that hour when he had hoped to triumph, some impalpable and vindictive being was coming against him, gathering forces against him in its vague world. But he shook himself free of it with an effort of reason and continued to caress her hand. He did not question her again for he felt that she would tell him of herself. Her hand was warm and moist; it did not respond to his touch but he continued to caress it just as he had caressed her first letter to him that spring morning.

"It was in the winter," she said, "about the beginning of the winter when I was going to leave my grandmother's and come up here to the convent. And he was ill at the time in his lodgings in Galway and wouldn't be let out and his people in Oughterard were written to. He was in decline, they said, or something like that. I never knew rightly."

She paused for a moment and sighed.

"Poor fellow," she said. "He was very fond of me and he was such a gentle boy. We used to go out together, walking, you know, Gabriel, like the way they do in the country. He was going to study singing only for his health. He had a very good voice, poor Michael Furey."

"Well; and then?" asked Gabriel.

"And then when it came to the time for me to leave Galway and come up to the convent he was much worse and I wouldn't be let see him so I wrote a letter saying I was going up to Dublin and would be back in the summer and hoping he would be better then."

She paused for a moment to get her voice under control and then went on:

"Then the night before I left I was in my grandmother's house in Nuns' Island, packing up, and I heard gravel thrown up against the window. The window was so wet I couldn't see so I ran downstairs as I was and slipped out the back into the garden and there was the poor fellow at the end of the garden, shivering."

"And did you not tell him to go back?" asked Gabriel.

"I implored him to go home at once and told him he would get his death in the rain. But he said he did not want to live. I can see his eyes as well as well! He was standing at the end of the wall where there was a tree."

"And did he go home?" asked Gabriel.

"Yes, he went home. And when I was only a week in the convent he died and he was buried in Oughterard where his people came from. O, the day I heard that, that he was dead!"

She stopped, choking with sobs, and, overcome by emotion, flung herself face downward on the bed, sobbing in the quilt. Gabriel held her hand for a moment longer, irresolutely, and then, shy of intruding on her grief, let it fall gently and walked quietly to the window.

She was fast asleep.

Gabriel, leaning on his elbow, looked for a few moments unresentfully on her tangled hair and half-open mouth, listening to her deep-drawn breath. So she had had that romance in her life: a man had died for her sake. It hardly pained him now to think how poor a part he, her husband, had played in her life. He watched her while she slept as though he and she had never lived together as man and wife. His curious eyes rested long upon her face and on her hair: and, as he thought of what she must have been then, in that time of her first girlish beauty, a strange friendly pity for her entered his soul. He did not like to say even to himself that her face was no longer beautiful but he knew that it was no longer the face for which Michael Furey had braved death.

Perhaps she had not told him all the story. His eyes moved to the chair over which she had thrown some of her clothes. A petticoat string dangled to the floor. One boot stood upright, its limp upper fallen down: the fellow of it lay upon its side. He wondered at his riot of emotions of an hour before. From what had it proceeded? From his aunt's supper, from his own foolish speech, from the wine and dancing, the merry-making when saying good-night in the hall, the pleasure of the walk along the river in the snow. Poor Aunt Julia! She, too, would soon be a shade with the shade of Patrick Morkan and his horse. He had caught that haggard look upon her face for a moment when she was singing *Arrayed for the Bridal*. Soon, perhaps, he would be sitting in that same drawing-room, dressed in black, his silk hat on his knees. The blinds would be drawn down and Aunt Kate would be sitting beside him, crying and blowing her nose and telling him how Julia had died. He would cast about in his mind for some words that might console her, and would find only lame and useless ones. Yes, yes: that would happen very soon.

The air of the room chilled his shoulders. He stretched himself cautiously along under the sheets and lay down beside his wife. One by one they were all becoming shades. Better pass boldly into that other world, in the full glory of some passion, than fade and wither dismally with age. He thought of how she who lay beside him had locked in her heart for so many years that image of her lover's eyes when he had told her that he did not wish to live.

Generous tears filled Gabriel's eyes. He had never felt like that himself towards any woman but he knew that such a feeling must be love. The tears gathered more thickly in his eyes and in the partial darkness he imagined he saw the form of a young man standing under a dripping tree. Other forms were near. His soul had approached that region where swell the vast hosts of the dead. He was conscious of, but could not apprehend, their wayward and flickering existence. His own identity was fading out into a grey impalpable world: the solid world itself which these dead had one time reared and lived in was dissolving and dwindling.

A few light taps upon the pane made him turn to the window. It had begun to snow again. He watched sleepily the flakes, silver and dark, falling obliquely against the lamplight. The time had come for him to set out on his journey westward. Yes, the newspapers were right: snow was general all over Ireland. It was falling on every part of the dark central plain, on the treeless hills, falling softly upon the Bog of Allen and, farther westward, softly falling into the dark mutinous Shannon waves. It was falling, too, upon every part of the lonely churchyard on the hill where Michael Furey lay buried. It lay thickly drifted on the crooked crosses and headstones, on the spears of the little gate, on the barren thorns. His soul swooned slowly as he heard the snow falling faintly through the universe and faintly falling, like the descent of their last end, upon all the living and the dead.

# James Stephens

## *The Triangle*

Nothing is true for ever. A man and a fact will become equally decrepit and will tumble in the same ditch, for truth is as mortal as man, and both are outlived by the tortoise and the crow.

To say that two is company and three is a crowd is to make a very temporary statement. After a short time satiety or use and wont has crept sunderingly between the two, and, if they are any company at all, they are bad company, who pray discreetly but passionately for the crowd which is censured by the proverb.

If there had not been a serpent in the Garden of Eden it is likely that the bored inhabitants of Paradise would have been forced to import one from the outside wilds merely to relax the tedium of a too-sustained duet. There ought to be a law that when a man and a woman have been married for a year they should be forcibly separated for another year. In the meantime, as our lawgivers have no sense, we will continue to invoke the serpent.

Mrs. Mary Morrissy had been married for quite a time to a gentleman of respectable mentality, a sufficiency of money, and a surplus of leisure—Good things? We would say so if we dared, for we are growing old and suspicious of all appearances, and we do not easily recognise what is bad or good. Beyond the social circumference we are confronted with a debatable ground where good and bad are so merged that we cannot distinguish the one from the other. To her husband's mental attainments (from no precipitate, dizzy peaks did he stare; it was only a tiny plain with the tiniest of hills in the centre) Mrs. Morrissy extended a courtesy entirely unmixed with awe. For his money she extended a hand which could still thrill to an unaccustomed prodigality, but for his leisure (and it was illimitable) she could find no possible use.

The quality of permanency in a transient world is terrifying. A permanent husband is a bore, and we do not know what to do with him. He cannot be put on a shelf. He cannot be hung on a nail. He will not go out of the house. There is no escape from him, and he is always the same. A smile of a certain dimension, moustaches of this inevitable measurement, hands that waggle and flop like those of automata—these are his. He eats this way and he drinks that way, and he will continue to do so until he stiffens into the ultimate quietude. He snores on this note, he laughs on that, dissonant, unescapable, unchanging. This is the way he walks, and he does not know how to run. A predictable beast indeed! He is known inside and out, catalogued, ticketed, and he cannot be packed away.

Mrs. Morrissy did not yet commune with herself about it, but if her grievance was anonymous it was not unknown. There is a back-door to every mind as to every house, and although she refused it house-room, the knowledge sat on her very hearthstone whistling for recognition.

Indeed, she could not look anywhere without seeing her husband. He was included in every landscape. His moustaches and the sun rose together. His pyjamas dawned with the moon. When the sea roared so did he, and he whispered with the river and the wind. He was in the picture but was out of drawing. He was in the song but was out of tune. He agitated her duly, surreptitiously, unceasingly.  She questioned of space in a whisper—"Are we glued together?" said she. There was a bee in a flower, a burly rascal who did not care a rap for any one; he sat enjoying himself in a scented and gorgeous palace, and in him she confided:

"If," said she to the bee, "If that man doesn't stop talking to me I'll kick him. I'll stick a pin in him if he does not go out for a walk."

She grew desperately nervous. She was afraid that if she looked at him any longer she would see him. To-morrow, she thought, I may notice that he is a short, fat man in spectacles, and that will be the end of everything. But the end of everything is also the beginning of everything, and so she was one half in fear and the other half in hope. A little more and she would hate him, and would begin the world again with the same little hope and the same little despair for her meagre capital.

She had already elaborated a theory that man was intended to work, and that male sloth was offensive to Providence and should be forbidden by the law. At times her tongue thrilled, silently as yet, to certain dicta of the experienced Aunt who had superintended her youth, to the intent that a lazy man is a nuisance to himself and to everybody else; and, at last, she disguised this saying as an anecdote and repeated it pleasantly to her husband.

He received it coldly, pondered it with disfavour, and dismissed it by arguing that her Aunt had whiskers, that a whiskered female is a freak, and that the intellectual exercises of a freak are—He lifted his eyebrows and his shoulders. He brushed her Aunt from the tips of his fingers and blew her delicately beyond good manners and the mode.

But time began to hang heavily on both. The intellectual antics of a leisured man become at last wearisome; his methods of thought, by mere familiarity, grow distasteful; the time comes when all the arguments are finished, there is nothing more to be said on any subject, and boredom, without even the covering, apologetic hand, yawns and yawns and cannot be appeased. Thereupon two cease to be company, and even a serpent would be greeted as a cheery and timely visitor. Dismal indeed, and not infrequent, is that time, and the vista therefrom is a long, dull yawn stretching to the horizon and the grave. If at any time we do revalue the values, let us write it down that the person who makes us yawn is a criminal knave, and then we will abolish matrimony and read Plato again.

The serpent arrived one morning hard on Mrs. Morrissy's pathetic pressure. It had three large trunks, a toy terrier, and a volume of verse. The trunks contained dresses, the dog insects, and the book emotion—a sufficiently enlivening trilogy! Miss Sarah O'Malley wore the dresses in exuberant rotation, Mr. Morrissy read the emotional poetry with great admiration, Mrs. Morrissy made friends with the dog, and life at once became complex and joyful.

Mr. Morrissy, exhilarated by the emotional poetry, drew, with an instinct too human to be censured, more and more in the direction of his wife's cousin, and that lady, having a liking for comedy, observed the agile posturings of the gentleman on a verbal summit up and down and around which he flung himself with equal dexterity and satisfaction—crudely, he made puns—and the two were further thrown together by the enforced absences of Mrs. Morrissy, into a privacy more than sealed, by reason of the attentions of a dog who would climb to her lap, and there, with an angry nose, put to no more than temporary rout the nimble guests of his jacket. Shortly Mrs. Morrissy began to look upon the toy terrier with a meditative eye.

It was from one of these, now periodical, retreats that Mrs. Morrissy first observed the rapt attitude of her husband, and instantly life for her became bounding, plentiful, and engrossing.

There is no satisfaction in owning that which nobody else covets. Our silver is not more than secondhand, tarnished metal until some one else speaks of it in terms of envy. Our husbands are barely tolerable until a lady friend has endeavoured to abstract their cloying attentions. Then only do we comprehend that our possessions are unique, beautiful, well worth guarding.

Nobody has yet pointed out that there is an eighth sense; and yet the sense of property is more valuable and more detestable than all the others in combination. The person who owns something is civilised. It is man's escape from wolf and monkeydom. It is individuality at last, or the promise of it, while those other ownerless people must remain either beasts of prey or beasts of burden, grinning with ineffective teeth, or bowing stupid heads for their masters' loads, and all begging humbly for last straws and getting them.

Under a sufficiently equable exterior Mrs. Morrissy's blood was pulsing with greater activity than had ever moved it before. It raced! It flew! At times the tide of it thudded to her head, boomed in her ears, surged in fierce waves against her eyes. Her brain moved with a complexity which would have surprised her had she been capable of remarking upon it. Plot and counterplot! She wove webs horrid as a spider's. She became, without knowing it, a mistress of psychology. She dissected motions and motives. She built theories precariously upon an eyelash. She pondered and weighed the turning of a head, the handing of a sugar-bowl. She read treason in a laugh, assignations in a song, villainy in a new dress. Deeper and darker things! Profound and vicious depths plunging stark to where the devil lodged in darknesses too dusky for registration! She looked so steadily on these gulfs and murks that at last she could see anything she wished to see; and always, when times were critical, when this and that, abominations indescribable, were separate by no more than a pin's point, she must retire from her watch (alas for a too-sensitive nature!) to chase the enemies of a dog upon which, more than ever, she fixed a meditative eye.

To get that woman out of the house became a pressing necessity. Her cousin carried with her a baleful atmosphere. She moved cloudy with doubt. There was a diabolic aura about her face, and her hair was red! These things were patent. Was one blind or a fool? A straw will reveal the wind, so will an eyelash, a smile, the carriage of a dress. Ankles also! One saw too much of them. Let it be said then. Teeth and necks were bared too often and too broadly. If modesty was indeed more than a name, then here it was outraged. Shame too! was it only a word? Does one do this and that without even a blush? Even vice should have its good manners, its own decent retirements. If there is nothing else let there be breeding! But at this thing the world might look and understand and censure if it were not brass-browed and stupid. Sneak! Traitress! Serpent! Oh, Serpent! do you slip into our very Eden, looping your sly coils across our flowers, trailing over our beds of narcissus and our budding rose, crawling into our secret arbours and whispering-places and nests of happiness? Do you flaunt and sway your crested head with a new hat on it every day? Oh that my Aunt were here, with the dragon's teeth, and the red breath, and whiskers to match! Here Mrs. Morrissy jumped as if she had been bitten (as indeed she had been) and retired precipitately, eyeing the small dog that frisked about her with an eye almost petrified with meditation.

To get that woman out of the house quickly and without scandal. Not to let her know for a moment, for the blink and twitter of an eyelid, of her triumph. To eject her with ignominy, retaining one's own dignity in the meantime. Never to let her dream of an uneasiness that might have screamed, an anger that could have bitten and scratched and been happy in the primitive exercise. Was such a task beyond her adequacy?

Below in the garden the late sun slanted upon her husband, as with declamatory hands and intense brows he chanted emotional poetry, ready himself on the slope of opportunity to roll into verses from his own resources. He criticised, with agile misconception, the inner meaning, the involved, hard-hidden heart of the poet; and the serpent sat before him and nodded. She smiled enchantments at him, and allurements, and subtle,

subtle disagreements. On the grass at their feet the toy terrier bounded from his slumbers and curved an imperative and furious hind-leg in the direction of his ear.

Mrs. Morrissy called the dog, and it followed her into the house, frisking joyously. From the kitchen she procured a small basket, and into this she packed some old cloths and pieces of biscuit. Then she picked up the terrier, cuffed it on both sides of the head, popped it into the basket, tucked its humbly-agitated tail under its abject ribs, closed the basket, and fastened it with a skewer. She next addressed a label to her cousin's home, tied it to the basket, and despatched a servant with it to the railway-station, instructing her that it should be paid for on delivery.

At breakfast the following morning her cousin wondered audibly why her little, weeny, tiny pet was not coming for its brecky.

Mrs. Morrissy, with a smile of infinite sweetness, suggested that Miss O'Malley's father would surely feed the brute when it arrived. "It was a filthy little beast," said she brightly; and she pushed the toast-rack closer to her husband.

There followed a silence which drowsed and buzzed to eternity, and during which Mr. Morrissy's curled moustaches straightened and grew limp and drooped. An edge of ice stiffened around Miss O'Malley. Incredulity, frozen and wan, thawed into swift comprehension and dismay, lit a flame in her cheeks, throbbed burningly at the lobes of her ears, spread magnetic and prickling over her whole stung body, and ebbed and froze again to immobility. She opposed her cousin's kind eyes with a stony brow.

"I think," said she, rising, "that I had better see to my packing."

"Must you go?" said Mrs. Morrissy, with courteous unconcern, and she helped herself to cream. Her husband glared insanely at a pat of butter, and tried to look like someone who was somewhere else.

Miss O'Malley closed the door behind her with extreme gentleness.

So the matter lay. But the position was unchanged. For a little time peace would reign in that household, but the same driving necessity remained, and before long another, and perhaps more virulent, serpent would have to be requisitioned for the assuagement of those urgent woes. A man's moustaches will arise with the sun; not Joshua could constrain them to the pillow after the lark had sung reveille. A woman will sit pitilessly at the breakfast table however the male eye may shift and quail. It is the business and the art of life to degrade permanencies. Fluidity is existence, there is no other, and for ever the chief attraction of Paradise must be that there is a serpent in it to keep it lively and wholesome. Lacking the serpent we are no longer in Paradise, we are at home, and our sole entertainment is to yawn when we wish to.

# James Stephens

## The Blind Man

He was one who would have passed by the Sphinx without seeing it. He did not believe in the necessity for sphinxes, or in their reality, for that matter—they did not exist for him. Indeed, he was one to whom the Sphinx would not have been visible. He might have eyed it and noted a certain bulk of grotesque stone, but nothing more significant.

He was sex-blind, and, so, peculiarly limited by the fact that he could not appreciate women. If he had been pressed for a theory or metaphysic of womanhood he would have been unable to formulate any. Their presence he admitted, perforce: their utility was quite apparent to him on the surface, but, subterraneously, he doubted both their existence and their utility. He might have said perplexedly—why cannot they do whatever they have to do without being always in the way? He might have said—Hang it, they are everywhere, and what good are they doing? They bothered him, they destroyed his ease when he was near them, and they spoke a language which he did not understand and did not want to understand. But as his limitations did not press on him neither did they trouble him. He was not sexually deficient, and he did not dislike women; he simply ignored them, and was only really at home with men. All the crudities which we enumerate as masculine delighted him—simple things, for, in the gender of abstract ideas, vice is feminine, brutality is masculine, the female being older, vastly older than the male, much more competent in every way, stronger, even in her physique, than he, and, having little baggage of mental or ethical preoccupations to delay her progress, she is still the guardian of evolution, requiring little more from man than to be stroked and petted for a while.

He could be brutal at times. He liked to get drunk at seasonable periods. He would cheerfully break a head or a window, and would bandage the one damage or pay for the other with equal skill and pleasure. He liked to tramp rugged miles swinging his arms and whistling as he went, and he could sit for hours by the side of a ditch thinking thoughts without words—an easy and a pleasant way of thinking, and one which may lead to something in the long run.

Even his mother was an abstraction to him. He was kind to her so far as doing things went, but he looked over her, or round her, and marched away and forgot her.

Sex-blindness carries with it many other darknesses. We do not know what masculine thing is projected by the feminine consciousness, and civilisation, even life itself, must stand at a halt until that has been discovered or created; but art is the female projected by the male: science is the male projected by the male—as yet a poor thing, and to remain so until it has become art; that is, has become fertilised and so more psychological than mechanical. The small part of science which came to his notice (inventions, machinery, etc.) was easily and delightedly comprehended by him. He could do intricate things with a knife and a piece of string, or a hammer and a saw; but a picture, a poem, a statue, a piece of music—these left him as uninterested as they found him: more so, in truth, for they left him bored and dejected.

His mother came to dislike him, and there were many causes and many justifications for her dislike. She was an orderly, busy, competent woman, the counterpart of endless millions of her sex, who liked to understand what she saw or felt, and who had no happiness in reading riddles. To her he was at times an enigma, and at times again a simpleton. In both aspects he displeased and embarrassed her. One has one's sense of property, and in him she could not put her finger on anything that was hers. We demand continuity, logic in other words, but between her son and herself there was a gulf fixed, spanned by no bridge whatever; there was complete isolation; no boat plied between them at all. All the kindly human things which she loved were unintelligible to him, and his coarse pleasures or blunt evasions distressed and bewildered her. When she spoke to him he gaped or yawned; and yet she did not speak on weighty matters, just the necessary small-change of existence—

somebody's cold, somebody's dress, somebody's marriage or death. When she addressed him on sterner subjects, the ground, the weather, the crops, he looked at her as if she were a baby, he listened with stubborn resentment, and strode away a confessed boor. There was no contact anywhere between them, and he was a slow exasperation to her—What can we do with that which is ours and not ours? Either we own a thing or we do not, and, whichever way it goes, there is some end to it; but certain enigmas are illegitimate and are so hounded from decent cogitation.

She could do nothing but dismiss him, and she could not even do that, for there he was at the required periods, always primed with the wrong reply to any question, the wrong aspiration, the wrong conjecture; a perpetual trampler on mental corns, a person for whom one could do nothing but apologise.

They lived on a small farm, and almost the entire work of the place was done by him. His younger brother assisted, but that assistance could have easily been done without. If the cattle were sick, he cured them almost by instinct. If the horse was lame or wanted a new shoe, he knew precisely what to do in both events. When the time came for ploughing, he gripped the handles and drove a furrow which was as straight and as economical as any furrow in the world. He could dig all day long and be happy; he gathered in the harvest as another would gather in a bride; and, in the intervals between these occupations, he fled to the nearest public-house and wallowed among his kind.

He did not fly away to drink; he fled to be among men—then he awakened. His tongue worked with the best of them, and adequately too. He could speak weightily on many things—boxing, wrestling, hunting, fishing, the seasons, the weather, and the chances of this and the other man's crops. He had deep knowledge about brands of tobacco and the peculiar virtues of many different liquors. He knew birds and beetles and worms; how a weazel would behave in extraordinary circumstances: how to train every breed of horse and dog. He recited goats from the cradle to the grave, could tell the name of any tree from its leaf; knew how a bull could be coerced, a cow cut up, and what plasters were good for a broken head. Sometimes, and often enough, the talk would chance on women, and then he laughed as heartily as anyone else, but he was always relieved when the conversation trailed to more interesting things.

His mother died and left the farm to the younger instead

of the elder son; an unusual thing to do, but she did detest him. She knew her younger son very well. He was foreign to her in nothing. His temper ran parallel with her own, his tastes were hers, his ideas had been largely derived from her, she could track them at any time and make or demolish him. He would go to a dance or a picnic and be as exhilarated as she was, and would discuss the matter afterwards. He could speak with some cogency on the shape of this and that female person, the hat of such a one, the disagreeableness of tea at this house and the goodness of it at the other. He could even listen to one speaking without going to sleep at the fourth word. In all he was a decent, quiet lad who would become a father the exact replica of his own, and whose daughters would resemble his mother as closely as two peas resemble their green ancestors—so she left him the farm.

Of course, there was no attempt to turn the elder brother out. Indeed, for some years the two men worked quietly together and prospered and were contented; then, as was inevitable, the younger brother got married, and the elder had to look out for a new place to live in, and to work in—things had become difficult.

It is very easy to say that in such and such circumstances a man should do this and that well-pondered thing, but the courts of logic have as yet the most circumscribed jurisdiction. Just as statistics can prove anything and be quite wrong, so reason can sit in its padded chair issuing pronouncements which are seldom within measurable distance of any reality. Everything is true only in relation to its centre of thought. Some people think with their heads—their subsequent actions are as logical and unpleasant as are those of the other sort who think only with their blood, and this latter has its irrefutable logic also. He thought in this subterranean fashion, and if he had thought in the other the issue would not have been any different.

Still, it was not an easy problem for him, or for any person lacking initiative—a sexual characteristic. He might have emigrated, but his roots were deeply struck in his own place, so the idea never occurred to him; furthermore, our thoughts are often no deeper than our pockets, and one wants money to move anywhere. For any other life than that of farming he had no training and small desire. He had no money and he was a farmer's son. Without money he could not get a farm; being a farmer's son he could not sink to the degradation of a day labourer; logically he could sink, actually he could not without endangering his own centres and verities—so he also got married.

He married a farm of about ten acres, and the sun began to shine on him once more; but only for a few days. Suddenly the sun went away from the heavens; the moon disappeared from the silent night; the silent night itself fled afar, leaving in its stead a noisy, dirty blackness through which one slept or yawned as one could. There was the farm, of course—one could go there and work; but the freshness went out of the very ground; the crops lost their sweetness and candour; the horses and cows disowned him; the goats ceased to be his friends—It was all up with him. He did not whistle any longer. He did not swing his shoulders as he walked, and, although he continued to smoke, he did not look for a particular green bank whereon he could sit quietly flooded with those slow thoughts that had no words.

For he discovered that he had not married a farm at all. He had married a woman—a thin-jawed, elderly slattern, whose sole beauty was her farm. How her jaws worked! The processions and congregations of words that fell and dribbled and slid out of them! Those jaws were never quiet, and in spite of all he did not say anything. There was not anything to say, but much to do from which he shivered away in terror. He looked at her sometimes through the muscles of his arms, through his big, strong hands, through fogs and fumes and singular, quiet tumults that raged within him. She lessoned him on the things he knew so well, and she was always wrong. She lectured him on those things which she did know, but the unending disquisition, the perpetual repetition, the foolish, empty emphasis, the dragging weightiness of her tongue made him repudiate her knowledge and hate it as much as he did her.

Sometimes, looking at her, he would rub his eyes and yawn with fatigue and wonder—There she was! A something enwrapped about with petticoats. Veritably alive. Active as an insect! Palpable to the touch! And what was she doing to him? Why did she do it? Why didn't she go away? Why didn't she die? What sense was there in the making of such a creature that clothed itself like a bolster, without any freedom or entertainment or shapeliness?

Her eyes were fixed on him and they always seemed to be angry; and her tongue was uttering rubbish about horses, rubbish about cows, rubbish about hay and oats. Nor was this the sum of his weariness. It was not alone that he was married; he was multitudinously, egregiously married. He had married a whole family, and what a family.

Her mother lived with her, her eldest sister lived with her, her youngest sister lived with her—and these were all swathed about with petticoats and shawls. They had no movement. Their feet were like those of no creature he had ever observed. One could hear the flip-flap of their slippers all over the place, and at all hours. They were down-at-heel, draggle-tailed, and futile. There was no workmanship about them. They were as unfinished, as unsightly as a puddle on a road. They insulted his eyesight, his hearing, and his energy. They had lank hair that slapped about them like wet seaweed, and they were all talking, talking, talking.

The mother was of an incredible age. She was senile with age. Her cracked cackle never ceased for an instant. She talked to the dog and the cat; she talked to the walls of the room; she spoke out through the window to the weather; she shut her eyes in a corner and harangued the circumambient darkness. The eldest sister was as silent as a deep ditch and as ugly. She slid here and there with her head on one side like an inquisitive hen watching one curiously, and was always doing nothing with an air of futile employment. The youngest was a semi-lunatic who prattled and prattled without ceasing, and was always catching one's sleeve, and laughing at one's face—and everywhere those flopping, wriggling, petticoats were appearing and disappearing. One saw slack hair whisking by the corner of one's eye. Mysteriously, urgently, they were coming and going and coming again, and never, never being silent.

More and more he went running to the public-house. But it was no longer to be among men, it was to get drunk. One might imagine him sitting there thinking those slow thoughts without words. One might predict that the day would come when he would realise very suddenly, very clearly, all that he had been thinking about, and, when this urgent, terrible thought had been translated into its own terms of action, he would be quietly hanged by the neck until he was as dead as he had been before he was alive.

# James Stephens

## *Desire*

### I

He was excited, and as he leaned forward in his chair and told this story to his wife he revealed to her a degree or a species of credulity of which she could not have believed him capable.

He was a level-headed man, and habitually conducted his affairs on hard-headed principles. He had conducted his courtship, his matrimonial and domestic affairs in a manner which she should not have termed reckless or romantic. When, therefore, she found him excited, and over such a story, she did not know how just to take the matter.

She compromised by agreeing with him, not because her reason was satisfied or even touched, but simply because he was excited, and a woman can welcome anything which varies the dull round and will bathe in exclamations if she gets the chance.

This was what he told her.

As he was walking to lunch a motor car came down the street at a speed much too dangerous for the narrow and congested thoroughfare. A man was walking in front of him, and, just as the car came behind, this man stepped off the path with a view to crossing the road. He did not even look behind as he stepped off. Her husband stretched a ready arm that swept the man back to the pavement one second before the car went blaring and buzzing by.

"If I had not been there," said her husband, who liked slang, "you would have got it where the chicken got the axe."

The two men grinned at each other; her husband smiling with good-fellowship, the other crinkling with amusement and gratitude.

They walked down the street and, on the strength of that adventure, they had lunch together.

They had sat for a long time after lunch, making each other's acquaintance, smoking innumerable cigarettes, and engaged in a conversation which she could never have believed her husband would have shared in for ten minutes; and they had parted with a wish, from her husband, that they should meet again on the following day, and a wordless smile from the man.

He had neither ratified nor negatived the arrangement.

"I hope he'll turn up," said her husband.

This conversation had excited her man, for it had drawn him into an atmosphere to which he was a stranger, and he had found himself moving there with such pleasure that he wished to get back to it with as little delay as possible.

Briefly, as he explained it to her, the atmosphere was religious; and while it was entirely intellectual it was more heady and exhilarating than the emotional religion to which he had been accustomed, and from which he had silently lapsed.

He tried to describe his companion; but had such ill success in the description that she could not remember afterwards whether he was tall or short; fat or thin; fair or dark.

It was the man's eyes only that he succeeded in emphasising; and these, it appeared, were eyes such as he had never before seen in a human face.

That also, he amended, was a wrong way of putting it, for his eyes were exactly like everybody else's. It was the way he looked through them that was different. Something, very steady, very ardent, very quiet and powerful, was using these eyes for purposes of vision. He had never met anyone who looked at him so comprehendingly; so agreeably.

"You are in love," said she with a laugh.

After this her husband's explanations became more explanatory but not less confused, until she found that they were both, with curious unconsciousness, in the middle of a fairy-tale.

"He asked me," said her husband, "what was the thing I wished for beyond all things."

"That was the most difficult question I have ever been invited to answer," he went on; "and for nearly half an hour we sat thinking it out, and discussing magnificences and possibilities."

"I had all the usual thoughts; and, of course, the first of

them was wealth. We are more dominated by proverbial phrases than we conceive of, and, such a question being posed, the words 'healthy, wealthy, and wise' will come, unbidden, to answer it. To be alive is to be acquisitive, and so I mentioned wealth, tentatively, as a possibility; and he agreed that it was worth considering. But after a while I knew that I did not want money."

"One always has need of money," said his wife.

"In a way, that is true," he replied, "but not in this way; for, as I thought it over, I remembered, that we have no children; and that our relatively few desires, or fancies, can be readily satisfied by the money we already have. Also we are fairly well off; we have enough in the stocking to last our time even if I ceased from business, which I am not going to do; and, in short, I discovered that money or its purchasing power had not any particular advantages to offer."

"All the same!" she murmured; and halted with her eyes fixed on purchasings far away in time and space.

"All the same!" he agreed with a smile.

"I could not think of anything worth wishing for," he continued. "I mentioned health and wisdom, and we considered these; but, judging myself by the standard of the world in which we move, I concluded that both my health and knowledge were as good as the next man's; and I thought also that if I elected to become wiser than my contemporaries I might be a very lonely person for the rest of my days."

"Yes," said she thoughtfully, "I am glad you did not ask to be made wise, unless you could have asked it for both of us."

"I asked him in the end what he would advise me to demand, but he replied that he could not advise me at all. 'Behind everything stands desire,' said he, 'and you must find out your desire.'"

"I asked him then, if the conditions were reversed and if the opportunity had come to him instead of to me, what he should have asked for; not, as I explained to him, in order that I might copy his wish, but from sheer curiosity. He replied that he should not ask for anything. This reply astonished, almost alarmed me at first, but most curiously satisfied me on considering it, and I was about to adopt that attitude—"

"Oh," said his wife.

"When an idea came to me. 'Here I am,' I said to myself, 'forty-eight years of age: rich enough; sound enough in wind and limb; and as wise as I can afford to be. What is there now belonging to me, absolutely mine, but from which I must part, and which I should like to keep?' And I saw that the thing which was leaving me day by day; second by second; irretrievably and inevitably; was my forty-eighth year. I thought I should like to continue at the age of forty-eight until my time was up."

"I did not ask to live for ever, or any of that nonsense, for I saw that to live for ever is to be condemned to a misery of boredom more dreadful than anything else the mind can conceive of. But, while I do live, I wish to live competently, and so I asked to be allowed stay at the age of forty-eight years with all the equipment of my present state unimpaired."

"You should not have asked for such a thing," said his wife, a little angrily. "It is not fair to me," she explained. "You are older than I am now, but in a few years this will mean that I shall be needlessly older than you. I think it was not a loyal wish."

"I thought of that objection," said he, "and I also thought that I was past the age at which certain things matter; and that both temperamentally and in the matter of years I am proof against sensual or such-like attractions. It seemed to me to be right; so I just registered my wish with him."

"What did he say?" she queried.

"He did not say anything; he just nodded; and began to talk again of other matters—religion, life, death, mind; a host of things, which, for all the diversity they seem to have when I enumerate them, were yet one single theme."

"I feel a more contented man to-night than I have ever felt," he continued, "and I feel in some curious way a different person from the man I was yesterday."

Here his wife awakened from the conversation and began to laugh.

"You are a foolish man," said she, "and I am just as bad. If anyone were to hear us talking this solemn silliness they would have a right to mock at us."

He laughed heartily with her, and after a light supper they went to bed.

## II

During the night his wife had a dream.

She dreamed that a ship set away from the Polar Seas on an expedition in which she was not sufficiently interested to find out its reason. The ship departed with her on board. All that she knew or cared was that she was greatly concerned with baggage, and with counting and going over the various articles that she had brought against Arctic weather.

She had thick woollen stockings. She had skin boots all hairy inside, all pliable and wrinkled without. She had a great skin cap shaped like a helmet and fitting down in a cape over her shoulders. She had, and they did not astonish her, a pair of very baggy fur trousers. She had a sleeping sack.

She had an enormous quantity of things; and everybody in the expedition was equipped, if not with the same things, at least similarly.

These traps were a continuous subject of conversation aboard, and, although days and weeks passed, the talk of the ship hovered about and fell continually into the subject of warm clothing.

There came a day when the weather was perceptibly colder; so cold that she was tempted to draw on these wonderful breeches, and to fit her head into that most comfortable hat. But she did not do so; for, and everybody on the ship explained it to her, it was necessary that she should accustom herself to the feeling, the experience, of cold; and, she was further assured, that the chill which she was now resenting was nothing to the freezing she should presently have to bear.

It seemed good advice; and she decided that as long as she could bear the cold she would do so, and would not put on any protective covering; thus, when the cold became really intense, she would be in some measure inured to it, and would not suffer so much.

But steadily, and day by day, the weather grew colder.

For now they were in wild and whirling seas wherein great green and white icebergs went sailing by; and all about the ship little hummocks of ice bobbed and surged, and went under and came up; and the grey water slashed and hissed against and on top of these small hillocks.

Her hands were so cold that she had to put them under her armpits to keep any warmth in them; and her feet were in a worse condition. They had begun to pain her; so she decided that on the morrow she would put on her winter equipment, and would not mind what anybody said to the contrary.

"It is cold enough," said she "for my Arctic trousers, for my warm soft boots, and my great furry gloves. I will put them on in the morning," for it was then almost night and she meant to go to bed at once.

She did go to bed; and she lay there in a very misery of cold.

In the morning, she was yet colder; and immediately on rising she looked for the winter clothing which she had laid ready by the side of her bunk the night before; but she could not find them. She was forced to dress in her usual rather thin clothes; and, having done so, she went on deck.

When she got to the side of the vessel she found that the world about her had changed.

The sea had disappeared. Far as the eye could peer was a level plain of ice, not white, but dull grey; and over it there lowered a sky, grey as itself and of almost the same dullness.

Across this waste there blew a bitter, a piercing wind that her eyes winced from, and that caused her ears to tingle and sting.

Not a soul was moving on the ship, and the dead silence which brooded on the ice lay heavy and almost solid on the vessel.

She ran to the other side, and found that the whole ship's company had landed, and were staring at her from a little distance off the ship. And these people were as silent as the frozen air, as the frozen ship. They stared at her; they made no move; they made no sound.

She noticed that they were all dressed in their winter furs; and, while she stood, ice began to creep into her veins.

One of the ship's company strode forward a few paces and held up a bundle in his mittened hand. She was amazed to see that the bundle contained her clothes, her broad furry trousers; her great cosy helmet and gloves.

To get from the ship to the ice was painful but not impossible. A rope ladder was hanging against the side, and she went down this. The rungs felt hard as iron, for they were frozen stiff; and the touch of those glassy surfaces bit into her tender hand like fire. But she got to the ice and went across it towards her companions.

Then, to her dismay, to her terror, all these, suddenly, with one unexpressed accord, turned and began to run away from her; and she, with a heart that shook once and could scarcely beat again, took after them.

Every few paces she fell, for her shoes could not grip on the ice; and each time that she fell those monsters stood and turned and watched her, and the man who had her clothes waved the bundle at her and danced grotesquely, silently.

She continued running, sliding, falling, picking herself up, until her breath went, and she came to a halt, unable to move a limb further and scarcely able to breathe; and this time they did not stay to look at her.

They continued running, but now with great and greater speed, with the very speed of madmen; and she saw them become black specks away on the white distance; and she saw them disappear; and she saw that there was nothing where she stared but the long white miles, and the terrible silence, and the cold.

How cold it was!

And with that there arose a noiseless wind, keen as a razor.

It stung into her face; it swirled about her ankles like a lash; it stabbed under her armpits like a dagger.

"I am cold," she murmured.

She looked backwards whence she had come, but the ship was no longer in sight, and she could not remember from what direction she had come.

Then she began to run in any direction.

Indeed she ran in every direction to find the ship; for when she had taken a hundred steps in one way she thought, frantically, "this is not the way," and at once she began to run on the opposite road. But run as she might she could not get warm; it was colder she got. And then, on a steel-grey plane, she slipped, and slipped again, and went sliding down a hollow, faster and faster; she came to the brink of a cleft, and swished over this, and down into a hole of ice and there she lay.

"I shall die!" she said. "I shall fall asleep here and die. . . ."

Then she awakened.

She opened her eyes directly on the window and saw the ghost of dawn struggling with the ghoul of darkness. A greyish perceptibility framed the window without, but could not daunt the obscurity within; and she lay for a moment terrified at that grotesque adventure, and thanking God that it had only been a dream.

In another second she felt that she was cold. She pulled the clothes more tightly about her, and she spoke to her husband.

"How miserably cold it is!" she said.

She turned in the bed and snuggled against him for warmth; and she found that an atrocity of cold came from him; that he was icy.

She leaped from the bed with a scream. She switched on the light, and bent over her husband.

He was stone dead. He was stone cold. And she stood by him, shivering and whimpering.

# James Stephens

## *Hunger*

### I

On some people misery comes unrelentingly. It comes with such a continuous rage that one might say destruction had been sworn against them and that they were doomed beyond appeal, or hope.

That seemed to her to be the case as she sat, when her visitor had departed, looking on life as it had moved about her; and she saw that life had closed on her, had crushed her, and that there was nothing to be said about it, and no one to be blamed.

She was ten years married, and she had three children. One of them had fallen when he was a baby, and had hurt his back so badly that the dispensary doctor instructed her not to let him walk for a few years.

She loved all her children, but this child she loved greatly; for she had to do more for him than for the others. Indeed she had to do everything for him, and she did not grudge doing it. He was the eldest and he was always with her. The other youngsters were with her as screamings, as demands, to be attended to and forgotten, but he was with her as a companion eye, a consciousness to whom she could talk and who would reply to her, and who would not, could not, by any means get into mischief.

Her husband was a house-painter, and when work was brisk he got good wages: he could earn thirty-five shillings a week when he was working.

But his work was constant only in the summer months: through the bad weather there was no call for him, for no one wanted house-painting done in the winter; and so the money which he earned in the fine months had to be stretched and made to cover the dead months.

Nor were these five months to be entirely depended upon: here and there in a week days would be missed, and with that his Society dues had to be paid, for he would pay these though he starved for it.

## II

Wages which have to be stretched so lengthily give but the slenderest sum towards a weekly budget. It was she who had to stretch them, and the doing of it occupied all the time she could spare for thinking.

She made ends meet where nothing was but ends, and they met just over the starvation line.

She had not known for years what it was like not to be hungry for one day; but life is largely custom; and neither she nor her husband nor the children made much complaint about a condition which was normal for them all, and into which the children had been born.

They could scarcely die of hunger for they were native to it. They were hunger. There was no other hunger but them: and they only made a noise about food when they saw food.

If she could have got work how gladly she would have taken it! How gladly she would have done it! Sweated work! Any work! so it brought in if it was no more than a few coppers in the day. But the children were there, three of them, and all were young and one was a cripple.

Her own people, and those of her husband, lived, existed, far away in the country. They could not take the children off her hands. She could not give a neighbour anything to look after them while she went out working. She was held to them as fast as if she were chained to them; and, for to think in such cases is only to be worried, there was no use in thinking about it. She had already all the worry she could deal with, and she wanted no more.

She remembered a tale that she had laughed at, when she was young, about a woman who had been circumstanced as she was now. This woman used to put her two children into a box, for she had to go out every day to work in order that she might feed them; and she kept them in the box so that they might not injure themselves during her absence.

It was a good idea, but the children came out of the box hunchbacks, and so stunted in their growth that it might be said they never grew thereafter. It might have been better for the children, and easier for them, if they had died; anyhow, their mother died, and the poor little oddities went to the workhouse; and must all their lives have got all the jeers which their appearance sanctioned.

There was nothing to be done; even her husband had long ago given up thinking of how this could be arranged; and although she still, and continually, thought about it, she knew that nothing could be done.

### III

Her husband was a jolly man; he used to make up lists of the gigantic feeds they would have when the ship came home (what ship he did not say, nor was it understood that he expected one), and he or she or the children would remind each other of foods which had been left out of his catalogue; for no food of which they knew the name could justly be omitted from their future.

He was a robust man, and could have eaten a lot had he got it. Indeed he had often tempted his wife to commit an act of madness and have one wild blow-out; for which, as she pointed out to him, they would have to pay by whole days of whole starvation, instead of the whole days of semi-hunger to which they were accustomed.

This was the only subject on which they came nigh to quarrelling, and he brought it forward with fortnightly regularity.

Sometimes she went cold at the thought that on some pay-day he might go in for a wild orgy of eating, and perhaps spend half a crown. Less than that sum could not nearly fill him; and the double of it would hardly fill him the way he needed to be filled; for he wanted to be filled as tightly as a drum, and with such a weight and abundance of victual that he could scarcely be lifted by a crane.

But he was an honourable man, and she knew that he

would not do this unless she and the children were with him and could share and go mad with him. He was very fond of them, and if she could have fed him on her own flesh she would have sacrificed a slice or two, for she was very fond of him.

## IV

The mild weather had come, and he got a cut in his hand, which festered and seemed stubbornly incurable. The reason was that the gaunt man was not fed well enough to send clean blood down to doctor his cut hand. In the end he did get over it; but for three weeks he had been unable to work, for who will give employment to a man whose hand looks like a poultice or a small football?

The loss of these three weeks almost finished her.

The distinguishing mark of her family had been thinness, it was now bonyness.

To what a food-getting fervour was she compelled! She put the world of rubbish that was about her through a sieve; and winnowed nourishment for her family where a rat would have unearthed disappointment.

She could not beg; but she did send her two children into the street, and sometimes one of these got a copper from a passing stranger. Then, like the call of a famished crow who warns his brothers that he has discovered booty, that youngster gave out a loyal squeal for his companion; and they trotted home with their penny. The sun shone on the day they got a penny; on the days when they got nothing the sun might bubble the tar and split the bricks, but it did not shine.

Her man returned to his work, and if she could hold on they would be able to regain the poverty of a few months previously, but which now beamed to her as a distant, unattainable affluence.

She could hold on, and she did; so that they tided feebly across those evil days; and came nigh at last to the longed-for scarcity which yet was not absolute starvation; and whereby they could live in the condition of health to which they were accustomed, and which they recognised and spoke of as good health.

They could not absolutely come to this for at least a year.

Provision had still to be made for the lean months to come; the winter months; and more than three weeks' wages which should have been skimmed in this precaution had been unprofitable, had not existed. The difference had to be made up by a double skimming of the present wage; which must also pay the present necessities, and recoup the baker and grocer for the few weeks' credit these shop people had given her.

In all, their lot for a long time was not to be envied, except by a beast in captivity: and envied only by him because he lusts for freedom and the chance of it as we lust for security and the destruction of chance.

### V

The winter came—the winter will come though the lark protest and the worm cries out its woe—and she entered on that period with misgiving, with resolution, and with a facing of everything that might come.

What bravery she had! What a noble, unwearying courage; when in so little a time, and at so small a pain, she might have died!

But such an idea did not come to her head. She looked on the world, and she saw that it was composed of a man and three children; while they lasted she could last, and when they were done it would be time enough to think of personal matters and her relation to things.

Before the summer had quite ended, e'er autumn had tinted a leaf, the war broke out; and with its coming there came insecurity. Not to her, not to them. They had no standard to measure security by. It came to the people who desire things done, and who pay to have doors varnished or window-frames painted. These people drew silently but resolutely from expense; while he and she and the children sunk deeper into their spending as one wallows into a bog.

The prices of things began to increase with a cumulative rapidity, and the quality of things began to deteriorate with equal speed. Bread and the eater of it came to a grey complexion. Meat was no more. The vegetables emigrated with the birds. The potato got a rise in the world and recognised no more its oldest friends. Nothing was left but the rain; and the rain came loyally.

They, those others, could retrench and draw in a little their horns; but from what could she retreat? What could she avoid? What could she eliminate, who had come to the bare bone and shank of life? The necessity for the loaf comes daily, recurs pitilessly from digestion to digestion, and with the inexorable promptitude of the moon the rent collector wanes and waxes.

They managed.

She and he managed.

Work still was, although it was spaced and intervalled like a storm-blown hedge. Here was a week and there another one, and from it they gleaned their constricted existence.

They did not complain; for those who are down do not complain. Nor did they know they were down. Or, knowing it, they did not admit their downness. For to front so final a fact is to face with naked hands a lion; and to admit is to give in. Is to be washed away. To be lost and drowned. To be anonymous; unhelpable; alive no more; but debris, or a straw which the wind takes and sails, or tears, or drifts, or rots, to powder and forgetfulness.

A bone in the world of bones! And they gnawed these bones until it seemed that nothing moved in the world except their teeth.

## VI

The winter came, and his work stopped as it always did in that season.

He got jobs cleaning windows. He got jobs at the docks hoisting things which not Hercules nor the devil himself could lift. But which he could lift, or which his teeth and the teeth of his children detached from the ground as from foundations and rivetings.

He got a job as a coalman; and as a night-watchman sitting in the angle of a black street before a bucket of stinking coal, which had been a fire until the rain put it out. To-day he had a job; but to-morrow and for a week he had none.

With what had been saved, skimmed, strained from the summer wages; with what came from the jobs; with the pennies that the children unearthed from strangers as though they dug in those loath souls for coin, they lived through the winter, and did not feel that they had passed through an experience worthy of record, or that their endurance might have been rewarded with medals and a pension.

They were living, as we all manage, amazingly, to live: and if others had an easier time that was their chance. But this was their life, and there were those who were even worse off than they were.

For they paid the rent! And, when that was done, what a deed had been accomplished! How notable an enemy circumvented!

## VII

The spring came; but it brought no leaves to their tree. The summer came; but it did not come to them; nor warn them of harvest and a sickle in the yield.

There was no building done that summer; the price of material had gone up and the price of wages. The contractors did not care for that prospect, and the client, remembering taxes and the war, decided to wait.

And her husband had no work!

Almost he had even given up looking for work. He would go out of the house and come into the house and go out of the house again; and he and she would look at each other in a dumb questioning.

It was strange how he had arranged with himself not to look at the children. How he had even arranged that their whimperings should seem to be inaudible, and their very presences invisible! And they, having raked his coming as with search-lights, and discovering that he brought nothing, looked at him no more.

They looked at her. They projected themselves to her, about her, upon her, into her. . . .

A wolf-mother, thus badgered and possessed, would have escaped from her young by mercifully or unmercifully slaughtering them. But she still could preserve her soul, her tenderness. Yet, if a whole infinity of tenderness seemed to be preserved for the children, a major, a yet more marvellous, tenderness was reserved for her man—it was without words, without action. It was without anything whatever. It was itself alone. Unproven, unquestioned, unending. To be perceived, received, only by the soul, and from the soul, or not to be received or perceived at all.

Sometimes she would say—not that she had anything to say, but to ease her husband's heart with a comradely word—

"Any chance to-day, do you think?"

And he would reply:

"Chance!"

And he would sit down to brood upon that lapsing word.

They were not angry; they had not the blood to be angry with; for to be wrathful you must be well fed or you must be drunk.

The youngest child died of an ill which, whatever it was at the top, was hunger at the bottom; and she grew terrified. She heard that there was work to be had in the Munition Factories in Scotland, and by some means she gathered together the fare and sent her husband across the sea.

"Write, if you can," said she, "the minute you get a place."

"Yes," he replied.

"And send us what you can spare," she said. "Send something this week if you can."

"Yes," he said.

And he went away.

And she went into the streets to beg.

## VIII

She left the boy behind in his chair, and brought the other little one with her.

She was frightened, for one can be arrested for begging. And she was afraid not to beg, for one can die of hunger.

How well she knew those streets! and yet she did not know them in this aspect! These were atrocious streets!

She got a penny here and a penny there, and she bought bread. Sometimes even she bought a twist of tea. She could manage until the end of the week; until her man sent the money.

She had thoughts of singing at the corners of streets, as she had so often seen done by the tone-less, ashen-faced women, who creak rusty music at the passer, and fix him with their eyes. But she was ashamed; and no song that she could remember seemed suitable; and she only could remember bits of songs; and she knew that her voice would not work for her, but that it would creak and mourn like a rusty hinge.

Her earnings were small, for she could not get in touch with people. That too is a trade and must be learned. They recognised her at a distance as a beggar, and she could only whisper to the back of a head or a cold shoulder.

Sometimes when she went towards a person that person instantly crossed the road and walked for a while hastily.

Sometimes people fixed upon her a prohibitive eye and she drew back from them humbled; her heart panting and her eyes hot at the idea that they took her for a beggar.

At times a man, without glancing at her, stuck a hand in a pocket and gave her a penny without halting in his stride.

One day she got twopence; one day she got sixpence; one day she got nothing.

But she could hold out to the end of the week.

## IX

The end of the week came, but it brought no letter.

"It will come to-morrow," she said.

"He is in a strange country," she thought in panic. "He must have missed the post, God help him!"

But on the next day there was no letter; nor any letter on the day after; and on the day that succeeded to it there was no letter.

"He . . . !" she said.

But she could not speculate on him. She knew him too well, and she knew that this was not he; he could no more leave them in the lurch than he could jump across Ireland in one jump.

"He has not got work," she said.

And she saw him strayed and stranded; without a hand; without a voice; bewildered and lost among strangers; going up streets and down streets; and twisting himself into a maze; a dizziness of loneliness and hunger and despair.

Or, she said:

"The submarines had blown up the ship that was coming with the money."

The week went by; another came, and still she did not hear from him. She was not able to pay the rent.

She looked at the children; and then she looked away from them distantly to her strayed husband; and then she looked inwardly on herself, and there was nothing to see.

She was down.

No littlest hope could find a chink to peer through. And while she sat, staring at nothing, in an immobile maze of attention, her mind—she had no longer a heart, it had died of starvation—her mind would give a leap and be still; and would leap again, as though an unknown, wordless action were seeking to be free; seeking to do something; seeking to disprove stagnation, and powerlessness, and death; and a little burning centre of violence hung in her head like a star.

She followed people with her eyes, sometimes a little way from her feet, saying to herself:

"The pockets of that man are full of money; he would rattle if he fell."

Or:

"That man had his breakfast this morning; he is full of food to the chin; he is round and tight and solid, and he weighs a ton."

She said:

"If I had all the money of all the people in this street I should have a lot of money."

She said:

"If I owned all the houses in this street I should have a lot of money."

The rent collector told her imperatively that she must leave at the end of the week, and the children called to her for bread, clamorously, unceasingly, like little dogs that yap and whine and cannot be made to stop.

X

Relief kitchens had been started in various parts of the city, but she only heard of them by chance; and she went to one. She told a lady in attendance her miserable tale, and was given the address of a gentleman who might assist her. He could give her a ticket which would enable her to get food; and he might be able to set her in the way of earning what would pay the rent.

This lady thought her husband had deserted her; and she said so, without condemnation, as one states a thing which has been known to happen; and the poor woman agreed without agreeing, for she did not believe it.

But she did not argue about the matter, for now that she accepted food, she accepted anything that came with it, whether it was opinions or advice. She was an acceptor, and if she claimed to possess even an opinion it might jeopardise her chance of getting anything.

She set out for the house of the gentleman who could give her the ticket which would get her food to bring home to the children.

He lived at some distance, and when she got to his house the servant told her he had gone to his office; at his office she was informed that he had gone out. She called three times at the office, and on the third time she was told that he had come in, but had gone home.

She trudged to his house again; and would have been weary, but that her mind had lapsed far, far, from her trudging feet; and when the mind is away the body matters nothing.

Where was her mind? At times it was nowhere. It was gone from her body and from material things. It might be said to have utterly quitted that tenement, and to be somehow, somewhere, refuged from every fear, havened from every torment and eased of every memory that could deject it. She was life and a will; or, if these are but one, she was the will to be, obscure, diligent, indefatigable.

And then, again, as the opening of a door, her mind, laden with recollections of time and space, of deeds and things and thwartings, was back in the known and incredible room, looking at the children, listening to them, consoling them; telling them that in a little while she should be home again, and that she would bring them food.

They had not eaten anything for—how long was it? Was it a year? Had they ever eaten? And one of them was sick!

She must get back. She had been away too long. But she must go forward before she could go back.

She must get the ticket which was food and hope and a new beginning, or a respite. Then she should be able to look about her. The children would go to sleep; and she could plan and contrive and pull together those separated and dwindling ends.

She came to the gentleman's house. He was in, and she told him her story, and how her case was desperate.

He also believed that her husband had deserted her; and he promised to write by that night's post to find out the truth about the man, and to see that he was punished for his desertion.

He had no tickets with him; he had used them all, for the hungry people in Dublin were numerous; work was slack everywhere, and those who had never before applied for assistance were now obliged to do so by dreadful necessity. He gave her some money, and promised to call at her room on the following day to investigate her case.

She went homewards urgently, and near home she bought bread and tea.

When she got in the crippled boy turned dull, dumb eyes upon her; and she laughed at him excitedly, exultantly; for she had food; lots of it, two loaves of it.

But the other child did not turn to her, and would not turn to her again, for he was dead; and he was dead of hunger.

## XI

She could not afford to go mad, for she still had a boy and he depended on her with an utter helpless dependence.

She fed him and fed herself; running from him in the chair to that other in its cot, with the dumb agony of an animal who must do two things at once, and cannot resolve which thing to do.

She could not think; she could hardly feel. She was dulled and distressed and wild. She was weakened by misery and tormented by duties; and life and the world seemed a place of busynesses, and futilities, and unending, unregulated, demands upon her.

A neighbour, hearing that persistent trotting over her head, came up to the room to remonstrate, and remained to shed for her the tears which she could not weep herself. She, too, was in straits, and had nothing more to give than those tears; and the banal iterations which are comfort because they are kindness.

Into this place the gentleman called on the following day to investigate, and was introduced to a room swept almost as clean of furniture as a dog kennel is; to the staring, wise-eyed child who lived in a chair; and to the quiet morsel of death that lay in a cot by the wall.

He was horrified, but he was used to sights of misery; and he knew that when things have ceased to move they must be set moving again; and that all he could do was to remove some of the impediments which he found in the path of life, so that it might flow on before it had time to become stagnant and rotten.

He took from the dry-eyed, tongue-tied woman all the immediate worry of death. He paid the rent, and left something to go on with as well; and he promised to get her work either in his house or at his office, but he would get her work to do somehow.

## XII

He came daily; and each day, in reply to her timid question as to her husband, he had nothing to say except that enquiries were being made.

On the fifth day, he had news, and he would have preferred any duty, however painful, to the duty of telling her his news.

But he told it, sitting on the one chair; with his hand over his eyes, and nothing of his face visible except the mouth which shaped and spoke sentences.

The munition people in Scotland reported that a man of the name he was enquiring for had applied for work, and had been taken on a fortnight after his application. The morning after he began work he was found dead in a laneway. He had no lodgings in the city; and at the post-mortem examination it was found that he had died of hunger and exposure.

She listened to this tale; looking from the gentleman who told it to her little son who listened to it. She moistened her lips with her tongue; but she could not speak, she could only stammer and smile.

The gentleman also sat looking at the boy.

"We must set this young man up," said he heavily. "I shall send a doctor to look him over to-day."

And he went away all hot and cold; beating his hands together as he walked; and feeling upon his shoulders all the weariness and misery of the world.

# Padraic Colum

## *Eilis: A Woman's Story*

I found Eilis in my aunt's house one autumn evening, and she told me this story. Eilis was knitting stockings for the household. She arose and welcomed me when I came in, and I shook hands with her without realising who the woman was.

My aunt was baking bread for the men who were coming in from the fields, and I went over to where she was at the fire. "Had you any luck with your fishing?" my aunt asked me.

"None at all," I said, "and your man will think less of me than ever now."

My aunt spoke to the woman knitting. "Myles says that the student here has too much dead knowledge to be any good," she said.

"Your man never thought much of them that are fond of books," the woman replied.

"You ought to give Eilis a book," my aunt said to me; "she is very fond of reading." I took down a book from my store at the window and brought it to Eilis. It was "The Story of Ireland."

"God will reward you," she said. "One gets an indulgence for lending a good book." I was struck by the way she said this and by her eager manner. I took a low stool and sat by her.

She had been reading a story in the summer, and she began to tell me the story eagerly. It was commonplace enough as written, probably a story out of some English newspaper, but Eilis told it as a folk-tale, and it became full of color and wonder. I knew by her gesture and by her care for the good word that she had listened to the poets and had heard the talk of scholars. She had the old culture, I thought, so I spoke to her in the Irish I was learning. But after we had exchanged some phrases, she said, as she took up her work, "Acushla, it's a long time since I spoke the Gaelic. The words are like the words of my old songs; I can hardly bring them to mind."

I knew her for Eilis Nic Ghabhrain—Elish MacGovern, as the people now called her. The MacGovern name had associations for me, for it was connected with that culture which the country people still hold, fragments of some long-descended civilization, Celtic or what you will. Phelim MacGovern, the brother of Eilis, was, to my mind, a good representative of this peasant culture. He lived at the time when the peasants were making an entry into affairs. A nation had been born in the shadow of past defeats and was beginning to stir. As yet the struggle was for a little security, a little knowledge, a little toleration. The tenant-farmers of Ireland were closing up for the bitter struggles against feudal privilege; they had not enough detachment to realise the nation. Phelim MacGovern, a poet and a scholar, understood the national idea, but this understanding brought him into frequent conflict with interests that were growing up in his community. He was often the object of powerful satire, for his neighbours delighted in a vigorous presentation of certain humours, and Phelim was always good material. However, he was a personality to the people, and it was likely that tradition would leave him a personality to their children. His poems are still in the minds of some of the older people of the Midlands. "The Lament for William Conroy, who was transported" is the best of Phelim MacGovern's poems.

He had met his end long before my meeting with Eilis, his sister, who was now an old woman. It was a tragic end, but it does not concern this story. I knew Phelim for a while when he was an old man. He used to repeat Latin poetry for me, and passages from the Irish version of the Iliad. His sister, too, had brought something down from this culture of the old days.

I gave more attention now to Eilis. There was grace and charm about this woman of eighty. Generally the older women in this part of the country have the manner that comes from a fine tradition; they have, too, the repose that comes with age, the acceptance, the trust. Eilis had these, and some other graces as well; a happy laugh, a gesture that seemed out of her girlhood, something wayward. My aunt was minding the bread, and the children were quiet. Eilis had quieted them. She remained watchful of the children, and now and then she would speak to them, or give them some task.

"Indeed, it was our house you were in, the day you stood out of the rain," said Eilis, "and it was my daughter you saw. It is desolate now, my house, for it's too far away from people. My daughter married a man from the town, a dark man. I don't understand him at all, and how could I, for he's not like another. He takes no notice of the land and has no care for it. I don't think he understands it at all. He'd say, 'Here's a paper for the reading woman,' or, 'Make room for the learned woman,' by way of making a mock of me.

"I think I'm like little Margaret here, who does be longing for a house by the roadside, the way she could be watching the people pass. Often, in my own mind, I see the house I was born in. It was white and high, in the friendly county of Fermanagh. There were trees around the house, and inside there was room after room. I had a room for myself in that house. Hadn't I the courage to leave the place where I was a girl, and to come here with a strange man, marrying away, and so far from my own people?

"The people here are good, and over-good, and Michael Conroy, my husband, was the best of them all. A man that wouldn't let me break a sod of turf across my knee, he took such care of me. It's no wonder I got fond of him, though for a long time my girl's heart was back in Fermanagh. Troubles grew up there. It's a long time ago now, and I don't think you ever heard about the happenings there. An election brought the troubles on. A man from the people went up against the landlord, and the gentry tried to frighten the people about voting for him. My father was asked to vote for the landlord, but he wouldn't go with that party at all. They broke him of his lands, and they put him out of his house, and they destroyed his trade with that. For my father had rich lands, and they were the greatest loss maybe, but I can't help thinking of the house that was so white and so fine. There were trees around it, as I told you, and you would have to open seven gates before you came to the door. Twelve of my father's children could sit down at his table. Eighteen persons worked in his house, for my father was a weaver by trade, getting good money for their work and their yarn. My father's father, and seven fathers beyond that, had lived there, and eight women of our name had kept fire on that hearth. And, maybe, the thorn-bushes that the travelling-man told me about are growing out of that hearth now. God have mercy on the people whose hearts and hands were against that house!

"Michael Conroy was good to me, and he was good to my people. When my father was broken of his lands he had his trade still. Michael built him a house behind our own, so that my father could have a place to work in. My father lived there, at the back of us, and he began to get the custom of the neighbours around. But he was broken in his strength, and it wasn't months before he got bad in health. In a while it came to the priest's turn, and my father was anointed. I said to my man, 'If my father is to die, I would like him to die under our roof.' Michael stood up, the man who never denied me anything, and he went to the door. Something put it into my mind to go over to him again. 'It will bring a blessing to our children,' I said. He went out.

"In a while Michael was back. He carried my father across the fields. 'Sister,' said he (he always called me sister), 'wipe the sweat off my face.' My father was on his back, and I wiped the sweat off my man's face. We put my father to bed, and he died in the night. The week after that Michael Conroy, my husband, was buried.

"There was no child, and there was no blessing on the house. I ran away from the house for the comfort I could get from my mother. She was living with a son of hers in the County Cavan. Many's the time after that my head was on her lap. I could hear the people say: 'She's too young to be a widow; she'll have to marry again if it was only for the sake of the fields.' Then my uncle went to Michael's place, and he got the fields ready. He couldn't get hands enough to spread the manure. He came back and told my mother that I'd have to marry. I suppose the pain was wearing away. My uncle went to the priest, and between them they got a good man for me. In a year I was married again, and back in Michael's house."

Eilis spoke to the children, and then went on with her knitting in silence. "Well, since that everything I saw was good, except we'd be lonesome at times when someone would die. I wonder are the young so kind? I often think that the world has knocked the friendship out of the people.

"And now I'll tell you why I was so loth to leave the County of Fermanagh. I wasn't fond of Michael Conroy; indeed, I didn't think of him at all when he came to our place in the beginning. Besides, the boy wanted more of a fortune with me than my father was willing to give. The match was broken off three times for the difference of five pounds, and when he went away that time I thought I had seen the last of Michael Conroy. One Sunday morning I was coming from early Mass, and my comrade girls were with me. I saw the cars before our door, and the crowd of strangers, and I knew that the Longford people had come back. My mother was watching out for me. She drew me aside, and she brought me into the barn. 'Conroy agrees, and your father agrees,' she said, 'but Eilis, my heart, I know that it's Shaun Gorman you're fond of. I'll send for him,' she said, 'and in God's name let the two of you go away together. You could go to his people, and the Gormans will be strong enough to mind you.' 'Mother,' said I, 'let me do my father's bidding.'"

"Was your mother wrong?" I asked. It was so far back now I could ask her. "Were you in love with Shaun Gorman?"

"I was, and greatly in love with him," she said.

"Was he fond of you?" I asked.

"How are we to know the heart of a man?" she said. "Shaun Gorman would be up to see the first smoke rising out of our house. He knew every scallop in the thatch, he had watched to see me at the door so often."

"And why wouldn't you take your mother's counsel and go with him?"

"I told it to my mother and we standing there in the barn. 'Mother,' I said, 'I'll tell you everything, and then we'll go to the people who have come for me. Mother, Shaun Gorman and myself planned to run off together. Do you remember when Maurya, the servant girl, went over to Shaun's house, and I went for her, in the evening? When I went out of this house I brought all I cared for with me, and I was to go with Shaun Gorman that night. But when I came to the ditch between his fields and our own, my knees failed, and I couldn't pass. I made the sign of the Cross, and I tried again, and again my knees were loosened. Then I said a prayer to the Virgin Mary, and after I said it every limb of me trembled. I sat down, and I could hear the moving of the horse that was to carry us to Shaun's people. The horse was before the door of his house. There was only a ditch between Gorman and myself, but the will of God was against it all. I rose up and came away. Maurya came back by herself, and when she came into the house she said to me, "Shaun Gorman has done with you, Eilis MacGovern, for this night you betrayed him." Shaun doesn't believe that now,' I said to my mother. After a while I put myself in his way, and I told him how it was with me. All he said was, 'It's no matter to me now; it's all over now.'

"I didn't think loath of leaving the sweet County of Fermanagh, where every face had something to say of Shaun Gorman. I heard the voices making a bargain. Then I heard Michael Conroy's, and I liked the kindness in that voice. I took my mother's hand, and the two of us went into the house."

# Padraic Colum

## *The Death of the Rich Man*

It was a road as shelterless and as bare as any road in Munster. On one side there was a far-reaching bog, on the other side little fields, cold with tracts of water. You faced the Comeragh hills, bleak and treeless, with little streams across them like threads of steel. There was a solitary figure on the road, a woman with bare feet and ragged clothes. She was bent and used a stick; but she carried herself swiftly, and had something of a challenge in her face. Her toothless mouth was tightly closed, her chin protruded, wisps of hair fell about her distrustful eyes. She was an isolated individual, and it would be hard to communicate the sensations and facts that made up her life.

Irish speakers would call the woman a "shuler." The word is literally the same as "tramp," but it carries no anti-social suggestion. None of the lonely cabins about would refuse her hospitality; she would get shelter for the night in any one of them—the sack of chaff beside the smouldering fire, the share in the household bit. But though she slept by their fires and ate their potatoes and salt, this woman was apart from them, and apart from all those who lived in houses, who tilled their fields, and reared up sons and daughters; she had been moulded by unkind forces—the silence of the roads, the bitterness of the winds, the long hours of hunger. She moved swiftly along the shelterless roads, muttering to herself, for the appetite was complaining within her. There was on her way a certain village, but before going through it she would give herself a while of contentment. She took a short pipe out of her pocket and sought the sheltered side of a bush. Then she drew her feet under her clothes and sucked in the satisfaction of tobacco.

You may be sure the shuler saw through the village, though her gaze was across the road. Midway on the village street there was a great house; it was two stories above the cottages, and a story higher than the shops. It was set high above its neighbours, but to many its height represented effort, ability, discipline. It was the house of Michael Gilsenin, farmer, shopkeeper, local councillor. "Gilsenin, the Gombeen man," the shuler muttered, and she spat out. Now the phrase "Gombeen man" would signify a grasping peasant dealer, who squeezed riches out of the poverty of his class, and few people spoke of Michael Gilsenin as a Gombeen man; but his townsmen and the peasants around would tell you that Michael Gilsenin had the open hand for the poor, and that he never denied them the bag of meal, nor the sack of seed-potatoes; no, nor the few pounds that would bring a boy or girl the prosperity of America. To the woman on the ditch Michael Gilsenin was the very embodiment of worldly prosperity. It was said, and the shuler exclaimed on Heaven at the thought, that Michael's two daughters would receive dowries of a thousand pounds each. Michael had furnished the new chapel at a cost of five hundred pounds; he had bought recently a great stock of horses and cattle; he had built sheds and stables behind his shop. And Michael Gilsenin had created all his good fortune by his own effort. The shuler wondered what bad luck eternal justice would send on his household to balance his prosperity. And in her backward-reaching mind, the shuler could rake out only one thing to Michael's discredit. This was his treatment of Thady, his elder brother. It was Thady who had owned the cabin and the farm on which the Gilsenins had begun their lives. Michael had reduced his grasping and slow-witted brother to subordination, and he had used his brother's inheritance to forward himself. In forwarding himself Michael had forwarded the family, Thady included, and now, instead of life in a cabin, Thady had a place in a great house. Michael was old now, the shuler mused, he was nearly as old as herself. It was well for those who would come after him. His daughters had dowries that made them the talk of the county, and his son would succeed to stock, farms, and shop. The shuler stretched out her neck and looked down the road and on to the village street. She saw the tall grey building, the house of stone with the slated roof and the many windows. And she saw a man hobbling out of the village. He had two sticks under him, for he was bent with the pains. The man was Thady Gilsenin, Michael's brother.

Thady Gilsenin was grudging and hard-fisted to the beggars, but he always stayed to have speech with them. His affinities were with these people of the roads. By his hardness and meanness, by his isolation and his ailments, he was kin to the shuler and her like. She quenched the pipe, hid it under her clothes, and waited for Thady Gilsenin.

\* \* \* \* \*

He stood before her, a grey figure leaning on two sticks. His hands were swollen with the pains, their joints were raised and shining.

"Well, ma'am," said Thady, "you're round this way again, I see."

"My coming won't be any loss to you, Thady Gilsenin," the shuler returned.

Thady turned round and looked back at the big house.

"And how is the decent man, your brother?" asked the shuler, "and how are his daughters, the fine growing girls?"

"His fine daughters are well enough," said Thady, turning round.

"There will be a great marriage here some day," said the shuler, "I'm living on the thought of that marriage."

"It's not marriage that's on our minds," Thady said, in a resigned way.

The shuler was quick to detect something in his tone.

"Is it death?" she asked.

"Ay, ma'am, death," said Thady. "Death comes to us all."

"And is it Michael that is likely to die?"

"Michael himself, said Thady.

This to the tramp was as news of revolution to men of desperate fortune. The death of Michael Gilsenin would be a revolution with spoils and without danger. She was thrilled with expectancy, and she said aloud: "O God, receive the prayers of the poor, and be merciful to Michael Gilsenin this day and this night! May angels watch over him! May he receive a portion of the bed of heaven! May he reign in splendour through eternity! Amen, amen, amen!" And crying out this she rose to her feet. "I'm going to his house," she said. "I'll go down on my two knees and I'll pray for the soul of Michael Gilsenin, the man who was good to the poor." She went towards the village, striking her breast and muttering cries. Thady stood for a moment, looking after her; then he began to hobble forward on his two sticks. They were like a pair of old crows, hopping down the village, towards the house of Michael Gilsenin.

\* \* \* \* \*

She could never have imagined such comforts and conveniences as she saw now in the chamber of the dying man. There was the bed, large enough to hold three people, with its stiff hanging and its stiff counterpane, its fine sheets, its blankets and quilt, its heap of soft pillows. There was the carpet warm under her own feet, and then the curtains to the window that shut out the noise and the glare. A small table with fruit and wine was by the bed, and a red lamp burnt perpetually before the image of the Sacred Heart, and so the wasting body and the awakening soul had their comfort and their solace. Michael's two daughters were in the room. They stood there broken and listless; they had just come out of the convent and this was their novitiate in grief. The shuler noted how rich was the stuff in their black dresses, and noted, too, their white hands, and the clever shape of their dresses. As for the dying man, she gave no heed to him after the first encounter. He was near his hour, and she had looked too often upon the coming of death.

They gave her a bed in the loft, and she lay that night above the stable that was back of the great house. She had warmed herself by the kitchen fire, and had taken her fill of tea, and now she smoked and mused, well satisfied with herself. "This night I'm better off than the man in the wide bed," she said to herself. "I'm better off than you this night, Michael Gilsenin, for all your lands and shops and well-dressed daughters. I'm better off than you this night, Michael Gilsenin, for all your stock and riches. Faith, I can hear your cattle stir in the sheds, and in a while you won't even hear the rain on the grass. You have children to come after you, Michael Gilsenin, but that's not much, after all, for they'll forget you when they've come from the burial. Ay, they will in troth. I've forgotten the man that lay beside me, and the child that I carried in my arms." She pulled a sack over her feet and knees and up to the waist, and sleep came to her on the straw. But she was awake and felt the tremor through the house, when Death came and took his dues. From then onward her sleep was broken, for people had come and horses were being brought out of the stable. Once old Thady came out, and the shuler heard him mutter about the loss in hay and oats.

When she came down to the yard she saw a well-dressed young man tending his horse. One of Michael's daughters came and stood with the young man, and the two walked earnestly together. The shuler knelt down on a flag and began sobbing and clapping her hands. She was working up to a paroxysm, but gradually, for she wanted to attract the attention of the pair without distressing them overmuch. The girl went indoors and the young man followed her. The shuler saw two empty bottles; they were worth a penny. She hid them under her dress and went into the house. She made her way to the front door, passing by many. People of importance were coming, and in such an assembly something surely would be gained. She stood by the street door and watched the great people come—priests, doctors, lawyers, shopkeepers, and councillors. She stood there like an old carrion bird. Her eyes were keen with greed, and her outstretched hand was shaking. She heard old Thady saying, "Now, thank God, we can be clear for the day of the fair. I was thinking that he would still be with us on the fair day, and we would have to close the shop, and that would be a great loss to us. Now we can have everything cleared off in time. God be good to Michael's soul."

# Padraic Colum

## *The Slopes of Tara*

A young crow, perched on a branch outside, barked insistently into a human habitation. Perhaps the internal conditions aroused the young crow's indignation. There were damp places on the floor where the rain came through the thatch; in one corner there was a bed with a ragged, miscellaneous covering. The room was filled with smoke, and the occupant was eating his breakfast off the top of a chest. He was seated on a box.

After a while the articulation of the crow took his interest, and he turned on the bird an eye that was remarkably like its own—a small, blue, penetrating eye. He finished his breakfast, put a cap on, and for a while surveyed the world from his doorway.

Before him were the lifeless grazing tracts of the County Meath. Formerly there had been a garden before the house that he was now the sole occupant of, and a cherry tree still growing showed that the place had once its grace and its cultivation. But the garden was gone back to the wild, and the house was an unsightly ruin. The man at the door was short of figure, and ragged of garb. His gaze was restless, and his quick, ever-moving glances reminded one of the looks of nature's smaller creatures, the rabbits and the squirrels. The man's mind also had gone back from discipline. He looked rather ruffianly, but there was humour in his face, quick judgment, and some practical wisdom. His cheek-bones were high, and his forehead projected, making a type that, as some people think, shows a strong imagination, joined to an active and sanguine temperament.

The tumble-down house was solitary. Once the district was inhabited, but the place had been cleared of men and women, and had been given over to cattle. The man at the door was a survival from a vanished population. He was known by the name of Shaun, and he had employment on one of the grazing-tracts. Now, closing his door, he went off on his day's vocation.

Near his path a shoot of briar raised itself in the air. It was fresh, slender, and green. Shaun regarded it, and spoke out of his constant meditation. "The young girl is like the shoot of briar," he said, "for a while she's free and lightsome, and in another while she's without freshness and near enough to the ground." He picked up his stock and rambled away.

He worked to strengthen a fence, and then he brought a crowd of young cattle into a far pasture. Steadily they went through the grass while the pageant of sun, cloud, and shadow crossed the fields. He lay on the ground and gave his mind to a familiar romance.

Far away there was a rocky rise with some structure upon it. The legend of the place was part of Shaun's dream. The walls there were raised for the pleasure of a woman. A man had sworn that his bride would have a turret out of which she could watch the ships on the seas of Ireland. The ravens built in the tower now, he knew, but he did not moralise on this.

His delight was in the splendour and success of that man who had brought the woman there. No woman who kissed his mouth could ever take the kiss of another man—no other kiss but Farnie's kiss could she take. And Farnie was born to no estate although he had the spirit and the manner of a noble. He could win any woman, for he had "a diplume for coortin'." First there came to him a woman who had two score town-lands. Then Farnie had blood-horses under him, and hounds to follow, and his own lands to ride across. The wife who had brought him these riches died, but Farnie was not left long to himself. A woman took his fancy and she had Cromwell's spoils for her dowry. Her brother would keep Farnie away, but one night he brought his horse under her window, and she came down to him, and they rode away together. He got five-score town-lands with that woman. Now Farnie had seven-score town-lands, and all that he willed he could do, and all that he longed for he could possess. And then when the second woman died, Farnie's fancy was taken by another. She was young, a girl just, and she had no riches, but she had a beauty like the beauty that went out of Ireland when the foreigners came in. And it was to pleasure her that Farnie built the turret that Shaun looked towards now. He mixed the mortar with the bullock's blood and new milk, so that the walls might stand for a thousand years. But the woman never climbed the stair within, and the couple never slept inside the walls.

And now the cattle grazed upon the slopes of Tara. Furze bushes grew upon the mounds that marked the Banqueting Hall of the Kings, putting above the green their heaps of golden blossoms. There once the chiefs of the Fianna and the nobles of the Royal House feasted to the espousal of Grania, the king's daughter, and Fionn, the great captain. Grania drugged the ale, and while the elders slept she offered herself for wife to each of the young men who were most spoken of—to Oscar, to Coalite, and at last, to the most expert and the most beautiful of them all—to Dermott O'Duibhne. Then away the pair went together, and for long the wild and waste places of Ireland hid them from the wrath of Fionn.

Over the fields grew the sadness of vanishing light. Shaun stole away from the farmhouse where he had been given a meal. He took the road to the town, for he liked to draw away from the silence and the shadow, and his soul was lonely for some coloured and wonderful experience. Near the town he encountered part of a returning hunt. He saw a few silent people on horseback, and then he was surrounded by a silent-footed pack. He shrank from the dogs, and the silent, stealthy forms slipping through the evening seemed like a terror that had missed him.

Outside the town there were men in groups, and Shaun went up and stood amongst them. Before, when he was in this town, he caught sight of a beauty, and he thought that the men here might have some tidings of her. They were unenlightened. They played cards and they made jokes about one another, and they talked to him mockingly. He had been talking to this one and that one, and to the whole company of them. But it suddenly came over him that he must preserve the secret that he had—the secret of the beauty that he had seen. He watched the game they played and was silent, and when the game was finished he went from the men and into the chapel.

There were few people in the chapel, and the candles on the altar were not yet lighted. Shaun remained near the door, and kept his eyes on the organ loft. The Sunday before he had heard a voice singing up there, and he had seen a face and figure between the lighted candles. There was a young girl there; her hair was brighter and softer than the candles' flame.

The rosary began and went on to the litany, but there was no music from the organ. The candles that had been lighted on the altar were quenched now, and the people began to leave, their devotions over. The tolling of the bell outside made Shaun restless. He went out and into the street. Then he shifted through the town, shy and curious. He watched a soldier go into a house where there was a dance, and then he waited to speak with a ballad-singer, who had "The Lament of Hugh Reynolds."—

> By the loving of a maid,
> One Catherine MacCabe,
> My life it is betrayed; she's a dear maid to me.
>
> And now my glass is run,
> And my hour it is come,
> And I must die for love and the height of loyalty
> I thought it was no harm
> To embrace her in my arms,
> And to take her from her parents; she's a dear maid to me.

He was being drawn to a place of friendliness, but for a long time the wild shyness of his nature kept him abroad. At last he found himself before the place that he was drawn to—a trim house at the outskirts of the town. Within, someone was playing on the violin. Shaun waited, and when the music stopped he knocked at the door. The door was opened readily, as though a visitor had been expected, and Nora Kavanagh, the friendly personage to whom Shaun was drawn, stood there. Nora said, "Shaun, come in." She was not one of Shaun's admirations, but her friendly spirit made him devoted to her. He said, "Miss Nora, I'm ashamed to go into your nice house." He said this although he wanted to meet with some friendliness that night. "You must come in, Shaun, I'm expecting someone else, but there's no one with me yet." She brought him within and made him sit down. Nora was neat and precise, rather like one of the friendly, witty nuns one often meets in Irish convents; she was friendly to the odd characters that were about the place; their sayings and doings made a comedy that was always diverting to her.

"I found a plant with a grand flower to it," said Shaun, "and I'd have brought it to you only I thought you'd like to see it growing." His gaze roved about the room. He saw the violin that Nora had left down, and he brought his eyes to her face. "I'll bring it to you, root and all," he said, "and maybe you'll play a tune for me." She took up the violin and began to play.

The music brought back to him the loneliness of the empty fields. There was a green rath with trees growing upon it. Somebody was playing for a dance. But nobody could dance to that tune. It would be such a dance as he had never seen—the music was calling people out of the rath. He saw one who came out. Her face was pale like a star in a lake, and her beautiful hair swept about her. Others were coming out of the darkness; they were mounted on fine horses . . .

The tune ended suddenly; a quick knock had come to the door, and Nora went to open it. When she came in again she had another with her. It was the girl of his vision, and Shaun recovered his sense of actuality only when she turned away from him. Maybe Farnie's last love was like her, a slender girl with all her life in her face, and different from the full-blown beauties that Farnie had gathered in his day.

She leaned forward in the chair Nora had given her, and she regarded the dreamer with friendly interest. He became shy and uneasy, because he saw himself as an unkempt creature. He rose up and sidled to the door. He refused to eat; Nora, knowing that she might not press him, let him go. "I saw you before, miss," he said to the girl as he was going out. "I saw you before, but you were far away." Then he went, and when she came back to the room with Nora, the girl felt somehow lonely after the strange little creature who had gone out.

As for Shaun, he went along the darkened road in a state of mind that was half satisfaction, half bewilderment. Woman had ceased to be an abstract creature, the ornament of the story, the spoil of the strong hand. Between himself and the beautiful growing girl he felt the hundred ties of race. He was the servitor who drove the swine into the woods, and she was the daughter of a prince, but still they were related, and her beauty was part of his dream and his glory.

The music that Nora had played seemed to come to him again as he crossed the fields. He heard a voice that called "Shaun, Shaun!" He knew that he was under an enchantment, for the fields that he knew so well now had no mark, no boundary. A sudden wind rustled in the grass. Shaun crouched down, and a company of riders drew towards him. The heads of the riders were bare, but across their brows there were thin bands of gold. The one who rode in front had on him a green mantle of a King. A rider turned his face to Shaun and cried out in a clear voice: "He has seen her, the man in the grass has seen her." But the clear voice that Shaun heard did not arouse the one who wore the green mantle. With bowed head the King rode on.

Then Shaun took up a handful of grass and threw it across his shoulder. He saw the landmarks, and the way through the night to his cabin. He made his way across the silent fields.

# Padraic Colum

## *Three Men*

He presented cards on which, under his name, was the inscription, "Secretary and Founder of the Eblana Literary Society." Professionally he was a photographer: in outdoor seasons he went to castles that were visited by sightseers, demesnes that were open to the public, and sylvan places that people made trips to, and photographed groups and couples; in the winter he went to schools and photographed pupils in their classes—especially in First Communion and Confirmation classes; incidentally he had a photographing business in the town, but citizens who called at his premises usually found him taking tea after having come back from an expedition, or taking tea preparatory to going on one. He was a stocky man with a bush of hair and beard and eyes that glinted and glanced behind spectacles.

He called on Anthony Tisdil. Taking the card offered him, Anthony Tisdil read:

> HOWARD TODD-GRUBB
> SECRETARY AND FOUNDER OF
> THE EBLANA LITERARY SOCIETY

Anthony Tisdil rubbed his forehead. These two fellow townsmen who had never before met socially talked about generalities.

Anthony Tisdil was discovered in the sitting-room of the house in which he lodged. Howard Todd-Grubb's glinting eyes took in the features of the sitting-room. On the walls were four coloured photographs representing idyllic scenes. On a table was a book with impressive covers—*Gladstone and His Contempo-*

*raries* was its title: the physiognomies of the statesmen who were contemporaries were often looked at by visitors, especially that of Daniel O'Connell with his hand within his vest. On the sideboard within a glass case was an owl: he had ruffled feathers and glazed eyes—a bird of night indeed. In the grate were pleated coloured papers. The chairs were plush-covered. There was also a horsehair sofa: on the edge of this Anthony Tisdil had been sitting.

The reason for his being in the sittingroom and the reason for his being called upon by Howard Todd-Grubb were connected. Anthony Tisdil had been in a railway collision the day before. He had come out of it unscathed. But his superiors in the office had given him a few days' leave of absence, and his landlady, out of sympathy with one who had undergone such an ordeal, and in recognition of the importance he had attained through it, had invited him (for the second time in his residence of twenty years) to occupy the sitting-room. His name had appeared in the account of the collision that was given in this morning's papers, and the Secretary and Founder of the Eblana Literary Society was calling upon him as upon an important, an exceptional man. Anthony Tisdil was about fifty: he was a little man with hair plastered across a bald streak on the crown of his head, with a scrubby moustache, a round face, and slightly protuberant eyes. He wore a brown coat which curved around his hips, black trousers, and very good elastic boots.

"Mr. Todd-Grubb," he said.

"The Eblana Literary Society," said Howard Todd-Grubb.

Anthony Tisdil rubbed his hand across his forehead. He had an inclination towards doing this when he was disturbed or bewildered.

"I have called to ask you to be one of our audience tonight," said the Secretary and Founder of the Eblana Literary Society. "You are now a man of mark in our town. I congratulate you on your miraculous escape."

Anthony Tisdil coughed and prepared to tell him about this escape, but found he had not the complete attention of his visitor. "Our distinguished—our very distinguished—fellow-townsman, Loftus Mongan, is going to let us have the privilege of hearing an address from him to-night," he said. His hands were on the back of a chair; he leaned across and addressed Anthony Tisdil, who had again seated himself on the edge of the sofa. "I have no hesitation in saying it will be epoch-making. It will embody his reflections on the future of our country—his lifetime's reflections, I may say. He will deliver it himself—Loftus Mongan in person, Mr. Tisdil. Naturally I think this is a great event for the Society of which I am Secretary and Founder. You have never been to one of our meetings?"

Anthony Tisdil admitted that he had not.

"Then come, Mr. Tisdil," said Howard Todd-Grubb warmly. "This is a special invitation, and for a special occasion."

Anthony Tisdil stooped down to pick something off the floor. The veins on his forehead were noticeable. He murmured something that seemed to be in the nature of an assent. Howard Todd-Grubb took his hand, shook it heartily, and then let himself out of the room.

At the same hour Loftus Mongan, M. A., had entered the shop of H. MacCabe, Provision Merchant. A heavy walking stick was held firmly in his hand, a shabby overcoat was on his short, broad figure, and he wore a silk hat with a well-worn brim. He carried exercise-books in his hand and held a bag which bulged with some learned material. Holding stick and bag and books he spoke to H. MacCabe in a distinct voice and with clear enunciation, the voice of an educated man who was well used to delivering himself. Loftus Mongan said:

"This is the first afternoon I have been out of my rooms, and I rejoice in this salubrious weather. My studies kept me confined, but I have hope that I shall be able to go forth like a lion refreshed—or, rather I should say, like a giant refreshed—we must keep to the exact quotation, Mr. MacCabe. When our respected young townsman who is now the Treasurer of the State of Maryland used to come to me for lessons, I always impressed upon him the necessity for exactness of statement. I had a letter from him the other day, and he assured me that it was that exactness more than anything else that enabled him to rise to his present exalted position. I must say that with a position such as he has attained to in the New World he is a credit to all of us. A namesake of yours, too, Mr. MacCabe. Well, and did you read today's journals yet? My opinion is that the government means to break with us, Mr. MacCabe."

Thereupon Loftus Mongan delivered himself on a political topic. He was listened to respectfully, for he was a learned man and a Protestant Nationalist. Then he sank his resonant voice to a low but clear whisper:

"What is the smallest quantity of lard you sell?"

"A pennyworth."

"I shall trouble you for a pennyworth then. I have fish for dinner to-day, and my housekeeper will only cook them with lard." H. MacCabe put some lard upon a scale.

He had tubs of lard, slabs of butter, lumps and humps and hunks of cheese, barrels of pigs' heads, hams, gams, crubeens, flitches of bacon, sausages, white puddings, black puddings, pork-steaks, kidneys, tumbled rashers, and fatty ends of flitches of bacon. Although he had written over his shop "direct wine and spirit importer," and "licensed for consumption on the premises," H. MacCabe remained the Provision Merchant. He was never more himself than when he was slashing bacon with a huge and greasy blade. His wrapper was always greasy and always bore traces of his breakfast egg. His cheeks had the whiteness of sides of bacon, and his hands looked like meats that had not been thoroughly cured. He was a big, active, red-headed man, and one might wonder what enthusiasm or devotion kept him behind a counter in a space as wide as a railway carriage. Up and down this corridor he moved, wrapping up quarter pounds of butter and half pounds of rashers, and slicing bacon with his remarkable knife. He hummed as he made his adroit cuts.

"These ends of bacon now—I remember I purchased some before, and my housekeeper found them of use. Would you put up—well, less than half a pound—for me?"

The Merchant put up three rashers and the pennyworth of lard for Loftus Mongan, M.A. One rasher was fat, one extremely lean, and the other looked as if it had been in pickle.

"Is that all, Mr. Mongan?"

"I have been told to make a trial of one of your penny squares of bread. Please give it to me somewhat stale. And how much does it all come to?"

"Four pence."

"Four pence! Dear me, what a lot can be got for money nowadays! You provision-dealers can be making very little."

"Nothing at all, Mr. Mongan—nothing at all, sir."

"What would you say to a measure of protection for this country?"

"I favour it because I understand that the Danes intend to give us no quarter." H. MacCabe spoke of the Danes, not as actual commercial competitors, but as vague and powerful oppressors. For him the nobles of Denmark still dowered their daughters with lands in Ireland.

Loftus Mongan put the rashers, the lard, and the bread into the bag he carried. It had been empty. Then with his stick placed under his arm, the bag and the exercise-books in his hand, he faced the provision dealer, the eyes under his shaggy brows confident again.

"More than one letter on the subject of free trade and protection has appeared in the public press over the signature of Loftus Mongan, M.A." he said.

"I know that, Mr. Mongan," said the Merchant.

"It is one of the subjects in which I take a great interest."

"I wish they were all as knowledgeable as yourself, Mr. Mongan."

"I have hardly any hopes of knowledge being cultivated in this part of the country—no hopes at all, I may say, Mr. MacCabe." He sank his voice to a whisper again. "How much do you think I am charging for lessons—English composition, arithmetic, Latin—two evenings a week?"

The Merchant leaned forward with interest now that commercial relations were the topic. "Tell me, Mr. Mongan," he said.

"Two shillings and sixpence—a bare half-crown. And how many pupils do you suppose I'm getting at that?"

"I couldn't say."

"Well, it doesn't matter. But if I did not have other means, my income would be small. I may tell you, Mr. MacCabe, that I am willing to take pupils of all ages. The man whose education has been neglected will be as sympathetically trained by me as the youth who has just entered a seminary. And pupils of the humblest social grade will be received. In my rooms." He laid his stick across the counter and looked into the Merchant's face. "I should be obliged if you would mention it, Mr. MacCabe. Many think that I only give instruction to bank clerks and constabulary-men going up for promotion. But I should be glad to teach the rudiments to anyone—for the sake of our town, you know. Those whose education has been neglected and those of a lower social grade will be sympathetically instructed by me. Good-bye to you." He took up his stick and strode out of the shop. His walk was quick and he swung his stick as he went along.

He marched past where Anthony Tisdil, still in the

sitting-room, was perusing and re-perusing a page in a journal. He had propped it against the covers of *Gladstone and His Contemporaries*, and, seated under the ruffled owl, was taking in sentences, was pondering on them. A man could always make some assertion of his will—that was the matter of the argument that so weighed with him. He read about clerks in an office. Their actions became part of routine, and it soon happened that they came to have as little power of assertion as horses have. But, generally speaking, every day, and indeed every portion of the day, a man had a chance of asserting his will. At this moment his landlady's sister brought tea in. He drank two cups, eating a slice of toast and a slice of bread and butter. Then he perceived that his action was part of routine and had nothing to do with his will. Did he or did he not want tea at the moment? He could not tell. He always drank tea at this hour on a Saturday when he was at home, taking two cups with a slice of toast and a slice of bread and butter. But now he began to be afraid that his action was part of routine. However, he finished his tea.

Re-perusing the page, it was borne in on him that the first effort towards its restoration was in the assertion of the will: one might begin upon small affairs—compel oneself to write a postcard, or restrain oneself from reading a newspaper in the train. From that one should go on to deal with larger issues. . . . But what stuck in Anthony Tisdil's mind and gave him matter to ponder on was the comparison between a man and a horse. A man could assert his will, a horse could not. In the beginning, as a young colt, the horse did assert his will, but after a while he was broken of the habit, and his action became what was termed automatic. It soon became impossible for a horse to assert his will at all.

He used to be treated with more respect by the fellows and the juniors in the office. Was it because everything he did was now part of routine that he was being treated with a lessened consideration? Other fellows weren't treated as he was being treated, after all. The other day, for instance. He had been working with his head bent, and had felt a pressure on his back. A junior, hardly a year in the place, a North of Ireland fellow named McConigal, had laid a paper on his back and was making some notes on it. He was quite cool about his action; he just said he hadn't seen any place on the desk, and he wanted to enter a name for a football team. But McConigal wouldn't be so cheeky with any of the other fellows—he knew that now. Well, when he went back to the office he would assert his will on McConigal and the likes of him.

That morning Anthony Tisdil had wakened up at the regular hour. Then he realized that he did not have to go to the office, and he was pleased to think that he did not have to make a scramble to get the train and that the day was his own. He read an account of the collision in the papers and he saw his own name there—he was referred to as "Mr. Anthony Tisdil." When he went down to the railway-station people looked at him with curiosity and interest. This unusual day had prepared him to be interested in the question that the journal had given a page to. Usually Anthony Tisdil paid no attention at all to what he happened to read. But not having his habitual work before him, and seated in the unfamiliar surrounding of Mrs. Brophy's sitting-room, what was said in the article became real to him, like the voice of Burtt, his immediate superior.

His landlady's sister came into the room. She wanted to know would Mr. Tisdil go down and play a game of draughts with Mr. Brophy.

Anthony Tisdil rose to go. Then he realized that playing that game of draughts would be automatic action; he had been playing draughts with George Brophy every evening for some months. "Tell Mr. Brophy I'm not playing to-night," he said. "But he has the board all ready, Mr. Tisdil." Anthony hesitated. Then he said, "No, I can't go down. I've—I've a place that I have to go to to-night." It was then, after his landlady's sister had left the room, that he decided to go to the meeting of the Eblana Literary Society. He had no desire to hear Loftus Mongan and no interest in the future of the country or anything of the kind. But he was going to do something that would break the routine of his evenings. He took up *Gladstone and His Contemporaries*, deciding that he would read through the pages until the time came for him to go to the meeting of the Eblana Literary Society.

The click of billiard-balls could be heard from the more frequented room below when the door of the Eblana Literary Society's premises was left open. It was open for a while after Anthony Tisdil had come in. There were three other arrivals: two young men who were at a table on which was a lighted lamp, and a man who was seated at the far end of the room, on the end of a bench. The Secretary and Founder of the Eblana

Literary Society had not yet appeared.

Anthony Tisdil recognized the two young men: they were Daniel Meeney and Ignatius Greally. They were playing a game of cards. Daniel Meeney played as if he thought it was the grandest thing in the world to be able to oblige Ignatius Greally with that particular card. He rubbed his hands, not as Anthony Tisdil rubbed them, but by way of subdued applause. His hair was brushed back from his forehead; his features were distinct and good. Such features, lighted up with such decorous enthusiasm, were to be seen in the local church on the tinted statue of Saint Michael. He finished the game and stood up from the table.

"That was a nice game, Mr. Greally," he said (there was just a suspicion he said "dat").

The figure seated on the end of a bench at the back of the room was that of a blind man. "Will Mr. Loftus Mongan be here?" he asked, when Anthony seated himself in the middle of the bench above his.

Anthony Tisdil said that he understood that Loftus Mongan would very shortly arrive.

"He's a grand man, Mr. Loftus Mongan," said the blind man. "He made a speech last year and it was the best I ever listened to. I skipped in here because Mr. Mongan himself told me that he was going to make another speech to-night. He's a grand man, and very simple with the poor people, I must say." The blind man wore an ancient ulster with huge capes to it and a wide-brimmed hat. He could be very bitter to those who treated him as a beggar, but, as a matter of fact, he received charitable contributions from the well-to-do in the town. He was recommended to them on account of piety. But the same blind man never made any attempts to conceal his ill-temper and his ill-will. Now he knocked on the floor with his stick. "I'm a long time here," he said.

It was then that Howard Todd-Grubb came amongst them. Anxious to be rid of the cares of office for the evening so that he might be free to devote all of his attention to Loftus Mongan's address, he appointed Daniel Meeney secretary pro tem. He welcomed Anthony Tisdil to the Eblana Literary Society, and introduced the two young men to him. Then he and the secretary pro tem. arranged the table for the speaker's convenience. "The proceedings will begin soon," the secretary pro tem. announced.

"I'm a long time here," said the blind man.

The secretary pro tem. assured him that he would not have long now to wait.

"Of course, I'm only a member of the public," said the blind man assertively, "but I came here to hear Mr. Loftus Mongan—why not, to be sure?"

Howard Todd-Grubb now lighted candles: he placed one on the table at the other side of the lamp, and two on the mantelpiece over the big empty grate. The blind man, feeling that illumination, perhaps, said "I suppose this is Mr. Loftus Mongan now."

But it was Lowry Muldoon who entered. His stiff black hair was upright, and his black eyes were jumping in his head at the sensation he was about to create.

"Did you see my miracle?" he cried. "God! Did any of you see my miracle?"

"What's the miracle, Lowry?" asked Ignatius Greally.

Lowry Muldoon stuck his hands in the pockets of an old Norfolk jacket that he wore, and swaggered across the room. "Give me a cigarette, somebody," he said. "The best miracle that ever was known in Ireland. The stigmata, you know. In all Irish papers. In the French papers, too, I believe. I invented it."

He puffed at the cigarette he had lighted at a candle, and swaggered around the room in high delight with himself. Invented the local miracle! Yes, Lowry Muldoon had invented it. There was no Maggie Halloran, although everyone in the district was convinced that the child was a neighbour of theirs. Wishing to have the local journal quoted in the Dublin dailies Muldoon had written an account of an imaginary miracle with startling headlines above it. The announcement that he now made was a shock to all in the room of the Eblana Literary Society.

The blind man muttered his disapprobation.

"You'll get sacked off your paper for this," said Ignatius Greally.

"Indeed, I won't. I'm running the paper myself. Hempson has been drinking since Christmas."

"Will you read anything to us to-night, Mr. Muldoon?" asked the secretary pro tem.

Howard Todd-Grubb, who was standing at the door and looking down the stairway, intervened. "We have reserved the evening for a discussion of the address that Loftus Mongan is going to deliver," he declared.

But Lowry Muldoon had already taken a paper out of the

inside pocket of his coat. "I have something with me. I don't know if it will do. Listen to this . . . "

"The proceedings will not begin until Loftus Mongan . . . "

But Lowry Muldoon had taken a place at the table, holding the pages of his manuscript in his hand. A grey-haired young man with a remarkably smooth face came in just then. He stood near the door. Folding his arms, he took the attitude of a listener. This attitude imposed on the others, all except the blind man, the mood of an audience. Lowry Muldoon began:

"Every smoker has had experience of the last match. Not uncommonly it is something like the following:—a windy road, a traveller remote from towns, a match-box almost empty, and a keen desire for tobacco. The traveller attempts his pipe, and lights match after match, and each in turn is blown out before he can use it. Soon comes the last match of all. This he nurses so tenderly that the wax or wood ignites thoroughly, and he lights his pipe. Overjoyed at his good fortune, he holds the flame to the fury of the wind, and still it burns steadily. He takes the pipe from his mouth and apostrophises the match. 'You little beast,' he says, 'you'll burn now, will you, when I don't want you any longer? Then burn you shall, right to the end!' Thus holding it at arm's length he watches it burn. It shortens and shortens. At length he drops it upon the ground where it flickers for a moment or two, and expires. Then, he puts his pipe into his mouth again, and lo! it is out."

"Is there much more of it?" asked the secretary pro tem., Howard Todd-Grubb having again gone out to watch for the approach of Loftus Mongan.

"Eight pages," said Lowry Muldoon.

"It's all right, I think. You can read it when the discussion is over," said the obliging secretary pro tem.

"No arrangement can be made until we have Mr. Loftus Mongan amongst us," said Howard Todd-Grubb. "I think he is approaching." He went to the door.

But the person whom he ushered in a moment later was not Loftus Mongan. She was a spinster, middle-aged and energetic-looking, who had a piece of worn fur around her neck and a bright ribbon in her hat, and a long black rigid-seeming coat. She was Miss Sears, who kept the lodging-house in which Loftus Mongan stayed; she was the person he had in mind when he spoke of "my housekeeper." Miss Sears had come to inform the Society that Mr. Loftus Mongan could not be with them that night.

"Do I hear that he is not coming after all?" the blind man asked Anthony Tisdil.

Anthony Tisdil said that he understood that Mr. Loftus Mongan was unable to come.

"Dear, dear, dear! What brought me out at all to-night?" said the blind man.

Anthony Tisdil, noticing that Miss Sears had presented Howard Todd-Grubb with a roll of manuscript, told him that the society was going to have the paper read to them in any case.

"Oh, murther, it's himself we want to hear," said the blind man bitterly.

Loftus Mongan was ill and confined to bed. Speaking from a seat which she had taken, Miss Sears informed the Society that he had been taken ill with cramps in the stomach. He was in agony. She had wanted him to lie down, but nothing would do him but get the papers ready for the Literary Society's meeting. Up to the last minute he had intended to be present. But when she had heard him say that he had become dizzy, she had taken the papers out of his hands and had come along with them. Mr. Loftus Mongan had sent a message by her asking Mr. Todd-Grubb to get one of the gentlemen present to read his address. And, if they would permit her, she would remain while it was being read, and bring back a report of how it had been received.

The secretary pro tem. stated that a rule of the Society disallowed their having females present during their proceedings. Thereupon Howard Todd-Grubb proposed that the rule should be suspended, so that Miss Sears might remain during the reading of Loftus Mongan's paper. The proposal was agreed to, and Miss Sears, who had stood up during the short discussion upon the motion, seated herself on one of the back benches. Lowry Muldoon having gone out when the interest in his essay expired, there were present the secretary pro tem., Daniel Meeney, Ignatius Greally, Anthony Tisdil, the young grey-haired man with the smooth face, the blind man, Miss Sears, and, of course, Howard Todd-Grubb. The secretary and founder of the Eblana Literary Society stood with his elbow upon the mantelpiece, and in the light of the candles his glasses gleamed, heightening the expectancy that was in the room.

But at the moment when the conscientious secretary pro

tem. was picking open the tape that was around the roll of manuscript, another member entered the room. He was Charles Hempson, the editor of the local paper in which the first account of the imaginary miracle had been given. He was purple-nosed, and wore a soiled white waistcoat. He left the door open, and the knocking and clicking of billiard-balls was very audible as Daniel Meeney pronounced the title of Loftus Mongan's paper: "Citizenship in the Future State."

In less than ten minutes after this title had been pronounced, Anthony Tisdil, Ignatius Greally, and the blind man, after an initial, momentary eagerness, had fallen into a gloomy stupor. Miss Sears remained upright and impassive in attitude and manner. Charles Hempson, tilting his chair back as he sat in it, squeezed his head in his hand from time to time in a significant and ostentatious manner. But the grey-haired young man manifested complete approval of what was being read. And Howard Todd-Grubb, seated near the reader, nodded his head, his spectacle glinting in a remarkable manner.

Why Howard Todd-Grubb did not himself undertake the reading of the address on Citizenship in the Future State will remain a mystery. But it was evident that his unfamiliarity with Loftus Mongan's caligraphy made the secretary pro tem. read the manuscript haltingly. After a ten minutes' reading he began to show dismay at the number of pages that were still in his hand, and time and time again he gave the impression that, in his judgment, he was dealing with an undiminishable quantity. It was evident that not Idea, but Number, was his preoccupation. A time came when he had to be prompted by Howard Todd-Grubb, who took a place beside him and even read over the reader's shoulder. Then there were two voices delivering passages from the manuscript and occasionally giving divergent readings. As read by the secretary pro tem. with the assistance of the secretary and founder of the Eblana Literary Society, the address was undeniably long. Pythagoras, Berkeley, and Burke were the philosophers quoted in it.

At last Daniel Meeney laid the last page on the back-turned pages before him as Howard Todd-Grubb, wiping his spectacles, looked expectantly at the audience before him.

"I think we may say that the Eblana Literary Society thanks Mr. Loftus Mongan," he said, as Miss Sears came to take the manuscript off the table.

"In my opinion," said the young man with the grey hair,

"we have listened to a very remarkable—a very profound work."

"In what way remarkable?" Charles Hempson interjected.

"In its general conception, first of all," said the grey-haired young man.

"Excuse me," said Charles Hempson, "But you know nothing about conceptions, general or otherwise."

It was evident that Charles Hempson had more to say, but he waited. He now sat with the chair turned around, his arms leaning on the back of it. He held the attention of the society.

"I have told this young man in effect that he is no better than a fool," he said. "He is a fool because he speaks on a subject he knows nothing about."

"Mr. Meeney," said the young man, "I ask are Mr. Hempson's remarks in order?"

"In order? No, I think not. He. Hempson, I'll have to remind you that you are not in order."

"There was one passage that I seemed to get a glimmering of an idea out of," said Charles Hempson deliberately, "and that was a passage on the last two pages of that magnitudinous manuscript. May I ask the secretary to read us that passage once more?"

All present, even the fatigued secretary pro tem., were now stirred up and eager. Howard Todd-Grubb snatched up the manuscript which Miss Sears had not yet taken into her possession, and gave a clear and ringing delivery to the last pages of the manuscript. These passages were by way of peroration; they had little—in fact they had nothing to do with the general idea of the paper which, some pages before, had been rounded off and completed. Loftus Mongan had wanted to convey a sense of a coming dawn in the country: he had written those passages that very morning; it had happened that his sleep had been broken, and he had been actually present at the phenomenon described.

"Is it not the fable of the poets," Howard Todd-Grubb read, "that birds sing at a certain hour in a way that is different from their song at other times? That hour is long before light. You hear the voice of one bird and then the voices of the choir. You rise and draw back your curtains. The stars are apparent in the sky, and the wind of night is above the voices of the birds, the dog, unaware that his watch is near over, barks. And still goes up that murmurous song. One bird sings distinguishably. But the song that goes up is like the sound of the leaves of the forest, or the falling of raindrops, or the hum of bees. It is as if all the birds were in one nest and, with necks raised and dewy wings spread out, were singing, or rather, were murmuring a song. It is as if the birds consecrated to this light the beginnings out of which have come their several songs. The murmur goes on and on, the star is in the sky, the dog barks, the gas-lamps of the country-town gleam. It gets brighter. The wind has no longer the wail of the night. The dog is satisfied with the honesty of the day and ceases to bark. The geese waken up and cackle. The morning song of the birds now ceases. And so it is with us who are here. The wail of the wind is around us; the voices of dogs and geese are the only ones that are heeded. But we shall give forth a melody again. And amongst us there will be one clear voice that shall be heeded."

Howard Todd-Grubb read these lines with fervour, declaiming them a little, but without any gesture. At one side of him stood Miss Sears, at the other, Daniel Meeney: she looked like a landlady who has supplied a reckoning and who knows that not one jot nor tittle can be taken from it; he looked like a man who had been aroused from listlessness, but who was about to sink back into listlessness again. Ignatius Greally, Anthony Tisdil, and the blind man were attentive. The young grey-haired man made no manifestation, but it was plain from his expression that nothing need have been added to the effect that had been produced. But Charles Hempson, his chair tilted back, his thumbs stuck in the arm-holes of his soiled white waistcoat, looked as insolent as before.

"Fine—very fine!" said the grey-haired young man.

"Fine—very fine, indeed!" said Charles Hempson. "Our friend has described the feelings of a man wakening up after hitting the booze for a fortnight. I think some of us know the state described. But I shall say to the gentleman who has perpetrated the work, 'I don't think we can do anything for you, sir.'"

Howard Todd-Grubb lost control of himself. "I think I speak on behalf of the decent members of this society," he said, "and I speak as founder and secretary of it, and speaking as founder and secretary and on behalf of the decent members, I say that we will not be able to tolerate Mr. Hempson's presence at any more of our meetings."

"The members of the society are invited to make a criticism of works put before them," said Charles Hempson. "Am I to understand that when the Society says criticism, it means fulsome adulation?"

"No, sir," said the founder and secretary of the Eblana Literary Society.

"Mr. Hempson!" said Miss Sears reprovingly.

Mr. Hempson addressed the secretary pro tem. "May I draw your attention to the fact that there are females present during the proceedings," he said.

"The rule was suspended to permit Miss Sears to be present during the reading of Loftus Mongan's paper," said Daniel Meeney.

"But not to join in the debate, I presume."

"No, not to join in the debate," said Daniel Meeney.

"Very well. Then I hope I shall be permitted to continue."

All the time Charles Hempson had been speaking, the blind man had been tapping the floor with his stick and clicking his tongue by way of protest. "Is there to be nothing but argufying?" he kept saying. "Why didn't Mr. Loftus Mongan come in?"

"Mr. Loftus Mongan shouldn't demean himself by coming to such a place," Miss Sears said, oblivious of the fact that speech was debarred her in that assembly.

"I'm only a member of the public," said the blind man, "but I want to tell you that Mr. Hempson is always making trouble. Didn't I hear him at a Board of Guardians' Meeting last year? He was that overbearing while they were reading Mr. Loftus Mongan's oration that I couldn't make out at all what it was about."

"Neither could your betters, my good man," said Charles Hempson.

"Mr. Hempson," said Miss Sears, "this poor man may have come to misfortune, but he is a well educated man—anybody can see that."

"Leave him alone—leave him alone," said the blind man. "But I'll tell you this—the Society will have no respect in this town as long as no member will put a hand on that man to turn him out."

"To turn me out?" exclaimed Charles Hempson, standing up from the chair.

"Is there no one here who will rid the Society, who will rid Loftus Mongan of this mocker?" Howard Todd-Grubb exclaimed. "I cannot deal with him on account of my glasses."

Anthony Tisdil rose up. In Howard Todd-Grubb's voice there was appeal, and appeal had not been made to him for many a long day. Perhaps his intention was merely to place himself at the side of the Secretary and Founder of the Eblana Literary Society and give him the support of a man who had been in a railway collision. As soon as he stood up, "Sit down, my man," said Charles Hempson to him.

Then Anthony Tisdil went towards him. The grey-haired young man had opened the door, perhaps with the intention of inducing the editor to make an exit. Anthony Tisdil pitched himself upon Charles Hempson. Now the editor was not steady on his legs (he had been leaning on the back of a chair) and the impact of Anthony's body made him lurch towards the door. At the threshold there was a struggle. Making an effort Anthony Tisdil thrust his man out. He plucked himself from Hempson's clawing hands and got back into the room. The grey-haired young man shut fast the door.

"Open the door! Damn you, open the door for me," came from the man outside.

All the occupants of the room except the blind man stood before the door: "The door will not open to you, Charles Hempson, mocker," Howard Todd-Grubb declared. There was a rattling at the door; a call from downstairs was heard; Charles Hempson's steps were listened to as they descended the stairway. But still Miss Sears remained on guard at the door.

"I move that the best thanks of the Eblana Literary Society be returned to our distinguished and courageous guest for his effort in combating the ferocious opposition to Loftus Mongan's address, and that the Society inform Loftus Mongan of that effort." It was Howard Todd-Grubb made the motion. It was seconded by the secretary pro tem. and supported by the grey-haired young man (it was disclosed that his name was Peter-Paul Duffy). The blind man said, "Hear Hear!" tapping the floor with his stick. As for Anthony Tisdil, he was overcome by the effort he had made. He sank into the chair at the table. Ignatius Greally emptied a glass of water on his head. He sat there, his head bent mechanically wiping the back of his neck where the water was dampening his collar.

"Hush," said Miss Sears at the doorway, "somebody is coming up the stairs. I firmly believe that it is Mr. Mongan himself."

"Is Mr. Mongan coming himself?" asked the blind man hopefully.

And when Miss Sears opened the door Loftus Mongan was actually there. He entered, massive with his thick-set figure, his silk hat, his walking-stick. He looked like a man who had been replenished. In a minute his hat and overcoat were off and his stick was laid in a corner. He took no account of the statement that his paper had been read by the secretary pro tem. He unrolled the manuscript he had taken out of Miss Sears's hands, and began his address.

His voice was resonant, although now and again there was a croak of hoarseness in it. As he went on Ignatius Greally looked at Daniel Meeney as if he were thunderstruck to think that the reading of an address could convey so little of its substance and spirit. The sectary pro tem., picking up the pages as they swept out of the hand of the reader, read them with startled interest. Peter-Paul Duffy was rapt by it all; occasionally he wrote a note on his shirt-cuff. Howard Todd-Grubb preserved his equanimity; it was as he had divined through Daniel Meeney's reading; he nodded from time to time to mark his acceptance of salient passages. The difference between the address as read by the secretary pro tem. and as delivered by the author was the difference between despondency and flashing hope. The blind man's face was lighted up as if he looked on the sun again. As for Anthony Tisdil he was caught and held by a title that Loftus Mongan introduced early into his address and frequently made use of—"The Illuminati." All that was to be achieved was to be achieved through the Illuminati. And the Illuminati were those present who were sharing in the thoughts that were being delivered by Loftus Mongan. Miss Sears was not visibly moved; she sat on a bench at the door, her hands in her lap, her eyes closed tightly.

With the first words of Loftus Mongan's address something had come near—so near that the opening of the door might bring it amongst men. That something was a future in which life was ennobled. Dignity and high reward adhered to every labour. Everyone had influence in creating a state that was great and respected. Loftus Mongan's belief in his fellow-men—especially in such of them as surrounded him at the moment—banished disbelief and distrust. The Illuminati were those present. Anthony Tisdil, by virtue of being there, was one of the Illuminati. After the peroration about the birds singing in the dawn there were words spoken to the Illuminati directly. They were as a call to them. Loftus Mongan laid the papers on the table and walked up and down the room.

He inquired about the reception that his address had had on its first reading. He heard about Charles Hempson's mocks and gibes. Then he heard about Anthony Tisdil's heroic intervention. Anthony was made known to him. He took Anthony's hand.

Lowry Muldoon burst in. "Somebody give me a cigarette," he said. It was felt by members present that he was an emissary of the enemy, and his reception was a guarded one. Ignatius Greally tendered him the cigarette; he lit it at an expiring candle and paced about the room. People were leaving the billiard-room below.

"Where is Charles Hempson?" Loftus Mongan asked.

"In the billiard-room, snoring drunk," said Lowry Muldoon. "Give me your manuscript," he said. "I'll put it in the *Standard* this week. I'll write the headings for it myself."

"I have something better to do with my manuscript, sir," said Loftus Mongan.

"It is the best offer I can make," said Lowry Muldoon. The lamp on the table flickered and went out. A candle went out. Lowry Muldoon tried to re-light his cigarette, and snuffed out another candle. Exits began. Miss Sears took the hand of the blind man and led him down the stairway. Peter-Paul Duffy made a respectful good-night to Loftus Mongan and went out. Lowry Muldoon took Ignatius Greally and Daniel Meeney by the arms and pushed them along. "You'll have to get me a pint," he said.

"Come, Mr. Tisdil, join us; be one of the Illuminati," Loftus Mongan said, as he took Anthony's arm. "What could I say when I met the rest of them?" Anthony Tisdil asked. "There are not so many of us as yet; in fact, there is only myself and my friend, Howard Todd-Grubb. Take your place side by side with us." "Oh, if there's only you and Mr. Todd-Grubb, I wouldn't mind joining," said Anthony Tisdil. "It's fellows I'd be afraid of." He thought of Burtt in the office. Burtt nor the others would ever know that he belonged to this wonderful band of transformers. But it would be in his own mind, and that would help him to stand up to Burtt and the others. "Give me your hand; take Mr. Todd-Grubb's hand; we will join together on this bridge," said Loftus Mongan. They stood on the bridge and the river flowed below them, and Anthony Tisdil thought of a line of poetry, "I stood on the bridge at midnight," and he was elevated by the thought that poetry was appropriate to the situation in which he was. "The Illuminati have come into existence," said Loftus Mongan. "The Illuminati have come into existence," exclaimed Howard Todd-Grubb fervently. The blind man's stick was heard tapping the pavement as he went towards wherever his domicile was. "Good luck to you, Mr. Mongan," he said as he heard a voice that he recognized. "It was grand, grand." Anthony Tisdil felt that he was one of three who had perceptible grandeur about them—The Illuminati.

# Seumas O'Kelly

## *The Building*

### I

Martin Cosgrave walked up steadily to his holding after Ellen Miscal had read to him the American letter. He had spoken no word to the woman. It was not every day that he had to battle with a whirl of thoughts. A quiet man of the fields, he only felt conscious of a strong impulse to get back to his holding up on the hill. He had no clear idea of what he would do or what he would think when he got back to his holding. But the fields seemed to cry out to him, to call him back to their companionship, while all the wonders of the resurrection were breaking in fresh upon his life.

Martin Cosgrave walked his fields and put his flock of sheep scurrying out of a gap with a whistle. His holding and the things of his holding were never so precious to his sight. He walked his fields with his hands in his pockets and an easy, solid step upon the sod. He felt a bracing sense of security.

Then he sat up on the mearing.

The day was waning. It seemed to close in about his holding with a new protection. The mood grew upon him as the shadows deepened. A great peace came over him. The breeze stirring the grass spread out at his feet seemed to whisper of the strange unexpected thing that had broken in upon his life. He felt the splendid companionship of the fields for the master.

Suddenly Martin Cosgrave looked down at his cabin. Something snapped as his eyes remained riveted upon it. He leapt from the mearing and walked out into the field, his hands this time gripping the lapels of his coat, a cloud settling upon his brow. In the centre of the field he stood, his eyes still upon the cabin. What a mean, pokey, ugly little dirty hovel it was! The thatch was getting scraggy over the gables and sagging at the back. In the front it was sodden. A rainy brown streak reached down to the little window looking like the claw of a great bird upon the walls. He had been letting everything go to the bad. That might not signify in the past. But now—

"Rose Dempsey would never stand the like," he said to himself. "She will be used to grand big houses."

He turned his back upon the cabin near the boreen and looked up to the belt of beech trees swaying in the wind on the crest of the hill. How did he live there most of his life and never see that it was a place fashioned by the hand of Nature for a house? Was it not the height of nonsense to have trees there making music all the long hours of the night without a house bedside them and people sleeping within it? In a few minutes the thought had taken hold of his mind. Limestone—beautiful limestone—ready at hand in the quarry not a quarter of a mile down the road. Sand from the pit at the back of his own cabin. Lime from the kiln beyond the road. And his own two hands! He ran his fingers along the muscles of his arms. Then he walked up the hill.

Martin Cosgrave, as he walked up the hill, felt himself wondering for the first time in his life if he had really been foolish to have run away from his father's cabin when he had been young. Up to this he had always accepted the verdict of the people about him that he had been a foolish boy "to go wandering in strange places." He had walked along the roads to many far towns. Then he had struck his friend, the building contractor. He had been a useful worker about a building house. At first he had carried hods of mortar and cement up ladders to the masons. The business of the masons he had mastered quickly. But he had always had a longing to hold a chisel in one hand and a mallet in the other at work upon stone. He had drifted into a quarry, thence to a stone-cutting yard. After a little while he could not conceal his impatience with the mere dressing of coping stones or the chiselling out of tombstones to a pattern. Then he saw the man killed in the quarry. He was standing quite near to him. The chain of the windlass went and the poor man had no escape. Martin Cosgrave had heard the crunch of the skull on the boulder, and some of the blood was spattered upon his boots. He was a man of tense nerves. The sight of blood sickened him. He put on his coat, left the quarry, and went walking along the road.

It was while he walked along the road that the longing for his home came upon him. He tramped back to his home above Kilbeg. His father had been long dead, but by his return he had glorified the closing days of his mother's life. He took up the little farm and cut himself off from his wandering life when he had fetched the tools from his lodgings in the town beside the quarries.

By the time Martin Cosgrave had reached the top of the hill he had concluded that he had not, after all, been a foolish boy to work in far places. "The hand of God was in it," he said reverently with his eyes on the beech trees that made music on the crest of the hill.

He made a rapid survey of the place with his keen eyes. Then he mapped out the foundation of the building by driving the heel of his boot into the green sod. He stepped back among the beech trees and looked out at the outlined site of the building. He saw it all growing up in his mind's eye, at first a rough block, a mere shell, a little uncertain and unsatisfactory. Then the uncertainties were lopped off, the building took shape, touch after touch was added. Long shadows spread out from the trees and wrapped the fields. Stars came out in the sky. But Martin Cosgrave never noticed these things. The building was growing all the time. There was a firm grasp of the general scheme, a realisation of what the building would evolve that no other building ever evolved, what it would proclaim for all time. The passing of the day and the stealth of the night could not claim attention from a man who was living over a dream that was fashioning itself in his mind, abandoning himself to the joy of his creation, dwelling longingly upon the details of the building, going over and, as it were, feeling it in every fibre, jealous of the effect of every stone, tracing the trend and subtlety of every curve, seeing how one touch fitted in and enhanced the other and how all carried on the meaning of the whole.

When he came down from the hill there was a spring in Martin Cosgrave's step. He swung his arms. The blood was coursing fast through his veins. His eyes were glowing. He would need to make a map of the building. It was all burned clearly into his brain.

From under the bed of his cabin he pulled out the wooden box. It had not been opened since he had fetched it from the far town. He held his breath as he threw open the lid. There they lay, the half-forgotten symbols of his old life. Worn mallets, chisels, the head of a broken hod with the plaster still caked into it, a short broad shovel for mixing mortar, a trowel, a spirit level, a plumb, all wrapped loosely in a worn leather apron. He took the mallets in his hand and turned them about with the quick little jerks that came so naturally to him. Strength for the work had come into his arms. All the old ambitions which he thought had been stifled with his early manhood sprang to life again.

As he lay in his bed that night Martin Cosgrave felt himself turning over and over again the words in the letter which Rose Dempsey had sent to her aunt, Ellen Miscal, from America. "Tell Martin Cosgrave," the letter read, "that I will be back home in Kilbeg by the end of the spring. If he has no wish for any other girl I am willing to settle down." Beyond the announcement that her sister Sheela would be with her for a holiday, the letter "brought no other account." But what an account it had brought to Martin Cosgrave! The fields understood—the building would proclaim.

Early in the morning Martin Cosgrave went down to Ellen Miscal to tell her what to put in the letter that was going back to Rose Dempsey in America. Martin Cosgrave walked heavily into the house and stood with his back against the dresser. He turned the soft black hat about in his hands nervously and talked like one who was speaking sacred words.

"Tell her," he said, "that Martin Cosgrave had no thought for any other person beyond herself. Tell her to be coming back to Kilbeg. Tell her not to come until the late harvest."

Ellen Miscal, who sat over the sheet of writing paper on the table, looked up quickly as he spoke the words. As she did so she was conscious of the new animation that vivified the idealistic face of Martin Cosgrave. But he did not give her time to question him.

"I have my own reasons for asking her to wait until the harvest," he said, with some irritation.

He stayed at the dresser until Ellen Miscal had written the letter. He carried it down to the village and posted it with his own hand, and he went and came as gravely as if he had been taking part in some solemn ritual.

II

That day the building was begun. Martin Cosgrave tackled the donkey and drew a few loads of limestone from the nearby quarry. Some of the neighbours who came his way found him a changed man, a silent man with his eager face set, a man in whose eyes a new light shone, a quiet man of the fields into whose mind a set purpose had come. He struggled up the road with his donkey-cart, his hand gripping the shaft to hasten the steps of the slow brute, his limbs bent to the hill, his head down at the work. By the end of the week a pile of grey-blue stones was heaped up on the crest of the hill. The walls of the fields had been broken down to make a carway. Late into the night when the donkey had been fed and tethered the neighbours would see Martin Cosgrave moving about the pile of grey-blue stones, sorting and picking, arranging in little groups to have ready to his hands. "A house he is going to put up on the hill," they would say, lost in wonder.

The spring came, and with it all the strenuous work on the land. But Martin Cosgrave went on with the building. The neighbours shook their heads at the sight of neglect that was gathering about his holding; they said it was flying in the face of Providence when Martin Cosgrave weaned all the lambs from the ewes one day, long before their time, and sold them at the fair to the first bidder that came his way. Martin Cosgrave did so because he wanted money and was in a hurry to get back to his building.

"What call has a man to be destroying himself like that?" the neighbours asked each other.

Martin Cosgrave knew what the neighbours were saying about him. But what did he care? What thought had any of them for the heart of a builder? What did any of them know beyond putting a spade in the clay and waiting for the seasons to send up growing things from the seed they scattered by their hands? What did they know about the feel of the rough stone in the hand and the shaping of it to fit into the building, the building that day after day you saw rising up from the ground by the skill of your hand and the art of your mind? What could they in Kilbeg know of the ship that would plough the ocean in the harvest bearing Rose Dempsey home to him? For all their ploughing and their sowing, what sort of a place had any of them led a woman into? They might talk away. The joy of the builder was his. The beech trees that made music all day beside the building he was putting up to the sight of all the world had more understanding of him than all the people of the parish.

Martin Cosgrave had no help. He kept to his work from such an early hour in the morning until such a late hour of the night that the people marvelled at his endurance. But as the work went on the people would talk about Martin Cosgrave's building in the fields and tell strangers of it at the markets. They said that the like of it had never been seen in the countryside. It was to be "full of little turrets and the finest of fancy porches and a regular sight of bulging windows." One day that Martin Cosgrave heard a neighbour speaking about the "bulging windows" he laughed a half-bitter, half-mocking laugh.

"Tell them," he said, "that they are cut-stone tracery windows to fit in with the carved doors." These cut-stone windows and carved doors cost Martin Cosgrave such a length of time that they provoked the patience of the people. Out of big slabs of stone he had worked them, and sometimes he would ask the neighbours to give him a hand in the shifting of these slabs. But he was quick to resent any interference. One day a stone-cutter from the quarry went up on the scaffold, and when Martin Cosgrave saw him he went white to the lips and cursed so bitterly that those standing about walked away.

When the shell of the building had been finished Martin Cosgrave hired a carpenter to do all the woodwork. The woodwork cost money. Martin Cosgrave did not hesitate. He sold some of his sheep, sold them hurriedly, and as all men who sell their sheep hurriedly, he sold them badly. When the carpentry had been finished, the roofing cost more money. One day the neighbours discovered that all the sheep had been sold. "He's beggared now," they said.

The farmer who turned the sod a few fields away laboured in the damp atmosphere of growing things, his mind filled with thoughts of bursting seeds and teeming barns. He shook his head at sight of Martin Cosgrave above on the hill bent all day over hard stones; whenever he looked up he only caught the glint of a trowel, or heard the harsh grind of a chisel. But Martin Cosgrave took no stock of the men reddening the soil beneath him. Whenever his eyes travelled down the hillside he only saw the flock of crows that hung over the head of the digger. The study of the veins of limestone that he turned in his hands, the slow moulding of the crude shapes to their place in the building, the rhythm and swing of the mallet in his arm, the zest with which he felt the impact of the chisel on the stone, the ring of forging steel, the consciousness of mastery over the work that lay to his hands—these were the things that seemed to him to give life a purpose and man a destiny. He would whistle a tune as he mixed the mortar with the broad shovel, for it gave him a feeling of the knitting of the building with the ages. He pitied the farmer who looked helplessly upon his corn as it was beaten to the ground by the first storm that blew from the sea; he was upon a work that would withstand the storms of centuries. The scent of lime and mortar greeted his nostrils. When he moved about the splinters crunched under his feet. Everything around him was hard and stubborn, but he was the master of it all. In his dreams in the night he would reach out his hands for the feel of the hard stone, a burning desire in his breast to put it into shape, to give it nobility in the scheme of a building.

It was while Martin Cosgrave walked through the building that Ellen Miscal came to him with the second letter from America. The carpenter was hammering at something below. The letter said that Rose Dempsey and her sister, Sheela, would be home in the late harvest. "With all I saw since I left Kilbeg," Rose Dempsey wrote, "I never saw one that I thought as much of as Martin Cosgrave."

When Ellen Miscal left him, Martin Cosgrave stood very quietly looking through the cut-stone tracery window. The beech trees were swaying slowly outside. Their music was in his ears.

Then he remembered that he was standing in the room where he would take Rose Dempsey in his arms. It was here he would tell her of all the bitter things he had locked up in his heart when she had gone away from him. It was here he would tell her of the day of resurrection, when all the bitter thoughts had burst into flower at the few words that told of her return. It was that day of great tumult within him that thought of the building had come into his mind.

When Martin Cosgrave walked out of the room the carpenter and a neighbour boy were arguing about something at the foot of the stairs.

"It's too steep, I'm telling you," the boy was saying.

"What do you know about it?"

"I know this much about it, that if a little child came running down that stairs he'd be apt to fall and break his neck."

Then the two men went out, still arguing.

Martin Cosgrave sat down on one of the steps of the stairs. A child running down the steps! His child! A child bearing his name! He would be prattling about the building. He would run across that landing, swaying and tottering. His little voice would fill the building. Arms would be reaching out to him. They would be the soft white arms of Rose Dempsey, or maybe, they would be the arms that raised up the building—his own strong arms. Or it might be that he would be carrying down the child and handing him over the rails there into the outspread arms of Rose Dempsey. She would be reaching out for the child with the newly-kindled light of motherhood in her eyes, the passion of a young mother in her welcoming voice. A child with his very name—a child that would grow up to be a man and hand down the name to another, and so on during the generations. And with the name would go down the building, the building that would endure, that would live, that was immortal. Did it all come to him as a sudden revelation, springing from the idle talk of a neighbour boy brought up to work from one season to another? Or was it the same thing that was behind the forces that had fired him while he had worked at the building? Had it not all come into his life the evening he stood among his field with his eyes on the crest of the hill?

Ah, there had been a great building surely, a building standing up on the hill, a great, a splendid building raised up to the sight of all the world, and with it a greater building, a building raised up from the sight of all men, the building of a name, the moulding of hearts that would beat while Time was, a building of immortal souls, a building into which God would breathe His breath, a building which would be heard of in Heaven, among the angels, through all the eternities, a building living on when all the light was gone out of the sun, when oceans were as if they had never been, a name, a building, living when the story of all the worlds and all the generations would be held written upon a scroll in the lap of God. . . . The face of the dreamer as he abandoned himself to his thoughts was pallid with a half-fanatical emotion.

The neighbours were more awed than shocked at the change they saw increasing in Martin Cosgrave. He had grown paler and thinner, but his eyes were more tense, had in them, some of the neighbours said, the colour of the limestone. He was more and more removed from the old life. He walked his fields without seeing the things that made up the old companionship. His whole attitude was one of detachment from everything that did not savour of the crunch of stone, the ring of steel on the walls of a building. He only talked rationally when the neighbours spoke to him of the building. They had heard that he had gone to the money-lender, and mortgaged every perch of his land. "It was easy to know how work of the like would end," they said.

One day a stranger was driving by on his car, and when he saw the building he got down, walked up the hill, and made a long study of it. On his way down he met Martin Cosgrave.

"Who built the house on the hill?" he asked.

"A simple man in the neighbourhood," Martin Cosgrave made answer, after a little pause.

"A simple man!" the stranger exclaimed, looking at Martin Cosgrave with some disapproval. "Well, he has attempted something anyway. He may not have succeeded, but the artist is in him somewhere. He has created a sort of—well, lyric—in stone on that hill. Extraordinary!"

The stranger hesitated before he hit on the word lyric. He got up on his car and drove away muttering something under his breath.

Martin Cosgrave could have run up the hill and shouted. He could have called all the neighbours together and told them of the strange man who had praised the building.

But he did none of these things. He had work waiting to his hand. A hunger was upon him to feel his pulse beating to the throb of steel on stone. From the road he made a sweep of a drive up to the building. The neighbours looked open-mouthed at the work for the days it went on. "Well, that finishes Martin Cosgrave anyway," they said.

Martin Cosgrave rushed the making of the drive; he took all the help he could get. The boys would come up after their day's work and give him a hand. While they worked he was busy with his chisel upon the boulders of limestone which he had set up on either side of the entrance gate. Once more he felt the glamour of life—the impact of forging steel on stone was thrilling through his arms, the stone was being moulded to the direction of his exulting mind.

When he had finished with the boulders at the entrance gate the people marvelled. The gate had a glory of its own, and yet it was connected with the scheme of the building on the hill palpably enough for even their minds to grasp it. When the people looked upon it they forgot to make complaint of the good land that was given to ruin. One of them had expressed the general vague sentiment when he said, "Well, the kite has got its tail."

In the late harvest Martin Cosgrave carried up all the little sticks of furniture from his cabin and put it in the building. Then he sent for Ellen Miscal. When the woman came she looked about the place in amazement.

"Well, of all the sights in the world!" she exclaimed.

Martin Cosgrave was irritated at the woman's attitude.

"We'll have to make the best of it," he said, looking at the furniture. "I will be marrying Rose Dempsey in the town some days after she lands."

"Rose would never like the suddenness of that," her aunt protested. "She can be staying with me and marrying from my house."

"I saw the priest about it," Martin Cosgrave said impatiently. "I will have my way, Ellen Miscal. Rose Dempsey will come up to Kilbeg my wife. We will come in the gate together, we will walk in to the building together. I will have my way."

Martin Cosgrave spoke of having his way in the impassioned voice of the fanatic, of his home-coming with his bride in the half-dreamy voice of the visionary.

"Have your way, Martin, have your way," the woman said. "And," she added, rising, "I will be bringing up a few things to put into your house."

III

Martin Cosgrave spent three days in the town waiting the arrival of Rose Dempsey. The boat was late. He haunted the railway station, with hungry eyes scanned the passengers as each train steamed in. His blood was on fire in his veins for those three days. What peace could a man have who was waiting to get back to his building and to have Rose Dempsey going back with him, his wife?

Sometimes he would sit down on the railway bench on the platform, staring down at the ground, smiling to himself. What a surprise he had in store for Rose! What would he say to her first? Would he say anything of the building? No, he would say nothing at all of the building until they drove across the bridge and right up to the gate! "Rose," he would then say, "do you remember the hill—the place under the beech trees?" She was sure to remember that place. It was there they had spent so much time, there he had first found her lips, there they had quarrelled! And Rose would look up to that old place and see the building! What would she think? Would she feel about it as he felt himself? She would, she would! What sort of look would come into her face? And what would he be able to tell her about it at all? . . . He would say nothing at all about it; that would be the best way! They would say nothing to each other, but walk in the gate and up the drive across the hill, the hill they often ran across in the old days! They would be quite silent, and walk into the house silently. The building, too, would be silent, and he would take her from one room to another in silence, and when she had seen everything he would look into her eyes and say, "Well?" It would be all so like a wonder story, a day of magic! . . . Martin Cosgrave sprang from the bench and went to the edge of the platform, staring down the long level road, with its two rails tapering almost together in the distance. Not a sign of the train. Would it never come in? Had anything happened to the boat? He walked up and down with energy, holding the lapel of his coat, saying to himself, "I must not be thinking of things like this. It is foolishness. Whatever is to happen will happen, and that's all about it. I am quite at ease, quite cool!"

At last it came, steaming and blowing. Windows were lowered, carriage doors flew open, people ran up and down. Martin Cosgrave stood a little away, tense, drawn, his eyes sweeping down the people. Suddenly something shot through him; an old sensation, an old thrill, made his whole being tingle, his mind exult, and then there was the most exquisite relaxation. How long it was since he felt like this before! His eyes were burning upon a familiar figure of a girl in a navy blue coat and skirt, her back turned, struggling with parcels, helped by the hands of invisible people from within the carriage. Martin Cosgrave strode down the platform, eagerness, joy, sense of proprietorship, already in his stride.

"Rose!" he exclaimed while the girl's back was still turned to him.

His voice shook in spite of him. The woman turned about sharply.

Martin Cosgrave gave a little start back. It was not Rose Dempsey, but her sister, Sheela. How like Rose she had grown!

"Martin!" she exclaimed, putting out her hand. He gave it a hurried shake and then searched the railway carriage with burning eyes. The people he saw there were all strangers, tired-looking travellers. When he turned from the railway carriage Sheela Dempsey was rushing with her parcels into a waiting-room. He strode after her. He looked at the girl. How unlike Rose she was after all! Nobody—nobody—could ever be like Rose Dempsey!

"Where is Rose?" he asked.

Sheela Dempsey looked up into the face of Martin Cosgrave and saw there what she had half-dreaded to see.

"Martin," she said, "Rose is not coming home."

Martin Cosgrave gripped the door of the waiting-room. The train whistled outside and glided from the station. He heard a woman's cheerful voice cry out a conventional "good-bye, good-bye," and through the window he saw the flutter of a dainty handkerchief. A truck was wheeled past the waiting-room. There was the crack of a whip and some cars rattled away over the road. Then there was silence.

Sheela Dempsey walked over to him and laid a hand upon his shoulder. When she spoke her voice was full of an understanding womanly sympathy.

"Don't be troubling over it, Martin," she said, "Rose is not worth it." She spoke her sister's name with some bitterness.

Vaguely Martin Cosgrave looked into the girl's eyes. He read there in a dim way what the girl could not say of her sister.

It was all so strange! The waiting-room was so bare, so cold, so grey, so like a sepulchre. What could Sheela Dempsey with all her womanly understanding, with all her quick intuition, know of the things that happened beside her? How could she have ears for the crashing down of the pillars of the building that Martin Cosgrave had raised up in his soul? How could she have eyes for the wreck of the structure that was to go on through all the generations? What thought had she of the wiping out of a name that would have lived in the nation and continued for all time in the eternities, a tangible thing in Heaven among the Immortals when the stars had all been burned out in the sky?

Martin Cosgrave drove home from the railway station with Sheela Dempsey. He sat without a word, not really conscious of his surroundings as they covered the miles. The girl reached across the side-car, touching him lightly on the shoulder.

"Look!" she exclaimed.

Martin Cosgrave looked up. The building stood in the moonlight on the crest of the hill. He bade the driver pull up, and then got down from the car.

"Who owns the house?" Sheela Dempsey asked.

"I do. I put it up on the hill for Rose."

There was silence for some time.

"How did you get it built, Martin?" Sheela Dempsey asked, awe in her tone.

"I built it myself," he answered. "I wonder has Rose as good a place? What sort of a building is she in to-night?"

Martin Cosgrave did not notice the sudden quiver in the girl's body as he put the question. But she made no reply, and the car drove on, leaving Martin Cosgrave standing alone at the gate of the building.

The faint sweep of the drive lay before him. It led his eyes up to the crest of the hill. There it was standing shadowy against the sky, every delicate outline clear to his vision. The beech trees were swaying beside it, reaching out like great shapeless arms in the night, blurred and beckoning and ghostly. A little vein of their music sounded in his ears. How often had he listened to that music and the things it had sung to him! It made him conscious of all the emotion he had felt while he had put up the building on the hill.

The joy of the builder swept over him like a wave. He was within the rising walls again, his hands among the grey-blue shapes, the measured stroke of the mallet swinging for the shifting chisel, the throb of steel going through his arms, the grind of stone was under his hands, the stone dust dry upon his lips, his eyes quick and keen, his arms bared, the shirt at his breast open, his whole body tense, tuned, to the desire of the conscious builder. . . . Once more he moved about the carpet of splinters, the grateful crunch beneath his feet, his world a world of stubborn things, rejoicing in his power of direction and mastery over it all. And always at the back of his mind and blending itself with the work was the thought of a ship forging through the water at the harvest, a ship with white sails spread to the winds. Had not thought for the building come into his mind when dead things sprang to life in the resurrection of his hopes?

Martin Cosgrave turned away from the gate. He walked down where the shadow of the mearing was faint upon the road. He turned up the boreen closed in by the still hedges. He stumbled over the ruts. He stood at the cabin door and looked up at the sky with soulless eyes. The animation, the inspiration, that had vivified his face since the building had been begun had died. The face no longer expressed the idealist, the visionary. His eyes swept the sky for a purpose. It was the look of the man of the fields, the man who had thought for his crops, who was near to the soil.

He had not looked a final and anxious, a peasant look, at the sky from his cabin-door in the night since he had embarked upon the building. He was conscious of that fact after a little. He wondered if it was a vague stirring in his heart that made him do it, a vague craving for the old companionship of the fields this night of bitterness. They were the fields, the sod, the territory of his forefathers, the inheritance of his blood. Who was he that he should put up a great building on the hill? What if he had risen for a little on his wings above the common flock?

The night air was heavy with the scent of the late dry harvest and all that the late dry harvest meant to the man nurtured on the side of a wet hill. The sheaves of corn were stooked in his neighbour's fields. Yesterday he had sacrificed the land to the building; to-morrow he would sacrifice the building to the land. Martin Cosgrave knew, the stars seemed to know, that a message, a voice, a command, would come like a wave through the generations of his blood sweeping him back to a common tradition. The cry for service on the land was beginning to stir somewhere. It would come to him in a word, a word sanctified upon the land by the memory of a thousand sacrifices and a thousand struggles, the only word that held magic for his race, the one word—Redemption! He looked up at the building, made a vague motion of his hand that was like an act of renunciation, and laughed a laugh of terrible bitterness.

"Look," he cried, "at the building Martin Cosgrave put up on the hill!"

He moved to the cabin-door, his feet heavy upon the uneven ground as the feet of any of the generation of men who had ever gone that way before. He pressed the cabin-door with his fist. With a groan it went back shakily over the worn stone threshold, sticking when it was only a little way open. All was quiet, black, damp, terrible as chaos, inside. Martin Cosgrave hitched forward his left shoulder, went in sideways, and closed the crazy door against the pale world of moonlight outside.

# Seumas O'Kelly

## *The Haven*

The long journey over the bog was tiring to the men. They sat about, melancholy and silent, for the hours it lasted. Hike trudged along in the path on the bank, stumbling over the rough ground, muttering and praying as he went. Calcutta kept his sentry by the funnel. The Boss hummed monotonously as he wandered about the boat.

There was a little movement, signs of revived interest in the world, as the brown bogland began to merge in the green pastures. A man whistled when they made the wooded places. The boat seemed to glide faster under the great boughs of the overhanging trees. The hoofs of the horse sounded sharp from the granite road, houses sprang up on the landscape, men were to be seen on the hillsides, carts rumbled along the roads. There was a bend in the canal; the men strained their eyes to round it, for round that bend was civilisation and *The Haven*.

First, the eyes of the men caught the red tiles crowning the roof; slowly the entire roof came to view, then the yellow gable with the open window, the well-known front, with its dark green paint edged with thin gold lines, folded itself out, and the white lettering over the door, "*The Haven*," shone to the hungry eyes of the crew. Even Hike, the driver, had been known to raise his head at that bend of the canal.

The boat glided up to the limestone landing-place, and nowhere was she steered with a more delicate tiller. Calcutta stepped lightly ashore, a rope in his hand, wound it about the waiting stump, and the boat, straining hard, was brought to a stand-still. As he unwound the rope from the stump he wiped his dry mouth with his hand, and raised friendly eyes to *The*

*Haven*. At the same moment the grotesque figure left the tiller, the Boss came from behind the funnel, both their feet touching the ground with military precision. Hike was leading the unyoked horse away to the stables below the village, the cross-bolt jolting on the great haunches of the brute. As the crew of three crossed the road to *The Haven*, the Boss hummed pleasantly, his eyes on Calcutta's fingers as they jingled some coppers.

Hanks of onions and some brushes made a drapery around the door, swaying in the breeze. When the men stepped into the shop it exhaled a scent of seeds. They were ranged about in bags. The mouth of one sack was folded back. A farmer stood over it, turning a tuber in his hand, his mind given up to the good things of the season. A woman in a grey shawl was handling some pieces of bacon on the counter, her pale, cold eyes filled with that battle-light which shortens the lives of shop assistants in wayside places.

Crockery ware, tins of biscuits, white firkins of lard, yellow pyramids of cheeses rose out of the dimly-lighted spaces overhead. But the men from the boat passed through the oak-stained partition, with high lights of coloured glass. Behind this gilded place was the sanctuary they sought.

It was a long, narrow bar. The counter was high, and of oak. The display of galleries of bottles gave an air of opulence to the place that pleased the men. The girth of the golden-hooped barrels was reassuring. The men sat down on an aesthetic form, facing this display, their feet in sawdust, their hearts filled with the goodness of *The Haven*.

A dark-haired young man stood at professional attention behind the counter, his hand resting lightly on the cream-coloured handle of the patent cork-puller. Some little feathers clung to his hair. His eyes had a suggestion of bleariness. He left the impression of one who had risen early and hurriedly in some lofty attic. His complexion had moved down to the lower reaches of the jaws. It lingered there in a faded purple glory.

A spare, thin person, with drooping shoulders, was standing at the counter, looking vaguely into a pint measure half-emptied. His thoughts were plainly regretful; he did not even look up when Calcutta ordered the first round. When the men got the measures in their hands they looked into them and forgot the long journey over the bog. The Boss stretched his legs out luxuriously before him, his heels tearing two little dark streaks in the sawdust on the floor.

The wall opposite the bar was taken up with stuff that seemed to flow over from the business outside. Great black pots were hanging from holdfasts. Coils of ropes, wire-netting, milk-strainers, tin cans, hay-rakes, reaping hooks, scythes, packages of sheep-dipping powder, reached up to the ceiling. They suggested husbandry, even industry. Opposite to them blazed the shelves of bottles, the barrels with the great golden hoops about their girths.

But the sense of these antagonisms was lost on the men. They had their backs steadily upon the symbols of industry. The second measure was already in their hands, their fingers about the glasses in a mild sort of ecstasy, devotional eyes upturned to the blazing shelves opposite, a holy silence upon them.

The oak-stained door of the partition swung open on its noiseless springs, and a few men came in. They were from another boat that had just arrived. The driver had the whip, which he never used, looped about his body. One of the group took a stride down the floor, his limbs well apart, rubbed his chin with his hand, gazed contemplatively upon the barman for a little and then ordered, as if in an afterthought, the most obvious of drinks.

One of these men wore an oil-coat of great capacity. The outlines of his figure were barge-like. His face peered out from under a pilot-hat with that intense gaze ahead acquired by those long afloat. The other men knew him to be one who had been at ferry work at the mouth of a river. Circumstances had compelled him to drift into the more secluded reaches of the canal. He was now in charge of a turfboat. The men admired the manner in which he disposed of his first drink.

"Now, men, time is passing. Come along," he said, his oil-coat flapping about him as he swung out.

Nobody followed.

A door leading to an unexpected yard and many stores was pushed open, and a man with a sack tied apron-fashion about him came in. He was a carpenter. He ordered some nails. While the assistant outside went to fetch them, the carpenter, in an expert double shuffle of the feet, moved down to the end of the bar where the light was most romantic. Simultaneously the barman found the same centre, had a glass filled; it hopped by his hand on to the counter, got caught on the same hop by the carpenter, and its contents had vanished down his ready throat before the boatmen had realised what had happened. The nails a moment later were handed in from outside, and the voice of the carpenter was heard in the yard calling out to his apprentice: "Tommy, buck up; what's delaying you?" Then there was the sound of planks falling from a cart.

"Terrible treatment to give the blessed drink," one of the boatmen said, resuming contemplation of his own measure.

A young lad danced in, with an Irish terrier at his heels, bringing with him a whiff of tar and guano. The men knew him to be a sort of god—the son of the owner of *The Haven*. He had been going about all day, listening to the forbidden talk of the workmen, rat hunting with the terrier, cutting notches with his penknife in unlawful places. He tilted the elbow of an arm that held a foaming measure, and disappeared under a flap in the counter.

The skipper with the pilot-hat returned with some lock-keepers. He accepted refreshment at their request. Then he said: "Now, men, time is passing. Come along," and went out again.

Nobody followed.

A young girl, leading a small child by the hand, passed through to some inward and private recess of *The Haven*. The heads of all the men jerked up and followed the female vision as it passed. Their eyes remained upon the thick black hair, tied with a bright ribbon as it fell down her back. As they gazed upon it they knew that according to the calendar and the custom of the country this hair should long ago have been put up. They knew then that the vision was one who wanted to remain suspended in her youth by the hair of her head.

"The youngest sister of the proprietor," one of the men having local knowledge said. "Brought in to mind the children."

The barman had looked after the vision with a certain pensive complexion on the lower reaches of the jaws. The Boss of *The Golden Barque* wondered vaguely if the raven-haired barman would succeed.

The man in the pilot-hat returned, beaming cheerfully around him. He had fetched some carters. One of them sang out the inevitable order. The skipper of the turf boat did what was expected of him. Then he went through the partition as breezily as before, saying: "Now, men, time is passing. Come along."

Nobody followed.

The men sat in a long silence on the form. There was a

great peace in the place. A brass kettle sang softly over a spirit-lamp. Some flies buzzed overhead. The barman sat down and resumed his reading of a romance entitled, "Anastasia and the Duke." The golden silence was only broken now and again by the soft palpitation of a throat down which a drink was passing. Then a voice said: "What did he say?"

"He said, 'Time is passing.'"

The silence was resumed. The kettle sang and the flies buzzed overhead. Then there was a group at the end of the form. It was followed by another spell of silence, during which the breathing of the barman, as he stooped over his book, became quite audible, for the romance had reached the chapter in which Anastasia stood in deadly peril of the amours of the Duke.

"What did you say?" The question was droned out from the shadows. The man at the end of the form turned his head round slowly and said:

"I say, who cares a curse for time?" and bringing round his head he hitched his back well up against the wall.

The proprietor passed through *The Haven*. The barman plunged his hands into a basin of water, and made a great show of washing glasses, his mind brought back with violence from the great scene of Anastasia's temptation. The proprietor was natty, fingering his waxed moustache, his head slightly stooped, his appearance preoccupied.

"Good-day to the men," he said, without looking up. A moment later his voice was heard in the yard, sharply calling out some orders.

After some time the silence was again broken.

"A great man," one of the group said, taking a pull at his measure.

"A great man," another agreed, after some reflection. Then, after a long pause:

"Aye, a great man"; and the vague person who had all this time, in marked isolation, been meditating over his glass, woke up, finished his potion, and went out, wiping his lips with the back of his hand.

At the partition he met the man with the pilot-hat, who was followed by an assortment of ex-boatmen and carters. He broke into a splendid smile as a carter gave the inevitable order.

"Now, men, time is passing," he said, reaching out for the first filled measure. It vanished.

The partition door was opened timidly, and the haggard

face of Hike peered in. Then he slunk down by the men to the extreme end of the counter. There he drank his measure with his back to the others. Calcutta followed his movements with a gleam in his eyes. The Boss frowned, then they all stood up as if in protest.

They spat on the sawdust and hitched their trousers about their loins with the air of men who were bracing themselves to once more face a difficult world. Then they passed through the partition.

The woman in the grey shawl was still leaning over the counter, but the bacon had been put aside, and now her thin hands were carefully feeling over some skeins of wool thread. The assistant was still waiting on her, a look of stupour on his exhausted face.

The men stepped out from *The Haven*, a faint odour of onions following them across the road. Skirting the road was the yellow water of the canal. Drawn up against the bank were some laden boats, looking picturesque in the clear light of the spring day.

When they got on board *The Golden Barque*, the Boss paced up and down the deck while the others lay about, smoking. Presently Hike came out of *The Haven*, and passed sullenly down the road. Suddenly the voice of Calcutta rang out, commanding, insolent.

"Hike!" he shouted.

At the word Hike stood, obedient as a soldier who had been called to attention. A hoarse laugh of derision greeted his action.

Then the Boss saw the grotesque figure of Hike swing about on the road. His face, malicious and repulsive, leered up at the boat from between the humps on his shoulders. The large eyes shone with a sinister light as they were raised to the figure of Calcutta. The lips of the long mouth parted, showing some immense yellow teeth. There was something demoniacal, hellishly ugly and wicked, in the expression of Hike. The Boss noticed that Calcutta sprang to his feet from the box on which he had been reclining.

Hike came over to the bank just below *The Golden Barque*, the leer sustained on his face.

"You thought you had her, didn't you?" he demanded of Calcutta. "She was to stay with you for ever, wasn't she? You were such a beauty nobody was ever to come between you." The voice of Hike was thick with an ugly emotion.

Calcutta measured the figure of the half dwarf, and spat down at him. "Go away and scratch your humps, you spawn of a dromaderry," he cried.

"You were so happy together, weren't you?—a pair of cooing doves?" Hike drawled, covering and uncovering his yellow teeth. "She wouldn't look at anyone else at all! No man would do for her but yourself! She loved you, did Mollie the Mermaid!"

At the name, Calcutta leapt to the side of the boat, but the Boss confronted him there.

"Go to the cabin," he commanded.

"Let me down to the cripple," Calcutta shouted. "I'll shake hands with him."

But Hike had moved away, his bullet-shaped head quivering between his humped shoulders, his queer cackle of a laugh dying down the road to the village.

Calcutta, his body twitching, went down to the cabin and drank several mugs of water in rapid succession, then threw himself on his back on the bunk, his blazing eyes riveted on the beam a few places above him, his lusty voice breaking out into a series of ribald songs, one following the other to the same out-of-tune air without any pause.

The Boss stood over the hatch for some time, listening to the rumble that filled the cabin beneath, Calcutta's vocalism so violent that all words were quite incoherent. Slowly the voice got into a sort of chant, and the words became understandable. Calcutta, glaring at the beam above him was roaring:

> Oh, oh, oh, I rowled me love in the new-mown hay,
> I rowled me love in the new-mown hay,
> I rowled me love in the new-mown hay,
> Oh, oh, oh, when the cocks they crew in the maurnin!

The boss wondered where Calcutta had got his songs; perhaps in the Black Hole. The Boss kicked the lid on to the opening into the cabin, and then resumed his own tramp about the deck of *The Golden Barque*, wondering, and wondering in vain, as the quiet night settled over the peaceful place, why two men should hate each other so bitterly. He was unable to decide whether it was very tragical or very comical that the memory of a woman should keep ever green their bitterness. One man, the Boss knew, held in his memory that which brought him visions of a white angel in shining joy and glory in heaven; the other man, whose voice now rumbled weirdly beneath, remembered so much of his passion that he exultingly figured her as burning in hell for all eternity.

The Boss gave it up.

"We must unload to-morrow," he said, his eyes roving over the cargo.

# Seumas O'Kelly

## *The Derelict*

The Boss of *The Golden Barque* was very pleased when he was able to resume business on her deck. He was likewise pleased that the man with the pock-marked face had disappeared and that Billy the Clown was available to fill his place. Billy the Clown was obviously a companionable person, interested in almost everything, and sometimes the Boss liked to talk. He explained to Billy that he always experienced a heavy bilious attack when forced to leave *The Golden Barque* for other craft on the canal. There was, he said, some quality in the timbers of *The Golden Barque* which cured him immediately he got aboard her.

He was anxious to impress this knowledge upon Billy as they voyaged through a very pleasant country, great trees hanging over the canal, sweeping green pastures visible between them, red and white cows browsing on the rich grass lands. Billy was mildly putting the point that one canal boat was as like another canal boat as one crow was like another crow or one Chinaman like another Chinaman. Tut-tut! The Boss would not—could not—hear of it. The comparison, as Billy put it slyly for the Boss, "didn't hold water." Canal boats, to the intelligence of the Boss, were full of individuality "as young hares"—it was Billy again who suggested the comparison. The Boss went on talking of canal boats with an intimacy and lack of humour which made of them human things. Calcutta listened, hanging over a pile of soap boxes, and having yawned went back to his vigil by the funnel, his smouldering eyes showing their eternal gleam of ugly hatred, watchfulness, as they became fastened on Hike, who stumbled and prayed on the bank.

The Boss had reached the topic of the ages of boats when

he hit on the affair of the Derelict. Had Billy the Clown ever heard of the Derelict? Billy the Clown had never heard of the Derelict. What was more, Billy the Clown declared he had no interest whatever in derelicts, in old ruins, tomb-stones, fairy raths, or mummies. He did not care if he never saw another Round Tower.

"The Derelict is not a boat," broke in the Boss. "It is a man."

"A live man?" Billy asked cautiously.

"Yes, a live man." The Boss swung the rudder a little to one side. "He's alive yet, too. He was the first Boss of *The Golden Barque*, and the reason I drew him down was because we're coming to his place and you'll be apt to see him."

They went on quietly for some time, the bubble of the water sounding pleasantly on the timbers of *The Golden Barque*, the country growing more and more serene, the banks given up to the quacking of little parties of white and fawn ducks. The Boss went on talking after a little while, but his voice had such a pleasant drone, and Billy felt so sure that what he talked about no more mattered than the bubble of the water at the prow of the boat, that he did not really break the beautiful peace, the exquisite sense of idleness of the whole place. He was speaking for quite a long time before Billy became conscious that he had worked his way back again to the ages of canal boats.

No, he was saying, *The Golden Barque* was a youthful thing compared to certain other old trick-o'-the-loops to be met with. Why did the Boss say that? He raised his fat hand as he put the question. He had his proof of it. The Boss brought down his fat hand with a clinch on the shaft of the tiller when he said he had his proof of it. He was always bringing forth great proofs of unimportant things, always clinching points that did not matter. But as he went on references to the Derelict became more and more frequent. Billy gathered, after a long time, after he had dropped off and leisurely caught him up again, that the Derelict was a name put upon one James Vasey, that James Vasey was the first man to put the nose of *The Golden Barque* to the water, and that as James Vasey was still a living if an old man, that, therefore, *The Golden Barque* could not possibly be as old as people might very well take her to be.

James Vasey—or the Derelict—was not always an old man no more than anybody else, the Boss insisted. There was a time when he was a young man, as young as anybody else if it went to that. Why did the Boss say that? The fat hand went up. When the Boss brought down the fat hand on the tiller a drake with a rich green and white head, a sheen of gold glinting over it, stood up on the bank, spread out his wings and shouted out shamelessly that he was as good a drake as any other drake that had ever led a line of ducks up the canal.

The Boss, ignoring him, brought forward his proof that the Derelict was once as young as anybody else; the weight of evidence in support of this stupendous assertion lay in the fact that once upon a time from the deck of that boat, from the very spot where the Boss had now planted his flat feet, James Vasey, the Derelict, had cast amorous eyes upon a young girl with a rich bloom on her cheeks. Not alone that, but *The Golden Barque* had been known to lie with her bow to the bank waiting patiently for James Vasey, the Derelict, who had risked his position as Boss of the boat by drawing her up there and bidding the men shut their mouths while he went in pursuit of a young female up a bohreen. If the Derelict was not as young as anybody else, how could he do a thing like that? And why did the Boss say the Derelict had gone up a bohreen after a young girl? He said it because he had proof of it. That proof lay not alone in the existence of James Vasey, the Derelict, but in the continued existence of the bohreen, or laneway, up which he had taken eager strides in auld lang syne. What was more, that very day that was in it the Boss would point out with his own hand the very and the identical bohreen up which the Derelict had coursed the time the hot fancy took him for the panting young female. And why did he say he could point it out with his own hand? Because—

And the Boss went on with his interminable proofs about nothing; a group of geese on the bank suddenly broke into a hearty quack of laughter which was taken up by other groups along the canal until the whole waterway was ringing with it.

They came to the romantic bohreen in the course of the day. The Boss came up the deck of the boat on his flat web-like feet to point it out to Billy. Nothing in the shape of a vehicle had passed through that bohreen, or by-road, for years. It was covered with scutch-grass, briars, dock leaves, nettles, Robin-run-the-hedge. Over this hearty growth the hedges each side had struggled until they had caught hands, embraced, hugged each other, became one tangle of shoots and leaves. It was more like a jungle than a bohreen. As luck would have it, out of this jungle an old man came prowling as the boat passed. The grizzled, long, lined face, the wisps of shaggy hair about the jaws, the head that hung level between the drooping shoulders, the small, sharp eyes, a certain furtiveness in their expression, the claw-like, nervous hands, gave him an entirely animal appearance. There was a crackling of brambles as he emerged from his den.

"Good morrow, James," the Boss sang out.

"Good morrow, Martin," the old man answered. He trembled with ague as he followed the boat on the bank, hobbling along like one who was accustomed to and took pleasure in a difficult effort.

"What way is the health, James?"

"I'd be right enough only the compression on the chest. It takes the wind from me in the night." He wheezed as he spoke.

"Well, keep the heart up. It is the heart that tells at the last."

"The heart is very sound with me, Martin. Did you see any trace of a *puckhaun* as you came along?"

"No, sorra trace, James. Are you missing the goat?"

"I am. He's a devil. My melt is broke striving for to keep him within bounds. A fortune he is costing me in ropes. Buck-leaping this way and that, until I pray to the Lord that he might brain himself against the ditch. I don't know where to turn for him now, for the four quarters of the world are forninst me."

The boat was gone by, the old institution not able to keep up any longer, his claw up to his wheezing chest. Further conversation was not possible. Billy could not help looking back at the old figure of the man on the bank, his gaze wandering helplessly about. Billy found it hard to imagine him as commander—the first commander—of *The Golden Barque*. But as a Derelict he was complete and magnificent.

"He has no interest in the canal now," Billy said to the Boss. "His mind is given up to the lost *puckhaun*."

"Don't think that," the Boss said. "That old fellow could not live a mile from the canal. He's down every day to see the boats going by. The life has a hold of him yet, and it will keep him until they put the band of death about his jaw."

They went on for some time in silence. The figure of the old man hobbling on the bank grew fainter. The Boss began to moralise. "Mind you," he said, "the canal has a call. The old soldier has a taste for the barracks, the farmer has nature for the fields, and the sailor can converse with the winds. That old fellow, James Vasey, has the same love for the canal as the water rat hid in the rushes."

The Boss began to hum in his monotonous voice as he fondled the shaft of the tiller, the same shaft that James Vasey had fondled years gone by.

"Did you take stock of that little house beside the bohreen?" he asked after a time.

Billy told the Boss it was almost his trade to take stock. He remembered the house as a little wreck of a place, roofless, the shoulder of the doorway that survived blackened, two square window spaces gaping beside it like eye cavities in the head of a skull.

But the Boss had another memory of it. His description was laboured. All the same he made a picture of it in time. Billy began to see the thatch on the roof, the smoke coming out of the chimney, the panes of glass shining in the windows, neat, white screens behind them; some order in the front, even a sanded path, and roses clustering about the doorway. The figure of a young girl busying herself about the house, trim and alert, followed; then the manner in which James Vasey began to follow her movements, to make note of her charms, and to throw sheep's eyes from the deck of *The Golden Barque*. It culminated in the pulling up of the boat and the scandal given to the crew by the chasing of the young girl up the bohreen. But James Vasey's enterprise prospered. The young girl liked the way he adventured, and she smiled on his advances.

The Boss liked to dwell on the subsequent developments. As he did so he more and more fell into the love tradition of the novelette. He closed his case with a "lived happy ever after" ring in his voice.

But Billy the Clown was left with the impression that the thing worth telling in James Vasey's life remained untouched. An under-current of contempt for the hero of the romance now and again betrayed itself in the manner of the Boss. While he was squeezing the first commander of *The Golden Barque* into an affair of rose and water he could not altogether help remembering him for something else. With pressure it came out in bits and scraps. Let us put them together.

The married life of James Vasey was the married life of all boatmen. He turned up at home when he could. He had a great joy in the little home beside the canal. The parents of the girl whom he had married died in course of time, leaving the place to James Vasey. A son and a daughter were born to him. The son went away to Liverpool and never returned. It was said of him that he turned out a bad lot. The daughter went to America. She kept in touch with the homeland. They had letters from her frequently. They expressed a crude but sincere affection for the parents. It was a lonely life that the old people dragged out in the home by the bohreen. This loneliness fell more heavily on the mother, for James Vasey had the distraction of his life and work on the canal.

It was, however, a great shock and a great change to him when his wife died after a few weeks' illness. James Vasey wrote to his daughter in America announcing the death of her mother. The memory of the lonely old man no doubt moved the girl, and she returned to Ireland. She brought some money with her. With it they were able to secure a little land and a little stock. The daughter was a good woman, a capable manager, and they were able to live in certain comfort. When the time came that James Vasey left *The Golden Barque* for ever, unable for further work, they had the little place to fall back upon. It was then he came to be known to his former fellow-voyagers as the Derelict.

It was the opinion of the Boss that the Derelict had always been a miser. His manner of securing tobacco and other little luxuries in life at the expense of other boatmen was cited as proof of this. It may be true, but it was also true that James Vasey had no opportunity of amassing wealth. His profession did not permit of it. But his passion for loans of tobacco, together with his failure to keep up his individual end of the expense of enjoyments in *The Haven*, had made him unpopular among the democracy of the canal.

He had actually scraped together a sum of ten pounds. The knowledge of this he had kept secret even from his own daughter. As he grew older, we may take it that he handled the money with twitching hands, a cackle in the old voice; that he fondled and doted over it in secret like the theatrical old man in "Les Cloches de Corneville." If he did not rise to that dramatic enthusiasm, we may take the more homely view that he tied it in the corner of an old stocking, hiding it away in various places like a cat with a kitten. He would probably die with it under his pillow, obsessed with his secret, fighting death at the last in defence of his hoard—only for what happened.

It was a night in early winter. The foliage had fallen from the trees, the wind swept the leaves in a heap in the bohreen. They made a stir there like impatient souls that wanted to be at rest. The canal gave an air of chilliness to the landscape, the desolation of the bog-land to the west looked like an open wound in the side of the country. The dismal note of a curlew overhead was like a voice from some suffering land. A drooping shoot of a rambler-rose fell over from the porch and made a constant swaying beside one of the windows of the Derelict's home. All was silence within. It was his custom, and the custom of his daughter, to go early to bed and to be early about. The hours of the night went by in a great peace, save for a dull glow by the kitchen hearth that stealthily made its way to the brown heap of sods by the wall.

At this time the Derelict was troubled with the first stages of his asthma. The "compression on his chest" made his sleep restless as the early dawn approached. He became troubled with his cough. It persisted, until at last it robbed him of his sleep. He drew his old frame up in the bed, pushing his shoulders up on the pillows, and barked for some time. He grew conscious that the atmosphere was heavy, that it was difficult for him to get his breath.

"Sara," he called out to his daughter. There was no response.

The air became more stifling. He struggled out of the bed, and it took him some time, for his thin legs were stiff and reluctant. He called his daughter's name again. He grumbled when she did not answer. Like all hard workers, Sara Vasey slept soundly. There was no sign of her stirring in the little room at the other end of the house.

The Derelict struggled to the door leading to the intervening kitchen and opened it. The place was filled with smoke, heavy, pungent smoke. Through it a wisp of light descended from the roof to the floor, shedding some sparks when it struck the ground. He stood looking at it for some time stupidly. Then a crackle over the chimney and another drift of sparks caught his eyes. He gave a little cry, turned back, groped for his clothes, and went out into the kitchen. A noise with ominous little cracks and snaps grew in volume until it made a dull hum, as he made for the front door and passed out through the porch.

A cutting wind passed him and filled the kitchen, and he saw flames driven across the rafters. He drew on some of his clothes, his gums hammering against each other, his hands trembling. He was grumbling and crying as he hobbled around to the window of his daughter's room. He cracked his knuckles on the glass.

"Sara!" he cried. A spurt of flame ate its way through the thatch above him, and he drew back with a cry.

Then his daughter came rushing out of the porch in her night-dress, calling on his name.

"Father!" she called out, "are you safe?" She rushed at him, hugging him in her arms hysterically, holding him in her arms protectingly from this calamity that had suddenly overtaken them in the quiet of the winter's night. It was while his daughter held him in her arms, and that he gazed in fear over her shoulder at the burning house, that the mind of the Derelict jumped back to the memory of his money.

"Sara," he said, "I'm safe and you are safe."

"Thank God, thank God," she cried, her teeth chattering, her eyes on the flames licking the thatch.

"But I left something behind me, daughter." He drew back from her embrace. He began to wring his hands. "I'm lost, I'm surely lost if I don't get the little stock of money."

"The stock of money?" She had never heard of it until now.

"Yes, daughter. I had a little bit put by. It is in the tin trunk under the bed."

"Oh father!"

"I thought that maybe you might reach it. You are active on the limbs, Sara. Save that much for me."

"But look at the smoke, the flames. I stumbled in the kitchen coming out. It was like a dead weight pressing me down."

"Sara, before it is too late. My God, my little store of money! What matter is anything else!"

"Let us call the neighbours. Maybe something could be done."

"The neighbours!" the old man exclaimed, looking about him with sudden fear. Then he turned on his daughter, resentment in his voice. "Is it to bring Tom Nolan to this place and tell him of my money? Damnation! Oh, I'll go in myself."

He made some steps towards the house, whining in a low voice.

"Father, don't attempt to go in. You will be burned," the girl said, going to his side.

"Oh, my God!" he cried, "the flames are making for the room. It is designedly. Look at the wind blowing them along the straw. My little money will be lost . . . I minded it well all the years. . . . Sara, don't give it to say you let it be destroyed before my eyes . . . Do as I bid you!" A note of command, hardness, crept into his voice. The girl drew back from him.

"Do you hear me?" he shouted. His voice changed to one of sudden desperation. She only shrank the further from him. He hobbled after her. She made an effort to avoid him. He clutched her night-dress, then buried his hard fingers in the flesh of her arms.

"Damn you," he cried, "I will make you do my liking. Don't you see the way the flames are making for the room?"

She clung about his neck. His breathing was hard, his eyes riveted upon the burning thatch as his face hung over her shoulder.

"Let it go, father. It can't be saved now. I did not know you had it."

The words only stung the Derelict to new fury. A glowering, wolfish look came into his eyes. He pushed the clinging girl back from him. "Let the lock of money go, is it?" he shouted. "Is that the respect you have for my earnings? In with you and bring it out to me."

"Later on, father."

"Later on! The house will be burned to the floor. I will be a ruined man for ever."

"It will be saved in the trunk."

"It can't . . . It is in notes: fine crisp notes that I know the feel of in my hands. . . . I could tell them in the darkness of the night. They were as known to me as the nails on my fingers."

His voice had risen to a hoarse cackle. He pushed the girl before him as he spoke. She clasped her hands in despair, then turned to break away from him.

He lurched after her. A strand of her loose hair flew behind her as she went. This he clutched, and she shrieked, bending her knees as the pressure from the hair brought her to a stop. When he laid his hands on the girl's arms again she was sobbing. They were on the verge of the smoke that enveloped the house in dense vapour. He pushed her forward, and they were two vague figures struggling in the smoke. A flock of wild birds wheeled overhead, crying in their strange voices, then vanished into the night.

"Father, for pity's sake! You are foolish, mad." The girl appealed to him.

"My little stock of money!" he cried. He gave her a drive

in front of him. She stumbled against the porch of the house. A blast of wind sent the smoke from about them in long, sinuous streaks, clearing a space. In that space he saw for a moment the white figure of his daughter, her face ghastly in the vivid yellow glare from the house. He thought he caught a look of defiance, scorn, hatred, in her eyes. She made a quick movement, and he concluded that she was about to escape him. He raised an angry arm, his fist closed.

"By God Almighty!" he shouted. The fist remained above his head for a moment, then fell to his side, for the white figure had vanished through the porch to the house.

He stood there, mumbling and shivering, his eyes still wolfish. The noise of a crackling beam inside made him limp away, whining. He cleared the smoke, then turned back to the house with a cry.

"Sara!" he called, "what is delaying you? Come on quick with the money. The flames will be upon it."

There was no reply. He limped around to the window of the room, his suspenders streeling behind him, his trousers hanging about his quivering, crooked, half-naked limbs, a human Derelict against a background of flames that were thick enough for hell.

"Sara!" he shouted at the window. He pushed his ashen-lined face close to the glass. He had a confused sense of a clouded interior with struggling shafts of flame through it. He burst in the little window. A rush of thick smoke struck him in the eyes, filled his mouth. He drew back, gasping.

"God, it will kill me," he cried. "What is delaying her at all? Has she put her hands to my money?"

With a new horror in his mind, he struggled back to the window. As he did so he heard, above the low boom in the house, the sharp noise of the tin trunk being drawn across the floor. He gave a little triumphant cry. "Blessings on you, girl," he cried. He clapped his thin hands, staggering about in the smoke in a weird movement that was a tragical parody of a dance of delight. The tears were streaming down his face. "Sara," he said, "you were always the good daughter. There was never one like you; for goodness and for bravery you were the best. Your mother in Heaven is directing you this night. May every blessing be showered upon you—for you are the one that will save my little store of money."

A cry that was half a scream, half a moan, broke from the

house. He stood stupefied for a while, then staggered to the window. He saw a figure vaguely inside, then a hand made a blind drive at the window. He was alert in a moment. He knew the hand was trying to push the notes to him through the window. He raised his arm and made a grab, but the hand inside never reached beyond the inner ledge of the window. It scraped along the wall and vanished. There was a thud of a body falling in a dead fleshy weight and then a sudden touch of light made the whole place jump to his gaze, vivid as a horrible nightmare. He shrieked, clawing the wall of the window with his hands, his nails tearing the hot mortar from the stones.

"Sara!" he cried. "Give me the money. What is wrong with you? Hell to your soul, give out my money. Look at them leaping upon the bed like devils. What has come over you at all?"

He was still clawing the wall when footsteps came running to the house. He felt a hand on his shoulder and, turning round, saw Tom Nolan, his next neighbour.

"James, what on God's earth has happened?"

"My place is in a blaze. I am destroyed, Tom. The world will have pity for me."

"Where is Sara?"

"She's within in the room, Tom. I was striving to direct her. What way will I be at all after this? I'll be destroyed for ever."

Tom Nolan did not wait for any more. He went through the door. The old man limped after him, paused at the porch, passed it, mumbling, whining.

"Tom," he said, "wait for me. I'll be with you now." He made little circles in front of the porch, hobbling on his old limbs, his hands pulling the streeling trousers up upon them. But he never ventured any further. Tom Nolan staggered through the porch, a white burden in his arms.

"James!" he shouted, "I found her lying under the window."

The old man followed him as he brought the girl beyond the range of the smoke and heat, then suddenly fell upon the limp figure. He took up one of the dangling arms, running his quivering fingers along it until he reached the hand. The hand was open and empty. The old man dropped it with a low wail. Tom Nolan left the inert figure of the girl on the grass. She looked black and terrible, some of her half-burned nightgown still smoking, in the light that was now breaking over the eastern sky. The old man pounced upon the other arm; it was blackened down from the elbow.

"I'm afraid, James, she's burned," Tom Nolan said.

But James Vasey, the Derelict, was not listening. He turned up the scorched hand. The fist was tightly closed. He endeavoured to open it, falling on his knees beside the figure of the girl.

"Let out of it, you bitch!" the old man shouted. He got his bony knuckles between the fingers of the closed fist and screwed them about, his eyes blazing, his gums beginning to hammer together again, a dribble falling from between his lips, his whole face twitching as it leered over the helpless figure. The neighbour who saw that sight at the dawn was too stupefied to speak.

At last the fist was forced open. A little crisp ashes, with no semblance to the original paper notes, lay in the palm. They jumped up when the pressure upon them was released. A vagrant wind blew them from the girl's hand along the wet grass. The Derelict knew, in spite of his delirium, what had happened. He knew that there were only two five pound notes in the tin box, and he knew that they had been burned while the girl endeavoured to pass them to him through the window. His old frame quivered, he moaned like one in mortal pain, he rose from the ground beating his hands together, the sweat streaming all over his face. Then with a shout he fell on his face on the ground, his hands blindly tearing at the ashes of the lost treasure, his furious drives burying it in the red clay of the earth, the figure of the girl lying all the time quietly in the shining grass.

\* \* \* \* \*

Sara Vasey recovered, but went about for the rest of her life with a right arm useless from the elbow down. The Derelict, her father, also recovered. Everything in the house by the canal was lost. Tom Nolan gave them all the shelter they needed until they were able to re-arrange their manner of life. The people, however, noted a great strangeness in the manner of Sara Vasey. She was given to brooding, silence, sudden and—to her neighbours—unaccountable bursts of hysterical weeping—and avoided her father as much as possible.

When the affairs of the little farm and a new cottage were set to rights she bought her ticket back to America. She went suddenly, quietly, without any send-off or leave-taking. The Derelict did not know she was going. One morning when he wakened up he found himself alone in the house.

The neighbours said Sara Vasey was an unnatural daughter.

\* \* \* \* \*

When Billy the Clown heard this story of the Derelict—in different words—from the Boss he had a vivid memory of the old animal who had come prowling out of his jungle, his mind troubled over the loss of his goat.

"Who christened him the Derelict?" Billy asked.

"Calcutta," the Boss replied.

Billy looked at the figure of Calcutta, black and slender and sinister, against the pale light of the sky. Billy walked up to him.

"Shake," he said, putting out his hand.

Calcutta, a little bewildered, shook, then his head swung round the funnel, his dull eyes bent on Hike, and Billy noted the tobacco spit which sang like a bullet in the direction of the hunched driver.

# Seumas O'Kelly

## Both Sides of the Pond

### I

Mrs. Donohoe marked the clearness of the sky, the number and brightness of the stars.

"There will be a share of frost to-night, Denis," she said.

Denis Donohoe, her son, adjusted a primitive bolt on the stable door, then sniffed at the air, his broad nostrils quivering sensitively as he raised his head.

"There is ice in the wind," he said.

"Make a start with the turf to the market to-morrow," his mother advised. "People in town will be wanting fires now."

Denis Donohoe walked over to the dim stack of brown turf piled at the back of the stable. It was there since the early fall, the dry earth cut from the bog, the turf that would make bright and pleasant fires in the open grates of Connacht for the winter months. Away from it spread the level bogland, a sweep of country that had, they said, in the infancy of the earth been a great oak forest, across which in later times had roved packs of hungry wolves, and which could at this day claim the most primitive form of industry in Western Europe. Out into this bogland in the summer had come from their cabins the peasantry, men and women, Denis Donohoe among them; they had dug up slices of the spongy, wet sod, cut it into pieces rather larger than bricks, licked it into shape by stamping upon it with their bare feet, stacked it about in little rows to dry in the sun, one sod leaning against the other, looking in the moonlight like a great host of wee brown fairies grouped in couples for a midnight dance in the carpet of purple heather. Now the time had come to convert it into such money as it would fetch.

Denis Donohoe whistled merrily that night as he piled the donkey cart, or "creel," with the sods of turf. Long before daybreak next morning he was about, his movements quick like one who had great business on his hands. The kitchen of the cabin was illuminated by a rushlight, the rays of which did not go much beyond a small deal table, scrubbed white, where he sat at his breakfast, an unusually good repast, for he had tea, homemade bread and a boiled egg. His mother moved about the dim kitchen, waiting on him, her bare feet almost noiseless on the black earthen floor. He ate heartily and silently, making the Sign of the Cross when he had finished. His mother followed him out on the dark road to bid him good luck, standing beside the creel of turf.

"There should be a brisk demand now that the winter is upon us," she said hopefully. "God be with you."

"God and Mary be with you, mother," Denis Donohoe made answer as he took the donkey by the head and led him along the dark road. The little animal drew his burden very slowly, the cart creaking and rocking noisily over the uneven road. Now and then Denis Donohoe spoke to him encouragingly, softly, his gaze at the same time going to the east, searching the blank sky for a hint of the dawn to come.

But they had gone rocking and swaying along the winding road for a long time before the day dawned. Denis Donohoe marked the spread of the light, the slow looming up of a range of hills, the sweep of brown patches of bog, then grey and green fields, broken by the glimmer of blue lakes, slopes of brown furze making for them a dull frame.

"Now that we have the blessed light we won't feel the journey at all," Denis Donohoe said to the donkey.

The ass drew the creel of turf more briskly, shook his winkers and swished his tail. When they struck very sharp hills Denis Donohoe got to the back of the cart, put his hands to the shafts, and, lowering his head, helped to push up the load, the muscles springing taut at the back of his thick limbs as he pressed hard against the bright frosty ground.

As they came down from the hills he already felt very hungry, his fingers tenderly fondling the slices of oaten bread he had put away in the pocket of his grey homespun coat. But he checked the impulse to eat, the long jaw of his swarthy face set, his strong teeth tight together awaiting the right hour to play their eager part. If he ate all the oaten bread now—splendid, dry, hard stuff, made of oat meal and water, baked on a gridiron—it would leave too long a fast afterwards. Denis Donohoe had been brought up to practise caution in these matters, to subject his stomach to a rigorous discipline, for life on the verge of a bog is an exacting business. Instead of obeying the impulse to eat Denis Donohoe blew warm breaths into his purple hands, beat his arms about his body to deaden the bitter cold, whistled, took some steps of an odd dance along the road, and went on talking to the donkey as if he were making pleasant conversation to a companion. The only sign of life to be seen on earth or air was a thin line of wild duck high up in the sky, one group making wide circles over a vivid mountain lake.

Half way on his journey to the country town Denis Donohoe pulled up his little establishment. It was outside a lonely cottage exactly like his own home. There was the same brown thatch on the roof, a garland of verdant wild creepers drooping from a spot at the gable, the same two small windows without any sashes in the front wall, the same narrow rutty pathway from the road, the same sort of yellow hen cackling heatedly, her legs quivering as she clutched the drab half door, the same scent of decayed cabbage leaves in the air. Denis Donohoe took a sack of hay from the top of the creel of turf, and spread some of it on the side of the road for the donkey. While he did so a woman who wore a white cap, a grey bodice, a thick woollen red petticoat, under which her bare lean legs showed, came to the door, waving the yellow hen off her perch.

"Good day to you, Mrs. Deely," Denis Donohoe said, showing his strong teeth.

"Welcome, Denis. Won't you step in and warm yourself at the fire, for the day is sharp, and you are early on the road?"

Denis Donohoe sat with the woman by the fire for some time, their exchange of family gossip quiet and agreeable. The young man was, however, uneasy, glancing about the house now and then like one who missed something. The woman, dropping her calm eyes on him, divined his thoughts.

"Agnes is not about," she said. "She started off for the Cappa Post Office an hour gone, for we had tidings that a letter is there for us from Sydney."

"A letter from her sister?"

"Yes. Mary is married there and doing well."

Denis Donohoe resumed his journey.

At the appointed spot he ravenously devoured the oaten bread, then stretched himself on his stomach on the ground and took some draughts of water from a roadside stream, drawing it up with a slow sucking noise, his teeth chattering, his eyes on the bright pebbles that glittered between some green cress at the bottom. When he had finished the donkey also laved his thirst at the spot.

He reached the market town while it was yet morning. He led the creel of turf through the straggling streets, where some people with the sleep in their eyes were moving about. The only sound he made was a low word of encouragement to the donkey.

"How much for the creel?" a man asked, standing at his shop door.

"Six shilling," Denis Donohoe replied, and waited, for it was above the business of a decent turf-seller to praise his wares or press for a sale.

"Good luck to you, son," said the merchant, "I hope you'll get it." He smiled, folded his hands one over the other, and retired to his shop.

Denis Donohoe moved on, saying in an undertone to the donkey, "Gee-up, Patsy. That old fellow is no good."

There were other inquiries, but nobody purchased. They said that money was very scarce. Denis Donohoe said nothing; money was too remote a thing for him to imagine how it could be ever anything else except scarce. He grew tired of going up and down past shops where there was no sign of business, so he drew the side streets and laneways, places where children screamed about the road, where there was a scent of soapy water, where women came to their doors and looked at him with eyes that expressed a slow resentment, their arms bare above the elbows, their hair hanging dankly about their ears, their voices, when they spoke, monotonous, and always sounding a note of tired complaint.

On the rise of a little bridge Denis Donohoe met a red-haired woman, a family of children skirmishing about her; there was a battle light in her wolfish eyes, her idle hands were folded over her stomach.

"How much, gossoon?" she asked.

"Six shilling."

"Six devils!" She walked over to the creel, handling some of the sods of turf. Denis Donohoe knew she was searching a constitutionally abusive mind for some word contemptuous of his wares. She found it at last, for she smacked her lips. It was in the Gaelic. "*Spairteach!*" she cried—a word that was eloquent of bad turf, stuff dug from the first layer of the bog, a mere covering for the correct vein beneath it.

"It's good stone turf," Denis Donohoe protested, a little nettled.

The woman was joined by some people who were hanging about, anxious to take part in bargaining which involved no personal liability. They argued, made jokes, shouted, and finally began to bully Denis Donohoe, the woman leading, her voice half a scream, her stomach heaving, her eyes dancing with excitement, a yellow froth gathering at the corners of her angry mouth, her hand gripping a sod of the turf, for the only dissipation life now offered her was this haggling with and shouting down of turf sellers. Denis Donohoe stood immovable beside his cart, patient as his donkey, his swarthy face stolid under the shadow of his broad-brimmed black hat, his intelligent eyes quietly measuring his noisy antagonists. When the woman's anger had quite spent itself the turf was purchased for five shillings.

Denis Donohoe carried the sods in his arms to the kitchen of the purchaser's house. It entailed a great many journeys in and out, the sods being piled up on his hooked left arm with a certain skill. His route lay through a small shop, down a semi-dark hallway, across a kitchen, the sods being stowed under a stairway where cockroaches scampered from the thudding of the falling sods.

Women were moving about the kitchen, talking incessantly, fumbling about tables, always appearing to search for something that had been lost, one crooning over a cradle that she rocked before the fire. The smell of cooking, the sound of something fatty hissing on a pan, brought a sense of faintness to Denis Donohoe, for he was ravenously hungry again.

He stumbled awkwardly in and out of the place with his armfuls of brown sods. The women moved with reluctance out of his way. Once a servant girl raised the most melancholy pair of wide brown eyes he had ever seen, saying to him, "It always goes through me to hear the turf falling in the stair-hole. It reminds me of the day I heard the clay falling on me father's coffin, God be with him and forgive him, for he died in the horrors."

By the time Denis Donohoe had delivered the cartload of

turf the little donkey had eaten all the hay in the sack. In the small shop Denis purchased some bacon, flour and tea, so that he had only some coppers to bring home with him. After some hesitation he handed back one penny for some biscuits, and these he ate as soon as he set out on the return journey.

The little donkey went over the road through the hills on the way back with spirit, for donkeys are good homers. Denis Donohoe sat up on the front of the cart, his legs dangling down beside the shaft. The donkey trotted down the slopes gayly, the harness rattling, the cart swaying, jolting, making an amazing noise.

The donkey cocked his ears, flecked his tail, even indulged in one or two buckjumps, as he rattled down the hilly roads. Denis Donohoe once or twice leaned out over the shaft, and brought his open hand down on the haunch of the donkey, but it was more a caress than a whack.

The light began to fade, the landscape to grow more obscure. Suddenly Denis Donohoe broke into song. They were going over a level stretch of ground. The donkey walked quietly. The quivering voice rang out over the darkening landscape, gaining in quality, and in steadiness, a clear light voice, the notes coming with the instinctive intonation, the perfect order of the born folk singer. It was some old Gaelic song, a refrain that had been preserved like the trunks of the primeval oaks in the bogs, such a refrain as might claim kinship with the Dresden *Amen*, sung by generations of German peasants until at last it reached the ears of Richard Wagner, giving birth to a classic. As he sang Denis Donohoe raised his swarthy face, his profile sharp against the pale sky, his eyes, half in rapture, like all folk singers, ranging over the hills, his long throat palpitating, swelling and slackening like the throat of a bird quivering in song. Then a light from the sashless windows of Mrs. Deely's cabin shone faintly and silence again brooded over the place. When he reached the cabin Denis Donohoe dismounted and walked into the kitchen, his eyes bright, his steps so eager that he became conscious of it and pulled up at once.

Mrs. Deely was sitting by the fire, her knitting needles busy. Denis Donohoe sat down beside her. While they were speaking a young girl came from the only room in the house, and, crossing the kitchen, stood beside the open fireplace.

"Agnes had great news from Australia from Mary," Mrs. Deely said. "She enclosed the price of the passage from this place to Sydney."

"I will be making the voyage the end of this month," the girl herself added.

There was an awkward silence, during which Mrs. Deely carefully piloted one of her needles through an intricate turn in the heel of the sock.

"Well, I wish you luck, Agnes," Denis Donohoe said at last, and then gave a queer odd little laugh, a little laugh that made Mrs. Deely regard him quickly and seriously. She noticed that he had his eyes fixed on the ground.

"It will be a great change from this place," the girl said, fingering something on the mantelpiece. "Mary says Sydney is a wonderful big city."

Denis Donohoe slowly lifted his eyes, taking in the shape of the girl from the bare feet to the bright ribbon that was tied in her hair. What he saw was a slim girl, her limbs showing faintly in the folds of a cheap, thin skirt, a loose, small shawl resting on the shoulders, her bosom heaving gently where the shawl did not meet, her profile delicate and faint in the light of the fire, her eyes, suddenly turned upon him, being the eyes of a girl conscious of his eyes, her low breath the sweet breath of a girl stepping into her womanhood.

"Well, God prosper you, Agnes Deely," Denis Donohoe said after some time, and rose from his seat.

The two women came out on the road to see him off. He did not dally, but jumped on to the front of the cart and rattled away.

Overhead the sky was winter clear, the stars merry, eternal, the whole heaven brilliant in its silent, stupendous song, its perpetual *Magnificat*; but Denis Donohoe made the rest of the journey in a black silence, gloom in the rigid figure, the stooping shoulders, the dangling legs; and the hills seemed to draw their grim shadows around his tragic ride to the lonely light in his mother's cabin on the verge of the dead brown bog.

II

There was a continuous clatter of conversation that rose and fell and broke like the waves on the beach; there was the dull shuffling of uneasy feet on the ground, the tinkling of glasses, the rattle of bottles, and over it all the half hysterical laugh of a tipsy woman. Above the racket a penetrating, quivering voice was raised in song.

Now and again bleary eyes were raised to the stage, shadowy in a fog of tobacco smoke. The figure on the boards strutted about, made some fantastic steps, the face pallid in the streaky light, the mouth scarlet as a tulip for a moment as it opened wide, the muscles about the lips wiry and distinct from much practice, the words of the song coming in a vehement nasal falsetto and in a brogue acquired in the Bowery. The white face of the man who accompanied the singer on the piano was raised for a moment in a tired gesture that was also a protest; in the eyes of the singer as they met those of the accompanist was an expression of cynical Celtic humour; in the smouldering gaze of the pianist was the patient, stubborn soul of the Slav. The look between these entertainers, one from Connacht the other from Poland, was a little act of mutual commiseration and a mutual expression of contempt for the noisy descendants of the Lost Tribes who made merry in the place.

A Cockney who had exchanged Houndsditch for the Bowery leered up broadly at the Celt prancing about the stage. He turned to the companion who sat drinking with him, a tall, bony half-caste, her black eyes dancing in a head that quivered from an ague acquired in Illinois.

"'E's all ryght, is Paddy," said the voice from Houndsditch. He pointed a thumb that was a certificate of villainy in the direction of the stage.

"Sure," said the coloured lady, whose ancestry rambled back away to Alabama. She looked up at the stage with her bold eyes.

"I know him," she said, thoughtfully.

"And I like him," she added grinning.

"We all like him. He's one of the boys."

"Wot price me?" said the Houndsditch man.

"Oh, you're good, too," said the coloured lady. "Blow in another cocktail, honey." She struck her breast where the uneasy bone showed through the dusky skin. "I've a fearful thirst right there."

Little puckers gathered about the small, humorous eyes of the Cockney as he looked at her. "My," he said, "you 'ave got a thirst and a capacity, Ole Sahara!"

The coloured lady raised the cocktail to her fat lips, and as she did so there was a sudden racket, men shouting, women clapping their hands, the voice of the tipsy woman dominant in its hysteria over the uproar. The singer was bowing profuse acknowledgments from the stage, his eyes, sly in their cynical humour, upon the face of the Slav at the piano, his head thrown back, the pallor of his face ghastly.

The lady from Alabama joined in the tribute to the singer.

"'Core, 'core," cried Ole Sahara, raising her glass in the dim vapour. "Here's to Denis Donohoe!"

# Seumas O'Kelly

## *The Weaver's Grave*

### I

Mortimer Hehir, the weaver, had died, and they had come in search of his grave to Cloon na Morav, the Meadow of the Dead. Meehaul Lynskey, the nail-maker, was first across the stile. There was excitement in his face. His long warped body moved in a shuffle over the ground. Following him came Cahir Bowes, the stone-breaker, who was so beaten down from the hips forward, that his back was horizontal as the back of an animal. His right hand held a stick which propped him up in front, his left hand clutched his coat behind, just above the small of the back. By these devices he kept himself from toppling head over heels as he walked. Mother earth was the brow of Cahir Bowes by magnetic force, and Cahir Bowes was resisting her fatal kiss to the last. And just now there was animation in the face he raised from its customary contemplation of the ground. Both old men had the air of those who had been unexpectedly let loose. For a long time they had lurked somewhere in the shadows of life, the world having no business for them, and now, suddenly, they had been remembered and called forth to perform an office which nobody else on earth could perform. The excitement in their faces as they crossed over the stile into Cloon na Morav expressed a vehemence in their belated usefulness. Hot on their heels came two dark, handsome, stoutly-built men, alike even to the cord that tied their corduroy trousers under their knees, and, being gravediggers, they carried flashing spades. Last of all, and after a little delay, a firm white hand was laid on the stile, a dark figure followed, the figure of a woman whose palely sad face was picturesquely, almost dramatically, framed in a black shawl which hung from the crown of the head. She was the widow of Mortimer Hehir, the weaver, and she followed the others into Cloon na Morav, the Meadow of the Dead.

To glance at Cloon na Morav as you went by on the hilly road, was to get an impression of a very old burial-ground; to pause on the road and look at Cloon na Morav was to become conscious of its quiet situation, of winds singing down from the hills in a chant for the dead; to walk over to the wall and look at the mounds inside was to provoke quotations from Gray's Elegy; to make the Sign of the Cross, lean over the wall, observe the gloomy lichened background of the wall opposite, and mark the things that seemed to stray about, like yellow snakes in the grass, was to think of Hamlet moralising at the graveside of Ophelia, and hear him establish the identity of Yorrick. To get over the stile and stumble about inside, was to forget all these things and to know Cloon na Morav for itself. Who could tell the age of Cloon na Morav? The mind could only swoon away into mythology, paddle about in the dotage of paganism, the toothless infancy of Christianity. How many generations, how many septs, how many clans, how many families, how many people, had gone into Cloon na Morav? The mind could only take wing on the romances of mathematics. The ground was billowy, grotesque. Several partially suppressed insurrections—a great thirsting, worming, pushing and shouldering under the sod— had given it character. A long tough growth of grass wired it from end to end, Nature, by this effort, endeavouring to control the strivings of the more daring of the insurgents of Cloon na Morav. No path here; no plan or map or register existed; if there ever had been one or the other it had been lost. Invasions and wars and famines and feuds had swept the ground and left it. All claims to interment had been based on powerful traditional rights. These rights had years ago come to an end—all save in a few outstanding cases, the rounding up of a spent generation. The overflow from Cloon na Morav had already set a new cemetery on its legs a mile away, a cemetery in which limestone headstones and Celtic crosses were springing up like mushrooms, advertising the triviality of a civilisation of men and women, who, according to their own epitaphs, had done exactly the two things they could not very well avoid doing: they had all, their obituary notices said, been born and they had all died. Obscure quotations from Scripture were sometimes added by way of apology. There was an almost unanimous expression of forgiveness to the Lord for what had happened to the deceased. None of this lack of humour in Cloon na Morav. Its monuments were comparatively few, and such of them as it had not swallowed were well within the general atmosphere. No obituary notice in the place was complete; all were either wholly or partially eaten up by the teeth of time. The monuments that had made a stout battle for existence were pathetic in their futility. The vanity of the fashionable of dim ages made one weep. Who on earth could have brought in the white marble slab to Cloon na Morav? It had grown green with shame. Perhaps the lettering, once readable upon it, had been conscientiously picked out in gold. The shrieking winds and the fierce rains of the hills alone could tell. Plain heavy stones, their shoulders rounded with a chisel, presumably to give them some off-handed resemblance to humanity, now swooned at fantastic angles from their settings, as if the people to whose memory they had been dedicated had shouldered them away as an impertinence. Other slabs lay in fragments on the ground, filling the mind with thoughts of Moses descending from Mount Sinai and, waxing angry at sight of his followers dancing about false gods, casting the stone tables containing the Commandments to the ground, breaking them in pieces—the most tragic destruction of a first edition that the world has known. Still other heavy square dark slabs, surely creatures of a pagan imagination, were laid flat down on numerous short legs, looking sometimes like representations of monstrous black cockroaches, and again like tables at which the guests of Cloon na Morav might sit down, goblin-like, in the moon-light, when nobody was looking. Most of the legs had given way and the tables lay overturned, as if there had been a quarrel at cards the night before. Those that had kept their legs exhibited great cracks or fissures across their backs, like slabs of dark ice breaking up. Over by the wall, draped in its pattern of dark green lichen, certain families of dim ages had made an effort to keep up the traditions of the Eastern sepulchres. They had showed an aristocratic reluctance to take to the common clay in Cloon na Morav. They had built low casket-shaped houses against the gloomy wall, putting an enormously heavy iron door with ponderous iron rings—like the rings on a pier by the sea at one end, a tremendous lock—one wondered what Goliath kept the key—finally cementing the whole thing up and surrounding it with spiked iron railings. In these contraptions very aristocratic families locked up their dead as if they were dangerous wild animals. But these ancient vanities only heightened the general democracy of the ground. To prove a traditional right to a place in its community was to have the bond of your pedigree sealed. The act of burial in Cloon na Morav was in itself an epitaph. And it was amazing to think that there were two people still over the sod who had such a right—one Mortimer Hehir, the weaver, just passed away, the other Malachi Roohan, a cooper, still breathing. When these two survivors of a great generation got tucked under the sward of Cloon na Morav its terrific history would, for all practical purposes, have ended.

II

Meehaul Lynskey, the nailer, hitched forward his bony shoulders and cast his eyes over the ground—eyes that were small and sharp, but unaccustomed to range over wide spaces. The width and the wealth of Cloon na Morav were baffling to him. He had spent his long life on the look-out for one small object so that he might hit it. The colour that he loved was the golden glowing end of a stick of burning iron; wherever he saw that he seized it in a small sconce at the end of a long handle, wrenched it off by a twitch of the wrist, hit it with a flat hammer several deft taps, dropped it into a vessel of water, out of which it came a cool and perfect nail. To do this thing several hundred times six days in the week, and pull the chain of a bellows at short intervals, Meehaul Lynskey had developed an extraordinary dexterity of sight and touch, a swiftness of business that no mortal man could exceed, and so long as he had been pitted against nail-makers of flesh and blood he had more than held his own; he had, indeed, even put up a tremendous but an unequal struggle against the competition of nail-making machinery. Accustomed as he was to concentrate on a single, glowing, definite object, the complexity and disorder of Cloon na Morav unnerved him. But he was not going to betray any of these professional defects to Cahir Bowes, the stonebreaker. He had been sent there as an ambassador by the caretaker of Cloon na Morav, picked out for his great age, his local knowledge, and his good character, and it was his business to point out to the twin gravediggers, sons of the caretaker, the weaver's grave, so that it might be opened to receive him. Meehaul Lynskey had a knowledge of the place, and was quite certain as to a great number of grave sites, while the caretaker, being an official without records, had a profound ignorance of the whole place.

Cahir Bowes followed the drifting figure of the nail-maker over the ground, his face hitched up between his shoulders, his eyes keen and gray, glint-like as the mountains of stones he had in his day broken up as road material. Cahir, no less than Meehaul, had his knowledge of Cloon na Morav and some of his own people were buried here. His sharp, clear eyes took in the various mounds with the eye of a prospector. He, too, had been sent there as an ambassador, and as between himself and Meehaul Lynskey he did not think there could be any two opinions; his knowledge was superior to the knowledge of the nailer. Whenever Cahir Bowes met a loose stone on the grass quite instinctively he turned it over with his stick, his sharp old eyes judging its grain with a professional swiftness, then cracking at it with his stick. If the stick were a hammer the stone, attacked on its most vulnerable spot, would fall to pieces like glass. In stones Cahir Bowes saw not sermons but seams. Even the headstones he tapped significantly with the ferrule of his stick, for Cahir Bowes had an artist's passion for his art, though his art was far from creative. He was one of the great destroyers, the reducers, the makers of chaos, a powerful and remorseless critic of the Stone Age.

The two old men wandered about Cloon na Morav, in no hurry whatever to get through with their business. After all they had been a long time pensioned off, forgotten, neglected, by the world. The renewed sensation of usefulness was precious to them. They knew that when this business was over they were not likely to be in request for anything in this world again. They were ready to oblige the world, but the world would have to allow them their own time. The world, made up of the two grave-diggers and the widow of the weaver, gathered all this without any vocal proclamation. Slowly, mechanically as it were, they followed the two ancients about Cloon na Morav. And the two ancients wandered about with the labour of age and the hearts of children. They separated, wandered about silently as if they were picking up old acquaintances, stumbling upon forgotten things, fathering up the threads of days that were over, reviving their memories, and then drew together, beginning to talk slowly, almost casually, and all their talk was of the dead, of the people who lay in the ground about them. They warmed to it, airing their knowledge, calling up names and complications of family relationships, telling stories, reviving all virtues, whispering at past vices, past vices that did not sound like vices at all, for the long years are great mitigators and run in splendid harness with the coyest of all the virtues, Charity. The whispered scandals of Cloon na Morav were seen by the twin gravediggers and the widow of the weaver through such a haze of antiquity that they were no longer scandals but romances. The rake and the drab, seen a good way down the avenue, merely look picturesque. The grave-diggers rested their spades in the ground, leaning on the handles in exactly the same graveyard pose, and the pale widow stood in the background, silent, apart, patient, and, like all dark, tragic looking women, a little mysterious.

The stonebreaker pointed with his quivering stick at the graves of the people whom he spoke about. Every time he raised that forward support one instinctively looked, anxious and fearful, to see if the clutch were secure on the small of the back. Cahir Bowes had the sort of shape that made one eternally fearful for his equilibrium. The nailer, who, like his friend the stonebreaker, wheezed a good deal, made short, sharp gestures, and always with the right hand; the fingers were hooked in such a way, and he shot out the arm in such a manner, that they gave the illusion that he held a hammer and that it was struck out over a very hot fire. Every time Meehaul Lynskey made this gesture one expected to see sparks flying.

"Where are we to bury the weaver?" one of the grave-diggers asked at last.

Both old men laboured around to see where the interruption, the impertinence, had come from. They looked from one twin to the other, with gravity, indeed anxiety, for they were not sure which was which, or if there was not some illusion in the resemblance, some trick of youth to baffle age.

"Where are we to bury the weaver?" the other twin repeated, and the strained look on the old men's faces deepened. They were trying to fix in their minds which of the twins had interrupted first and which last. The eyes of Meehaul Lynskey fixed on one twin with the instinct of his trade, while Cahir Bowes ranged both and eventually wandered to the figure of the widow in the background, silently accusing her of impatience in a matter which it would be indelicate for her to show haste.

"We can't stay here for ever," said the first twin.

It was the twin upon whom Meehaul Lynskey had fastened his small eyes, and, sure of his man this time, Meehaul Lynskey hit him.

"There's many a better man than you," said Meehaul Lynskey, "that will stay here for ever." He swept Cloon na Morav with the hooked fingers.

"Them that stays in Cloon na Morav for ever," said Cahir Bowes with a wheezing energy, "have nothing to be ashamed of—nothing to be ashamed of. Remember that, young fellow."

Meehaul Lynskey did not seem to like the intervention, the help, of Cahir Bowes. It was a sort of implication that he had not— he, mind you,—had not hit the nail properly on the head.

"Well, where are we to bury him, anyway?" said the twin, hoping to profit by the chagrin of the nailer—the nailer who, by implication, had failed to nail.

"You'll bury him," said Meehaul Lynskey, "where all belonging to him is buried."

"We come," said the other twin, "with some sort of intention of that kind." He drawled out the words, in imitation of the old men. The skin relaxed on his handsome dark face and then bunched in puckers of humour about the eyes; Meehaul Lynskey's gaze, wandering for once, went to the handsome dark face of the other twin and the skin relaxed and then bunched in puckers of humour about *his* eyes, so that Meehaul Lynskey had an unnerving sensation that these young grave-diggers were purposely confusing him.

"You'll bury him," he began with some vehemence, and was amazed to again find Cahir Bowes taking the words out of his mouth, snatching the hammer out of his hand, so to speak.

"—where you're told to bury him," Cahir Bowes finished for him.

Meehaul Lynskey was so hurt that his long slanting figure moved away down the graveyard, then stopped suddenly. He had determined to do a dreadful thing. He had determined to do a thing that was worse than kicking a crutch from under a cripple's shoulder; that was like stealing the holy water out of a room where a man lay dying. He had determined to ruin the last day's amusement on this earth for Cahir Bowes and himself by prematurely and basely disclosing the weaver's grave!

"Here," called back Meehaul Lynskey, "is the weaver's grave, and here you will bury him."

All moved down to the spot, Cahir Bowes going with extraordinary spirit, the ferrule of his terrible stick cracking on the stones he met on the way.

"Between these two mounds," said Meehaul Lynskey, and already the twins raised their twin spades in a sinister movement, like swords of lancers flashing at a drill.

"Between these two mounds," said Meehaul Lynskey, "is the grave of Mortimer Hehir."

"Hold on!" cried Cahir Bowes. He was so eager, so excited, that he struck one of the grave-diggers a whack of his stick on the back. Both grave-diggers swung about to him as if both had been hurt by the one blow.

"Easy there," said the first twin.

"Easy there," said the second twin.

"Easy yourselves," cried Cahir Bowes. He wheeled about his now quivering face on Meehaul Lynskey.

"What is it you're saying about the spot between the mounds?" he demanded.

"I'm saying," said Meehaul Lynskey vehemently, "that it's the weaver's grave."

"What weaver?" asked Cahir Bowes.

"Mortimer Hehir," replied Meehaul Lynskey. "There's no other weaver in it."

"Was Julia Rafferty a weaver?"

"What Julia Rafferty?"

"The midwife, God rest her."

"How could she be a weaver if she was a midwife?"

"Not a one of me knows. But I'll tell you what I do know and know rightly: that it's Julia Rafferty is in that place and no weaver at all."

"Amn't I telling you it's the weaver's grave?"

"And amn't I telling you it's not?"

"That I may be as dead as my father but the weaver was buried there."

"A bone of a weaver was never sunk in it as long as weavers was weavers. Full of Raffertys it is."

"Alive with weavers it is."

"Heavenly Father, was the like ever heard: to say that a grave was alive with dead weavers."

"It's full of them—full as a tick."

"And the clean grave that Mortimer Hehir was never done boasting about—dry and sweet and deep and no way bulging at all. Did you see the burial of his father ever?"

"I did, in troth, see the burial of his father—forty year ago if it's a day."

"Forty year ago—it's fifty-one year come the sixteenth of May. It's well I remember it and it's well I have occasion to remember it, for it was the day after that again that myself ran away to join the soldiers, my aunt hot foot after me, she to be buying me out the week after, I a high-spirited fellow morebetoken."

"Leave the soldiers out of it and leave your aunt out of it and stick to the weaver's grave. Here in this place was the last weaver buried, and I'll tell you what's more. In a straight line with it is the grave of—"

"A straight line, indeed! Who but yourself, Meehaul Lynskey, ever heard of a straight line in Cloon na Morav? No such thing was ever wanted or ever allowed in it."

"In a straight direct line, measured with a rule—"

"Measured with crooked, stumbling feet, maybe feet half reeling in drink."

"Can't you listen to me now?"

"I was always a bad warrant to listen to anything except sense. Yourself ought to be the last man in the world to talk about straight lines, you with the sight scattered in your head, with the divil of sparks flying under your eyes."

"Don't mind me sparks now, nor me sight neither, for in a straight measured line with the weaver's grave was the grave of the Cassidys."

"What Cassidys?"

"The Cassidys that herded for the O'Sheas."

"Which O'Sheas?"

"O'Shea Ruadh of Cappakelly. Don't you know anyone at all, or is it gone entirely your memory is?"

"Cappakelly *inagh*! And who cares a whistle about O'Shea Ruadh, he or his seed, breed and generations? It's a rotten lot of landgrabbers they were."

"Me hand to you on that. Striving ever they were to put their red paws on this bit of grass and that perch of meadow."

"Hungry in themselves even for the cutaway bog."

"And Mortimer Hehir a decent weaver, respecting every man's wool."

"His forehead pallid with honesty over the yarn and the loom."

"If a bit broad-spoken when he came to the door for a smoke of the pipe."

"Well, there won't be a mouthful of clay between himself and O'Shea Ruadh now."

"In the end what did O'Shea Ruadh get after all his striving?"

"I'll tell you that. He got what land suits a blind fiddler."

"Enough to pad the crown of the head and tap the sole of the foot! Now you're talking."

"And the devil a word out of him now no more than anyone else in Cloon na Morav."

"It's easy talking to us all about land when we're packed up in our timber boxes."

"As the weaver was when he got sprinkled with the holy water in that place."

"As Julia Rafferty was when they read the prayers over her in that place, she a fine, buxom, cheerful woman in her day, with great skill in her business."

"Skill or no skill, I'm telling you she's not there, wherever she is."

"I suppose you want me to take her up in my arms and show her to you?"

"Well then, indeed, Cahir, I do not. 'Tisn't a very handsome pair you would make at all, you not able to stand much more hardship than Julia herself."

From this there developed a slow, laboured, aged dispute between the two authorities. They moved from grave to grave, pitting memory against memory, story against story, knocking down reminiscence with reminiscence, arguing in a powerful intimate obscurity that no outsider could hope to follow, blasting knowledge with knowledge, until the whole place seemed strewn with the corpses of their arguments. The two gravediggers followed them about in a grim silence; impatience in their movements, their glances; the widow keeping track of the grand tour with a miserable feeling, a feeling, as site after site was rejected, that the tremendous exclusiveness of Cloon na Morav would altogether push her dead man, the weaver, out of his privilege. The dispute ended, like all epics, where it began. Nothing was established, nothing settled. But the two old men were quite exhausted, Meehaul Lynskey sitting down on the back of one of the monstrous cockroaches, Cahir Bowes leaning against a tombstone that was half-submerged, its end up like the stern of a derelict at sea. Here they sat glaring at each other like a pair of grim vultures.

The two grave-diggers grew restive. Their business had to be done. The weaver would have to be buried. Time pressed. They held a consultation apart. It broke up after a brief exchange of views, a little laughter.

"Meehaul Lynskey is right," said one of the twins.

Meehaul Lynskey's face lit up. Cahir Bowes looked as if he had been slapped on the cheeks. He moved out from his tombstone.

"Meehaul Lynskey is right," repeated the other twin. They had decided to break up the dispute by taking sides. They raised their spades and moved to the site which Meehaul Lynskey had urged upon them.

"Don't touch that place," Cahir Bowes cried, raising his stick. He was measuring the back of the grave-digger again when the man spun round upon him, menace in his handsome dark face.

"Touch me with that stick," he cried, "and I'll—"

Some movement in the background, some agitation in the widow's shawl, caused the grave-digger's menace to dissolve, the words to die in his mouth, a swift flush mounting the man's face. A faint smile of gratitude swept the widow's face like a flash. It was as if she had cried out, "Ah, don't touch the poor old, cranky fellow! you might hurt him." And it was as if the grave-digger had cried back: "He has annoyed me greatly, but I don't intend to hurt him. And since you say so with your eyes I won't even threaten him."

Under pressure of the half threat, Cahir Bowes shuffled back a little way, striking an attitude of feeble dignity, leaning on his stick while the grave-diggers got to work.

"It's the weaver's grave, surely," said Meehaul Lynskey.

"If it is, said Cahir Bowes, "remember his father was buried down seven feet. You gave in to that this morning."

"There was no giving in about it," said Meehaul Lynskey. "We all know that one of the wonders of Cloon na Morav was the burial of the last weaver seven feet, he having left it as an injunction on his family. The world knows he went down the seven feet."

"And remember this," said Cahir Bowes, "that Julia Rafferty was buried no seven feet. If she is down three feet it's as much as she went."

Sure enough, the grave-diggers had not dug down more than three feet of ground when one of the spades struck hollowly on unhealthy timber. The sound was unmistakable and ominous. There was silence for a moment. Then Cahir Bowes made a sudden short spurt up a mound beside him, as if he were some sort of mechanical animal wound up, his horizontal back quivering. On the mound he made a superhuman effort to straighten himself. He got his ears and his blunt nose into a considerable elevation. He had not been so upright for twenty years. And raising his weird countenance, he broke into a cackle that was certainly meant to be a crow. He glared at Meehaul Lynskey, his emotion so great that his eyes swam in a watery triumph.

Meehaul Lynskey had his eyes, as was his custom, upon one thing, and that thing was the grave, and especially the spot on the grave where the spade had struck the coffin. He looked stunned and fearful. His eyes slowly withdrew their gimlet-like scrutiny from the spot, and sought the triumphant crowing figure of Cahir Bowes on the mound.

Meehaul Lynskey looked as if he would like to say something, but no words came. Instead he ambled away, retired from the battle, and standing apart, rubbed one leg against the other, above the back of the ankles, like some great insect. His hooked fingers at the same time stroked the bridge of his nose. He was beaten.

"I suppose it's not the weaver's grave," said one of the grave-diggers. Both of them looked at Cahir Bowes.

"Well, you know it's not," said the stonebreaker. "It's Julia Rafferty you struck. She helped many a one into the world in her day, and it's poor recompense to her to say she can't be at rest when she left it." He turned to the remote figure of Meehaul Lynskey and cried: "Ah-ha, well you may rub your ignorant legs. And I'm hoping Julia will forgive you this day's ugly work."

In silence, quickly, with reverence, the twins scooped back the clay over the spot. The widow looked on with the same quiet, patient, mysterious silence. One of the grave-diggers turned on Cahir Bowes.

"I suppose you know where the weaver's grave is?" he asked.

Cahir Bowes looked at him with an ancient tartness, then said:

"You suppose!"

"Of course, you know where it is."

Cahir Bowes looked as if he knew where the gates of heaven were, and that he might—or might not—enlighten an ignorant world. It all depended! His eyes wandered knowingly out over the meadows beyond the graveyard. He said:

"I do know where the weaver's grave is."

"We'll be very much obliged to you if you show it to us."

"Very much obliged," endorsed the other twin.

The stonebreaker, thus flattered, led the way to a new site, one nearer to the wall, where were the plagiarisms of the Eastern sepulchres. Cahir Bowes made little journeys about, measuring so many steps from one place to another, mumbling strange and unintelligible information to himself, going through an extraordinary geometrical emotion, striking the ground hard taps with his stick.

"Glory be to the Lord," cried Meehaul Lynskey, "he's like the man they had driving the water for the well in the quarry field, he whacking the ground with his magic hazel wand."

Cahir Bowes made no reply. He was too absorbed in his own emotion. A little steam was beginning to ascend from his brow. He was moving about the ground like some grotesque spider weaving an invisible web.

"I suppose now," said Meehaul Lynskey, addressing the marble monument, "that as soon as Cahir hits the right spot one of the weavers will turn about below. Or maybe he expects one of them to whistle up at him out of the ground. That's it; devil a other! When we hear the whistle we'll all know for certain where to bury the weaver."

Cahir Bowes was contracting his movements, so that he was now circling about the one spot, like a dog going to lie down.

Meehaul Lynskey drew a little closer, watching eagerly, his grim yellow face, seared with yellow marks from the fires of his workshop, tightened up in a sceptical pucker. His half-muttered words were bitter with an aged sarcasm. He cried:

"Say nothing; he'll get it yet, will the man of knowledge, the know-all, Cahir Bowes! Give him time. Give him until this day twelve month. Look at that for a right-about-turn on the left heel. Isn't the nimbleness of that young fellow a treat to see? Are they whistling to you from below, Cahir? Is it dancing to the weaver's music you are? That's it, devil a other."

Cahir Bowes was mapping out a space on the grass with his stick. Gradually it took, more or less, the outline of a grave site. He took off his hat and mopped his steaming brow with a red handkerchief, saying:

"There is the weaver's grave."

"God in Heaven," cried Meehaul Lynskey, "will you look at what he calls the weaver's grave? I'll say nothing at all. I'll hold my tongue. I'll shut up. Not one word will I say about Alick Finlay, the mildest man that ever lived, a man full of religion, never at the end of his prayers! But, sure, it's the saints of God that get the worst of it in this world, and if Alick escaped during life, faith he's in for it now, with the pirates and the body-snatchers of Cloon na Morav on top of him."

A corncrake began to sing in the nearby meadow, and his rasping notes sounded like a queer accompaniment to the words of Meehaul Lynskey. The grave-diggers, who had gone to work on the Cahir Bowes site, laughed a little, one of them looking for a moment at Meehaul Lynskey, saying:

"Listen to that damned old corncrake in the meadow! I'd like to put a sod in his mouth."

The man's eye went to the widow. She showed no emotion one way or the other, and the grave-digger got back to his work. Meehaul Lynskey, however, wore the cap. He said:

"To be sure! I'm to sing dumb. I'm not to have a word out of me at all. Others can rattle away as they like in this place, as if they owned it. The ancient good old stock is to be nowhere and the scruff of the hills let rampage as they will. That's it, devil a other. Castles falling and dunghills rising! Well, God be with the good old times and the good old mannerly people that used to be in it, and God be with Alick Finlay, the holiest—"

A sod of earth came through the air from the direction of the grave, and, skimming Meehaul Lynskey's head, dropped somewhere behind. The corncrake stopped his notes in the meadow, and Meehaul Lynskey stood statuesque in a mute protest, and silence reigned in the place while the clay sang up in a swinging rhythm from the grave.

Cahir Bowes, watching the operations with intensity, said:
"It was nearly going astray on me."

Meehaul Lynskey gave a little snort. He asked:
"What was?"

"The weaver's grave."

"Remember this: the last weaver is down seven feet. And remember this: Alick Finlay is down less than Julia Rafferty."

He had no sooner spoken when a fearful thing happened.

Suddenly out of the soft cutting of the earth a spade sounded harsh on tinware, there was a crash, less harsh, but painfully distinct, as if rotten boards were falling together, then a distinct subsidence of the earth. The work stopped at once. A moment's fearful silence followed. It was broken by a short, dry laugh from Meehaul Lynskey. He said:

"God be merciful to us all! That's the latter end of Alick Finlay."

The two grave-diggers looked at each other. The shawl of the widow in the background was agitated. One twin said to the other:

"This can't be the weaver's grave."

The other agreed. They all turned their eyes upon Cahir Bowes. He was hanging forward in a pained strain, his head quaking, his fingers twitching on his stick. Meehaul Lynskey turned to the marble monument and said with venom:

"If I was guilty I'd go down on my knees and beg God's pardon. If I didn't I'd know the ghost of Alick Finlay, saint as he was, would leap upon me and guzzle me—for what right would I have to set anybody at him with driving spades when he was long years in his grave?"

Cahir Bowes took no notice. He was looking at the ground, searching about, and slowly, painfully, began his web-spinning again. The grave-diggers covered in the ground without a word. Cahir Bowes appeared to get lost in some fearful maze of his own making. A little whimper broke from him now and again. The steam from his brow thickened in the air, and eventually he settled down on the end of a head-stone, having got the worst of it. Meehaul Lynskey sat on another stone facing him, and they glared, sinister and grotesque, at each other.

"Cahir Bowes," said Meehaul Lynskey, "I'll tell you what you are, and then you can tell me what I am."

"Have it whatever way you like," said Cahir Bowes. "What is it that I am?"

"You're a gentleman, a grand oul' stonebreaking gentleman. That's what you are, devil a other!"

The wrinkles on the withered face of Cahir Bowes contracted, his eyes stared across at Meehaul Lynskey, and two yellow teeth showed between his lips. He wheezed:

"And do you know what you are?"

"I don't."

"You're a nailer, that's what you are, a damned nailer."

They glared at each other in a quaking, grim silence.

And it was at this moment of collapse, of deadlock, that the widow spoke for the first time. At the first sound of her voice one of the twins perked his head, his eyes going to her face. She said in a tone as quiet as her whole behaviour:

"Maybe I ought to go up to the Tunnel Road and ask Malachi Roohan where the grave is."

They had all forgotten the oldest man of them all, Malachi Roohan. He would be the last mortal man to enter Cloon na Morav. He had been the great friend of Mortimer Hehir, the weaver, in the days that were over, and the whole world knew that Mortimer Hehir's knowledge of Cloon na Morav was perfect. Maybe Malachi Roohan would have learned a great deal from him. And Malachi Roohan, the cooper, was so long bedridden that those who remembered him at all thought of him as a man who had died a long time ago.

"There's nothing else for it," said one of the twins, leaving down his spade, and immediately the other twin laid his spade beside it.

The two ancients on the headstones said nothing. Not even *they* could raise a voice against the possibilities of Malachi Roohan, the cooper. By their terrible aged silence they gave consent, and the widow turned to walk out of Cloon na Morav. One of the grave-diggers took out his pipe. The eyes of the other followed the widow, he hesitated, then walked after her. She became conscious of the man's step behind her as she got upon the stile, and turned her palely sad face upon him. He stood awkwardly, his eyes wandering, then said:

"Ask Malachi Roohan where the grave is, the exact place."

It was to do this the widow was leaving Cloon na Morav; she had just announced that she was going to ask Malachi Roohan where the grave was. Yet the man's tone was that of one who was giving her extraordinarily acute advice. There was a little half-embarrassed note of confidence in his tone. In a dim way the widow thought that, maybe, he had accompanied her to the stile in a little awkward impulse of sympathy. Men were very curious in their ways sometimes. The widow was a very well-mannered woman, and she tried to look as if she had received a very valuable direction. She said:

"I will. I'll put that question to Malachi Roohan."

And then she passed out over the stile.

III

The widow went up the road, and beyond it struck the first of the houses of the nearby town. She passed through faded streets in her quiet gait, moderately griefstricken at the death of her weaver. She had been his fourth wife, and the widowhoods of fourth wives had not the rich abandon, the great emotional cataclysm, of first, or even second, widowhoods. It is a little chastened in its poignancy. The widow had a nice feeling that it would be out of place to give way to any of the characteristic manifestations of normal widowhood. She shrank from drawing attention to the fact that she had been a fourth wife. People's memories become so extraordinarily acute to family history in times of death! The widow did not care to come in as a sort of dramatic surprise in the gossip of the people about the weaver's life. She had heard snatches of such gossip at the wake the night before. She was beginning to understand why people love wakes and the intimate personalities of wakehouses. People listen to, remember, and believe what they hear at wakes. It is more precious to them than anything they ever hear in school, church, or playhouse. It is hardly because they get certain entertainment at the wake. It is more because the wake is a grand review of family ghosts. There one hears all the stories, the little flattering touches, the little unflattering bitternesses, the traditions, the astonishing records, of the clans. The woman with a memory speaking to the company from a chair beside a laid-out corpse carries more authority than the bishop allocuting from his chair. The wake is realism. The widow had heard a great deal at the wake about the clan of the weavers, and noted, without expressing any emotion, that she had come into the story not like other women, for anything personal to her own womanhood—for beauty, or high spirit, or temper, or faithfulness, or unfaithfulness—but simply because she was a fourth wife, a kind of curiosity, the back-wash of Mortimer Hehir's romances. The widow felt a remote sense of injustice in all this. She had said to herself that widows who had been fourth wives deserved more sympathy than widows who had been first wives, for the simple reason that fourth widows had never been, and could never be, first wives! The thought confused her a little, and she did not pursue it, instinctively feeling that if she did accept the conventional view of her condition she would only crystallise her widowhood into a grievance that nobody would try to understand, and which would, accordingly, be merely useless. And what was the good of it, anyhow? The widow smoothed her dark hair on each side of her head under her shawl.

She had no bitter and no sweet memories of the weaver. There was nothing that was even vivid in their marriage. She had no complaints to make of Mortimer Hehir. He had not come to her in any fiery love impulse. It was the marriage of an old man with a woman years younger. She had recognised him as an old man from first to last, a man who had already been thrice through a wedded experience, and her temperament, naturally calm, had met his half-stormy, half-petulant character, without suffering any sort of shock. The weaver had tried to keep up to the illusion of a perennial youth by dyeing his hair, and marrying one wife as soon as possible after another. The fourth wife had come to him late in life. She had a placid understanding that she was a mere flattery to the weaver's truculent egoism.

These thoughts, in some shape or other, occupied, without agitating, the mind of the widow as she passed a dark shadowy figure through streets that were clamorous in their quietudes, painful in their lack of all the purposes for which streets have ever been created. Her only emotion was one which she knew to be quite creditable to her situation: a sincere desire to see the weaver buried in the grave to which the respectability of his family and the claims of his ancient house fully and fairly entitled him to. The proceedings in Cloon na Morav had been painful, even tragical, to the widow. The weavers had always been great authorities and zealous guardians of the ancient burial place. This function had been traditional and voluntary with them. This was especially true of the last of them, Mortimer Hehir. He had been the greatest of all authorities on the burial places of the local clans. His knowledge was scientific. He had been the ground savant of Cloon na Morav. He had policed the place. Nay, he had been its tyrant. He had over and over again prevented terrible mistakes, complications that would have appalled those concerned if they were not beyond all such concerns. The widow of the weaver had often thought that in his day Mortimer Hehir had made his solicitation for the place a passion, unreasonable, almost violent. They said that all this had sprung from a fear that had come to him in his early youth that through some blunder an alien, an inferior, even an enemy, might come to find his way into the family burial place of weavers. This fear had made him what he was. And in his later years his pride in the family burial place became a worship. His trade had gone down, and his pride had gone up. The burial ground in Cloon na Morav was the grand proof of his aristocracy. That was the coat-of-arms, the estate, the mark of high breeding, in the weavers. And now the man who had minded everybody's grave had not been able to mind his own. The widow thought that it was one of those injustices which blacken the reputation of the whole earth. She had felt, indeed, that she had been herself slack not to have learned long ago the lie of this precious grave from the weaver himself; and that he himself had been slack in not properly instructing her. But that was the way in this miserable world! In his passion for classifying the rights of others, the weaver had obscured his own. In his long and entirely successful battle in keeping alien corpses out of his own aristocratic pit he had made his own corpse alien to every pit in the place. The living high priest was the dead pariah of Cloon na Morav. Nobody could now tell except, perhaps, Malachi Roohan, the precise spot which he had defended against the blunders and confusions of the entire community, a dead-forgetting, indifferent, slack lot!

The widow tried to recall all she had ever heard the weaver say about his grave, in the hope of getting some clue, something that might be better than the scandalous scatter-brained efforts of Meehaul Lynskey and Cahir Bowes. She remembered various detached things that the weaver, a talkative man, had said about his grave. Fifty years ago since that grave had been last opened, and it had then been opened to receive the remains of his father. It had been thirty years previous to that since it had taken in his father, that is, the newly dead weaver's father's father. The weavers were a long-lived lot, and there were not many males of them; one son was as much as any one of them begot to pass to the succession of the loom; if there were daughters they scattered, and their graves were continents apart. The three wives of the late weaver were buried in the new cemetery. The widow remembered that the weaver seldom spoke of them, and took no interest in their resting place. His heart was in Cloon na Morav and the sweet, dry, deep aristocratic bed he had there in reserve for himself. He had never, that the widow could recall, said anything about the site, about the signs and measurements by which it could be identified. No doubt, it had been well known to many people, but they had all died. The weaver had never realised what their slipping away might mean to himself. The position of the grave was so intimate to his own mind that it never occurred to him that it could be obscure to the minds of others. Mortimer Hehir had passed away like some learned and solitary astronomer who had discovered a new star, hugging its beauty, its exclusiveness, its possession to his heart, secretly rejoicing how its name would travel with his own through heavenly space for all time—and forgetting to mark its place among the known stars grouped upon his charts. Meehaul Lynskey and Cahir Bowes might now be two seasoned astronomers of venal knowledge looking for the star which the weaver, in his love for it, had let slip upon the mighty complexity of the skies.

The thing that is clearest to the mind of a man is often the thing that is most opaque to the intelligence of his bosom companion. A saint may walk the earth in the simple belief that all the world beholds his glowing halo; but all the world does not; if it did the saint would be stoned. And Mortimer Hehir had been as innocently proud of his grave as a saint might be ecstatic of his halo. He believed that when the time came he would get a royal funeral—a funeral fitting to the last of the line of great Cloon na Morav weavers. Instead of that they had no more idea of where to bury him than if he had been a wild tinker of the roads.

The widow, thinking of these things in her own mind, was about to sigh when, behind a window pane, she heard the sudden bubble of a roller canary's song. She had reached, half absent-mindedly, the home of Malachi Roohan, the cooper.

## IV

The widow of the weaver approached the door of Malachi Roohan's house with an apologetic step, pawing the threshold a little in the manner of peasant women—a mannerism picked up from shy animals—before she stooped her head and made her entrance.

Malachi Roohan's daughter withdrew from the fire a face which reflected the passionate soul of a cook. The face cooled as the widow disclosed her business.

"I wouldn't put it a-past my father to have knowledge of the grave," said the daughter of the house, adding, "The Lord a mercy on the weaver."

She led the widow into the presence of the cooper.

The room was small and low and stuffy, indifferently served with light by an unopenable window. There was the smell of old age, of decay, in the room. It brought almost a sense of faintness to the widow. She had the feeling that God had made her to move in the ways of old men—passionate, cantankerous, egoistic old men, old men for whom she was always doing something, always remembering things, from missing buttons to lost graves.

Her eyes sought the bed of Malachi Roohan with an unemotional, quietly sceptical gaze. But she did not see anything of the cooper. The daughter leaned over the bed, listened attentively, and then very deftly turned down the clothes, revealing the bust of Malachi Roohan. The widow saw a weird face, not in the least pale or lined, but ruddy, with a mahogany bald head, a head upon which the leathery skin—for there did not seem any flesh—hardly concealed the stark outlines of the skull. From the chin there strayed a grey beard, the most shaken and whipped-looking beard that the widow had ever seen; it was, in truth a very miracle of a beard, for one wondered how it had come there, and having come there, how it continued to hang on, for there did not seem anything to which it could claim natural allegiance. The widow was as much astonished at this beard as if she saw a plant growing in a pot without soil. Through its gaps she could see the leather of the skin, the bones of a neck, which was indeed a neck. Over this head and shoulders the cooper's daughter bent and shouted into a crumpled ear. A little spasm of life stirred in the mummy. A low, mumbling sound came from the bed. The widow was already beginning to feel that, perhaps, she had done wrong in remembering that the cooper was still extant. But what else could she have done? If the weaver was buried in a wrong grave she did not believe that his soul would ever rest in peace. And what could be more dreadful than a soul wandering on the howling winds of the earth? The weaver would grieve, even in heaven, for his grave, grieve, maybe, as bitterly as a saint might grieve who had lost his halo. He was a passionate old man, such an old man as would have a turbulent spirit. He would surely—. The widow stifled the thoughts that flashed into her mind. She was no more superstitious than the rest of us, but—. These vague and terrible fears, and her moderately decent sorrow, were alike banished from her mind by what followed. The mummy on the bed came to life. And, what was more, he did it himself. His daughter looked on with the air of one whose sensibilities had become blunted by a long familiarity with the various stages of his resurrections. The widow gathered that the daughter had been well drilled; she had been taught how to keep her place. She did not tender the slightest help to her father as he drew himself together on the bed. He turned over on his side, then on his back, and stealthily began to insinuate his shoulder blades on the pillow, pushing up his weird head to the streak of light from the little window. The widow had been so long accustomed to assist the aged that she made some involuntary movement of succour. Some half-seen gesture by the daughter, a sudden lifting of the eyelids on the face of the patient, disclosing a pair of blue eyes, gave the widow instinctive pause. She remained where she was, aloof like the daughter of the house. And as she caught the blue of Malachi Roohan's eyes it broke upon the widow that here in the essence of the cooper there lived a spirit of extraordinary independence. Here, surely, was a man who had been accustomed to look out for himself, who resented the attentions, even in these days of his flickering consciousness. Up he wormed his shoulder blades, his mahogany skull, his leathery skin, his sensational eyes, his miraculous beard, to the light and to the full view of the visitor. At a certain stage of the resurrection—when the cooper had drawn two long, stringy arms from under the clothes—his daughter made a drilled movement forward, seeking something in the bed. The widow saw her discover the end of a rope, and this she placed in the hands of her indomitable father. The other end of the rope was fastened to the iron rail of the foot of the bed. The sinews of the patient's hands clutched the rope, and slowly, wonderfully, magically, as it seemed to the widow, the cooper raised himself to a sitting posture in the bed. There was dead silence in the room except for the laboured breathing of the performer. The eyes of the widow blinked. Yes, there was that ghost of a man hoisting himself up from the dead on a length of rope reversing the usual procedure. By that length of rope did the cooper hang on to life, and the effort of life. It represented his connection with the world, the world which had forgotten him, which marched past his window outside without knowing the stupendous thing that went on in his room. There he was, sitting up in the bed, restored to view by his own unaided efforts, holding his grip on life to the last. It cost him something to do it, but he did it. It would take him longer and longer every day to grip along that length of rope; he would fail ell by ell, sinking back to the last helplessness on his rope, descending into eternity as a vessel is lowered on a rope into a dark, deep well. But there he was now, still able for his work, unbeholding to all, self-dependent and alive, looking a little vaguely with his blue eyes at the widow of the weaver. His daughter swiftly and quietly propped pillows at his back, and she did it with the air of one who was allowed a special privilege.

"Nan!" called the old man to his daughter.

The widow, cool-tempered as she was, almost jumped on her feet. The voice was amazingly powerful. It was like a shout, filling the little room with vibrations. For four things did the widow ever after remember Malachi Roohan—for his rope, his blue eyes, his powerful voice, and his magic beard. They were thrown on the background of his skeleton in powerful relief.

"Yes, father," his daughter replied, shouting into his ear. He was apparently very deaf. This infirmity came upon the widow with a shock. The cooper was full of physical surprises.

"Who's this one?" the cooper shouted, looking at the widow. He had the belief that he was delivering an aside.

"Mrs. Hehir."

"Mrs. Hehir—what Hehir would she be?"

"The weaver's wife."

"The weaver? Is it Mortimer Hehir?"

"Yes, father."

"In troth I know her. She's Delia Morrissey, that married the weaver; Delia Morrissey that he followed to Munster, a raving lunatic with the dint of love."

A hot wave of embarrassment swept the widow. For a moment she thought the mind of the cooper was wandering. Then she remembered that the maiden name of the weaver's first wife was, indeed, Delia Morrissey. She had heard it, by chance, once or twice.

"Isn't it Delia Morrissey herself we have in it?" the old man asked.

The widow whispered to the daughter:

"Leave it so."

She shrank from a difficult discussion with the spectre on the bed on the family history of the weaver. A sense of shame came to her that she could be the wife to a contemporary of this astonishing old man holding on to the life rope.

"I'm out!" shouted Malachi Roohan, his blue eyes lighting suddenly. "Delia Morrissey died. She was one day eating her dinner and a bone stuck in her throat. The weaver clapped her on the back, but it was all to no good. She choked to death before his eyes on the floor. I remember that. And weaver himself near died of grief after. But he married secondly. Who's this he married secondly, Nan?"

Nan did not know. She turned to the widow for enlightenment. The widow moistened her lips. She had to concentrate her thoughts on a subject which, for her own peace of mind, she had habitually avoided. She hated genealogy. She said a little nervously:

"Sara MacCabe."

The cooper's daughter shouted the name into his ear.

"So you're Sally MacCabe, from Looscaun, the one Mortimer took off the blacksmith? Well, well, that was a great business surely, the pair of them hot-tempered men, and your own beauty going to their heads like strong drink."

He looked at the widow, a half-sceptical, half admiring expression flickering across the leathery face. It was such a look as he might have given to Dergorvilla of Leinster, Deirdre of Uladh, or Helen of Troy.

The widow was not the notorious Sara MacCabe from Looscaun; that lady had been the second wife of the weaver. It was said they had led a stormy life, made up of passionate quarrels and partings, and still more passionate reconciliations. Sara MacCabe from Looscaun not having quite forgotten or wholly neglected the blacksmith after her marriage to the weaver. But the widow again only whispered to the cooper's daughter:

"Leave it so."

"What way is Mortimer keeping?" asked the old man.

"He's dead," replied the daughter.

The fingers of the old man quivered on the rope.

"Dead? Mortimer Hehir dead?" he cried. "What in the name of God happened him?"

Nan did not know what happened him. She knew that the widow would not mind, so, without waiting for a prompt, she replied:

"A weakness came over him, a sudden weakness."

"To think of a man being whipped off all of a sudden like that!" cried the cooper. "When that's the way it was with Mortimer Hehir what one of us can be sure at all? Nan, none of us is sure! To think of the weaver, with his heart as strong as a bull, going off in a little weakness! It's the treacherous world we live in, the treacherous world, surely. Never another yard of tweed will he put up on his old loom! Morty, Morty, you were a good companion, a great warrant to walk the hills, whistling the tunes, pleasant in your conversation and as broad-spoken as the Bible."

"Did you know the weaver well, father?" the daughter asked.

"Who better?" he replied. "Who drank more pints with him than what myself did? And indeed it's to his wake I'd be setting out, and it's under his coffin my shoulder would be going, if I wasn't confined to my rope."

He bowed his head for a few moments. The two women exchanged a quick, sympathetic glance.

The breathing of the old man was the breathing of one who slept. The head sank lower.

The widow said:

"You ought to make him lie down. He's tired."

The daughter made some movement of dissent; she was afraid to interfere. Maybe the cooper could be very violent if roused. After a time he raised his head again. He looked in a new mood. He was fresher, more wideawake. His beard hung in wisps to the bedclothes.

"Ask him about the grave," the widow said.

The daughter hesitated a moment, and in that moment the cooper looked up as if he had heard, or partially heard. He said:

"If you wait a minute now I'll tell you what the weaver was." He stared for some seconds at the little window.

"Oh, we'll wait," said the daughter, and turning to the widow, added, "Won't we, Mrs. Hehir?"

"Indeed we will wait," said the widow.

"The weaver," said the old man suddenly, "was a dream."

He turned his head to the women to see how they had taken it.

"Maybe," said the daughter, with a little touch of laughter, "Maybe Mrs. Hehir would not give in to that."

The widow moved her hands uneasily under her shawl. She stared a little fearfully at the cooper. His blue eyes were clear as lake water over white sand.

"Whether she gives in to it, or whether she doesn't give

in to it," said Malachi Roohan, "it's a dream Mortimer Hehir was. And his loom, and his shuttles, and his warping bars, and his bobbin, and the threads that he put upon the shifting racks, were all a dream. And the only thing he ever wove upon his loom was a dream."

The old man smacked his lips, his hard gums whacking. His daughter looked at him with her head a little to one side.

"And what's more," said the cooper, "every woman that ever came into his head, and every wife he married, was a dream. I'm telling you that, Nan, and I'm telling it to you of the weaver. His life was a dream, and his death is a dream. And his widow there is a dream. And all the world is a dream. Do you hear me, Nan, this world is all a dream?"

"I hear you very well, father," the daughter sang in a piercing voice.

The cooper raised his head with a jerk, and his beard swept forward, giving him an appearance of vivid energy. He spoke in a voice like a trumpet blast:

"And I'm a dream!"

He turned his blue eyes to the widow. An unnerving sensation came to her. The cooper was the most dreadful old man she had ever seen, and what he was saying sounded the most terrible thing she had ever listened to. He cried:

"The idiot laughing in the street, the King looking at his crown, the woman turning her head to the sound of a man's step, the bells ringing in the belfry, the man walking his land, the weaver at his loom, the cooper handling his barrel, the Pope stooping for his red slippers—they're all a dream. And I'll tell you why they're a dream: because this world was meant to be a dream."

"Father," said the daughter, "you're talking too much. You'll over-reach yourself."

The old man gave himself a little pull on the rope. It was his gesture of energy, a demonstration of the fine fettle he was in. He said:

"You're saying that because you don't understand me."

"I understand you very well."

"You only think you do. Listen to me now, Nan. I want you to do something for me. You won't refuse me?"

"I will not refuse you, Father; you know very well I won't."

"You're a good daughter to me, surely, Nan. And do what

I tell you now. Shut close your eyes. Shut them fast and tight. No fluttering of the lids now."

"Very well, Father."

The daughter closed her eyes, throwing up her face in the attitude of one blind. The widow was conscious of the woman's strong, rough features, something good-natured in the line of the large mouth. The old man watched the face of his daughter with excitement. He asked:

"What is it that you see now, Nan?"

"Nothing at all, Father."

"In troth you do. Keep them closed tight and you'll see it."

"I see nothing only—"

"Only what? Why don't you say it?"

"Only darkness, Father."

"And isn't that something to see? Isn't it easier to see darkness than to see light? Now, Nan, look into the darkness."

"I'm looking, Father."

"And think of something—anything at all—the stool before the kitchen fire outside."

"I'm thinking of it."

"And do you remember it?"

"I do well."

"And when you remember it what do you want to do—sit on it, maybe?"

"No, Father."

"And why wouldn't you want to sit on it?"

"Because—because I'd like to see it first, to make sure."

The old man gave a little crow of delight. He cried:

"There it is! You want to make sure that it is there, although you remember it well. And that is the way with everything in this world. People close their eyes and they are not sure of anything. They want to see it again before they believe. There is Nan, now, and she does not believe in the stool before the fire, the little stool she's looking at all her life, that her mother used to seat her on before the fire when she was a small child. She closes her eyes, and it is gone! And listen to me now, Nan—if you had a man of your own and you closed your eyes you wouldn't be too sure he was the man you remembered, and you'd want to open your eyes and look at him to make sure he was the man you knew before the lids dropped on your eyes. And if you had children about you and you turned your back and closed your eyes and tried to remember them you'd want to look at them to make sure. You'd be no more sure of them than you are now of the stool in the kitchen. One flash of the eyelids and everything in this world is gone."

"I'm telling you, Father, you're talking too much."

"I'm not talking half enough. Aren't we all uneasy about the world, the things in the world that we can only believe in while we're looking at them? From one season of our life to another haven't we a kind of belief that some time we'll waken up and find everything different? Didn't you ever feel that, Nan? Didn't you think things would change, that the world would be a new place altogether, and that all that was going on around us was only a business that was doing us out of something else? We put up with it while the little hankering is nibbling at the butt of our hearts for the something else! All the men there be who believe that some day The Thing will happen, that they'll turn round the corner and waken up in the new great Street!"

"And sure," said the daughter, "maybe they are right, and maybe they will waken up."

The old man's body was shaken with a queer spasm of laughter. It began under the clothes on the bed, worked up his trunk, ran along his stringy arms, out into the rope, and the iron foot of the bed rattled. A look of extraordinarily malicious humour lit up the vivid face of the cooper. The widow beheld him with fascination, a growing sense of alarm. He might say anything. He might do anything. He might begin to sing some fearful song. He might leap out of bed.

"Nan," he said, "do you believe you'll swing round the corner and waken up?"

"Well," said Nan, hesitating a little, "I do."

The cooper gave a sort of peacock crow again. He cried:

"Och! Nan Roohan believes she'll waken up! Waken up from what? From a sleep and from a dream, from this world! Well, if you believe that, Nan Roohan, it shows you know what's what. You know what the thing around you, called the world, is. And it's only dreamers who can hope to waken up—do you hear me, Nan; it's only dreamers who can hope to waken up."

"I hear you," said Nan.

"The world is only a dream, and a dream is nothing at all!

We all want to waken up out of the great nothingness of this world."

"And, please God, we will," said Nan.

"You can tell all the world from me," said the cooper, "that it won't."

"And why won't we, Father?"

"Because," said the old man, "we ourselves are the dream. When we're over the dream is over with us. That's why."

"Father," said the daughter, her head again a little to one side, "you know a great deal."

"I know enough," said the cooper shortly.

"And maybe you could tell us something about the weaver's grave. Mrs. Hehir wants to know."

"And amn't I after telling you all about the weaver's grave? Amn't I telling you it is all a dream?"

"You never said that, Father. Indeed you never did."

"I said everything in this world is a dream, and the weaver's grave is in this world, below in Cloon na Morav."

"Where in Cloon na Morav? What part of it, Father? That is what Mrs. Hehir wants to know. Can you tell her?"

"I can tell her," said Malachi Roohan. "I was at his father's burial. I remember it above all burials, because that was the day the handsome girl, Honor Costello, fell over a grave and fainted. The sweat broke out on young Donohoe when he saw Honor Costello tumbling over the grave. Not a marry would he marry her after that, and he sworn to it by the kiss of her lips. 'I'll marry no woman that fell on a grave,' says Donohoe. 'She'd maybe have a child by me with turned-in eyes or a twisted limb.' So he married a farmer's daughter, and the same morning Honor Costello married a cattle drover. Very well, then. Donohoe's wife had no child at all. She was a barren woman. Do you hear me, Nan? A barren woman she was. And such childer as Honor Costello had by the drover! Yellow hair they had, heavy as seaweed, the skin of them clear as the wind, and limbs as clean as a whistle! It was said the drover was of the blood of the Danes, and it broke out in Honor Costello's family!"

"Maybe," said the daughter, "they were Vikings."

"What are you saying?" cried the old man testily. "Ain't I telling you it's Danes they were. Did anyone ever hear a greater miracle?"

"No one ever did," said the daughter, and both women clicked their tongues to express sympathetic wonder at the tale.

"And I'll tell you what saved Honor Costello," said the cooper. "When she fell in Cloon na Morav she turned her cloak inside out."

"What about the weaver's grave, Father? Mrs. Hehir wants to know."

The old man looked at the widow; his blue eyes searched her face and her figure; the expression of satirical admiration flashed over his features. The nostrils of the nose twitched. He said:

"So that's the end of the story! Sally MacCabe, the blacksmith's favourite, wants to know where she'll sink the weaver out of sight! Great battles were fought in Looscaun over Sally MacCabe! The weaver thought his heart would burst, and the blacksmith damned his soul for the sake of Sally MacCabe's idle hours."

"Father," said the daughter of the house, "let the dead rest."

"Ay," said Malachi Roohan, "let the foolish dead rest. The dream of Looscaun is over. And now the pale woman is looking for the black weaver's grave. Well, good luck to her!"

The cooper was taken with another spasm of grotesque laughter. The only difference was that this time it began by the rattling of the rail of the bed, travelled along the rope, down his stringy arms dying out somewhere in his legs in the bed. He smacked his lips, a peculiar harsh sound, as if there was not much meat to it.

"Do I know where Mortimer Hehir's grave is?" he said ruminatingly. "Do I know where me rope is?"

"Where is it, then?" his daughter asked. Her patience was great.

"I'll tell you that," said the cooper. "It's under the elm tree of Cloon na Morav. That's where it is surely. There was never a weaver yet that did not find rest under the elm tree of Cloon na Morav. There they all went as surely as the buds came on the branches. Let Sally MacCabe put poor Morty there; let her give him a tear or two in memory of the days that his heart was ready to burst for her, and believe you me no ghost will ever haunt her. No dead man ever yet came back to look upon a woman!"

A furtive sigh escaped the widow. With her handkerchief she wiped a little perspiration from both sides of her nose. The old man wagged his head sympathetically. He thought she was the long dead Sally MacCabe lamenting the weaver! The widow's emotion arose from relief that the mystery of the grave had at last been cleared up. Yet her dealings with old men had taught her caution. Quite suddenly the memory of the handsome dark face of the grave-digger who had followed her to the stile came back to her. She remembered that he said something about "the exact position of the grave." The widow prompted yet another question:

"What position under the elm tree?"

The old man listened to the question; a strained look came into his face.

"Position of what?" he asked.

"Of the grave."

"Of what grave?"

"The weaver's grave."

Another spasm seized the old frame, but this time it came from no aged merriment. It gripped his skeleton and shook it. It was as if some invisible powerful hand had suddenly taken him by the back of the neck and shaken him. His knuckles rattled on the rope. They had an appalling sound. A horrible feeling came to the widow that the cooper would fall to pieces like a bag of bones. He turned his face to his daughter. Great tears had welled into the blue eyes, giving them an appearance of childish petulance, then of acute suffering.

"What are you talking to me of graves for?" he asked, and the powerful voice broke. "Why will you be tormenting me like this? It's not going to die I am, is it? Is it going to die I am, Nan?"

The daughter bent over him as she might bend over a child. She said:

"Indeed, there's great fear of you. Lie down and rest yourself. Fatigued out and out you are."

The grip slowly slackened on the rope. He sank back, quite helpless, a little whimper breaking from him. The daughter stooped lower, reaching for a pillow that had fallen in by the wall. A sudden sharp snarl sounded from the bed, and it dropped from her hand.

"Don't touch me!" the cooper cried. The voice was again restored, powerful in its command. And to the amazement of the widow she saw him again grip along the rope and rise in the bed.

"Amn't I tired telling you not to touch me?" he cried.

"Have I any business talking to you at all? Is it gone my authority is in this house?"

He glared at his daughter, his eyes red with anger, like a dog crouching in his kennel, and the daughter stepped back, a wry smile on her large mouth. The widow stepped back with her, and for a moment he held the women with their backs to the wall by his angry red eyes. Another growl and the cooper sank back inch by inch on the rope. In all her experience of old men the widow had never seen anything like this old man; his resurrections and his collapse. When he was quite down the daughter gingerly put the clothes over his shoulders and then beckoned the widow out of the room.

The widow left the house of Malachi Roohan, the cooper, with the feeling that she had discovered the grave of an old man by almost killing another.

V

The widow walked along the streets, outwardly calm, inwardly confused. Her first thought was "the day is going on me!" There were many things still to be done at home; she remembered the weaver lying there, quiet at last, the candles lighting about him, the brown habit over him, a crucifix in his hands—everything as it should be. It seemed ages to the widow since he had really fallen ill. He was very exacting and peevish all that time. His death agony had been protracted, almost melodramatically violent. A few times the widow had nearly run out of the house, leaving the weaver to fight the death battle alone. But her commonsense, her good nerves, and her religious convictions, had stood to her, and when she put the pennies on the weaver's eyes she was glad she had done her duty to the last. She was glad now that she had taken the search for the grave out of the hands of Meehaul Lynskey and Cahir Bowes; Malachi Roohan had been a sight, and she would never forget him, but he had known what nobody else knew. The widow, as she ascended a little upward sweep of the road to Cloon na Morav, noted that the sky beyond it was more vivid, a red band of light having struck across the grey blue, just on the horizon. Up against this red background was the dark outline of landscape, and especially Cloon na Morav. She kept her eyes upon it as she drew nearer. Objects that were vague on the landscape began to bulk up with more distinction.

She noted the back wall of Cloon na Morav, its green lichen more vivid under the red patch of the skyline. And presently, above the green wall, black against the vivid sky, she saw elevated the bulk of one of the black cockroaches. On it were perched two drab figures, so grotesque, so still, that they seemed part of the thing itself. One figure was sloping out from the end of the tombstone so curiously that for a moment the widow thought it was a man who had reached down from the table to see what was under it. At the other end of the table was a slender warped figure, and as the widow gazed upon it she saw a sign of animation. The head and face, bleak in their outlines, were raised up in a gesture of despair. The face was turned flush against the sky, so much so that the widow's eyes instinctively sought the sky too. Above the slash of red, in the west, was a single star, flashing so briskly and so freshly that it might have never shone before. For all the widow knew, it might have been a young star frolicking in the heavens with all the joy of youth. Was that, she wondered, at what the old man, Meehaul Lynskey, was gazing. He was very, very old, and the star was very, very young! Was there some protest in the gesture of the head he raised to that thing in the sky; was there some mockery in the sparkle of the thing of the sky for the face of the man? Why should a star be always young, a man aged so soon? Should not a man be greater than a star? Was it this Meehaul Lynskey was thinking? The widow could not say, but something in the thing awed her. She had the sensation of one who surprises a man in some act that lifts him above the commonplaces of existence. It was as if Meehaul Lynskey were discovered prostrate before some altar, in the throes of a religious agony. Old men were, the widow felt, very, very strange, and she did not know that she would ever understand them. As she looked at the bleak head of Meehaul Lynskey up, against the vivid patch of the sky, she wondered if there could really be something in that head which would make him as great as a star, immortal as a star? Suddenly Meehaul Lynskey made a movement. The widow saw it quite distinctly. She saw the arm raised, the hand go out, with its crooked fingers, in one, two, three quick, short taps in the direction of the star. The widow stood to watch, and the gesture was so familiar, so homely, so personal, that it was quite understandable to her. She knew then that Meehaul Lynskey was not thinking of any great things at all. He was only a nailer! And seeing the Evening Star sparkle in the sky he had only thought of his workshop, of the bellows, the irons, the fire, the sparks, and the glowing iron which might be made into a nail while it was hot! He had in imagination seized a hammer and made a blow across interstellar space at Venus! All the beauty and youth of the star frolicking on the pale sky above the slash of vivid redness had only suggested to him the making of yet another nail! If Meehaul Lynskey could push up his scarred yellow face among the stars of the sky he would only see in them the sparks of his little smithy.

Cahir Bowes was, the widow thought, looking down at the earth, from the other end of the tombstone, to see if there were any hard things there which he could smash up. The old men had their backs turned upon each other. Very likely they had had another discussion since, which ended in this attitude of mutual contempt. The widow was conscious again of the unreasonableness of old men, but not much resentful of it. She was too long accustomed to them to have any great sense of revolt. Her emotion, if it could be called an emotion, was a settled, dull toleration of all their little bigotries.

She put her hand on the stile for the second time that day, and again raised her palely sad face over the graveyard of Cloon na Morav. As she did so she had the most extraordinary experience of the whole day's sensations. It was such a sensation as gave her at once a wonderful sense of the reality and the unreality of life. She paused on the stile, and had a clear insight into something that had up to this moment been obscure. And no sooner had the thing become definite and clear than a sense of the wonder of life came to her. It was all very like the dream Malachi Roohan had talked about.

In the pale grass, under the vivid colours of the sky, the two grave-diggers were lying on their backs, staring silently up at the heavens. The widow looked at them as she paused on the stile. Her thoughts of these men had been indifferent, subconscious, up to this instant. They were handsome young men. Perhaps if there had been only one of them the widow would have been more attentive. The dark handsomeness did not seem the same thing when repeated. Their beauty, if one could call it beauty, had been collective, the beauty of flowers, of dark, velvety pansies, the distinctive marks of one faithfully duplicated on the other. The good looks of one had, to the mind of the widow, somehow nullified the good looks of the other. There was too much borrowing of Peter to pay Paul in their well-favoured features. The first grave-digger spoiled the illusion of individuality in the second grave-digger. The widow had not thought so, but she would have agreed if anybody whispered to her that a good-looking man who wanted to win favour with a woman should never have so complete a twin brother. It would be possible for a woman to part tenderly with a man, and, if she met his image and likeness around the corner, knock him down. There is nothing more powerful, but nothing more delicate in life than the valves of individuality. To create the impression that humanity was a thing which could be turned out like a coinage would be to ruin the whole illusion of life. The twin grave-diggers had created some sort of such impression, vague, and not very insistent, in the mind of the widow, and it had made her lose any special interest in them. Now, however, as she hesitated on the stile, all this was swept from her mind at a stroke. That most subtle and powerful of all things, personality, sprang silently from the twins and made them, to the mind of the widow, things as far apart as the poles. The two men lay at length, and exactly the same length and bulk, in the long, grey grass. But, as the widow looked upon them, one twin seemed conscious of her presence, while the other continued his absorption in the heavens above. The supreme twin turned his head, and his soft, velvety brown eyes met the eyes of the widow. There was welcome in the man's eyes. The widow read that welcome as plainly as if he had spoken his thoughts. The next moment he had sprung to his feet, smiling. He took a few steps forward, then, self-conscious, pulled up. If he had only jumped up and smiled the widow would have understood. But those few eager steps forward and then that stock stillness! The other twin rose reluctantly, and as he did so the widow was conscious of even physical differences in the brothers. The eyes were not the same. No such velvety soft lights were in the eyes of the second one. He was more sheepish. He was more phlegmatic. He was only a plagiarism of the original man! The widow wondered how she had not seen all this before. The resemblance between the twins was only skin deep. The two old men, at the moment the second twin rose, detached themselves slowly, almost painfully, from their tombstone, and all moved forward to meet the widow. The widow, collecting her thoughts, piloted her skirts modestly about her legs as she got down from the narrow stonework of the stile and stumbled into the contrariness of Cloon na Morav. A wild sense of satisfaction swept her that she had come back the bearer of useful information.

"Well," said Meehaul Lynskey, "did you see Malachi Roohan?" The widow looked at his scorched, sceptical, yellow face, and said:

"I did."

"Had he any word for us?"

"He had. He remembers the place of the weaver's grave." The widow looked a little vaguely about Cloon na Morav.

"What does he say?"

"He says it's under the elm tree."

There was silence. The stone-breaker swung about on his legs, his head making a semi-circular movement over the ground, and his sharp eyes were turned upward, as if he were searching the heavens for an elm tree. The nailer dropped his underjaw and stared tensely across the ground, blankly, patiently, like a fisherman on the edge of the shore gazing over an empty sea. The grave-digger turned his head away shyly, like a boy, as if he did not want to see the confusion of the widow; the man was full of the most delicate mannerisms. The other grave-digger settled into a stolid attitude, then the skin bunched up about his brown eyes in puckers of humour. A miserable feeling swept the widow. She had the feeling that she stood on the verge of some collapse.

"Under the elm tree," mumbled the stonebreaker.

"That's what he said," added the widow. "Under the elm tree of Cloon na Morav."

"Well," said Cahir Bowes, "when you find the elm tree you'll find the grave."

The widow did not know what an elm tree was. Nothing had ever happened in life as she knew it to render any special knowledge of trees profitable, and therefore desirable. Trees were good; they made nice firing when chopped up; timber, and all that was fashioned out of timber, came from trees. This knowledge the widow had accepted as she had accepted all the other remote phenomena of the world into which she had been born. But that trees should have distinctive names, that they should have family relationships, seemed to the mind of the widow only an unnecessary complication of the affairs of the universe. What good was it? She could understand calling fruit trees fruit trees and all other kinds simply trees. But that one should be an elm and another an ash, that there should be name after name, species after species, giving them peculiarities and personalities, was one of the things that the widow did not like. And at this moment, when the elm tree of Malachi Roohan had raised a fresh problem in Cloon na Morav, the likeness of old men to old trees—their crankiness, their complexity, their angles, their very barks, bulges, gnarled twistiness, and kinks— was very close, and brought a sense of oppression to the sorely-tried brain of the widow.

"Under the elm tree," repeated Meehaul Lynskey. "The elm tree of Cloon na Morav." He broke into an aged cackle of a laugh. "If I was any good at all at making a rhyme I'd make one about that elm tree, devil a other but I would."

The widow looked around Cloon na Morav, and her eyes, for the first time in her life, were consciously searching for trees. If there were numerous trees there she could understand how easy it might be for Malachi Roohan to make a mistake. He might have mistaken some other sort of tree for an elm—the widow felt that there must be plenty of other trees very like an elm. In fact, she reasoned that other trees, do their best, could not help looking like an elm. There must be thousands and millions of people like herself in the world who pass through life in the belief that a certain kind of tree was an elm when, in reality, it may be an ash or an oak or a chestnut or a beech, or even a poplar, a birch, or a yew. Malachi Roohan was never likely to allow anybody to amend his knowledge of an elm tree. He would let go his rope in the belief that there was an elm tree in Cloon na Morav, and that under it was the weaver's grave—that is, if Malachi Roohan had not, in some ghastly aged kink, invented the thing. The widow, not sharply, but still with an appreciation of the thing, grasped that a dispute about trees would be the very sort of dispute in which Meehaul Lynskey and Cahir Bowes would, like the very old men that they were, have revelled. Under the impulse of the message she had brought from the cooper they would have launched out into another powerful struggle from tree to tree in Cloon na Morav; they would again have strewn the place with the corpses of slain arguments, and in the net result they would not have been able to establish anything either about elm trees or about the weaver's grave. The slow, sad gaze of the widow for trees in Cloon na Morav brought to her, in these circumstances, both pain and relief. It was a relief that Meehaul Lynskey and Cahir Bowes could not challenge each other to a battle of trees; it was a pain that the tree of Malachi Roohan was nowhere in sight. The widow could see for herself that there was not any sort of a tree in Cloon na Morav. The ground was enclosed upon three sides by walls, on the fourth by a hedge of quicks. Not even old men could transform a hedge into an elm tree. Neither could they make the few struggling briars clinging about the railings of the sepulchres into anything except briars. The elm tree of Malachi Roohan was now non-existent. Nobody would ever know whether it had or had not ever existed. The widow would as soon give the soul of the weaver to the howling winds of the world as go back and interview the cooper again on the subject.

"Old Malachi Roohan," said Cahir Bowes with tolerant decision, "is doting."

"The nearest elm tree I know," said Meehaul Lynskey, "is half a mile away."

"The one above at Carragh?" questioned Cahir Bowes.

"Ay, beside the mill."

No more was to be said. The riddle of the weaver's grave was still the riddle of the weaver's grave. Cloon na Morav kept its secret. But, nevertheless, the weaver would have to be buried. He could not be housed indefinitely. Taking courage from all the harrowing aspects of the deadlock, Meehaul Lynskey went back, plump and courageously to his original allegiance.

"The grave of the weaver is there," he said, and he struck out his hooked fingers in the direction of the disturbance of the sod which the grave-diggers had made under pressure of his earlier enthusiasm.

Cahir Bowes turned on him with a whithering, quavering glance.

"Aren't you afraid that God would strike you where you stand?" he demanded.

"I'm not—not a bit afraid," said Meehaul Lynskey. "It's the weaver's grave."

"You say that," cried Cahir Bowes, "after what we all saw and what we all heard?"

"I do," said Meehaul Lynskey, stoutly. He wiped his lips with the palm of his hand, and launched out into one of his arguments, arguments, as usual, packed with particulars.

"I saw the weaver's father lowered in that place. And I'll tell you, what's more, it was Father Owen MacCarthy that read over him, he a young red-haired curate in this place at the time, long before ever he became parish priest of Benelog. There was I, standing in this exact spot, a young man, too, with a light moustache, holding me hat in me hand, and there one side of me—maybe five yards from the marble stone of Keernahans—was Patsy Curtin that drank himself to death after, and on the other side of me was Honor Costello, that fell on the grave and married the cattle drover, a big, loose-shouldered Dane."

Patiently, half absent-mindedly, listening to the renewal of the dispute, the widow remembered the words of Malachi Roohan, and his story of Honor Costello, who fell on the grave over fifty years ago. What memories these old men had! How unreliable they were, and yet flashing out astounding corroborations of each other. Maybe there was something in what Meehaul Lynskey was saying. Maybe—but the widow checked her thoughts. What was the use of it all? This grave could not be the weaver's grave; it had been grimly demonstrated to them all that it was full of stout coffins. The widow, with a gesture of agitation, smoothed her hair down the gentle slope of her head under the shawl. As she did so her eyes caught the eyes of the grave-digger; he was looking at her! He withdrew his eyes at once, and began to twitch the ends of his dark moustache with his fingers.

"If," said Cahir Bowes, "this be the grave of the weaver, what's Julia Rafferty doing in it? Answer me that, Meehaul Lynskey."

"I don't know what's she doing in it, and what's more, I don't care. And believe you my word, many a queer thing happened in Cloon na Morav that had no right to happen in it. Julia Rafferty, maybe, isn't the only one that is where she had no right to be."

"Maybe she isn't," said Cahir Bowes, "but it's there she is, anyhow, and I'm thinking it's there she's likely to stay."

"If she's in the weaver's grave," cried Meehaul Lynskey, "what I say is, out with her!"

"Very well, then, Meehaul Lynskey. Let you yourself be the powerful man to deal with Julia Rafferty. But remember this, and remember it's my word, that touch one bone in this place and you touch all."

"No fear at all have I to right a wrong. I'm no backslider when it comes to justice, and justice I'll see done among the living and the dead."

"Go ahead, then, me hearty fellow. If Julia herself is in

the wrong place somebody else must be in her own place, and you'll be following one rightment with another wrongment until in the end you'll go mad with the tangle of dead men's wrongs. That's the end that's in store for you, Meehaul Lynskey."

Meehaul Lynskey spat on his fist and struck out with the hooked fingers. His blood was up.

"That I may be as dead as my father!" he began in a traditional oath, and at that Cahir Bowes gave a little cry and raised his stick with a battle flourish. They went up and down the dips of the ground, rising and falling on the waves of their anger, and the widow stood where she was, miserable and downhearted, her feet growing stone cold from the chilly dampness of the ground. The twin, who did not now count, took out his pipe and lit it, looking at the old men with a stolid gaze. The twin who now counted walked uneasily away, bit an end off a chunk of tobacco, and came to stand in the ground in a line with the widow, looking on with her several feet away; but again the widow was conscious of the man's growing sympathy.

"They're a nice pair of boyos, them two old lads," he remarked to the widow. He turned his head to her. He was very handsome.

"Do you think they will find it?" she asked. Her voice was a little nervous, and the man shifted on his feet, nervously responsive.

"It's hard to say," he said. "You'd never know what to think. Two old lads, the like of them, do be very tricky."

"God grant they'll get it," said the widow.

"God grant," said the grave-digger.

But they didn't. They only got exhausted as before, wheezing and coughing, and glaring at each other as they sat down on two mounds.

The grave-digger turned to the widow.

She was aware of the nice warmth of his brown eyes.

"Are you waking the weaver again tonight?" he asked.

"I am," said the widow.

"Well, maybe some person—some old man or woman from the country—may turn up and be able to tell where the grave is. You could make inquiries."

"Yes," said the widow, but without any enthusiasm, "I could make inquiries."

The grave-digger hesitated for a moment, and said more

sympathetically, "We could all, maybe, make inquiries." There was a softer personal note, a note of adventure, in the voice.

The widow turned her head to the man and smiled at him quite frankly.

"I'm beholding to you," she said and then added with a little wounded sigh, "Everyone is very good to me."

The grave-digger twirled the ends of his moustache.

Cahir Bowes, who had heard, rose form his mound and said briskly, "I'll agree to leave it at that." His air was that of one who had made an extraordinary personal sacrifice. What he was really thinking was that he would have another great day of it with Meehaul Lynskey in Cloon na Morav to-morrow. He'd show that oul' fellow, Lynskey, what stuff Boweses were made of.

"And I'm not against it," said Meehaul Lynskey. He took the tone of one who was never to be outdone in magnanimity. He was also thinking of another day of effort to-morrow, a day that would, please God, show the Boweses what the Lynskeys were like.

With that the party came straggling out of Cloon na Morav, the two old men first, the widow next, the grave-diggers waiting to put on their coats and light their pipes.

There was a little upward slope on the road to the town, and as the two old men took it the widow thought they looked very spent after their day. She wondered if Cahir Bowes would ever be able for that hill. She would give him a glass of whiskey at home, if there was any left in the bottle. Of the two, and as limp and slack as his body looked, Meehaul Lynskey appeared the better able for the hill. They walked together, that is to say, abreast, but they kept almost the width of the road between each other, as if this gulf expressed the breach of friendship between them on the head of the dispute about the weaver's grave. They had been making liars of each other all day, and they would, please God, make liars of each other all day to-morrow. The widow, understanding the meaning of this hostility, had a faint sense of amusement at the contrariness of old men. How could she tell what was passing in the head which Cahir Bowes hung, like a fuchsia drop, over the road? How could she know of the strange rise and fall of the thoughts, the little frets, the tempers, the faint humours, which chased each other there? Nobody— not even Cahir Bowes himself—could account for them. All the widow knew was that Cahir Bowes stood suddenly on the road.

Something had happened to his brain, some old memory cell long dormant had become nascent, had a stir, a pulse, a flicker of warmth, of activity, and swiftly as a flash of lightning in the sky, a glow of lucidity lit up his memory. The immediate physical effect on Cahir Bowes was to cause him to stand stark still on the road, Meehaul Lynskey going ahead without him. The widow saw Cahir Bowes pivot on his heels, his head, at the end of the horizontal body, swinging round like the movement of a hand on a runaway clock. Instead of pointing up the hill homeward the head pointed down the hill and back to Cloon na Morav. There followed the most extraordinary movements—shufflings, gyrations—that the widow had ever seen. Cahir Bowes wanted to run like mad away down the road. That was plain. And Cahir Bowes believed that he was running like mad away down the road. That was also evident. But what he actually did was to make little jumps on his feet, his stick rattling the ground in front, and each jump did not bring him an inch of ground. He would have gone more rapidly in his normal shuffle. His efforts were like a terrible parody on the springs of a kangaroo. And Cahir Bowes, in a voice that was now more a scream than a cackle, was calling out unintelligible things. The widow, looking at him, paused in wonder, then over her face there came a relaxation, a colour, her eyes warmed, her expression lost its settled pensiveness, and all her body was shaken with uncontrollable laughter. Cahir Bowes passed her on the road in his fantastic leaps, his abortive buck-jumps, screaming and cracking his stick on the ground, his left hand still gripped tightly on the small of his back behind, a powerful brake on the small of his back.

Meehaul Lynskey turned back and his face was shaken with an aged emotion as he looked after the stonebreaker. Then he removed his hat and blessed himself.

"The cross of Christ between us and harm," he exclaimed. "Old Cahir Bowes has gone off his head at last. I thought there was something up with him all day. It was easily known there was something ugly working in his mind."

The widow controlled her laughter and checked herself, making the sign of the Cross on her forehead, too. She said:

"God forgive me for laughing and the weaver with the habit but fresh upon him."

The grave-digger who counted was coming out somewhat eagerly over the stile, but Cahir Bowes, flourishing his stick, beat him back again and then himself re-entered Cloon na Morav.

He stumbled over the grass, now rising on a mound, now disappearing altogether in a dip of the ground, travelling in a giddy course like a hooker in a storm; again, for a long time, he remained submerged, showing, however, the eternal stick, his periscope, his indication to the world that he was about his business. In a level piece of ground, marked by stones with large mottled white marks upon them, he settled and cried out to all, and calling God to witness, that this surely was the weaver's grave. There was scepticism, hesitation, on the part of the gravediggers, but after some parley, and because Cahir Bowes was so passionate, vehement, crying and shouting, dribbling water from the mouth, showing his yellow teeth, pouring sweat on his forehead, quivering on his legs, they began to dig carefully in the spot. The widow, at this, re-arranged the shawl on her head and entered Cloon na Morav, conscious, as she shuffled over the stile, that a pair of warm brown eyes were, for a moment, upon her movements and then withdrawn. She stood a little way back from the digging and waited the result with a slightly more accelerated beating of the heart. The twins looked as if they were ready to strike something unexpected at any moment, digging carefully, and Cahir Bowes hung over the place, cackling and crowing, urging the men to swifter work. The earth sang up out of the ground, dark and rich in colour, gleaming like gold, in the deepening twilight of the place. Two feet, three feet, four feet of earth came up, the spades pushing through the earth in regular and powerful pushes, and still the coast was clear. Cahir Bowes trembled with excitement on his stick. Five feet of a pit yawned in the ancient ground. The spade work ceased. One of the grave-diggers looked up at Cahir Bowes, and said:

"You hit the weaver's grave this time right enough. Not another grave in the place could be as free as this."

The widow sighed a quick little sigh and looked at the face of the other grave-digger, hesitated, then allowed a remote smile of thankfulness to flit across her palely sad face. The eyes of the man wandered away over the darkening spaces of Cloon na Morav.

"I got the weaver's grave surely," cried Cahir Bowes, his old face full of a weird animation. If he had found the Philosopher's Stone he would only have broken it. But to find the weaver's grave was an accomplishment that would help him into a wisdom before which all his world would bow. He looked around triumphantly and said:

"Where is Meehaul Lynskey now; what will the people be saying at all about his attack on Julia Rafferty's grave? Julia will haunt him, and I'd sooner have anyone at all haunting me than the ghost of Julia Rafferty. Where is Meehaul Lynskey now? Is it ashamed to show his liary face he is? And what talk had Malachi Roohan about an elm tree? Elm tree, indeed! If it's trees that is troubling him now let him climb up on one of them and hang himself from it with his rope! Where is that old fellow, Meehaul Lynskey, and his rotten head? Where is he, I say? Let him come in here now to Cloon na Morav until I be showing him the weaver's grave, five feet down and not a rib or a knuckle in it, as clean and beautiful as the weaver ever wished it. Come in here, Meehaul Lynskey, until I hear the lies panting again in your yellow throat."

He went in his extraordinary movement over the ground, making for the stile all the while talking.

Meehaul Lynskey had crouched behind the wall outside when Cahir Bowes led the diggers to the new site, his old face twisted in an attentive, almost agonising emotion. He stood peeping over the wall, saying to himself:

"Whisht, will you! Don't mind that old madman. He hasn't it at all. I'm telling you he hasn't it. Whisht, will you! Let him dig away. They'll hit something in a minute. They'll level him when they find out. His brain has turned. Whisht, now, will you, and I'll have that rambling old lunatic, Cahir Bowes, in a minute. I'll leap in on him. I'll charge him before the world. I'll show him up. I'll take the gab out of him. I'll lacerate him. I'll lambaste him. Whisht, will you!"

But as the digging went on and the terrible cries of triumph arose inside Meehaul Lynskey's knees knocked together. His head bent level to the wall, yellow and grimacing, nerves twitching across it, a little yellow froth gathering at the corners of the mouth. When Cahir Bowes came beating for the stile Meehaul Lynskey rubbed one leg with the other, a little below the calf, and cried brokenly to himself:

"God in Heaven, he has it! He has the weaver's grave."

He turned about and slunk along in the shadow of the wall up the hill, panting and broken. By the time Cahir Bowes had reached the stile Meehaul Lynskey's figure was shadowily dipping down over the crest of the road. A sharp cry from Cahir Bowes caused him to shrink out of sight like a dog at whom a weapon had been thrown.

The eyes of the grave-digger who did not now count followed the figure of Cahir Bowes as he moved to the stile. He laughed a little in amusement, then wiped his brow. He came up out of the grave. He turned to the widow and said:

"We're down five feet. Isn't that enough in which to sink the weaver in? Are you satisfied?"

The man spoke to her without any pretence at fine feeling. He addressed her as a fourth wife should be addressed. The widow was conscious but unresentful of the man's manner. She regarded him calmly and without any resentment. On her part there was no resentment either, no hypocrisy, no make-believe. Her unemotional eyes followed his action as he stuck his spade into the loose mould on the ground. A cry from Cahir Bowes distracted the man, he laughed again, and before the widow could make a reply he said:

"Old Cahir is great value. Come down until we hear him handling the nailer."

He walked away down over the ground.

The widow was left alone with the other grave-digger. He drew himself up out of the pit with a sinuous movement of the body which the widow noted. He stood without a word beside the pile of heaving clay and looked across at the widow. She looked back at him and suddenly the silence became full of unspoken words, of flying, ringing emotions. The widow could see the dark green wall, above in the band of still deepening red, above that the still more pallid grey sky, and directly over the man's head the gay frolicking of the fresh star in the sky. Cloon na Morav was flooded with a deep, vague light. The widow scented the fresh wind about her, the cool fragrance of the earth, and yet a warmth that was strangely beautiful. The light of the man's dark eyes was visible in the shadow which hid his face. The pile of earth beside him was like a vague shape of miniature bronze mountains. He stood with a stillness which was tense and dramatic. The widow thought that the world was strange, the sky extraordinary, the man's head against the red sky a wonder, a poem, above it the sparkle of the great young star. The widow knew that they would be left together like this for one minute, a minute which would be as a flash and as eternity. And she knew now that sooner or later this man would come to her and that she would welcome him. Below at the stile the voice of Cahir Bowes was cackling in its aged notes. Beyond this the stillness was the stillness of heaven and earth. Suddenly a sense of faintness came to the widow. The whole place swooned before her eyes. Never was this world so strange, so like the dream that Malachi Roohan had talked about. A movement in the figure of the man beside the heap of bronze had come to her as a warning, a fear, and a delight. She moved herself a little in response, made a step backward. The next instant she saw the figure of the man spring across the open black mouth of the weaver's grave to her.

A faint sound escaped her and then his breath was hot on her face, his mouth on her lips.

Half a minute later Cahir Bowes came shuffling back, followed by the twin.

"I'll bone him yet," said Cahir Bowes. "Never you fear I'll make that old nailer face me. I'll show him up at the weaver's wake to-night!"

The twin laughed behind him. He shook his head at his brother, who was standing a pace away from the widow. He said:

"Five feet."

He looked into the grave and then looked at the widow, saying:

"Are you satisfied?"

There was silence for a second or two, and when she spoke the widow's voice was low but fresh, like the voice of a young girl. She said:

"I'm satisfied."

# Daniel Corkery

## *Vanity*

### I

From that great mountain-wall which divides Cork from Kerry great spurs of broken and terraced rock run out on the Cork side like vast buttresses; and in the flanks of these great buttresses are round-ended glens, or cooms, as they are called in Irish. Those on the northern flanks of such spurs are gloomy beyond belief.

The dwellers in these cold valleys are of such an austere, puritanic type that the exception among them who is given to the vanities of the world shows out with indescribable, if unholy lustre. In Lyrenascaul old Diarmuid Mac Coitir was such a man; it may be more correct to say, had been such a man, for he was now of great age and confined to his bed. In the little dark back-room—it was dark because a sheer slab of rock, grey, lichened, and damp, rose up behind the house—he passed the long hours of day and night. Between the darkness of the room itself and the darkness that was coming over his eyes, there was not much difference for him now between day and night, except that in the day he could still hear the little stir of life—very little indeed it was—that went on around the miserable bit of a farm, which he had made over to his son. In the few other houses that clung against the sides of Lyrenascaul there were here and there other bed-ridden ancients; these you beheld with their beads in their hands, night as well as day, and a certain pallor, a quiet peacefulness that lay always on their features, told you they had long since put this world aside and were now calmly awaiting the call to the next world. Diarmuid had never been of the same mind as these; and instead of that great calmness of theirs, it would be a thick sort of smile would come slowly crawling over his features, sometimes holding them for quite long spells.

He lived there with his wife, who was almost as old as himself and as unworldly as he was worldly; and the only other person in the house was their only remaining son, the still unmarried Michael, now an old man himself, one too who had inherited much of the worldliness and hardness of the ancient who day after day lay bed-ridden in the little dark back-room.

Into that out-of-the-world coom—it was miles from any main road—it was seldom a stray newspaper from Cork or Dublin made its way. You might even to-day live there a long six months and not see one; and I am told that many people easily remember the time when no papers at all entered, with their strange tales of the outside world. Old Diarmuid could not read (indeed his son could hardly do as much) but even if he could what interest would he have found in the news of a world he had never been in, more especially when that news would consist of a series of unrelated facts, with, for him, no yesterday, no to-morrow? News of fairs and markets he might have fathomed, if there were any such. There usually was not. In every paper, however, that chanced to find its way into that forgotten world, there would be a series of paragraphs that always came home to him and gripped his thoughts—these were the death notices. For many years these notices were such a novelty that he learned each of them by heart from some other person's reading, and would recite the latest to his gossips, and compare it with ones he had earlier learned, and go on to speak of the difference between one which mentioned that a Requiem Mass had been sung and one which was content with the modest: R.I.P.

At that stage he was, when, without warning, he was one day struck with a stroke of paralysis. He took to his bed. One evening he sat up, thinking of what had befallen him. He called to his son:

"Hi!" he said, "Michael, Michael!"

Michael had been chopping furze to give as food to their poor sorry nag; he came in, chopper in hand:

"Well?"

"Tell me this, Michael, if 'twas dead you found me this day, or any other day, would you put a little biteen of a notice in the paper—just a little biteen of a wan with R.I.P. at the end of it?"

Michael looked at him and noticed how strong and sturdy he was. He smiled, not sweetly or lovingly. He threw an eye around the dark, almost empty little house, he took a step to the open door and glanced with scorn at the scraggy patch of land that was their farm; he came back and said:

"Isn't it well you deserve it from me?"

"Don't be hard, Michael, boy, there's a good time coming; you won't have to face what I had to face, the struggling with landlords, and the law—the law, that would leave a rich man poor and a poor man broken. Give me your word, Michael, boy, when it pleases God to call me you'll put a little biteen of a notice in the paper so that—"

"I won't then give you me word. An old man like you, 'tis something else should be troubling you besides having your name stuck in the paper and you cold on the bed—" And then, just as he was about to begin his furze-chopping again, he called out:

"Was there ever anyone from Lyrenascaul in the paper and he dead?"

"That's why!" said the old man, sitting up suddenly, while quite a glow came back into his heavy face.

Not long after there did really happen to be a death-notice from Lyrenascaul in the paper. It was American gold put it there. Old John Kevane had died. The news had been leisurely enough sent to his son in America. A few days after its arrival there the notice appeared in the Cork and Dublin papers—cabled from America! Whereupon old Diarmuid Mac Coitir renewed his importunity, not, however, with more success, "There's a great fear of you dying, a great fear indeed!" his son would answer, and pass the thing off as a joke.

II

It was long after midnight when the old man heard his son's horse-and-cart jolting up the rock-strewn bohereen. In that dead hour he could hear it even when a great way off. He had not expected Michael earlier, he had been at Inchigeela fair. Some little brightness came into the dull face to hear the sound of the wheels. That fair day used to be a bright feature in his own life in the days now gone for ever; he thought it meant the same for his son, as in some measure it did; and with each recurrence of the event some little trace of his old alertness would struggle up in the old man's face, and that unlovely smile was sure to follow. After long waiting he heard the son putting up his horse. He entered and his face was a great broad smile.

"'Tis a queer thing I'm after hearing this day," he said to his father.

"What was it?" and the old man scanned his son's face, rather pleased, perhaps, as well as a little jealous, to find in it the excitement and jollity of strong drink.

"What was it?" he said.

"Well, then, 'tis this: I'm after learning, and from good authority, that if yourself and herself died together on the wan day on me I'd get a notice in the paper for the same money as if it was only one of ye was in it!" And he sat on a stool, with one gaiter dangling in his hand, and he laughed stupidly, and with such loudness as seemed sacrilegious in that solemn mountain glen, in that great darkness and silence.

"Wouldn't ye do it, and I promise ye, ye'd get it—the notice!"

"Do what?"

"Die, the pair of ye, on the wan day!"

The old man growled at him and turned away. The son went off in a great fit of laughter. Likely enough his horse had often heard him laugh that night as he came the long twenty-seven miles of bogland and mountain. And the great joke held him for several weeks!

Although he had answered not a word, this new idea took possession of the old man's mind. But whereas formerly in those odd moments when in imagination he would behold his neighbours passing the paper which contained his own death-notice from hand to hand, he always felt nothing but joy and pride, now there was in the dream some shadowy fear he could not fathom, could not put aside. There was certainly no feeling of pride left in him. In fact he soon came to trying to avoid the vision; it had now, however, become part of himself, so keenly had he desired it, so frequently had he indulged it. He could not avoid it. At any moment of great stillness it would suddenly stand before him—a group of his neighbours—old Padraig Lynch, old Tadhg Cremin, old Steve Casey, with his one eye, old Morty Shea, with his high, white forehead and glasses—there they were, all gathered together around the Master while he read out to them "At their son's residence in Lyrenascaul, at an advanced age, Jeremiah and Mary Cotter. . . . " Ah! that was it: there were now always the two names coupled together in the death-notice he beheld his neighbours reading. Yet in spite of his new-sprung hatred he couldn't banish the vision, couldn't prevent its reappearance at the most unexpected hours.

If he woke up in the still night what else was there for him to think about? In fact it seemed as if he had been waked up for the one purpose of seeing the vision, as if indeed the vision had been waiting for him to awaken. In great and terrifying clearness there was Morty Shea, that calm, saintly-looking man with the white forehead and the glasses, there was Steve Casey, with the one eye, a black slit where the other should be, listening, intently listening; there, too, was—. All joy had passed away out of old Diarmuid's mind.

When his wife, who was now almost ninety, he himself was ninety-three, brought in a ponny of milk to him he would strain whatever sight he had left to look slyly up in her face; he would also pass his hand over hers—he was glad if it felt distinctly hotter or distinctly colder; he was depressed if it seemed the same as his own. He would make sly inquiries of his son as to how she was in health.

It was another fair day, a mellow harvest-golden day in September; the son was again from home. He would not be home till late. Towards evening the old woman brought in some milk and home-made bread to the bed-ridden man. They had nothing to say to one another. They were too old. She waited till he had finished, she then carried out the vessels again. He settled himself for a comfortable sleep; he would then wake up refreshed and be ready to receive the news of the fair; it had become a point of honour with him to be awake on such occasions. He had not been long asleep when he awoke with a curious tingling sensation, and there was that terrible vision once again, the same faces, the same attitudes. And he was disturbed. He should not have awakened so soon.

"Maire!" he called out in his wheezy voice.

There was no sound, except the water running down that slab of rock behind the house.

"Maire! Maire!"

Even while he called, it was of his own fear he was thinking. And then, horribly real—the people in the vision began to move, a hand was lifted, an eye turned—

* * * * *

"Don't forget the R.I.P., Master," said their son. "If that wasn't in it he wouldn't be satisfied, even how long we made it."

"I have R.I.P. in it."

"Read it now."

"At their son's residence, Lyrenascaul, Jeremiah and Mary—"

# Daniel Corkery

## *The Cobbler's Den*

### I
#### The Trump of Doom

In every close-knitted nest of lanes you will find a sort of guest-house—a chosen spot where the gossips meet. It may be a little huxter's shop, or a little newspaper shop, a barber's shop, or, best of all, a cobbler's workroom.

If you went even casually into John Ahern's little cobbler's shop—it had once been a shop anyway, for the counter still remained—you would feel almost at once that you had arrived at one of those belated guest-houses. First of all, you leant over the counter and he looked up at you from his stool—a kindly-eyed man, with a head entirely bald, except for a fuzzy-wuzzy top-knot in front, that seemed to announce somehow the innocence that was in him. But before long you were inside the counter, seated on a crazy stool at the fire, and he had wheeled round his bench to be able to gossip with greater comfort.

The Blind Man would then come in. He spent his days going from door to door, encumbered with a stick and an accordeon. The stick he never seemed to use, the accordeon he never played; yet on a good day he would bring back eighteen-pence. He was a quiet, happy man who loved his pipe. Although he might have passed the day in the most noisy part of the city, he would sit quite silent of an evening at John Ahern's fireside, as if he had only risen from his bed and had not yet heard the day's news.

And then Maggie Maw would come in. She spoke too much, far too much; but when she took it too far entirely you could say to her, and keep on saying it, Maggie Maw, Maggie Maw, and so get her out, raging mad. She was a dealing woman. From wholesale chinaware stores she would buy for little or nothing chipped ware and odd cups and saucers, and this merchandise she took from house to house and exchanged for soiled or torn clothes which, in turn, she bartered for cash. She was worn to a shadow; but it was not her bartering had worn her away; it was her spirit. This you knew if you saw how she tumbled headlong into whatever argument would be going on at John Ahern's. There was scarcely a night that would not finish by her flinging out of the house with fire in her eyes—victorious or, for the moment, routed.

Very quietly she would come in; she always came in very quietly—passionate people are either dead or blazing. But at her appearance a change would come over us all; John Ahern would begin to talk and to hammer on his lap-iron like anything, this was to get up his courage; and the Blind Man's head would begin to move about more jerkily: when he took the pipe from his mouth and held it poised an inch or two away from his lips, the storm had begun.

This night when she came in, the cobbler was in the midst of some old rambling stories he had about the floods that used to rise up in the centre of the city in other years. Dead cows, he said, he had seen floating in the streets, as well as great trees and empty boats. And he had seen a hen-coop on one occasion. But the worst flood of all was the one that swept a poor watchman off his feet as he turned a corner, and drowned him.

"Maybe 'twas a big flood," said Maggie, "but it wasn't as big a flood as was in me Uncle Din's time."

"'Twas bigger, Maggie," the shoemaker replied, calmly.

"It couldn't be bigger," returned Maggie, just as calmly.

"'Twas bigger, Maggie, I seen the two of them."

"How could it be bigger? What was it but a rain flood? Didn't I often hear tell?"

"'Twas a tide flood, Maggie, everywan knows that."

"How could it be a tide flood, in the name of goodness? Catch a watchman not to know if a tide flood wasn't coming—unless he was a country boy, and no wan ever seen a watchman that was a country boy."

"'Twas a rain flood and a tide flood together, I'm telling ye," said the cobbler, giving the boot-sole a terrible bang.

"Well, that's the best of all," said Maggie, with that pertinacity of hers which always made us wild, "a rain flood and a tide flood together, and me brave boy of a watchman, born and reared in the Marsh, not to know that neither wan nor the other was coming!—well, Mr. Ahern, you must think we're terrible greenhorns altogether. Of course I'm not saying that we aren't, because we all know what you think of us; but praise be to God 'tisn't to you we'd be coming if 'twas a character we'd be wanting and—"

But a little barefooted boy had come in to see if Mr. Field's boots were done, and as Maggie noticed how he was staring up at her, she thought it better to turn away and poke the fire and at last to sit down. The Blind Man put the pipe again into his mouth and leaned back against the wall.

When the little boy had gone out, the cobbler remained bent over his work for quite a long time; but Maggie was busy with her thoughts—even the Blind Man could feel that.

"The flood in me Uncle Din's time, 'twas awful altogether," she began, quite simply, "'twas how the weirs bursted; and of course no wan was prepared for a thing like that. Maybe the people living near the bridge, although I never heard tell of anywan living there, maybe they heard the roaring of all the water coming down; but not a living soul was thinking of a flood that night. They were all in their beds with the first sleep over them—only for Jim Costello wouldn't there be hundreds and thousands of them drownded—a flood like that rising up unbeknownst!"

The Blind Man took his pipe from his lips—an action that encouraged Maggie more than one might imagine; her brain worked the quicker for it.

"Jim Costello was sleeping on the ground floor, and 'twas a noise again the window he heard that woke him, and he sat up and he said, 'Cush, cush,' thinking that maybe it was a cat; but, lo and behold you, there it was again, rubbing and leaving; and so he pulled the blind aside, and he saw a light moving, and there were voices speaking to wan another. But the queer thing was he didn't see any water, for what was he doing but looking through the branches of a tree—'twas a floating tree was rubbing again the glass all the time. All at wanst the tree said Swish! and away it went sailing for itself, and then he could see the lantern shining in the water, and when he put his foot out of the bed, 'twas into cold water he put it. He called out to the people in the boat, and they came over and took him off; but just when he was in it, he said; 'Wait a while, now, men; I won't be long,' and he went back into his little caboose of a room again, and they waited, thinking 'twas something good he was gone back for; but sure it wasn't; what did he come out with but his connopium."

"His what?" said the Blind Man.

"His connopium, he was in a band the boys had. Well, they pushed away through the floods, and there wasn't a sign of life anywhere, only blackness and misery all around them, with the houses dark, and all fast asleep. 'Tis right we give them a chance for their lives, anyway,' said Jim, and with that he blew into his connopium terrible strong, and, to make it sound like the last day, he played up 'Arise ye dead and come to Judgment!'"

"My God!" said the Blind Man.

"Yes indeed, sir, 'Arise ye dead and come to Judgment!' was what the poor souls heard, and maybe some of them dreaming and some of them sick and sore."

"But they were all saved?"

"Hundreds and thousands; but sure some of them were never the same afterwards." She said this rising up from her chair and pulling her shawl about her.

"Never the same, sir," she repeated.

"They warn't!" said the shoemaker, under his breath.

"'Tis to this good man I'm talking, sir," said Maggie, indicating the inoffensive Blind Man, and she left us, rather more self-satisfied than usual.

After a pause the Blind Man said:

"What's a connopium?"

John Ahern raised up his head and looked bothered for a moment; then enlightenment came into his eyes:

"There's no such thing," he said, drawing hard at the waxed hemp, saying "Ha! ha!" breathily in the dint of exertion. Then there was another pause; and again the Blind Man spoke:

"That tune, 'Arise ye dead and come to Judgment,' must be grand, but I never heard it?"

"Hard for ye."

"How so-a?"

"There's no such tune; you couldn't believe daylight from that wan," said the shoemaker.

## II
### The Heiress

The shoemaker came in with the light of discovery in his eyes; he was both happy and excited. The Blind Man and myself were waiting for him, and I was now more than glad at not having gone away; for when that light is in a person's countenance it is a cruel thing if he must keep his story all to himself. Besides, a story of something that has just happened is always better than an old story you have heard before. By the way in which he delayed over beginning his tale, we knew he thought much of it. He was evidently very pleased to have us there to listen to him.

"Leave me alone! Leave me alone!" he was saying as he tied on his apron, although we hadn't as yet questioned him about the matter at all. "Leave me alone!" he said again as he sat down on his bit of a stool; and "Well! Well!" he muttered, as he looked through his glasses at a pair of boots that had come in since he went out; he didn't see a bit of these two raggy boots he held in his hand, soles up. All this, of course, was acting. At last he had to make a beginning:

"Do you know what I'm after seeing?" he said, looking straight at us.

"We do not," we said.

"Maggie Maw," he answered, "and she arm-in-arm with the Heiress!"

"Go on!" we said, surprised.

"Yes, indeed, on the Grand Parade."

And then he went into the whole matter. The point of his discovery was that Maggie Maw—we had often heard her—had been the most outspoken and vigorous scorner of all those who had been seen to make up to the Heiress, now that she was an heiress and had ceased to be an apple woman. Old the Heiress was, old and withered, a small little thing, a quiet but not unhappy woman so long as her trade was apple-selling in the open-air market-place. There she used to sit, her apples spread around her in great heaps, and if no one was buying she made the time pass by humming old songs that had been street songs when she was a little girl. We had never known that she had a brother in America until the news came one fine morning that he had died and left his sister heiress to half a brand-new American city. Of course the will was disputed both in the Irish and

American law-courts, as such wills always are—and altogether there was a heap of trouble, the days, the months, the years passing on meanwhile, and feeble wits getting older and feebler. Far and wide poor old Judy Brien, honest woman, became known as the Heiress, and her picture appeared in the newspaper; it was no wonder then people had made up to her; and these people were scorned by us who had known poor Judy all our lives, but of course none of us scorned them as Maggie Maw did: fire would come into her eyes as she spoke of them. And now here was Maggie Maw herself making up to the Heiress! The like of it was never known. The shoemaker awaited her with shining eyes; and we waited to see what would happen.

At last she came in; and immediately the shoemaker began:

"Wisha, Maggie," he said, "maybe you could give a poor struggling shoemaker the lend of a ten-pound note?" And he winked at us.

"Maybe 'tis two of them the poor man will be getting, if he waits for it," she answered, settling herself down, and looking around at us, as if she had said something very clever. There was a little rest then; but the shoemaker began again:

"Mrs. Cullinane," he said to her, "maybe when you get the chance, you'll recommend a man you've known all your life to the grand ladies—the grand ladies who'd be able to give him a decent penny for his work?"

She knew then he was up to something. She cried out:

"In the name of goodness, Mr. Ahern, tell me what it is ye're driving at, at all, at all?"

"Mrs. Cullinane," he answered, "I'm driving at nothing, only we're honoured by the grand company we're keeping this holy and blessed night!"

How it would have ended I don't know; but then a very queer thing happened: Just as John Ahern let it out that he had seen her walking arm-in-arm with the Heiress, and just as she cried out, "'Tis a shame for ye; leave the poor creature alone; I tell you I wouldn't swop my own station in life with that poor distracted woman this night,"—just as she said this, in walked the Heiress herself! We hadn't a word in us. Though the courts, it was said, allowed her a few shillings a week until their decision would be made, the poor woman had become quite old-looking and feeble, her hands were crooked and skinny, and her face pinched with the hunger and cold. It was a great pity she ever heard of this American money at all: her mind was going. We made room for her at the fire, and she spread her blue hands out to the heat of it.

She seemed greatly disturbed. There she sat gazing at the heart of the fire, not speaking a word, nor understanding a word of what we were saying. It was likely she was thinking of the one thing always. Maggie Maw had said "Sh!" as soon as she came in the door; then she rose and pinched the Blind Man and told him who the visitor was, and after that we had great trouble in keeping up some sort of conversation.

Yes, not one word of our gossip did the Heiress pay attention to. Maggie Maw, good-hearted soul as she was, would hand her the snuff-box or bid her draw in to the fire—and a fine fire it was, for the Heiress's boots began soon to steam in front of it— they were sodden from her wanderings in the guttery streets. And generally Maggie treated her as you'd see a mother treating a child that was beginning to get better after a long sickness.

At ten o'clock the Heiress got up and went out as silently as she had come in, our eyes following her to the door.

It took us some time to get back to our joking. At last, however, we saw the shoemaker hold out a little tin box of tacks he had to Maggie Maw, as if it were a box of the best snuff. Without stopping to look at it, she put it away in the middle of whatever she was saying to the Blind Man. Then the cobbler said, mimicking the gentle way in which she had spoken to the Heiress:

"Maybe you'd draw in to the fire, ma'am, you're after travelling a power and all, to judge be the state of your boots." She got cross with him.

"Mr. Ahern," she said, "maybe you didn't see the tears running down the cheeks of that poor misfortunate creature?"

"Go on, now, Maggie," he said, trying to put her off.

"'Tis no lie," she said.

"There were no tears," he said.

"There was."

"Was she swinging on her stool, back and forwards?" said the Blind Man.

"She was so-a!" said Maggie.

"The poor thing," said the Blind Man, "is it how she's after hearing she's not the real heiress at all?"

"'Tis worse than that."

"In the name of God, how could it be worse?"

"Well, 'tis worse, 'tis far worse!"

"Go 'long, Maggie, go 'long with you!" said the shoemaker, as if he was ashamed of her lies.

"'Tis worse I'm telling you," she repeated.

They kept it up that way, the two of them, until the Blind Man had to put out his stick straight before him:

"Stop now, all of ye, stop! stop! I say, and let us hear what the woman has to say."

Well, then they stopped, and Maggie after settling her hair began:

"And I coming down the Parade who did I see on before me but herself—"

"Ah!" the shoemaker said, not caring if she stopped again.

"Don't mind your Ah's or your Oh's, if you please, sir, or I'll rise up this minute and walk out that door!"

Not one of us said a word; and Maggie went on:

"There she was, walking on before me, and I hardly knew her, 'cause it wasn't her own natural walk at all she had, but a grand sort of walk, with her head stuck up in the air, like them painted damsels on the stage that you'd see going around with little pug-dogs in their arms—well, there she was walking along like wan of them: 'Glory be to God,' I says to myself, 'is it how the poor thing is going out of her mind entirely?' and so I followed along through the crowd, and leave me tell you, 'tis around her the crowd was going, for she wouldn't get out of the way for any of them, not she—"

Maggie took breath here, and then she turned towards the Blind Man, touching his arm: "Would you believe me, sir, I forgot where I was going with following her. God knows I followed her like you'd follow a poor foolish man who would have a drop of drink in him, afraid he'd do some harm to himself—"

"Go on with the story," said the Blind Man; his poll was back against the wall, and his face was staring at the ceiling.

"Sudden-like she stops; and there was a grand closed-up motor car standing beside the pathway; and over she steps, and in she gets, as quick as lightning, and bangs in the door after her. 'Hey!' says one of them news-boys to the driver—he was sitting half-asleep in the front of the car—'Hey!' he says, 'look at who's after going in!'—and just then out of the shop comes the grand lady who owned the motor. Ah, 'tis then there was the confusion, and nobody but meself there to explain the ins and outs of the whole affair, and I trying to talk to three or four people at the one time. If you please, she didn't want to come out! 'Who are ye?' she says. 'Go 'way,' she says, 'I don't know wan of ye,' she says—"

"Look at that for you!" said the Blind Man.

"'Drive on,' she says. Well, sir it was I got her out, and a hard job I had to keep her out of the hands of the police—"

"And was that the time I saw ye?" said the shoemaker.

"It was then, and though she's an heiress an' all, I'm not one bit sorry for what I done—so there!"

"'Tis how she thought she had the money in her fist—oh dear!" said the Blind Man.

"As I'm after saying, I wouldn't swop with her this night," said Maggie Maw.

"Is there anything worse than being mad?" questioned the Blind Man.

We couldn't say.

"There is," he said, "'tis worse to be half-mad."

"How so-a?" said John Ahern.

"Because 'tis only the people who are half-mad knows they're mad at all—"

"That's a fact, anyway."

"If that poor woman was swinging backwards and forwards on her stool, like Maggie says she was, the tears were running down her face all right—and no wonder."

"And to think," says Maggie Maw, "all the singing she used to have in her and she selling her handful of apples on the Square—"

"That's what herself was thinking of and she sitting there to-night—" the Blind Man broke in.

"What makes you say that?"

"What else brought her back to the old spot?" he answered.

"Praise be to God," said Maggie, looking up at his calm face, "the blind do be very wise," and then she added, "well, God leave us the senses anyway, money or no money."

### III
#### The Wake

"In spite of all," said Maggie, "that Hannah Gillane is a

proud wan, and the spirit's not broke in her."

"She was always proud," said John Ahern.

"She was; but 'tisn't everywan would be proud after suffering such a power and all as she's after suffering."

"She's after suffering a lot, God knows; there she is now with neither chick nor child—and such a lot of them there one ten years ago."

We kept still a moment; and then Maggie Maw said:

"Supposing you or me or anywan else in the lane got news home that our last boy was lying dead beyond in America, what would be the first thing we'd do?"

We didn't answer; we knew our ideas wouldn't satisfy Maggie.

"I'll tell you," she continued, "ye'd call a neighbour in—thanks be to God, the lane, bad and all as it is, isn't without a kind neighbour yet—well, ye'd call a neighbour in; and then another neighbour, that would be just after hearing the news, would come in, and then ye'd have a good cry over the boy—God between us and all harm—and 'twould do everywan a world of good."

"'Twould that," said the shoemaker, his head bent on the boot that was caught between his knees.

"But what does she do?—Not a word out of her to man or mortal; but on with her bonnet, and out with the purse, and she fastens the door behind her, and away she goes—business-like to the last and buys everything that's fitting and decent for a Christian wake—think of that, and the boy lying dead, and maybe buried, beyond in America—thousands upon thousands of miles away!"

At this point, the Blind Man came in, put his stick in a corner, and lighted his pipe. While he was settling himself, Maggie's eyes were bent on the fire, and there was a look of great activity in them.

"'Tis of Hannah Gillane we're talking, sir," she said to the Blind Man when he was settled.

"God help her," he took the pipe from his mouth, "'tis she have the great sorrow this night."

"But did ye hear tell what happened at the wake?—maybe ye didn't?"

"What wake?"

"The wake over the boy in America."

"She hadn't a wake surely?"

"She had then, and a good wake."

"Oh my!"

"But leave me tell ye."

We made ourselves comfortable. We had heard whispers in the lane; now we were about to hear the full and all of it; after all there was no one like Maggie; when she told you a story there was no fear you'd hear it better elsewhere; nothing ever escaped her.

"Well, at the beginning, leave me tell ye, 'twas such a terrible lonesome thing to see the four candles lighting on their four cold plates—and lovely plates they were—and the room done up, so spotless and shining you could take your meals off the floor, and the bed laid out, and, God help us! nothing on it! 'Twas the lonesome look of the bed was the worst; as I say, I shivered—"

"No wonder," said the shoemaker.

"And no real corpse I ever seen made me shiver—isn't that strange?"

"I can believe you."

"Well, there were four or five market-women sitting in the room, one here and another there, and not a word out of them; and there was herself, with her white, stony face, and her best clothes on her, and she going about, cold and independent, and she saying: 'Maybe ye'd rather a drop of wine.'"

"Oh my! Oh my!" said the Blind Man, picturing it all.

"Yes, indeed; you'd think 'twas a heart of stone she had. God knows 'twas as much as I could do to keep without coming away again; but sure that would be a frightful thing to do."

"'Twould indeed."

"'Whatever'll come of it, I'll take a chair, anyway,' I said, and I sat down in a quiet little corner, away from anyone. Well, there we were, sitting silent for a long time, and then, little by little, we got to talking of one thing and another; but all the same what was I doing but counting up the hours. Every time I heard Shandon strike, and we were so silent-like, I heard every quarter of it—I'd say: 'I'll stay another half-hour, and that's all.'"

"It must be terrible on you."

"'Twas, cold and lonesome and sad, and all on account of that empty bed. But maybe herself had something to do with it, too, for now—'erra leave me alone, 'tisn't like human nature at all she is—"

"That's true anyway."

"Is she now?—with her white face, and her slow eyes, and not a tear out of them. No wonder we were afraid to leave the second word out of us for fear we'd say something would offend her. And what happened in the end—well, 'twas all her own fault in a way."

"How so-a?"

"I'll tell you, then,—because when people are happy and talking they don't drink half as much as they do when they're gloomy and silent—hushed-up-like in themselves, nothing to do but drink the drink that's put before you—and let me tell you, 'twas good drink, too—I'll say that for her."

"So you may."

"After a while, when we were getting a little nice in ourselves, we began to find our tongues all right, and then there was talk and plenty of it, and, indeed, maybe too much of it. Anyway, 'twas after getting to be like any ordinary Christian wake—except for the bed, of course—and there was Shandon striking out the hours fine and bold, and not one of us thinking of stirring."

"But herself?"

"The same as ever, not a word out of her."

"God help her," said the Blind Man.

"We were nearly after forgetting her by this. All of a sudden, as will happen at the best of wakes, the talk stopped, and there was no one ready to keep it going; 'twas very awkward, you know, and so at last poor Moll Meany—(she was very salubrous in herself, let me tell you) what does she do but look up towards the bed, and sure I suppose she couldn't see the wall, not to mind the bed; looks up at the bed, and blinks her little eyes at it, and says, like as if it was any ordinary, homely wake: 'Isn't it the handsome corpse he is!'"

"She did!" said the Blind Man.

"Would you believe me, we all looked up at the head of the bed before we knew what we were doing! When I thought of what we were after doing, well, I felt I'd go down through the ground with shame."

"But herself?"

"Up she gets, mad and tearing, and she whiter than ever—'Out with ye,' she says, 'ye pack of tipplers, ye pack of tipplers, ye pack of dirty tipplers!' 'Twasn't long or lazy we were making for the door—all except poor Moll herself—between us we had to bring her down; and 'twas a job we had with that fierce woman pitching us to the dogs and calling on her dead boy to take her away from us! Wasn't that a terrible thing?"

"A terrible thing, right enough," said the shoemaker.

"'Twas—and do you know I'd be ashamed to meet that woman in the lane now, I couldn't face her, I'd be afraid."

"You needn't then," said the Blind Man, "'tisn't of you or Moll Meany that woman is thinking."

IV
The Forgiveness

There was a sort of hub-bub in the lane, a quiet sort of hub-bub, people going from door to door, and stopping in the street to talk with one another. And it was all on account of what the Night Watchman had said about Theig Gorman, the mason. It wouldn't have mattered in the least if it were about anyone else he had said it; since it was about Theig, however, it filled us with wonder, for he was like no one else in the place. He had been, as long as any of us remembered, living with his sister in a little house in a corner of The Alley. It was the only house in the place that had geraniums in the window, it was the only house that kept no lodgers. Neither he nor she troubled anyone, and no one troubled them: they lived quietly and alone. He was a hard, bitter old man, and she was a quiet, devout woman, who spent much of her time in the Franciscan Church. And so for long periods, he being so hard and forbidding-looking, and she so quiet and silent, you would not hear even their names mentioned, not to mind hearing any news about them. For all that, no boy or girl ever grew up in the lane without coming to know that there was some mystery about the dark, silent man who lived in the nicely-kept house in The Alley, without coming to know also that the mystery was whether or not Theig Gorman was a married man.

Beyond this the young people never went; they began to grow old, the question remaining as dark as ever. If he were a married man, there was no one to say that he had ever seen the wife or knew where she lived or whether she had not long since died. The little house with the geraniums in the window kept its secret.

This evening it was the Blind Man began—he said:

"After all the years I'm going around the lanes, I couldn't swear this moment he's a married man; maybe he's not, maybe 'tis only a rumour that got out sometime about him, and that he only laughed at it in the beginning, and after a while—"

"Don't you know very well that Father Lenihan asked him the question plump and plain—?"

"Well, an' if he did, what answer did he get?"

"'Meaning no disrespect, Father,' he says, "tis so long ago I can't tell'—that's what he said."

"And what would a person take out of that?"

"That he was married once upon a time, anyway?"

"But how could a man forget whether he was married?"

"Maybe he didn't forget?"

"And the world and all knows that that poor sister of his came from America to keep house for him, and he still a young man, for that's forty year ago, if 'tis a day."

"Very well, and what brought her home? Believe you me there was something very strange behind all that—a young man to bring his sister home from America to keep house for him, and she earning good money over there!"

"Wisha! if he was married itself, no blame to anyone for going away from him, for he was always a sour, crabbed sort of man—" It was a stray customer of John Ahern's said this, and the Blind Man didn't like it.

"But was he always sour and crabbed?"

"Erra, he was, ever and always," said John himself.

And then Maggie Maw came in, grave, yet shining, a light in her eyes. The first word she said was: "I have it all!" And so we made room for her—our own Maggie.

"Now, for the love of God, don't let one of ye say hum nor haw out of ye, for 'tis the queer, outlandish thing is after happening in this lane: last night it happened and we all asleep in our beds!"

Up the shoemaker straightened his back and looked at us:

"I knew I heard something," he said, staring us all in the face.

"You did not!" said Maggie, and she stared back at him, with fire in her eyes. Soon enough his head went down:

"Maybe I didn't," he said, beginning again to work silently.

"Theig Gorman is a married man," said Maggie, after a while.

"Go on!" we said, all of a heap. The Blind Man took his pipe from his lips, John Ahern nodded his head as if to say "I knew it, I knew it."

"Married in Tralee town, forty years ago, come next September," Maggie added.

And again the shoemaker nodded, as if he knew that, too; and Maggie caught sight of him doing so:

"Mr. Ahern," she said, "maybe you'll tell us where his wife was all these long, forty years?"

But he was trying too hard to pull out a nail that had gone in crooked, to answer her; he was a poor fool of a man, at the best.

"Where was she, Maggie?" said the Blind Man, quietly.

"Running mad in the wilds of Kerry—there's a damsel for you!" she answered, flinging up her head.

There never was such a story.

"Maybe I'm too hard on her; but it seems she was a barmaid in some house there, and me young mason from Cork— he wouldn't be more than twenty then, I suppose—took up with her, and married her. Well, when the job was done, when the convent was built, and me mason thinking of bringing home his bride, lo and behold you, me lady escapes and there's no tidings of her!"

"Hoity-toity," said John Ahern.

"Neither tale nor tidings of her. The poor man comes home to his empty shell of a house, and has to write off to America, begging and imploring his sister to come home and live with him, and save him from the lodging-house keepers. And so she did. And she earning good money and all at the gusseting, up she gets and comes home, and keeps house for her brother, and he a sour and a bitter man that would be getting worse and worse as the years went by. Well, if there's anywan will be rewarded by the God above for doing her duty, 'tis that girl Hetty Gorman, though 'tis an old woman she is now, by the same token."

"She is that—you could tell it by the way she walks," said the Blind Man.

"Well, sir," Maggie took up her tale again, "the years go by—well and good; but first I ought to tell you that Theig himself went down to Tralee, all the way, three times he went down, looking for her, and all in vain: even the priests couldn't help him; me fine lassie wouldn't be said by man or mortal, only take her fling as long as she was young and handsome. He soon got sick of it, trying to bring the wanderer home; I can vouch for it myself he didn't sleep a night out of his little house in the corner for the last thirty-seven years."

"Are you sure of that now?" said the shoemaker, foolishly. Maggie raised up her eyes and was about to say something very saucy when the Blind Man said: "Go on, Maggie," quietly and gravely; he was not a bit like John Ahern, he was now probably thinking of how very different from his expectation these long years of marriage had turned out for the mason. The thoughtful tone of his voice solaced Maggie, and she went on with more life and earnestness:

"At last after forty years, to make a long story short, the Missioners—the Redemptorists—and sure they're the hardest of all, come to Tralee. The tents are set up outside the chapel. The lights are blazing. The chapel is crowded to the doors, morning and evening and all day long; and everyone is talking about the mission, and back-biting the people who aren't taking advantage of it; and every morning the Missioners go round the lanes to the houses of the real bad ones—"

"Maybe they caught herself?"

"They did, as nice as tuppence; and they heard out her story, and they wouldn't promise her one bit of satisfaction till she'd go up to Cork and see whether her lawful husband was alive or dead; and in case he was alive, she was to ask his forgiveness and go and live with him if so he'd choose. And so she done. Over the mountains she came—who knows but she walked it?—anyway, and we all in here last night, saying our say, she steals up the lane outside, a poor rag of a woman, a poor sop off of the roads, not knowing what was before her, up the lane she steals and in by the house in the corner. She knocks at the door. Poor Hettie takes her in; himself was out. For a long time she can't speak with the fit of coughing that was on her, and the fright, too, maybe. Anyway, she outs with her story, and Hettie says to her:

"'Tis business for himself; you must wait till he comes home!'"

"Now, here's a queer thing. Nor bite nor sup would she take, only asked and implored to be let alone, sitting before the fire, and the tails of her old skirt steaming, and the cough racking her, and when the fit would be over, nodding her head and shaking herself back and forward and not saying a word. The livelong night poor Hettie went about her business, sweeping the floor, or what not, and maybe killing the poor soul with the sight of the nice clean little house and all the comfort was waiting her all the years if only she thought well to come home to it."

"That's right, Maggie," said the Blind Man.

"What else could the misfortunate creature do only cry down her two eyes?" she then questioned us, with strong faith in her own insight.

"You're right, Maggie," said the Blind Man, again.

"'Twas near twelve o'clock when himself came up the lane. The two of them could hear his heavy boots pounding the paving stones. 'That's himself,' said Hettie. The poor thing took with a tremble. 'Lave me out,' she says, and up she jumps and makes for the door like a cat. But Hettie came between her and the door—them quiet women do be very brave, 'As ye came so far, 'tis as good for ye to see himself,' she says, and just then they heard Theig outside. Back the poor wanderer jumps again and curls up before the fire on the bit of a stool with her back to them all, and pulls the shawl over her head. And in walks the man-of-the-house! He came in heavy and silent, like he is always. Hettie says nothing. He says nothing. He looked at the poor thing, and thought 'twas how she was some poor traveller having a heat of the fire. At last he takes the candlestick and has his foot on the first step of the stairs and is going up to bed when Hettie says, very calm-like, 'Theig,' she says, 'ye'd better talk to your lawful wedded wife.' Erra, you'd think he was struck. He took one step into the room, and over with him to the poor trembling creature, and he drags the shawl back off to her head, and holds the candle into her face, and then he jumps back and he ups with his fist and says: 'Get out! Get out!' he roars at her, and he hardly able to say that same with the smother of rage he was in.

"She didn't stir. He didn't know what to do then. 'Get out of it,' he roared at her again. She didn't stir, only clung against the wall. There wasn't a sound out of her. He had the middle of the floor all to himself. He turned to his faithful sister:

'Hettie,' he says, 'what brought her in?'

'The Grace of God,' she answers."

"Look at that!" said the Blind Man, "the Grace of God."

"He wouldn't be pacified. He sprang at the door, and

nearly tore it down off its hinges in his hurry to open it; and he says:

'Out with you, ye—, or there'll be human blood split on the thrashold of this house this night!'

"The poor drudge got up, and pulled her shawl over her head, and gave one look at Hettie, meaning to ask her to intercede for her—'You'll forgive her, Theig?' Hettie says, calm-like again.

"'Never, so help me!' said the wild man, and out he flings her, not caring whether she fell or stood, and he bangs the door behind her, and goes up to bed without a word out of him.

"Well, that Hettie Gorman is a wise woman. She knew her place better than to open that door after he banging it like that. She just held her tongue and when she was ready, up she goes to her bed."

"And then the Night Watchman—" began the shoemaker.

"Go on, Mr. Ahern," said Maggie, folding her arms. He couldn't go on without spoiling it. He made a sign of submission, and Maggie went on:

"In the middle of the night, just before the dawn came in, poor Hettie woke up, for she thought she was after hearing a moaning. She tried to put it out of her head. She couldn't. And then it came again. She lit her candle. 'What am I to do, in the Name of God?' she says. And the terrible moaning came up again. She got up then and went to her brother's door; she thought he'd be asleep. My dear, she found him sitting up in his bed, as white as a ghost, and he scared, and his eyes standing in his head. He could hardly talk to her.

'Did ye hear it?' he said.

'I did,' she said.

'Is it of this world?' he says, watching her face.

"What was he thinking but maybe the woman threw herself into the tide after the terrible things he said to her.

"'Forgive her, Theig,' says Hettie, putting her hand on his poor old head.

"''Tis she's crying, you're sure?' he says.

"''Tis herself, and she's fasting, and falling with the weakness that's on her.'

"'Tell her I forgive her, only to have her go away out of this.'

"Down Hettie comes; but the poor thing, clung up against

the door like an old cat in the morning, wouldn't take the forgiveness from any lips except his own—the priests wouldn't believe her. So up comes Hettie again:

"'Put your head out that window, and say the one word, and leave the poor soul go away in peace.'

"He did that. 'I forgive you,' he says, 'all and everything, only go away in the Name of God, and don't trouble me ever again.'

"'I'm thankful,' she says, and away she went like a ghost.

"And mind you even that much couldn't happen unknownst. Who should be passing on his rounds but the Night Watchman, and he hears the words coming down in the night—'Only go away in the Name of God, and don't trouble me any more'—and he sees the poor shadow of a woman gliding away, and he thinks and thinks, and blabs the whole story all over the place—God forgive him."

\* \* \* \* \*

That is one of the nights in the Cobbler's Den I remember most distinctly, for Maggie's tale took a long, long time to tell, and when it was over the Blind Man stood up and said:

"Glory be to God, it must be very late—I never heard the lanes so silent," and on that word we all listened and sure enough there wasn't a stir.

"I declare," said the shoemaker, "'tis after twelve!" And so we all stood up, Maggie saying "I'll be kilt"—and made, all of us, for the door. But Maggie pushed us back again as soon as we reached it—"Whisht! Whisht!" she said. And sure enough we heard the sound of a sleepy old horse-and-car coming over the cobbles, and we saw the lantern shining as it moved along. Well, we stood silent in the dark old hall-way, and we saw an old scotch car, piled with Theig Gorman's furniture, go by, and there were all Hettie's geraniums, packed together into a table that was turned upside down. A gas-lamp was shining on them, and the flowers were nodding and shaking as the car jolted.

"That's all the fault of that Watchman, God forgive him," said Maggie again. Theig Gorman went to live in the North Side, and we knew him no more.

## V
### The Revenge

When Maggie came in she said: "The last of the Riordans is dead—God be merciful to her soul."

"'Tis a happy release," said John Ahern.

"Well, 'tis; but in spite of everything, and the hard name and all, the Riordans are an old stock in these parts, and 'tis only natural that a person would be sorry after them."

"Nora Riordan was never the same after Jer. Madigan's funeral."

"She wasn't, how could she?"

"That's twenty-five years ago," said the Blind Man.

"'Tis, and more," said the shoemaker, and he took a mouthful of tacks, as if there was no more to be said.

"'Tis twenty-five years next month, the twelfth," was Maggie's way of confirming quietly the Blind Man's estimate.

"'Tis more," said the shoemaker, as well as he could, without looking up.

"'Tis twenty-five years, neither no more nor less," said Maggie, again with that quietness which invites any amount of argument. The Blind Man put his stick out straight in front of him; it was his way of ruling:

"What does a few years matter to her now and she dead?" he said.

"Or a few pounds?" said John Ahern.

I knew that Nora Riordan was Mrs. Kenneally's maiden name; in the Cobbler's Den old neighbours never lost their maiden names; in these lanes the very children will speak of their mothers as Nora Kelly or Julia Murphy, and at a certain stage of growth are often puzzled over their own names. But my memory did not go back twenty-five years, and so I did not remember Jer. Madigan's funeral.

I beseeched them to let the telling of it to Maggie, knowing that we would never get to the end of it if it was John Ahern or the Blind Man undertook it. For Maggie Maw could not be kept quiet; she would interrupt them at every second word, putting in little things they would have forgotten; the only chance, then, of hearing it outright from start to finish, was to give it altogether to herself. After a moment's pause, she would begin as if the story lay ready before her mind; perhaps she used to be turning such things over and over—she was not able to read. She began in a hard voice:

"The woman that's now lying a corpse—God be merciful to us all—in the Dead House of the Union—'tis she was the hard woman and the able dealer. She could make money out of the stones, as the saying is. What good did it do her?— The devil a ha'p'orth! No doubt she made it honest, but she made it hard. What she made out of the shop—I call that honest money—though 'twas money made out of drink itself. But what she made by other means, *by other means*, well, that's what got her the hard name. Listen, till you hear it, child."

Maggie would call anyone "child" on occasion.

"There was one thing—she kept the best of whiskey—that can't be denied; and she kept a snug house, with a good fire in it, and a red blind on the window, that would be shining down the lane, shining red in the black pools of water at night-time when the gas would be lighting inside it. 'Twas a great help to her— the name the house had for the good stuff. There wasn't a better-known shop in the parish. It was only out of your own door and into Miss Nora's. If you had a visitor, or if it was a marriage, or a death, or a christening, or a boy coming home from the sea or what not—well, 'twas into Miss Nora's with everywan—our second home it was. But for all that, 'twasn't out of the house she made her money: 'twas this way: If you had an old father with a cough, or an old mother with a fatty heart, or a poor child wouldn't live to be a man—well, she'd come at the blind side of you and insure him or her—as the case may be—with a dead-man for a few pence in the week, or maybe a shilling, and then in a year or two or three there'd be my brave Miss Nora getting her twenty, or thirty, or maybe her forty pounds from the insurance company, neat and clean into her hands! When anybody in the place died, what we used to say was: 'There's a score of pounds for Miss Nora!' And so it would turn out.

"That's how she made her money, the most of it, and not out of the house at all; and sure 'twas a mean and stingy way, and a way that couldn't try (thrive) with anyone. She insured Kate Madigan's old father, old Jer. Madigan, as well as anyone else, expecting he'd die in a year or two; but sure he didn't die in ten years, not to mind two! There she was, paying and paying until she was sick and tired of it; to make it worse the poor old man turned daft in the end, went about laughing and smiling and showing his teeth at everyone, and talking about nothing else, up and down the lane, only how Nora Riordan was waiting for him to die and he not going to die at all! He got that small with the age that when he'd go into her house, his head wouldn't hardly reach up to the counter; and there he'd stand, not caring who'd be in the shop, looking up at her, and laughing, and he saying:

"'I'm geh, geh, geh!'"

"That's so," said the Blind Man, "'I'm geh!' that's what he used to say."

"Child," Maggie began again, "that was his way of saying 'I'm dead, dead, dead!' making game of her, you know, he'd be; and after saying that, he'd come out, laughing like a poor idiot, and go up and down the lane again, telling everyone the great joke he was after playing on Miss Nora. My dear, she was belled all over the parish."

"Well, it went on like that, year after year; but faith'n she never gave in; she kept on paying her shilling a week, and at last in the middle of one of the hardest winters we ever had in these parts, after a terrible wild and stormy night, poor Kate Madigan found her old father stiff and cold in his bed. And, signs on it, she hadn't a penny in the house! Not a penny to wake him or bury him. What could she do but go down to Miss Nora's and explain her case? And so she did. And what did Miss Nora say? 'He's dead—is he? Well, he wasn't in much of a hurry anyway!' That's what she said; and not one brown copper would she give poor Kate. She wouldn't even offer her the loan of it. Kate was a poor harum-scarum of a woman, and that hard answer made her frantic; indeed it made all of us frantic. I remember well myself the talk and the arguing, as it spread around the lane, and I remember hearing Kate herself calling down the curse of God on the Riordans, all that ever came and went of them and all that would ever come. I don't say that was right, but I remember it; there she was, standing all alone in the middle of the lane, her hair wild and streaming, and her shawl in a wisp, and the rain falling on her, and the night coming down, and she never caring a brass pin, and all of us pitying her, and peeping out of the doors, and waiting to know how 'twould all end. I needn't tell you Miss Nora never came near the door at all. She was too respectable, my dear. But at last poor Kate stopped up, sudden and sharp, in the middle of a fit of screaming, and out loud she says: 'I know what I'll do,' and away in home she went. And we all said 'She's distracted, poor thing—God guide her this night.'"

"That's so," said the Blind Man, "distracted she was."

"The day for the funeral came. There we were, snapping up our poor piece of a dinner to have it over us, and peeping out the window at the same time for fear we might be late. The coffin, a poor shell of a thing that would hardly hold together during the journey, the coffin went up to her top room all right; we all saw it; but beyond the coffin not another sign of a funeral did anyone see up the lane or down the lane. There wasn't a hearse nor a car nor a carriage nor a bit of linen nor a black band nor anything else whatsomever. Well, at last, and we taking our drink of tea, we saw all the men moving towards the house; and there sure enough was the coffin up on their shoulders, ready to start. Wherever they came from, a multitude of people had gathered round. There they were, a black mass of them around the coffin on every side. Down comes poor Kate Madigan herself, as harum-scarum looking as ever, her hair flying in the wind—and a bad wintry day it was. She stands in the middle of them, and up she stretches her hand, and her arm bare to the elbow—'Round the block, men!' she says, like a general giving his commands. And so they began to move, herself after the coffin, and her shawl back over her head. No hearse, no anything, only the coffin up on their shoulders and the crowds moving behind it. Well, they went up the Alley, around Coppinger's Lane, down Galwey's Lane, out under the archway, and along through Hatton's Court, and that brought them straight in front of Miss Nora's house. When they came near it, Kate Madigan catches the two ends of her shawl in her hands and stretches it from her on both sides, and up she lifts her voice, and begins keening poor Jer. that was up in front of her in the coffin. She was that loud and wild in her screaming that dead and all as he was, you wouldn't know how he could keep himself from hearing her. 'You left me to pull and to drag!' she says, 'You left me to pull and to drag in a world of deceivers!' Everyone knew the meaning she had in them words. And those that didn't were very soon told it, I can tell you. On they passed; and Miss Nora all the time was inside, as stiff as a statue, and her face like marble, and she not daring to come and take a peep out through the window. On they passed, and they came at last back to where they started from, and maybe they thought to stop. Well, if they did, up again goes Kate Madigan's arm, and her fingers working with hate—'Round again, men,' she says, and they obeyed her without a word.

"The crowds of the world were after them. I saw them myself this time and they coming out under the archway, and 'twas how they burst through it, burst through it like water out of a spout, and the coffin swinging to the right and to the left, and faith'n 'twas little peace the poor patient inside in it was getting, between the jolting and the noise and the cries and poor Kate's keening. Again they went by Miss Nora's, and the house kept as silent as before. But if it did, there was poor Kate screaming like a witch, worse than the last time; she was after losing all control of herself by this; and when they reached the end she cries out again. 'Round wanst more!' Well, she won! The third time, there was Father Long standing in the archway, and he blocked their passage, and he spoke quietly to poor Kate, for he saw she was in no fit state to be reasoned with, and he told her to take the coffin into the house again for the night, and that next day there'd be a hearse sent up and everything else was fitting. She consented. And so 'twas done. And only the next day did we learn that the second time the cries came outside her window, Miss Nora fell down in a dead mag—still to the world, and had to be lifted up to bed. Well, as Johnny here says, she was never the same afterwards. And there she's dead now above in the Hospital after all the money she made, and the grand family she reared and buried."

"'Tis no good to be too covetous," said John Ahern.

"'Tisn't," said the Blind Man, "pinching and screwing up for the future, and sure when the future comes there's the Will of God there before us, the same as ever. If It means us to be made, we'll be made; if It means us to be poor, we'll be poor; if It—"

"If It means us to be blind we'll be blind," said the foolish shoemaker. The Blind Man was staggered, but he was good enough for him.

"And if It means us to be a cobbler, a cobbler we'll be!" he answered, and he stood up the same as if he wasn't after saying anything at all. But Maggie Maw had to stick half of her shawl into her mouth and run.

## VI
### Maggie's Way

When it failed John Ahern to get poor Bridgie Heffernan away from the quay wall, to get her away from it and so avoid seeing the dreadful sight she would see if she remained, it was I who was sent to try to do what he had failed to do.

"She's clung again' them, and she neither saw me nor heard me when I spoke to her," John Ahern had explained.

"You only asked her the one time?" the Blind Man questioned.

"The one time, and that itself was a great trial out of me, you don't know the look she have on her."

I found Bridgie still clung against the bars of the slip, the slip from which her little boy, the only child she had left, had made his way into one of the empty fishermen's boats that always lie anchored there, and so had come by his death. With a bit of packing-case he had paddled her out to where his uncle's boat—the Lurline—lay moored in mid-stream, and then in getting from one boat into the other he had fallen between the two and was drowned. That is how his companions explained it, and no doubt they were right. Well, there now was the mother, her bony work-worn hands clutching the iron bars, staring with mad eyes at the dragging operations that went on in the middle of the river. In the boat were three men: a large-bodied policeman filled all the stern, doing nothing it seemed except weighting the boat; the drowned boy's uncle, Jack Heffernan, in his thick fisherman's woollens, handled the rope to which the stroke-haul was fixed, while his son, Jim, grasping a long pole, stood ready to catch the body when it would have come near the surface. It was to prevent her from seeing the recovery of the dead body of her only child that we were trying to get Bridgie Heffernan away from the slip.

The work went on in silence now, in slowness, too, but when six hours earlier they began it, there was noise enough, hurry, too, people on either riverside shouting directions and advice. One could not imagine how the body could have escaped the hooks so long, considering that it was quite certain where the boy had been drowned. Yet escape the hooks it did, and unpleasant imaginations had begun to disturb the minds of those people who had been looking on a long time. What must it have been for the mother! She had become so silent and wild-looking that she stood now in the centre of a little cleared space, people watching her from behind or peeping at her sideways out of the corners of their eyes. When I saw that cleared space and noticed the wild white look she had about the eyes, I knew that I, too, should fail, and my heart sank. Little by little, however, I pushed through the crowds and at last got near her:

"Bridgie," I said, "there's John Ahern after wetting a cup of tea for you."

What I will not forget is the way she turned her head to see who had spoken, and then how she opened and shut her mouth a few times, moistening her lips with her tongue, as one might do after a long sleep. And her brows worked a little, as if she were trying to recollect what had been said to her:

"Bridgie," I said again, "John Ahern is after wetting a cup of tea for you—" but before I had got half through the words she had turned away, and her eyes were now fixed again on the men in the boat. I lingered by her for some time, and remember noticing how you would not remark the sun shining on the water if it wasn't for the boat and the men in it. On them alone it seemed to shine, on the boat, the men, and on the white bright drops of water that were falling from the rope as Jack Heffernan hauled it in or dragged it along. But when you raised your eyes, there was the statue of the Blessed Virgin on the Dominican Church shining like gold, and beyond it and above it was Shandon Steeple shining, too; and all the windows in the houses on that closely-built hillside were flashing back the sun like signals or burning like flares. It was a golden, sunny evening.

When I looked again at Bridgie she seemed not to be seeing anything at all; listening she seemed to be, listening intently. Then I felt she wouldn't notice if I slipped away.

In John Ahern's there was a little crowd awaiting me. They wanted to question me. I forestalled them:

"Is Maggie after coming?" I said.

"No—there's no trace of her anywhere;—well—you didn't succeed?"

"Leave me alone for God's sake," I said, "and let us all sit down or scatter away out of this until Maggie comes."

"Did you speak to her at all?" said John Ahern.

He had his new coat still on him, and he looked very awkward, standing up, instead of sitting down, not knowing what to do with himself.

"You know very well I asked her." I was getting cross with them.

"Maggie Maw is never where she's wanted; that woman would break your heart sometimes," he said.

Someone else took up the talk:

"Another evening she'd be in and out like an old hen."

"Did ye try the market?"

"What's the use of saying that? I declare to God I'm sick and tired of answering that self-same question."

"You're right," said the Blind Man to me, "'twould be better for us to sit down and not to be losing our tempers; it might be better for you, John, to take off your coat and go on with your work."

"I will not go on with my work," he answered; he had often given the little lad who now lay in the river a penny for taking a finished job to the owner. "I will not go on with my work—what a thing I'd do!"

"Well," the Blind Man said again, "you might as well; there's no one but Maggie will get that poor creature to leave her post, by all I hear."

John Ahern would have answered back, but just then poor Bridgie Heffernan herself, the poor woman we had been talking about, appeared in the doorway: "Excuse me, neighbours," she said, and turned to look behind her, as if she didn't know what else to do or say; and there behind her, to our astonishment, was Maggie herself, her two hands steering the poor distracted creature along, just as you'd have to guide a blind man up a narrow gangway.

"You'll excuse us, John," said Maggie then, "you'll excuse us for making so free."

We thought that a rather queer thing for her to say; but anyway she had done what we had failed in, she had got the woman away from the quayside. And so we trusted that her way was right. We pushed back and made room; and over to the table she piloted the distracted woman—and a quiet soul that poor Bridgie Heffernan always was—sat her down at it, poured her out a cup of tea, poured one out, too, for herself, and without another word they began to drink it. We kept our eyes away from them, and John Ahern took off his coat and hung it up, slipped on his apron, and sat down to his bench; the Blind Man took out his pipe and emptied it on the hob. And the meal went on, almost in dead silence, for a little while; suddenly, however,

Bridgie looked around at us, a half-eaten piece of bread in her hand, and nodded, with a curious look in her eyes, once or twice at John Ahern. He nodded back. Then she said, breaking out suddenly into rapid speech:

"If you want e'er a little boy to run a message for you, or tidy up the place, a little boy you'd like to have on the same floor with you, or maybe 'tis an apprentice itself you'd be wanting, and sure he's nearly old enough for that same, maybe you won't forget my little Paddy, sir?"

"I won't forget him, ma'am," answered John Ahern, bravely enough, for all his astonishment. She nodded again at him, as if more than thankful, and then turned to the Blind Man (he was sitting perfectly still, a bit of a penknife stuck in the bowl of his pipe), and said, again with the same hurried speech:

"And you, sir, God knows 'tis often I gave you my heart's pity and you going along through the crowds without one with you or a word out of you, and if he'd be any company to you, or any help at all, there's that little boy of mine—a willing little child, and you'd like to hear him speaking, although he has no more sense for a boy of his age—"

We saw Maggie suddenly stand up; we didn't know why: she had nodded at someone who had thrust a head in the doorway. She took the broken piece of bread from Bridgie's hand, just as you'd do to an infant who had got tired of a crust; she then settled the shawl around her, took her arm and said:

"We'll be going home now, if you don't mind, Bridgie."

We knew then that the signal through the doorway meant that the body had been recovered. Poor Bridgie was staring at Maggie, quite dazed it seemed. Trying to gather her wits, she said:

"Home?"

"That's your place, ma'am," Maggie returned. And then maybe the poor bothered woman saw the tears running silently down from Maggie's eyes, for at that moment she came to herself and you'd think her heart would break.

\* \* \* \* \*

"Look at that!" said the shoemaker, when they were gone.

"Maggie's a great little 'oman!" said the Blind Man, "how did she do it?"

"No, but to get her to eat—that's what's puzzling me."

"'Tis queer," said the Blind Man.

"'Tis queer, and damn queer, too," said the shoemaker, "none of us could do it."

"'Tisn't that at all I mean."

"Well, what do you mean, so-a?"

"'Tis this: now there's us, we have a Maggie in this lane, and in the next lane or the next lane to it, maybe they have a Maggie Maw of their own—who knows? We don't know about their Maggie Maw, and they don't know about ours. Isn't that queer enough for you?"

"'Tis," said John Ahern, he was staring through his glasses up at the Blind Man, trying to follow what he was saying.

"The name of that policeman you were telling me about, John, and Jack Heffernan's name and Jim's name, too—they'll all be in the paper, and right, too; but will you find Maggie's name in it?"

"You will not," we answered, in one voice.

"You will not," he went on, "and I say she's after doing something none of them could do."

"That's so."

"Those grand ladies that do be going about, poking their noses into our little places, they're very knowledgeable right enough; could any of them do what Maggie is after doing this evening, and she neither able to read or write?"

"They could not," said John Ahern.

"They could not," said I.

"Faith'n, they couldn't," said the Blind Man.

# Daniel Corkery

## *Carrig-an-Afrinn*

### I

Dunerling East was its name, the model farm in all that countryside. Only after many years it had come to be so; and Michael Hodnett, the farmer who had made it so, lay fast asleep in his armchair on the right-hand side of the front door. As of its own weight his big strong-looking head had sunken itself deep into his deep chest. The sunshine of the October afternoon was depositing itself lavishly upon him, thickening upon him, it seemed, while slumber bound him there, so huge and lumpish, so inert, so old and fallen. Dunerling East just now was looking more model-like than ever before. The house itself had had all its sashes, its doors, its timber work painted afresh; its blinds and curtains had been renewed; its ivy growths trimmed; and the whole farm, even its farthest fields and screening thickets, spoke of the same well-being, the same skilful management. The sleeper might lawfully take his rest, his spirit had so indisputably established itself everywhere within the far-flung mearings. Even were he to pass away in his sleep, and stranger folk as reckless as might be, to come into possession of the land, many years must needs go by before Dunerling East became hail-fellow-well-met with the farms round about it, shaggy and scraggy as they were, waterlogged in the bottoms and bleached or perished on the uplands, unsheltered by larch or beech.

All this cleaning up had been done in preparation for the first coming together, after many years, of all or nearly all that were left of the family. The arrival of Stephen Hodnett, the third youngest son, from the States had been the occasion. He had brought with him his young wife, and, as well, an elder sister of hers, a young widow, for whose distraction indeed the voyage had been undertaken. Of all the sons of the house this son, Stephen, perhaps had done best: he was now manager of a large bakery store in New York. But the brother next to him in years, Finnbarr, had done well too. He was come, also accompanied by his wife, from Kerry, where he managed a very successful creamery. The son to whom the care of the farm had fallen, to whom indeed the farm now legally belonged, Nicholas by name, had maintained it in the condition to which his father, this old man asleep in the chair, had brought it; perhaps he had even bettered it, but, of course, the land had been got into good heart long before it fell to his turn to till it. Nicholas, though older than Stephen or Finnbarr, had never married: he would wait until his father's death. The only other son of the house was up in Dublin—Father Philip Hodnett, a curate in St. Multose's parish. He was the one living member who was not at present in Dunerling East. Within the house lurked somewhere the eldest living of all the old man's family, Ellen, the second child born to him. She looked old enough to be the mother of those mentioned, even of Nicholas, the eldest of them. She was sixty and looked more. Her cheeks were thin and haggard, colourless, her hair grey, and her eyes stared blankly at the life moving before them as if it were but an insipid and shadowy thing when compared with what moved restlessly, perhaps even disastrously, within the labyrinths of her own brain. On her the mothering of the whole family had fallen when Michael Hodnett buried his wife in Inchigeela.

From the feet of the sleeping figure the ground fell away downwards to a bracken-covered stream. Beyond the bracken it rose again; much more suddenly however, so suddenly indeed that the red earth showed in patches through the tangled greenery. Those reddish patches looked like corbels supporting the cornice-like ledge of the upward-sloping grazing grounds above. Just now, along that sun-drenched ledge, a procession of shapely deep-uddered cattle was moving from left to right, the beasts in single file or in pairs or groups, deliberately pacing. Thirty-one milkers were to pass like that, making for the unseen bridgeway across the stream in the hollow. Presently they would dip from sight and again be discovered in the tree-covered passage trailing up towards the milking sheds, the rich sunshine catching their deep-coloured flanks and slipping swiftly and suddenly from their horns and moving limbs. Anyone who had ever come to know how deeply the sight of that afternoon ritual used to thrill the old man, now so sunken in his sleep, could hardly forbear from waking him to witness it.

Behind the cattle sauntered Nicholas. His head was bent, and in his right hand a sliver from a sally tree lazily switched the cattle along. Although a working day, he was dressed in his Sunday clothes. His gaiters were new, rich brown in colour, and had straps about them; his boots also were new and brown. All day since morning his visitors, his brothers Stephen and Finnbarr and their people, had been away motoring in the hills towards the west—around Keimaneigh and Gougane Barra— and he had found the idle day as long as a week. "Stay where you are," he had said to one of the labourers who were digging out potatoes in the fields behind the house; "stay where you are, and I'll bring them in," and he was glad of the chance to go through the fields one after another until he was come to where the impatient cattle were gathered, anxious and crying, about the fastened gate. Their time for milking was overdue, and they needed no urging towards the sheds. When they were safe across the bridge he left them to themselves: by that time the first of them were already headbound in the stalls. Closing a gate behind them he made diagonally up the sloping field. At his approach his father suddenly raised his head.

"'Tisn't Sunday?" he said, and then, recollecting himself: "They haven't come back yet?"

"Any moment now," Nicholas answered. He then turned his back on him and gazed across the countryside where a couple of roads could be picked out. The weather had been very fine for some weeks and little clouds of sunny dust wavered above them.

"Are the cows in?"

"I'm after bringing them across."

"Is Finn after looking at them?"

"Yes, he'd get rid of the Kerry, he said."

"Didn't I tell you! Didn't I tell you!"

He had filled up with passionate life. As he blurted out the words, he raised his heavy stick in his blob of a hand. Nicholas glanced away from him, and again searched the countryside with his eyes:

"They won't be long now; 'tis as good for us to be going in!"

He put his arm beneath his father's. He lifted him. The old man's right foot trailed uselessly along the ground. But his thoughts were on the cows:

"'Tis often I do be thinking on the two beasts we had and we coming hither from Carrig-an-afrinn. Scraggy animals, scraggy, splintery things."

II

Mrs. Muntleberry, the young American widow, and her sister, Stephen's wife, were both thoughtful gentle women; it was plain in their quiet eyes, their quiet faces. After the meal, homely in its way, but good, they now sat bent forward earnestly staring at the old man who was keeping himself so alert and upright in their midst, ruling the roomful with word, gesture, glance. Of his power of work, of his downrightness, they had, of course, often heard from Stephen: in Stephen himself they had found something of the same character: until to-day, however, they had not realised how timid in him were the strong traits of his father's character. They had been motoring in a world of rock-strewn hillsides; they had swung into glens that struck them cold, so bleak they were, so stern-looking even in the softest tide of the year. Carrig-an-afrinn they had not actually passed through: it would have meant threading slowly up many twisting narrow hillside bohereens in which their car could scarcely turn: perhaps also Stephen had not cared to have them actually come upon the bedraggled homestead—little else than a hut—from which the Hodnetts had risen. They had, however, gone as close to it as the main road allowed them, had seen, and felt almost in their bones, the niggardliness of life among those hillsides of tumultuously tumbled rocks. That wayfaring in bleak places had brought them to understand Stephen's father; even if he were no different this evening, had remained as he had been ever since their arrival—drowsing between sleep and waking, mumbling old songs, sometimes losing count of who they were—they would nevertheless because of this day's excursioning have more deeply understood the tough timber that was in him. But all the evening he had been quite different. The names of old places, of old families, had been in the air about him. He grew young to hear them, to bethink himself of them. They had aroused him. Stephen had forgotten many of them.

He would say, "'Tis north from Inchimore," and his father had enough to catch at: "'Tis the Sweenys were north of Inchimore. 'Tis Keimcorravoola you're thinking of." And of itself either the place name or the family name was enough to spur the old man's brain to all manner of recollections. So it had been with him all the evening, alert as they had never seen him, a new man, and not a bit modest about his powers when young, whether at fighting or hurley or farming. His stick was in the air about their heads: and once without warning he had brought it down on the table, making them all leap to their feet and grab at the dancing tea things—down with all his force lest they should not clearly understand how final had been the stroke with which he had felled a Twomey man in a faction fight at Ballyvourney. And when in speaking of some other ancient wrestling bout he referred to his adversary's trunk, how he had clasped it and could not be shaken off, the two women looked at himself, alert yet lumpish before them, noted his body's girth and depth, and felt that "trunk" was indeed the right word to use of such bodies.

Finn's wife, the Kerry woman, was enjoying it heartily. Her Kerry eyes, deep hazel in colour, were dancing to watch the old man's antics, grotesque and unashamed, were dancing also to note the quiet, stilly, well-schooled Americans opening the doors of their minds to comprehend adequately this rough-hewn chunk of peasant humankind. The expression coming and going on the faces of the three sons, she also enjoyed. She watched to see how they took every gross countryside word and phrase that would unconcernedly break from the old man's lips. Her own Finn she held for the cleverest of them because he had the gift of slipping in some contrary word that would excite his father to still more energetic gestures or more emphatic expletives.

In time old Hodnett had exhausted the tale of the great deeds of his prime: a gentler mood descended on him: "Like you'd shut that door, or like you'd tear a page out of a book and throw it from you, I put an end to all that folly and wildness. Listen now, let ye listen now, this is what happened and I coming over here from Carrig-an-afrinn."

## III

He told them how on that day, which of all the days of his long life stood most clearly before his mind, he had made swiftly home from the fair at Macroom. Michael, his eldest son, a boy of about sixteen years at the time, had hastened down from the potato field on hearing the jolting of the returning cart. As usual with him he examined his father's face. He was at first relieved and then puzzled to discover from it that his father had scarcely taken any drink during that long day of absence from home, of boon companionship in the town. More than that, his father was going about in a sort of constraint, as if he had had something happen to him while away, or had come upon some tidings which now must be dwelt upon within himself. Yet he did not seem gloomy or rough, and he could be gloomy enough and rough enough when the fit was on him. Often and often after a long day in Macroom, he had turned in from the road, flung the reins on the horse's back, and without preface begun to heap maledictions on the head of the villain pig buyers from Cork with whom he had been trafficking. To-day he was different:

"Is Johnny above?" he questioned his son as he loosed the horse from the shafts. The boy nodded.

"Up with you then. Up with you while there's light in it."

The boy, climbing up to where he had left old Johnny, who was helping them to dig out the potatoes, was still wondering over the mood his father had returned in.

"What is he after getting?" the labourer asked him.

"Four ten."

"He'd get more in Dunmanway last Friday."

"He's satisfied. He says he is."

Before long they saw himself coming through the gap. "What way are they up along there?" he asked them, nodding his head towards the sloping ridges they had been digging.

"Small enough then," his son answered.

The father stooped and picked up one of the potatoes. He began to rub it between his finger and thumb.

"They'll be different in Dunerling East," his son said, complacently tossing his head.

As if that were the last thing he had expected to come from the boy's lips his father looked sharply at him.

Dunerling East was the farm he had been for several

weeks negotiating the purchase of. It was ten miles away towards the east, ten miles farther from the hardness of the mountains, the cold rains, the winds, the mists. In those ten miles the barren hills that separate Cork from Kerry had space to stretch themselves out, to die away into gentle curves, to become soft and kind. So curiously his father had looked at him the boy wondered if something had not happened to upset the purchase. He was not surprised when his father peering at him under his brows, spoke to him in a cold voice:

"The potatoes might be better. The grass too. And the cattle. Only the Hodnetts might be worse."

Michael glanced at the labourer, then back at his father. He found him still skinning the potato with his hard thumb. But he could also see, young and all as he was, that his thought was not on the potato, big or little. The labourer had once more bent to his digging; and Michael, withdrawing his eyes slowly from his father's face, spat on his hands and gripped the spade: yet he could not resist saying:

"They're poor return for a man's labour."

He scornfully touched the potatoes hither and thither with the tip of his spade, freeing them from the turfy earth, black and fibrous. They were indeed small.

The father seemed careless of their size. He stood there, a solid piece of humankind, huge, big-faced, with small round eyes, shrewd-looking, not unhumourous. He said: "If I hadn't that fifty pound paid on it, I'd put Dunerling East out of my mind."

He turned from them and made for the gap through which he had come. They questioned each other with their eyes and then stared after the earnest figure until the broken hillside swallowed it up.

It was a soft, still evening. Here and there a yellow leaf fell from the few scattered birch trees growing among the rocks which, on every side, surrounded the little patch of tilled earth. A robin was singing quietly, patiently—the robin's way. The air was moist; and because a break in the weather seemed near, they worked on, the two of them, until they could no longer see the potatoes. Then Johnny straightened his back, lit his bit of a pipe and shouldered his spade. Together both of them, taking long slow strides, made down towards the house. Suddenly the boy said:

"Look at himself!"

They saw him standing upright on one of the numerous ledges of rock which broke up through the surface of their stubble field. He had his back towards them. He was staring downwards, overlooking his own land, towards the straggling road, staring intently, although little except the general shape of the countryside could now be distinguished.

"Is it? Is it him at all, do you think?" old Johnny asked.

"'Tis sure," Michael answered. Then he cried out, sending the vowels travelling:

"Ho-o! Ho-o!"

His father turned and after a pause began to make towards them. Awkwardly they awaited him; they did not know what to say. He said:

"'Tis at Carrig-an-afrinn I was looking."

Carrig-an-afrinn was the name of the whole farm, a large district, mostly a hillside of rock and heather; they were standing in Carrig-an-afrinn: but they understood that what he had been looking at was Carrig-an-afrinn itself—the Rock of the Mass, the isolated pile of rock by the roadside from which the ploughland had got its name.

They walked beside him then.

"I'm after hearing a thing this day I never knew before," he said, and then stopping up and examining their faces he added:

"'Tis what I heard: in any place where a Mass was ever celebrated an angel is set on guard for ever and ever."

"'Twould be a likely thing," the old labourer said.

"I never heard tell of it," Michael said.

"Myself never heard tell of it," his father snapped out.

"'Twould be a likely thing," old Johnny said again, "remembering the nature of the Mass."

"Who was it told you?"

"One who was well able!"

The three of them turned and looked downwards towards the rough altar-like pile of rock where Mass used to be said secretly for the people in the penal days when it was felony to celebrate Mass in public. Only the pile of rock was visible, and that not distinctly, so thick the light had become.

"You know very well that Mass was said there hundreds and hundreds of times."

The father spoke to his son almost as if he had been contradicting him. He received no reply. Then he added in a suddenly deepened voice:

"Likely that place is thick with angels."

The labourer uncovered his head without a word.

In stillness they stood there on the lonely hillside; and in the darkening rocks and fields there was no sound, except of small things stirring at their feet. After a few seconds, the farmer faced again for the house. Without thought, it seemed, he avoided the rocky patches. Indeed even at midnight he could have walked unperplexed through those rock-strewn fields. The others heard his voice coming to them in the dusk over his shoulder:

"'Tis a strange thing that I never heard of that wonder until I'm just leaving the place for good and all. A strange thing; and it frightens me."

When they found themselves free of the fields and in the *poirse*, or laneway, that led up to their yard, he said again with sudden passion:

"'Tis a small thing would make me break the bargain."

The boy flared up:

"A queer thing you'd do then."

"Queer!"

"It may be years and years before we have the chance of buying a place like Dunerling East."

He spoke the name as if that of itself were worth the purchase money.

"Carrig-an-afrinn is not a bad farm at all."

At this Michael burst out:

"Johnny, do you hear him? And he raging and swearing at them rocks as long as I remember—raging and swearing at them as if they were living men and they against him! And he praying to God to take us out of it before his eyes were blinded with the years. And now he'd stay in it!"

Of that incident and of the night that followed it, the old man, forty-four years after, remembered every detail—every word spoken and every thought that disturbed his rest.

## IV

Having given them to understand all that has been here set down, he went on: "I tell ye, I didn't shut an eye that night, only thinking and thinking and I twisting and turning in my bed. When I looked back through the years and thought of what a poor place Carrig-an-afrinn was—there was scarcely a poorer—'twas little less than a miracle to have me able to buy out a big place like this—a place that had been in the grip of the gentry for hundreds and hundreds of years. And up to that I always thought that I had no one to thank for it but myself—the strength of my own four bones, but after what I was told in Macroom that day, how did I know but that maybe it was in Carrig-an-afrinn itself the luck was? and that good fortune would follow whoever lived in it like good Christians, and that maybe secret friends would help them, and they at the ploughing or waiting up in the nights for a calf to come, or a young foal or a litter of bonamhs itself? Who knows? Who knows? And what puzzled me entirely was that I should be ignorant of all that until the very day, as you may say, I was settled on leaving it. It frightened me. While we were in Carrig-an-afrinn no great sickness befell us or misfortune, except a horse to break his leg or a cow to miscarry or a thing like that; and I thought of all the strong farmers I was after seeing in my time, and they having to sell off their places and scatter away with themselves into Cork or Dublin, or maybe to America itself. Sure this place itself, if ye saw it when we came hither, the dirty state 'twas in, the land gone back, exhausted, and the house and sheds broken, everything in wrack and ruin—'tisn't with a light heart ye'd undertake it. But of course only for that I couldn't have bought it all at all. So I said to myself, and I listening to the clock ticking at the foot of the bed, I'm undertaking that big place, and maybe 'twon't thrive with me. And if it fails me, where am I? That's what I said. If it fails me, where am I? I tell ye, I was broken with thinking on it. And all the time, and this is the queerest thing of all, I heard someone saying, 'Carrig-an-afrinn, Carrig-an-afrinn. Carrig-an-afrinn, Carrig-an-afrinn.' And not once nor twice nor three times, but all the night long, and I thinking and thinking. Of course, there was no one saying it at all, only maybe the beating of my own heart to be like a tune. But I was afraid. I thought maybe music might come rising up to me out of the *cummer*, and it thronged with angels, or a great light come striking in at the window. And sure enough at last I started up and I cried out, 'There it is! There it is!' But 'twas no unnatural light at all, only the dawn of the day breaking in on top of me. 'Tis how I was after dozing off for a little while unknown to myself, and I woke up suddenly in confusion and dread.

"That morning and I rising up, my limbs were like wisps of straw. I was terrified of the long day before me, and that's the worse way a man can be. But when I came out and stood in the broad sun, and 'twas a morning of white frost, I drew in the air to myself, and I took courage to see my poor animals grazing so peacefully on the hill, just like what you see in a picture. If the big farms broke the men that were born to softness and luxury, Dunerling East wouldn't break me, and I reared hard and tough! That's what I said, with great daring in my breast.

"Not long after that we moved our handful of stock east to this place. I laughed to picture the two scraggy beasts, and all the deep feeding of Dunerling East to themselves. And that same evening myself and Michael, Michael that's dead, God rest him, went over and hither and in and out through the length and breadth of this estate and round by the boundary ditch; and 'tis a thing I will not forget till my dying day what he said to me, my son Michael, that same evening, and we killed from the exertion. He stopped and looked up at me before he spoke:

"'Look,' he said, 'why have you your hands like that?'

"My two hands, clenched, and stiff, *stiff*, like you'd have them in a fight, watching your opponent, watching to catch him off his guard, or for fear he'd spring on you. That's how I had my hands. And 'twas natural for me to have my hands like that, for what I was saying to myself was: I'll break it! I'll break it! And I was saying that because if I didn't break it I was sport for the world. Like a bully at a fair I was, going about my own land the first day I walked it!"

In recalling the labours of his prime he had become a new man. When they looked at him they saw not the stricken old creature whose days were now spent in the drowsy sun, but the indomitable peasant who had wrung enough from the rocks of Carrig-an-afrinn to buy out Dunerling East from the broken gentry, and who then had reclaimed Dunerling East from its hundred years of neglect. When he could not find words to fit his thought his left eye would close tight, and one big tooth, that he still retained in his upper gum, would dig itself into his lower lip, until the struggling words came to him. And they noticed that his two hands had clenched themselves long before he needed them clenched to illustrate how it was he had tackled the reclamation of the sluggish marshlands of Dunerling East. His own sons quailed before him. The two Americans had drawn together, shoulder touching shoulder: they watched him across the table with wide eyes, their faces drawn. The creamery manager from Kerry dared no longer to put in his jocose word. He wished rather to be able to draw off the old man's mind from this renewal of the unrelenting warfare of his manhood. But no such word could he find: his father was abroad in a passion of fictitious energy: it would indeed be a potent word that could stay or hinder him. Every now and then the timbers of the heavy chair groaned beneath the movement of his awkward carcase. He was unconscious of it. It meant as little to him as his own exposing of the shifts, the meanness, the overreaching, the unintentional tyranny he had practised while he worked out his dream.

"My poor boy, Michael," he went on, "was the first to go. He was great for the work. For a boy that was slight and tender I never saw the equal of him. 'Twas how he had great spirit. A word was worse to him than a whip. When we'd be cutting the deep grass in the inches, half a dozen of us all in a line, and he'd fall behind, being young and soft, I'd say to him, 'Ah, Michael,' I'd say, 'God be with the little fields of Carrig-an-afrinn, you could cut them with a scissors'; that would bring him into line I tell ye. The poor boy. 'Twas pleurisy he got first; and we thought nothing of it: maybe we didn't take it in time. But what chance was there to be taking him into Macroom to the doctor, or from one holy well to another? The time he died too, it could not be a worse time. Herself was bringing in little Stephen into the world—and before she was rightly fit the harvest was upon us; and 'twas the first real good harvest we got out of Dunerling East. When I looked at it standing I said: "Tis my doing and my boy's doing, and my boy is dead!' But herself was better than any man in a harvest field. Maybe she overworked herself. She wasn't the one to give in. The day she was laid in Inchigeela 'tis well if I didn't curse the day I came hither from Carrig-an-afrinn. Father O'Herlihy was standing by. 'The Lord giveth and the Lord taketh away,' he said, and his hand on my shoulder, and 'twas all I could do to say 'Amen' to that. There I was with a houseful of them about me and only herself, that poor thing inside, only herself to do a ha'p'orth for them. I don't blame her for being as she is—knitting, knitting, knitting, or looking into the fire and thinking—I don't blame her at all. What she went through after that, pulling and hauling and slashing and digging, 'twould kill half a parish. Up at four in the morning getting the pigs' food ready, or the mash for the calves; and milking the cows, and keeping the children from mischief. The only other girl I had, she was second after Nicholas there, I lost her just when she was rising to be of use to me. 'Twas a fever she got from drinking bad water. And the two boys I lost after that, one of them was the terror of the countryside. He turned against herself inside; he was wild and fiery. Mind you, he dared me to my face. He said what no son of mine ever said to me. I won't repeat it. I won't repeat it. The eyes were blazing in his head. The delicacy was showing in him. The brains of that kind is a terror. He went off with himself and left me in the lurch. And then he came back—one twelvemonth after—and 'tis like herself inside he was. Only bitter, and the health wasted. The same as any labouring boy he walked in to me. Not a shirt to his back, or what you could call a shirt. He shamed me, the way he was. And he dying on his feet. 'Twas a dead man was patrolling the fields for months before he took to the bed entirely. And I daren't say a word to him because he had a tongue would raise blisters on a withered skull. The other poor boy, his name was Laurence, was a handsome boy. Everybody used to say he'd make a handsome priest. But sure at that time I couldn't dream of such a thing. It takes a power of money to make a priest. He died of pneumonia, and not a thing to happen to him only a bit of a pain in his side. Only for that I hadn't time to be thinking on it I'd be saying there was a curse on top of us; but no, because year after year the produce was getting better and better; and in spite of all the sickness and deaths and funerals—and funerals are the greatest robbers of all—the money began to rise up on me, and I could get in the help when I wanted it—'tis often I had a score of men at the harvesting, besides what neighbours would come of themselves. Those there (he nodded at his three sons, all of them sitting with bowed heads, with pipes in their mouths, not daring to break across his speech)—those there, they only knew the end of the story. Ah boys, ah boys, the softness comes out of the hard, like the apple from the old twisted bough, and 'tis only the softness ye knew of. And then in the end of it all, the great change in the laws came about and I bought out the land and 'twas my own, as you may say. The day I signed for it, a sort of lowness came over me, and I remembered my poor dead boy saying, and he my first born, 'Look how you're holding your hands!' Let ye listen to me now; I cried down my eyes to my own self that night because herself was in the clay. That poor soul inside, you might as well be talking to a cock of last year's hay, dull with the weather and the sun, you'd only get 'yes' and 'no' for an answer. And the rest—those here—were too young. What I did was: to send over for old Johnny, old Johnny I would have helping me an odd time in Carrig-an-afrinn, to come over to me, that I wanted him. God knows all I wanted him for was to keep me in talking against that terrible fit of darkness and loneliness would fall on me again. He came over and together we walked the land, every perch of it. He knew what sort it was when we came hither, and 'tis he was the man could tell the difference. What he said was, now, let ye listen, let ye listen to what he said, and he only a poor ignorant man: 'After all, 'twas only a rush in your hand!' Now that was what a wrestler would say of another in the old times, 'He was only a rush in my hands,' meaning by that that he had no trouble in breaking him. That was great praise and yet it couldn't rouse me for I was after walking the land field after field; and one field I found was the same as another. That's a strange thing to say. Maybe 'tis how I was old and I coming hither. 'Twas in Carrig-an-afrinn I grew up. There was never a man drove a handful of cattle of his own rearing to a fair that hadn't some favourite among them; and he sees the dealers come round them and strike them and push them, and knock them about, and he knows that they are all the same to him, that he sees no difference between one and the other, except one to be riper than another, or a thing like that. And 'twas so with me. I walked my fields and one was the same as another. There was no corner of them that I could make for when the darkness would fall on me. I knew 'twould be different in Carrig-an-afrinn. And that's what I was thinking of when old Johnny said to me that after all Dunerling East was like a rush in my hands. I opened my heart to him. I told him I felt like the steward of the place, and not like the owner of it. He said 'twasn't right for me to be saying a thing like that, and 'tis down on my two knees I should be and I thanking God, but that the heart of man was only a sieve. The very next day and I still going about like that, counting up the great improvements I was after making since I came in, and arguing with myself, and yet dissatisfied with myself, I wandered up the hillside opposite, and whatever turn I gave or however the sun was shining, 'twas about four o'clock in the evening, I saw Doughill and Douse rising up in the west and snug away down at the foot of Doughill I saw a little shoulder of a hill, and 'Honour of God,' I said, 'if that isn't Carrig-an-afrinn itself!' Let ye listen to me, I fell down on my knees in thanksgiving like a pagan would be praying to the sun! And from that day forward I had a spot of land to turn to when the black fit would fall on me. Mind you, 'twas a good time I found it, for while I was breaking the place and wrestling with it I didn't think of anything else, only to be going ahead and going ahead. But 'twas different when I could pay for the help, and I had time to look around, and the rent wasn't half what it used to be. Ah, the soft comes out of the hard, and the little lambs from the hailstones. If Dunerling East is a good property now 'twas many the hot sweat fell into the sods of its ridges. But sure them that could witness to that, they're all dead, except that poor thing inside, God help her; and 'tis she took the burden as well as the next."

## V

His voice fell and the glow of exaltation vanished from his features.

"They're all dead?" Mrs. Muntleberry said, quietly.

"Dead!" the old man answered her, and having said it, his head kept on moving slightly up and down to some pulse in his brain.

"Then these," she said again, and indicated the three sons with her eyes, "these are a second crop."

"A second crop," he said, "except that poor creature inside."

They found it hard to break the silence that had fallen on them. Earlier in the evening both Stephen and Finnbarr had been, as one might say, themselves—Stephen, the baker manager, a hustler, and Finn, the creamery manager, not unable to hustle also. But as the story went on, and though they had heard it all in a fragmentary way before, they had scattered from the homestead without ever having made themselves one clear unified picture of what coming hither from Carrig-an-afrinn had meant for their father. They had never seen him clearly as one who would not be beaten, no matter who by his side fell worsted in the struggle. Only the oldest of them, Nicholas, the farmer, could recall any of the dead, and he was a soft quiet creature, strong of body, but inactive of brain. The one mood, however, had come upon all three; they were not much different from what they had been before they had scattered, from what they had been when Ellen would still them by whispering the one word: 'Himself.'

It was Finn who first rose. He went and lightly beat the inverted bowl of his pipe against the bars of the fire grate. Then drawing with his strong lips through the empty stem, head in the air, he took a few steps towards the window and drew back one of the heavy curtains. The colour, the glow had gone from the day. Instead there were now everywhere filmy veils of mist. Beyond the sunken stream the hillside looked near and the screens of trees, ash and beech, seemed tall and unsubstantial: in the twilight softness the homely features of farming and cattle trafficking were hidden away. The scene was gracious and tender. They all stared through the window.

"It looks fine, so it does," Finn said.

"It does; it looks fine," his wife added, letting the words die away.

The old man was listening.

"'Tis what a traveller said, and he a man that had recourse to all the places in the world, 'tis what he said: that it had the appearance of a gentleman's place out and out."

Mrs. Muntleberry turned and let her eyes rest softly on his face:

"Still you liked Carrig-an-afrinn too?"

He lifted his head; such words he had not expected: "Ah, ma'am, ah, ma'am," he said, making an effort to move his trunk so that he might face her directly, "Carrig-an-afrinn, Carrig-an-afrinn, the very name of it, the very name of it!" And he stared at her with a fixity of expression that frightened her, stared at her in blank hopelessness of saying even the first word of all the words that rioted within him. He recovered. He swept his hand across his brow, toying with his hair. "They tell me Pat Leary, who's there ever since we came hither—there's only the one year between us—they tell me he sits in the *cummer* an odd hour at the foot of the rock where the Chalice used to stand. His work is done. He'll catch hold of plough nor snaffle no more, same as myself. 'Tis a great comfort to him to sit there."

She was sorry she had brought Carrig-an-afrinn back to his thoughts.

"The heart is a sieve," she said, watching him to see how

he'd take old Johnny's word. But he was not so easily moved from mood to mood.

"You saw it to-day?" he questioned earnestly. "You saw it to-day?"

"We went quite close to it. Did we see the Rock itself? Did we, Stephen?"

Stephen said as boldly as he could:

"Oh yes, we went quite close to it."

"Ah, ma'am, Nicholas there, some day he's going to pack me into the motor car; and over with us to see it. It can't be long I have to stay."

Before he had finished, almost indeed at the first word, Nicholas had risen and quietly taken down a shabby-looking old violin from the top of a heavy cupboard that stood in the corner. While they all looked at him he tuned it without a word, and to him tuning was no easy task. Then he stretched his two long legs out from the chair and began to play.

The instrument was almost toneless, and the player almost without skill. He played the old songs of the countryside, going straight from one to another, from a *caoine* to a reel, from a love song to a lively rattle about cattle-dealing or horse racing. Nerveless, toneless, yet the playing was quiet; and it was the music itself, and not the instrument or musician was in the fiddler's mind. After a while this the Americans noticed. Then the scratching, the imperfect intonation, the incongruous transition from melody to melody disturbed them but little. He played on and on; and they were all thankful to him. The room darkened, but the sky was still bright. At last he lowered the fiddle, a string needed to be tightened. The others at once broke into talk. Mrs. Muntleberry was nearest to Nicholas. She had her eyes on the instrument. He noticed how at the word "Carrig-an-afrinn" which was again on the lips of the old man, her head had raised itself. He whispered to her, without taking his eyes off his task:

"He'll never see Carrig-an-afrinn again."

"No?" she whispered back, with a little gasp of surprise.

"Nor nobody else," he went on; "they're after blasting it away to make the road wider: 'tis how two lorries couldn't pass on it. I'm in dread of my life he'll find it out. 'Twould be terrible."

She turned her eyes on the old man's face. The music had restored him again to confidence. His eyes were glowing. He had re-established his mastery. "Let ye listen, let ye listen to me," he was saying.

# Daniel Corkery

## *A Looter of the Hills*

### I

I told the woman that her little girl was now recovered and that there was no need for a further visit. In quiet thankfulness she accompanied me down the rickety stairs, and suddenly, and entirely by way of impulse, said: "Doctor, there's another poor patient here, and you ought to have a look at him. His name is Phil Donaghy." With that she tapped on a door I had not noticed in a sort of recess at the bottom of the stairs. As if she had expected no reply she had put her fingers on the handle when the door opened: she said at once:

"Oh! I didn't know you were with him, Nora. I'm after asking the doctor here to have a look at him: 'twill do him no harm."

Nora, a decent-looking soul, started and gaped at us, and I, knowing the pieties of such people, said at once: "The room will do well enough. And himself, too."

Of late I have been noticing that so surely as that close-wedged mass of tenement houses, crouching there in the shadow of St. Michael's, rises to my memory or actually comes into view from some terrace on the hills, it is this Phil Donaghy, the patient I was then to become acquainted with, that emerges from it as an individual. That network of lanes and alleys, lying in the skirts of the bleak-looking ungainly church, is his background. They are scarcely six feet wide, these lanes, and the houses in them are so high in the old-fashioned way, that they feel even narrower still. The houses cling to one another in ramshackle groups like a lot of tipsy sailormen, some of them tossing their heads, some of them gone in the pins, others sodden and dull, while others again are gay with all manner of patchings, stains and weatherings. The footpaths by which one navigates the district are hardly a foot in width, paved with cobblestones, as also are most of the lanes themselves; and when you leave these pathways and turn into the hallways you find but little difference. One trusts oneself to a dark twisting passage along which one feels with the feet cautiously; flooring, soundless with rottenness, is beneath them, or flags, or, it may be, common earth. They are so long, these passages, they shoot forward so fiercely, turn sharply aside, shoot forward again, that one imagines oneself as burrowing under the old church itself, for piles and piles of crazy masonry seem to surround one on every side and to be over the head as well.

The room I was led into was large enough, very ill-lighted however. The window was hidden away behind driftings of lace curtains that had gone the colour of a negro. I gingerly put one of them aside and saw that the little yard into which the window looked was like a dripping well sunken into that mass of burrowed masonry. The sky I could not see, but an expiring gleam of light falling down the greenish mouldy walls hinted of it. That yard was indeed a dismal prospect. I turned from it and found my patient hunched over a lifeless bit of fire in the grate. When he raised his undetermined face to me, the eyes melancholy, the brows lifted, I could think only of an empty shop.

"Stand up, my man," I said; and when he did so, resting limply on the back of a chair, I noticed the huge limbs, the huge awkward-looking trunk, and I knew for certain there was peasant blood in him.

"Out in the air," I said cheerily, "out in the air is the place for you—what else have you to do?"

His eyes sharpened, searching me with some effort at keenness. Not only that, but the kindly creature who had been tidying the place for him—she was his brother's wife, and lived on an upper floor—looked up quickly at me as if I had said some surprising thing! In a moment she was all words: "That's what I tell him, Doctor. He should rouse himself!" And she caught him by the sleeve: "You should rouse yourself, Phil. Isn't that what I'm always saying to you? A thousand times, Doctor, I said as much to him myself. And what harm but there's not a foot of the country that he doesn't know by heart. He used to be forever scouring it, ever and ever; but that was before his mother died on him."

The lump of manhood turned its slow eyes upon her and said—I know not what.

She looked from his face to mine:

"Yes, Doctor, that's right. 'Tis long before 'twill be forgotten—how we buried her, the flowers—"

I knew then where I was. That very funeral, six months earlier I had come upon it as it threaded the lanes. Crowds of people followed it, with some sort of hidden excitement playing through them, and the coffin was entirely hidden in flowers and greenery—not the fast-bound wreaths, shapely and meagre, that florists supply to order, but a wild profusion of branches, flowers, and leaves, heaped and gaudy.

II

Only for that his mother had come from the heart of the country she could never possibly have lived to be over eighty years of age in such surroundings. Up to that age she had been a busy woman, attending to the housework, shopping, going to Mass, taking her place in all the doings of the laneway. Then she had a stroke, as the people say, losing control of her right side, more or less. From that out the dark room, with the bed in the corner, was her kingdom. No more housework, no more shopping, or Mass, or Retreats, or Missions, or anything. Then, as will happen, the recollections of her simple childhood came more and more to the surface. To her overgrown half-wit of a son she would say:

"There's no knowing the damage a goat will do. The goat we had, it went into Colonel Seeve's place one morning before a soul was up, and it tore down and destroyed all the lovely shrubs in the lawn! What did it care about handsome places! And it came home and laid down, and had a lovely sleep for itself! Look at that for you! And not a mortal knowing where it was after spending the day. But when 'twas found out—oh, then there was murder!"

Or she might say to him—to him who was true child of the city's heart:

"Sheep's milk is so thick you couldn't drink it without

putting water in it. Now there's lots of people don't know that sheep have any milk at all. The people of this lane now, Betty outside, or Johnny Mahony, they never saw sheep's milk at all. Sitting there they were, and they downfaced me when I said that people used to drink sheep's milk and goat's milk too."

Or again, although his world had never been any other than the laneways and the wharves:

"Up in the dark of the morning we'd be, boiling the potatoes for them. And maybe then someone would say, 'Do you hear that? That's the Linehans.' 'Tis the way we'd be listening to know if the others were taking the road. And one after another we'd hear them coming from all quarters. You'd think some of them hadn't gone to bed at all at all. Away to the fair with them then: into Macroom; and 'twould be the dark of night when they'd come back. Over the mountains they'd go: there are places there would frighten you to look at them."

At another time she would be still further back in her childhood: "Gathering brosna in the wood we'd be; and we'd be all right so long as the daylight held; but the place would get cold and still, and we'd be listening to know if anything was stirring; and we'd say we had no right to stay so long, and we'd run home with ourselves. But all the same maybe we'd stay longer the next evening or the evening after."

As if to aid her in this recovery of her childhood's far-off life in far-off places the film on her eyeballs thickened, more and more hiding away from her the dismal surroundings into which her many years had narrowed. When, unconsciously, she had ceased the struggle to keep tally of what was going on about her, when her eyes had gone utterly dark, her head lifted itself higher and higher, the features relaxed, her face brightened, took on the appearance of a sky in which the winds have died and the clouds vanished—frank, open and serene, lighted from within.

Beside her was another simple nature, this gom of a son of hers, who was lucky if he poked out two days' work in a week. Only when there was a rush of shipping at the jetties did the stevedore beckon him to take his place in the run of corn-baggers or timber-heavers. For the most part, he loitered in his mother's room drinking in her chatter of a world he had never known. Who could say what images he made himself from the rambling gossip! Anyway he began to explore the countryside round about, one day taking to the hills on either side of the city, on another threading the river valley to the west. It was not long until in that darkened room buried under, lost among, those piles of crumbling masonry there were to be heard two voices instead of one speaking of the green hillsides: "Little lambs they were, jumping about their mothers. Lively. Awful game. Look! Look, can't ye!" And if the aged eyes could no longer actually see his clumsy antics, his six-foot friskings, they could most certainly make themselves pictures of lambs that were as white as snow and pastures that were green and deep. Or it might be a braver vision he had raised for her:

"At the top of the field he turns them round . . . "

"The headland, Phil boy, the headland."

"Turns them round; and the tackling and chains goes rattling: 'Whoa! Hack! Back you! Back, I tell you!' And one of them puts his head up in the air. And he opens his jaws. You'd think he'd take a bit out of the air or the clouds! And the other fellow puts his head down, down, into his chest, like a magistrate in the court. And he drags them round like that—'Whoa! Come out of it!' And all the seagulls and crows!"

"But 'tis hard work, ploughing is," she'd answer, "and after a day of it, if the ground was heavy, you'd be only fit to throw yourself in the bed, like a log of wood. Isn't it often I seen them! Often and often!"

Because his nature was simple and passionate it was his way to act out his thought; and, listening in the dim passage outside the door of their room you might hear coming from within, the swish of a scythe or the whirr of a reaping machine or the gossip of a group of gleaners or the unrestrained argument of a group of cattle-dealers at a fair. For, little by little, he had ventured farther and farther from the dens of the city and grown knowledgeable of the life of the countryside. It was a common thing with him now to rise long before the dawn that he might enjoy the spectacle of a fair. Sometimes he was paid a couple of shillings for assisting in the driving of the cattle, at a headlong pace, into the city to catch a steamer or train. But indeed, whatever he thought of it himself, it was not for the sake of the odd shillings he hung about the earnest bargainers like that; it was rather to find food for his own hungry mind and heart that in turn he might feed that other hungry mind and heart imprisoned in the slumland of the city. She as well as himself had benefit of all he saw and heard in his excursions.

One day he had lain stretched for hours on a grassy bank gazing lazily at the mowers in the meadow. That evening his mother grabbed him to her suddenly and buried her nostrils in his clothes:

"That's a good smell. So 'tis. So 'tis. A good smell. A good smell."

After a day of cattle-driving the smell of the beasts was to her a delight, as indeed was anything at all that renewed for her the impressions life had made on her virgin soul eighty years before. He began to loot the hillsides for her sake. Armfuls of wild flowers he brought her, whole branches of blossoming trees or masses of trailing woodbine. In autumn he came garlanded with boughs of crab apple, tangles of fruity briars or even half a sheaf of corn. She would bury her nose in them, play with them, plucking the fruit and thorning her fingers while she did so.

### III

Late one night in the springtime her daughter-in-law heard stirrings in the old woman's room. She went to her: "Mother," she whispered through the darkness, "what's the matter? Is it how ye can't sleep or what?"

"Nothing child, nothing is the matter. What a goose you are! Don't be rising like that getting cold for yourself."

The voice ceased suddenly, the stirrings had again begun. The young woman groped on the table and lit the candle. She found a live lamb in the grip of the old woman. The animal was struggling to escape from the claw-like ancient hands.

Things had gone too far; there was a scene. The half-wit had only little to say while they threatened him with the law.

"I'm no robber. I never stole anything. I was going to take it back. Nobody would miss it. I gave it milk. I covered it with my coat. I never stole nothing!"

After that day the two of them, mother and son, had again to fall back on the wild flowers, the hawthorn and crab blossom, which fortunately were now plentiful along the hedges. Into the midst of the lane-dwellers as they sat at nightfall at their doorways, the harmless giant would break, his basketing arms letting the wilful blossoms fall as he moved along with odours in his wake. They would raise their nostrils and smile, sometimes wistfully, or shake their heads, remembering old times and places.

## IV

Of a morning in autumn Nora roused her husband impatiently. As her custom was she had, first thing, gone to the bedside of the old woman. She was now returned:

"Something is after happening," she said to him.

"What's up with you? Is it Nanny?" Then he sat up quickly. "You're shaking."

"The two of them is missing!"

"Merciful Father!"

When he had dressed himself, was come with her to the empty room—litter of birdcages, of withered boughs, of branches dry and crackling as it was—she said to him: "I knew they were up to something. They had their heads together. That's what they were planning. And sniggering. Laughing at us."

"I'll break his neck for him! I keep a home for him, and that's the thanks I get. Nothing but annoyance and trouble."

The room soon filled with the neighbours, councils were held: the police, it was decided, had better be sent for. They best could trace them. In the police station telephones were set ringing; telegrams dispatched; hospitals communicated with. All, however, without result. Alone or accompanied by a young policeman, Tom went from place to place, everywhere noticing as soon as the matter had been explained, a thinnish sort of smile break over the faces of the officials. And he felt ashamed of himself.

"You have tried them all, you say?"

"Every one of them; and the Poorhouse too."

"Well, there's the river."

Tired out, embittered too, he came home and told his wife what the police sergeant had said.

"Don't say it—don't say it, Tom," she said, her finger on his wrist, "'tis before my mind the livelong day! We were hard on them; we were hard on them!"

"No, no. We gave them their own way in everything, too much of it."

Towards nightfall they heard an authoritative voice in the hallway; tremblingly they opened. It was the same sergeant. He looked at them—as his habit was—for a long time steadily and in chill silence. They felt miserably guilty. He asked them many sidelong questions, as also was his way, before explaining to them the simple matter that a horse and cart had been stolen from a farmer's yard a mile outside the city. No one in the lane, however, had heard any sound of a cart; and anybody else might have taken it as well as this half-wit of theirs. The telephones, the wires, were, however, all at work again, so he informed them; and before long they would surely have news. Yet no news arrived.

Late that night Tom and his wife and a neighbour sat in silence, dispirited, fearful of they knew not what. The neighbour had tired of urging them to make their minds at ease, to go to bed, to be ready for whatever would be sent to them; no more than that could he say to comfort them. Yet the silence irked them all; so that at last the wife rose up and began to set about some homely task. Tom too raised his head from his long brooding. "Do you know, I think I can tell where they're gone to? Come, Dinny, come with me. We'll get the ambulance from the Corporation."

The sleeping Corporation watchman did not wish to set out on a wild-goose chase. They had to threaten him; if the aged woman was found dead from exposure her death would be laid at his door, he would hear about it.

The motor ambulance drove through the silent streets, making a great clatter. Into the country with them, mile after mile. Towards the west they made, then northwards, cutting into the heart of the hills. Yet in spite of the excellent lamps they had they could make only slow progress, for none of them knew the country when they were a score of miles distant from it; all they knew was the direction. The steady whirr of the engine comforted them, and they began less and less to fear the unforeseen. They wondered at the great silence, the great blank spaces of the sky as the darkness drew away. The sun rose up on their right, and they saw wisps of mist hanging from juts of rocks or laid astray along the hedges. The increasing warmth of the sun was sweet to them, yet Tom widened his eyes as he caught the tumultuous singing of the birds. Their morning rapture promised that everything would be the same, but he was quietly saying to himself that nothing ever again would be the same, and his look was piteous.

At last they quenched their lamps: the landscape was flooded with brightness. They climbed along the side of a straggling belt of ruined woodland; they made the ridge; descending, they swung round on to a bridge that crossed a foaming torrent diminished after the summer yet still very loud.

Before them lay a broad valley with wide meadows and sloping fields of corn, unexpectedly rich and soft-looking in the heart of those craggy hills. But their eyes had scarcely scanned its features when they noticed down below them in the middle of the dust-white road a solitary farm cart standing perfectly still, its shadow laid sharply upon the dust. So still the picture they made—horse, cart, shadow, and the solitary clumsy figure gazing towards them as if he had heard the noise of the car from afar off, it struck them the group must have been as stilly as that for hours. Without a word they slowed down as they approached. The poor fool looked at them as if he had expected them. He gave them no time to question him.

"She was all right, not a bit afraid, talking, talking, asking me everything. She never stopped, only asking me everything. I'm telling you she was as game as paint till she heard that river there and it giving tongue out of it."

What could they say to him?

They brought her home and never again did the gift of consciousness descend upon her. After seventy years of absence she anyway once again had breathed her native air, had heard the voice of her native vale, its birds and its waters, enough perhaps to give her blind eyes to see its fields heavy with harvest, and its households as she had known them in her childhood.

Her son—the melancholy fit will pass. He will again take to wandering on the hills, gazing at the flowers thick-strewn in the hedges, or gaping at the young things playing about their dams, his mind all a confusion, yet not uncomforted.

# Daniel Corkery

## *The Priest*

### I

Because Father Reen had been reading all day the rain had meant but little for him. Since breakfast time he had not been disturbed, his housekeeper even had not entered, and he had reached an age, he was sixty-two, when a day of unbroken quiet was the best of holidays. Yet any more of the quietness might have taken the edge off his pleasure. In the afternoon, just in good time it seemed, an uncertain sunbeam floated tremulously across the pages of his book; quite unexpectedly, it had stolen in through the still streaming window panes. Father Reen, his mouth suddenly opening, raised his head and stared with his blue eyes, large and clear, across the river valley towards the mountains. He noticed that, even as he looked, hedgerow, branch, and rocky height were emerging through the saturated air, were taking form, unsubstantial still, yet no longer broken in outline. His house was in a good place for the afternoon sunshine; it stood on a rise of ground above the river and looked to the south-west. The soil was sandy, the paths in the garden well kept and kind to the feet; before long, in the mild November sunshine, he was pacing to and fro the full length of his little place. Between this pleasant place in the sun, and the study he had just come from, he had grown into the custom of passing nearly all his free time—too much of it, as he often told himself, for it meant further and further withdrawal from the life of the village, the life of his parish; but then where in the parish was such life to be come upon as he could profitably make use of? He was conscious that in this parish of his, as in many another round about it, there was, speaking from either social or cultural point of view, neither an upper class nor even a middle class—there was only a peasant class that had only comparatively recently emerged from penury, a class that needed spurring, that needed leadership, and that was not finding it. He had long since reasoned out that the time had come for the building up of a middle class, an upper class too, on native lines, to take the place of those that had failed; but as often however as this thought came to him he smiled, for he certainly was not one of those who get things put to right. Now, however, breathing the fresh air, which was chilly enough to make quick walking necessary, he fortunately was free from the thought of all this. Beyond the feel of the fresh air in his nostrils he was free almost from sensation. Film after film of moisture he saw lifting, dissipating themselves in the effulgence of the sun, leaving the wide river valley, the hundred thousand rocky scars and ridges that encumbered it, sharply drawn, one against another, if as yet without colour, a succession of grey tones. But the swollen river made no response to the light above it, for its waters had become stained, were heavy after the scourings from the fords and inches. He could see it tumbling along.

Whenever in his pacing he faced the west his eye traversed not only the river but the village beyond it. He saw the evening smoke of its homely fires ascending, each spire of it alive with the sunshine streaming through it. He had been so long in the place, first as curate and then as parish priest, that he had got into the way of whispering to himself such pet phrases as: My valley, my river, my river, my hills. This afternoon, the ascending smoke spires taking his eye. My people! was the phrase that possessed his lips. It seemed touched with the memory of emotion rather than with any living warmth. He had scarcely uttered the words when he stopped up in his pacing, for in that single patch of open village street that was visible to him, he saw a horseman swinging steadily along, making, he was certain, towards the bridge, towards this hillside, towards this house of his.

II

In less than a half-hour Father Reen was riding alone

across the bridge and through the village, faced towards the west, towards Kilmony, a ploughland ten miles away on the farthest edge of his far-flung parish, where, the messenger had informed him, an old man was nearing his end.

Anyhow there would be no more rain. The sky was clearing, the wind was swung round towards the north. Now the sun was hidden behind a barricade of cloud, cold grey in colour, and thick, that rested all along the horizon, shafts of rich light ascending from behind it to the height of heaven. The sun would not show itself again; and the moment it was gone one would feel how hard the night was turning to frost. Father Reen was conscious of this as he made on at a good pace. Yes, the air would become colder and colder, the landscape barer and barer, harder and harder in its features. The village, which he had come through, was wind-swept enough, was hard enough and niggard enough in all its ways, yet it did not lack for trees in various groupings, nor for clipped bushes, shapely hedges, flower plots. And he remembered how, as he passed through, he had heard an outburst of reckless laughter from the stragglers in the forge—their meeting place as long as he could remember. He knew he would come on no other group of gossips as loud voiced or as merry as they: nor on hedgerow trees or clipped hedges or any flowers. Already he was aware of the denuded character of the landscape about him, every feature of it sharp and bare; he foresaw all the long roads and byways, little cared for, stone-strewn, with their surfaces swept away, deep-channelled by the rain torrents from the hills; and, very insidiously, uneasiness intruded on his peace of mind, not induced so much by the discomfort of the roads ahead of him as by the thought of Kilmony itself, to which they led—a place where the people were still living in wretched cabins, on the poorest fare, without a notion of giving attention to, or spending a penny on, anything except the direst necessaries of life—a place where he hardly ever remembered an old person to die without the lust of property troubling the spirit almost to the beginning of the agony. Against the fear that this foreknowledge aroused in him he struggled; he shook his head at it, he set his teeth, he grasped the reins more firmly, consciously giving himself to the onward rhythm of the gallop.

Already, he felt, there was thin frost forming on the pools beneath his horse's hoofs. And what a bite in the north-west as it blew across the marches and the reedy lakes! Soon the stars would begin to come forth sparkling with frost. Everywhere now slabs of rock, pinnacles of rock, hillsides of rock; and not a tree anywhere, not a bush even; scarcely a sign of humanity, hardly a human being. On an upland farm he had seen a boy driving a few scraggy beasts diagonally up a sloping field to the stall. Now, across the inch, he saw an old man bent under a huge mass of bogland cow-fodder, making for a gap—and between man and boy there were miles, it seemed, of rock and heather, of such desolation as hindered the growth of any community spirit, which, of itself, would little by little, induce a finer way of living. My people! My people! he thought, so good, so sinless, even so religious, yet so hard, so niggardly, so worldly, even so cruel; and again he blamed himself for not starting, for not forwarding some plan or other—sports or story-telling, or dancing or singing or reading or play-acting—anything that would cut across and baffle that lust of acquisitiveness which everywhere is the peasant's bane. My people! My people! My people! and then: If only I were young again! But this, he chided himself, was but self-deception. What was really wrong with him, he told himself, was that he had unconsciously withdrawn himself from them, with those hard ways of theirs. They were leaderless, at least in the social sense. They had no initiative—yet he had left them to themselves lest—yes, that was it—lest—he was like a doctor falling into age, afraid to use any except the safest remedies—lest complications might ensue—yes, that was the phrase. But it was true he was ageing. And the best day he ever was he had not been one of those blessed people who get things done. Anyway, his duty as a priest—that, O thanks be to God, he had never neglected, so far as he knew.

It was dark night when he turned up the hillside on the ridge of which lay Kilmony—a place where every household was intermarried with every other household. Pluckily his horse stepped up the broken ground, his forehoofs smiting the rocky shelvings, impatient for footing. When the ascent became a little easier Father Reen raised his head and saw the crest of the hill swarthy and sharp against the grey cloudless sky, darker than it, full of roughnesses, of breaks and points, a restless line running east and west with here and there a bright star fallen upon it. He knew he was at the right place. Beyond that ridge, he remembered, were immense slowly-rising uplands abandoned to nature, miles on miles, where sheep were driven to pasture at the end of springtime, and left to themselves the length of summer, where turf was dug out, but where no attempt at tillage had ever been made. On his right he now noticed a haphazard group of gables; some of them had once been whitened, and these helped still to separate the whole group from the beetling background. He heard a gate opened, and dimly he made out a tall figure in the middle of the road—it was indeed little more than a rough pathway—standing against the sky awaiting him.

### III

"Am I at Miah Neehan's?" he asked.

"Yes, Father. You're better get off here, the yard isn't too clean in itself."

He dismounted, and already he felt the wind cold on his sweaty limbs.

"I'm in time?" he questioned.

"Good time. In good time," he was answered, and then he heard the voice raised:

"Isn't it a wonder one of ye wouldn't hold a lamp for Father Reen?"

There was but a dull glimmer of light in the interior of the dwelling: he saw it reflected in the dung pit which, in the old-fashioned way, occupied most of the yard. By peering he made out the causeway of large boulders running through the mire to the doorway. All was just as he had expected. It was one of those places, now happily rare, over which the spirit of the bad old times, as the people say, still seemed to brood, a place where necessity was served, and that only. Among the dark figures in the doorway he saw movement—the effect of a harshly spoken word of his guide—and he was glad, for the sweat was chilly on his limbs. He saw now a flannel-coated middle-aged man emerge, shielding the lamp from the wind with a corner of his wrapper. He made towards him, and by the time he reached the threshold the figures were all withdrawn again into the interior. There were both men and women, but the faces of the women were so deeply hidden within the hoods of their cloaks that all he could see of them was a pale gleam. They were seated by the walls, but the men were standing haphazardly about or leaning their shoulders wherever they could find support. Tall and spare, a mountainy breed, their heads were lost in the darkness that hung beneath the ancient thatch. The fire on the hearth was uncared for; and not a word was passing among those present. He saluted them, his hat in his hand, and waited until the lamp had been again hung on its accustomed nail.

"Where is he?" he said.

There was a slight pause before the reply came: "Inside, Father."

Before he entered the lower room, the only other room in the house, he turned towards where the voice had spoken, saying: "Are his affairs settled, are they in order?"

No answer coming, he turned towards the man who had held the lamp for him, looking at him questioningly, but he, throwing down his eyes, slunk away into the midst of the others. He raised his voice then:

"Are his affairs in order?"

Just then, the man who had welcomed him on the roadway, he had since been seeing after the horse, entered hurriedly, looking like one who had been anxious whether those within might not have been scanting the courtesies. A voice in the semi-darkness, a woman's voice, met him:

"Father Reen wants to know are his affairs settled?"

"Oh yes; that's all right. In good order. In good order. You needn't give yourself any uneasiness about that, Father."

He spoke loudly, challengingly, the priest felt, to those about them in the room. Indeed he had scarcely finished when one of the tallest of the men flung himself from his place and strode across the room to the doorway where he took his station, his back to those within, his eyes staring out into the black night. "Sit down, sit down, Jack. Be easy." He who had answered the priest's question it was who spoke, with the carelessness of contempt, it seemed, rather than in any spirit of good fellowship. But the man in the doorway answered him, flinging round his head suddenly and angrily:

"I'm all right here—just here where I am."

It appeared to Father Reen the two were fairly matched. "Very well, very well. Please yourself. Come on in, Father."

A woman's voice said:

"Tim, you'd want a second candle within."

"You're right. One is a poor light on these occasions." He soon had a lighted candle in his hand, showing the way.

"Come on in, Father. Everything is ready for you. Quite ready."

## IV

Father Reen was alone with the dying man. In the squalid room, the rickety contrivance of a bed, the ancient coverings, the stained walls, the tainted air, he again found all he had expected to find. Above all he found his thought realised in the head thrown weakly back upon the pillow, the eyes of which had fastened on him at the moment of entrance. He could feel how grimly the old man's will—he was ninety-one years of age—had been exerted, had been struggling against the craving of the worn-out body for rest, for the lapse of consciousness. He drew near to the bedside, seated himself at its edge, and noticed how the old eyes were searching the spaces of the room; he then heard the dry and wearied voice speaking with a distinctness that of itself alone would acquaint one with the triumph of the will over every other faculty in the old man's soul:

"Whisper, Father, is that door shut?"

The priest rose, made certain that the door between them and the crowd of descendants and relatives outside was fastened, then seating himself again said:

"'Tis all right."

"Whisper," the old head was reaching up to his face, "I'm destroyed, destroyed with them, with them in and out to me all day, all night too, in and out, in and out, watching me, and watching each other too."

\* \* \* \* \*

It was a long time before he was satisfied he had done all he could, and could do no more, for that struggling soul, which, he was sure, would enter the next world before the night was out. But the moment he had caught sight of the old face, the tight wisdom of it, the undefeated will in it, the clasp on the lips, the firm old chin, and then the hard-shut fist like a knob on the scraggy forearm that would lift and threaten and emphasize—he knew what was before him—that he would have to call up all the resources of his own brain and will, having asked help from on high, and wrestle, and wrestle, and wrestle to dislodge that poor old peasant's handful of thoughts from that which had been their centre and stay for seventy or eighty years—the land, the farm, as he called it—a waste of rock and shale, bog and moor, that should never at all have been brought under the spade. He had more than his farm to stay his thoughts upon: as earnest of his long and well-spent life he had his dirty bank-book under his pillow with eighty pounds marked in it to his credit. No sooner was Father Reen aware of this than he knew that it would be easier almost to wrench one of the rocks in the fields abroad from its bed than to wrench that long-accustomed support from the old man's little world of consciousness without shattering it to insanity. Yet this at last Father Reen felt he had succeeded in doing; he thought he found a new look coming into the old man's eyes, overspreading his brow, some expression of hard-won relief, some return of openness, of simplicity, that may not have been there since early manhood; in the voice he thought he found some new timbre, some sudden access of tenderness, of sweetness; and, more surely telling of the new scale of values suddenly come upon by that old battler in a rough world, a flood of aspirations broke impetuously from the trembling lips: "Jesus Christ, O welcome, O welcome; keep near me, I'm not worthy, I'm not worthy, but welcome. O Blessed Mother, pray for me, now, now"—a flood onward and never-ending once it had started at all; and Father Reen noticed how the two fists, twin knobs, equally hard and small, were pressed fiercely down upon the brows, side by side, covering the eye sockets, hiding almost the whole of the rapt countenance, except the moving chin. Limbs and all, the old peasant had become one knot of concentration, and the thought of what he was leaving behind him was not any longer its secret.

## V

When Father Reen re-entered the larger room, the living room, he found the crowd in the self-same positions as when he had gone from them; and he felt that not a syllable had passed between them. Tim, that master mind of the group, the man who had led him to the old man's bedside—he was one of the old man's grandsons—had the middle of the earthen floor to himself. He blurted out, almost with a touch of levity in his voice: "You had a job with him."

A murmur of sudden and indignant surprise broke from those against the walls. Father Reen shot one glance at the speaker, he could not help it, the fall from the plane he had been moving in was so terrible—and the man, suddenly realising his fault, made some hopeless, mollifying gesture with a limp hand, speaking no word, however. His wife, as Father Reen perceived, came forward, saying: "Would Father Reen take some little refreshment? We could make a cup of tea? 'Tis a long journey is before you."

He motioned her from him, making for the door: he wanted with all his heart to be in the saddle and away under the stars.

## VI

It took some little time to get the horse ready. He then had to lead it down that steep decline beneath the crest of the hill. As he did so he noticed a glimmer of light above him on the right hand side. He had noticed no house there when ascending; he would not have noticed it now only that he caught a high-pitched babble of talk above him, and, looking round, had spied the dim gleam of a window. As he looked he saw a flash of light—the door had opened—and he heard an angry passionate outburst: "I'll have the law of him! I'll have the law of him!"

The door was suddenly shut to. There remained the angry onward confusion of talk and the dull glimmer in the tiny window. It was a son's house or a grandson's house, surely; and there was many another house in the neighbourhood thinking the same thought this night. Law, yes, and years and years of it over those stony fields and that dirty bank-book. But this much, he told himself, he had known from the moment of entering that crowded living room.

That remembrance quickened his blood. With almost a touch of savagery he urged his beast forward the moment he found his legs gripping its belly. The hard roads invited it. They, with the frozen pools all along them, were bright enough to see by; there was also the tangle of starshine hanging somehow in the middle air above the landscape. For one no longer young he rode wildly, but then the Reens from time immemorial had been eager horsemen. When he came down on to the level ground he broke into a hard gallop; and when, after an hour's going, he had won to the better-kept road beside the lakes he rode as if for a high wager. He was flying not from Kilmony so much as from that fund of reflections all he had witnessed there had aroused in him. That terrible promiscuity of rock, the little stony fields that only centuries of labour had salvaged from them, the unremitting toil they demanded, the poor return, the niggard scheme of living; and then the ancient face on the pillow, the gathering of greedy descendants—he had known it all before; for years the knowledge of how much of a piece it all was had kept his mind uneasy. He knew he would presently be asking himself: Where do my duties end? And this hard riding of his was but an effort to baffle that inveterate questioning. He rode like a man possessed. If the rhythm of the riding, the need for alertness, the silence of the black, stark landscape, the far-stretching lakes, the mass of starshine in the air, weakened at moments the urgency of the question, it overwhelmingly leaped upon him, that question did, whenever he passed a lonely farmhouse clung against its slab of protecting rock at the base of a cliff, or espied one aloft on some *leaca* or other, betrayed to the night by the lamp still dimly burning. Each and every one of them seemed to grab at his very heart pleading for some human succour that their inmates could not name. And all the time the hoofs of his animal were beating out from the frozen road in perfectly regular rhythm: My people! My people! My people!

# Liam O'Flaherty

## *Spring Sowing*

It was still dark when Martin Delaney and his wife Mary got up. Martin stood in his shirt by the window a long time looking out, rubbing his eyes and yawning, while Mary raked out the live coals that had lain hidden in the ashes on the hearth all night. Outside, cocks were crowing and a white streak was rising from the ground, as it were, and beginning to scatter the darkness. It was a February morning, dry, cold and starry.

The couple sat down to their breakfast of tea, bread and butter, in silence. They had only been married the previous autumn and it was hateful leaving a warm bed at such an early hour. They both felt in a bad humour and ate, wrapped in their thoughts. Martin with his brown hair and eyes, his freckled face and his little fair moustache, looked too young to be married, and his wife looked hardly more than a girl, red-cheeked and blue-eyed, her black hair piled at the rear of her head with a large comb gleaming in the middle of the pile, Spanish fashion. They were both dressed in rough homespuns, and both wore the loose white frieze shirt that Inverara peasants use for work in the fields.

They ate in silence, sleepy and bad humoured and yet on fire with excitement, for it was the first day of their first spring sowing as man and wife. And each felt the glamour of that day on which they were to open up the earth together and plant seeds in it. So they sat in silence and bad humour, for somehow the imminence of an event that had been long expected, loved, feared and prepared for, made them dejected. Mary, with her shrewd woman's mind, munched her bread and butter and thought of . . . Oh, what didn't she think of? Of as many things as there are in life does a woman think in the first joy and anxiety of her mating. But Martin's mind was fixed on one thought. Would he be able to prove himself a man worthy of being the head of a family by doing his spring sowing well?

In the barn after breakfast, when they were getting the potato seeds and the line for measuring the ground and the spade, a cross word or two passed between them, and when Martin fell over a basket in the half-darkness of the barn, he swore and said that a man would be better off dead than . . . But before he could finish whatever he was going to say, Mary had her arms around his waist and her face to his. "Martin," she said, "let us not begin this day cross with one another." And there was a tremor in her voice. And somehow, as they embraced and Martin kept mumbling in his awkward peasant's voice, "pulse of my heart, treasure of my life," and such traditional phrases, all their irritation and sleepiness left them. And they stood there embracing until at last Martin pushed her from him with pretended roughness and said: "Come, come, girl, it will be sunset before we begin at this rate."

Still, as they walked silently in their raw-hide shoes, through the little hamlet, there was not a soul about. Lights were glimmering in the windows of a few cabins. The sky had a big grey crack in it in the east, as if it were going to burst in order to give birth to the sun. Birds were singing somewhere at a distance. Martin and Mary rested their baskets of seeds on a fence outside the village and Martin whispered to Mary proudly: "We are first, Mary." And they both looked back at the little cluster of cabins, that was the centre of their world, with throbbing hearts. For the joy of spring had now taken complete hold of them.

They reached the little field where they were to sow. It was a little triangular patch of ground under an ivy-covered limestone hill. The little field had been manured with seaweed some weeks before, and the weeds had rotted and whitened on the grass. And there was a big red heap of fresh seaweed lying in a corner by the fence to be spread under the seeds as they were laid. Martin, in spite of the cold, threw off everything above his waist except his striped woollen shirt. Then he spat on his hands, seized his spade and cried: "Now you are going to see what kind of a man you have, Mary."

"There now," said Mary, tying a little shawl closer under her chin. "Aren't we boastful this early hour of the morning? Maybe I'll wait till sunset to see what kind of a man have I got."

The work began. Martin measured the ground by the southern fence for the first ridge, a strip of ground four feet wide, and he placed the line along the edge and pegged it at each end. Then he spread fresh seaweed over the strip. Mary filled her apron with seeds and began to lay them in rows, four, three, four. When she was a little distance down the ridge Martin advanced with his spade to the head eager to commence.

"Now in the name of God," he cried, spitting on his palms, "let us raise the first sod!"

"Oh, Martin, wait till I'm with you!" cried Mary, dropping her seeds on the ridge and running up to him. Her fingers outside her woollen mittens were numb with the cold, and she couldn't wipe them in her apron. Her cheeks seemed to be on fire. She put an arm round Martin's waist and stood looking at the green sod his spade was going to cut, with the excitement of a little child.

"Now for God's sake, girl, keep back!" said Martin gruffly. "Suppose anybody saw us trapesing about like this in the field of our spring sowing, what would they take us for but a pair of useless, soft, empty-headed people that would be sure to die of the hunger. Huh!" He spoke very rapidly, and his eyes were fixed on the ground before him. His eyes had a wild, eager light in them as if some primeval impulse were burning within his brain and driving out every other desire but that of asserting his manhood and of subjugating the earth.

"Oh, what do we care who is looking?" said Mary; but she drew back at the same time and gazed distantly at the ground. Then Martin cut the sod, and pressing the spade deep into the earth with his foot, he turned up the first sod with a crunching sound as the grass roots were dragged out of the earth. Mary sighed and walked back hurriedly to her seeds with furrowed brows. She picked up her seeds and began to spread them rapidly to drive out the sudden terror that had seized her at that moment when the first sod was turned up and she saw the fierce, hard look in her husband's eyes, that were unconscious of her presence. She became suddenly afraid of that pitiless, cruel earth, the peasant's slave master, that would keep her chained to hard work and poverty all her life until she would sink again into its bosom. Her short-lived love was gone. Henceforth she was only her husband's helper to till the earth. And Martin, absolutely without thought, worked furiously, covering the ridge with black earth, his sharp spade gleaming white as he whirled it sideways to beat the sods.

Then as the sun rose the little valley beneath the ivy-covered hills became dotted with white frieze shirts, and everywhere men worked madly without speaking and women spread seeds. There was no heat in the light of the sun, and there was a sharpness in the still thin air that made the men jump on their spade hafts ferociously and beat the sods as if they were living enemies. Birds hopped silently before the spades, with their heads cocked sideways, watching for worms. Made brave by hunger they often dashed under the spades to secure their food.

Then when the sun reached a certain point all the women went back to the village to get dinner for their men, and the men worked on without stopping. Then the women returned, almost running, each carrying a tin can with a flannel tied around it and a little bundle tied with a white cloth. Martin threw down his spade when Mary arrived back in the field. Smiling at one another they sat under the hill for their meal. It was the same as their breakfast, tea and bread and butter.

"Ah," said Martin, when he had taken a long draught of tea from his mug, "is there anything in this world as fine as eating dinner out in the open like this after doing a good morning's work? There, I have done two ridges and a half. That's more than any man in the village could do. Ha!" And he looked at his wife proudly.

"Yes, isn't it lovely," said Mary, looking at the black ridges wistfully. She was just munching her bread and butter. The hurried trip to the village and the trouble of getting the tea ready had robbed her of her appetite. She had to keep blowing at the turf fire with the rim of her skirt, and the smoke nearly blinded her. But now sitting on that grassy knoll, with the valley all round glistening with fresh seaweed and a light smoke rising from the freshly turned earth, a strange joy swept over her. It overpowered that other feeling of dread that had been with her during the morning.

Martin ate heartily, revelling in his great thirst and his great hunger, with every pore of his body open to the pure air. And he looked around at his neighbours' fields boastfully, comparing them with his own. Then he looked at his wife's little round black head and felt very proud of having her as his own. He leaned back on his elbow and took her hand in his. Shyly and in silence, not knowing what to say and ashamed of their gentle feelings, for peasants are always ashamed of feeling refined, they finished eating and still sat hand in hand looking away into the distance. Everywhere the sowers were resting on little knolls, men, women and children sitting in silence. And the great calm of nature in spring filled the atmosphere around them. Everything seemed to sit still and wait until midday had passed. Only the gleaming sun chased westwards at a mighty pace, in and out through white clouds.

Then in a distant field an old man got up, took his spade and began to clean the earth from it with a piece of stone. The rasping noise carried a long way in the silence. That was the signal for a general rising all along the little valley. Young men stretched themselves and yawned. They walked slowly back to their ridges.

Martin's back and his wrists were getting a little sore, and Mary felt that if she stooped again over her seeds that her neck would break, but neither said anything and soon they had forgotten their tiredness in the mechanical movement of their bodies. The strong smell of the upturned earth acted like a drug on their nerves.

In the afternoon, when the sun was strongest, the old men of the village came out to look at their people sowing. Martin's grandfather, almost bent double over his thick stick, stopped in the lane outside the field and, groaning loudly, he leaned over the fence.

"God bless the work," he called wheezily.

"And you, grandfather," replied the couple together, but they did not stop working.

"Ha!" muttered the old man to himself. "Ha! He sows well and that woman is good, too. They are beginning well."

It was fifty years since he had begun with his Mary, full of hope and pride, and the merciless soil had hugged them to its bosom ever since each spring without rest. But he did not think of that. The soil gives forgetfulness. Only the present is remembered in the spring, even by the aged who have spent their lives tilling the earth; so the old man, with his huge red nose and the spotted handkerchief tied around his skull under his black soft felt hat, watched his grandson work and gave him advice.

"Don't cut your sods so long," he would wheeze, "you are putting too much soil on your ridge." "Ah, woman! Don't plant a seed so near the ridge. The stalk will come out sideways."

And they paid no heed to him.

"Ah," grumbled the old man, "in my young days, when men worked from morning till night without tasting food, better work was done. But of course it can't be expected to be the same as it was. The breed is getting weaker. So it is."

Then he began to cough in his chest and hobbled away to another field where his son Michael was working.

By sundown Martin had five ridges finished. He threw down his spade and stretched himself. All his bones ached and he wanted to lie down and rest. "It's time to be going home, Mary," he said.

Mary straightened herself, but she was too tired to reply. She looked at Martin wearily and it seemed to her that it was a great many years since they had set out that morning. Then she thought of the journey home and the trouble of feeding the pigs, putting the fowls into their coops and getting the supper ready and a momentary flash of rebellion against the slavery of being a peasant's wife crossed her mind. It passed in a moment. Martin was saying, as he dressed himself:

"Ha! My soul from the devil, it has been a good day's work. Five ridges done, and each one of them as straight as a steel rod. Begob, Mary it's not boasting to say that ye might well be proud of being the wife of Martin Delaney. And that's not saying the whole of it, my girl. You did your share better than any woman in Inverara could do it this blessed day."

They stood for a few moments in silence looking at the work they had done. All her dissatisfaction and weariness vanished from Mary's mind with the delicious feeling of comfort that overcame her at having done this work with her husband. They had done it together. They had planted seeds in the earth. The next day and the next and all their lives, when spring came they would have to bend their backs and do it until their hands and bones got twisted with rheumatism. But night would always bring sleep and forgetfulness.

As they walked home slowly Martin walked in front with another peasant talking about the sowing, and Mary walked behind, with her eyes on the ground, thinking.

Cows were lowing at a distance.

# Liam O'Flaherty

## *The Tramp*

There were eight paupers in the convalescent yard of the workhouse hospital. The yard was an oblong patch of cement with the dining-room on one side and high red-brick wall on the other. At one end was the urinal and at the other a little tarred wooden shed where there was a bathroom and a wash-house. It was very cold, for the sun had not yet risen over the buildings that crowded out the yard almost from the sky. It was a raw, bleak, February morning, about eight o'clock.

The paupers had just come out from breakfast and stood about uncertain what to do. What they had eaten only made them hungry and they stood shivering, making muffs of their coat-sleeves, their little black woollen caps perched on their heads, some still chewing a last mouthful of bread, others scowling savagely at the ground as they conjured up memories of hearty meals eaten some time in the past.

As usual Michael Deignan and John Finnerty slouched off into the wash-house and leaned against the sink, while they banged their boots on the floor to keep warm. Deignan was very tall and lean. He had a pale melancholy face and there was something the matter with the iris of his right eye. It was not blue like the other eye, but of an uncertain yellowish colour that made one think, somehow, that he was a sly, cunning, deceitful fellow, a totally wrong impression. His hair was very grey around the temples and fair elsewhere. The fingers of his hands were ever so long and thin and he was always chewing at the nails and looking at the ground, wrapped in thought.

"It's very cold," he said in a thin, weak, listless voice. It was almost inaudible.

"Yes," replied Finnerty gruffly, as he started up and heaved a loud sigh. "Ah—" he began and then he stopped, snorted twice to clear his nose, and let his head fall on his chest. He was a middle-sized, thick-set fellow, still in good condition and fat in the face, which was round and rosy, with grey eyes and very white teeth. His black hair was grown long and curled about his ears. His hands were round, soft and white, like a schoolmaster's.

The two of them stood leaning their backs against the washstand and stamped their feet in a moody silence for several minutes and then the tramp, who had been admitted to the hospital the previous night, wandered into the wash-house. He appeared silently at the entrance of the shed and paused there for a moment while his tiny blue eyes darted around piercingly yet softly, just like a graceful wild animal might look through a clump of trees in a forest. His squat low body, standing between the tarred doorposts of the shed with the concrete wall behind and the grey sky overhead, was after a fashion menacing with the power and vitality it seemed to exude. So it seemed at least to the two dejected, listless paupers within the shed. They looked at the tramp with a mournful vexed expression and an envious gleam in their eyes and a furrowing of their foreheads and a shrinking of their flesh from this fresh dominant coarse lump of aggressive wandering life, so different to their own jaded, terror-stricken lives. Each thought, "Look at the red fat face of that vile tramp. Look at his fierce insulting eyes, that stare you in the face as boldly as a lion, or a child, and are impudent enough to have a gentle expression at the back of them, unconscious of malice. Look at that huge black beard that covers all his face and neck except the eyes and the nose and a narrow red slit for the mouth. My God, what throat muscles and what hair on his chest, on a day like this too, when I would die of cold to expose my chest that way!"

So each thought and neither spoke. As the tramp grinned foolishly—he just opened his beard, exposed red lips and red gums with stray blackened teeth scattered about them and then closed the beard again—the two paupers made no response. The two of them were educated men, and without meaning it they shrank from associating with the unseemly dirty tramp on terms of equality, just as they spent the day in the wash-house in the cold, so as to keep away from the other paupers.

The tramp took no further notice of them. He went to the

back of the shed and stood there looking out of the door and chewing tobacco. The other two men, conscious of his presence and irritated by it, fidgeted about and scowled. At last the tramp looked at Deignan, grinned, fumbled in his coat pocket, took out a crumpled cigarette and handed it to Deignan with another grin and a nodding of his head. But he did not speak.

Deignan had not smoked a cigarette for a week. As he looked at it for a moment in wonder, his bowels ached with desire for the little thin, crumpled, dirt-stained roll of tobacco held between the thumb and forefinger of the tramp's gnarled and mud-caked hand. Then with a contortion of his face as he tried to swallow his breath he muttered, "You're a brick," and stretched out a trembling hand. In three seconds the cigarette was lit and he was inhaling the first delicious puff of drug-laden smoke. His face lit up with a kind of delicious happiness. His eyes sparkled. He took three puffs and was handing the cigarette to his friend when the tramp spoke.

"No, keep it yerself, towny," he said in his even, effortless, soft voice. "I've got another for him."

And then when the two paupers were smoking, their listlessness vanished and they became cheerful and talkative. The two cigarettes broke down the barriers of distrust and contempt between themselves and the tramp. His unexpected act of generosity had counteracted his beard and the degraded condition of his clothes. He was not wearing a pauper's uniform, but a patched corduroy trousers and numbers of waistcoats and tattered coats of all colours, piled indiscriminately on his body and held together not by buttons but by a cord tied around his waist. They accepted him as a friend. They began to talk to him.

"You just came in for the night?" asked Deignan. There was still a condescending tone in the cultured accents.

The tramp nodded. Then after several seconds he rolled his tobacco to the other cheek, spat on the floor and hitched up his trousers.

"Yes," he said, "I walked from Drogheda yesterday and I landed in Dublin as tired as a dog. I said to myself that the only place to go was in here. I needed a wash, a good bed, and a rest, and I had only ninepence, a piece of steak, a few spuds, and an onion. If I bought a bed they'd be all gone and now I've had a good sleep, a warm bath, and I still have my ninepence and my grub. I'll start off as soon as I get out at eleven o'clock and maybe walk fifteen miles before I put up for the night somewhere."

"But how did you get into the hospital ward?" asked Finnerty, eyeing the tramp with a jealous look. The cigarette had accentuated Finnerty's feeling of hunger, and he was irritated at the confident way the tramp talked of walking fifteen miles that day and putting up somewhere afterwards.

"How did I get in?" said the tramp. "That's easy. I got a rash on my right leg this three years. It always gets me into the hospital when I strike a workhouse. It's easy."

Again there was a silence. The tramp shuffled to the door and looked out into the yard. The sky overhead was still grey and bleak. The water that had been poured over the concrete yard to wash it two hours before still glistened in drops and lay in little pools here and there. There was no heat in the air to dry it.

The other six paupers, three old men with sticks, two young men, and a youth whose pale face was covered with pimples, were all going about uncertainly, talking in a tired way and peering greedily in through the windows of the dining-room, where old Neddy, the pauper in charge of the dining-room, was preparing the bread and milk for the dinner ration. The tramp glanced around at all this and then shrugged his shoulders and shuffled back to the end of the wash-house.

"How long have you been in there?" he asked Deignan.

Deignan stubbed the remainder of his cigarette against his boot, put the quenched piece in the lining of his cap and then said, "I've been here six months."

"Educated man?" said the tramp. Deignan nodded. The tramp looked at him, went to the door and spat and then came back to his former position:

"I'll say you're a fool," he said quite coolly. "There doesn't look to be anything the matter with you. In spite of your hair, I bet you're no more than thirty-five. Eh?"

"That's just right about my age, but—"

"Hold on," said the tramp. "You are as fit as a fiddle, this is a spring morning, and yer loafing in here and eating yer heart out with hunger and misery instead of taking to the roads. What man! You're mad. That's all there's to it." He made a noise with his tongue as if driving a horse and began to clap his hands on his bare chest. Every time he hit his chest there was a dull heavy sound like distant thunder. The noise was so loud that Deignan could not speak until the tramp stopped beating his chest. He stood wriggling his lips and winking his right eye in irritation against what the tramp had said and jealousy of the man's strength and endurance, beating his bare hairy chest that way on such a perishing day. The blows would crush Deignan's ribs and the exposure would give him pneumonia.

"It's all very well for you to talk," he began querulously. Then he stopped and looked at the tramp. It occurred to him that it would be ridiculous to talk to a tramp about personal matters. But there was something aggressive and dominant and yet absolutely unemotional in the tramp's fierce stare that drove out that feeling of contempt. Instead Deignan felt spurred to defend himself. "How could you understand me?" he continued. "As far as you can see I am all right. I have no disease but a slight rash on my back and that comes from underfeeding, from hunger and . . . depression. My mind is sick. But of course you don't understand that."

"Quite right," said Finnerty, blowing cigarette smoke through his nostrils moodily. "I often envy those who don't think. I wish I were a farm labourer."

"Huh." The tramp uttered the exclamation in a heavy roar. Then he laughed loudly and deeply, stamped his feet and banged his chest. His black beard shook with laughter. "Mother of Mercy," he cried, "I'll be damned but you make me laugh, the two of you."

The two shuffled with their feet and coughed and said nothing. They became instantly ashamed of their contemptuous thoughts for the tramp, he who a few minutes before had given them cigarettes. They suddenly realized that they were paupers, degraded people, and contemptible people for feeling superior to a fellow-man because he was a tramp. They said nothing. The tramp stopped laughing and became serious.

"Oh, the last job I had was a solicitor's clerk," murmured Deignan, biting his nails. "But that was only a stopgap, I can't say that I ever had anything permanent. Somehow I always seemed to drift. When I left college I tried for the Consular Service and failed. Then I stayed at home for a year at my mother's place in Tyrone. She has a little estate there. Then I came to Dublin here. I got disgusted hanging around at home. I fancied everybody was pitying me. I saw everybody getting married or doing something while I only loafed about, living on my mother. So I left. Landed here with two portmanteaux and eighty-one pounds. It's six years ago next fifteenth of May. A beautiful sunny day it was too."

Deignan's plaintive voice drifted away into silence and he gnawed his nails and stared at the ground. Finnerty was trying to get a last puff from the end of his cigarette. He was trying to hold the end between his thumbs and puckered up his lips as if he were trying to drink boiling milk. The tramp silently handed him another cigarette and then he turned to Deignan.

"What did ye do with eighty-one quid?" he said. "Did ye drink it or give it to the women?"

Finnerty, cheered by the second cigarette which he had just lit, uttered a deep guffaw and said, "Ha, the women blast them, they're the curse of many a man's life," but Deignan started up and his face paled and his lips twitched.

"I can assure you," he said, "that I never touched a woman in my life." He paused as if to clear his mind of the horror that the tramp's suggestion had aroused in him. "No, I can't say I drank it. I can't say I did anything at all. I just drifted from one job to another. Somehow, it seemed to me that nothing big could come my way and that it didn't matter very much how I spent my life, because I would be a failure anyway. Maybe I did drink too much once in a while, or dropped a few pounds at a race meeting, but nothing of any account. No, I came down just because I seemed naturally to drift downwards and I couldn't muster up courage to stop myself. I . . . I've been here six months . . . I suppose I'll die here."

"Well, I'll be damned," said the tramp. He folded his arms on his chest, and his chest heaved in and out with his excited breathing. He kept looking at Deignan and nodding his head. Finnerty who had heard Deignan's story hundreds of times with numberless details shrugged his shoulders, sniffed and said: "Begob, it's a funny world. Though I'm damn sure that I wouldn't be here only for women and drink."

"No?" said the tramp. "How do you make that out?"

"No, by Jiminy," said Finnerty, blowing out a cloud of blue smoke through his mouth as he talked. "I'd be a rich man today only for drink and women." He crossed his feet and leaned jauntily back against the washstand, with his hands held in front of him, the fingers of the right hand tapping the back of the left. His fat round face, with the heavy jaw, turned sideways towards the doorway, looked selfish, stupid and cruel. He laughed and said in an undertone, "Oh boys, oh boys, when I come to think of it." Then he coughed and shrugged his shoulders. "Would you believe it," he said turning to the tramp, "I've spent five thousand pounds within the last twelve months? It's a fact. Upon my soul I have. I curse the day I got hold of that money. Until two years ago I was a happy man, I had one of the best schools in the south of Ireland. Then an aunt of mine came home from America and stayed in the house with my mother and myself. She died within six months and left mother five thousand pounds. I got it out of the old woman's hands, God forgive me, and then. . . . Oh well," Finnerty shook his head solemnly, raised his eyebrows and sighed. "I'm not sorry," he continued, leering at a black spot on the concrete floor of the wash-house. "I could count the number of days I was sober on my fingers and thumbs. And now I'd give a month of my life for a cup of tea and a hunk of bread." He stamped about clapping his hands and laughing raucously. His bull neck shook when he laughed. Then he scowled again and said, "Wish I had a penny. That's nine o'clock striking. I'm starving with the hunger."

"Eh? Hungry? The tramp had fallen into a kind of doze while Finnerty had been talking. He started up, scratched his bare neck and then rummaged within his upper garments mumbling to himself. At last he drew forth a little bag from which he took three pennies. He handed the pennies to Finnerty. "Get chuck for the three of us," he said.

Finnerty's eyes gleamed, he licked his lower lip with his tongue and then he darted out without saying a word.

In the workhouse hospital a custom had grown up, since goodness knows when, that the pauper in charge of the dining-room was allowed to filch a little from the hospital rations, of tea, bread, and soup, and then sell them to the paupers again as extras at nine o'clock in the morning for a penny a portion. This fraudulent practice was overlooked by the ward-master; for he himself filched all his rations from the paupers' hospital supply and he did it with the connivance of the workhouse master, who was himself culpable in other ways and was therefore prevented by fear from checking his subordinates. But Finnerty did not concern himself with these things. He dived into the dining-room, held up the three pennies before old Neddy's face and whispered "Three." Neddy, a lean wrinkled old pauper with a very thick red under-lip like a negro, was standing in front of the fire with his hands folded under his dirty check apron. He counted the three pennies, mumbling, and then put them in his pocket. During twenty years he had collected ninety-three pounds in that manner. He had no relatives to whom he could bequeath the money, he never spent any and he never would leave the workhouse until his death, but he kept on collecting the money. It was his only pleasure in life. When he had collected a shilling in pennies he changed it into silver and the silver in due course into banknotes.

"They say he has a hundred pounds," thought Finnerty, his mouth dry with greed, as he watched Neddy put away the pennies. "Wish I knew where it was. I'd strangle him here and now and make a run for it. A hundred pounds. I'd eat and eat and eat and then I'd drink and drink."

The tramp and Deignan never spoke a word until Finnerty came back, carrying three bowls of tea and three hunks of bread on a white deal board. Deignan and Finnerty immediately began to gulp their tea and tear at the bread, but the tramp merely took a little sip at the tea and then took up his piece of bread, broke it in two, and gave a piece to each of the paupers.

"I'm not hungry," he said. "I've got my dinner with me, and as soon as I get out along the road in the open country I'm going to sit down and cook it. And it's going to be a real spring day, too. Look at that sun."

The sun had at last mounted the wall. It was streaming into the yard lighting up everything. It was not yet warm, but it was cheering and invigorating. And the sky had become a clear pure blue colour.

"Doesn't it make ye want to jump and shout?" cried the tramp, joyously stamping about. He had become very excited, seeing the sun.

"I'm afraid I'd rather see a good dinner in front of me," muttered Finnerty with his mouth full of bread.

"What about you, towny?" said the tramp, standing in front of Deignan. "Wouldn't ye like to be walking along a mountain road now with a river flowing under yer feet in a valley and the sun tearing at yer spine?"

Deignan looked out wistfully, smiled for a moment dreamily and then sighed and shook his head. He sipped his tea and said nothing. The tramp went to the back of the shed. Nobody spoke until they had finished the bread and tea. Finnerty collected the bowls.

"I'll take these back," he said, "and maybe I might get sent over to the cookhouse for something."

He went away and didn't come back. The tramp and Deignan fell into a contemplative doze. Neither spoke until the clock struck ten. The tramp shrugged himself and coming over to Deignan, tapped him on the arm.

"I was thinking of what you said about . . . about how you spent your life, and I thought to myself, 'Well, that poor man is telling the truth and he's a decent fellow, and it's a pity to see him wasting his life in here.' That's just what I said to myself. As for that other fellow. He's no good. He's a liar. He'll go back again to his school or maybe somewhere else. But neither you nor I are fit to be respectable citizens. The two of us were born for the road, towny. Only you never had the courage of your convictions."

The tramp went to the door and spat. Deignan had been looking at him in wonder while he was talking and now he shifted his position restlessly and furrowed his forehead.

"I can't follow you," he said nervously and he opened his mouth to continue, when again he suddenly remembered that the man was a tramp and that it would not be good form to argue with him on matters of moral conduct.

"Of course ye can't," said the tramp, shuffling back to his position. Then he stuck his hands within his sleeves and shifted his tobacco to his other cheek. "I know why you can't follow me. You're a Catholic, you believe in Jesus Christ and the Blessed Virgin and the priests and a heaven hereafter. You like to be called respectable and to pay your debts. You were born a free man like myself, but you didn't have the courage . . . "

"Look here, man," cried Deignan in a shocked and angry voice, "stop talking that rubbish. You have been very kind about—er—cigarettes and food, but I can't allow you to blaspheme our holy religion in my presence. Horrid. Ugh."

The tramp laughed noiselessly. There was silence for several moments. Then the tramp went up to Deignan, shook him fiercely by the right arm and shouted in his ear, "You're the biggest fool I ever met." Then he laughed aloud and went back to his place. Deignan began to think that the tramp was mad and grew calm and said nothing.

"Listen here," said the tramp. "I was born disreputable. My mother was a fisherman's daughter and my lawful father was a farm labourer, but my real father was a nobleman and I knew it when I was ten years old. That's what gave me a disreputable outlook on life. My father gave mother money to educate me, and of course she wanted to make me a priest. I said to myself, I might as well be one thing as another. But at the age of twenty-three when I was within two years of ordination a servant girl had a child and I got expelled. She followed me, but I deserted her after six months. She lost her looks after the birth of the child. I never clapped eyes on her or the child since." He paused and giggled. Deignan bit his lip and his face contorted with disgust.

"I took to the road then," said the tramp. "I said to myself that it was a foolish game trying to do anything in this world but eat and sleep and enjoy the sun and the earth and the sea and the rain. That was twenty-two years ago. And I'm proud to say that I never did a day's work since and never did a fellow-man an injury. That's my religion and it's a good one. Live like the birds, free. That's the only way for a free man to live. Look at yourself in a looking-glass. I'm ten years older than you and yet you look old enough to be my father. Come, man, take to the road with me today. I know you're a decent fellow, so I'll show you the ropes. In six months from now you'll forget you were ever a pauper or a clerk. What d'ye say?"

Deignan mused, looking at the ground.

"Anything would be better than this," he muttered. "But . . . Good Lord, becoming a tramp! I may have some chance of getting back to respectable life from here, but once I became a tramp I should be lost."

"Lost? What would you lose?"

Deignan shrugged his shoulders.

"I might get a job. Somebody might discover me here. Somebody might die. Anything might happen. But if I went on the road . . . " He shrugged his shoulders again.

"So you prefer to remain a pauper?" said the tramp with an impudent, half-contemptuous grin. Deignan winced and he felt a sudden mad longing grow within his head to do something mad and reckless.

"You're a fine fellow," continued the tramp, "you prefer to rot in idleness here with old men and useless wrecks to coming out into the free air. What man! Pull yourself together and come over now with me and apply for yer discharge. We'll foot it out together down south. What d'ye say?"

"By Jove, I think I will!" cried Deignan with a gleam in his eyes. He began to trot excitedly around the shed, going to the door and looking up at the sky, and coming back again and looking at the ground, fidgeting with his hands and feet. "D'ye think, would it be all right?" he kept saying to the tramp.

"Sure it will be all right," the tramp kept answering. "Come on with me to the ward master and ask for your discharge."

But Deignan would not leave the shed. He had never in all his life been able to come to a decision on an important matter.

"Do you think, would it be all right?" he kept saying.

"Oh damn it and curse it for a story," said the tramp at last, "stay where you are and good day to you. I'm off."

He shuffled out of the shed and across the yard. Deignan put out his hand and took a few steps forward.

"I say—" he began and then stopped again. His brain was in a whirl thinking of green fields, mountain rivers, hills clad in blue mists, larks singing over clover fields, but something made him unable to loosen his legs, so that they could run after the tramp.

"I say—" he began again, and then he stopped and his face shivered and beads of sweat came out on his forehead.

He could not make up his mind.

# Liam O'Flaherty

## The Outcast

*"I am the Good Shepherd"* (Jesus Christ)

The parish priest returned to the parochial house at Dromullen, after a two months' holiday at the seaside resort of Lisdoonvarna.

He returned fatter then he went, with immense red gills and crimson flakes on his undulating cheeks, with pale blue eyes scowling behind mountainous barricades of darkening flesh and a paunch that would have done credit to a Roman emperor.

He sank into the old easy chair in the library with a sumptuous groan. He was tired after the journey. He filled the chair and overflowed it. His head sank into his neck as he leaned back and the neck-flesh eddied turbulently over the collar of his black coat, toppling down behind in three neat billowing waves. He felt the elbow-rests with his fat white palms caressingly. Great chair! It had borne his weight for ten years without a creak. Great chair! Great priest!

His housekeeper stood timorously on the other side of the table, with her hands clasped in front of her black skirt, a lean, sickly woman with a kind white face. She had followed him in. But she was afraid to disturb the great man so soon after his arrival.

He sighed, grunted, groaned, and made a rumbling internal noise from his throat to his midriff. Then he said "Ha!" and shifted his weight slightly. He suddenly raised his eyebrows. His little eyes rested on the housekeeper's twitching hands. They shot upwards to her pale face. His mouth fell open slightly.

"Well?" he grunted in a deep, pompous voice. "Trouble again? What is it?"

"Kitty Manion wants to see ye, Father?" whispered the housekeeper.

"Foo!" said the priest. He made a noise in his mouth as if he were chewing something soft. He grunted. "I heard about her," he continued in a tone of oppressed majesty. "I heard about the slut.... Yes, indeed.... Ough!... Show her in."

The housekeeper curtsied and disappeared. The door closed without a sound. The white handle rolled backwards with a faint squeak. There was silence in the library. The priest clasped his paunch with both hands. His paunch rose and fell as he breathed. He kept nodding his head at the ground. Two minutes passed.

The door opened again without a sound. The housekeeper pushed Kitty Manion gently into the library. Then the door closed again. The white handle squeaked. There was a tense pause. The parish priest raised his eyes. Kitty Manion stood in front of him, at the other side of the table, two paces within the door.

She had a month-old male child at her breast. His head emerged from the thick, heavy cashmere shawl that enveloped his mother. His blue eyes stared impassively, contentedly. The mother's eyes were distended and bloodshot. Her cheeks were feverishly red. Her shawl had fallen back on to her shoulders like a cowl, as she shifted it from one hand to another in order to rearrange her child. Her great mass of black hair was disordered, bound loosely on the nape of her neck. Her neck was long, full, and white. Her tall, slim figure shivered. These shivers passed down her spine, along her black-stockinged, tapering calves and disappeared into her high-heeled little shoes. She looked very beautiful and innocent as only a young mother can look.

The priest stared at her menacingly. She stared back at him helplessly. Then she suddenly lost control of herself and sank to her knees.

"Have pity on me, Father," she cried. "Have pity on me child."

She began to sob.... The priest did not speak. A minute passed. Then she rose to her feet once more. The priest spoke.

"You are a housemaid at Mr. Burke's, the solicitor."

"I was, Father. But he dismissed me this morning. I have no place to go to. No shelter for me child. They're afraid to take me in in the village for fear ye might . . . Oh! Father, I don't mind about mesel', but me child. It . . . "

"Silence!" cried the priest sternly. "A loose tongue is an ill omen. How did this happen?"

She began to tremble violently. She kept silent.

"Who is the father of yer child, woman?" said the priest slowly, lowering his voice and leaning forward on his elbows.

Her lips quivered. She looked at the ground. Tears rolled down her cheeks. She did not speak.

"Ha!" he cried arrogantly. "I thought so. Obstinate slut. I have noticed you this long while. I knew where you were drifting. Ough! The menace to my parish that a serpent like you . . . Out with it!" he roared, striking the table. "Let me know who has aided you in your sin. Who is he? Name him. Name the father of your child."

She blubbered, but she did not speak.

"For the sake of your immortal soul," he thundered, "I command you to name the father of your child."

"I can't," she moaned hysterically. "I can't, Father. There was more than one man. I don't know who . . . "

"Stop, wretch," screamed the priest, seizing his head with both hands. "Silence! Silence, I command you. Oh my! Oh! Oh!"

The child began to whimper.

"Jesus, Mary, and Joseph," muttered the girl in a quiet mutter.

The priest's face was livid. His eyes were bloodshot. His paunch trembled. He drew in a deep breath to regain control of himself. Then he stretched his right hand to the door with the forefinger pointed.

"Go!" he thundered, in a melancholy voice. "Begone from me, accursed one. Begone with the child of your abomination. Begone."

She turned slowly, on swaying hips, to the door, with the foot movements of one sinking in a quagmire. She threw back her head helplessly on her neck and seized the door-handle. The handle jingled noisily. The door swung open and struck her knee. She tottered into the hall.

"Away with you," he thundered. "Begone from me, accursed one."

The housekeeper opened the hall door. She was thrusting something into the girl's hands, but the girl did not see her. As soon as she saw the open air through the doorway, she darted forward with a wild cry. She sprang down the drive and out into the road.

She paused for a moment in the roadway. To the right, the road led to the village. To the left, it led to the mountains. She darted away to the left, trotting on her toes, throwing her feet out sideways and swaying from her hips.

It was an August day. The sun was falling away towards the west. A heat mist hung high up in the heavens, around the dark spurs of the mountains.

She trotted a long way. Then she broke into a walk as the road began to rise. It turned and twisted upwards steeply towards the mountains, a narrow white crust of bruised limestone curling through the soft bog-land. The mountains loomed up close on either side. . . . There were black shadows on the grey granite rocks and on the purple heather. Overhanging peaks made gloomy caverns that cast long spikes of blackness out from them. Here and there the mountains sucked their sides inwards in sumptuous curves, like seashell mouths. Long black fences raced majestically up the mountain sides and disappeared on far horizons over their peaks, with ferocious speed. The melancholy silence of a dead world filled the air.

The melancholy silence soothed the girl. It numbed her. She sat down to rest on the stunted grass by the roadside. She cast one glance at the valley behind her. She shuddered. Then she hugged her baby fiercely and traversed its tiny face with kisses. The baby began to cry. She fed him. Then he fell asleep. She arose and walked on.

She was among the peaks, walking along a level, winding stretch of road that led to the lake, the Lake of Black Cahir. A great dull weariness possessed her being. Her limbs trembled as she walked. Her heart began to throb with fear. Her forehead wrinkled and quick tremors made her shiver now and again. But she walked fiercely on, driven forward towards the lake in spite of her terror.

She reached the entrance to the valley where the lake was. She saw the lake suddenly, nestling cunningly behind an overhanging mossy-faced cliff, a flat white dot with dark edges. She stood still and stared at it for a long time. She was delirious. Her eyes glistened with a strange light.

Then she shivered and walked slowly downwards towards the lake bank, stopping many times to kiss her sleeping child. When she reached the rocky bank and saw the deep, dark waters, she uttered a cry and darted away. The child awoke and began to cry. She sat down and fondled him. He ceased crying and beat the air feebly with his hands. She kissed him and called to him strange words in a mumbling voice.

She took off her shawl, spread it on a flat, smooth rock, and placed the child in it. Then she tied the shawl into a bundle about the child. She placed the bundle carefully against another rock and knelt before it. Clasping her hands to her breast, she turned her face to the sky and prayed silently.

She prayed for two minutes, and then tears trickled down her cheeks, and she remained for a long time staring at the sky without thinking or praying. Finally she rose to her feet and walked to the lake bank quickly, without looking at her baby. When she reached the brink, she joined her hands above her head, closed her eyes, and swayed forward stiffly.

But she drew backwards again with a gasp.

Her child had crowed. She whirled about and rushed to him. She caught him up in her arms and began to kiss him joyously, laughing wildly as she did so.

Laughing madly, wildly, loudly, she rushed to the bank.

She threw back her head. She put the child's face close against her white throat, and jumped headlong into the lake.

# Liam O'Flaherty

## The Fall of Joseph Timmins

It was Sunday evening. Mr. Joseph Timmins sat by his wife's bedside. His wife, Louisa, who had become a confirmed invalid of late, was lying flat in bed, with her shoulders propped against pillows. She was reading aloud an article from *The Irish Rosary*. The article dealt with the "Persecution of the Church of Mexico."

Although it was cold outside it was very stuffy in the room. The window was shut and there was a fire. Mrs. Timmins required a warm room for her ailment. It was the heat that first began to make Mr. Timmins discontented as he sat listening. Then the tiresome crackling of the fire made him feel bored and his winter underclothing, which he had just begun to wear, irritated his flesh. Finally he became aware of his wife's rasping and sanctimonious voice and his heart poured out all its rebellious hatred against her.

He stole a glance at her lean, withered, spectacled face, at her clammy yellow hands, at her sunken undeveloped breasts, shaped like a flat board against the bedclothes and he realized acutely that he was fifty years old, without ever having been loved. So a pained dissatisfied expression came into his nervous face and he began to think of her with hatred. Until then he had listened to her reading without grasping the meaning of the words. Now he heard them acutely and hated them, their meaning and the persecuted Church, which represented his unhappiness. The Church was his wife, with her unsexed body and the spectacles on her nose and her horror of the marriage bed.

The sudden upheaval in his mind was all the more violent because it terrified his conscience and he was too weak either to act upon it or to repress it. Indeed he called weakly upon the Blessed Virgin to save him from this sin, but the devil of unrest and concupiscence held his paltry personality within strong chains, so that he heard his thoughts actually shouting in his mind and he sat listening to them, incapable of resistance.

Indecent memories made him flush, and yet they made him hate her all the more and feel ashamed of his cowardice. He remembered how in the first year of their marriage, she had terrified him by her modesty. Yes, she had lain, twenty-five years ago, in that very same bed, their marriage bed. She had turned all the holy pictures to the walls, sprinkled him with holy water and begun to make an act of contrition when the marriage was about to be consummated. It was like being married to a nun or setting up house in a church.

And all these barren years, without children and even without sin. . . . The devil now suggested to his mind, shouted it out, that even sin, strong lustful sin, would have fertilized the arid desert of his life. It would have freed him from her clammy hands and her undeveloped breasts that were shaped against the bedclothes like a flat board.

And he himself . . . what was he? What did he look like in the mirror, one day after his bath, when he saw himself naked? A puny thin man with a beard streaked with grey, a nervous pale face twitching, eyes that had a monk's womanfear in them and bony thighs like an old man.

Word by word, slowly, she enumerated the tortures they were suffering, the bishops and priests of Mexico and her dry lips seemed to find pleasure in the recital of their suffering, in the laceration of their whipped flesh. For their loins had never known a woman. And he, listening, rejoiced wickedly, for those atheists were crashing through the walls of steel that had bound his cowardice and with imaginary bullets he slew hordes of bishops and dashed their gourds of holy water into cesspools and smashed the holy pictures with hammers and spat upon the tablets of contrition. He heard cries of lust and triumph and he mingled with the conquering atheistic soldiers, gouging the eyes of monks and violating nuns.

It was horrible. His irritated skin grew hot and moist with perspiration. He made a sound with his lips, like a hiss of pain. He clenched his hands together and stretched them downwards stiffly towards his thighs.

Suddenly his wife stopped reading, put the magazine

on the bed and looked at him. She looked at him down her nose over her spectacles. Her eyes, shining through the fire-brightened glasses, were cold and cruel like the eyes of a miser. They had in them all the meanness and the cruelty and the aridity of perverted sanctity, the joylessness of the woman who has killed her mother instinct, the hatred of the parasitic soul that withers the sap of nature with its clammy touch.

"Joseph," she said, in her dry, harsh, old-maid's voice, "is it too much for you, dear?"

Her voice made him start, but he did not look at her. He merely relaxed his hands and let his body go limp. Her voice silenced the devilish voice of rebellion in his mind. Like an automatic machine his conscience registered a mortal sin, the sin of taking pleasure in obscene thoughts. Her voice made him feel conscious of her power over him and of his own weakness. Just as a schoolboy when he hears the voice of the Dean of Studies, remembers his lessons with fear; so Mr. Timmins remembered his work as a director of an insurance company and also the religious societies to which he belonged, especially the one for saving street women "from the scarlet sin of their unhappy life" as his wife called it. These labours and duties rose up before his mind, big and perpetually unfinished and it became obvious to him that life should mean nothing to him beyond these labours, for which he would be rewarded in the next world.

"Yes," he said, in a childish feminine voice, "it's rather horrible, what people . . . I mean . . . things are turning out rather . . . it's unrest, I suppose and . . . science."

Then he found courage to look at her, because, with a sudden twist, his mind had become like hers, a mind hostile to rebellion and to the desires of the flesh; only with the difference that his mind was more violent and passionate than hers and it would now like to gouge out the eyes of the atheistic soldiers and burn all Protestants and heretics in a big fire. Whereas her mind, behind the cruel cold eyes, watched suffering and torment without movement and saw that they were good.

Her eyes turned wearily and contemptuously from her husband's nervous twitching face. She sighed and said wearily:

"Science, thy name is sin. No, Joseph, it's not science, but the coming of Antichrist. I can feel it in the growing generation. It's truly horrible, but I can even see signs in your nephew that he is becoming a prey to the immoral teachings of the College of Science. He laughs immoderately and yawns when I talk to him of his religious duties. He makes too free with the servants."

His eyes wandered from her face as she spoke. They rested on her undeveloped breasts that were like a flat board against the bedclothes. In a flash he smelt the sun-baked plains of Mexico and saw bronzed horsemen galloping with screaming nuns on the pommels of their gaudy saddles. "The curse of the cinema," she had said. The hot voluptuous sun and the stretching long-grassed golden plains made his flesh throb where the new underclothing grated against it. He shuddered and said almost angrily:

"I am at the end of my patience. Unless he mends his ways.... Well, it's hard ... my dead brother's son ... and we ... God didn't bless us with children, but ... nothing but ruin can come of the company he keeps ... his drinking and if what I hear is true ... women."

"Women," said Mrs. Timmins, "you haven't told me anything about ... "

"My dear," said Mr. Timmins, "I didn't want to disturb ... I'm not certain and in your condition ... "

"Joseph," said Mrs. Timmins. "You must put your foot down. At once. It's your weakness that's responsible. He must leave the college at once. Take him into your office."

Mr. Timmins began to speak, but he became inarticulate and he wrung his hands. His face became crimson. He was trying very hard to feel violent against his nephew, but all the time he felt the impact of hot voluptuous sunrays against his irritated flesh and he had visions of wild lawless men in rolling golden plains, herding women.

There was a knock at the door. Then the parlourmaid entered.

"Dinner is served, sir," she said. "Will you have your beef-tea now, ma'am?"

"Yes," said Mrs. Timmins. "And I think I'll try a little chicken, Kitty. A little breast."

"Yes, ma'am. Do you want some more coal on the fire?"

"Do."

While the maid was at the coal-shuttle, Mr. Timmins got up and kissed his wife reverently on the forehead. Her skin was yellow and clammy. His lips quivered as they touched her skin. She called him back from the door, waited until the parlourmaid had left the room and then said in a very severe tone:

"You must speak to him. Don't let me have to do it."

Then Mr. Timmins went out hurriedly. He hurried without being aware of it, fondling the tip of his little thin beard and moving his lips. When he turned the corner and came to the stairhead he realized the cause of his hurried movements. The parlourmaid was tripping down in front of him. Immediately he flushed and thought of the golden rolling plains, the swishing of the long grass and the flying hoofs of the sweating horses. Everything hot under the boiling sun. His lips grew dry as he went down the stairs in the wake of the comely silken legs and saw, resisting, conscious-stricken, the curve of her body and the undulating glossy hair rising from her soft white neck. And he saw that she was young and soft and round and fresh, like a young flower wet with dew, opening out its honeyed cup to a wandering bee.

The maid went off across the hallway towards the kitchen. It was dim there where she disappeared and her tall straight figure, swaying voluptuously at the hips, became alluring among the shadows. When she disappeared something began to burn in his chest, for a few moments only, a pang of mingled joy and sadness. It was queer, both unpleasant and violently intoxicating.

He passed the dining-room door and went into the drawing-room to look for his nephew. The drawing-room was empty. He went through to the dining-room. His nephew was standing at the side-board and he put down something hurriedly that clinked. Mr. Timmins flared up at once.

"Drinking?" he said, in a low tense voice.

The nephew turned round, calmly sticking a coloured handkerchief into his outside breast pocket. He was a young man of twenty, low-sized and powerfully built. His face had already become slightly coarse. His strong neck, his curly dark hair and the contemptuous expression of his grey eyes made him attractive, in the way that stupid, strong men are attractive.

"Hello, Uncle Joe," he said carelessly in a deep bass voice. "What's the matter? Everybody takes a pick-me-up before dinner now. I don't feel up to scratch. That match yesterday was a bit tough."

"I have a few words to say to you, Reggie," said Mr. Timmins.

"What about?" said the nephew.

The parlourmaid entered with the soup. They took their seats, facing one another across the table. Mr. Timmins watched his nephew's eyes. The nephew smiled slyly at the parlourmaid and he looked at Mr. Timmins with a vacant stare and fiddled with his napkin. As the parlourmaid leaned over his shoulder with the soup, Mr. Timmins again felt that sensation of something burning in his chest. The maid left the room. Mr. Timmins put down his spoon and began to speak furiously.

"She insists on your leaving the College of Science," he said, "and I must own . . . well, I quite agree with her. For your father's sake, Reggie . . . Well, I tried my best to . . . give you your own way and to . . . What return do you make? What's going to become of you, I say? Twice during the past week I have been approached by friends. Yes. Mrs. Turnbull stopped me in the street, waved her umbrella in my face and accused you of dragging her Andrew into the ways of the devil. Do you think I hear nothing? I'm told everything, even about your champagne dinner at Jammet's with a common bookmaker."

The nephew broke bread and said calmly:
"That was on a bet, uncle. Ye can't expect a man . . . "
"A man," said Mr. Timmins. "You call yourself a man. I would forgive you for squandering my money if it was for a good purpose. I'm not mean. Your father left me a sacred trust. Lord have mercy on him, his ways were not mine and he died penniless. But I'm not mean. God didn't bless us with children. What I have is yours. But it's a hopeless and miserable end to a life of labour and . . . and self-denial to think that . . . Eh? What's going to become of you? She says I'm weak and it's time. What can I do? Have you no conscience? Football, drink and bad company are no fitting preparation for the . . . Do you or do you not want to?"

The nephew pushed away his empty plate and put his arms on the table.

"Listen, Uncle Joe," he said calmly.
"Sit properly in my presence," said Mr. Timmins angrily.
"Oh, all right," said the nephew, "ye might let us have a meal in peace. There's something I wanted to ask you about only I'll wait till afterwards. Ye know it's bad for yer digestion talking during meals. I heard Dr. . . . "
"Silence!" shouted Mr. Timmins.
"Very well, only . . . "
"Silence," whispered Mr. Timmins, blushing and shaking his fist. He heard the maid's footsteps. Mr. Timmins did not look towards the maid. Neither did he think of her. He an-

swered her severely when she asked him if his untouched soup had not been to his liking. He felt a meaningless anger that he had not experienced for years. Hosts of things contributed to produce this anger, trivial things like his new underwear and his wife's yellow skin, weighty things like the consciousness of his own arid years that had never known the softness and subtle passion of love. And he wanted revenge, violent and immediate, a breaking forth that would shatter everything, even his own life and his hope of Paradise.

His appetite was gone, but he wanted to drink. He wanted to go to the sideboard, put a decanter to his lips and spill it down his throat. But he was afraid of his nephew. The young brute. Just like his dead father, who had got drunk on the night after his young wife's funeral and had to be brought home from an improper house.

"He has something to say to me," thought Mr. Timmins. "Very well. Nothing he can say will alter my determination to get even with this young ruffian. He's laughing at me. Upon my soul he is."

Not a word was spoken for the remainder of the meal. The nephew ate ravenously, utterly indifferent to the twitching, angry countenance of his uncle sitting opposite him. Mr. Timmins made a pretence of eating, but each mouthful stuck in his throat. The sound of the maid's footsteps excited him now, just as the contour of her figure had done in the hallway. And under cover of the new silent anger that had hardened his soul, he conceived an extraordinary and intoxicating desire to . . . Each time she bent over him he thought of it with almost diabolical pleasure. There was a soft sweet scent from her hair and even from her white apron when she bent over him. The starched apron crinkled, pressed out of shape by her bending supple figure. He was acutely conscious of every sound and movement she made and of her shape, even though he didn't look at her. When they were finished their coffee, Mr. Timmins said:

"You may leave the table. I'll hear what you have to say in the drawing-room."

The nephew grunted and went out. Mr. Timmins looked about him stealthily and fondled the tip of his beard. Then he drank two large glasses of port in rapid succession. His head became giddy for a moment. Then he grew exalted. A melancholy sensation that was very pleasant overcame him. Walking very erect, with his hands clasped beneath his shoulder-blades, he went into the drawing-room. The nephew was standing by the fire, leaning his arm on the mantelpiece, with his head bent. He tapped the fender with his toe.

"Well," said Mr. Timmins.

The nephew looked up and folded his arms.

"I owe some money," he said. "It's got to be paid or I'm ruined."

"Money," said Mr. Timmins.

"Yes," said the nephew in a hoarse voice. "A Jew. He won't wait. I put him off for two months. It's fifty quid."

Mr. Timmins walked backwards into a chair and sat down.

"Not a cent," he said, in a calm voice through his teeth. "Not one penny of my money are you going to get. Do you hear?"

"Very well," said the nephew, shrugging his shoulders. "Only he'll come down on you."

"Not a penny," repeated Mr. Timmins.

Suddenly the nephew thrust his head forward and muttered angrily:

"D'ye think it's any pleasure to me to spend yer rotten money or to live in this deadhouse? Why didn't ye let a fellah have a bit o' fun in the house? Where am I to go except to a pub when I want to talk to the lads? There never was anything here only the lives of the saints and novenas to the Holy Ghost an' castin' my father's name at me. God damn the two of ye. Take it or leave it. I know the dodge. But ye're not gettin' me into yer office. I'd rather go to Liverpool and work as a navvy and fry a steak on a shovel. I've got my strength an' I'm not dependin' on you for my lodging."

Beating his broad chest with his clenched fists and muttering something under his breath, he walked heavily out of the room and banged the door after him.

For a long time after he had gone, Mr. Timmins sat with his mouth open, without thought. Still without thinking he went into the dining-room and went to the sideboard. He poured out a measure of brandy and tossed it off. He paused, shivered and filled out another measure rather unsteadily. As he was slowly raising it to his lips the maid entered to clear the table. He started and looked her boldly in the face.

Although she had been in the house for six months, this was the first time that he had looked her in the face. The liquor had lent him new eyes and they saw that her face was willing and as bold as his own turbulent desires. She had a handsome face with a skin the colour of milk. Her eyes were quick and passionate. They did not flinch or get excited under his gaze. They were not innocent. Her lips were avaricious. He could bargain with them. He saw and understood all this, because it seemed that the devil had lent him a new brain with the new eyes. He smiled on her. She answered him with another smile and then she said respectfully, as she put a tray on the table:

"I'm afraid you didn't find the dinner to your liking this evening, sir."

Mr. Timmins fluttered his fingers a trifle drunkenly.

"That doesn't matter a bit. Funny, I don't know your name."

"Kitty, sir."

"Kitty, Ahem! Yes. Kitty. Isn't there a song 'Oh, Kitty, will you marry me?' I think I heard it somewhere."

The parlourmaid bent her head, shot a glance at him from under her drooping lashes and laughed slyly. Mr. Timmins flushed and tried to laugh also, but his lips were dry. His head became full of hot vapour and his limbs became loose. Without knowing what he was doing, he went towards her and held out his hand. Without looking, she caught his hand and put it away gently from her waist. He left the dining-room, raising his feet high off the floor. He staggered into the arm-chair by the fire in the drawing-room and stared into the fire, contemplating in ecstasy the fantastic visions that swam into his mind through clouds of vapour.

As if to conceal the lovely, sinful visions from his wife, he suddenly became enraged with God and with his neighbours and with the societies of which he was a member. He showered unuttered blasphemies and curses on them all and sneered contemptuously on all the monkish men and skinny women that lived around him in smug, silent houses. He cursed the folly of his past life, his unspent departed youth and the misery of a Heaven in such company. With glee he shattered with a wish all that he had fought to gain in the hereafter, by penance and the curbing of his nature.

And in this mood he became cunning and laughed slyly to himself, seeing the cunning profligacy of his nephew, as a cunning predatory bee, stealing the honey that fools had gathered and left untouched. And he decided to do likewise, to be cunning also, without belief, a hypocrite, a profligate.

As he rose unsteadily to his feet, he heard a voice say within him:

"My age does not matter. Nor my bony thighs. I have money, I can buy her. Lots of she things. They gave girls to old Solomon."

He walked to the door leading into the dining-room on tiptoe and saw her bending over the empty tablecloth with a crumb-brush. He made a sound with his lips. She looked up. He smiled. She glanced towards the door that led into the hallway and then looked coldly into his face. He beckoned to her. She did not move and her face looked indignant, but his new cunning saw something in her eyes and lips that made him hurry forward to her round the table. He put his arm round her motionless body and began to whisper into her ear. She kept saying something to which he did not listen, and then he began to shower kisses on her neck, her forehead and her hair. With his trembling hands he pressed her to him, crushing her against the table. And she murmured, struggling to free herself:

"Not here, sir. We'll be seen."

The door banged. She gasped and broke loose. Dazed, with his arms stretched out, Mr. Timmins looked up. His nephew was standing at the door. The maid was hurrying out the other door into the hallway. The nephew's eyes followed her. Then they turned to Mr. Timmins. Mr. Timmins saw them change slowly from wonder to mocking glee.

In a flash the vapours vanished from his brain and he felt a lassitude in all his limbs. He felt old and weak and helpless and ugly; withered and poor.

"Excuse me, Uncle Joe," said the nephew. "I came in to . . ."

"Yes," interrupted Mr. Timmins, sinking into a chair. "You came for that money. How much was it, did you say?"

# Brinsley MacNamara

## *The Smiling Faces*

### I

There were so many, in her time, who had come and sat in the same way in her bar that, for perhaps too long, Miss Cunningham was disinclined to regard too seriously the case of Thomas Weldon. It could not possibly be that he had his eye on herself, for although she was a well-to-do woman with this nice, thriving business, and two lovely farms, as well, on the outskirts of the village of Clunnen, no one ever thought that way of her now.... These possessions might easily have built up a certain sense of allurement about her in the far-back past, but now she was old and quiet in herself, maintaining her grip upon life only, it would seem, by her constant and cautious attention to her business. It was the very reason, in a way, why she had come to notice particularly the case of Thomas Weldon, as she moved about her establishment continuously, talking to her customers, humouring them, concerned about them, even when it came to giving advice that might be a bit against herself sometimes.

Thomas Weldon had grown upon her of late, for he seemed to be always and ever sitting there by her counter now, talking to herself and Essie Kelch, the barmaid. If she ever had any notion of marrying herself, Thomas Weldon might easily have been the sort of man she would have chosen. But the idea of her ever marrying! Oh, not at all! Never! Yet he was a nice man still, a real settled sort of a man anyway until this, until he had begun to come here so often, for no other purpose, as it had suddenly appeared to her, than to talk the few timid words he customarily spoke to Essie Kelch while in her presence. Essie

Kelch indeed! A good attentive girl who brought a nice bit of custom here of an evening by her pleasant little way, but the idea of marrying Essie Kelch! The cheek of these young ones nowadays anyway! But she had spoken to her, quietly, which was her habit, yet with the right kind of meaning behind her words:

"I suppose he does be even trying to flirt with you, when there's no one else here, and I'm not in the bar?"

"Oh, not at all, Miss Cunningham. Is it a man like him? Why, I'm sure he never even once thought of the like in his whole life."

She had watched most carefully after that, and had noticed several times how the quiet eyes of Thomas Weldon had strayed from her in eagerness, often while she was in the very middle of some of her most entertaining accounts of the secret histories of County Meath families, and became entangled in that curious network of a smile which would always seem to be gathered over the smiling face of Essie....

Ah, how well she had guessed?

If it had ever gone further than that, she firmly resolved that such occasions should not so easily present themselves for the future.

II

"But sure you all say that," said Essie.

"Who all? I never said it before, so I didn't," said Thomas Weldon, in his halting, heavy way, yet pleadingly.

"But the lads from Castleconnor and Mullaghowen and Garradrimna! Oh, many and many's the time I've heard it."

"And you used to be talking to all them lads like to me?"

"I used, what else?"

"D'ye tell me now?"

"D'ye think I'm eight years here and never spoke to a boy in my life? And they in and out here every second in the day...."

A snatch of conversation like this would fall between them in the infrequent intervals between the appearance and the disappearance of customers, and if Miss Cunningham chanced to be out of the bar for as long as a few seconds; and with this he had to be satisfied.

The end of the night that had held for him just such a little bit of magic would be the lonesome road home past the ruined archway at Clonarney, that was called "Smiling Bess," and which in other days he had not had the courage to pass on really dark nights, but he did not care now. . . . He could feel brave and forceful now. After the Road of the Elms there was the long boreen down to the neat house in his comfortable nest of fields. He could feel the softness of his rich land about him as he went into the lonely house and lit the candle. A woman would be lovely here. . . . Essie Kelch, for instance, would be lovely here. . . .

And so he would sit lonely with his thoughts until the night was nearly done and the dawn had come. But sure not one of Weldons had ever married like this. Indeed, in his own very family down all the years he had been waiting for his sisters to be settled, he had heard the word mentioned, heard them say of some wayward girl: "Well, bad luck to her smiling face anyway, and see how she got round him in the heel of the hunt!"

His own sisters had not been like that at all, but quiet, settled girls, even before they were properly settled, and so he had had to wait for what appeared a great length of time until they were off his hands, and it was this waiting, more than anything else, that had made him so timid, speaking no word to any girl, thinking of no girl until now. . . . Only what would his sisters say, his severe and sedate and comfortably married sisters say to a "one" like that, a barmaid? Even long dead Weldons would turn in their graves. What good would she be for the wife of a farmer with the light ways in her after she being grinning across the counter at men all her life? Wouldn't anyone, living or dead, think he was mad entirely? They would, oh, they would! Begad, there was no use in making an eeget of a fellow's self altogether. . . .

But in the fields a few hours later, the smiling face of Essie would appear. Essie would seem to call him. The Weldons had ever been good farmers. They had brought these fields, these fields of his, to beauty, to lovely smiles on summer days, with which he had enriched his soul till now, till *she* had come, with her face before him always, coming between him and the face of the fields. And all the tenderness he had aforetime given to the land. Ah, where was it now? Yet there was "something" all about him, in the trees and the quickening clay, in the wide stretch of the windy sky and over all the world.

But soon a brightness that was its own shadow, too, would have fallen for him upon the day, and he would be feeling that he must clean himself and hurry early into Clunnen this evening. . . . And it always took him such a long time now, the cultivation of his appearance. . . . In a way, it was harder work than when he had devoted himself to the land. . . .

### III

"I don't like the way that poor man is goin' on at all. Setting his land on the 'eleven months system,' and letting his bit of oats rot with neglect, like the way he did last year."

Miss Cunningham was saying this to Essie now more than a year after she had first "noticed it."

"Oh, sure he's getting to be a rale ould eeget anyway. I don't know what's come over him. . . . If only he would say what seems to be in his mind itself. . . . But sitting there with his elbows on his knees always, and he thinking and brooding to himself. . . . "

"You shouldn't be taking much notice of him anyway."

"I won't, Miss Cunningham, and that's as sure as you're there."

After such a word out of Miss Cunningham's continuous and concerned mood of advice, Essie always tried to be as "cold" as she could, by keeping her face as much averted as possible when speaking to Thomas Weldon.

Ah, why was she doing that, he would think. If only she knew. . . . If only she could feel the sadness and then the fire that came into him whenever he heard her talking and laughing and skitting with lads from Castleconnor in the little sitting-room off the bar whither she had carried their drinks on a tray, and where he could not see her or them. For often he had heard her giggling richly in there. Oh, it was tearing him to pieces . . . murdering him!

That summer saw the almost complete neglect of his farm. But Miss Cunningham could do nothing to stop it. He was quiet and harmless, never raising his voice in her house, never getting drunk, only safely, moodily, and with not a word out of him, his eyes quietly in pursuit of the laughing eyes of Essie. Oh, but he was going from bad to worse. It was said that he had his nice place mortgaged up to the hilt. He had become neglectful, even of his appearance, and, seeing him now, one would nearly laugh outright at the idea of connecting his name with that of little, laughing Essie.

He moved more moodily through autumn evenings, often feeling, as he passed by "Smiling Bess," that there could be a great cruelty, surely, in smiling faces, that maybe Essie, when she laughed in the bar, or in the sitting-room now, was maybe only laughing at him. . . . What was it brought him such a feeling as he passed the sinister archway at Clonarney? The woman's head, so fantastically ornamented like the head of a Gorgoneion; what could it mean to him? Yet he could never pass it now without feeling some dread. . . . And still, strangely, on his homeward way, he would often return the road to repass it. Why was the thing doing this to him, with its smile like that of one who had led men to their doom in the days gone by?

One night that was darker than usual, and upon the occasion of such a return along the road to Clunnen, he stopped to search for the face of "Smiling Bess" through the gloom. This night, beyond all others, she had called him! And for what? He could scarcely see her. But, beyond the stillness of his troubled mind, he heard the sound of suppressed laughter from one side of the archway. He could just see a confused group, but he knew what it was—a man with a girl in his arms. . . . Suddenly they seemed to have become aware of his presence. There was no sound at all. Above, the smiling face of Gorgoneion grinned on. It was Essie in someone's arms! He could see their bicycles leaning against the other side of the archway. Oh, aye, it was one of the Castleconnor lads. . . . To think that he had let this happen!

And there, in that moment, the resolve to which, heretofore, he had been unable to summon himself was born. . . . He could not let it go over him another single day. He would tell her to-morrow. She did not know, the poor, little thing, that she had nearly ruined him. Surely she must have guessed that the only "love" conversation he had ever had with her was a proposal. But she had not seen. He had "axed" her in his queer, timid way, and she had only shown by her conduct that she refused him—for the time being. But to-morrow he would tell her! He would tell her to-morrow. The long spell of his quietness would be broken, and she would know then how much . . . how terrible big was his love for her. He would carry her home to his little neglected place in the fields, and all would be beautiful again . . . her smiling face . . . the smiling face of the fields.

But above him now, monstrous through the darkness, the face of "Smiling Bess." . . . He hurried away, that face in his eyes, and in his ears what he took to be the sound of laughter. . . .

IV

The next morning, he heard, the postman, or someone passing early out of Clunnen, had told him, that Miss Cunningham had passed peacefully away in the night-time. Ah, that was sad, the poor old thing!

He went into Clunnen, as he had purposed, only to find, in the natural course, that "Miss Cunningham's" was closed and shuttered. And for three days, until the funeral, he went into Clunnen, but never into one of the other houses. They might say what they liked of him! They would know now that he was no drunkard, but only one with lovely feelings always.

He saw Essie at the funeral, in a little black hat that suited her, crying over Miss Cunningham's grave. And he cried too. A nice woman, Miss Cunningham! She had never said a word to him, although he must have been more or less disgusting to her, sitting there, day in, day out. And he felt this of her now, although she had prevented him from "axing" Essie properly. . . . But to think that he must wait longer, now that he had at last made up his mind. . . . Yet he waited, waited in patience, his great resolve still further exciting him, until the shop opened again, and, in the temporary employment of the executors of the late Miss Cunningham, Essie appeared as usual in the bar.

He was again standing looking at her, saying polite and sympathetic things about the departed. . . . But the words were rushing upon him now, after the silent years. . . . When would she give up speaking about the virtues of Miss Cunningham so that he might decently tell her? . . . But, even still, she was saying things that he had not the heart to interrupt, the kindliest things about Miss Cunningham.

He had not spoken to a soul since her death, so immersed had he been in his tremendous resolve. He had not heard the rumour that, as a reward for her faithful services, Miss Cunningham had willed Essie the house and the two farms, and a considerable sum of money. Yet even if he had heard of it, the full significance of such news might not have dawned on him.

At long last, when Essie began to speak of other things, he had the opportunity. And the words burst from him, a long-pent-up stream.... He scarcely knew what he said, but he asked her surely to marry him over and over again.... He said all the lovely things to her that he had wanted to say for so long.

"How well you never came to ask me until now?" she said. "Think of all the years I have spent here slaving, when I'd have loved to get out of it and be mistress of my own place. And you spent and spent, wasting and wasting, coming in here. And now to think that you have the cheek to ask me when you have everything spent, and when you know well that I'm coming in for this place and the two farms, and any amount of money...!"

His very face looked speechless as he stared at her bewildered:

"Ah, no, I never heard, not a word, I never heard, not a single word, and that's as sure as you're there."

"Ah, you never heard? Do you think I'll believe that for a story? And isn't that why you're asking me to marry you now, and for no other reason at all?"

"Ah, no, it isn't. It isn't surely."

And then he spoke of it no more.... There fell a great quietness upon his mind, a quiet like of old, before he had begun to come here. Let her think of him what she liked! Her words were hard, and she did not understand. He felt now that she might never be able to understand... So where was the use? He was trembling as he stood there by his drink at the counter. She was not the same girl now. Oh, no, nor never again....

"Don't you know well I'm engaged to that Castleconnor lad anyway?"

He knew now, of course, and then he did not seem to want to know, for he remained dead silent. He seemed to remain a long time there imprisoned in himself, until he was roused by hearing, from beyond what seemed a great distance, Essie laughing in the sitting-room.... It was the very same as the laughter he had heard by the archway of "Smiling Bess." The Castleconnor lad was in there with her now, and they were going to be married....

He was already in the moment of his second great resolve. ... Ah, yes. It was the thing that should be done, the right thing now. He moved towards the door of the room, surprised the while how easy it was to do this now. . . .

"Excuse me," he said, walking right in and surprising Essie upon the young man's knee, "but I was going home, and it's how I didn't like to go without wishing yous a great dale of joy. . . ."

He did not know whether he had shaken hands with the young man or not, or how he had left the room, for already he was out of the house and far down the road. It did not seem so hard to pass the face of "Smiling Bess" now, for it appeared that it might be a long time before he should pass it in the day-time or dark again. He was going like some truant lover towards his own fields now. But would they understand? Maybe they would understand. The dumbness that had been upon him, and the waiting and waiting, until he had lost. He would be always telling them of that now until maybe they might smile once more.

This, surely, was his third and more certain resolve—to make them smile again. . . .

But he had wasted himself and them. He was not the man he had been, nor were they the fields the Weldons had left him.

. . . Make them smile again. . . . If they broke into laughter at him altogether, what kind of laughter must it be?

That would be his life now, he thought, to prevent this from coming. He must hold himself and give himself to that battle. The people would laugh at him, maybe, but the fields. . . . Ah, no, they could never have the heart to do it. But he had thought the same way once of Essie. . . . And yet . . . and yet, because of her, the fields were lovelier and kindlier than ever before.

It was her face still that he saw in them, and maybe she would never . . . never laugh at him again.

And if that could be, then "Smiling Bess" might hold no terror for him any more.

# Brinsley MacNamara

## *The Sisters*

### I

Whenever I remember the sisters, I see them always in the evening sitting in their quiet cottage by the lakeside. There could never be any question about the love of the sisters for one another, because about the time they were laying the foundations of their story I knew them well, and so came to have knowledge of the beautiful things they had done for one another, the constancy of one, I thought, being but a reflection of the constancy of the other. Indeed, so rich and fine was the sympathy into which their beings flowed that, frequently, I was forced to think of them as one person. The elder was called Rachel, the younger, Rebecca, and one of the few things about them that I never quite came to know was just why the names of women in the Bible had been chosen for their names, unless perhaps someone of their family had had foreknowledge that these two daughters of their people were destined to link those names again with all that is beautiful, and noble in womanhood. And yet this thought did not immediately strike me when I met Rebecca, who was the first of the sisters I came to know. She was living away from her sister in another part of the country, and she told me she was very lonely.

"Oh, I'm so lonely without Rachel," she said, "so awfully, dreadfully lonely."

It was not for me, a stranger to all the implications of her life, suddenly to feel how much her sister meant to her, yet I remember now that I was considerate, and listened with attention

until she had told me more:
"If only you knew Rachel, the poor thing, you would see exactly what I mean and feel about her exactly as I do."

Then she went on to tell me how much, or, at least, to signify as best she might, all that her sister meant in her life. It seemed to me a very beautiful affection which superseded even sisterhood.

"This," said I to myself, "is something new in human friendship, and it may preserve me, God be thanked, from cynicism, if only I extend to it some of that interest which I have already almost completely squandered down many byeways of disillusionment."

It was not so easy at first to maintain my interest, my almost concern, as it had already become, without running the risk of betraying an attitude that must border dangerously upon the offence of curiosity. For there was a certain native subtlety set constantly, an unconscious fortification around the mind of Rebecca, making it proof always against my insinuating attacks. Yet there were times when the look in her eyes would betray her soul to me, but, in the act of looking far, I would suddenly be interrupted, my vision blinded by the ringing flash of her laugh, which, curiously, held at once the qualities of light and sound. Always it would be that way when I seemed to be coming near her soul, for this same jolly laugh would never fail to come at the end of the long silence she would have maintained throughout the look, as if she, too, had retreated from a possible glimpse of her own soul, just barely succeeding in returning to life, after a perilous moment, through the miracle of her laugh. Sometimes I felt that the great personal concern which had come to her naturally through the affliction of womanhood had superadded the power of a double bondage, for she would be always thinking of her sister. At the end of that long, sad look, which was the accompaniment of her thoughtful moments, perhaps there was another face which reached up to hers for succour and for sympathy.

Then something flashed, with a force that almost startled me, out of her silence, her somewhat mysterious way.

"Rachel is elder than I!"

I was suddenly, yet perhaps prematurely, jubilant in the hope that this might be the first glimmering of the light breaking through the trees at the end of the dark forest of her soul, and yet upon her return to silence, this word she had said to me only hung a darker curtain around her life, although her innermost self was already separated by many veils from me. And, attempting to puzzle out this speech, I was only the more deeply mystified into further separation. Rebecca still successfully eluded me. Then, somewhere in the midst of much talking, she spoke a few more words which had a ring of significance that reached to my very soul, where it lay quiet and listening, always listening and quiet whenever I talked with Rebecca.

"I'd give anything to see Rachel married."

And, as I looked into the eyes of Rebecca in the peaceful place where she spoke these words, one corner of at least one veil was lifted and I saw something which in this, the excited moment of the discovery, I was much surprised to think had escaped me. Rebecca was not so young, perhaps, as her ringing laugh had led me to believe, and flashing back to me through this new glimpse of her were her very own words—"Rachel is elder than I." Then, somehow, although I had never seen her in the flesh I could see Rachel clearly, a sad-faced, almost hopeless girl, her age exceeding that of Rebecca by even more than the number of years that was between them, a girl whose face and figure stood in urgent need of artifice and adornment. Led further now even thus timidly, almost, as one might say, half accidentally, my mind went questioning further down the inquisitive byeway it had taken. Somehow, I could not help feeling that the unwedded state of Rachel had, maybe, more than its share in helping to maintain the strange, strong bond which continuously united the separated sisters.

A few days later, as I talked with Rebecca, and while some joke about the question of marriage sprang up between us, she laughed in such a way as I had not hitherto heard her. It was the quality of music again commingled with that of a sudden cloud, as it were, that was full of sorrow falling upon her laugh towards the end of its harmonious scintillation. It expressed for my enlightenment regarding her something I really wanted to know far more explicitly than if she had said it. It seemed to say, indeed I was very certain that it said:

"Oh, yes; of course, I would like to be married, and there is one who greatly desires it, but somehow I do not think it would be just the proper thing for me to do—before Rachel, I mean. She's the eldest, and it might frighten her. It might put her against marrying altogether. She might only want to come and live with me, then, and be a kind of second mother to the children."

It was queer how the heartiest ring of her laugh seemed to struggle back, even in spite of me, into this fancy of mine.

## II

So much of both of us now flashed continuously before one another in our conversation that I often wondered whether or not I knew her far better than this other man who had asked her to marry him. At least I knew why she was waiting, and perhaps he did not know. And yet, perhaps, it was just the kind of thing she would be telling him, because it was a thing she had not told me, seeing that I had had to tell it to myself. And, although she had never told me, I knew so well that she loved him dearly. Thus was it given more particularly to me to feel for her in my knowledge of all the love that troubled her. She was waiting for the sake of love. If she waited longer she might soon be as old as Rachel now was. And I had seen that Rachel was old—so old, indeed, as to be now almost past all hope of marriage. She was waiting, waiting, but would the young man, who must now so frequently whisper his love to her, love her as greatly if that day should come or then want to whisper more? . . . I knew that the life of Rebecca was hovering dangerously, and her merry laugh always hung perilously now upon the brink of tears. Although this thought sprang more and more often, it was harder and harder to think of her as some day weeping only. Many little things were coming to show that the crisis of her life was crushing in, and that now she was not waiting nobly, but merely in affright, for the shadow to fall.

For instance, one May evening as I sat in a pleasant garden by the lakeside, I saw Rebecca walking with her lover. My eyes wandered continually from the book I was reading to watch them, yet not in flippant curiosity, but filled rather with a great concern for the ultimate happiness of Rebecca. There seemed to be a constraint upon their movements, and, in spite of myself, I imagined them to be talking of Rachel. Sometimes they stopped dead upon the path, as if arrested and imprisoned in the silence that had come upon them. I knew that Rachel was, for all the bond of love that tied them, becoming more powerfully significant in the life of Rebecca, and maybe, after all I had already thought, towards no happy ending. Then her lover and she sat down upon an old stone seat some distance from me. Their faces were like the faces of people in a cinema picture as they talked on, and the expressions upon their faces from moment to moment held more meaning for me, than, perhaps, if I could have heard what they were saying. I blessed the inventors of the "silent drama" for having given me the opportunity of acquiring the trick of reading this kind of emotional expression.... There passed before me much of the story of which Rebecca was the heroine.... But I knew, from the almost pathetic incompleteness of the look upon their faces, that this film-play of a story from real life was still unfinished when the lovers rose to go. Another and perhaps the final reel of the story had still to be unwound before me, and I felt that my interest in it must rise ever higher and higher as it flickered to its end.

However, soon after the passage of the portion I had witnessed in the garden, came a gap of reality which almost meant to me the spoiling of the whole picture. For a long while, only one figure moved upon the screen, the figure of Rebecca herself, but her very loneliness made her slightest movement full of meaning. It seemed better for the time being that she had already gone some distance out of my life, so that I might see her more clearly in her true relation to herself, and I was watchful now with an almost joyous, vibrant watchfulness, because my eyes were no longer blinded by the magical quality, which flashed out from her laugh when it was gay, or fell down from it, as from a lowering cloud, when it was sad. Perhaps it was because she had so often told me, without any words, that her love had eased her loneliness that she must know how I felt every tremor of her feelings, and that a meeting between us could only effect an intensification that must end for her in a flood of tears. The gap of uneventfulness in the picture grew at length to possess a certain excitement in the thought that it must soon be filled and, maybe, by a sudden multiplicity of happening. He was gone from her and she was lonely, and what could happen now? He had gone from her because she had waited ... waited for Rachel to get married first.... And Rachel had not married, while she was now as old as Rachel had been when she had begun to wait, just because she had thought that Rachel was getting a little too old, perhaps, for marriage, but still hoped to see her married first. And now Rebecca had lost her lover, and Rachel was still unmarried.

It was a realisation to sigh about and be regretful over. Yet hope remains unlost for ever, and there was something surely, which might again kindle bright in the life of Rebecca. There was her love of Rachel, her sister. . . . It would be very beautiful indeed if ever they came together to part no more. And, somehow, I felt that this must be the ending of the story I had been watching so long in silence upon the screen of my much-concerned fancy.

### III

When Rachel came, and I, who had learned to know this hitherto invisible character, I who had almost seen her, too, through very strength of my gazing, was in no wise disappointed. She was old, so old, when one remembered that she was a girl still and had not married. She was artfully adorned, but not all the trouble she had gone to could hide the fingermarks of Father Time. Soon he must have her by the throat, and then what lingered of her comeliness should be no more. And seeing this—for who that looked could help but see—Rebecca beside her appeared so young even when one remembered that she was still a girl and had not married. This was the immediate first impression, but it began to fade from my mind when I saw the sisters, Rachel and Rebecca, walking in the cool of the evenings, down one or another of the lanes which led past the lake from their little cottage. Their arms would be about one another, and they would be always talking, for there is much that loving sisters may talk about, even in one of the quiet places of the world. As they came home through the dusk, I often met them, and found it difficult to distinguish Rachel from Rebecca, or Rebecca from Rachel, so alike were they in build, so much did they resemble one another even in almost every feature.

Puzzled about this, my mind sometimes urged itself further down untravelled byeways of speculation. I felt that, inevitably, the portion of the lives of the sisters, which had gone to shape the story my mind had made was coming to an end now, and that, henceforth, whatever between them, their lives might make, must only be as little bits of one chapter—their story's ending. And, consequent upon this enforcement of reality by my thought of them, I desired greatly to know at least a little of what they must be saying to one another out of all the talking they were having how.

So I was glad when they invited me to tea in their quiet cottage by the lakeside, on one of my last evenings in that part of the world. I could not help feeling a sense of clash which would seem to have arisen before I came into the room. The shadow of it was all across the face of Rebecca, more particularly about her eyes, from which tears would seem recently to have fallen, and there was a stillness upon all the movements of the sisters, a frigid reserve upon their words. I could not suddenly detect evidence of the great affection I had been led to believe in, to such an extent that it now almost implicated me. It was disappointing to a distressing degree, but I, who had come to know so much about the mud of earth, found a certain comfort from this admission to myself of the triumph of reality. . . . The fading of the rose that blossoms from romance only to become of the dust again. The thought began to tremble in my mind that love is sometimes a thing of remoteness, rather than always of intimacy, and does not bear admixture with the grievous quality of real life; so even the love of the sisters had not been sufficient to conquer the strength of this fundamental affliction. We did not blithely draw into pleasant conversation. It seemed as if we had suddenly been fixed in a new and surprising relation to one another, which possessed almost a sense of pain. We were speaking little because our lives of a sudden had been abridged, as it were, by the thing that had not been done. . . . It was simply because Rachel had not married, in the first place, and to know why she had not married was not far to seek. The reason flowed sadly from her look at me across the table—she was most pitifully plain-looking. The features of Rebecca, although possessing an indisputable similarity, were still softened by comeliness. This was how I had always seen her, but now, as I looked in the clearer light that was shining around us, I thought that her features were becoming rapidly sharpened into the angularity, the ugliness and oldishness of the features of Rachel. . . . I remembered how I had been unable to distinguish them from one another in the dusk.

Our talk fell downward. There were long silences. Rachel had most to say, as if anxious to maintain some show of blamelessness. There were moments when she appeared even younger than Rebecca, who would heave a great sigh now and then, and look with a gaze of pitiful wonder into the fire.

I felt almost sorry for having come here, even though I had come to say good-bye. Rebecca rose out of her silence, and, going to the overmantel, gazed long at her own face as she tried to rebuild her hair. Rachel fell silent now, as if compelled by some remembered thought of Rebecca that made her half sorry for what she had just been feeling.

I had come to the ending at long last, and I saw with sorrow that this, of the present, was to be the dominant colour of their lives down the years to be. . . .

I rose quietly, and, with a few poor words of excusing, went out of the cottage by the lakeside, and out of the lives of Rachel and Rebecca.

# Brinsley MacNamara

## *In the Window*

### I

She used to be always sitting there in the window. With such remarkable constancy, indeed, did she occupy her position that it seemed as if she might be taken to be a constituent portion of the window, as a structure, a kind of stained glass figure set there in immovable scrutiny in the very middle of Garradrimna.

"Old Nellie Nowlan and she with the two eyes of her, forever set for a squint at a body, whether one would be passing up or passing down."

In this remark, which she continually compelled, was she fixed in the mind of Garradrimna, just as resolutely as she had fixed herself in the window. Yet there must have been a time, however, far distant, when Nellie Nowlan had been very young. There must have been a time when she had long wavy hair and shining eyes and a laugh that rang like silver on the air. Yet somehow people were not inclined to remember that time, but, in the chill of their forgetfulness, it was the period she herself most fondly remembered.

Here, in this very room where she made dresses for all the women of Garradrimna, she had been a remarkable character in the midst of the other girls with whom she worked. It was here that her personality had developed itself along a certain line. There was something unique about her way of summing a situation; in her way of placing a personality or a scene before the mind's eye of others; in her way of giving a whole chapter or private history through the aptness of a term; in her gift for coining a nickname. As they sat there at their sewing she would be the first to glance out at a passer-by. His or her significance was at once remarked upon by Nellie Nowlan, for she was, as it were, the interpreter of the little peep-show which was represented by the window.

"Who's that, Nellie?" two or three of them would say, without lifting their heads from the place where they sat humming as they turned their machines. Then Nellie would tell them. Sometimes, a few words would be sufficient to describe the passer-by, but, occasionally, she would laugh in a wise, quiet way as if she knew more.

"Oh, do tell us the story, Nellie!" one of the others would say.

Then their exclamations of invitation and approval would echo as a chorus.

"Nellie is the one can give the fine turn to an account."

"Indeed, you might say she's the one can get well into the mind of a person."

"She's the one can size up a situation, so she can!"

Thus, as the mind of Nellie fed upon their praise, life came to hold for her only a comic significance, and so it was that, as she gazed out of the window in quest of objects of amusement for her sisters, her mind was continually sped by some humorous or satirical impulse. As time went on she developed a slight curl at the corners of her mouth, which showed that her reputation as a critic of manners in Garradrimna had been justly bestowed. Gradually there arose among the people of the village a certain combative spirit in regard to her. They exhibited their dislike of her as best they might, over invitations to dances and other social gatherings, from which she came to be entirely excluded.

"We don't want to invite people that'll only be taking off things to be grinning about them to-morrow or next day."

In this phrase was embodied the feeling which set the people of Garradrimna in enmity to Nellie Nowlan. In the beginning she had met their offensive with a certain amount of scorn, her criticism often having the effect of completely spoiling a dance. But behind all her manifestations of satirical delight were the beginnings of a certain bitterness that she should be missing participation in such scenes, which, although slight, perhaps disappointing in themselves, mean much to any girl who is young, as she still was. One or other of the girls with whom she worked often went to a dance to which she had not been invited, and would bring back a full report of everything that had occurred. Very often little things happened of which the participants did not desire publication. And it was through Nellie Nowlan that the most widespread publicity was effected, for there she would be, coming all through the next day, with a wide smile on her face, to gaze after them as they went by the window.

Gradually, the enmity that existed towards her extended to every one of the young men. She effected a fine disdain of all of them, yet, in her secret heart, she longed many a time for the company and the affection of some one of them. And not so very slowly, and not without a certain sadness in their passing, the years were slipping by.

II

Now and then a girl of her long acquaintance would disappear from the sewing-room, having married, perhaps, a comfortable man, and now and then she would be faced with the amazing miracle of a marriage for love. But no matter what wonderful turn of Fate might be behind it, there was something in the mere fact of any marriage which caused her to survey anew the reality of her own life. Consequently was it that her interest in marriage exceeded all other interests. Just as soon as the rumour of such an event went abroad she became excited.

Then there occurred the coming of the girl to the sewing-room for her wedding-dress. Nellie, as the forewoman of the establishment, would be called upon to talk the proposed dress over and over with the girl, and, even as she talked, with a gaiety suitable to the occasion, her thoughts crept ever downwards. It was so hard to picture the other suitably arrayed in the proudest moment of womanhood while that moment would seem to be receding from her continually. Thus was she driven to show an abnormal interest in marriage and in the circumstances surrounding it. Her mind became concentrated upon it to a degree that was unhealthy, considering the little bitter turn that mind was presently taking. While she talked so confidentially to the girls who came for the fine raiment which was to furnish the grandest day of their lives, she flew very near to having a certain hatred for them which caused the twist of her nature to become more pitifully apparent in her daily interpretation of the little peep-show of the window.

From satire, distinguished by a certain amount of humour, this endeavour of her mind became altogether bitter, turning to positive hatred and malevolence when she saw a marriage proposed or achieved, especially when she saw it achieved. This was the spectacle evoking a moment of pride, which cut her to the soul—the girl, married and radiant in the dress she had made for her, going off proudly for the honeymoon with her man. It was then that her tongue claimed its distinction in the things she said of the newly-married pair. Her harangue would grow bitter and passionate in the glimpse it gave of her own disappointment and her lonely ending. It was the gift of talk she possessed that had brought her to this sad possibility. Yet in the moment of her sorrow it did not become softened in abasement, but, rather, intensified in blind enmity. It was hateful to listen to her as she talked, but the girls in the sewing-room had always the satisfaction of seeing her weep bitterly by way of conclusion to her spell of excitement. The people of Garradrimna were not aware of this, but only of the ugly, obvious side of her character, and knew her only as "ould Nellie Nowlan, the gabster, that bees always running to the window and you passing by."

It was surprising that at this period they should describe her as being old, for, although there was beginning to appear a certain repose even in the twist of her facial muscles towards laughter, she still showed that interest in all goings-on which had made her well hated in Garradrimna. Yet, surely, she was no longer young. She had seen most of the girls of her generation come to this room for their dresses and seen them move down from the chapel on their way to Dublin with their men. All her school-mates were gone, but, even during the course of their passing, there had been something to atone for the offence it appeared against her. There had been glad talk about childish things when they came with their parcels of material to leave the order for their dresses, and, somehow, it had helped to brighten the darkness that their purpose represented for her. But now a different aspect of all this was appearing. The girls coming to the room were almost unknown to her. They were, for the most part, younger sisters of those girls she had known. Sometimes, they spoke of their nieces. Out of their talk there leaped to the mind of Nellie Nowlan the thought that some of these must be quite big girls now; soon some of them might be coming to this room, even as their mothers before them, her intimates, had come!

### III

A terrible sadness came to her as she allowed her mind to dwell on this thought. Its achievement would represent the final disaster of her life, and would be something she could never be able to bear. There was vast punishment in the very notion of it. Then, suddenly she realised, in a brilliant moment, that she had never tried very hard to win a man. True, her curious attribute had more or less forbade such an endeavour, but the truth was clear that she had never tried. She had merely busied herself as a critic of marriage and all the circumstances surrounding marriage. And yet if she had really set her mind on it, it would have been very easy to have arranged a marriage somehow. Her mother had died and left her the house and this business of dressmaking. Indeed, many a young man who had looked hopefully towards the house had had his hopes finally blasted by suddenly catching sight of her sitting there in the window. If she had happened to live anywhere excepting in the main street, where the large window of her work-room afforded a finer means of scrutiny than any other house in Garradrimna, many a young man might have come long ago to whisper soft words to her on the doorstep in the twilight of quiet evenings, and she might have gone proudly to the chapel many years since with her man in a lovely wedding-dress she had made for herself, while she could say of herself that she was still young. It was a lovely dress surely. She had given to its production all she knew of the art of decorating the female form until it was a very beautiful thing indeed. And through the long years that it had not been called into use she had continued to decorate it in the lonely evenings after the other girls had gone from the sewing-room. Far into the night she would remain there crying over it, until the brightness it continually recalled would seem to be not altogether faded from her mind. It might be still possible for her to enter into that state which was her perpetual dream. But it would be hard for her to find a match among the young men of Garradrimna, because there was not a single young man in his generation that she had not "read" from time to time, and her "reading" had been published broadcast. But her mind was sustained by the romantic thought that, some day, a rich, grand, young man might come riding by like a hero out of a story—a stranger from some far place to carry her away.

Now, gradually, a change had come upon the character of her vigil in the window. Although it was no longer one of anxious, critical scrutiny, it was in this light that it was viewed by the people who went up and down the street, for a reputation once made in Garradrimna was a thing that lasted for ever. The only people who had pity for Nellie Nowlan were the married women who had been her schoolmates.

"Isn't she wearing her age badly, the poor thing?" they would say to one another, as they went past the window. The pity of her ageing became more apparent when people saw her attempting to defeat the years by decking herself out in gaudy dresses. It was said that she wasted her time in making dresses for herself instead of attending to the needs of her customers. They grew into a state of wonderment and perpetual conjecture as to what the future of Nellie Nowlan might be.

Then the miracle she had longed for began to happen. A young man, a shop boy, had come to Garradrimna from some distant town, and taken up a position in the shop just opposite the sitting-room. He was an unusual young man, and he dressed with a splendour which was marvellous considering the grime of the shop and the salary he had come to earn there. It may have been this fact of his sharply contrasted neatness, considering her calling, which attracted her, but his first day in Garradrimna had not advanced many hours when "old Nellie Nowlan" was hopelessly in love with Austin Ivory, which was the young man's name. That day she never left the window. Once or twice, when he came to the door, his roving eye had wandered her way. The result had been a smile, which she returned with all the graciousness she could summon, a very wonderful smile, indeed, for it held all the yearnings of romance which had been denied fulfilment through the years. After all her weary waiting there had come to her this one wonderful day.

Now Austin Ivory was coming more frequently to the door, and she was calling the other girls in their turns to her side and saying: "Isn't he lovely, musha! isn't he lovely?"

## IV

She began to experience a new torment. Her annoyance hitherto, after all, had been merely annoyance, but the thoughts and suspicions which came to her now were as the wounds of some extended form of torture. She was so fearfully anxious to preserve this promise of admiration which she had fondly fancied in the eyes of Austin Ivory. From the first glance he had thrown towards her she had taken him to be the young man out of a book who was to bring her love. And yet, as she saw him settle into the ways of Garradrimna, an ache that was akin to hunger filled her continually. She knew that the people would be telling him about her and how she had spent her life in talking bitterly. It would be a continual struggle to maintain her innocent charm in his eyes.

Consequently, she was all the more surprised when she saw him come to the door of the shop to smile at her frequently during the glad days. Gradually they had become acquainted, as everyone soon became in Garradrimna. . . . Then there came, quite unaccountably, the turning point of her life. The great winter dance was being held in Garradrimna, and, as a mark of appreciation of his entry into their midst, the committee of the dance had made him their secretary. Now, for many a year, they had left her out of the list of the invited because of her reputation, and it was one of the most surprising moments of her life when a complimentary ticket for the dance reached her one fine morning. It was addressed to her by him, in his own grand handwriting.

Later in the day, as she sat there laughing excitedly in the window, she almost fainted when she saw him crossing the street to speak to her. It was about the dance, she knew for certain from the very first moment she saw him leaving the doorstep. Indeed, himself and herself anyway had the running of it, as you might say, he with his task of selecting those to be invited, and she with the making of dresses for those who were. They were a notable pair surely.

It was grand to hear him talking, not a bit like anyone else she had ever heard speak in Garradrimna, so eloquent, and his talk so full of laughter and loveliness. And it was given to her in this moment to know the crowning joy of her life. She thought at first that he was only joking when he so boldly invited her to accompany him to the dance, but when she saw that he was serious she almost wept for delight. She accepted gladly, all the coyness of her girlhood returning to make her excitement a most joyous thing to behold. It seemed a most wondrous compensation for all the long, empty years of her yearning. It seemed the very gladdest thing to imagine that he had selected her from all the girls of Garradrimna for this honour.

Yet, for all the incisive and bitter wisdom with which she had probed the causes of things in the village, it was not given her to glimpse the dark workings of Austin Ivory's mind. He had set himself to gain a footing in Garradrimna and to be his own master. He had a few pounds in the Bank, and Nellie Nowlan had a nice house, and a thriving little business, and he might start some other business in conjunction with it, which would help him towards comfort and the realisation of his plans. Of course, a little further down the street was Miss Diana Deering, who had a public house of her own and a fine way of going on. But he was sufficiently wise to realise that, for the present at least, such an ambition was far beyond him, and he did not wish to waste time upon what might prove, after much striving, to be merely a fruitless endeavour.

Nellie had no thoughts of such things in the days that led up to the dance. Her wisdom, so darkly streaked with experience, had been obliterated by the brightness of her dream. So consumed was she by a great yearning for the moment of triumph the dance represented that she could just barely fetch up strength to turn the machine. She was making a gorgeous dress for the dance, and all the girls said she would look lovely when she came to wear it. But all the time she could not help wondering what kind of success Diana Deering would make in her new dress.

## V

Now, therefore, was she immediately tortured into conflict with this young girl. She looked so young and lovely here in this human show place. Not so herself, poor Nellie Nowlan, who had spent the greater part of her life in turning ugly criticisms of such places off her tongue. She now seemed curiously ashamed of all the bitter things she had said about all the dances that had been held in Garradrimna. Musha! what was there to be bitter about, she now thought with regret—what was there to give so much cause for talk in the few years a girl knows the summer of her good looks. Herself, maybe, and another girl, with a young man between them, a few moments of pleasure and glad longing, with their accompaniment of a great deal of talk and some sad misgiving. That was life, and it all passed so clearly before her eyes now, all of it that she had missed. She had not entered into the life around her, although that would have been only natural, seeing that it was the life into which she had been born and of which she might have been expected to form a part.

She had set herself up as an uplifted critic of the same life, and that, certainly, was a queer thing to have done. She was beginning to be scorched by her punishment now. . . . Here she was so very lonely now in the very middle of this room in the very middle of Garradrimna. He had not taken her out for a dance although he had brought her here. At the other end of the room he was flirting with Diana Deering. Then she saw that glad young couple whirl round and round while she remained so lonely, sitting so stiff and quiet there with no one coming near her at all. It was a fine piece of punishment surely, but Garradrimna knew how to punish well. . . . Yet a few who were not altogether without feeling began to wonder what had brought her here. Surely she might have known that it must be this way with her after all the talk she had had. Why, their mothers had often told them of the way she used to talk of the girls who went to dances. And, just fancy she had the cheek to come here. It was a "charity" to see her sitting there, a very withered wallflower indeed. Oh, yes, she must be feeling it now. But why had she come here at all? There were only two people in the room who knew this, and these two were herself and Austin Ivory. She had set her eyes on him beyond all the young men she had ever seen, and he had thought of her house as a suitable place of business in which he might eventually become master of Garradrimna. But now he had forgotten both Nellie Nowlan and her house in the light of a larger opportunity. He was giving all his attention to Diana Deering. He never even looked in the direction of Nellie, and all Garradrimna was delighted with him, because he had made himself the instrument of their revenge upon her. Under ordinary circumstances they might have envied him, but now all wished him success with Diana, and said it would be the grand match indeed!

They never saw her slipping away, but a few girls passing home from the dance saw a light in the sewing-room, and could not resist the temptation to look in through a little hole in the blind. Nellie Nowlan was in there, looking ghastly in the mixture of daylight and candle-light. She was doing a strange thing. She was cutting the dress she had worn at the dance into little strips, and these she was again cutting into smaller pieces, which in turn she was tearing into shreds and burning in the grate. The odour of burning silk filled all the room. It was her sad, symbolic act of renunciation, like something a girl might do before entering a convent. . . . And there was another dress. Oh God! There was another dress! It would be harder, surely, to burn that.

A few weeks later, when the little pageant of the wedding of Austin Ivory with Diana Deering went by, there were a great many people watching, not the procession down from the chapel but the window, to see the effect upon Nellie Nowlan. However, she was not in the window, nor was she to be seen later when they went by the window, which was open, talking in high voices of the marriage, so that she might hear.

If only they had known all, the cruelty of Garradrimna might have been fully satisfied, because it was seen and remarked upon that she did not remain working in the sewing room, on that or succeeding evenings, after the other girls had gone.

At length they grew to wonder what she could have been working at so late for so many years, and why she had abandoned it.

And it remained a mystery.

# Elizabeth Bowen

## *Her Table Spread*

Alban had few opinions on the subject of marriage; his attitude to women was negative, but in particular he was not attracted to Miss Cuffe. Coming down early for dinner, red satin dress cut low, she attacked the silence with loud laughter before he had spoken. He recollected having heard that she was abnormal—at twenty-five, of statuesque development, still detained in childhood. The two other ladies, in beaded satins, made entrances of a surprising formality. It occurred to him, his presence must constitute an occasion: they certainly sparkled. Old Mr. Rossiter, uncle to Mrs. Treye, came last, more sourly. They sat for some time without the addition of lamplight. Dinner was not announced; the ladies, by remaining on guard, seemed to deprecate any question of its appearance. No sound came from other parts of the Castle.

Miss Cuffe was an heiress to whom the Castle belonged and whose guests they all were. But she carefully followed the movements of her aunt, Mrs. Treye; her ox-eyes moved from face to face in happy submission rather than expectancy. She was continually preoccupied with attempts at gravity, as though holding down her skirts in a high wind. Mrs. Treye and Miss Carbin combined to cover her excitement; still, their looks frequently stole from the company to the windows, of which there were too many. He received a strong impression someone outside was waiting to come in. At last, with a sigh they got up: dinner had been announced.

The Castle was built on high ground, commanding the estuary; a steep hill, with trees, continued above it. On fine days the view was remarkable, of almost Italian brilliance, with that constant reflection up from the water that even now prolonged the too-long day. Now, in continuous evening rain, the winding wooded line of the further shore could be seen and, nearer the windows, a smothered island with the stump of a watchtower. Where the Castle stood, a higher tower had answered the island's. Later a keep, then wings, had been added; now the fine peaceful residence had French windows opening on to the terrace. Invasions from the water would henceforth be social, perhaps amorous. On the slope down from the terrace, trees began again; almost, but not quite concealing the destroyer. Alban, who knew nothing, had not yet looked down.

It was Mr. Rossiter who first spoke of the destroyer—Alban meanwhile glancing along the table; the preparations had been stupendous. The destroyer had come today. The ladies all turned to Alban: the beads on their bosoms sparkled. So this was what they had here, under their trees. Engulfed by their pleasure, from now on he disappeared personally. Mr. Rossiter, rising a note, continued. The estuary, it appeared, was deep, with a channel buoyed up it. By a term of the Treaty, English ships were permitted to anchor in these waters.

"But they've been afraid of the rain!" chimed in Valeria Cuffe.

"Hush," said her aunt, "that's silly. Sailors would be accustomed to getting wet."

But, Miss Carbin reported, that spring there *had* already been one destroyer. Two of the officers had been seen dancing at the hotel at the head of the estuary.

"So," said Alban, "you are quite in the world." He adjusted his glasses in her direction.

Miss Carbin—blonde, not forty, and an attachment of Mrs. Treye's—shook her head despondently. "We were all away at Easter. Wasn't it curious they should have come then? The sailors walked in the demesne but never touched the daffodils."

"As though I should have cared!" exclaimed Valeria passionately.

"Morale too good," stated Mr. Rossiter.

"But next evening," continued Miss Carbin, "the officers did not go to the hotel. They climbed up here through the trees to the terrace—you see, they had no idea. Friends of ours were staying here at the Castle, and they apologized. Our friends invited them in to supper . . . "

"Did they accept?"

The three ladies said in a breath: "Yes, they came."

Valeria added urgently, "So don't you *think*—?"

"So tonight we have a destroyer to greet you," Mrs. Treye said quickly to Alban. "It is quite an event; the country people are coming down from the mountains. These waters are very lonely; the steamers have given up since the bad times; there is hardly a pleasure-boat. The weather this year has driven visitors right away."

"You are beautifully remote."

"Yes," agreed Miss Carbin. "Do you know much about the Navy? Do you think, for instance, that this is likely to be the same destroyer?"

"*Will they remember?*" Valeria's bust was almost on the table. But with a rustle Mrs. Treye pressed Valeria's toe. For the dining-room also looked out across the estuary, and the great girl had not once taken her eyes from the window. Perhaps it was unfortunate that Mr. Alban should have coincided with the destroyer. Perhaps it was unfortunate for Mr. Alban too.

For he saw now he was less than half the feast; unappeased, the party sat looking through him, all grouped at an end of the table—to the other, chairs had been pulled up. Dinner was being served very slowly. Candles—possible to see from the water—were lit now; some wet peonies glistened. Outside, day still lingered hopefully. The bushes over the edge of the terrace were like heads—you could have sworn sometimes you saw them mounting, swaying in manly talk. Once, wound up in the rain, a bird whistled, seeming hardly a bird.

"Perhaps since then they have been to Greece, or Malta?"

"That would be the Mediterranean fleet," said Mr. Rossiter.

They were sorry to think of anything out in the rain tonight.

"The decks must be streaming," said Miss Carbin.

Then Valeria, exclaiming "Please excuse me!" pushed her chair in and ran from the room.

"She is impulsive," explained Mrs. Treye. "Have *you* been to Malta, Mr. Alban?"

In the drawing-room, empty of Valeria, the standard lamps had been lit. Through their ballet-skirt shades, rose and lemon, they gave out a deep, welcoming light. Alban, at the ladies' invitation, undraped the piano. He played, but they could see he was not pleased. It was obvious he had always been a civilian, and when he had taken his place on the piano-stool—which he twirled round three times, rather fussily—his dinner-jacket wrinkled across the shoulders. It was sad they should feel so indifferent, for he came from London. Mendelssohn was exasperating to them—they opened all four windows to let the music downhill. They preferred not to draw the curtains; the air, though damp, being pleasant tonight, they said.

The piano was damp, but Alban played almost all his heart out. He played out the indignation of years his mild manner concealed. He had failed to love; nobody did anything about this; partners at dinner gave him less than half their attention. He knew some spring had dried up at the root of the world. He was fixed in the dark rain, by an indifferent shore. He played badly, but they were unmusical. Old Mr. Rossiter, who was not what he seemed, went back to the dining-room to talk to the parlour maid.

Valeria, glittering vastly, appeared in a window.

"Come *in!*" her aunt cried in indignation. She would die of a chill, childless, in fact unwedded; the Castle would have to be sold and where would they all be?

But—"Lights down there!" Valeria shouted above the music.

They had to run out for a moment, laughing and holding cushions over their bare shoulders. Alban left the piano; they looked boldly down from the terrace. Indeed, there they were: two lights like arc-lamps, blurred by rain and drawn down deep in reflection into the steady water. There were, too, ever so many portholes, all lit up.

"Perhaps they are playing bridge," said Miss Carbin.

"Now I wonder if Uncle Robert ought to have called," said Mrs. Treye. "Perhaps we have seemed remiss—one calls on a regiment."

"Patrick could row him out tomorrow."

"He hates the water." She sighed. "Perhaps they will be gone."

"Let's go for a row now—let's go for a row with a lantern," besought Valeria, jumping and pulling her aunt's elbow. They produced such indignation she disappeared again—wet satin skirts and all—into the bushes. The ladies could do no more: Alban suggested the rain might spot their dresses.

"They must lose a great deal, playing cards throughout an evening for high stakes," Miss Carbin said with concern as they all sat down again.

"Yet, if you come to think of it, somebody must win."

But the naval officers who so joyfully supped at Easter had been, Miss Carbin knew, a Mr. Graves, and a Mr. Garrett: *They* would certainly lose. "At all events, it is better than dancing at the hotel; there would be nobody of their type."

"There is nobody there at all."

"I expect they are best where they are . . . Mr. Alban, a Viennese waltz?"

He played while the ladies whispered, waving the waltz time a little distractedly. Mr. Rossiter, coming back, momentously stood: they turned in hope: even the waltz halted. But he brought no news. "You should call Valeria in. You can't tell who may be round the place. She's not fit to be out tonight."

"Perhaps she's not out."

"She is," said Mr. Rossiter crossly. "I just saw her racing past the window with a lantern."

\* \* \* \* \*

Valeria's mind was made up: she was a princess. Not for nothing had she had the dining-room silver polished and all set out. She would pace around in red satin that swished behind, while Mr. Alban kept on playing a loud waltz. They would be dazed at all she had to offer—also her two new statues and the leopard-skin from the auction.

When he and she were married (she inclined a little to Mr. Garrett) they would invite all the Navy up the estuary and give them tea. Her estuary would be filled up, like a regatta, with loud excited battleships tooting to one another and flags flying. The terrace would be covered with grateful sailors, leaving room for the band. She would keep the peacocks her aunt did not allow. His friends would be surprised to notice that Mr. Garrett had meanwhile become an admiral, all gold. He would lead the other admirals into the Castle and say, while they wiped their feet respectfully: "These are my wife's statues; she has given them to me. One is Mars, one is Mercury. We have a Venus, but she is not dressed. And wait till I show you our silver and gold plates . . . " The Navy would be unable to tear itself away.

She had been excited for some weeks at the idea of marrying Mr. Alban, but now the lovely appearance of the destroyer put him out of her mind. He would not have done; he was not handsome. But she could keep him to play the piano on quiet afternoons.

Her friends had told her Mr. Garrett was quite a Viking. She was so very familiar with his appearance that she felt sometimes they had already been married for years—though still, sometimes, he could not realize his good luck. She still had to remind him the island was hers too . . . Tonight, Aunt and darling Miss Carbin had so fallen in with her plans, putting on their satins and decorating the drawing-room, that the dinner became a betrothal feast. There was some little hitch about the arrival of Mr. Garrett—she had heard that gentlemen sometimes could not tie their ties. And now he was late and would be discouraged. So she must now go half-way down to the water and wave a lantern.

But she put her two hands over the lantern, then smothered it in her dress. She had a panic. Supposing she should prefer Mr. Graves?

She had heard Mr. Graves was stocky, but very merry; when he came to supper at Easter he slid in the gallery. He would teach her to dance, and take her to Naples and Paris . . . Oh, dear, oh, dear, then they must fight for her; that was all there was to it . . . She let the lantern out of her skirts and waved. Her fine arm with bangles went up and down, up and down, with the staggering light; the trees one by one jumped up from the dark, like savages.

\*   \*   \*   \*   \*

Inconceivably, the destroyer took no notice.

Undisturbed by oars, the rain stood up from the water; not a light rose to peer, and the gramophone, though it remained very faint, did not cease or alter.

In mackintoshes, Mr. Rossiter and Alban meanwhile made their way to the boat-house, Alban did not know why. "If that goes on," said Mr. Rossiter, nodding towards Valeria's lantern, "they'll fire one of their guns at us."

"Oh, no. Why?" said Alban. He buttoned up, however, the collar of his mackintosh.

"Nervous as cats. It's high time that girl was married. She's a nice girl in many ways, too."

"Couldn't we get the lantern away from her?" They

stepped on a paved causeway and heard the water nibble the rocks.

"She'd scream the place down. She's of age now, you see."

"But if—"

"Oh, she won't do that; I was having a bit of fun with you." Chuckling equably, Mrs. Treye's uncle unlocked and pulled open the boat-house door. A bat whistled out.

"Why are we here?"

"She might come for the boat; she's a fine oar," said Mr. Rossiter wisely. The place was familiar to him; he lit an oil-lamp and, sitting down on a trestle with a staunch air of having done what he could, reached a bottle of whisky out of the boat. He motioned the bottle to Alban. "It's a wild night," he said. "Ah, well, we don't have these destroyers every day."

"That seems fortunate."

"Well, it is and it isn't." Restoring the bottle to the vertical, Mr. Rossiter continued: "It's a pity you don't want a wife. You'd be the better for a wife, d'you see, a young fellow like you. She's got a nice character; she's a girl you could shape. She's got a nice income." The bat returned from the rain and knocked round the lamp. Lowering the bottle frequently, Mr. Rossiter talked to Alban (whose attitude remained negative) of women in general and the parlourmaid in particular . . .

"*Bat!*" Alban squealed irrepressibly, and with his hand to his ear—where he still felt it—fled from the boat-house. Mr. Rossiter's conversation continued. Alban's pumps squelched as he ran; he skidded along the causeway and balked at the upward steps. His soul squelched equally: he had been warned, he had been warned. He had heard they were all mad; he had erred out of headiness and curiosity. A degree of terror was agreeable to his vanity: by express wish he had occupied haunted rooms. Now he had no other pumps in this country, no idea where to buy them, and a ducal visit ahead. Also, wandering as it were among the apples and amphoras of an art school, he had blundered into the life room: woman revolved gravely.

"Hell," he said to the steps, mounting, his mind blank to the outcome.

He was nerved for the jumping lantern, but half-way up to the Castle darkness was once more absolute. Her lantern had gone out; he could orientate himself—in spite of himself—by her sobbing. Absolute desperation. He pulled up so short that, for balance, he had to cling to a creaking tree.

"Hi!" she croaked. Then: "You *are* there! I hear you!"

"Miss Cuffe—"

"How too bad you are! I never heard you rowing. I thought you were never coming—"

"Quietly, my dear girl."

"Come up quickly. I haven't even seen you. Come up to the windows—"

"Miss Cuffe—"

"Don't you remember the way?" As sure but not so noiseless as a cat in the dark, Valeria hurried to him.

"Mr. Garrett—" she panted. "I'm Miss Cuffe. Where have you been? I've destroyed my beautiful red dress and they've eaten up your dinner. But we're still waiting. Don't be afraid; you'll soon be there now. I'm Miss Cuffe; this is my Castle—"

"Listen, it's I, Mr. Alban—"

"Ssh, ssh, Mr. Alban: *Mr. Garrett has landed.*"

Her cry, his voice, some breath of the joyful intelligence, brought the others on to the terrace, blind with lamplight.

"Valeria?"

"Mr. Garrett has landed!"

Mrs. Treye said to Miss Carbin under her breath, "Mr. Garrett has come."

Miss Carbin, half weeping with agitation, replied, "We must go in." But uncertain who was to speak next, or how to speak, they remained leaning over the darkness. Behind, through the windows, lamps spread great skirts of light, and Mars and Mercury, unable to contain themselves, stooped from their pedestals. The dumb keyboard shone like a ballroom floor.

Alban, looking up, saw their arms and shoulders under the bright rain. Close by, Valeria's fingers creaked on her warm wet satin. She laughed like a princess, magnificently justified. Their unseen faces were all three lovely, and, in the silence after the laughter, such a strong tenderness reached him that, standing there in full manhood, he was for a moment not exiled. For the moment, without moving or speaking, he stood, in the dark, in a flame, as though all three said: "My darling . . ."

\* \* \* \* \*

Perhaps it was best for them all that early, when next day

first lightened the rain, the destroyer steamed out—below the extinguished Castle where Valeria lay with her arms wide, past the boat-house where Mr. Rossiter lay insensible and the bat hung masked in its wings—down the estuary into the open sea.

PR 8876 .S56 1993

Short stories from the Irish Renaissance

CANISIUS COLLEGE LIBRARY
BUFFALO, N.Y.